I0760830

The Love Birds

COMPLETE SERIES

KATIE EAGAN SCHENCK

The characters and events portrayed in this book are fictitious. Any similarity to real persons, living or dead, is coincidental and not intended by the author.

ISBN-13: 9781965807903

Cover design by: SelfPubBookCovers.com/ RLSather

When Cardinals Appear

Dedication

In loving memory of my grandmother, Marie McRorie.

Chapter One

Whoever said you can't go home again clearly never faced the arduous task of closing out their late mother's estate. I felt that in my bones as I entered my childhood home and shut the door behind me before collapsing against it with a groan.

There were no direct flights from Seattle, where I'd just completed my master's, to Baltimore. After braving two layovers, crowded airports, and what felt like the longest drive ever with a talkative taxi driver, I breathed a sigh of relief at the quiet stillness of the house. Returning to Cedar Haven was not my choice, but a part of me was glad to be home.

I left my suitcases by the door then shrugged out of my wool coat. Moonlight filtered in through the windows, but otherwise, the house was dark. Flicking on a light switch, I turned toward the living room. Little had changed since I'd left six months ago.

Well, that wasn't completely true. The hospital bed was gone and with it the IV pole that had supplied my mother with the sweet elixir of pain relief. Also missing was the annoying, repetitive beeping that kept time with her heartbeat. I shook my head. What I would have given to hear that obnoxious beep again. The noise and her labored breathing had at least provided proof that she still lived.

I squeezed my eyes shut, fighting to suppress the ache in my chest. It had been a hell of a year. When I took off the spring semester last year to help my mom after her diagnosis, I never thought I would be planning her funeral six months later.

I crossed the room to my mother's worn-out red couch, which contrasted nicely with the soft-pink cherry blossoms she and I had sponge painted on the wall behind it, a memory I would always treasure. The day of my parents' divorce, she insisted we needed to liven up the place. My father never would have let her paint something so "girly," as he would say, on the walls of a common area. In defiance, she'd roped me into helping her, and we'd spent a Sunday afternoon dripping paint all over the hardwood and laughing at ourselves.

The ache in my chest spread. She'd found a way to make a dark day bright but only after she'd extracted a promise from me. The promise was one I risked breaking by my mere presence in our house, in my hometown. But it was her fault I'd returned, so I supposed she couldn't hold it against me if my fulfillment of that promise was delayed.

Sinking down into the lumpy cushions, I let my eyes sweep the room. The flat-screen television my older brother, Steven, had insisted on installing hung on the opposite wall, gathering dust. Had he stopped by at all to check on the house? If he had, it didn't surprise me to find he hadn't done much cleaning. When we were growing up, he used to pay me part of his allowance to clean his room.

With a sigh, I pushed off the couch and headed to the kitchen. Picture frames dotted the walls, right where Mom had left them. Family portraits from before the divorce hung by the stairs, and framed collages of school pictures were on full display in the hall. As I moved deeper into the house, my annoyance grew as I realized how little Steven had bothered to do in my absence. A groan rumbled in my throat. Only then did it dawn on me what a monumental task I was undertaking as the personal representative of the estate.

My phone vibrated in my pocket—James had texted to make sure I arrived safely. *Should I text him back?* I hesitated before pushing the call button, needing to hear a familiar voice after a day surrounded by strangers.

James answered on the first ring. "Hey, honey. How was your trip?"

"Long and exhausting, but I'm here." I turned on the light in the kitchen. The oval oak table was covered with faded crayon marks, and the six cushioned chairs surrounding it featured a faded flower pattern.

"Is it weird to be back there?"

I rolled out one of the chairs and plopped down. "Yes and no. The quiet is almost unnatural, but it still *feels* like home." Mom's kitchen had always been simple, homey. A calendar from the year before was pegged to the wall beside a useless old phone, disconnected years ago. Mom insisted on keeping the misplaced relic in honor of bygone times.

"I get that. I wish I could have come with you."

"It's fine. You needed to get settled before you start your new job on Monday." I ground my teeth and winced at the ache in my jaw. It served me right for lying. He could have joined me. The "new job" was only a transfer from Seattle to Los Angeles, and they'd offered him a flexible start date in light of the move. He simply chose the earliest one.

The front door opened, and an unmistakable male voice bellowed, "Hello?"

"Listen, can I call you later? Steven's here, and we've got some things to discuss."

"Well, I've got a call with Germany at four tomorrow morning, so I need to get to bed soon."

"Okay." My heart sank, but there was no point in pressing the issue. Despite it being only six o'clock on the West Coast, I knew that any pushback would lead to an argument. "Call me when you get home."

"I'll do my best. Bye, babe. Love you."

"I love—" My phone beeped three times in my ear, indicating he'd already disconnected. I slammed my phone down onto the table. Once again, James failed to recognize how much I needed him. I didn't know why I expected anything different. I was used to it.

"Lanie?" Steven called. "Where are you?"

"In the kitchen."

I stood as Steven barreled in, dropped his briefcase, and engulfed me in a bear hug. "Man, am I glad to see you! How's it going, little sis?"

I extricated myself as delicately as possible from his vise grip, bristling at the nickname. "Don't call me that."

"I can't help it if you're both shorter and younger." Steven gave an impish grin. "Why didn't you call me from the airport? I could've given you a ride."

His hazel eyes, lighter than mine, held a note of suspicion, and I forced myself to focus on the changes in his appearance to hide my annoyance. We shared the same dirty-blond hair, though his was closely trimmed on the sides and longer on top. The one thing that hadn't changed was his height. He stood a good foot taller than me, something he inherited from our father, hence my annoying nickname.

"I'm sorry. I wasn't sure when you typically got off work." Although that wasn't technically the truth, I hoped to avoid trying to explain my desire to have a few minutes alone in Mom's house because I feared it would sound like I didn't want to see him.

"I'm the boss, so I can take off whenever I need to." He arched an eyebrow. "Dad was home, though, and he's retired. You could've asked him."

I nodded. My father and I had argued a lot recently, and the last thing I needed was a never-ending drive alone with him on which he could interrogate me about my life choices.

"Was the ceremony nice?" Steven asked.

The tension in my shoulders relaxed at the subject change. "It was okay. I didn't know any of the other graduates. But some of my friends came, and James."

"I'm sorry I couldn't be there. Setting up the office has taken all of my time and money."

"No worries." I turned away to hide my face. I understood why he and Dad hadn't come, but that didn't make it hurt any less. It might have helped alleviate some of the pain from Mom's absence to have the rest of my family there. But I didn't say that. Graduation was over a month ago, and I didn't want to argue. Besides, I hadn't come home for Christmas, so I supposed we were even.

I stepped over to the refrigerator and peered inside. It had recently been stocked with the bare necessities: milk, eggs, cheese, and coffee creamer. I smiled. While Steven hadn't bothered with the upkeep of the house, at least he'd had the forethought to buy some supplies.

After closing the refrigerator door, I turned back to him. "Have you opened yet?"

"Oh yeah. We took on a few small clients in November and had a grand opening right after New Year's." His face broke into a broad grin. "It was the biggest party Cedar Haven has seen in years."

"I'll bet." I struggled to keep the sarcasm out of my voice. My hometown wasn't exactly known for being party central. I checked the cabinets next. Mom's everyday plates were neatly stacked, and glasses shimmered in the kitchen light. From the looks of things, he hadn't started packing. I stifled a groan. Looked like I would have my work cut out for me in preparing the house for sale. Perhaps not starting my new job until May was a good thing. I was really out of my element and had no idea how long it would take to finalize the sale of the house and the rest of Mom's estate.

"I suppose congratulations are in order. How does it feel to have a master's degree?"

"Not much different, to be honest. I'm sure that'll change once I start teaching." I closed the cabinet door and faced him, leaning against the granite counter.

"Speaking of." Steven cleared his throat, and my stomach clenched. "Are you sure you want to live all the way out in California? Can't you find something here?"

I glared at him. "Been talking to Dad?"

Steven widened his eyes in faux innocence. "Why would you assume that?"

"Because he's been hounding me about moving home since I left." I rubbed my temples with my forefingers, hoping to stop the headache that was forming behind my eyes. "And as I'm sure he told you, I'm not coming back. James helped me find the perfect job. It's an entire school dedicated to children with special needs. We're going to find a place together."

"Okay, but your family is here." Steven crossed his arms over his chest. He resembled Dad when he did that. His forbidding posture and furrowed brow was totally a Max McAllister stance.

"Can we not talk about this right now?" *Or ever.* "I just got here." If I was being honest, I struggled with my own reasoning sometimes, which meant I would have an even harder time trying to articulate it to my family, who loved everything about Cedar Haven. My main aversion to moving home revolved around Mom's dreams for me to have a better life and the promise I'd made to her. But the house and the town also held too many memories. They were painful reminders of all I'd lost and people I would rather forget. If I stayed, the ghosts of my past would haunt me, and I wasn't sure I could live with that.

Steven's face softened. "I'm sorry. It's just... You know, Dad and I would love to have you home." He picked up his briefcase then opened it on the kitchen table. "Anyway, I wanted to drop off the paperwork for the house and Mom's will. You should be familiar with it, as it's the same stuff I emailed you a few months ago."

Oh no. My mouth went dry.

"There's also a docket sheet that includes court dates for

probate," Steven continued, oblivious to my growing discomfort. "You'll need to attend those." He set out a separate stack. "I've already spoken to John over at Peak Realty, and he gave me the documentation for the house. We'll need to have it assessed, both for value and any necessary repairs."

Keeping my eyes on the documents, I tucked my hair behind my ears, my stomach squeezing. While I'd received his emails, I hadn't actually looked at anything he sent.

"I wish I understood why Mom made me executor," I said, trying to quell the growing panic. "You're the lawyer, after all. It makes more sense for you to handle her estate."

"I'm sure she had her reasons." Though his expression remained impassive, I detected a slight bitterness in his tone. He put a hand on my shoulder and gave me an awkward pat. "Like I said, this should all be familiar to you. All you need to do is sign." When I shifted my weight to my other foot, he finally seemed to notice my change in demeanor. "You did read the emails I sent, right?"

"Well..." I hedged.

His head fell back as he stared at the ceiling. "Seriously, Lanie? I sent everything to you back in August."

"I was busy with school."

"Your semester ended before Christmas." He shot me a pointed look. "Which means you've had almost a month without classes."

"I-I was packing." Even I could hear how flimsy the excuses sounded. I stared at the floor, avoiding his gaze. The truth was, every time I'd tried to open the attachments and review the information he'd sent, I'd become overwhelmed with grief, and I'd shut down my computer. I couldn't deal. Avoidance had become my new modus operandi.

With a sigh, he pinched the bridge of his nose. "I should have known something was up when you didn't ask any follow-up questions after confirming receipt of my emails. It's bad enough we postponed this while you were finishing grad school, but now you've given us a deadline of May." He shook his head. "Or really April to give you time to get back to the West Coast to settle in before your new job starts."

"I'm here now." My hands on my hips, I lifted my chin. "How long could it possibly take?" I hoped I sounded more confident than I felt. If the state of the house was any indication, it would take a lot of time and effort.

"There are court deadlines we need to meet." After riffling through the stacks on the table, he thrust a document at me. "This is the calendar of court dates. I set all of this up under the apparently incorrect assumption you were on top of things."

My chest tightened as I scanned the paper. He was right, but I sure as hell wasn't going to tell him that. "What about the house?" I waved a hand at the unpacked kitchen. "You didn't need me to clean or pack up all of Mom's stuff."

"I was a little preoccupied with setting up my law practice." Steven glowered at me, and I resisted the urge to shrink away from him. "And for your information, I cleared my calendar for Friday so we could start sorting Mom's things and prep the house for sale."

"Oh." My defiance deflated, and I hung my head. "I'm sorry."

"It is what it is." He glanced at his watch. "Listen, it's late, and I know you're tired. Why don't you get settled, and you can look these over this evening. We can meet at my office tomorrow morning around ten to go over it all. How does that sound?"

I blew out a breath. Some time alone was exactly what I needed. After traveling all day, I could use some downtime, though I had no idea how I would get through all that paperwork in a single night.

Steven gave me a quick hug before he left. As I stared at the documents, a sinking feeling hit my belly.

I'll feel better once I've unpacked and grabbed a bite to eat. I went to the front hall and gathered my suitcases before climbing the stairs to my old room. It was exactly as I had left it, with posters covering the walls, a netted hammock full of stuffed animals hanging in one corner, and my bookcases overflowing with all my favorite stories, including every book Jane Austen had ever written. Mom had planned to turn my room into a craft haven once I went off to college, but between my summer visits and then Mom's cancer diagnosis, things had changed.

Really, my insistence that Mom not overexert herself had put a pin in most of her plans. Melody McAllister was always a force to be reckoned with. Even as the cancer weakened her physically, mentally, she remained strong and determined. Maybe stubborn was a better descriptor. I smiled and shook my head, remembering how exasperated some of the nurses were when Mom insisted on doing things for herself despite how difficult those tasks were for her. But my smile faded as quickly as it had appeared. At the end of the day, all the determination in the world hadn't been enough to save Mom.

I set my suitcases on the bed and unpacked my clothes. Leaving grad school had been rather anticlimactic. Graduation wasn't the same without Mom there. It was a quieter affair than I'd expected. After taking the spring semester off to care for Mom, I'd had to catch up on my studies. My friends had all graduated in May, which meant very few people came to celebrate. Mom had always been so proud of her children's accomplishments, and I could almost picture her in the crowd, cheering louder than anyone else.

Tears pricked behind my eyelids, and I blinked them back. I didn't have time to fall apart. First things first, I needed to fulfill my duties and settle Mom's estate. Maybe once I returned to the West Coast, I'd finally find time to grieve.

After setting up my toiletries in the bathroom, I yawned and stretched. The thought of sifting through legal documents drained what little energy I had left, but I needed to make up for the time I'd lost avoiding the task. If I didn't take care of it that night, Steven would kill me.

I went downstairs and grabbed one of the stacks and a snack before climbing upstairs to my room. As I read through the boring legalese, my eyelids drooped, and I lay back on the pillow to rest for a moment.

~

The sunlight streaming through the curtains woke me, and I blinked bleary eyes at my surroundings. *Where am I?* Instead of seeing the pristine walls of my Seattle bedroom, I found myself staring at demotivational posters my brother had given me as a joke when I was a teen. Each one depicted an inspirational scene such as a guy climbing a mountain at sunrise or a bear catching a fish, but underneath was a cynical quote or emoji. I loved them.

Rubbing my eyes, I tried to remember how I got there. Had I slept through the night?

Mom! I scrambled out of bed, sending papers flying, and rushed to the living room, only to find it empty and silent. The reality of what I'd lost crashed over me again, and I stumbled to the couch. *That* was why I couldn't stay there. If the promise to my mother wasn't enough to drive me away, the painful reminders alone would spur me to go. Even if I moved clear across town, I would never be able to move far enough away for the memories to dissipate. Seattle hadn't been far enough. California wouldn't be far enough, either, but at least it was a fresh start.

When I regained my composure, I returned to my room and gathered the papers I'd scattered in my panic. I took them to the kitchen, where the other stack still sat on the table, mocking me. I swore it grew overnight. The microwave clock said it was seven in the morning, which meant I had only three hours to sort through everything before I needed to leave to meet Steven at his office.

"Before I dive into this mess, I need coffee!" I set a mug in the Keurig, added a dark-roast pod, and pressed the start button. The air filled with the delicious aroma of roasted hazelnut. An unopened box of cherry toaster pastries was in the cabinet. Fortified with food and caffeine, I prepared to breach Paper Mountain.

After what seemed like hours, I finally finished signing the real estate forms and took a break to sip my lukewarm coffee. The kitchen had a large window on the back wall, which overlooked the small yard. Mom had kept bird feeders on the deck, and they had sat empty since she died. All the birds must have moved on to more plentiful homes.

As I gazed out at the quiet wintry morning, a spot of red caught my eye. I stood and walked toward the window, fascinated by such a bright color against the barren, snow-covered landscape. A little cardinal flitted around the railing of the deck. It was the only wildlife out that early, as even the squirrels seemed to be hibernating in their warm dens.

The cardinal stopped moving, and its small black eyes met mine. We gazed at each other for some time. Its vibrant red feathers reflected the first rays of the sun. Without thinking, I lifted my hand to open the window, startling the bird, and it flew away.

I shook my head and returned to the table. While I couldn't explain it, my steps were a little lighter, and I drank the rest of my coffee before rinsing the mug in the sink. I hadn't reviewed the will yet, but I'd run out of time. *Oh well.* If I didn't get through everything before I needed to leave, I would just go through it with Steven at his office. The important thing was getting the house on the market. Until it sold, we couldn't finalize the rest of the estate.

After one more glance out the window to see if the cardinal had returned, I went upstairs. I chose a dark-blue sweater and a pair of slacks—a respectable outfit for visiting a lawyer's office, even if said lawyer was my brother.

With great care, I put everything Steven had left into the respective folders, slid the folders into a bag, bundled up for the cold, and walked out to Mom's old car. As I approached, I wondered if it had been driven at all since I left for school. I climbed behind the wheel, dropped the bag in the passenger seat, and started the engine. The morning air was frigid, and my damp hair formed icicles as I waited for the car to warm. I cranked up the heat, knowing it probably wouldn't put a dent in the cold before I reached Steven's office.

I backed down the driveway and onto the small cul-de-sac that held my childhood home. Most people were heading to work, and I waved at a couple of neighbors. Old Cassandra Winters was out in her bathrobe and slippers, grabbing the paper. My heart rate kicked up its rhythm, and I swallowed then shook my head with a scoff. As children, Steven and I were convinced Ms. Winters was a witch. Mom often sent us over with baked goods, and her house always had an overpowering scent of sage. Ms. Winters had two cats, one gray and one black, who enjoyed swirling around our legs in an almost menacing manner, as if the cats wanted to trip us.

As I pulled onto Main Street, I saw the same quaint little shops and restaurants that had been there since I was young. Collins Hardware Store sat on the corner of Main Street and Chesapeake Way, though it looked like it had recently received a fresh coat of paint. Betty's Boutique Salon was already hopping with elderly women coming in for their weekly shampoos and sets. I sighed. When was Cedar Haven going to join the twenty-first century?

My car suddenly jolted and made a popping sound. *What the—?* I pulled over on the shoulder and got out. The driver's-side tire was flat. A quick glance behind me confirmed I had driven over a pothole.

Great. Just what I needed on my first day back in town. I reached into the car and grabbed my cell phone.

"Hey, Lanie, are you on your way?"

"I was," I hissed. "But I just hit a pothole, and I've got a flat."

Steven sighed. "All right. I'll call over to Sanders's Tire and Auto and get someone out there to help you. Shouldn't take long."

"Can't you come get me?" I pleaded, cursing myself for never learning how to change a tire.

"Sorry, sis. I'm swamped this morning." When I didn't respond, he hurried on. "But I can take you out for lunch to make up for it."

My stomach knotted. The last thing I wanted was a possible run-in with the owner of the auto shop, but I wasn't sure how I could avoid it. "Okay. Well, thanks for calling them for me."

"No problem. I'll see you soon."

"Bye." I mumbled and shoved my phone into my pocket. Mr.

Sanders was a nice enough man, but having him fix my tire would be awkward. His son, Nate, and I were high school sweethearts, but we hadn't spoken since our awful breakup.

In retrospect, pledging to stay in a relationship before going away to college on the other side of the country had been a stupid move, but I was smitten with Nate and convinced we could survive the distance. Unfortunately, the distance was only one aspect of the odds against us. Between classes, new people, and the time zone difference, we barely made it through my first semester. When I came home for Christmas that year, we had a huge fight and broke up.

I couldn't recall what had caused the fight, but it didn't really matter. I was devastated. Since then, Nate and I had an unspoken agreement to avoid each other at all costs. When I came home last spring to care for my mom, I'd tried to be cordial the few times I saw him. But Nate wouldn't even look at me, which made no sense. He'd been the one to end things, after all, not the other way around.

The last time I saw him was at Mom's funeral, but he hadn't stuck around after the service. I caught only a glimpse of him as I followed the casket out of the church.

Knowing I had no other choice, I resigned myself to my fate and climbed back into the car. At least in a town so small, I shouldn't have a long wait. I figured it would be as good a time as any to look over the paperwork I hadn't gotten through.

I'd barely begun to review Mom's last will and testament when a loud rap on my window startled me. I looked up, and my stomach plummeted as I met a familiar set of dark-brown eyes. It was Nate, not his father, who'd come to rescue me. I tried not to notice the short length of the black hair I'd once loved to run my fingers through. Or the way his once-soft features had given way to a chiseled jawline.

His eyes widened, and his mouth dropped open. A plethora of emotions crossed his face before his full lips pressed in a grim line and his dark eyebrows knitted together. Was he really that upset to see me or just shocked that I was here? *Well, here goes nothing.*

I steeled myself for what I expected to be a most unhappy reunion. But hey, at least he couldn't avoid me. I opened the door and climbed out.

"Hey, Nate," I squeaked with an internal cringe. "It's, uh, been a while. How've you been?"

"Fine," Nate responded gruffly. He walked around the car, assessing the damage.

"How's your family?" Jeez, couldn't he throw me a bone? I was *trying* to be nice.

"Great. Do you have the spare?"

"Uh, sure, it should be in the trunk." So, he was going to be all business. Well, fine, then. Two could play that game. I walked around and opened the trunk for him before taking a step back and crossing my arms.

He pulled out the spare and inspected it. "It's flat too."

Ugh, seriously? My face warmed despite the bitter cold. It hadn't occurred to me to check anything in the car. Of course, I hadn't expected to end up with a flat tire either. The day was off to a spectacular start.

I struggled to maintain a cool and detached tone. "Sorry, this is my mom's old car. I'm not sure how much it's been used since I returned to Seattle in July... after she passed."

Nate finally raised his eyes to meet mine, and my attempt at indifference wavered when I saw how much they had softened with sympathy. A part of me preferred his gruff attitude. I hated pity.

He inclined his head toward the tow truck. "The truck's unlocked. Go get warm. I'll pull your car onto the bed and then take you to the shop."

I hesitated, thinking I should thank him or something. For what, I wasn't sure. Basic human kindness, perhaps? But Nate had already started moving the truck bed to an incline to load the car. Without another word, I grabbed my bags and climbed into the passenger seat of the tow truck. The cab was nice and toasty, which was a godsend after being out in the frigid air.

I glanced out the back window to watch Nate's progress and couldn't help admiring how much he had grown into himself in the last six years. He appeared to have bulked up quite a bit, though it was hard to tell through his thick winter coat. As he bent down to attach the chain to the car, his hands worked quickly, the chain rattling as he moved. Did he do this often? I hadn't expected him to have taken a job with his father, as he'd always talked about becoming a veterinarian. Then again, he might not have had much choice in the matter. His father had hinted on more than one occasion that he wanted Nate to take over the business.

He came over to the controls and pulled the car up the incline. Then he raised the bed onto the truck. After securing all four tires with straps, he climbed into the cab beside me, and put the truck in gear.

The pregnant silence between us made the once-comforting warm air stifling. Should I try to talk to him again? It might relieve some of the tension, but Nate hadn't said much since his arrival. Perhaps since he was no longer focused on getting the car onto his truck, he would be a little more amenable.

"How long have you been working for your father?"

"I don't work *for* my father." His expression darkened.

Um, okay, then. That had seemed like a safe and innocent question but whatever. I gave up trying to be civil and leaned back against the seat, crossing my arms.

He glanced at me. "My dad retired. I own the business now."

"Oh, wow. That's great! When did that happen?" I latched onto anything to alleviate the awkwardness.

"About a month after your mom..." He cleared his throat. "He had a heart attack."

"I'm so sorry. I hadn't heard." I reached out to him, but the look on his face told me he wouldn't welcome my touch, so I dropped my hand. "Is he okay?"

"He's better." Nate shifted in his seat. "But between the heart attack and your mother's passing"—his voice cracked on the last word—"I guess he realized life's too short and decided it was time to retire."

I bit my lip and turned away, blinking back a surge of tears. The news was hardly surprising. Mom's death had shaken the whole town, not to mention my entire life. All my plans for moving to California directly after graduation had been obliterated the moment I'd learned she had cancer. I'd never intended to return after she died, but her inexplicable decision to name me executor had further altered my course.

Squeezing my eyes shut, I swallowed a sob, but a rogue tear still managed to slip through my herculean efforts not to cry. I swiped my hand over my face to dash it away but not before Nate saw.

"I'm sorry," he murmured. "She was a good woman."

I whipped my head around, raising my eyebrows. Nate and Mom had never gotten along. In fact, Mom was thrilled when I came home crying about the breakup. Ha, what an understatement. If I'd let her, Mom probably would have thrown a party.

Some of Mom's animosity was perhaps my fault. At one point, I had considered postponing college. At the very least, I proposed starting locally at the community college before heading off to my dream school, when Nate could join me. But Mom put her foot down, threatening not to pay for any of it if I didn't go. She didn't want me to wait for "some guy," as she so eloquently put it, to pursue my dreams. I knew she was still bitter about the divorce, but her angry objections to Nate always felt misplaced. He'd never done anything to warrant her dislike, but I'd always assumed he just reminded her too much of my dad. Or our relationship reminded her too much of theirs. My parents were also high school sweethearts, and Mom never quite forgave herself for graduating high school and jumping into marriage.

She said she wanted a better life for me, and she made me promise to move as far away from Cedar Haven as possible and never to settle. That was what she felt she had done. She'd given up some of her dreams when she married my father. They were so young, and it was natural that she worried I was making the same mistake. In the end, she won. She convinced me to go to Seattle, but I defied her in one way. I stubbornly stood by my commitment to Nate. And we saw how that worked out.

As if he'd sensed my thoughts, his cheeks reddened. "Your mother and I…" He cleared his throat. "We made our peace."

"You did?" I couldn't believe my ears. They talked? When? While I was away? I stared at him, the questions burning in my throat, but Nate simply nodded and didn't elaborate.

"Well, that's something, I guess," I said. "With everything that happened, I never would've expected you to forgive her."

Nate frowned but kept his eyes on the road. "I never held any ill will toward your mother."

"Just toward me, then?" I covered my mouth with my hand. "I'm sorry. That wasn't fair."

He shrugged in what I assumed was meant to be a nonchalant way, but it came off stiffly. "It is what it is."

He scratched his eyebrow, a familiar gesture that demonstrated his discomfort. I hid a smile. We once shared such a strong connection that I could almost read his mind, and a part of me was thrilled that I could still read him so well, even after all this time.

We pulled into the shop's parking lot. He backed the truck in front of one of the bays and hopped out. I waited in the cab for him to finish unloading the car, but I jumped when he opened my door.

"There's some stuff you need to sign." Nate nodded to the small office. "Your brother said you were heading to see him. I can take you when you're done."

I grabbed my things and went inside. Not much had changed since Nate had taken over the business. My family had been coming to Sanders's Tire and Auto for as long as I could remember, both out of loyalty and because they were the only mechanic shop in town. As I stepped into the building, I spotted a seating area with some old chairs and an ancient television that was only capable of playing four channels. On the other side of the small room was a desk with a computer, printer, and phone. A man I vaguely recognized was on a call as I approached, and he held up a finger, indicating he would be with me shortly.

While I waited, I replayed the short conversation Nate and I had on the drive over. He and my mother had resolved their differences. I couldn't get over that unexpected revelation. What I wouldn't give to have been a fly on that wall.

"Ma'am?" the man at the counter called out.

I smiled and stepped forward. "My car was just brought in. A blue Ford Focus."

"No problem. Have you been here before?" he asked as he typed into the computer. His graying hair fell onto his forehead, and he shoved it out of his eyes.

"Um, it's been a few years, but I might be in the system. Or it might be under my mother's name. I'm Lanie McAllister."

The man's head shot up, and his green eyes took me in as if seeing me for the first time. I took a wary step back. There were only two reasons why my name would be familiar to this man: either he knew my mom, or he knew my history with Nate. Neither was a welcome possibility.

"Melody's daughter?" he asked.

"That's me," I chirped with feigned enthusiasm.

"I was sorry to hear about her passing. Did you move back to town?"

"Oh no. I'm just here to finalize her estate."

He harrumphed but said nothing else. I bristled. The noise reminded me of my father, whose tick often indicated his disapproval.

Just as I opened my mouth to give him a piece of my mind, the whir of the printer sounded beside him. He marked a couple of places on the paper and slid it over. "If you'll initial here and here and then sign right here, we can get you a new tire."

I scanned the document and filled in the sections he indicated then shoved it back across the counter. The man didn't even blink as he checked to see that I'd filled it out correctly.

Nate walked in through the back door and glanced at the paper. "Thanks for checking her in, Sam." He raised his eyes. "Are you ready to go?"

I nodded, and he opened the door. As I walked toward him, Sam gave a low chuckle, which did nothing to improve my opinion of him. Perhaps he was more familiar with my and Nate's history than he let on.

Nate led the way, but I froze when I saw the car he was headed toward. It was a '69 black Camaro convertible, a car with which I was well acquainted. He opened the passenger door and turned but frowned when he didn't see me directly behind him. My expression must have betrayed my thoughts because he smiled for the first time since he'd picked me up.

"I can't believe you still have this car," I finally said as I strolled over to him.

"She's in mint condition," Nate confirmed, a hint of pride in his voice.

I grinned as I climbed in and set my bags on the floor, feeling like I was stepping back in time. I recalled many evenings with Nate, cruising down back roads and stopping to take in the sunset over the water. It made me wish for a simpler time, before a broken heart and Mom's death completely altered my life.

He slid in, a warm smile pulling on his lips. He had always loved that car, and the change in his mood was palpable. We pulled out onto the road, and I relished the vibration of the rumbling engine as he switched gears. Something about that moment felt more like coming home than anything I'd experienced since my plane landed.

Within a few minutes, we pulled up in front of an unfamiliar building with a sign outside that said McAllister and Associates. What? We'd already arrived? I bit my lip and tried to get control of myself. *Get a grip, Lanie.* The man was giving me a ride, not taking me on a date. I pulled the bag into my lap.

"Well, thanks for the ride." I turned toward Nate with a forced smile. "And the rescue."

"No problem." He nodded toward the bag. "What's all that?"

"My mother's life, essentially." I opened the bag and gestured to one pile. "This is to put her house on the market. The rest is her will and other related documents."

"How long will you be in town?"

"Not long, I hope!" I met his gaze and realized a moment too late I'd suffered from foot-in-mouth syndrome for the second time that morning. The warmth he'd had moments ago disappeared in an instant.

"I hope it all works out for you," he said, his voice hard and cold.

"Nate, I didn't mean—"

"I'll call you when the car is ready." He stared at the road, and I took that as my dismissal.

"Thanks." I snuck one last glance at him, but he refused to look at me. As soon as I climbed out and closed the door, he merged onto the highway, leaving me alone on the sidewalk.

"Welcome home, Lanie," I whispered to myself.

Chapter Two

I WAITED FOR MY BROTHER TO FINISH A PHONE CALL. FOR someone who owned a small-town firm, he had gone to extra lengths to make it feel both professional and comfortable. It wasn't stuffy like some other offices were, and I could tell he had put a lot of thought into choosing the furniture and decor.

From the comfortable reception area with four high-back armchairs to the small oval coffee table covered with various legal magazines, it was clear he'd aimed for a friendly, professional vibe. A window at the front of the room looked out over a recently plowed Main Street. The receptionist's desk sat along the opposite wall, and a petite young woman with dark-brown hair typed rapidly, her brows pulled together in concentration. Though he was just starting out with only his receptionist and a paralegal, he'd left options for expanding, including an empty office for another lawyer—perhaps a partner someday.

Steven's door opened, and he stepped forward, all decked out in a black suit and blue tie. Did he have court later that day, or did he always dress that way? Mom had certainly instilled that we should always dress for work as if we were headed to church in our Sunday best.

"I'm glad to see you made it in one piece," Steven said as he engulfed me in a hug.

"Both the tire and the spare were flat since no one's driven it in six months." I narrowed my eyes as I leaned away from him. "Nate had to tow it to the shop."

"Sorry about that." Steven rubbed his neck. "It never crossed my mind to drive the car."

"I gathered as much," I muttered. Despite my annoyance, I couldn't blame Steven. He wasn't mechanically inclined. Dad had once tried to show him how to change the oil. After Dad completed the demonstration, Steven asked how much it would cost to have someone else do it.

"Nate, huh?" Steven arched an eyebrow. "I didn't expect him to handle it himself." Shoving his hands into his pockets, he rocked back on his heels. "How did, uh, that go?"

I glared at him. My unexpected and uncomfortable reunion, on the other hand, was entirely his fault. "Fine. No thanks for the warning."

"Sorry, sis. I really thought he'd send someone else."

I couldn't stay mad at him, and I didn't want to talk about my ex. "Should we get started?"

To my relief, he took the hint and led the way, indicating a seat for me on the other side of his desk as he sank into his chair. His office was just as nicely decorated as the reception area. Shelves lined the back wall, bowing in the middle from the weight of the law books. Behind his desk, he'd hung his framed degrees.

I struggled sometimes to process just how much Steven had grown up. My memories of the annoying older brother who would pull my pigtails and play silly pranks on me was hard to reconcile with the man sitting before me. He not only owned a successful law practice but was also engaged to marry his college sweetheart, who had all too willingly moved back to Cedar Haven to start her life with him. I smiled at the photo of him and Rose on his desk.

"Did you have a chance to look over the paperwork?" Steven asked.

"Mostly. I finished the real estate documents, but I've barely started the rest." I handed him the completed pile.

After flipping through it to confirm I'd signed on all the requisite pages, he knocked the papers together on the desk and into a neat stack. I removed the will from my bag and held it out to him, but he shook his head.

"I have my own copy here." He tapped a different pile on his desk. "Did you have any questions about the sale of the house?"

I shrugged. "It all seemed pretty straightforward. I appreciate that you were able to do a comparison of recent sales in the area to have a ballpark of the price."

"I didn't do anything. John down at Peak Real Estate handled all of that." He waved his hand dismissively. "He said the market's perfect for selling, and he expects the house will go quick. But before I give him the paperwork, I wanted to talk to you about cleaning out all of Mom's things." He folded his hands on the desk. "Many of the items Mom felt were valuable are covered in the will, but certain personal effects—such as her clothes, pictures, and the like—are to be divided between us. I know you and Mom were the same size, so I have no objection if you want to go through her clothes and take whatever you want. I figure we can donate the rest."

"That sounds fair," I agreed, trying to ignore the lump that formed in my throat.

"There is one thing of value she didn't bequeath that I think we should discuss," Steven continued. "Her car."

"I assumed we would sell that too," I said.

"While you're here, I figured you'd use it to get around. And then you're welcome to keep it if you want, but we would have to go through the process of changing the title to you."

"I don't think I want to drive it all the way out to LA."

His eyebrows drew together, but he didn't address the elephant in the room. "For now, let's just put it on the back burner. We can discuss it when we're closer to finalizing the rest of the estate."

I nodded and swallowed. I appreciated that he didn't pressure me —Dad was doing enough of that for both of them—but I suspected my brother would push the issue sooner or later. I hoped I could delay it as long as possible.

"She bequeathed the furniture in the master bedroom, as well as your old furniture, to you," Steven said, looking over a highlighted copy of our mother's will. "But I know you're not settled yet. I didn't know if you wanted to keep any of it, and I was thinking if you didn't want it, we could hold an estate sale. If you do want it, we could get a storage unit while we wait for the house to sell." He gestured toward the door of his office. "You haven't seen it yet, but the bookshelves from the living room are in my paralegal's office."

My stomach churned, and I took a deep breath. Steven had had a significant amount of time to process everything and had clearly studied the will. While part of me appreciated that he'd already started moving his share of Mom's things, another part resented the time he'd had to do it. His efforts meant we would have less to do to prepare the house for sale. At the same time, I'd worked my butt off to finish school and attempt to piece my life back together, but I'd had to put that on hold to come back and settle Mom's estate. It wasn't fair.

"Lanie?" Steven asked, drawing me back to the present. "Are you still with me?"

"I'm sorry. This is just a lot to take in."

His hazel eyes softened. "I know, and I realize you just got here, but we need to get Mom's house on the market as soon as possible. It's the largest part of her estate, and we can't finalize everything until it's disposed of."

I winced at his wording. It sounded clinical and detached, as if he were discussing a piece of trash and not our childhood home. But I shouldn't judge him. That was just "Steven the Lawyer" talking, and I knew he didn't mean anything by it. He was compartmentalizing everything just like I had at school. Taking a deep breath and letting it out slowly, I picked up my copy of the will and nodded at him to continue. It was going to be a long morning.

~

"Well, that was productive," Steven said hours later as he stacked the paperwork neatly on his desk and stretched. "There are still some details I think we need to review, but for now, we're in a good place."

With a weary smile, I rubbed the crick out of the back of my neck. I'd spent most of the morning with my head bent toward the paperwork in my lap. We'd gone through the entire will, making notes of specific bequests Mom had made as well as more general things we would need to divide between the two of us. It hurt my heart to see Mom's entire life reduced to a stack of pages.

Steven checked his watch. "I promised you lunch, and it's about that time. Any preference?"

I shook my head, still too muddled to think coherently. He reached across the desk and held out his hand, which I gratefully accepted.

"The worst is over," he assured me as he gave my hand a squeeze. "Most of this is just a formality. The house should be the last stressful part. Closing out the estate in probate will be easy, since she had such a detailed will drawn up." With that, he stood and shrugged into his black wool coat.

I scrambled into my peacoat and followed him out to the parking lot. We climbed into his car and drove in silence. When we pulled up in front of Bea's Diner, I hid a smile. I'd only come a handful of times since high school, but I wasn't surprised Steven had chosen it. We used to hang out there all the time, and he had even worked there briefly before heading off to college.

"This good?" Steven put the car in park and switched off the ignition.

"Perfect." We walked into the diner together. Unlike my childhood home, the diner was a place where I welcomed the familiarity. The old jukebox in one corner probably cost more in annual repairs than it was worth, but Bea refused to give it up. I couldn't blame her. It certainly added to the ambiance, and those old songs always comforted me whenever I needed them. After a bad test in high school or, later, when the nurse gave me more bad news about Mom's condition, I went there with a pocket full of quarters and played all my favorites, one after the other. Decorated in a fifties theme, the place had old records hanging on the wall, along with a plastic Elvis swaying his hips in time to the music. Each booth had its own miniature jukebox so that diners could purchase songs from their seats.

After finding a booth, I began flipping through the songs. I almost always ordered the same thing, so I didn't see the point in perusing the menu.

"Any idea when Mom's car will be ready?" Steven asked as he looked over the options.

With my eyes still on the song selection, I shrugged. "They didn't give me an estimate."

"I can drop you off at the shop after we eat if you want." He smirked at me over his menu. "It might be less awkward than having Nate pick you up."

I glared at him but didn't respond. I hadn't given much thought to how I would retrieve the car, but having Steven drop me off appealed to me more than riding with Nate again. Maybe I would get lucky and pick up the car while he was on his lunch break. Then I could avoid him entirely.

"As I live and breathe," a familiar voice called out. "Lanie McAllister!" Bea rushed over to our table, her gray curls bobbing under her hairnet.

I stood to embrace her.

"Welcome home, girl."

"Thanks, Bea. It's so good to see you."

"You're done with school, ain't ya?"

"I am."

"Oh, I wish your dear mother could have seen it." Bea's blue eyes grew misty. "She was so proud of both you kids."

I swallowed around the lump in my throat and struggled to respond. Steven took one look at me and stood as well.

"What, no hug for me?" he teased, giving me a small smile of understanding as I mouthed my thanks behind Bea's back.

"I see you every day," Bea retorted, waving him away. "Doesn't that fiancée of yours know how to cook?"

"She does, but she's usually exhausted after her shift at the hospital," Steven countered. "You know what it's like being on your feet all day."

Bea pursed her lips and nodded before turning to me. "So, what can I get you? Whatever you want, it's on the house."

"Aw, you don't have to do that," I protested as I sat down. "Steven's buying."

"In that case," Bea said with a twinkle in her eyes. She chuckled and nudged Steven's shoulder. "I'm just messing with you."

We ordered burgers and fries, our usual staple. After Bea left to put in our orders, Steven leaned back and stared at me. I squirmed in my seat. *Here it comes.*

"What?" I asked more defensively than I intended.

"I know you don't want to talk about it, but I wish you would at least consider moving home. Couldn't James find a job out here?"

Like that would ever happen. With a sigh, I turned my attention once more to the songs, avoiding his eyes. "I don't want to argue."

"It doesn't have to be an argument," Steven countered, spreading his hands on the table. "I want to understand your reasoning."

"Why do you care so much?"

"Because you're my sister, and I love you. I missed you while you were away." He ran a hand through his hair. "Besides, Rose and I moved here because we thought it was the best place to start our family. Her parents have returned to South Korea to take care of their parents, and with Mom gone, you and Dad are the only family I have left."

"It's not like you'll never see or hear from me again. We can set up weekly calls and plan visits."

"No offense, Lanie, but if your behavior while you were at school is any indication, I don't trust you'll keep in touch." He raised an eyebrow in challenge.

Ouch. He doesn't trust me? My teeth worried my lower lip. Deep down, I knew he had a point, though he could have approached it with a slight degree of tact. Aside from confirming that I'd received emails or sending back text responses in five words or less, I hadn't maintained regular contact with anyone from home. I already dreaded the dressing-down I expected to receive from my friends when they learned I was back.

Folding his hands on the table, he leaned forward. "Look, I get that you don't want to talk about it, and I'm not here to pressure you. I'd just like to have a better understanding of why you have to move so far away. California is as close to moving out of the country as you could possibly get."

"Hawaii is farther," I joked, trying to lighten the mood. It didn't work. My attention returned to the mini jukebox as I debated my next words. "James isn't a small-town kind of guy, and he's from the West Coast, so he prefers to stay out there. And the job is the perfect start for where I want to go. It'll give me the resources and skills to make a difference for these kids." Neither was a lie, not technically. Maybe it was lying by omission, but did that really count?

"But don't you think you could make more of a difference to children who are struggling in underfunded special education programs here?"

I dropped my gaze and stared at the table. Of course I'd considered that. *Struggled* with it was more like it. The school where I would teach was one of the top special education academies in the country, and as such, it was expensive and difficult to get into. Parents desperate to find the best education for their children waited years to be accepted. That meant some of the children who needed help the most were unable to access it. But even if I wanted to move home, which I definitely did not for a multitude of reasons, I couldn't. Not without breaking the promise I made to Mom. Besides, I'd already run into one of those reasons that morning and hoped to avoid repeat performances of the encounter.

"Does this have anything to do with Nate?" Steven asked as if he could read my mind.

"It has more to do with James," I replied, then I raised my eyes to meet his, trying to gauge if he could see through my half-truths. Seeing Nate that morning had shaken me more than I was willing to admit, even to myself. "But honestly, it's just this town." I waved a hand toward the window. "There are so many memories. I don't think I could bear it." I gave a one-shoulder shrug. "Besides, you know Mom always wanted something more for me. She never wanted me to settle."

I'd never told anyone else about the promise I'd made, not even Steven. When I fell in love with Nate, I'd kept it a secret because I had every intention of breaking the promise. And then after he dumped me, it seemed I would keep it whether I wanted to or not. With Mom gone, it felt even more imperative that I honor my word.

"Are you engaged?"

I blinked at his bluntness but shook my head. "We've talked about marriage, but I think James wanted to wait until everything was settled here. He doesn't want to overwhelm me when I already have enough on my plate. But once things calm down, I expect he'll ask."

"And I assume you'll accept?" Steven cocked his head, studying me.

"Sure," I said, unable to pull any enthusiasm into my voice. I hoped Steven wouldn't notice. "Why wouldn't I? After all, James was there for me when Mom died, and we both know how much she loved him."

"I guess I expected you would be more excited about the prospect of getting engaged." A laugh bubbled out of his throat. "If Rose had had your lackluster attitude about it, I never would have proposed!" His smile faded, and he ran his hand through his hair. "Look, if California is where you want to be, you have my full support. I'll even try to help you convince Dad that it's the best move for you." He rolled his eyes. "Though we both know that's a losing battle. But just... promise me you're not doing this out of some misplaced obligation, to either James or Mom."

Our food arrived, and I silently thanked the server for her impeccable timing. I couldn't look him in the eye and make that vow, not when my last one haunted me like a shadow I couldn't shake. What I'd told Steven was true enough. Mom did love James, not so much for who he was but for what he represented—my ticket out of town to the life she wanted for me. The one I promised her I would live. And after spending so much of my relationship with Nate fighting with Mom, it had been nice to be with someone who earned Mom's approval, regardless of how I felt about it.

James had spent Mom's last weeks with me. He'd stayed for the funeral, then he left and went backpacking in Europe to celebrate finishing his degree. It strained our relationship, and for a while, I considered breaking it off. When he returned to Seattle in the fall, he convinced me to stay with him by helping me study for exams and taking care of necessities like grocery shopping and running errands. His support during my last semester had more than made up for his absence in the months prior, or at least, that was what I told myself.

My phone buzzed. I listened to the voice message, meeting Steven's questioning look across the table. "Just James checking in."

"No word on the car, then?"

"Apparently not," I replied. "But I don't mind going over there and waiting. I can't imagine it will take much longer."

"I'll drop you off when we're done here."

"I'd appreciate that. Is there anything else we need to do today?"

Steven shook his head. "I think at this point, we just need to start preparing the house."

"I can work on Mom's clothes this afternoon, and then maybe this weekend, we can figure out the furniture."

"I'll come by the day after tomorrow," Steven said. "If there are any items neither of us want, we'll need to get them appraised and hold an estate sale. I'd like to do that as soon as possible."

I nodded glumly. Once again, my brother's businesslike approach to Mom's possessions grated on my emotions. I knew he meant well and that his efforts to move things along were just part of the process, but it was difficult for me to follow his lead. Perhaps I was being sentimental, but I thought there should be more reverence for the life our mother had led. An estate sale was just a fancy name for a yard sale, and it lacked dignity.

Bea stopped by our table briefly to say goodbye, then Steven and I bundled up before heading out into the bleak January weather. I prayed I wouldn't run into Nate while I waited at the mechanic's shop. His father had often spent much of his day in the small office above the garage, completing paperwork, and I crossed my fingers and hoped that Nate spent most of his time there as well.

"I'll text you when I'm on my way over," Steven said as he pulled into the parking lot.

"Sounds good. Thanks for lunch and the ride."

"No problem. Good luck with Nate," he replied with a hint of humor in his eyes.

I jumped out of the car and slammed the door. My annoyance at Steven melted when I entered the waiting area and Sam was at the desk. Nate was nowhere to be seen.

"Ms. McAllister," Sam said, picking up a plastic envelope and pointing it in my direction. "I was about to call you. We found some issues with your car, and we're going to need to keep it a few days."

"A few days?" I squeaked. I winced, and my chest tightened. What was I going to do for transportation in the meantime? I cleared my throat. There had to be some mistake. "What else is wrong with it?"

The door opened, and a different man entered from the garage. He had blue eyes and short brown hair and looked like he hadn't shaved in a week. A flush crept up my neck as he gave me an appreciative once-over.

"This is Jeff." Sam gestured to the man. "He can tell you more."

"Why don't you follow me, and I can show you what I've found," Jeff said as he held the door.

"I'm not sure I'll understand what I'm looking at," I mumbled. A quick glance around confirmed Nate was not in the bays either. The tension in my shoulders eased.

"No worries. I'll explain it as I go."

For the next several minutes, Jeff walked me around the car as he described the myriad of problems he'd found. When Jeff finished, my head was swimming.

"How much will this cost?" I asked, my voice unsteady. The estate would reimburse me for the repairs, but I estimated how much money I had in my bank account to cover the cost up front and guessed I might be a few hundred or so short.

"I'm sure I can waive the cost of labor for an old friend," a deep voice said behind me.

I spun around. Nate's dark-brown eyes held a hint of amusement, and my lips quirked up slightly in return. Maybe he was in a better mood.

"I couldn't ask that of you," I protested.

"You didn't ask, and it's not for you," Nate replied. "It's my understanding the estate will pay for any repairs, and I don't think it's necessary to charge labor and a tow for something your mother had no control over."

"Th-Thank you," I stammered as my cheeks burned. Of course, he was doing that in deference to Mom. Nothing more. "I appreciate that."

Nate clapped a hand on Jeff's back. "Jeff has already ordered the parts, and we should have your car ready in a few days."

I nodded then shifted uneasily. Without the car, how was I going to get home? Nate seemed to sense my discomfort.

"Something wrong?" he asked.

"It's just—" I shook my head. It wasn't his problem. I would figure something out. "Never mind. It's nothing."

He rubbed a finger over his eyebrow as if trying to determine whether I was lying. I gave a weak smile I hoped was convincing, and he shrugged.

"We'll call you when it's ready."

I walked through the waiting room and out the door, my mind reeling. *Now what?* I pulled up Uber on my phone, knowing full well I would never get someone out to the tiny town. Sure enough, the app reported no drivers available in my area.

Spectacular. There was yet another reason I didn't want to stay in the tiny nowheresville of Cedar Haven. Who didn't have Uber these days? A longing for Seattle swept over me. I missed the city for so many reasons, but public transit and multiple rideshare apps were among my top five at the moment.

Scrolling through my old contacts, I debated calling my friends, but I dreaded it. I hadn't spoken to any of them in months. When I'd first returned to the West Coast, they checked in on me regularly, but people would leave only so many unanswered voicemails before they gave up.

Cursing my antisocial behavior, I swallowed as I dialed, leaning against the building for support. My first two calls went to voicemail. Kristin Donnovan was an old theatre chum, and Leslie Wilson was a fellow teacher. I left messages for both of them without much hope of a response anytime soon.

My next contact was Mom, and I quickly scrolled away as a ripple of pain spread through my chest. I also skipped Rose, since I knew my future sister-in-law was working.

Next up was Toccara Jenson. We'd been friends since elementary school, and my heart filled with hope. Last I'd heard, Toccara had started her own business, which meant she could choose her hours. Of all my friends, she might be my best shot.

"Lanie?" Toccara answered, and I winced at the incredulous tone.

"Hi, Toccara. How are you?"

A brief silence followed, and I could almost sense the judgment pouring through the phone.

"Um, I'm fine. It's been a while."

"I-I know," I stammered. "I'm sorry about that. Things with school—well, you know how it is."

"Sure," Toccara said, though she didn't sound very convinced. "So, what's up?"

"I wanted to tell you I'm back in town." I paced the sidewalk in front of the mechanic's shop. "I'm home to settle my mom's affairs. And, um..." *There's really no great way to do this.* "Unfortunately, I had a bit of an accident with my mom's car this morning. It's in the shop. I was wondering if you might be able to come pick me up."

Another heavy silence. I crossed my fingers as I waited. I wished I had been more responsive to my friends over the last six months. Then I wouldn't be in such an awkward predicament.

"I'd love to help you out, Lanie, but I'm a bit tied up at the moment."

I rested my back against the wall and slid down. The sidewalk was cold and a little damp. I took a deep breath and forced a cheery tone. "No worries. I understand. Maybe we can catch up while I'm home."

"I'd love that!" Toccara said, and my chest tightened at how sincere she sounded. Maybe she would find a way to forgive me for being a terrible friend.

"Great! Well, check your schedule and let me know when you're free."

"Will do. Welcome home, Lanie."

I ended the call. There was only one person left I felt comfortable calling. I dialed Trudy Jackson, but I didn't hold out much hope.

Trudy was the only one of my friends who had taken the plunge and gotten married. I vaguely recalled receiving a birth announcement a few months ago.

"Lanie? Oh my goodness, girl, how are you?"

That was promising. "I'm home."

"You are? For good?"

"Uh, not exactly. I've got to take care of some things, like my mom's house, but probably for at least a couple of months. How are you?"

"I'm doing well. My little Davey is almost six months old now."

"Wow! I can't believe I haven't met him yet."

"You'll just have to come on by," Trudy said.

"About that..." I crossed my fingers again. "My mom's car is in the shop, and I'm kind of stranded. Any chance you might have a moment to come pick me up?"

"Girl, I wish I could, but Davey just went down for his nap, and I've got no one to watch him."

"Right." I closed my eyes as I realized I was stuck there for at least the foreseeable future.

"Wait, are you at Sanders's Auto?"

"Yeah, why?"

Trudy chuckled. "How awkward was that?"

"You have no idea," I murmured.

"I'm surprised Nate couldn't give you a ride home."

"I, uh, didn't ask him."

"Guess I can't blame you there." Trudy laughed. "Well, if you're still there in another hour or so, feel free to call me back. I can come after Davey wakes up."

Dear Lord, I hope I'm not here for that long. "Thanks, Trudy. I'd love to see you while I'm home."

"Definitely! You've gotta fill me in on what's been going on. Call me soon, okay?"

"Will do."

I pushed myself off the sidewalk. It was too cold to stay out there any longer, so I went into the waiting room. I texted Steven as a last-ditch effort, knowing full well he had a lot going on that afternoon. As expected, his response was less than encouraging.

Sam glanced up when I walked in but mercifully said nothing. I plopped into a chair, prepared to wait until Steven got off work or Trudy's son woke from his nap. My one saving grace was that Nate was nowhere in sight, though it would be hard to avoid him if I was stuck there for too long.

Chapter Three

About an hour into viewing a mind-numbing episode of one of those you-are-not-the-father shows, courtesy of the lack of channels on the ancient television in the waiting room, I watched a young woman enter with her son. I glanced up when they first came in but, when I saw it wasn't Steven, turned back to the endless drama on the screen.

Soon after they arrived, the waiting room erupted in chaos. The young mom struggled to respond to Sam's questions and simultaneously tried to console her son, who screeched and ran around the room.

I jumped up from my seat and approached the boy, but he scampered away, shaking his head and yelling incoherently. Without thinking, I kneeled on the floor and removed a toy from my purse. It was a small ball with a smiley face and rubbery hair sticking out of the top. When I worked with kids throughout my master's program, I'd learned to always keep an assortment of sensory toys with me. Meltdowns like that one were pretty common in my line of work.

I tossed the ball from hand to hand. The child continued to run in circles, screeching and pulling at his clothes, but when he got close to me, he turned and watched the ball.

Keeping my eyes on the ground, I rolled the ball to him. He picked it up and tugged at the hair then squeezed it. As he played with the toy, he stopped running around and quieted. He sat on the floor, rocking back and forth.

I softly hummed a simple melody, and the boy mimicked my tune. His mother shot me a grateful smile and finished her business with Sam. As I continued to hum quietly, the boy slowly stopped rocking, though his eyes never strayed from the toy. When his mother was done, she stepped over to us.

"You okay, buddy?"

The boy blinked at her but didn't respond. His mom went to take the toy away.

"He can keep it," I said quickly, keeping my voice low and soothing. "I always keep them on hand for my students."

"You're a teacher?" the woman asked.

"For special education," I said with a smile. "I'm familiar with these sorts of situations."

"Thank you for your help. My husband was supposed to be here by now, but I guess he got held up." A car pulled into a parking spot out front. "Ah, here he is now." She glanced back at Lanie. "Your students are lucky to have you." After she helped her son to stand, they left.

I stared after them, a strange heaviness filling my chest. My last semester hadn't involved any student teaching, and I missed working with my students. In Seattle, I'd found a position in an inner-city school. The children weren't as fortunate as the ones I would teach in LA. Somehow, I didn't think I would have the same opportunities for one-on-one interactions, and the thought caused a pang of regret.

"That was amazing." A familiar voice caused me to jump. I scrambled off the floor, brushing dirt from my pants.

"I-I didn't realize you were watching," I stammered, tucking my hair behind my ears. I supposed I was lucky he hadn't come out to the lobby sooner.

"I didn't want to interrupt." Nate moved closer. "How'd you know to do that?"

"It's what I went to school for." I gave what I hoped was a nonchalant shrug. "Though it's been a while since I worked with a child."

"You haven't lost your touch." His deep-brown eyes searched mine, and I shifted self-consciously. Seeming to realize he was staring, he cleared his throat and gestured to the waiting room. "But what are you still doing here?"

"Oh, um, I don't have a ride." When he didn't respond, I babbled to fill the silence. "I tried to find one, but no one was free."

"Why didn't you say so earlier?"

"I didn't want to bother you." I couldn't quite look him in the eye, fearing if I did, I would blurt out the truth. After putting my foot in my mouth twice that morning, I wasn't aiming for the third time being the charm.

He blew out a breath. "I can take you."

Just what I was trying to avoid. "Are you sure? I don't want to impose."

"It's no imposition. No sense in you sitting around here." He inclined his head to the office. "Let me grab my coat and wallet, and I'll meet you at the car." He left me standing in the lobby, debating whether I should make a quick run for it. Maybe I should take my chances in the bitter cold. Anything had to be better than another round of walking on eggshells with my ex.

But I knew I couldn't leave. Not only would it be rude, but it would also make things worse. I trudged out to the parking lot and leaned against his car to wait.

"It's unlocked," he called as he made his way toward me.

I blinked then rolled my eyes, grumbling under my breath about small-town trust.

Nate snorted. "Guess you forgot what that was like in Seattle."

I climbed into the car and buckled in. An uncomfortable silence settled between us as we left the parking lot. I vowed not to be the one to break it.

"I'm sorry," I blurted out a moment later when it became unbearable. I really needed to work on my resolve. "For being so flippant earlier about being back."

He shrugged. I waited for him to say more, but when he didn't, I glared out the window. *Great. He can't even accept my apology?* If that was what I could expect from him for the rest of the time I was at home, then I needed to make sure to hightail it back to the West Coast as soon as possible.

I stifled a sigh. Things used to be a lot easier. Our conversations once lasted for hours, but suddenly, we couldn't fill a ten-minute drive.

As soon as he'd parked in my driveway, I mumbled a quick thanks and jumped out, not even bothering to look at him. I raced to the door, hoping to put the whole awful experience behind me.

"Wait!" Nate cried out.

I stopped on the porch and spun around, bracing myself for whatever he was going to say.

He ran a hand through his hair. "Is this how it's going to be between us?"

Crossing my arms, I leaned back, assessing him. "I don't know. You tell me."

We stared at each other for a moment, and I resisted the urge to escape into the sanctuary of the house.

He pursed his lips and stepped forward. "I'm sorry about earlier too. I expect it's been overwhelming, coming back here."

"You don't know the half of it," I said, shuffling my feet. I took a deep breath, hoping a bit of honesty might help alleviate some of the iciness between us. "The truth is, I don't know how long I'll be back. We're putting the house on the market, and Steven talked about holding an estate sale." I pushed myself off the side of the house and placed a hand on the porch railing. "But it's not like I have anywhere to be right away. My job doesn't start until May."

His eyes widened. "You already have a job? Where?"

"I've accepted a position at a school in California."

A shadow crossed his face. "I guess you're a West Coast girl now."

"I don't know that I'd go that far." I forced a smile. "But I'm excited about it."

"Well, I hope it works out for you, then." He shoved his hands into his pockets and hunched his shoulders, essentially closing himself off to further conversation.

I took that as my cue. "I should go. I promised Steven I'd go through Mom's clothes today. Thanks for the ride." I started toward the door then turned back. "And for fixing the car."

"My pleasure."

Tears pricked behind my eyes, and I turned away before he could see them. I opened the door and slammed it behind me before collapsing against it.

The universe had a sick and twisted sense of humor. First, my mother chose me to be the executor of her estate, despite the fact that Steven was the oldest and a lawyer. Second, I had to leave the life she'd made me promise to live so I could go home and settle her affairs. Then, upon arriving home, I had not one but two uncomfortable run-ins with my ex-boyfriend, the man I'd thought I would spend the rest of my life with but who, instead, had broken my heart. And for reasons I didn't understand, he not only hated me but apparently could barely stand the sight of me.

I buried my face in my hands as I tried to stop the flow of tears that had started coursing down my cheeks. As if it weren't hard enough to come home. As if I weren't facing the awful task of sorting through my mother's life, in the house that held so many memories. *Nope.* Apparently, the universe needed to throw in constant reminders of the *other* reason I hated the town: Nate Sanders.

The sad thing was, I didn't even hate him. On the contrary, despite how things had ended, I'd tried to be cordial when I came back last spring. The few times I ran into him, he either changed course to avoid me or grunted his way through small talk, disappearing the moment someone else approached. Why he got to play the wounded party when *he* was the one who broke up with *me*, I would never know. But eventually, I gave up and avoided him right back. With my mother's car in his shop, however, that had ceased to be an option. We had to deal with each other, at least until he fixed the car.

Maybe I could avoid him in the meantime. I doubted I would be going anywhere for the next few days since I had so much to do at the house. And whenever the car was ready, I might be able to convince Steven to go get it. Or better still, Nate could just keep it. I could rent a car or beg, borrow, and steal rides. Whatever it took to avoid another awkward encounter.

After grabbing my phone, I scrolled through my contacts and clicked James's name, needing to vent to someone who might understand. But I stopped myself. He was in the middle of his workday and wouldn't appreciate an interruption. The last time I called him while he was working, we had a "discussion" that evening about his policy of not taking personal calls during office hours.

"Only call if it's a real emergency," he had said. "And even then, consider whether I'm the appropriate person to assist."

It sounded so clinical and detached, like he was reading straight from a dry employee manual. Since then, I'd avoided even texting him while he was at the office. I knew his job was important to him, but sometimes, I tired of playing second fiddle.

Pushing thoughts of Nate and James from my mind, I headed upstairs. I'd lost precious time sitting in the mechanic's shop, waiting for a ride. But as I stood in my mother's room, I struggled to decide which area to tackle first. Steven had made it clear we needed to get the house ready to sell as soon as possible. However, he was wedding planning with Rose that evening, which meant I was on my own for the night.

What I hadn't counted on, however, was how overwhelming the

task was. It wasn't the amount of clothing I had to go through; it was more the memories each item conjured. A soft gray cardigan hung off the back of the chair in front of Mom's vanity. Toward the end of her life, Mom alternated between hot flashes and freezing, and the cardigan had been the easiest way to regulate her temperature because she could slip it off and on without assistance. My heart squeezed at the memory, and for a moment, I imagined her sitting in front of the mirror on one of her good days, wrapped up in the sweater's warmth as she brushed her thinning blond hair. The skin on her hand was so pale, I could count her veins.

With a sigh, I entered Mom's closet and removed armfuls of clothes before laying them gently on the queen-sized bed. There were warm cashmere sweaters in mostly pink and blue, soft blue jeans, and sparkly sequined dresses in an array of colors. I'd grabbed a few large plastic bags from the kitchen on my way up for the clothes I would donate, but it was agonizing to put any items into them.

I pressed a dark-green sweater to my face and breathed in deep, relishing Mom's faded scent of lavender and peonies. It was one of Mom's favorite pieces because it brought out the green in her hazel eyes. I could almost picture Mom standing in front of her full-length mirror, tugging her sweater into place as she dressed for work, her blond hair in curlers on her head. Steven and I might have inherited Mom's hair color, but our thick locks were a product of our father.

I closed my eyes as a tear slipped down my cheek. Though I knew I would never wear that sweater, I couldn't quite part with it. I set it onto the pile of clothes I would keep.

Next, I picked up a dark-blue button-down dress featuring a heart-shaped lace cutout at the chest. Mom had loved that dress so much, she bought two. The other one was green. I held it up to myself as I stepped to the mirror. I imagined Mom standing behind me, wearing the green one, the fabric hugging her soft curves. I shook my head, and the image dissipated. I decided to keep the green dress and donate the blue one. Each item that went into the bags was placed with a tender reverence.

When all the clothes were sorted, I surveyed my work. Two full bags were tied up and ready to go to the local church. Mom would want it that way. She'd always helped the less fortunate and would be happy to see so many of her treasured possessions going to people in need in the community. While I tried to take comfort in that knowledge, I still had to swallow a lump in my throat.

My stomach growled, and I checked my watch, surprised to find it had taken me about three hours to sort everything. I went to the kitchen and assembled a snack tray of crackers, cheese, and pepperoni with a glass of white wine. Food in hand, I slipped into the living room and sat on the worn red sofa.

As if on cue, the ringtone for James sounded, and I smiled. He must have just gotten off work. "Hey, babe, thanks for calling."

"Of course," James said. "How was your day?"

"Ugh, not great." I proceeded to tell him about my experience with the flat tire, omitting the part about my ex coming to the rescue. I couldn't say why I kept that information to myself. A few hours ago, I would have poured my heart out to my boyfriend, uncomfortable conversations included. Maybe I was too emotionally exhausted to hash all that out again. Or maybe a part of me feared James would be jealous or worried, though he'd never displayed possessive behavior before.

"I'm so sorry. That sounds like quite an ordeal. I can't believe your brother didn't bother with upkeep while you've been away."

"I know, right?" I sipped my wine, feeling vindicated. "But what's done is done. I spent the rest of the afternoon going through my mom's clothes."

"I bet that was hard," he said in a soothing tone.

"It certainly wasn't the most fun thing to do." I tried to sound nonchalant. Clearing my throat, I changed the subject. "How's your new job?"

"It's amazing! I was put on a team working on this huge campaign, and everyone's been very welcoming," James gushed. He told me how awesome the team was and how happy he was at the firm. I tried to ignore the pang in my chest. He sounded so happy and full of life; I couldn't help feeling a little jealous. Why couldn't I be with him, starting our lives together instead of stuck in Cedar Haven, trying and failing to outrun the past that threatened to catch up with me?

My phone beeped, and Steven's name flashed on the screen. A strange but familiar panic set into my bones.

"I'm sorry, James, but Steven's calling. I've gotta go."

"Oh, okay. Well, I hope tomorrow goes better for you. I'll call you soon. Love you."

"Love you too." I clicked over to answer Steven. "What's wrong?"

"Wrong? Nothing's wrong," Steven replied, bewilderment coloring his voice.

I exhaled and covered my face with my hand. Would I ever stop fearing the worst? "Sorry. I've become accustomed to bad news every time the phone rings."

"I get it," Steven said. "But everything's fine. I was calling to see how your day went."

"Pretty well. I managed to sort through all of Mom's clothes."

"That's great," Steven said, but something sounded off in his voice.

"What is it?" I asked.

A deafening silence came from the other end, and my heartbeat quickened. Was my first instinct right?

"Look, I need you to promise you'll hear me out before you get mad, okay?"

I frowned. "Why would I be mad?"

"I asked Nate to help us with the furniture," he exclaimed in a rush.

"What?" My mouth fell open. *What the—* "Why would you do that?"

"There's a lot of furniture to move around," he retorted. "I'd like to break down the beds and move as much downstairs as possible to avoid having people traipsing through the house, messing it up right as it goes on the market. I also thought they could help stage the furniture you and I are keeping for when people come to see the house."

"But wasn't there anyone else you could have asked?" I moaned.

"Nate's guys literally lift heavy things for a living. And they'll do it for a couple of beers and some pizza. It seemed the most obvious choice."

I stared at the ceiling. There was no denying he had a point. It would cost a fortune to hire movers, especially on such short notice. But I didn't want to see Nate again. The car was one thing, and I wasn't above begging Steven to deal with it. But this?

"I can't believe you asked him without clearing it with me first." I tried to sound strong, though my voice trembled.

"Come on. It's just for a few hours."

"No, Steven. Mom made me executor, and I think this task should fall to me." I hated myself for pulling rank, but there was no way I was going to spend another afternoon in uncomfortable silence with Nate Sanders.

"Fine." Steven sounded sullen. "Then what do you suggest?"

I considered my options. "I'll call around tomorrow and price-check movers. And I'll reach out to some of my old friends. Maybe they know someone."

"Well, while you're calling around, you need to find an appraiser as well for anything we want to sell in the estate sale."

"Okay," I said with a resigned sigh. "I can do that too." For what felt like the millionth time, I questioned Mom's decision to make me executor.

"I do have someone in mind, if you're interested. As an attorney, I do work with them often." Steven's tone had moved from sullen to sarcastic.

"Please send me their information," I said, trying to appease him.

He was silent for a moment, and I checked to make sure the line hadn't disconnected.

“I’m sorry I couldn’t pick you up earlier. How much was the car?” Steven asked, and my shoulders relaxed at his friendlier tone.

“I don’t know yet. They said since it hasn’t been driven in months, there are a lot of repairs needed.”

“Do you need transportation in the meantime? Rose might be able to drive you around.”

“I’m not planning on going anywhere for a while,” I said. “But I’ll keep her in mind.”

We chatted about the day, then Steven had to go. I pulled up an app on my phone and searched for local movers before bookmarking the various sites. I hoped I would be able to find an affordable moving company, but I wasn’t above begging friends and neighbors. Anything to avoid spending more time with Nate.

The next day went by without incident. I continued to go through the house room by room. I also took a break to call the movers I’d reviewed the night before and get estimates. Steven’s assessment of the expense was accurate, and I feared Nate might be our best shot after all. But I wasn’t willing to admit defeat just yet.

I woke up early on Friday, ready to meet Steven to discuss the furniture. As I sat at the table, sipping my coffee, a flash of red caught my eye. A cardinal was perched on the back porch railing, looking in at me. Was it the same one I saw the morning after I’d arrived? I stood and took a few cautious steps toward the window, not wanting to scare it away. The cardinal cocked its head as if it wanted to speak. A smattering of black dots sat near its beak, like freckles, and its wing tips were tinged with black. Something about the bird’s presence was soothing, and the tension that I’d carried in my shoulders for the past few months eased. The front door slammed, and I jumped.

“Hallooo?” Steven bellowed.

“In the kitchen!” I called. When I turned back to the window, the cardinal was gone.

"Morning, sis," Steven sang out as he entered the room. He'd already removed his coat and pushed the sleeves of his dark-blue sweater up his arms. "Are you ready for a busy day?"

I smiled and nodded. "Where would you like to start?"

Steven looked around the kitchen. "First, I'd love to have another cup of coffee." He grabbed a mug from the cabinet and made himself a cup before adding cream and sugar. I returned to my seat at the table, and he joined me.

"I've gotten through most of the rooms and have divided up the items but figured you'd want to take a look," I said.

"That sounds like a good place to start. Once we've sorted through the small items, we can clean the furniture and make some decisions."

"I wasn't sure if you and Rose would want any of Mom's dishes or cookware." I gestured to the pots hanging from the ceiling and the pale-white cabinets where the everyday dishes were stored. "She kept the china in the divorce, so there's that too."

Steven squinted through the doorway to the dining room at the cherrywood china cabinet where the light-blue plates were displayed. "We don't have much need for such a fancy set."

"Wedding china certainly seems to be a thing of the past," I agreed. We'd used it only for holidays and special occasions. "You don't think Dad would want it?"

Steven snorted. "What would Dad use it for? He barely even uses real dishes these days, preferring the wonders of paper plates."

I didn't respond. Guilt needled my stomach. I hadn't seen my father since arriving back in town. At least I had the excuse of not having transportation, and truth be told, I'd expected him to come by the house. Steven hadn't mentioned whether Dad would be by that day. My father had been surprisingly helpful for the last few months of Mom's life, and they had parted on good terms. So I thought he would want to pitch in with cleaning up the house. Still, the last awful conversation I had had with him echoed in my mind whenever I thought about seeing him again, and I didn't regret his absence. Seeing him again was bound to be awkward, but I couldn't put it off forever. He was the only parent I had left.

"Maybe you should take it," Steven said, interrupting my thoughts. "California is full of famous people. Who knows? Perhaps one day, you'll have Brad Pitt over for dinner, and you wouldn't want him eating off some run-of-the-mill dish set."

"Hmm, I'm not sure if it's good enough for him," I replied, matching his teasing tone. "What about the pots and pans?"

Steven stood and wandered over to the pans hanging from the ceiling. His eyes narrowed as he scrutinized their quality. I understood why. Mom had loved to cook and continued using the pans well beyond their natural life.

"Honestly, I think these should probably be tossed," Steven finally said after he completed his examination.

I forced myself to nod, though it hurt my heart to do so. While I couldn't hold on to everything of Mom's, somehow, throwing away items she had lovingly touched every day felt wrong. It was as if, little by little, the small remaining pieces of my mother were being chipped away until all that remained were intangible memories.

"We can try to donate them, of course," he hurried on, and I worked to keep my emotions in check.

"It can't hurt to try."

That decided, we finished our coffee and went through each room of the house. There were many things I had set aside for Steven or charity that he seemed to think were too worn. Towels that had begun to sport small holes from overuse, sheets that had faded to pale remembrances of their former brightly colored selves. I couldn't help seeing it all as some twisted, painful metaphor for how my once vibrant and energetic mother had slowly faded away.

The morning passed quickly as we took stock of everything. I had a clipboard to keep track of it all. Once we were finished sorting, we packed up the items bound for donation and loaded them into Steven's pickup. By the time we had dropped everything off at the church, it was lunchtime, and Steven offered to stop by Bea's Diner. I readily agreed. All that work had made me hungry.

We entered the diner, and as I scanned the room for an empty booth, my eyes met Nate's dark-brown ones, and my heart skipped a beat. I glanced away, searching in vain for somewhere else to sit, but the lunch rush was in full swing, and the only available seats were at the breakfast bar. Unfortunately, Steven had seen Nate as well and was already making his way over to his table. I recognized a couple of guys from the shop and noted, without enthusiasm, their table had two empty seats.

"Nate!" Steven called out in greeting. "How's it going?"

"Good. It's going good," Nate replied. He nodded at the vacant chairs. "Would you two like to join us?"

Steven took the seat across from Nate, which left me the seat next to him. I shot a glare at my brother, but it wasn't fair to assume Steven was seating us together on purpose. I knew him well enough to know how oblivious he could be in such situations. As a matter of fact, it had taken him months to notice Rose was interested in him and even longer before he worked up the courage to ask her out.

"How's the house preparation going?" Nate directed his question to Steven.

"Pretty well, actually," Steven replied with a glance at me. "I think we're making good progress." He turned to the other men. "Did you close the shop for lunch?"

"Nah, taking a break," Jeff said. "Nate's buying as a thank-you for agreeing to help with your mom's house."

"Uh, about that." Steven grimaced. "Lanie is looking into movers."

"Why?" Jeff stared at me. "We not good enough for you?"

Warmth crept up my neck. *Gee, thanks for throwing me under the bus, Steven.* "It's not that, but as executor of the estate, I just want to make sure I handle things correctly." I swallowed as I snuck a glance at Nate, wondering if he bought my half-truth. The frown on his face suggested he didn't.

"Why would us helping out not be the correct way to handle things?" Nate asked, a touch of anger in his tone.

I thought fast. Why, indeed? I couldn't very well tell him that he was the main reason behind the change in plans and that avoiding him was my new life goal.

"She's probably afraid old Sam here will drop some precious breakable," Jeff joked, slapping Sam on the back.

"You're the one who has butterfingers," Sam retorted. "Wasn't it you who kept dropping a wrench yesterday?"

I forced myself to laugh along with the rest of the group, relieved the other guys hadn't taken it personally. But Nate's eyes never left my face, and I knew he wasn't buying it.

"Well, if you change your mind, let us know," Nate said.

I shifted in my seat. "Thanks. I appreciate that."

Truthfully, I *did* appreciate their willingness to pitch in. Knowing I wasn't doing everything alone kept me from feeling overwhelmed. But considering how awkward Nate and I were around each other, I didn't want to put us through that again. And I would consider us lucky if we survived lunch without it morphing into an uncomfortable situation.

Fortunately, the conversation turned to other things, and I perused the menu in peace. I was conscious of Nate sneaking glances at me when he thought I wouldn't see, but I tried to ignore him. Even if I wanted to know what those glances might mean, and I definitely did not, I had too much on my plate as it was without overanalyzing them.

"Thinking of trying something different?" Nate asked in a low voice.

I started at the sound then shook my head. "I'd love to say yes, but I think I'm too much of a creature of habit."

"Me too," Nate agreed, sliding his menu to the middle of the table. "Tell me more about your new job. You said you start in May?"

I stared at him, wondering why he was so interested in talking to me all of a sudden. The other day, he could barely even look at me.

"I'm supposed to be there for orientation in May. They have year-round school, and I'll start teaching in June for the summer semester." I side-eyed Steven. He'd said he was on my side, but I still didn't want to rub his nose in the reminder that I was leaving soon.

"Does Steven not know?"

"No, he knows, but he and my father hoped I would reconsider and move home."

"But you don't want to?"

"I have a job lined up," I replied, evading the question. "I'd be unemployed for who knows how long if I stayed here."

Nate stared at his hands for a while, and I hoped that meant he would return to ignoring me. I rummaged in my purse for coins, hoping to steal away to select a new song on the jukebox.

"I understand you have a job waiting for you," he said, drawing me back into conversation. "But I did want to let you know the middle school is hiring a teacher for their special education department. Mrs. Carlisle is planning to retire at the end of this year, and they'd like to bring someone in beforehand to make it a smooth transition for the kids."

I bit my lip. "I appreciate you letting me know."

"But you're not interested?"

I shut my eyes as I debated my next words. How many more times was I going to have this conversation? And why did Nate, of all people, care? Shouldn't he be thrilled at the thought of never seeing me again?

"It's not that. It's just—" I pressed my hands against the table as if bracing myself, though for what, I wasn't sure. "This place doesn't feel like home to me anymore. Not without my mom. There are too many memories."

"They're not all bad memories, right?"

Was he serious? After how he treated me yesterday, I was convinced he didn't have any good memories of me whatsoever. I glanced at him. His question sounded genuine, even if I couldn't understand why.

"No, not all of them." I exhaled sharply. "Being back here, I find it hard sometimes to remember she's gone. At school, it was different. I was so far behind, most of my time was spent catching up. And she only visited the one time, so there wasn't much out there to trigger any memories. But being here, in her house, sometimes I wake up and rush down to the living room to check on her, only to remember she's gone." I bowed my head. "I don't know that I would ever fully let go of that feeling if I stayed."

To my surprise, he reached over and gently took my hand in his. I froze, unable to pull away. The warmth coursing through our hands was all too familiar. Did he feel it too? Before I could say anything, the server arrived to take our order, and I took advantage of the distraction to snatch my hand back.

What was that all about? I breathed in and out, willing my heart rate to slow. He was just trying to comfort me. It didn't mean anything. Besides, it *couldn't* mean anything because I was with James.

But when the server left and Nate raised his eyes to look at me, with that sweet smile that never failed to melt my heart, I started reevaluating everything I thought I knew about Nate Sanders.

Chapter Four

"THANKS FOR LUNCH," SAM SAID AS STEVEN PAID THE BILL.

"Anytime." Steven turned to me. "Ready to go?"

I nodded and jumped up, desperate to put some distance between Nate and me. I couldn't get over my reaction to him holding my hand. Flushed cheeks and a pounding heart? What was wrong with me?

Deep down, I dreaded the answer, and I shook my head, trying to clear it. Of course, I would always have a soft spot for him. He was my first love, but that was it. I was with James, and we were preparing to start our new lives in California as soon as the estate business was finished. Still, I wondered whether there was something more to the way Nate had looked at me during lunch. Maybe things weren't as settled between us as they should be.

"See you all later." Steven waved to Sam, Jeff, and Nate then gestured for me to lead the way.

My thoughts spun around in my head as I headed to Steven's car. The last thing I needed was to waltz down memory lane. But on the drive home, I couldn't stop thinking about Nate and how everything that had once seemed so right had gone so horribly wrong.

It was funny how I'd gone to school with him for years and saw him every day but never took any notice of him. Then one day, Nate and I were paired to perform a scene from *Romeo and Juliet*. At first, it was awkward. Despite having several classes together, I didn't really know him. We'd been assigned the death scene, though our teacher had shortened it so that we were alone on stage. During rehearsal, we'd practiced both our lines and the actual dying part, but neither of us were comfortable practicing the farewell kisses Romeo and Juliet impart to each other before they die.

When it became clear we were running out of time, I broached the issue with Nate one day during rehearsal. To say he was uncomfortable with the topic was an understatement. I suggested that for Romeo's death, he could just kiss my cheek, and that for Juliet, I could turn from the audience and kiss near his mouth but not on it. Nobody would be able to tell the difference.

It sounded so simple in my head, but I hadn't allowed myself to consider the emotion involved, specifically my emotions. Because during those rehearsals, I'd gotten to know him more than I had during all our intervening years at school. And the more I knew, the more I liked until I was mortified to realize I had a full-fledged crush on my scene partner.

During our final rehearsal, I'd worked up the courage to give him a real kiss. We were alone in the auditorium, and I hesitated a beat after I said my line. His eyes fluttered open as he frowned at me, but he must have seen something in my face because he swallowed. And then… he nodded as if he knew exactly what I'd planned. What I'd intended to be a quick peck on the lips morphed into something much more meaningful as he lifted his hand and slid his fingers into my hair.

Things changed quickly after that. Our rehearsals had caused us both to become interested in acting, so we tried out for the spring play. He got the lead while I won a supporting role. That allowed us to spend most days together after school, and soon, we were inseparable.

Everything wasn't all hearts and flowers, though. Being in high school came with its own sources of drama. Nate had a jealous side, which sometimes clashed with my outgoing personality. But I was committed to Nate. We worked through our differences, convinced we could survive anything.

Even when my mother began to interfere, we held on to that belief. Mom's negative comments started innocently enough. A jibe here about Nate's future prospects, implying Nate couldn't afford to attend college. A snide remark there about being stuck in a small town. Then her comments became more blatant, especially after I made the mistake of telling her I might delay going away to college. I'd been accepted at my dream school in Seattle, but I didn't want to leave Nate. She not only reminded me of the promise I'd made to her, but she also began to criticize my relationship more openly.

Unfortunately, her attempts to break us up backfired. At first, I vacillated between ignoring her comments and defending Nate, but those tactics just led to further arguments. Finally, I got so fed up with her, I moved in with my dad for my last semester of high school, a choice I later regretted.

When I left for college, I thought everything was good between Nate and me. But the calls and texts became more sporadic as the months dragged on. I started suspecting he'd found someone else, and when we broke up over winter break, I demanded he tell me who it was. He swore there was no one else, that we'd just drifted apart. I could never quite bring myself to believe him.

As far as first loves went, I considered myself incredibly lucky, despite the way things ended. Nate had always been a man of few words, but what he did say was thoughtful. Though it took me a long time to break him out of his shell, the end result was worth it for the short time we were together.

"You're awfully quiet," Steven said as he pulled in front of the house.

I blinked as I was jolted back to the present. "Sorry, I was just thinking."

"I'm guessing being back has brought up a lot of old memories for you."

"You could say that again," I murmured as I climbed out of the car then unlocked the front door.

I went up to my room, needing a moment alone with my thoughts. The house was starting to feel emptier, and I didn't want to admit how painful that was. I wasn't sure if I would ever be ready to say goodbye to it, even if I didn't intend to return to Cedar Haven.

A knock sounded at my door, and I called out that it was open. Steven came in and sat down on my bed. He frowned as he looked around the room. It was the one place in the house that hadn't been touched, though I knew I would need to start packing soon.

"Have you scheduled the movers yet?"

I shook my head. "I called a few yesterday, but I was hoping to call a few more next week."

Steven's lips pressed together. "The appraiser I work with is available next week. I'd like to get everything moved once he's evaluated what we plan to sell so we can put the house on the market."

I gave an absent nod. That was good news, even if it didn't feel like it. Each step brought us closer to selling the house and finalizing the estate, which meant I could return to my real life.

"I invited Rose over for dinner tonight," Steven continued when I didn't respond. "I thought you might enjoy the company."

That caught my attention, and I gave him a warm smile. "It's been so long since I've seen her."

"She's missed you," Steven said. "I've got some stuff to take care of, but we'll be back in a little bit. Anything you need while I'm gone?"

I shook my head. Steven gave me a quick hug and left. Moments later, a car door slammed. I breathed a deep sigh of relief at being alone at last.

Climbing off my bed, I decided to wander into Mom's room. I pulled the cardigan off the vanity chair and slid my arms into it, relishing the faded scent of lavender and peonies. After so many busy days, I hadn't managed to get over my jet lag. I lay down on Mom's bed and curled into a ball, promising myself I would close my eyes for only a few minutes.

~

The front door crashed open, startling me awake. I stared around the darkened room, disoriented. When did I fall asleep? The faint scent of lavender touched my nose.

"Mom?" I whispered. Of course, there was no response. I rubbed my eyes, wishing I could remember my dream.

"Lanie!" Rose sang out from downstairs. "Where are you?"

"I'll be right down," I croaked, and I cleared my throat, which was thick with sleep. I turned on a light and stared at myself in the mirror, smoothing my dirty-blond hair before I went to greet my brother and future sister-in-law.

"It's been too long," Rose declared as she threw her arms around me.

I bit my lip, guilt sinking in my stomach like a brick. I'd meant to call Rose. But then, I'd meant to call everyone back home. I could blame it on my thesis, but as that wasn't the whole story, I kept silent.

The warm scent of jasmine filled my nostrils as we embraced. Rose had been a godsend during those last few months of caring for Mom. A nurse herself, Rose had managed to coordinate home care to give me periods of respite, and at my request, she translated the medical jargon the oncologist used.

As we stepped back from each other, Rose grasped my hands and gave a sympathetic smile. Her thick black hair fell in sheets on either side of her face, and her dark-brown eyes were hooded with long lashes.

"Rose, it's so good to see you. How have you been?"

"Busy!" Rose shrugged out of her coat before handing it to Steven. "I've been doing a lot of the wedding planning on my own while this one"—she nudged Steven with her elbow—"has been dealing with everything here."

"Well, the house will be on the market soon, and then I'll be all yours," Steven exclaimed, throwing his arm around his fiancée. "Though I thought my only job was to show up and say 'I do.'"

Rose rolled her eyes. "Men."

The doorbell rang, and Steven released Rose and went to answer it. I led the way to the kitchen and began setting the table with plates.

"How's it been, being home?" Rose asked as she got out glasses.

"It's been... difficult." I turned and leaned against the counter. "Did Steven tell you we had lunch with my ex today?"

"He did," Rose replied, her tone hesitant. "But he also said he thought it went well."

Before I could respond, Steven came into the kitchen, carrying multiple boxes. He set them on the table and opened every box. There were two pizzas, breadsticks, and chicken wings.

"Why did you order so much?" I asked. "It's just the three of us."

"There might be one more," Steven said cryptically.

"You didn't!" I cried out. Had he invited Nate for *dinner* too? I didn't think I could handle another awkward meal with him.

The front door opened, followed by heavy footsteps coming down the hall. Something about the sound was familiar, but I couldn't quite place it. I didn't have to wait long, however, before Max McAllister himself entered the room.

My father had always been a forbidding presence, earning the nickname *The Intimidator* from a few of his work buddies who were also avid NASCAR fans. He stood six foot four with broad shoulders and strong arms. Beyond his imposing physique, his bushy black eyebrows seemed to be permanently fixed into a grimace, so even when he smiled, he never quite gave off a happy disposition.

"Hey, Dad." Steven clapped our father on the back. "Glad you could make it."

Dad grunted in response as his brown eyes met mine. His expression darkened, but he allowed Steven to usher him to the table. Neither of us spoke to the other, but the tension between us was palpable.

How long till he brings up California? I snuck another glance at Dad's face. Based on his expression, I would bet about five minutes.

"Lanie, why don't you sit here?" Rose directed me to a seat away from Dad. I shot her a look of gratitude. While there was no avoiding him, I would take all the distance I could get.

Everyone took their seats and filled their plates. The room was silent save the rustling of boxes being moved or a chair scraping against the floor. My heart pounded painfully against my rib cage as the scent of pizza turned my stomach. I couldn't believe Steven had invited Dad to dinner without telling me. As if I hadn't had enough uncomfortable encounters for one day.

"So, what's the plan?" Rose asked.

"I've been calling around to movers, but so far, they're all either too expensive or not available," I began. "But Steven found an appraiser who can be here next week."

"You're going to pay for movers?" Dad frowned. "I'm sure the good people of Cedar Haven would be willing to pitch in."

"I already asked Nate if he and some of his guys could help." Steven shot a pointed look at me. "But *someone* didn't want to go that route."

Rose elbowed Steven, but Dad's frown only deepened, if that was possible. I bit back a sigh as I picked at my food.

"I don't know that Nate would have been my first choice either," Dad said.

My head shot up. As far as I was aware, only Mom had issues with Nate. Dad had never been anything but kind to my ex.

"Regardless of who we use, we need to get someone in soon," Steven said. "If we're going to have an estate sale, we should do that within the next month so we can get the house cleared out and on the market."

"What happens if some of Mom's things don't sell?" I asked.

"Whatever doesn't sell, we can donate," Steven said as he picked up a chicken wing. "We simply need to keep track of everything for closing out the probate case."

"Just let me know when the sale is and what time you want me." Dad lifted another slice of pizza onto his plate.

"You're coming?" Since he hadn't been by once while I'd been home, I figured he hadn't planned on getting involved.

"Steven asked me to help." Dad shrugged.

"We need the manpower," Steven said. "We don't want anyone slipping out without paying for things, and that will give you and me leave to help customers."

Steven and Rose finished their food and began clearing the table while my father and I lingered. For a while, we glowered at each other in silence, neither wanting to be the first to break it and thus admit defeat. Finally, Dad blew out a long breath.

"Why haven't you been by to see me?" His conversational tone had an unmistakable edge to it.

"Well, I don't have a car right now, for one."

"You couldn't find a ride?"

"There's nothing stopping you from coming here." I took a deep breath, willing myself to remain civil to avoid an argument. "But I'm glad you were able to come over tonight."

Dad harrumphed. "Good thing I did. Otherwise, I might not have seen you at all."

"I'm home for at least another month or so, Dad," I chided. "That's more than enough time for several visits." Rose turned from the sink and gave me a thumbs-up. At least my future sister-in-law understood what I was trying to accomplish.

"You could make more of an effort."

I bristled. *Seriously?* "I flew three thousand miles to be here. Is it too much to ask that you close the distance by driving a few?"

"I could," Dad said. "But I wasn't sure what welcome to expect."

"I don't know what to tell you. It didn't seem like you wanted to hear from me after our last call."

Dad shook his head. "You're the one who hung up on me."

With good reason. I glared at him. "Only after you called me a huge disappointment."

"You're twisting my words," Dad retorted, his eyes flashing. "I meant *your decision* was a disappointment."

Unbelievable! "Oh, really? Because that's not what I remember," I shot back, my hands shaking.

Dad sipped his soda. "Perhaps I was too harsh with you, but I think you're making a mistake."

And here we go. To my father's credit, he'd lasted much longer than I'd anticipated. Maybe he was mellowing out in his old age. Unfortunately, it wasn't enough to avoid the argument entirely.

"So you've said, on multiple occasions." I crossed my arms over my chest.

"And if you'd listen to me, maybe I wouldn't feel the need to reiterate my point."

I shoved back from the table. "I don't want to hear it!"

Dad stood and held up his hands, which might be viewed as a sign of surrender, but I knew better. "We need to talk about this."

"There's nothing more to say. You don't want me to move to California, and I don't want to move back here. We're at an impasse!"

"You're running away."

Heat crept up my neck as I worked to keep my temper in check. "I'm not running away from anything. I'm progressing, moving toward something. Why can't you see that?"

"What's in California that's so much better than here? Cedar Haven is full of people who love you and want the best for you." He tapped his hand on the table. "This is your home."

"No, Dad, it *was* my home. Soon, it'll belong to some stranger. We've been over this. My home is on the West Coast, where James and a new job are waiting for me. Why can't you understand that?"

He took a deep breath and shook his head. “What would your mother say?”

“She’d probably cheer me on,” I practically shouted, throwing my arms up. “She never wanted me to settle.” I opened my mouth to tell him about the promise she’d forced me to make, but then I thought better of it. He would find a way to twist that as well. “And who do you think you are, trying to speak for Mom? You didn’t even know her at the end.”

Dad recoiled as if I’d slapped him, and I regretted my words. I wasn’t being fair, and I knew it, but I’d long tired of having the same stupid argument. While my parents had been divorced for some time when Mom got sick, they had reconciled their friendship before she died. He had helped with transporting her to doctors’ appointments and visited her often during her last months.

Steven stepped forward as if to break Dad and me apart, but Rose put her hand on his shoulder. Her eyes met mine with an unspoken warning. Closing my eyes, I counted down from ten. When I was sure I wouldn’t lash out again, I looked at my father.

“I’m sorry,” I said, my shoulders hunched forward. “I shouldn’t have said that. Can we please drop this? I’m building my life in California, with James. Once we’ve settled Mom’s estate, I’m going, and nothing you do or say is going to convince me otherwise.”

I stared at him, daring him to keep pushing the issue. He blinked first, and the tightness in my chest eased. I’d won the battle, but the war was far from over.

“At least I know you got one thing from me,” Dad said with a wry smile. “My stubbornness.”

I laughed, mostly in shock. “Are you sure? Mom could be pretty stubborn too.”

“So what you’re saying is you got a double dose?” Steven asked with a smirk. He and Rose had come back to the table once the storm had passed.

“All right,” Dad conceded. “I’ll let it go for tonight, but we’re not done having this conversation.”

"We never are, Dad," I grumbled as I left the kitchen, seeking the sanctuary of my room. I could hear Dad and Steven hashing out details for the next week, and I needed a moment to decompress.

Sometimes, it bothered me that my dad and I weren't closer, particularly once he was the only parent I had left. But arguments like the one that night reinforced the reason our relationship was strained. He had a very narrow way of viewing the world, and he didn't like for that view to be challenged. By opting to move to the other side of the country, I was directly challenging it. To him, Cedar Haven was the only place worth living in. That wasn't to say he didn't enjoy traveling, but he always said the wonderful thing about traveling was going home at the end. He had expected that once I finished my "travels" at college, I would happily return. My refusal to do so had been a thorn in his side for months, and despite sticking to my guns, I'd yet to make any headway in convincing him to let it go.

Dad left soon after dinner, and I went back downstairs. Rose spent the rest of the evening gushing over her wedding plans and asking for my opinion on everything from the flowers to the food. I welcomed the distraction from all the talk of estate sales and probate court. Before they left, Rose invited me out for drinks the next night, and I readily agreed. Not having a car was starting to get to me.

The next day passed without incident. I begrudgingly started packing up my room. Or at least, I tried to. In truth, I spent more time flipping through old yearbooks or diaries I unearthed than actually packing, but it was the thought that counted. As evening fell, I prepared for a night out with Rose. I spent more time than I had in a while curling my blond locks and staring at myself in the mirror. Sometimes, I struggled to reconcile the changes I saw from the person I was before Mom got sick with the one currently reflected back to me. I'd never been a high-maintenance person, but I used to put more thought and effort into my appearance. While caring for Mom, I was too tired to bother. I always pulled my hair back into a messy bun to keep it out of my face, and I never bothered with makeup. It was strange, almost luxurious, to be sitting in front of the mirror, pampering myself.

At the same time, my skin prickled like I had something more pressing to do. It was a familiar feeling, one that had never fully gone away even after Mom died. Perhaps it would fade with time. Or perhaps the sense of foreboding, that perpetual waiting for the other shoe to drop, was something that would remain with me for the rest of my life.

As I finished applying lip gloss, the doorbell rang. I slid the makeup back into the drawer of the vanity and went to greet Rose. When I opened the door, I stumbled back at the sight of not only my future sister-in-law but a gaggle of my high school friends as well.

"Surprise!" they all cried out, their arms thrown open and their smiles wide.

"What the—" I gasped. "What are you all doing here?"

"I thought you could use a girls' night!" Rose exclaimed. "Steven helped me reach out to some old pals. They wanted to see you."

I surveyed the group, noting they were all dressed to the nines. My hand nervously smoothed the simple black dress I had picked out. Was I underdressed? But there weren't any upscale restaurants or bars in the tiny town of Cedar Haven. Definitely nothing resembling a night club.

"Well?" Rose pressed, her voice tinged with impatience. "What are you waiting for? Grab your coat and let's go!" That was followed by a chorus of agreement from the rest of the girls. I laughed and did as instructed.

An unfamiliar minivan sat in the driveway, and as I climbed in, I stifled another laugh at the haphazard attempt to clean up crumbs. Trudy was the only one of my friends who was married and had a kid. I recalled Trudy had said her son—Davey, was it?—had just turned six months old.

Leslie Wilson climbed in beside me as Trudy and Rose took over the front seat. Kristin Donnovan and Toccara Jenson were already buckling up in the back row. When I turned to look at them, they gave hesitant smiles.

"It's good to see you," Toccara said, the overhead light from the car highlighting her dark curls. Her deep-crimson coat brought out the reddish undertones in her complexion.

"Seriously, Lanie, it's been ages!" Kristin piped up beside her. Her rich black braids fell forward as she leaned closer. "How long are you home?"

"Not long, I'm afraid," I said. "Just long enough to settle my mom's affairs."

"Where will you go once that's done?" Leslie asked, her blue eyes curious as she turned and joined the conversation.

"I have a job waiting for me in California."

"And a boyfriend as well!" Rose quipped from the front seat. Her sleek black hair was pulled back into a low bun and secured with two sticks.

"Are you still with that guy from school?" Trudy asked as she turned the key in the ignition. Her hooded brown eyes met mine in the rearview.

"Yes, I'm still with James. We're getting a place together in LA," I said, smoothing my hair. In the meantime, James was crashing with some friends. He'd promised to wait until after I returned from Cedar Haven to look for a place.

"He was at your mom's funeral, wasn't he?" Kristin asked.

I nodded, swallowing around the sudden lump in my throat. With a shake of my head, I dispelled the memory. Not tonight. My friends had rallied to take me out and show me a good time, and I refused to let sad thoughts intrude on our fun.

"We'll just have to make the most of the time we have with you." Toccara's wide smile was warm, but it didn't quite touch her eyes. Guilt needled in my belly, knowing how terrible I had been at keeping in touch with my friends. They'd stopped by when I was home caring for Mom, usually with groceries or takeout. I'd lost count of how many casseroles Trudy had made. But I couldn't bring myself to answer their calls while at school. Compartmentalizing was the only way I'd been able to cope.

"I'm sorry I've been MIA this last year," I said. "But I'm sure I'll be back to visit."

"She'll be here for the wedding," Rose insisted, her small dark eyes sparkling as her cheeks brightened.

The car filled with oohs and aahs as we traveled along the dark highway out of town. I squinted out the window, searching for any hint of where we were going. Giving up, I refocused on the conversation occurring around me.

"When's the big day?" Trudy asked.

"September. It's usually a slower time for me at the clinic, and we'll be back from our honeymoon right before flu season." Rose's contagious laugh filled the car, prompting everyone else to join in.

Trudy slowed the car and turned onto a side road, causing me to peer curiously out the window. I still didn't recognize what little I could see of the scenery in the darkness.

"Where are we going?" I finally asked, trying to keep the apprehension from my voice.

The girls all exchanged conspiratorial glances. When no one volunteered any information, I racked my brain, trying to think of long-forgotten places I'd heard of in the surrounding area. Suddenly, the dark road gave way to the brilliant lights of a city, and I recognized where we were.

"We're going to the National Harbor?" I asked. Of all the possibilities, that wasn't one I'd considered. It was like a mini DC but without the long drive and expensive parking.

"They have quite a few nightclubs," Leslie explained with another conspiratorial look around the car. "We thought you should understand what you'll be leaving behind once you move out west."

"They've really built it up since I was last here," I murmured. The city seemed entirely out of place, caught between the river and the quiet suburbs, like the Emerald City at the end of the yellow brick road.

Trudy pulled into a parking garage, and we all filed out of her minivan. Toccara and Leslie linked arms with me, pulling me toward the sidewalk, as the rest of the girls filled in behind us. I was grateful for the pressure on my arms, as it allowed me to take everything in without worrying about tripping on a dip in the sidewalk.

I'd been there once or twice before when it was first built. The Gaylord Hotel had an ice show every year around Christmastime, and my parents had taken Steven and me before they split up. We had also gone ice skating and spent some time shopping around the town.

The group headed in the direction of Bobby McKey's, a dueling-piano bar, and I relaxed for the first time that evening. Seattle had a similar piano bar my friends and I enjoyed visiting. I smiled as the promise of an evening filled with laughter, drinks, and music lifted my spirits.

When we entered the bar, I blinked upon seeing they'd reserved a table. How long had they been planning this evening? I took a seat between Toccara and Rose. Leslie sat across from me at the round table with Kristen and Trudy beside her. I looked around, taking in each of my friends and the changes I had missed. Leslie's mousy-brown hair was shorter than I remembered, cut just past her chin. Kristen appeared to have lost weight, and her arms had more definition, like she had been hitting the gym. Trudy's features had softened from her recent pregnancy; the angles of her face were rounded. An air of wealth surrounded Toccara, from her perfectly manicured nails to her designer handbag. Her new business must be booming.

"Thank you all," I said. "Rose was right. I needed this."

Their faces lit up around the table, filling the void I had struggled with for so long. The moment was interrupted when the waitress came over to get our orders. While the show hadn't started yet, the air filled with anticipation as more people filtered into the club.

"Tell us more about your boyfriend," Trudy said. "I met him briefly at the funeral, but we didn't get a chance to talk."

"James has been amazing this last year," I said. Not wanting to worry anyone, I rushed on, forcing excitement I didn't feel into my voice. "He flew here right after graduation and stayed with me until Mom passed. I don't know what I would have done without him."

"So you guys are moving in together?" Rose asked. "Does that mean he already has a job lined up?"

"He got a position at a marketing firm based in LA right after he graduated and started at the end of last summer," I confirmed. "They have a branch in Seattle, and he worked there while I finished my last semester."

Our drinks arrived, and I took a long sip of the fruity cocktail. If the conversation continued to focus on my relationship, I would need the fortification.

"Will we hear wedding bells in your near future?" Toccara teased, stirring her frozen concoction with a straw.

An image of Nate flashed before my eyes when Toccara said "wedding," but it disappeared the moment I blinked. What was that? Everyone stared at me, and my cheeks flushed scarlet as I tried to articulate a response.

"Oooh, she's blushing!" Kristen exclaimed. "That means yes!"

I shook my head. "No, er, I mean, we've, uh, talked about it." My voice shook as words failed me. My mind had just conjured an image of Nate, and I couldn't imagine what that meant.

"Maybe once you're back out west, he'll propose," Leslie said. "He probably doesn't want to overwhelm you with everything else that's going on."

Though I was grateful for the subject change, her comments put everyone at the table in a somber mood. Their eyes filled with sympathy and concern as they assessed me. I shifted uncomfortably. Maybe I should have played up the potential proposal more, even though it was hard to feign excitement.

"How are you really doing?" Toccara asked, her dark eyes searching my face.

"It's been... difficult," I admitted, sucking in a ragged breath. "Especially being home. Living in her house." I closed my eyes and twirled my hair around my finger. "Sometimes, I wake up and rush downstairs to check on her only to be reminded she's not there." I coughed a bitter laugh. "I even think sometimes I can still hear the beeping of her heart monitor."

A hand closed over mine, and I opened my eyes to see Rose. The other girls reached across the table, and soon my hand was completely covered with the loving touches of my friends.

"I can't imagine what you're going through," Trudy said. The other girls glanced at one another and nodded. I forced a smile. I was the only one of my friends to have lost a parent.

I shook out my curls. "But Steven and I have made a lot of progress, and I think it'll get easier when I'm not living there anymore."

"If you need a break, you're welcome to stay with me," Kristen offered.

"I just might take you up on that." I released their hands and waved, trying to dispel the somber mood. "Ugh, I'm sorry. I don't mean to be such a downer. Tonight's supposed to be fun!"

While my declaration was met with a chorus of cheers and enthusiastic nods, I didn't miss the concerned looks being exchanged by my friends. Luckily for me, the lights dimmed, and the show began.

The rest of the night passed in a blur. Listening to familiar songs played on pianos and hearing the crowd sing along allowed me to let go of all my stress and worry, even if just for one night. My friends and I danced, sang, and took full advantage of the fruity drinks offered at the bar. A bachelorette party was underway, and my heart stuttered at the idea that one day soon, I might celebrate my own pending nuptials. But it wasn't James's face I saw in the vision, and that unsettled me.

Near midnight, we left the bar. Trudy had offered to be the designated driver, and she led the way to the parking garage, where her minivan waited. Though tired, I felt like a weight had been lifted from my shoulders that evening, and I was glad I had gone out. I promised myself to do better at keeping in touch with that wonderful group of friends.

Trudy dropped me off first, and everyone climbed out of the car to give me a hug. Rose's was the tightest and the longest, as if she hoped to imbue me with all of her love and warmth to carry me through the night.

"By the way, the school system is having a fundraiser this week to provide the kids with supplies for second semester," Rose said. "It'd be great if you could come and help out."

"That sounds like a distraction," I teased. "But one I need. Text me the details, and I'll be there."

Rose smiled and nodded then hopped into the vehicle. While I hadn't thought about what it would feel like to go back to the empty house alone, as I waved a last goodbye to the girls, a wave of nausea came over me.

With a heavy sigh, I unlocked the door and flicked on the hallway light. The silence was deafening after the loud music of the bar. I set my purse down on the bench by the door and stepped out of my shoes. Trudging across the floor in my stockinged feet, I headed to the kitchen, flipping lights on my way as if I could block out the melancholy darkness waiting inside me.

I grabbed a bottle of water from the fridge and sank into a chair at the kitchen table. After pulling the cap off, I gulped it down. The last thing I needed tomorrow was a hangover. After I had swallowed half of the bottle, I pulled out my phone. A missed call appeared on the screen. I tapped the voicemail, and James's familiar voice filled the room.

"Hey, babe. It's been a while since I heard from you, so I thought I'd check in. Hope everything is going well. Call me. Love you."

It was too late to call, even with the West Coast being three hours behind. James was an early to bed, early to rise kind of guy, and I knew he would already be asleep. It was just as well. I couldn't shake my discomfort at what had happened when my friends mentioned marriage. While I wasn't ready to marry James, I'd thought that was because I wasn't ready to marry anyone.

But seeing Nate's face unsettled me. Coupled with my reaction to him holding my hand at lunch the other day, I clearly had some things to sort out before I spoke with James again. More importantly, I hoped to resolve my feelings by the time I next saw Nate, which, if I had my way, wouldn't be anytime soon.

Chapter Five

SUNDAY MORNING DAWNED MUCH TOO EARLY AFTER THE late night before. My phone chimed, waking me. With a groan, I rolled over and tapped to open a group text from Trudy, which gave details about the fundraiser Rose had mentioned. A semiannual event for the local schools, it included an auction, and they were seeking donations.

I rubbed my eyes then reread her message. Mom had a few items I thought might work. And Steven would be thrilled to get rid of some things, especially if they went to a good cause.

Hey, Trudy, I can donate some odds and ends of my mom's. Where should I meet you?

After climbing out of bed with my phone, I padded down to the kitchen in search of coffee. My water chugging had staved off a hangover, but I was still bleary-eyed and exhausted from being out so late. As the coffee brewed, my phone pinged again.

Awesome, Lanie! Can you stop by the high school this afternoon?

In one text, she'd reminded me of my lack of transportation. A glance outside confirmed the weather wasn't conducive to walking, and even if it had been, it would be quite a walk, as the school wasn't nearby. Besides, I would need help carrying everything.

Ping. I glanced down, and my stomach dropped.

Hey, Nate here. I need to drop off my contribution as well. Happy to pick you up on the way, Lanie.

I set my phone down and grabbed the mug, gulping down the scalding liquid and instantly regretting it. My throat burned, and for a moment, I thought I might be sick. But I yanked a chair out and slid into it, laying my head on my hands. The nausea passed, and I took another tentative sip of coffee. Still too hot, but the warmth and caffeine helped to wake up my brain.

What should I do? On the one hand, I needed a ride, and Nate's offer was more than gracious, though I suspected he felt obligated since my car was still in his shop.

On the other hand, my attempts to avoid Nate had so far been unsuccessful, and agreeing to a ride would be the equivalent of admitting defeat. How many more awkward conversations could one person be expected to survive?

I weighed my options. Rose and Steven were both off that day. However, they were planning to visit a caterer for a tasting. While they could likely drop me off on their way, I would be stuck at the school until they were finished, giving the universe ample opportunity to throw Nate in my face again. Perhaps it would be better to accept my fate and meet him willingly. Then I would avoid any surprises like the other day at lunch.

Torn over what to do, I picked up my coffee and stepped to the window. My eyes swept over the backyard, taking in the shortening shadows as the sun rose in the sky. A familiar flash of red caught my attention, and I leaned toward the glass. The little cardinal was back, perched on the railing and staring right at me.

"Am I crazy to see him again?" I asked. The bird flitted closer and settled on a branch right outside the window. I'd never seen a cardinal so close before. The distinctive black dots resembling freckles were clear near its beak, confirming it was the same cardinal I'd seen before.

"It feels like a bad idea," I continued as the little bird flitted closer to the window.

"Maybe I should say no and take my chances with Steven and Rose." The bird cocked its head and chirped. Was it my imagination, or was there a hint of disapproval in the bird's song? Shaking my head, I tried to snap out of it, but something about the tilt of the bird's head and the way it fluffed its wings was eerily reminiscent of a look Mom used to give me.

Before I could process the resemblance, the bird flew away, and I was left disquieted. I ran a hand over my face. Great, I was talking to birds. Was I going crazy? I returned to the table and drained the last of my coffee. The weird resemblance between the cardinal and Mom meant nothing. My confusion over Nate was causing me to wish my mom was there. That was all. With that justification, I rinsed out the mug in the sink.

As I picked up my phone, Nate's message stared at me, waiting, mocking. With a sigh, I typed a message back, hoping I wouldn't live to regret it.

Sounds good. Thanks, Nate.

After confirming what time he would pick me up, I headed upstairs to get ready. About an hour later, I was sitting in the living room, awaiting his arrival and trying to ignore my pounding heart. How ridiculous. It'd been six years since we'd broken up. Shouldn't I have been over it by then? I'd thought I was, but the memory of the spark I felt when we'd touched haunted me. What was wrong with me?

The doorbell rang, pulling me from my thoughts. I pasted on a smile and opened the door, but one look at him caused the breath to catch in my throat. He wore a black leather jacket and jeans, his dark hair combed neatly back, still damp from a shower. His clothing accentuated his muscles much more than the bulky winter coat he had on the other day, confirming my earlier assessment he had filled out significantly since high school.

"Morning," he said with a shy smile. His eyes swept quickly over me, and I hated how pleased I was when he raised an appreciative eyebrow.

Nate offered his arm. "Ready?"

As I'll ever be. I grabbed my bag of donations and accepted his arm, carefully stepping out over the frozen ground.

"Thanks for giving me a ride," I said as I slid into his car.

"Figured it was the least I could do, since it's my fault you're stranded," he replied with an impish grin.

See? Obligation. Nothing more. Some of the tension in my shoulders eased, but I still had an awkward ride ahead. I glanced at him out of the corner of my eye. He seemed in a much better mood. Maybe it wouldn't be so bad after all.

"More like Steven's," I said with a shrug. "If he or my dad had bothered to drive the car once in a while, it wouldn't have so many issues."

"Can't argue with you there." Nate put the car into gear and backed down the driveway. As we pulled onto the street, my neighbor, Cassandra, went out to pick up her newspaper. I waved and blinked when Cassandra's wrinkly face broke into a smile as she waved back.

"Steven and I were convinced she was a witch when we were kids," I said.

"She's certainly a character," Nate agreed. "Whenever she comes to the shop, she brings a homemade gift. Sometimes, it's cookies, but then others, it's some sort of satchel filled with herbs to ward off evil spirits, bring good luck, or help find love." His cheeks flushed at his last comment. "Not sure any of it has worked for me."

"What? No hot dates?" I teased as Nate's blush deepened. "I find that hard to believe."

He glanced at me before turning his attention back to the road. "Believe what you want." His voice had an edge to it. Maybe I had gone too far. Just what I needed, to make things more uncomfortable.

"I'm sorry. I didn't mean anything," I murmured.

"Sorry. I know you didn't." Nate sighed. "Sore subject."

I stared at my hands, unsure of what to say. Part of me wanted to ask why he'd called it a sore subject. After all, he broke up with me, not the other way around. While he'd sworn that there was no one else, I'd often wondered if he'd lied to spare my feelings. Though I knew I shouldn't care, I itched to know if he was involved with anyone. But a huge elephant sat in the car between us, and neither of us wanted to be first to address it. The longer the silence dragged on, the more desperate I became to fill it.

"What made you decide to work at the shop?" I finally asked, praying I'd chosen a safe subject. "You always talked about being a vet."

"Well"—Nate's shoulders visibly relaxed—"I enjoy working on cars. And you know my dad wanted me to take over. When I finished my associate degree at the community college, I switched to a trade school to study automotive technology." He shot me a look. "Besides, I didn't have a lot of money, and not going to a West Coast school saved me a bundle on student loans."

Heat crept up the back of my neck. We were treading dangerously close to that elephant again. I thought fast, hoping to steer the conversation back to safe subjects.

"I'm sure your dad was happy to keep the business in the family."

"Of course he was." Nate rolled his eyes. "He wasn't planning on retiring immediately. I was going to transition into the role over time. But then he had his heart attack." He shook his head. "Following old dreams didn't seem as important anymore."

I turned toward the window and choked on a sudden onset of tears. I understood what he meant. Sometimes, the line between my dreams and what Mom wanted for me blurred. Guilt stirred inside my chest, and I snuck a quick glance at him. I wondered what Mom would say about my spending time with him. I didn't really need to ask because

Mom had made her feelings about Nate clear. Her words echoed in my head. *Promise me you won't settle here. Promise me you'll build your life as far away from this town as you can. Don't make my mistakes, Lanie.*

"You said you made your peace with my mom," I blurted out suddenly, forgetting my plan to stick to safe subjects. "What did you mean by that?"

"Nothing," he responded a little too quickly. He meticulously pulled into the parking lot of the school and avoided my gaze. "It's not important."

Before I could press the issue, he climbed out of the car and moved around it to open my door. His chivalry distracted me. When I stepped onto the pavement, he offered his arm again, and I took it gratefully, sliding the bag of donations onto my shoulder. The parking lot was plowed and salted, but the temperature had dropped below freezing the night before. I suspected black ice blended in with the pavement, and the last thing I needed was to slip and fall.

"What are you donating?" I inclined my head toward the folder in his hands.

"Coupons," he said with a wry grin. "Free oil changes, tire rotations, stuff like that." He nodded at my bag. "What about you?"

"Some old knickknacks of my mom's that Steven and I don't want and that don't have much value anyway."

When we reached the entrance, Nate held the door open, and we walked to the auditorium. The buzz of activity grew louder as we drew near, and a wave of nostalgia came over me. Nate and I had spent most of our relationship there. Over in the back corner, Nate had asked me to be his girlfriend. And the stage was where we'd shared our first kiss. I tried not to focus on those memories, but as I looked around the room, they were impossible to ignore. Nate tensed beside me. Was he remembering our time together as well? I shook my head and forced myself to focus. Trudy had taken over the stage and was directing people left and right to set up. School was closed for the Martin Luther King holiday the next day, which made that the perfect time to host the fundraiser, right before the new semester started.

"Lanie! Nate! Thank you so much for coming," Trudy exclaimed when she saw us. She rushed over and gave us each a brief hug. "What'd you bring me?"

Nate handed her his folder. "Coupons, as requested."

Trudy flipped through it quickly and beamed. "Thanks, doll." She turned to me.

"I've got some old figurines of my mom's and a few other trinkets that may spark some interest." I pulled out a few statuettes. "Unfortunately, I couldn't bring much because we have to wait for the appraiser, but I thought this would help."

"It's perfect," Trudy assured me. "I'll set these up over here. Feel free to have a look around."

"Do you mind?" I asked Nate. When he gave me a questioning gaze, I hurried on. "We don't have to stay if you have somewhere to be." I didn't want him to get the wrong idea.

"I'm free as a bird." Nate gave me a slow smile that made my traitorous heart skip a beat. "We can stay as long as you like."

I wandered around the different tables, noting Trudy had been busy that morning, setting up the area for bids. Homemade crafts were on one table, jewelry on another, and various other businesses had donated coupons like Nate did. Bea's Diner had donated a free dinner date, complete with a three-course meal, prime seating, and bottomless sodas. A laugh bubbled out of my throat before I could stop it. Nate had won a similar date for us during our senior year. We'd gone together on Valentine's Day, and it had been a fun evening, despite the cheesiness of the location.

"Something funny?" Nate asked.

"Just remembering a simpler time." I pointed at the coupon.

"Right. That was a fun night. They tried to make the diner seem like fine dining, but they didn't quite pull it off."

I looked up at him and saw the same wistfulness that filled my chest. My breath caught in my throat, and I spun away. The elephant had returned.

"Nate, it's nice to see you," a voice said behind us. We turned to find a petite older woman with a plump face and salt-and-pepper hair.

"Mrs. Carlisle, what a pleasant surprise. What brings you to school on a Sunday?" Nate asked.

"Thought I'd help with the fundraiser one last time before I retire," she said. "Ah, Lanie, how are you, dear?"

"I'm well, Mrs. Carlisle." *Oh no.*

"I'm glad I ran into you," Mrs. Carlisle continued. "I understand you've finished your degree in special education."

I gave a wary nod. I knew where the conversation was going, and my stomach churned with dread. A quick glance at Nate's clenched jaw confirmed he was following it to its natural conclusion as well.

"The school would like to hire my replacement before I leave." Mrs. Carlisle's kind smile only increased the nausea building within me. "I'm not sure if you've heard, but I'm retiring at the end of the year. Are you staying in Cedar Haven? If so, you should think about applying. I think you'd be a perfect fit."

I gulped, trying to suppress the panic rising in my chest. Nate refused to meet my gaze. *Awesome.* Yet another sore subject between us, though I couldn't understand why he cared whether I stayed. I thought he'd accepted my reasoning at lunch the other day. Apparently not.

"I'm actually not staying," I squeaked. *Ugh. Get a grip.* I cleared my throat. "I have a job waiting for me in California."

"Ah," Mrs. Carlisle said, her face falling "Congratulations on the position. We'll be sad to see you go, but I understand." She forced a smile. "It was lovely to see you both." After giving my shoulder a brief pat, she turned and walked away.

"I know you have a job waiting," Nate said, his tone clipped. "But an interview wouldn't kill you."

"What's the point when I've already accepted another position?"

I demanded with my hands on my hips. But my heart flip-flopped in my chest. I didn't want to have that conversation, well... ever, but especially not there, not in *that* room.

Nate finally looked at me, and his warring emotions were clear on his face. He took a deep breath and closed his eyes. When he opened them, they were calmer, though something still raged behind them.

"It's none of my business, of course," he began. "I just think you could do so much more here for kids who don't have the same opportunities as the ones at the school in LA."

I turned away and resisted the urge to rub my temples. He sounded like Dad, and it took a great deal of effort not to rail at him as I had my father the other night. Besides, as tired as I was of the argument, it wouldn't be fair to take my aggravation out on Nate. He wasn't aware of the unfair pressure my father was putting on me.

"I'm sorry," Nate said when I didn't respond. "It's not my place."

"It's okay." I sighed. "You're not the first person to make this argument. You probably won't be the last." I gave him a weak smile. "Are you ready to go?"

A shadow passed over Nate's face, but it was gone as quickly as it had come. Without a word, he nodded and offered his arm again, and we walked out of the school together. I reflected on the last time we'd left the school arm in arm like that. It was just after graduation, and I thought the world lay at our feet. I'd been so naïve. And though it had been years since our breakup, I couldn't ignore the overwhelming sense of loss that came over me as we crossed the parking lot.

"Are you okay?" he asked when we reached his car. The concern in his eyes caught me off guard. Again, I wondered why he cared.

"Just... thinking."

"It's weird, being back here." Nate stared behind us at the school.

"That's one way of putting it," I murmured. My heart ached, and all I wanted to do was return home and lick the wounds that had reopened after spending time with Nate. He might have said the words, but I knew that my decision to leave him for college had been the catalyst for our breakup. I was a fool to think we would make it. My mother was right. A sharp pain, like a knife, twisted in my gut.

He looked at me sharply. My face must have betrayed my thoughts because he rounded the car and tentatively wrapped his arms around me. The movement felt wrong and right all at the same time. Without thinking, I slid my arms around his waist, and he tightened his hold. He smelled the same, a mixture of Old Spice and Ivory soap.

"I'm sorry, Nate," I choked out, unsure whether he would understand my apology or where my memories had ended up.

"It's not your fault," he assured me, his hand stroking my hair.

I pulled back to see his face. "How can you say that? I'm the one who broke us."

As Nate shook his head, his eyes betrayed an emotion I couldn't place. I frowned and leaned closer. When he dropped his gaze, it hit me. He was hiding something.

"What is it?"

"Nothing."

I reached up and held his face in my hands, forcing him to look at me. "Tell me."

"It's nothing. Just forget it."

"Does this have to do with my mother?"

"Lanie." He said my name like a caress, his voice pleading. "Please, just let it go."

I held his face for a moment longer, ignoring the warmth coursing through my hands. When I released him, he sighed, whether in relief that I'd dropped it or because he felt that same warmth, I didn't know. I was also afraid to find out.

"Fine, I'll drop it... for now," I said, glaring up at him. And I meant it. Sooner or later, I would make him tell me whatever he was hiding, especially if it had to do with my mom.

He stepped back from me and opened the door. With one last glare in his direction, I climbed into the passenger seat, and he drove me home.

~

The next day, I lucked out in not needing to rely on Nate for a ride. Trudy herself picked me up for the fundraiser, and I vacillated between enjoying myself and wanting to hide. Between the condolences for my loss and the questions about my plans, I longed for the obscurity I'd had in Seattle, where I could walk through a crowd and disappear.

Of course, the one person I wished to talk to most avoided me for the entire event. Nate attended the fundraiser as well, but he was always one step ahead of me. Whenever I started to approach him, he would find an excuse to be somewhere else. Was he afraid I would start asking more questions about whatever he was hiding? Or was it as painful and awkward for him to be around me as it was for me to be around him? On the one hand, I appreciated that he gave me space, but on the other, his avoidance hurt more than I wanted to admit.

When I woke the day after the fundraiser, I had another visit from the cardinal. I'd thought by that point, with the lack of food in the yard, it would have moved on. But there it was, as bright and curious as ever, perched on the back railing, gazing in at me. It stayed longer that time, watching me go through my morning routine, but we were both startled when my phone rang.

I recognized the number from the shop. "Hello?"

"Hey, Lanie, it's Nate. Your mom's car is ready."

"Okay, great," I said with enthusiasm. I would no longer have to rely on the kindness of others to get around. But then reality hit, and I chewed on my bottom lip. How was I going to pick up the car?

"I can come pick you up if you'd like," Nate said as if reading my mind.

Ugh, another awkward ride with Nate. Just what I didn't need. Then again, maybe that was a good thing. He couldn't avoid me in the car. And I was tired of dancing around the elephant between us. I was stuck there for as long as it took to sell the house and settle the estate. I really didn't want to walk on eggshells every time I ran into him, which, in our tiny town, was sure to be often.

"You sure? I don't want to interrupt your workday."

"It's no problem. Is now a good time?"

"Yeah, that's fine. Thanks, Nate."

"Be there soon."

I got ready to go, vowing that I wouldn't let him weasel his way out of a difficult conversation again. We were both adults. There was no reason we couldn't at least tolerate each other.

When he arrived, I was waiting on the front porch. He jumped out of his car and opened the door, but I was already there. I didn't want to be distracted by his chivalry. With a curt nod, I slid into the car. He hesitated outside before climbing into the driver's seat.

"Thanks for the ride," I said.

"No problem. I'm sorry the repairs took so long."

I shrugged. "It's fine. Having no transportation gave me time to sort through my mom's things, and I've made a lot of progress."

"That's good to hear."

"I saw you at the fundraiser," I blurted, my voice accusatory.

He shot me a wary look. "I saw you too."

"Why didn't you say hello?"

Nate blew out a breath and ran a hand through his hair. "I wasn't sure if you wanted me to."

"Just because you're keeping something from me doesn't mean we can't be friends," I shot back.

He winced, and my resolve faltered. What right did I have to demand he tell me his secrets? Was my rabid curiosity really enough for me to justify treating him this way? What if whatever happened was something deeply personal? I wasn't being fair.

"I'm sorry," he replied before I could retract my words. "I shouldn't have avoided you." He braked at the stoplight and turned and looked at me. "I wasn't sure where we'd left things, and I didn't want to upset you."

"You could have just asked." I raised an eyebrow.

The light turned green, and he returned his attention to the road. "Next time, I will. I promise."

"I'm sorry too."

His eyebrows shot up. "What do you have to be sorry for?"

"Your relationship with my mother is none of my business," I said, though it pained me to do so. If Mom had wanted me to know whatever transpired between them, she would have told me. "I shouldn't have pressured you."

His throat moved as he swallowed, and his hands tightened on the steering wheel. Curiosity raged within me, but I pressed my lips together, mentally repeating the mantra that it wasn't my business.

"What will you do with your newfound freedom?" he asked in a clear attempt at a subject change.

I decided the gracious thing would be to follow his lead. "Not much. The appraiser is coming tomorrow to look over everything. Steven expects that will take most of the day." I glanced out the windshield. "And then I still need to find movers."

"No luck with your search?"

I shook my head. "Everywhere is so expensive. I didn't think it would be this difficult."

"The offer still stands for the guys and me to come by and help."

"I appreciate that," I said. And I did, but if we could barely get through a short errand without arguing, I didn't hold out much hope of doing so for an entire day. "But I'm sure I'll figure something out."

"All right," he said slowly. "But it might alleviate some of your stress to have that out of the way."

I hated that he was right. The house couldn't sell until we moved the furniture we were keeping and staged the rest. If I had any hope of getting back to the West Coast in the near future, I needed to get that over with and soon.

"You have a point."

"But?"

He always could see right through me.

I blew out a breath. "Won't it be awkward?"

He barked out a laugh that warmed my chest. "More awkward than it's been so far?"

With a grin, I nodded. "Fine. You win. If you guys are free, we're planning the move for Monday."

He pulled into the parking lot of the shop and slid the car into a free space. "I'll check with the guys and let you know, but I don't think it'll be a problem." He walked me to the building and held the door. "Sam will take care of you. I'll be in my office." Then he scurried away without another word.

I stared after him. While we still hadn't addressed the elephant, I considered the conversation a success. At least some if not all of the air had been cleared, and as I approached Sam, my steps were lighter.

Chapter Six

The next few days flew by. After the appraiser spent the better part of Wednesday at the house, Steven and I prepped as much as we could for the estate sale. He stopped by most nights to go through the rest of Mom's belongings. My brother treated the process much more clinically than I did, and sometimes, I wondered if he even noticed I was in the room.

Sunday night, Steven came over to remove his share of the smaller items. We sat in the living room, packing up boxes of old books, photo albums, and a few trinkets.

"Do you remember our last trip to Disney before Mom and Dad split up?" Steven asked as he flipped through old photos.

"When we all spent a day or so in the hotel, suffering from heat exhaustion?" I shook my head. "Who could forget?"

"I know it wasn't the best experience," Steven said, his voice low. "But it's one of my favorite memories."

I stared at him as if he'd grown two heads. "Seriously? Why?"

He shrugged as he flipped another page. "Hindsight, I suppose."

"Hindsight?"

When he looked at me, his hazel eyes were filled with sadness. "We didn't know then it would be our last family vacation." He looked at the album. "On the one hand, I wish it had turned out differently so we would have a better memory to share. But on the other, I think the fact it was so awful made it more meaningful, in a way. Instead of spending day after day trudging through the parks and standing in endless lines, we were forced to rest and spend time together with little to distract us."

I moved over to the couch and settled in beside him. Tucking my knees under me, I glanced at the photos. There was one of the four of us, standing in front of Cinderella's Castle. My parents had Mickey ears, Steven had bought a ridiculous Goofy hat, and I wore a tiara. The happy smiles hid the darkness beneath the surface. My parents' marriage had been on the brink of divorce for years. In some ways, that vacation was their last-ditch effort to stay together. In others, it seemed a fitting farewell.

"We did play a lot of board games," I said.

"And I've hated Monopoly ever since," Steven grumbled.

I giggled. "That's just because Dad is ruthless." Leaning back against the couch, I stared at the ceiling. "But no worse than Mom at Uno."

"Ugh! I forgot about that." Steven smacked his forehead and groaned. "I swear she hoarded those draw-four cards. And she always threw them down—"

"Right when one of us would yell 'Uno,'" Steven and I said simultaneously then laughed.

As he resumed packing the photo albums for Rose to look through for a wedding collage, I continued to mentally reminisce about that last vacation. Steven was right. Despite how awful it had been to get sick at Walt Disney World, that vacation had briefly made me believe everything would be okay. My parents had continued to try for another year before they finally separated.

"You know how you said you didn't know why Mom chose you

as the executor when you first got back?" Steven's voice broke into my thoughts.

"Yeah?"

He leaned back against the arm of the couch and looked at me. "I think she knew you needed to be here."

I raised an eyebrow. "For what?"

"Closure."

"What do you mean?"

With a deep breath, he continued, "Even though you were here for Mom when she was sick, I think the two of you tiptoed around a lot of issues. You two used to fight all the time. You even moved out and lived with Dad for your last semester of high school." He glanced at his hands. "But when she got sick, that stopped. Things changed. You dropped everything to come help her."

"She needed me," I protested.

Steven held up a hand. "I'm not finished."

I crossed my arms with a frown, unsure where the conversation was going.

"You were right to come home. She did need you, and I'm sorry I wasn't more helpful back then. It was difficult to visit while I clerked in Baltimore, but I wish I had done more." He fixed me with a probing look. "But come on, Lanie. Can you honestly tell me you and Mom hashed everything out before she died? When you first came home, I could see you were holding back, biting your tongue in favor of keeping the peace. Like if you bottled up all your anger at some of her comments, it would prevent her from getting worse."

Worrying my lip, I considered his words. I thought I'd hidden my emotions better than that but perhaps not. If my brother had seen through me so easily, did that mean Mom had as well?

"I just... I thought we'd have more time," I whispered. "I thought, once she got better, we'd—" A single tear slid down my cheek. "But she—she never—"

Steven pulled me into his arms as I struggled not to lose it.

"Shhh, it's okay, Lanie. I know." He rubbed my back as his voice cracked. "We all thought we'd have more time with her."

It was the first time since the funeral that I had seen my brother grieve. My arms tightened around him, and I hoped he felt as comforted by my embrace as I was by his. He was, after all, the only other person in the world who could truly understand what I was going through because of the loss we shared.

When we finally broke apart, red-eyed and sniffling, Steven gave me a watery grin. "This is why I wish you would stay in Cedar Haven. I can't bear to lose you too."

"I'm moving to California, not dying," I tried to joke, but my voice caught in my throat. I'd been so busy thinking of how hard it was for me to be home, but I hadn't stopped to think about what my brother was going through. While he had seemed to be doing well, maybe it was just a façade he put on to get through the day.

He snorted. "You know what I mean. It hasn't been the same while you've been gone these last six months. I missed you."

I nodded, not trusting myself to speak. I'd missed him too. The distance I gained when I returned to school helped push my grief to the back of my mind, but it'd been hard to be away from my family.

"You can always come visit me in LA," I said. "We could try out Disneyland, see how it compares."

"It won't. It's too small," Steven teased. "But I'm sure Rose and I will make it out there after the wedding craziness is over." He stretched and stood. "Speaking of, I should probably get on my way. She's been chomping at the bit to get these albums."

There was an unopened box on the floor by the couch. "What's in that one?"

Steven shrugged. "It looks like an old file box. Probably has old bills and whatnot. You can put it in a closet for now, and we'll take a look at it later."

As I helped Steven carry the boxes to his car, I couldn't stop thinking about what he'd said. Had Mom made me executor to force me back here to deal with everything we'd left unsaid? Was I being selfish by wanting to put this small town in the rearview? But Mom made me promise to leave, to never settle here. If she changed her mind, wouldn't she have told me?

~

I woke up the next morning with my heart in my throat. I went downstairs and grabbed a mug from the cabinet. The little sleep I'd had was filled with confusing dreams about Nate. With the mug in hand, I stepped over to the back window. My cardinal friend was flitting along the railing.

"Hello there." I waved. The cardinal cocked its head at me, displaying those familiar black dots near its beak. "Today is a big day. We're getting the house ready to sell."

The cardinal chirped and fluffed its wings as if it approved. Maybe it was hopeful the new owners would be better about filling the bird feeders. After he flew away, I finished my coffee then headed upstairs to get dressed.

When I returned, Steven was already at the kitchen table, waiting.

"Ready for this?" Steven asked with a grin.

"Ready as I'll ever be," I muttered. "What time will they be here?"

Steven checked his watch. "Any minute now."

I nodded absently as I went into the dining room and grabbed some newspaper. There were a few things I still needed to box up that I planned to keep. After grabbing a few of the moving boxes Steven had brought from his office, I slipped into Mom's room, wrapped some of Mom's treasured knickknacks, and placed them carefully into the box. The doorbell rang, and Steven's voice drifted up the stairs as he greeted the men. Packing up these items was the perfect excuse to be upstairs when they arrived. I needed a moment to compose myself before I saw Nate.

It bothered me more than it should have that he was hiding

something. Of course, he was under no obligation to tell me anything. I kept telling myself it wasn't my business, but when he'd mentioned making peace with Mom, he'd said it so matter-of-factly I couldn't help being curious. I wondered what had been said between them and when. Was it before Mom got sick?

As I lifted a small carousel horse replica, I sensed a presence behind me. I spun around and found Nate standing in the doorway, watching me with a peculiar expression on his face. When our eyes met, he straightened and ran a hand through his hair.

"Sorry, I didn't mean to startle you," he said. "Steven sent me up here to break down your mother's bed." He nodded to the stripped queen bed against the back wall.

"I can move this stuff out of here so I won't be in your way." I hastily stacked the remaining items into my arms to move to another room.

He touched my shoulder gently, and the wave of unexpected heat tingling down my arm almost caused me to drop everything. I glanced at him, and his face softened with the sweet smile that used to take my breath away.

"You're fine, Lanie. You're not in my way."

As I slowly faced him, the air separating us crackled with electricity. Gazing at him, I watched as the warmth in his eyes gave way to a fierce heat. My heartbeat quickened, and suddenly, I felt like I was sixteen again: a mix of nervousness, elation, and desire making me tongue-tied. Drawing a ragged breath, I realized I'd stopped breathing.

Nate blinked, and when his eyes refocused, the fire in them was gone. He reached out with a half smile and took a couple of items from my arms before setting them on top of the dresser.

"Do you need help with these?" he asked absently as he lifted a figurine.

I stared at the familiar item, a single dolphin jumping a wave. It was the last Christmas present Nate had given me before we broke up. I hadn't seen it in years. What was it doing here, among my mother's things?

I took it from him without thinking. "Where did you find this?"

"With the rest of the stuff you were wrapping," he replied, raising an eyebrow as he waved his hand over the assortment of knickknacks.

"I thought I lost it," I murmured as I turned the dolphin over in my hands. Such little dust had accumulated on it, almost as if it had been lovingly cared for in my absence. I wondered how it had gotten there and why I hadn't noticed it while sorting through everything before.

Nate was still staring at me, frowning, though whether from confusion or because he recognized the figurine as well, I didn't know.

"Do you remember this?" I asked.

"Remember it?" Nate scoffed. "Do you know how long I agonized over what to get you?" He shook his head with a rueful smile. "I went to so many stores. I looked at jewelry, electronics, clothing, just trying to find the perfect present. But when I walked into that Hallmark store and saw this, I knew I'd never find anything better."

"It really was perfect," I agreed, turning it over again. "I've always loved dolphins."

That Christmas, I gave him a football jersey of his favorite team. We hadn't been able to spend the day together due to plans with our respective families, but he had texted me a photo of his family in front of the tree, and he wore that jersey. My heart ached for that simpler time.

A throat cleared behind Nate, and both our heads shot up to find Steven standing in the doorway. I set the dolphin down and took a step back.

"I thought you came up here to break down the bed," Steven said, struggling to keep an amused grin from his face.

Nate nodded. "I was helping Lanie wrap up these breakable items. I didn't want to risk knocking anything over."

Steven quirked an eyebrow. "Mm-hmm, well, we need you downstairs when you're done." His assessing gaze made my cheeks burn before he turned and left us alone again.

"I really should move this stuff to another room," I hedged as I gathered the figurines once more. "It sounds like they need you downstairs."

Nate stopped my hand with his, and that familiar spark hit me all over again. "They can wait, Lanie. I'm happy to help." He picked up a figure of a little girl in a green dress and laid it in some newspaper then carefully wrapped it before placing it in the box.

Torn between wanting some distance and not wanting to offend him, I suppressed a sigh as I grabbed a sheet of newspaper and wrapped another item. I couldn't deny the packing was more efficient with two pairs of hands, and before I knew it, we were finished. Without speaking, we moved over to the bed, lifted the mattress, rested it against the wall, and followed up with the box spring. Then I watched as Nate knelt at the frame and unscrewed the bars.

His hands moved deftly as he worked, reminding me of how they felt on my shoulder. The spark that ripped through my body confused and thrilled me. But I didn't understand why I was having all those feelings whenever he was around. I've heard that old saying that people never forgot their first love, but it felt like more than just never forgetting him. The connection went much deeper, almost as if old feelings I had buried deep within for years were reawakening.

"Penny for your thoughts?" Nate's voice broke through my reverie, and I jumped. Not trusting myself to speak, I forced a smile and shook my head, hoping to hide the guilt churning in my stomach.

"I saw Mrs. Carlisle again," Nate said, his eyes flicking to mine briefly. "They're having a hard time finding a teacher to replace her."

"I'm sorry to hear that," I said flatly. All the warmth from a moment ago evaporated. I stood and walked over to the mattress before picking up one end. "We should get this downstairs."

A shadow passed briefly over Nate's face, but he nodded and went to the other side.

"After you," he said brusquely, causing my heart to sink a little. I didn't mean to blow him off, but I really wasn't in the mood for another conversation about staying there.

We carried the mattress, box spring, and bed frame downstairs to the space Steven had left for it. Then I ran upstairs to pack more items and get away from Nate. Whatever old feelings I was having weren't enough to keep me there, so there was no point in even entertaining them.

Hours later, I finally finished packing the last of my mother's knickknacks and headed downstairs to check on their progress. The couch was the only furniture remaining, as we had plans to donate it, but everything else was gone. They'd set up Mom's bed on the opposite side of the living room from the couch, right under the spot where the TV used to be. Steven and Nate must have removed it from the wall while I was upstairs.

I moved into the kitchen, looking for the guys and Steven. Voices floated into the room, and I stepped to the kitchen window. Nate and Steven were talking out on the back porch, and a slight feeling of déjà vu came over me as they stood by the railing where the cardinal had visited earlier that morning. While I couldn't make out what they were saying, I had a distinct feeling it had to do with me. Especially when Nate lowered his head, his expression pained.

Doesn't he see how hurt Nate is? My heart ached for him. Maybe I should have just eaten the costs of movers and not put Nate and myself through it all. Spending time together was bound to stir up the past, which wasn't healthy. We needed to move forward.

Before anyone caught me staring, I headed upstairs to make sure we hadn't missed anything. Seeing the house so bare caused a pang in my chest. That was my childhood home; I'd grown up within those walls. I walked to my room. How many times had I taken solace in that sanctuary? How many tears had I poured into those pillows?

How many laughs had echoed across the ceiling? A choked sob escaped my lips as tears sprang to my eyes.

"Lanie?" A voice came from behind me in the darkened hall. I quickly wiped away my tears and turned.

"Lanie, the guys are—" Steven stopped short. "Hey, are you okay?"

"I'm fine," I replied quickly. "The guys are what?"

"Heading out," Steven said, his eyes searching my face. "I can tell them goodbye for you."

"No, I'll be right down." I ducked into the bathroom, leaving Steven staring after me. With the door closed, I leaned heavily against it, taking deep breaths. I went to the sink and splashed cold water on my face, patting my eyes to help clear the red splotches. When I had hidden all traces of my grief, I sucked in one more deep breath and descended the stairs.

The guys were all suited up to head out into the cold winter air. I pasted a warm smile on my face as I looked them over. When my eyes met Nate's, he frowned, and my smile faltered. He always could read my emotions like the back of his hand.

"Thank you all so much for helping us get the house ready," I said, relieved that my voice sounded steady. Steven came over and threw his arm around me. "We appreciate everything you did today."

"It was nice to get out of the shop!" Jeff declared.

"Certainly smelled better," Sam joked.

"Well, maybe if you bathed more often, that wouldn't be a problem." Rob playfully smacked Sam on the back.

Not to be outdone, Sam turned and pulled Rob into a headlock while rubbing his fist on Rob's head. Rob hollered and struggled to pull away, and when Sam released him, he staggered back a few steps as he tried to smooth his hair. The rest of the guys laughed at the roughhousing, except for Nate. His eyes never left my face.

My phone rang, catching everyone's attention. I looked at it then up at Steven. "It's James. I'm sorry. I need to take this."

"Come on, Nate." Jeff put a hand on his shoulder. "Let's go grab a drink at The Point."

Nate started to protest, but something in Jeff's demeanor made him stop. His eyes met mine, and a dark cloud passed over his face before he followed the guys out the door.

I turned away and answered the phone.

"Lanie!" James's voice rang out. "I'm so glad I caught you. I feel like we've been playing phone tag for days. How are you?"

"I'm okay. The time zones are throwing me for a loop," I said. It was partially true, and James's preference for going to bed early certainly didn't help things.

"I get that," he said, his voice filled with sympathy. "Listen, I know you've got a lot going on, but I wanted to tell you I found the perfect apartment."

"You already found a place?" My stomach dropped, and I struggled to keep my voice even.

"Yeah. Look, I know we talked about me crashing with friends until you return and then we'd find a place together, but I think you're going to love what I found. It's a great complex with a gym and a pool, and the apartment has all the latest amenities. It's three bedrooms, which I know seems like a lot, but we could each have our own office."

I sank to the floor and covered my mouth with my hand, fighting a wave of nausea as James continued his ecstatic exclamations about the apartment. It was beginning to feel like my real life was moving on while I remained in some sort of limbo, tying up loose ends. I could see the logic in him apartment hunting without me, but the news still hit me like a ton of bricks. Especially since James wasn't known for being prudent when it came to financial decisions.

"Honey? Are you still there?"

"I'm here," I said, shaking my head as I tried to clear it. "That all sounds great, but are you sure we can afford it?"

James scoffed. "We'll figure it out."

That wasn't very comforting. I gnawed on the inside of my cheek as I debated my next words. "Do they at least have a website I could look at?"

"Of course they do. I'll email it to you, and we can talk more later after you have a chance to review everything. Sound good?"

It didn't seem like I had much of a choice. I closed my eyes and took a deep breath. "Thanks, James."

"No worries. I got you."

You've got me, but how about a budget? Perhaps I wasn't being fair, but James had a habit of jumping into things with both feet without fully thinking them through. I had asked him to wait for me to look for places to avoid that exact situation. From all the amenities he'd listed, I was pretty sure we were going to be in over our heads.

"How are things going?" James asked when I didn't respond.

I stood and stepped over to the front window. All the cars were gone save Mom's and Steven's. "It's been stressful."

"Any idea how much longer you'll have to be out there?"

"Actually, things are moving a lot quicker than I anticipated," I said. "Steven and I have divided up the furniture and other things. And today we had some help getting ready for the estate sale this weekend."

"Wow, that is fast. And good news. I miss you."

"I miss you too." I meant it, mostly. I missed having him to lean on, the way he distracted me from my pain just when I needed it most.

"Have you seen your dad yet?"

"I had dinner with him the other night."

"I'm glad to hear that. I know things have been rough between you two recently," James said with enthusiasm. "So, who helped you move the furniture?"

"Um, Steven asked a few guys he knows," I responded meekly. I didn't want to get into who the guys were right then. While I'd told James about Nate, I wasn't sure whether he would put two and two together. Something told me to keep that information to myself, at least for the moment.

"Well, that's nice. Hey, I'm sorry, hon, but I've gotta go. I'll send over the apartment complex's website. Give me a call after you take a look, okay?"

"I will. I love you."

"Love you, too, babe." My phone beeped three times, and I suddenly felt every mile of the distance between us.

"'A few guys I know,' huh?" Steven asked as he stepped back into the hallway. "That's not quite how I would describe them."

I leaned against the wall with one arm and pressed my forehead against it. "It just didn't feel like the right time to tell him."

"Is he aware your first love still lives here?"

"We've had the whole 'exes' conversation, but I'm not sure if he'd remember who Nate was." I pushed off the wall and walked by him into the kitchen. "It's been a long day."

"A long but productive day," Steven countered, following me. "I was thinking of ordering a pizza for dinner and inviting Rose to join us." He gave me a critical once-over. "Unless you're tired of people."

"That sounds nice, and I'd love to see Rose!"

"All right, I'll give her a call and put in the order. Pepperoni and pineapple?"

I nodded as I got a glass of water. Steven was right—it had been a productive day, and I was amazed at how fast we were accomplishing everything. If we were able to sell the house as quickly as we had readied it for sale, I would be back on the West Coast in no time. That knowledge should have made me happy, but for some reason, it didn't. To be fair, I had expected to be there a while, which was why I had told the principal of my new school I couldn't start until the summer. It would be nice to have some time off to relax and enjoy some downtime.

Between caring for Mom, finishing school, finding a job, and then dealing with Mom's estate, I hadn't had much time to just be. Then again, whenever I did have a moment to myself, it was harder to keep the crushing weight of grief at bay. I preferred to stay as busy as possible.

At least I would be with James, and maybe having some distance from Cedar Haven would help me to move on. Besides, I reasoned, I'd be busy enough setting up our new home and establishing myself in California. That last thought brought me up short. It shouldn't bother me so much that James was looking for a place without me, but it did. I wanted to be part of the process, especially to ensure he didn't get something out of our price range. Lately, my life felt out of control, like I was just going through the motions. Choosing where I would live gave me a sense of purpose and a tether to the future I wanted to create.

I stared out the kitchen window and watched as the shadows lengthened with the setting winter sun.

Chapter Seven

My trepidation about the apartment continued into the next morning. I was still stewing over it when the doorbell rang. Who on earth would be stopping by so early? With a sigh, I shoved away from the table and went to greet my visitor. My eyes widened when I opened the door and found my neighbor, Cassandra Winters, standing on the front porch, dressed in all black, her gray hair cascading down her shoulders. She held a picnic basket, and the tantalizing scent of baked goodies wafted through the air.

"Mrs. Winters," I said. "What a pleasant surprise."

"Good morning, Lanie." She held out the picnic basket. "I thought you might want something other than toaster pastries for a change."

I blinked. "How did you—?" But before I could continue, a cardinal landed on the porch railing.

"Well, hello there, little fella," Mrs. Winters cooed, holding out her finger to the bird. I half expected the cardinal to hop onto it. Maybe I'd been wrong all those years about my strange neighbor. Maybe she was really a Disney princess in disguise. The bird cocked its head and chirped. I recognized the black spots near its beak.

"That little bird has visited me almost daily since I've been home," I said, shivering as the frigid air cut right through my thin shirt. "Ah, where are my manners? Would you like to come in?"

Mrs. Winters glanced up, startled, as if she had forgotten I was there. "Actually, I think you need to come with me."

"What do you mean?" I tilted my head, frowning at the change in her tone.

"There's something I want to show you," she said. "Would you join me for a cup of tea?"

"That would be lovely, Mrs. Winters, but I—"

"Oh, my dear, I think you're old enough to call me Cassandra now." She gave a wink before spinning on her heel, startling the cardinal in the process. It flew overhead as she walked down the driveway. I debated whether to follow her, my blood chilling in my veins and not from the winter air. But curiosity got the better of me, so I quickly grabbed a coat and shoved my feet into my shoes before I hurried after my eccentric neighbor.

I hesitated on the porch, my muscles tense, but I took a deep breath and forced myself to step into the notorious home of the neighborhood witch. Even as an adult, I found that Cassandra's decor made me uneasy. Herbs hung from the ceiling, and the house still smelled like sage. The walls were painted in the rich colors of nature, a dark earthy brown in the hall giving way to a vibrant green in the kitchen. It felt like stepping into some enchanted forest instead of a house.

Cassandra indicated a seat. Sinking into it, I let my eyes dart around the room as I looked for evidence that would confirm my childish suspicions. While I didn't see a cauldron on the stove, I wouldn't have been surprised to find a broom perched in the corner, ready to take flight.

"I'm not going to turn you into a newt," she said with a chuckle.

I jumped at the sound of her voice then bowed my head sheepishly. "I'm sorry."

"Oh, it's all right. I can understand why you children were afraid of me all those years ago. I've been called worse than a witch," she replied with a mischievous gleam in her blue eyes. After filling the kettle, she set it on the stove to boil then reached into her oven and pulled out a tray of scones.

"Were you expecting company?" I asked.

"You never know." She set out two small plates then took the seat across from me. "I understand you're selling your mother's house."

"We have an estate sale this weekend, and then it will go on the market." At first, I nibbled at the scone, but the sweet, flaky pastry was too delicious, and before I knew it, I had gobbled up two.

The kettle whistled, and Cassandra stood and poured the water into two cups. She placed a bag of peppermint tea into one and handed it to me. After grabbing a sugar bowl, some honey, and spoons, she sat down again.

"I was so sorry I couldn't visit more often with Melody before she passed." Cassandra's eyes were moist with unshed tears. "She was kind to me. The baked goods she sent over with you kids were always a welcome treat."

"It's hard," I said, swallowing around the lump that formed in my throat. "Living there without her."

Cassandra slid her hand across the table, and I clasped it.

"Your mother will never truly leave you. She'll always be in your heart."

I forced a smile and cleared my throat. "You said you wanted to show me something?"

"Oh yes, it was about that little cardinal on your porch." She stood and stepped over to her small kitchen window, where a shelf was filled with books. "Ah, here it is." After setting it on the table, she flipped through to a faded black-and-white photo of a bird. "Cardinals are said to be visitors from heaven."

I leaned forward, staring at the page she pointed at. The cardinal in the photo looked exactly like my bird, though without its telltale red. Beneath the photo were stories, the stuff of old folklore and legends.

"As I said, your mother will never leave you." Cassandra pointed at another line on the page. "'Cardinals represent light during the darkest of nights, provide hope to the sorrowful, and are a source of warmth in winter's cold embrace.' Here, it says, 'Red cardinals are a sign that a departed loved one is attempting to connect.'" She sat down in her chair, letting her words sink in.

I shook my head, not for one minute believing any of it. Cardinals were just birds, and their presence was noticeable only because they were a vibrant red.

"It's just a coincidence," I insisted, even while a small kernel of hope grew in my heart. "The only thing that bird wants to communicate is it's past time to refill Mom's old feeders."

"If it were about food, the cardinal would have moved on long ago." Cassandra sipped her tea, regarding me over the lip of the cup. "You said you've seen it regularly since you've been home."

"Maybe it has a nest in our yard and doesn't want to travel in the cold," I argued. I wasn't a religious person, and that just sounded like one of those things people told one another as a source of comfort, a way to ease the pain of losing someone they loved.

"You can choose not to believe." She shrugged. "But I suspect that little bird has a purpose."

Lifting the cup to my lips, I barely tasted the tea. My mind was running through logical arguments against what she was saying. No way would I believe Mom was trying to communicate with me from beyond the grave. And even if she was, the only message I was getting from the visits revolved around Nate, since they always seemed to occur right before I saw him.

"But she hated Nate!" I blurted out, then I covered my mouth with my hand.

Cassandra cocked an eyebrow as she wrapped her hands around her cup. "Perhaps she has a message for you about this Nate." She pushed the plate of scones toward me. "Eat. You look pale."

I automatically reached for another scone and took a bite, not fully registering what I was doing. I didn't linger long in Cassandra's house, my unease increasing the more time I spent there. While my imagination was more grounded as an adult, her otherworldly demeanor still unsettled me. After thanking her for the scones and tea, I went to my house to prepare for the day. All the while, I tried to push Cassandra's crazy cardinal theory out of my mind.

It didn't work. I thought back over the times I'd seen the cardinal. The first was when the car got a flat tire and Nate came to rescue me. Then it appeared again before that awkward lunch at Bea's Diner when Nate told me about that job. It showed up a third time when he took me to drop off items for the fundraiser, and another visit happened right before he arrived to help with the move. And then I'd seen it that morning, so did that mean...?

I shook my head. I was being ridiculous. It was just a bird, not some messenger from the great beyond.

But then I thought back to what Steven had said the other night. He asked if Mom and I had really settled everything between us before she passed. I believed we had, at least as much as anyone could hope to. There would always be things I wished I'd said or done differently, but when she died, I felt we were on solid ground. Our relationship was never perfect, but I didn't have any regrets.

As I pretended to pack up my room, I glimpsed a photo stuck in the mirror frame that I'd never had the heart to take down. Nate and I were in formal attire. It was just before prom. We looked like we'd been caught kissing, but really, my friends had staged it in a way to get a better view of the back of my dress and hair.

Pulling it off the mirror frame, I studied it. Nate's eyes were looking at the camera, but mine were on him. His arms were wrapped tightly around me, and his smile was bright, but it didn't quite reach his eyes. I recalled my mother had stood nearby when this photo was taken. Even then, he stared at my mom with a wariness that broke my heart. But he'd told me they had made their peace. What did that mean? What did peace look like for Mom and Nate? And did it have something to do with why the cardinal visited me?

I put the picture back and pulled out my computer. James had sent the apartment information, and I decided it was as good a time as any to see what he'd found. When I clicked on the website, my stomach dropped. Just as I'd suspected, the cheapest apartment they offered was way more than I had planned to pay monthly. If I hadn't already done my own research, I might have accepted that it was just the price of housing in LA. But I knew better. While the apartments I had bookmarked to check out when I got back to the West Coast had fewer amenities, they were affordable.

With a sigh, I closed my eyes and rubbed my temples. Based on the number of exclamation points in James's email, he was excited about the complex, but the math just didn't add up. We could either rent that apartment or we could eat, but we couldn't do both. I supposed I could get a part-time job, but that seemed unnecessary when I had already found several apartment options that would work instead, even if they didn't have all the bells and whistles James raved about.

Maybe I should consider finding my own place. James and I had been together for years, and it made sense for us to take that next step and move in together. As I'd told Steven, he would likely propose once Mom's estate was no longer hanging over my head. It might not even make sense for us to get separate apartments, knowing we would be moving in together once we were married.

I cringed at the thought. Marriage. We'd discussed it at length, of course, but it had always seemed like some abstract thing we would get to eventually. But with grad school behind us, James had brought it up more frequently than before I went home. Part of me wasn't even sure I ever wanted to get married. It wasn't like I'd had the greatest example. My parents' divorce had been awful, but I reminded myself they were friends in the end.

But was it really marriage I was struggling with or a life with James? Did I even *want* to move to California? Sometimes, I wasn't sure. Because of my promise to Mom, my plan had always been to live somewhere other than Cedar Haven, and when the school in California offered me a position, it made the most sense.

I could stay in Cedar Haven, though I winced at the thought. The idea of breaking the promise to my mother hurt my very soul. And yet, there was a job there, still doing what I loved. Okay, sure, it would be significantly less money than I would make in California, but I could bunk with my dad for a while until I got settled.

Could I live in Cedar Haven with all the painful memories? Nate's question echoed in my head. *They're not all bad memories, right?* And he was correct. Over the past few days, I'd been reminded of happier times by going out with Rose and my friends then hanging out with Steven and reminiscing about our childhood. Even driving with Nate was a sweet echo of a time I wouldn't want to forget.

After navigating to the local middle school's web page, I found the job posting for Mrs. Carlisle's position. When I finished reading it over, I knew I was a perfect fit. My stomach knotted as I filled out the application, convinced my mother's ghost was about to pop out from some dark corner of the room to scold me for breaking my promise. But I reasoned that Mom also had always encouraged me to keep my options open. What better way to do that than to apply for the position? It couldn't hurt, and we miss one hundred percent of the chances we don't take, right?

Hours later, I drove to the school with a folder containing my résumé, transcripts, and letters of recommendation. Soon after I submitted the application, someone from the school called and asked me to interview. Well, I'd already gotten my feet wet, and my life didn't feel like mine anymore. Between James's decision to find us a home without my input, being stalked by a bird, and my confusion over Nate, I needed to take control of something in my life. Applying for the job was my way of doing just that. Besides, an interview didn't mean I would accept. It wouldn't stop me from going to California as planned. But it might provide an alternative to the life I thought I wanted.

What I didn't know was what my choice would mean for James and me. I loved him, or at least, I thought I did, but the apartment episode had made me realize that I hadn't been happy with him for a while. And his latest decision could have a huge impact on my life, at least financially. I promised myself I would talk to him about the situation before I made any rash decisions. One interview wasn't enough for me to upend all my plans, and besides, there was always a chance they would turn me down.

As I pulled into the parking lot of the school, I breathed easier at the sight of clear, dry pavement. The last thing I needed was to slide on black ice, face-first into a snowbank, when I wanted to make a good impression. Squaring my shoulders, I marched to the front of the building and rang the bell, ready for whatever future the decision might bring.

After the interview, I stopped by the grocery store to find something for dinner. It'd been ages since I last cooked. I gathered some basic ingredients while I decided what I wanted to make. When I rounded the corner after grabbing a pint of ice cream, I had to swerve to avoid a person striding toward me. A flash of dark hair caught my eye, and I turned. Nate's eyes widened as they met mine.

"I'm sorry. I didn't see you there," he said.

"It's my fault I was tearing down the aisle like the Indy 500," I quipped, glancing into his cart. "Frozen dinners?"

"What's wrong with that?" he demanded.

"It just screams 'bachelor,'" I replied with a wry smile.

"Well..." He waved his bare left hand. He peeked into my basket. "What are you getting?"

"Odds and ends, though I feel like cooking something tonight. Haven't decided what yet."

"Need suggestions?" he asked.

I raised an eyebrow. "Are you trying to procure an invite?"

"Maybe." That slow, heart-melting smile stole over his face. "If you're offering."

That was... unexpected. But I wasn't about to waste his good mood. "Hmm, I could be persuaded."

"How about we make a trade? You cook, and I'll buy your groceries?"

I wasn't one to turn down a free meal, even if I was technically paying for it with my labor. "It's a deal." I dumped my things into his cart and slid an arm through his elbow.

"When did you learn to cook?"

I bit my lip and stared at the ground. "My mom taught me some things growing up, but I guess I learned most of it through trial by fire when she was sick."

He patted my hand but didn't respond. Perhaps he didn't know what to say. As the awkward silence between us lengthened, I searched for a safe subject.

"I was thinking I'd make shepherd's pie."

"Sounds like the perfect meal for a cold winter's day," he agreed.

I blew out a breath, and we wandered through the rest of the store as I added to our supplies. To my surprise, the conversation flowed easily while we shopped. Nate paid, and I blinked at the cost, but when I opened my mouth to protest, he waved me off. Business must be good, though I supposed with it being winter, I likely wasn't the only person who had fought a pothole and lost.

We headed to my house, with Nate following in his car, and he helped carry the groceries inside. I poured two glasses of wine then turned on some music while I began preparing the meal. Singing along to the tune, I caught Nate staring at me and flushed at the intensity of his gaze. I suspected what he was thinking as the memory flashed through my mind as well—late nights on the phone when I'd serenaded him before he slipped off to sleep.

While I worked, I debated whether to tell him about the interview. On the one hand, he'd told me about the job in the first place, so it wouldn't be weird for me to share my news. On the other hand, I hadn't told anyone else, and somehow, I worried that telling Nate might imply I planned to stay. I wasn't sure why I thought he would care beyond my filling a potential void in the town's education system.

Once I slid the shepherd's pie into the oven, I lowered the volume of the music and took a sip of my wine, steeling myself. My heart thumped in my chest, but whether from excitement or nerves, I didn't know.

"I have something to tell you," I whispered conspiratorially, leaning toward him.

"What's that?" he whispered back, his eyes twinkling as he played along.

"I had an interview today," I said.

He blinked and raised an eyebrow. "An interview? For what?"

"Mrs. Carlisle's position," I replied with a wink before lifting my glass and gulping down more wine. Why had I just winked at him? What was I thinking? I supposed that was the problem—I wasn't thinking. The alcohol went straight to my head, which did little to help the situation.

"What?" Nate asked, his eyes wide. "You applied? When?"

"This morning." I smiled, though I wasn't sure what to make of his reaction. Shock etched across his face, but was it good or bad? And for that matter, why did I care?

Nate leaned back in his seat and stared at me in silence. I gave him a moment to process my news, but as the silence stretched on, everything started to itch, and I couldn't stop myself from fidgeting. Why wasn't he saying anything? Did I make a mistake in telling him? But he'd told me about the job, so shouldn't that be a good thing? Unless he didn't trust that I would follow through. My head was swimming, and I struggled to remember the last time I'd eaten. Was it the scones? I should have paced myself with the wine.

"What changed your mind?"

His words brought me back to the present, and I worked to keep my face neutral while my shoulders sagged in relief. Curiosity danced in his eyes, along with another emotion I couldn't place, but at least he didn't seem angry or upset.

"You wouldn't believe me if I told you." I laughed, shaking my head. "Let's just say a little bird told me I should."

He rubbed his chin, and a slow smile broke over his face, stealing my breath. But he still hadn't said what he thought, and that worried me.

I frowned. "Aren't you going to say anything?"

"I'm a little speechless," Nate admitted. He slid his hand across the table, and I tentatively placed mine in it. "And I'm not sure what's... safe to say."

I cocked my head. "Safe? What do you mean?"

"Just that, well, the other day, you wouldn't even consider applying, and now, you've applied and interviewed." He pulled away and ran his hand through his hair. "I guess I'm trying to understand what changed."

The oven timer beeped, and I jumped up to toss the rolls in the oven, grateful for the interruption. I wasn't sure how I should answer him. To blame it on James and the apartment felt childish and reckless. Besides, I wasn't even sure if Nate knew about James. We'd never talked about him.

And I couldn't very well tell him that my neighbor thought my mother's spirit was trying to communicate with me through a bird. My joke about it earlier had been more for my benefit than his.

When I returned to him, he stared at me with that same intensity again, and it was all I could do not to fidget. I decided that a half-truth was better than nothing.

"My dad is dead set on me staying in Cedar Haven," I said, forcing a smile. "And I feel like I owe it to him, as the only parent I have left, to at least see how that would work. I'm not making any promises, but it might get him off my back for a while."

"Did they say when they would make their decision?" Nate asked, and I breathed a little easier.

"As soon as possible." I shrugged. "But you know the government. I'm sure there are levels of approval they'd need to go through. It went well, though."

"I'm glad to hear it," Nate said. "If you stay, do you think you'll still sell the house?"

"Probably. I can't afford to buy Steven out of his share of the estate, and I don't know that I'll ever feel comfortable here without her." I took another sip of wine. "I haven't really thought about that. It was an impulse decision, and I hadn't expected to be interviewed so soon."

"I don't think they've had a lot of applicants," Nate said. "Not many people looking for small-town life these days. I'm glad you applied. It's good to have options."

I spun around at his words, and he gave me a wary look. Swallowing, I cleared my throat. "I'm sorry, it's... I... I, er, that's something my mom would say."

Nate sat perfectly still, and I had the distinct impression that he was choosing his next words carefully. All the air seemed to leave the room as I waited, wondering if he was about to reveal whatever secret he'd been keeping from me.

"Perhaps I heard her say it once or twice," Nate finally replied, his voice strained. "But it's a common saying."

I nodded, choosing not to force the issue. The oven timer went off behind me, and I bent to check dinner.

Nate stood and got plates and silverware while I set out the shepherd's pie and rolls on the table. I refilled our wineglasses, though the last thing I needed right then was more alcohol, and took a seat, gesturing for him to serve himself. After spooning out a healthy portion, he passed the spoon, grazing my fingers. His eyes met mine briefly before looking away.

"This is delicious." He scooped up a mouthful of mashed potatoes.

"Better than a TV dinner?" I teased.

"Not even in the same neighborhood."

"You never learned to cook?"

He shook his head. "I'm afraid the most I do is grill."

A laugh bubbled up in my throat. "Cooking is just grilling indoors."

"I disagree," he said as he reached for his wine. "There's something about burning something over an open flame that brings out the caveman in all of us."

I snorted. "'Burning something'? So what you're saying is, you're not good at grilling either?"

"Hey now, I said I grill. I never said how the food turned out!"

"Did you learn your skills from Max McAllister? He never met a hamburger he couldn't turn into a hockey puck."

"I don't believe I ever had the pleasure of your dad's, er, culinary experiments." His mouth twisted as he stumbled over the words, and I laughed again.

"Hmm, that's right." I pointed my fork at him. "You only enjoyed my mom's taco nights."

"When she set me up to see how many I would eat?" Nate glared at me. "Yeah, I haven't forgotten that."

I covered my mouth to hide my giggling, but his answering grin assured me he wasn't offended. That was what I missed the most since we'd broken up. The joking around, harmless teasing, and playful banter. Nate had always been closed off from the world, aside from a few close friends. But I had discovered a different side of him when we were together. His sense of humor and boisterous laughter warmed my insides.

He scraped his plate, clearly enjoying every last bite, and I hid a smile as warmth blossomed in my chest. I missed cooking. When I was back in Seattle, I'd never found the time to cook for James and me. We usually ordered takeout, as he had never learned to cook for himself.

"Well, since you made this amazing meal, it's only fair I do the dishes," he announced as he took his plate and mine to the sink.

"You don't have to do that." I stood to stop him.

"Nonsense. I was raised to do my part." He placed a hand on my shoulder and gently nudged me back into my seat. "Besides, I'm hoping I'll earn another invite in the future."

"You can count on it." My lips curled into a soft smile as I watched him fill the sink and begin washing the dishes. *I could get used to this.* I blinked at the thought, hoping to dispel it, but instead, a whole different future filled my mind. I pictured coming home to him after a long day at school, him washing the grease and grime off his hands before joining me in the kitchen while I made his favorite meal.

I shook my head, and the image vanished. What was wrong with me? Why had I allowed myself to entertain such a vision of my future? And more importantly, why was Nate in the starring role instead of James? What did that say about me?

"I need some fresh air." I rushed out of the kitchen, leaving Nate calling after me.

I stepped out onto the front porch, crossing my arms over my chest as the first bite of winter's chill cut through my thin shirt. Breathing in the crisp air, I closed my eyes. Perhaps it was only natural, being there without my mother to guide me, that I would fall into old habits. Maybe I was making too much out of nothing. So what if I still had feelings for Nate? It wasn't like I would act on them, especially since I had no evidence he felt the same way about me.

A moment later, the front door opened, and Nate slid in beside me. I could feel his eyes searching my face, and I worked to keep my expression neutral. He slipped his hands into the pockets of his pants and hunched his shoulders.

"It's freezing out here."

I nodded, not quite trusting myself to speak. My skin felt tight, my muscles tense at his closeness. It was one thing to admit that I still felt something for him, but it was quite another to have those feelings welling up in my chest while he stood next to me. I shoved them down and turned to him.

"Thanks for cleaning up," I said, forcing a smile.

"Thanks for dinner." His brows pulled together. "Are you... okay?"

"Of course. Why wouldn't I be?"

"You ran out of the kitchen and have been standing out here in the cold."

"The house was warm after the oven was on," I lied. "I needed to cool off a bit."

"Oh." His frown deepened as if he could see right through me. "Well, I guess I should go."

"Wait," I said, internally cringing. I should let him go. Spending time with him wasn't helping anything, but I didn't want to be alone. "Why don't you stay a minute and have another drink with me?"

He gave me a dubious look but nodded, and a small part of me filled with hope. I squashed that part. We were friends. At least, I hoped we were moving in that direction. And frankly, I needed all the friends I could get.

We went inside and sat on the couch, where we faced each other. A charity was coming to pick up the couch at the end of the week, and I savored the little time I had left with it. It was funny, the things we got attached to when someone we loved passed on. Some tangible items had no real monetary value but possessed such priceless sentiment.

He glanced at me with a teasing grin. "It's nice to sit here with you without the threat of yellow police tape."

I threw back my head and laughed so hard I almost spilled my wine. He caught my hand to steady the glass, and my eyes flew open as I met his gaze. The air seemed to surge with an electric intensity. But it didn't last as my cheeks flushed, and I pulled away.

"I forgot about that," I murmured. "Mom and her threats." I gave a weak smile. "You were always a good sport about her antics. The tacos, the police tape."

Nate shrugged, and I could feel his discomfort growing. I

supposed we were approaching one of the many elephants in the room. I stifled a sigh that quickly morphed into a yawn.

"I'm so sorry." I covered my mouth with my hand.

"It's fine. I know it's getting late." He stared at the floor, his lips pressed into a thin line. "I should be heading home. I've gotta open the shop early tomorrow."

We stood, and he set his glass in the kitchen before making his way to the front door. After shrugging into his coat, he surprised me when he grasped my hand and gently pulled me to him, wrapping his arms around me. My heart thudded as I rested my head against his broad chest.

Too soon, he pulled away enough to look at me, and a desire to press my lips to his took over me. But I knew better. I stepped away and opened the door. When I glanced back, he had a bemused look on his face as if he was overcome by the same pull.

He blinked and recovered. "Bye, Lanie. I'll see you later."

Instead of responding, I waved and closed the door behind him before leaning against it. I listened as his car door slammed and the engine sparked to life. A moment later, the wheels crunched on the snow-covered driveway. Then silence.

I couldn't put it into words, but somehow, I knew that things between us had changed that night. Whether that was a good thing or not, I suspected I would find out soon enough.

Chapter Eight

On the day of the estate sale, I woke up groggy and disoriented. I'd dreamed of my old apartment in Seattle, and I didn't recognize my childhood bedroom at first. As I sat up, everything rushed back to me, and I groaned when I remembered what day it was. I wasn't looking forward to the throngs who would be traipsing through my childhood home in a few hours.

Before my mom died, I considered myself an outgoing person, but in the last six months, I'd become more withdrawn and introverted. When I returned to school, I avoided social engagements, though I had the excuse of catching up on all the schoolwork I'd missed. Since I'd been home, preparing the house had kept me busy, but it was harder to escape socializing in such a small town.

Memories from the night before drifted through my mind. I'd enjoyed spending time with Nate, reminiscing about the past. I believed we were well on our way to being friends again. I hadn't realized just how comfortable I was with him until that hug at the end of the night. It felt like old times. Maybe too much like old times. At one point, I thought he might kiss me, and it scared me that part of me wanted him to.

I winced, silently rebuking myself. What about James? We were planning to move in together, for goodness' sake. What was I thinking? The truth was, I hadn't thought about James much at all yesterday. After my residual anger regarding the apartment had driven me to apply for a job I shouldn't want and didn't need, I hadn't given him a moment's consideration. That had to be a bad sign. Shouldn't I have at least told him about the job interview?

I pushed the thought from my mind and tried to focus on the day ahead. James and I would have plenty of time to talk later. Climbing out of bed with a heavy sigh, I straightened the covers then set out my outfit for the day. I chose a navy-blue pantsuit in hopes of appearing like a capable salesperson. More like a suit of armor against what was going to be an emotional day. While I'd made my peace with the things we weren't keeping, it wasn't going to be easy to watch them go to strangers. On the flip side, I expected the town to come out in full support. Perhaps seeing some familiar faces would lessen the blow.

When I stepped out of the shower a little while later, voices drifted up from the floor below. A quick peek out the window confirmed Steven had arrived. I quickly dressed, ran a brush through my hair, and pulled the damp strands into a ponytail.

"Well, good morning, sleepyhead," Steven called as I descended the stairs. "I tried calling you last night, but you didn't pick up."

"She was probably exhausted, poor thing." Rose's voice carried from the living room. "She hasn't had a chance to catch her breath since she arrived."

As I entered the living room, I caught Steven's eye, and he shrugged. "It had to be done, and since she's in such a hurry to get back to her West Coast lifestyle, it's good we're moving quickly."

Some might have taken offense at that last comment, but I knew my brother. He'd accepted my decision to move to California, but that didn't mean he wouldn't get a few digs in before I left.

"Could you stop talking about me like I'm not here?" I demanded, hands on my hips in mock anger.

"Somebody woke up on the wrong side of the bed," Steven teased.

I shot him a glare before I turned to see what they'd done with the downstairs. Steven and Rose had set up the room in a way that directed the flow of traffic. All of the items had price tags according to the appraisal they had received. My heart fractured as memories of each piece flooded my mind.

"Dad will be here soon," Steven continued, writing on his clipboard. "You can help Rose set up things in the kitchen."

I nodded absently, following Rose as instructed. The plan was to put Mom's china on full display. Some of the pots and pans had been deemed acceptable for sale, but we'd tossed most of them.

"Why don't you grab a cup of coffee and some food before we get started?" Rose indicated the box of doughnuts on the counter. I gave her a grateful smile and helped myself, standing over the sink to avoid getting crumbs everywhere.

"How are you feeling about today?"

I gave a noncommittal shrug. "I'm trying to stay indifferent, but it's difficult."

"I understand," Rose murmured softly. "After everything you've been through this last year, it's got to be hard to say goodbye."

"I think it's more I feel like I'm losing another part of my mom." I sipped my coffee as I surveyed the kitchen, committing every little detail to memory. "It'll be hard to leave all this behind."

"You're definitely set on moving, then?"

I gave her a wary look. "Why? Has someone told you differently?"

Rose's responding laugh was infectious. "Clearly, you know your family well."

"Steven says he's accepted my decision, but my dad..." I shook my head. "Part of me wonders if I'm making a mistake, but I feel like I have to at least try, you know?" I didn't mention the application and interview for the local teaching position. No reason to get anyone's hopes up. "I appreciate their concern, but I think it's for the best."

"And not even a certain someone will change your mind?" Rose asked innocently, but I saw right through her.

"Did Steven put you up to this?" I retorted with a glare.

"No. Like you said, he's accepted your decision." She grinned. "But I'm not blind. I've seen the way Nate looks at you."

"I don't know what you mean," I said, turning away from her. Lucky for me, Steven and my father entered at that moment. I wasn't ready to address my conflicting feelings toward Nate.

My dad gave me a nod before he walked over to the table and surveyed the china. He picked up various pieces and turned them in his hands, his eyes far away. I wondered if he was remembering happier times with Mom.

After cleaning the crumbs from my fingers, I moved next to Dad at the table. He had lifted a gravy boat and was fiddling with a small crack at its base. I touched his arm gently, and he turned to me with a sad smile.

"Your mother cracked this when she slammed it down on the table one Thanksgiving," he said, his eyes wistful. "I don't remember exactly what I did, but I do recall she was hopping mad with me."

When I rested my head on his shoulder, he set the dish down and wrapped his arms around me. We stood there together, lost in our memories, our ongoing argument about my plan to leave momentarily forgotten. It touched me to know that despite everything that had happened, my parents had never stopped loving each other. What their marriage had taught me, above all else, was that love wasn't enough. Good relationships required work, communication, and a hefty dose of humility.

I stifled a sigh as realization swept in. James and I needed to talk, and the sooner the better. If I planned to have a future with him, I needed to hear him out on the new apartment and discuss my concerns like a rational adult. Not jump feetfirst into a job opportunity just to prove I could. And who knew? Maybe talking to him would help me sort out whatever was going on between Nate and me, assuming there was anything going on. It could be all in my head.

"You'd better get started on pricing everything," my father whispered, pulling me back to the present as he extracted himself from our embrace. "You know how your brother is."

I nodded and turned to Rose. The men left the kitchen to continue preparing the rest of the house. Working with my future sister-in-law was exactly what I needed for the day. We shared a comfortable silence, only sporadically broken by a comment on an item here or a shared memory there. It was peaceful, and I appreciated the lack of unnecessary chatter.

Soon the sale began, and Steven opened the front door to welcome the customers. I blinked when I saw the line already waiting outside, but I recognized many of them. Dad stationed himself by the back door, managing the cash box and tablet with a card reader attached. Rose and Steven worked the floor, helping customers. They both had previous sales experience, and they were naturals.

I opted to stay in the kitchen, helping customers who wandered in but wanting to maintain a low profile. Some people sought me out to express their condolences, but most seemed to understand my need for solitude. I hoped the day would pass quickly and successfully.

"Thanks for staying, Rose," I said as we finished cleaning up from the sale. What few items remained were destined to be donated.

"No problem," Rose replied as she set a Sold sign on the kitchen table. "Got any plans tonight?"

"A night in my jammies with a glass of wine sounds like heaven."

"You two should go out," Steven said as he came into the room and surveyed our progress. "You've earned it."

"Don't you have plans?" I tried to disguise the desperation in my voice. I could use a quiet night at home after the exhausting day I'd just had.

"Nope, she's all yours," Steven said as he slipped an arm around

Rose and gave her a quick squeeze. "Tonight, Dad and I are helping load some of the furniture that sold." He gave me an appraising look. "Unless you want to help us, I suggest you two go have some fun."

"What do ya say, Lanie? I hear Seabreeze has karaoke," Rose suggested.

The last thing I wanted to do was spend a night listening to awful singing, but Rose looked so hopeful, I couldn't bring myself to turn her down. And karaoke night was one of the most popular events at the bar. I would be able to disappear into the crowd.

"Sure, sounds great," I said, forcing myself to sound enthusiastic.

"Perfect!" Rose exclaimed. "Let me just run home to change. Pick you up in an hour?" Rose embraced me without waiting for a reply and rushed out the door. With a resigned sigh, I trudged up the stairs to get ready.

I chose an off-the-shoulder pink dress that hugged me in all the right places. It wasn't exactly the best option for blending in, but after being so underdressed for Bobby McKey's the other night, I didn't want to risk it again. No chance of that in this dress. I curled my hair and applied a little makeup. Before I knew it, the front door opened, and Rose's voice drifted up the stairs.

I slid my feet into a pair of matching heels and met Rose in the hall. One look at Rose's outfit made me second-guess my choice. Had I overdone it? I pursed my lips. Did I care? The dress could be my armor, and something told me that tonight, I would need it.

Steven dropped us off at Seabreeze, which was already packed. Seeing all those people caused conflicting emotions to bubble up inside me. As we walked toward the bar, Rose linked our arms, and I was grateful for the support. The distinct sound of steel drums poured out from within, and I resisted the urge to roll my eyes. A Caribbean paradise, right in the middle of quiet Cedar Haven. Sometimes, the town tried way too hard to be something it wasn't.

Once inside, we searched the crowded place for empty seats, and my traitorous heart skipped a beat when I saw Nate. He sat at a table with a couple of the guys from the shop and a few women I didn't recognize. A burning sensation spread through my chest, and I froze. What was wrong with me? I had James, so I had no right to be jealous.

Before I could assess the feeling further, Nate's eyes met mine, and the slow smile that came over his face took my breath away. He had rolled up the sleeves of his shirt, and his well-defined arm was draped over the back of his chair. I gave him a shy smile in return then scurried after Rose to a booth along the wall of the bar.

"Thanks for coming out with me tonight," Rose said as we sat down. "I've been hoping to get a chance to talk to you alone."

"What's up?" I asked as I shrugged out of my coat and set it on the bench beside me.

"I know Steven has asked you to read a poem at our wedding, and initially, we weren't planning on having a bridal party, but I was wondering..." Rose's voice faltered.

I searched her face, frowning at her nervousness. "Yes?" I prompted, my curiosity getting the better of me.

"Would you be my maid of honor?"

"Oh my gosh, Rose! Of course, I would love to," I gushed. Rose's shoulders visibly relaxed as I grabbed her hand. "I'm even more excited for your wedding now!" I cocked my head. "But why were you so afraid to ask me?"

Rose blew out a breath. "It's just... with everything you have going on, I didn't want to add to your plate."

"But this is a fun thing, and I could use more of those."

The server came, and we ordered our drinks: a cosmopolitan for Rose and a Long Island iced tea for me. I needed something strong, especially if Rose had any plans to participate in karaoke.

While we waited for our drinks, we chatted about Rose's job and what I had missed while I was in Seattle. Through it all, I shamelessly snuck glances at Nate when Rose wasn't looking and was rewarded many times with another heart-stopping smile. The women at the table with him kept trying to engage him in conversation, but from what I could tell, he didn't pay them any attention. I hated how much that pleased me.

"That boy has got it bad," Rose said, catching me off guard.

"What? Who?"

"Don't look now, but Nate Sanders hasn't taken his eyes off you since we walked in."

Blood rushed to my cheeks as I dropped my gaze to the table. I was saved from a response when the server appeared with our drinks. I gulped down mine, hoping Rose would drop that line of conversation. Nobody knew about the dinner Nate and I had shared, but I knew that in such a small town, nothing stayed secret for long.

"Is something going on between you?" Rose pressed.

Oh boy. There's not enough alcohol in the world for this conversation. "N-No. Why would you think that?"

"Because you turned about five shades of red when I told you he was staring at you," Rose replied with an arched brow.

I sighed. If we kept making eyes at each other across the bar like that, it wouldn't be long before the whole town shared Rose's suspicions. The best thing to do would be to come clean and avoid any nefarious rumors.

"He, uh, I mean, we had dinner together the other night."

"Um, okay, and why am I just now hearing about this?" Rose demanded as she leaned forward, her sleek black hair curtaining her face.

"I haven't told anyone," I protested. "It was an impromptu thing. We ran into each other at the store, and I invited him over." Lifting my shoulders in what I hoped was a nonchalant shrug, I forced a smile. "No big deal."

"The way his eyes are burning holes into that dress of yours suggests otherwise."

That was no exaggeration because I could feel the heat of Nate's gaze from across the room. It took all my willpower not to sneak another glance in his direction. With a deep breath, I focused on Rose.

"If I tell you something, do you promise not to tell anyone? Not even Steven?" I pleaded.

Rose nodded, her brown eyes wide. How do I approach this? Was this even the right thing to do? Probably not, but I needed an outlet, a sounding board. Keeping my feelings bottled up wasn't helping anything. I racked my brain on how to broach the subject. Perhaps I should start where all the trouble began, with that darn bird.

"Do you believe in legends?" I blurted out.

Rose's brows knitted together, and I imagined that was the last thing my future sister-in-law had expected me to say.

"Legends? What do you mean? And what does this have to do with your ex?"

"Just"—I held up a hand—"answer the question. Do you think there's any truth to myths or legends? Folklore?"

Rose rested her pointed chin on her hand as she appeared to seriously contemplate my question. "I guess there's some truth to every legend, isn't there? It had to have started somewhere, right? So it's likely it began with a real story that took on mythical proportions over time." She fixed me in her steely gaze. "Please explain what the heck this has to do with Nate."

"I know this is going to sound crazy." I hesitated. "But I've been seeing this bird, a cardinal, often over the past several weeks. I went to see Mrs. Winters. You know, my mom's neighbor?"

"Oh my! Steven told me about her." She lowered her voice. "Isn't she a witch?"

"She's not, well—" Cassandra had never confirmed or denied her witchy reputation. Not that it really mattered. I waved my hand. "Anyway, she told me legend says cardinals are visitors from heaven."

"Visitors from... Wait, do you think your mom was reincarnated as a bird?" Rose asked incredulously as she signaled to the server to bring another round.

"Not exactly," I hedged. I wasn't explaining things very well.

"Cassandra says they represent a deceased loved one who's trying to make contact."

"All right. Let's say I buy this. What does your mom want to contact you about?" Rose asked. "This isn't Casper. She doesn't have any unfinished business that I'm aware of."

I threw back my head and laughed. "Wow, what a reference."

"I was a Devon Sawa fan back in the day," Rose said with a wink. "What do you think your mom wants, though?"

"The thing is," I continued, stirring what was left of my drink and struggling to find the right words. "The cardinal tends to show up right before I run into Nate."

"Oh? Did you see it today?"

"I think I saw it briefly this morning, but things were hectic, and I wasn't really paying attention."

Rose swallowed the last of her drink in silence as she digested everything I'd said. I silently pleaded with her to understand and not dismiss me as crazy. It mattered in that moment that someone believed me. I needed someone else to understand what I was going through.

"But... didn't your mom hate Nate?" Rose finally asked after the server had set down our drinks and removed the empty glasses.

"She did," I replied, and I couldn't hide the pain in my voice. "I never fully understood why other than that she and my dad were also high school sweethearts and she seemed to see my dad in him, but that's the part that doesn't make sense."

"Maybe she's warning you away from him?"

"It doesn't feel that way," I admitted. "And Cassandra suggested my mom might have had regrets."

"Ah, so she does have unfinished business, just like Casper," Rose quipped with a grin.

I snorted. "I suppose that's one way of looking at it."

"And how do you feel about Nate?"

I squirmed under Rose's scrutiny. "I, well—" But I was cut off by the sudden appearance of the man in question.

"Hello, Lanie." His voice, low and deep, sent my heart careening into overdrive.

"Fancy meeting you here," I replied, pulling my lips into an easy smile, which faltered when I met his gaze. His eyes were filled with that same fire from the other night.

"Would you like to join us?" Rose asked innocently as I shot her a death glare.

Nate didn't move, his eyes locked on me. Unsure what else to do, I scooted over on the booth's bench and patted the spot beside me. His slow smile caused another wave of heat to sweep over my face.

"Are you planning to do karaoke?" Rose directed her question at Nate while I resisted the urge to kick her under the table.

"I'm not much of a singer," Nate said with a chuckle. He turned his dark-brown eyes back to me. "But I wouldn't object to hearing you sing."

"Oh, I don't think so." I shook my head vehemently. "I don't sing in front of strangers." *Or exes.*

"You sang at your mother's funeral," Rose pointed out.

"That was different," I murmured, breathing deeply through the sudden pang of sadness at the memory. Nate gently laid a hand on mine, a move that didn't go unnoticed by Rose.

"It was a beautiful song," Nate told her, his voice sincere.

"I think you should sing, Lanie," Rose insisted.

"I'm going to need a few more of these if I'm going up there," I quipped, shaking my glass.

With a wicked grin, Rose waved our server over.

The laid-back atmosphere of the bar gave way to excitement as the stage was set up for karaoke. Cedar Haven didn't have much to offer, but karaoke night was a town favorite. I downed my drink quickly, hoping to imbue some liquid courage before I dared to climb up on stage in front of the town.

"All right, how's everyone doing tonight?" the DJ called out over the microphone. A chorus of cheers erupted in response.

"The sign-up sheet for karaoke is open now. Come on down and show us how much talent Cedar Haven has!"

Multiple people stood up and rushed to the front, but I made no move to join them.

"Come on, Lanie. Whatcha gonna sing for us?" Rose asked.

"I was thinking something fun, maybe '22' by Taylor Swift."

"Ooh, that sounds perfect!" Rose agreed and motioned for Nate to move. He slid out to let me pass. His encouraging smile did nothing to settle my nerves. Swallowing my fears and my pride, I teetered down to the stage, very aware of just how much alcohol was currently making its way through my system. After a cursory glance at the list, I signed my name along with my song choice. The DJ had Taylor Swift's newer albums as well. Maybe it was the alcohol, or maybe it was Nate's influence, but for whatever reason, I found myself signing up for a second song.

Most of the singers that night weren't half-bad, though I probably wouldn't have noticed, as I was too focused on my own performance. The closer it got to being my turn, the more my hands shook. At one point, Nate laid his hand over mine and gave a gentle squeeze, which did nothing to calm me down. If that kept up, I would pass out before I ever made it on stage.

"All right, all right, all right," the announcer said. "Next up, we have Cedar Haven's own Lanie McAllister performing Taylor Swift's '22.' Give it up for Lanie!"

More cheers came, the loudest ones from Rose and Nate, as I walked up to the stage. I concentrated on the screen, ignoring the crowd as I waited for the first notes to play. My first few lines were a little stiff, and I swayed to the music to try to loosen up. By the time I hit the chorus, I was in my element, flashing two fingers and dancing across the stage.

When it was over, my face flushed from both exertion and excitement. I took a quick bow and returned to my table. Nate and Rose greeted me with huge smiles.

"That was amazing!" Rose grabbed my hand. "Please tell me you'll do an encore."

"Well," I replied hesitantly. "There was one other song I signed up for."

"Which is?" Rose demanded.

"It's a surprise," I said with a sideways glance at Nate.

He raised an eyebrow but didn't comment.

We sat and enjoyed another round while others performed, then it was my turn again. Still riding the high from my earlier success, I felt less nervous about the performance. But I was apprehensive about the song I had chosen. For one thing, I didn't know it nearly as well as the last one, and for another, when I'd first heard it, it reminded me of Nate. To sing it with him sitting just a few feet from me would be a whole new experience.

Would he read anything into it? More importantly, did I want him to? Last night had felt like old times in so many ways, and I wasn't sure how to process those feelings I was having toward him. If he did read something into it, would he tell me? Was I about to ruin the tentative friendship we'd formed?

As the first notes of "The 1" began to play, I cleared my throat and swayed to the beat. I searched the crowd until I found him. He smiled encouragingly at me as I sang through the first verse, but when I arrived at the refrain, his brows pulled together briefly before his whole countenance softened. The song was about a past love, and the narrator talked about how she wished the relationship had lasted. How sad she was that things had ended between them and how nice it would have been if it had turned out differently.

I sang the last two lines with my whole heart. Cheers erupted from the other patrons, but I only had eyes for Nate.

When I returned to our table, Rose was ready to go. She had texted Steven to come pick us up. My stomach clenched in disappointment. I'd hoped to have a moment alone with Nate, but as I followed Rose to the door, he discreetly grabbed my hand and gave it a squeeze. A promise. Of what, I wasn't sure, but I hoped to find out more soon.

"What was that?" Rose demanded once we were outside and alone.

"What was what?"

"You know what." She crossed her arms. "That song. The way you looked at Nate. Lanie, what's going on? I know I've teased you about Nate, but I'd meant it as a joke. Now, I'm wondering if I was a lot closer to the mark." Shaking her head, she stared at me. "I thought you were with James?"

Her words were like a bucket of ice-cold water over the warmth of my high. She was right. *What am I doing?* Guilt settled in the pit of my stomach. I hadn't been thinking about James at all.

"I-I don't know," I moaned, covering my face with my hands. "I'm so confused."

Her face softened, and she put a hand on my shoulder. "I can't empathize, as I've never had any doubts about your brother, but I can sympathize. Do you still have feelings for Nate, or is this stemming from the cardinal?"

I stood there, unsure how to respond. Did I still love Nate? Perhaps the better question was, had I ever *stopped* loving Nate? Deep down, I knew I hadn't, but it wasn't the same as being in love with him. He was my first love, and as the saying went, "You never forget your first love." Was that all that it was? Was I pining for what might have been? What never could be?

"Both, maybe?" I finally said with a sigh. "Please don't tell Steven. I'm afraid he'd let it slip to Dad, and then I'd never hear the end of it. He has more than enough fodder for his campaign to convince me to stay. This would just add fuel to the flames."

"I've told your father he needs to let that go." Rose rolled her eyes. "But I promise I won't say a word to either of them."

Her eyes were so filled with pity, I couldn't bear to meet them.

"You need to figure this out and soon. Before someone gets hurt."

I nodded and dropped the subject as Steven's car pulled up. Rose slid into the passenger seat while I claimed the back seat. I looked forward to having some time alone with my thoughts. Rose was right. I was playing with fire, and someone, probably me, was going to get burned.

When I arrived home, I saw I had missed a call. Nausea swept through me when I saw it was James and not Nate. But maybe it was for the best. We needed to talk, and while it was too late to call him back, I did it anyway. I couldn't keep avoiding him.

"Lanie?" His voice was groggy, confirming I had woken him up. "It's late. Is everything okay?"

"I'm not sure," I mumbled.

"What's wrong?" he asked, and my heart broke a little at the sincere concern in his voice.

"I need to tell you something," I said, debating exactly what I wanted to say and how I wanted to say it.

"I'm listening."

"I—" An internal battle raged within me until I finally made a choice. "I applied for a job in Cedar Haven."

Coward. But I couldn't bring myself to tell him about Nate over the phone. We'd been together for all of our adult lives. He deserved better. We both did.

The silence on the other end did nothing to assuage my guilt. *What is he thinking?* The springs on his bed squeaked, and I could almost see him sitting up, rubbing his eyes, and trying to make sense of what I'd said.

"Why would you do that? You have a job here."

"I know." I covered my eyes with my hand. "It's just, the other day, when you told me you'd found us an apartment, I felt like my life was moving on without me. I needed to feel like I was in control of something. I'd heard about this job from some of my fr-friends." I winced as I stumbled over that word. "I thought I would keep my options open."

James exhaled slowly. I'd never hated myself more. First, I woke him up, then I couldn't even fess up to the real truth, the one that mattered. But I supposed that was fitting, since I wasn't even ready to admit that truth to myself.

"I thought you said you didn't want to move back there because it's too painful. I… I thought I was doing you a favor by finding us a place."

"I know, babe, and I appreciate it, but the place you found… It's too expensive." I blew out a breath. "I want to be part of the process."

"All right, well, we can wait until you're here, then. I just don't understand why you applied for a position there. You do still want to move in together, right?"

I closed my eyes, wishing I could give him a better answer. I wasn't sure about anything at that moment. Despite the issues we'd had recently, James had been a good boyfriend. We had a lot in common. But there had always been something missing, and that night, sitting beside Nate with my heart jackhammering in my chest, I realized the thing that was missing was passion. I didn't feel passionate about James. Sure, I cared about him, but how I felt didn't hold a candle to my feelings for Nate.

"I do," I assured him, and at that moment, I meant it. What I wasn't clear on was whether that would change. "I just—look, there's something I need to…"

"Hey, listen, you don't have to explain anything to me," James cut in. "I know you're having a rough time, what with your mom's estate and selling the house. If waiting to find a place until you're here will alleviate some of your burden, I totally get it."

"Thank you for understanding," I replied, sagging against the wall. The war going on inside me was wearing me down. "I'm sorry for waking you."

"Hey, I'm here for you. Whatever you need."

My eyes welled with tears, and I forced them back, desperately trying to keep my voice even. "Go back to sleep. I'll talk to you later."

"Good night, my love."

I winced as I ended the call. The truth had been right there on the tip of my tongue. Why hadn't I told him about Nate? I was all mixed up inside. My head fell back as I stared at the ceiling. What was I going to do now?

Chapter Nine

"You're coming to the Valentine's Day dance this weekend, aren't you, Lanie?" Rose asked as we sat together on my bed, pretending to pack. It was a convenient excuse for hiding from Steven and Dad as they continued preparing the house for sale. The real estate agent planned to list it the next morning, and I struggled to come to terms with the idea that someday soon, my childhood home would be in the hands of strangers.

"I'm not really a Valentine's Day person." I flipped through an old magazine I'd found when going through my desk drawers. "Besides, isn't it for couples and singles? My plus-one is on the other side of the country."

"It's for anyone who wants to attend," Rose replied with exasperation. "Come on. You have to go. You know it raises money for the fire department. Who cares what your relationship status is?"

"Ugh, this town has too many events!" I cried as I shut my eyes and mimed banging the back of my head against the wall.

"I heard Nate is going," Rose said a little too innocently as she flipped a page in her magazine. Her eyes flicked briefly to mine.

I kept my face blank, picking up the magazine again and feigning interest in an article. "I'm trying to keep my distance."

"Is that what you're doing?"

Glowering at Rose, I climbed off my bed and tossed the magazine into the trash. At the rate we were going, I would still be packing when the new owners moved in. How had I accumulated so much stuff in my short lifetime?

"Have you talked to him since karaoke?"

"No, as that would defeat the entire purpose of keeping my distance." I opened a drawer and pulled out a pile of papers, mostly old notebooks from my emo poetry phase. After shooting a quick glance over my shoulder, I paged through them, cringing at my angsty rhymes.

"Well, you shouldn't let it fester. Half the town saw the sparks flying between you two, and I imagine they'll be keeping a close watch on any interaction you may have at the dance."

"Which is why I have no intention of going," I retorted, debating what to do with the notebooks. Tear them up and save face, or save them for a laugh when I was back on the West Coast?

"Lanie," Rose said, her tone gentle.

With a sigh, I turned and looked at her.

"You need to talk to him. Things are clearly not as over between you two as I thought."

"As long as I'm with James, there can be nothing between Nate and me," I insisted. At least, that was what I kept telling myself.

I ripped out the most cringeworthy poems and shredded them before tossing the rest of the notebooks into a box. Upon opening the next drawer, I found a heavy book.

"Ooh!" Rose squealed. "I love old yearbooks." She waved her hands, gesturing for me to hand it to her. After I did, she flipped through the pages and skimmed the signatures, reading a few of particular interest aloud. "Oh my gosh! There's one from Nate in here."

I spun around. "Don't read that!"

"'Dear Lanie,'" Rose read, oblivious to my growing distress. "'I can't believe we're graduating soon. It's going to be hard when you go off to college in a few months, but I know we are meant to be together. We're strong, and we can survive the distance.' Wow. It's like a weird version of foreshadowing."

"Please stop," I whispered as I sank to the floor.

Rose closed the book and stood. "Hey, are you okay?"

I shook my head, willing myself not to cry. I knew that message by heart. While I was home caring for Mom, I'd found the yearbook and read the message over and over, desperately clinging to a happier time in my life. Even after our relationship's disastrous ending, I had never loved anyone as much as I'd loved Nate.

And even back then, I'd probably known that what I'd felt for Nate had never gone away. There were times when I was home last spring when I would go into town to buy groceries or pick up a prescription, and out of the corner of my eye, I would catch a glimpse of dark hair. Each time, I turned, my heart fluttering in my chest. It was almost never him, and the few times we had met, our conversations were brief and brutal. All that time, I thought what I felt was dread. But what if it was hope?

"I'm afraid I'm still in love with him," I murmured, not realizing I had spoken aloud.

"Oh, honey." Rose knelt on the floor, wrapping her arms around me and pulling me close.

I raised my eyes to meet Rose's. "I don't know what to do."

"What do you want to do?" Rose asked.

Leaning back against the bed, I sighed. "Part of me worries that I'm just setting us both up for heartbreak again." I rolled my head to look at her. "Even if I break things off with James, I still have that job in California waiting for me."

"I'm sure we could find you a job here. There's bound to be a teaching position at one of the schools."

I kept the news about my interview to myself, mostly so I didn't jinx it. But even if they offered me the position, it wasn't so simple. I still had my promise to my mother hanging over my head. The idea of ending things with James and choosing to stay in Cedar Haven made my skin tight and itchy. Would she ever forgive me if I broke my word? Or would she find a new way to haunt me, one that was less peaceful than a small red bird?

"You're thinking about your mom, aren't you?"

When I glanced at Rose, she was staring at me with a gentle smile. "Am I that transparent?"

"Yes," she said with a laugh, then her face sobered. "And no. I don't pretend to know every complicated detail about your relationship with your mom, but I've learned enough to understand the pressure she put on you." She laid a hand on my shoulder. "She also talked about it once or twice."

I raised my eyebrows. "She did? When? What did she say?"

"Oh, I don't remember the specifics. She wasn't very lucid at the time, but it was more her tone." Rose's eyes softened. "I think she regretted pushing you. She wanted you to be happy. By the end, she seemed to understand that what she thought would make you happy and what actually does are two very different things."

"I'm just so worried that I'll disappoint her." I covered my face in my hands. If seeing me stuck in a loveless marriage was her worst fear, then mine was breaking my promise and smashing her dreams for me.

"As long as you follow your heart, Lanie, I doubt you could ever do that."

I stared up at her, wishing I could believe that, but the truth was, I knew my mother better than that. Maybe she regretted some things when death came knocking, but I couldn't imagine she would ever release me from the promise I'd made.

Rose stood and moved toward my shelves with a box. I wanted to protest that I would take care of the books, but I stopped myself. If we didn't pack something, I might have to pay rent to the new owners.

She paused as a card fluttered out of one of the books. Her forehead creased as she stared at it.

"What's that?" I asked, going to my dresser and pulling out an armful of clothes.

"A business card." She turned to me, one hand on her hip. "For the therapist I recommended."

"Oh, yeah, um, about that," I said, avoiding her gaze.

"Did you even try to go?"

"Yes." I dropped the clothes onto the bed and crossed my arms. "I didn't like her."

"How many appointments did you have?"

"Just the one." At her expression, I rushed on. "But it was enough. Trust me." Turning back to the clothes on the bed, I continued, "Besides, I don't need therapy. I'm fine."

"Sure you are," Rose retorted sarcastically.

I ignored her, folding the clothes and packing them into a rubber bin I'd found in the attic. But I couldn't stop the memory of that awful appointment. Or the image of Dr. Grace Kelvin, with her spectacles halfway down her nose and her eyebrows raised in the most judgmental expression.

"What did she say that was so awful?" Rose asked, her tone gentler than before.

My fist clenched around the hem of a sweater, and I took several deep breaths before responding. "She thought I should confront Mom about all the things she did wrong before it was too late. Dr. Kelvin said that I was shoving my feelings deep down inside and not dealing with them in order to keep the peace."

Rose laid a hand on my shoulder. "And what about that was wrong?"

I whirled around, my mouth dropping open in shock. "How can you say that? I had mere months to spend with my mother, and you think I should have spent them in a constant battle?"

"No." She took the shirt from my hand and placed it in the box. "But I do think you're pushing your feelings away, even now that she's gone. You won't say an ill word about her, despite the fact that even I know there were unresolved issues between you."

My anger deflated, and I sank down onto the bed. "I'm not sure what good it would have done."

"Perhaps not, and maybe Dr. Kelvin was wrong to insist you confront your mom." She sat beside me. "But don't you think you owe it to yourself to work through those issues in a safe and professional environment? Dr. Kelvin can be harsh, but I do believe she saw what we all do, what simmers within you beneath the surface."

"I won't go back, not to her, anyway," I said. "If you have other recommendations, I'll consider them but not her."

"I understand." Rose patted my hand. "It may even be better if you go to someone outside of the community, who doesn't know you at all."

"And what am I supposed to talk about?" My tone was haughty, but I suspected even Rose could see that it was to mask my fear. What would I learn in therapy about my mother, about myself? What did I stand to lose with that knowledge?

"If you're not comfortable talking about your mom, you could talk about Nate, James, whether you should make California or Maryland your home." She shrugged. "It's your hour, but I do think you should try again."

"Fine." I finished packing up the pile of clothes on the bed before I removed another armful from the dresser. Talking about Nate almost sounded worse than discussing my complicated relationship with my mother. Almost.

"This may all be for nothing," I said, trying to lighten the mood. "Who says Nate still feels anything for me? It could all be in my head."

She gave me a dubious look. "Anyone who saw the two of you at karaoke wouldn't believe that for a second."

"But—"

"Well, you can always ask him," Rose cut me off. Her face brightened. "At the Valentine's Day dance!"

"You're relentless," I growled, but deep down, I knew she was right. Nate and I had been dancing around the elephant between us for long enough. Even if it turned out he felt nothing for me, it was better to know, wasn't it? And if that was the case, it would be good for me to have a shoulder to cry on, even if I was paying for that shoulder.

~

After the house went on the market, the real estate agent suggested we hold an open house. I thought the idea came rather last-minute, but Steven agreed. So I spent the week vacuuming the downstairs and clearing away the dust that had gathered. I also forced myself to finish packing my room. I couldn't put it off any longer.

Saturday morning, I woke early and checked to ensure the pamphlets the real estate agent had dropped off the day before were set out on the table in the hall. Steven was bringing muffins, scones, and coffee to be served to potential buyers, and I threw a tray of cookies into the oven for good measure. No one could resist the smell of freshly baked goods, and it might entice someone to make an offer on the spot. At any rate, it couldn't hurt.

My cardinal friend appeared, and I hoped that meant Nate would be at the dance that evening. After the conversation with Rose, I thought it was the best venue to have the talk we needed, though a part of me hoped he would show up at the open house. Either way, I felt that seeing the cardinal was a good omen. Maybe that night, I would finally make some sense of all the conflicting feelings I'd been having lately.

Steven arrived promptly at eight, his arms filled with bags of goodies and a box of freshly brewed coffee. I opened the door for him, and he sniffed the air appreciatively.

"Are you baking in here?" He moved toward the kitchen.

I followed close behind. "I thought it might help add to the appeal."

He smiled and grabbed some paper plates from the cabinet before setting out the various muffins on the counter. Should we have kept the kitchen table until after the house sold? I hadn't minded eating while standing up or carrying food to my room, but perhaps the table would have helped for staging purposes. I shook my head. It was too late.

"You don't have to stay, you know." Steven took one of the muffins and peeled back the paper. "People are just going to be wandering through the rooms and talking to their own agents, if they have one."

"I don't really have anywhere else to be."

He raised an eyebrow. "Aren't you going to the dance tonight? Don't you need to get your hair or nails done or something?"

I laughed. "I'm not going to the prom, Steven. It's just a dance."

He shrugged. "Well, Rose will be here later, and I figured the three of us could go together if you wanted."

"That works for me."

The open house was set to begin at nine, and I made sure I finished getting ready before people started arriving. Steven had brought folding chairs to make up for our lack of furniture.

A few minutes before nine, John, our real estate agent, arrived. I had met him briefly at the estate sale, but Steven had handled most of the real estate stuff. John stood in the living room, scrutinizing every detail with a furrowed brow. His dark hair was cut short, and his small eyes seemed to narrow each time they moved to another corner of the room. I hoped my cleaning hadn't been in vain, though if it didn't live up to his standards, I couldn't imagine what he'd thought of it before.

"When people arrive, try not to bombard them with information. Be available for any questions they might have, but otherwise, let them wander the house at their leisure." John turned to Steven. "I imagine we'll get an offer within a week or so."

"Good," Steven replied. "The sooner we can sell the house, the better."

A sharp pain twinged in my chest, but I forced a smile when John's dark gaze fell on me. No sense in him knowing how much it hurt me to see my childhood home sold. Besides, what else did I expect us to do with it? I was leaving, and Steven had already bought a place for him and Rose to live after they married.

People began drifting in about half past nine, and I kept the smile pasted on my face. I didn't recognize any of the potential buyers, which only served to increase my anxiety. But it made sense that someone outside of town would be interested. Everyone who already lived in Cedar Haven had a home, and I hadn't heard anyone say they were looking to buy.

Steven and John fielded most of the questions, which left me with a lot of time on my hands and not much to distract me. Maybe I should have found something else to do that day, but as the executor, I felt an obligation to be there.

Around noon, Nate entered the house with a frown as he scanned the room. When his eyes met mine, they lit up, and he crossed over to me.

"Good crowd," he said. "Any offers yet?"

I shook my head. "John thinks we'll get one within a week or two."

He glanced at me. "How do you feel about that?"

"I don't know." Were it anyone else, I might have lied. But Nate knew how hard being there was for me. I slipped my hand in his and gave him a squeeze. "Thanks for coming."

"Anything for you."

My heart skipped a beat, and I turned away. I still hadn't talked to either him or James, and I hated myself for it. Well, I'd planned to talk to Nate that night at the dance, but maybe right then was my chance. I opened my mouth to tell him everything when Steven joined us.

"Hey, Nate, thanks for stopping by. You wouldn't happen to be in the market for a new home, would you?"

Nate laughed and shook his head. "Even if I was, I couldn't afford this."

"Well, don't let Lanie here keep you hiding in a corner. We've got a great spread of baked goods in the kitchen." He put a hand on Nate's shoulder and led him away. Nate glanced at me, worry in his eyes, but he didn't resist Steven.

Part of me was glad for the moment to collect my thoughts, which made me a bigger coward. Why couldn't I just tell him? Even if he didn't feel the same, it was better to know that now before I blew up my whole life, wasn't it?

I mustered up my courage and headed to the kitchen, hoping to steal Nate away for a moment alone. But when I arrived, he was gone.

That evening, I picked out a simple red dress. I curled my hair and pulled half of it into a silver butterfly barrette. I was still puzzled about Nate's sudden departure earlier in the day, but I assumed he'd needed to return to the shop. Still, it was odd that he hadn't at least said goodbye.

As I reached into my jewelry drawer for a pair of earrings, my hand hovered over a small box. With hesitant fingers, I pulled it out and flipped it open, knowing full well what was inside: a silver locket with the initials NL engraved on its face. Nate had given it to me on the anniversary of our first date.

Let's not be too obvious. I placed the box back into the drawer. I grabbed a pair of earrings and started to close the drawer, but something told me to wear the locket. Shaking my head, I picked the box up and slipped the chain around my neck before I could change my mind. It did go well with the dress, and maybe it would give me the courage to tell Nate how I felt.

The front door opened, and Steven called for me. While I was happy to ride over with him and Rose, I hoped Nate would give me a lift home and I could broach the conversation then. After grabbing my purse and sliding my feet into a pair of red heels, I went downstairs.

"Well, well, well. Don't you look nice this evening." Steven smiled warmly. "Trying to impress someone?"

I rolled my eyes and slipped into my coat, gesturing for him to lead the way. After he flipped the porch light on, we headed to Steven's car. Rose sat in the passenger seat and gave me two thumbs up. I forced a smile as I climbed into the back seat.

"You look amazing!" Rose gushed.

"Thanks. So do you," I replied, reaching forward and giving Rose's arm a squeeze.

"And of course, I look awesome," Steven teased as he settled into his seat and backed the car down the driveway.

"As always, darling," Rose said sweetly, and I pretended to gag.

The drive to the fire station's hall was short, and I struggled to calm my pounding heart as we pulled into the parking lot. I didn't immediately see Nate's car, but since the whole town was there, that wasn't a surprise. Steven helped me out of his car, and I followed him and Rose into the hall.

Cedar Haven liked to go all out for their events, and the Valentine's Day dance was no exception. The hall was decorated with red and pink balloons. Rich ruby tablecloths were dotted with sequined hearts, and the lights were even shaded to give the room a warmer hue. I smiled wistfully. Despite my earlier grumbling, I had missed those events since going away to college. Even when I was home and caring for Mom, I hadn't had time to attend any town affairs. Growing up, I had a love-hate relationship with Cedar Haven's desire to celebrate every little thing. While holidays like Christmas and Halloween were normal, the town also put on a Presidents' Day play, a May Day celebration, and even a Flag Day parade. Sometimes, it felt a little too much, but I suddenly had a new appreciation for the town's eccentricities.

Trudy and her husband, Russell, sat at a table together, watching the crowds. I left Rose and Steven to go say hello. They greeted me with warm smiles as I took a seat next to Trudy.

"We thought we'd grab a table now, before the crowds take over," Trudy said. She gave me a brief once-over and a raised eyebrow. "You look spectacular."

"Thanks," I replied, a warm flush stealing over my cheeks. I tried to keep my excitement in check. So far, it seemed like the town's rumor mill hadn't caught on to Nate and me, and I hoped to keep it that way.

"Where's the baby tonight?" I asked Trudy, trying to distract myself, though my eyes kept sliding to the door.

"With my mom," Trudy replied with a smile. "She's been chomping at the bit to have an overnight with him, so I thought tonight would be perfect."

"And let me tell you, it's awesome to be off duty," Russell said, clinking his glass with Trudy's. "Parenthood is no joke." He drained his glass. "I'm going to get another one. You want one, babe?"

Trudy shook her head, having barely touched the drink in front of her. I saw that as an opportunity to scout the hall for Nate, and I jumped up to join Russell.

I ordered a glass of wine and tried to discreetly search the room. Rose and Steven were chatting with Bea. I had heard that Bea was cutting back on her hours at the diner and might be looking to sell it soon. Without any close family nearby, she didn't have anyone to take over. I hoped when the time came, someone in town would step up and keep the place the same.

Wine in hand, I started to make my way back to Trudy when I saw him. He stood near the entrance to the hall, talking to some of the guys from the shop. My heart in my throat, I placed the glass on an empty table then rushed over to him.

"Nate, I'm so glad you're here. I'd hoped to catch up with you at the open house, but you left without saying goodbye."

"Lanie," Nate replied, giving a brief nod.

I frowned. "Are you okay?"

"Fine. Excuse me. I forgot something in my car." He turned and stalked away.

For a moment, I stared at his retreating back, shocked at his cold and distant demeanor, then I raced after him.

"Wait!" He didn't turn, and I scrambled to catch up. When I finally did, I grabbed his arm. "Hey, what's going on?"

"Nothing. I told you, I forgot something." But he refused to meet my eyes.

"It looks like you're leaving."

He shrugged. "Maybe I am. There's no point in my being here."

"Why not? The whole town is here, and you're part of the town," I teased, but my joke fell flat. "Please tell me what's going on." I tried to sound firm, but my voice cracked, and I shivered—whether from the winter air or his frigid reception, I couldn't say.

His face softened. "Go back inside before you freeze."

"Come with me. I'd love to dance with you, like old times."

That struck a chord. His eyes darkened, and he pulled his arm free. "Maybe you should dance with your boyfriend."

I staggered back as the air left my lungs, like someone had punched me. "You know about James?"

"Your brother told me." His lips set in a grim line. "*You* should have told me."

He was right. Of course I should have told him. I knew why I hadn't, but I was too much of a coward to admit that to him, even then.

"It just never came up," I said with a shrug. What a terrible excuse.

He shook his head. "This whole time, I thought it was the job taking you to California, but it's not, is it? It's him."

"That's not true! I do have a job lined up." At his raised eyebrow, I blew out a breath. "But yes, James is part of it. He and I have plans to move in together."

Nate inhaled sharply, and I hurried on.

"But things have changed," I said. "These last few weeks, spending time with you, I realized—"

"I don't want to hear it, Lanie," he retorted, backing away from me.

"Nate, please!" I cried, grasping for something to make him understand. Lifting the locket, I held it out, and it glinted in the streetlights. "I wore this tonight for the same reason I sang you that song at karaoke."

His eyes widened when he recognized the locket. "B-But what about your boyfriend?" His tone was rough, and I could see the anger in his eyes dissipating as he stared at the necklace.

"I..." What *about* James? That was the question of the moment. I wasn't being fair to either man. There I was, trying to assure myself of Nate's feelings when I had someone waiting for me in California. How selfish could I possibly be?

Before I could formulate a response, a throat cleared behind me. As I whirled around, my hand flew to my mouth, and I gaped as a familiar figure stepped from the shadows.

"Hello, Lanie."

"James?" It came out more like a whisper. The shock of seeing him stole my breath.

He chuckled as he moved closer to us. His thick dark hair was parted to the side, though I struggled to make out his expression as the light played across his full beard. Pushing his glasses up his nose, he stuck out his hand to Nate.

"I don't believe we've met," James said, his tone cool.

Nate stared at his hand for a moment before he accepted it. I monitored their every moment, both men grim-faced as they shook hands. When they stepped back from each other, they both turned to me. I tried to arrange my features into a blank expression, but I wasn't sure I achieved it. Blood pounded in my ears as I processed the situation.

I swallowed the lump forming in my throat. "What are you doing here?"

James raised an eyebrow. "I came to surprise you."

Well, he'd certainly done that. I glanced at Nate, but his eyes were alighting with the anger that had just disappeared a moment ago. My only hope was to prove how surprised I was by James's sudden appearance, though the fact that I hadn't been up front about James's existence wasn't going to help things. But I would deal with that later.

"It's good to see you," I said, keeping my voice light but detached. "But I wish you had told me you were coming so I could've prepared."

James smirked. "That wouldn't have been much of a surprise, now would it?" He glanced from me to Nate. "After our last phone call, I was worried. Applying to a job here when you have the perfect position waiting for you in California?" He shook his head. "It just wasn't like you. I had a meeting with our DC office anyway and thought it might be nice to conduct it in person. So I booked a flight and figured I'd swing by to visit with you for the weekend."

The tightness in my shoulders eased ever so slightly. While he was in town, at least he wasn't staying long. After he met with the DC office on Monday, he would be back on a plane to California either Monday night or Tuesday morning.

As I processed all that, Nate shifted uncomfortably beside me. I opened my mouth to ask James to give us a minute, hoping I could salvage the conversation we were about to have. But before I could do so, Nate straightened his spine and turned to me.

"It sounds like you two have a lot to talk about," he said, his tone clipped. "I was just leaving anyway." He was stiff and formal as he inclined his head to James. "It was nice to meet you."

"You as well," James said as he came to my side and threw an arm over my shoulders. "Have a pleasant evening."

Nate looked at me then, and I silently pleaded with him to give me a chance to explain. But either he didn't understand the message I was trying to convey, or he didn't care because he spun on his heel and stalked away. A lump lodged in my throat. *Can this night get any worse?*

"Well, this wasn't quite the welcome I'd hoped for," James said, turning me away from Nate and heading toward his rental car. "Here I thought I'd arrive at the dance and you'd come running into my arms. Instead, I interrupt what sounded like a passionate lovers' quarrel."

Heat flooded my cheeks, and I pushed away from him. "You should have told me you were coming."

His expression darkened. "Why? Because I ruined your moment with him?"

When I didn't respond, he continued.

"That's your ex, isn't it? I thought the name sounded familiar. Is that why you applied for that position here?"

I stared at the ground, refusing to respond and confirm everything he'd said. Though I knew I had no right to be angry with him, a flush spread across my body, and my skin tingled. Maybe I wasn't angry. Maybe I was ashamed. No, that wasn't true either. I was angry, but the only person I was angry with was myself.

James ran a hand through his hair and sighed. "Look, we clearly need to talk, and I'd rather not do it in a parking lot while we both freeze. Can we go back to your house?"

With a nod, I opened the passenger door and climbed in. He went to the driver's side and joined me. We drove in silence, the darkness seeming to close in around us. I dreaded the conversation we were about to have.

I sent a text to my brother and Rose, letting them know I had gone home, but I neglected to mention James's arrival. It would only cause more questions I didn't want to answer. I was already facing two difficult conversations. No reason to add another one until it was absolutely necessary.

When we arrived at the house, I got out of the car and marched to the front door, not even bothering to help with James's luggage. Part of me hoped that he would leave it and drive back to DC, but I doubted he'd bothered to get a hotel. My family lived within commuting distance of the city, and I assumed James had planned to stay in Cedar Haven. Whether that would change remained to be seen.

Sure enough, he came in a moment later with his carry-on and a garment bag. He left both by the door and stared at the now-empty house. All that was left were the few things I would take with me. A recliner from my mother's bedroom sat in one corner. The worn-out red couch was gone.

I gestured to the chair, and I sank down onto the stairs. "You can sit there if you like."

He looked from the chair to me before he came over and sat beside me. There wasn't a lot of space on the steps. For a moment, neither of us said anything. I had no idea how to have that conversation or what I wanted to say. As if I wasn't confused enough, my mother's voice echoed in my head. *James is going places. He can take you with him and give you a life you've never dreamed of. Don't let him go. Whatever you do, hold on to that one.*

But was it fair to James, to me, to hold on to him? And did I need him to help me leave? I had gotten the California job on my own merit. I could easily find my own place in LA and still live those old dreams my mother and I had discussed, even without being in a relationship. Besides, what did it say about me if I stayed in a relationship just so I had a guaranteed ticket out of town?

"Do you still love him?" James asked, breaking the silence.

The question caught me off guard, though I couldn't imagine why. One thing I'd always appreciated about James was his directness. I never had to wonder what he thought or where we stood. He was honest and forthcoming, sometimes to a fault.

"I..." Answering that question was harder than I expected. Admitting my feelings to Rose was one thing, but to say them to my boyfriend, the man I was on the precipice of moving in with, was quite another. I swallowed. "I do."

The sentence held a certain irony that I hadn't intended. We weren't engaged, though up until recently, I'd expected we were heading that way. It was what my mom had hoped for, and I thought she was a little put out that James hadn't proposed before she died. But James knew I wasn't ready for marriage back then.

His face contorted as he processed my words. The dark anger in his eyes gave way to pain and sadness, and the hard line of his mouth morphed into a pout. Maybe I should have softened the blow—hemmed and hawed a bit or told him I wasn't sure—but with James, I tried to meet his directness with my own. While I didn't always succeed, I knew he wouldn't want me to spare his feelings. He wouldn't appreciate being placated.

"I see," he said, his voice hoarse. "And I assume that he's the reason you decided to apply for a position here?"

"He's part of it." Also true, though not the whole story. "But it's... complicated."

He waved his hand. "I've got all night."

We stared at each other as I struggled to formulate the words. Figuring that I didn't have much else to lose, I took a deep breath.

"As I told you on the phone, I applied to the position after you told me you found an apartment."

He shook his head. "I just don't understand why it was such a big deal for you."

"We were supposed to go apartment hunting together," I said. "You promised me you would wait until I got back."

"Are you serious?" He gaped at me. "I know what we said, but you had so much on your plate. The least I could do was to have a place for you to land, all ready when you returned."

For some women, his care and attention would seem like a blessing, but for me, it was just another example of an area of my life in which I had no control. I didn't know how to express that without sounding like I'd lost my mind, so I decided to just go with it.

"I appreciate what you were trying to do," I began. "But your actions chipped away at the one area in my life that was still mine." When he frowned at me, I sighed. "I didn't want to come back here."

I threw my arm out on that last word. "I had no desire to be my mom's executor, to go through her things like this, to settle her life like it was some legal transaction. Steven was the obvious choice for executor, but for reasons I may never understand, she picked me. And so, I had no other option but to come back here and face all the memories I've been trying to avoid."

A knot settled in my stomach, but I ignored it. "I held onto the knowledge that when I returned to the West Coast, I would finally be able to make the life I wanted for myself. We talked about getting an apartment together, and I was so looking forward to doing that *with* you, but then you told me you found one." I shut my eyes, taking deep breaths to control my temper. "And of course, it wasn't just any apartment. It had to have all these amenities that we'll probably never use. You chose something so far out of our price range, I expect we'd be living on ramen noodles for the next decade."

It dawned on me at that moment that the problem in my relationship with James was not me or James or even Nate. Our problem was compatibility. James and I had never fully been in sync. After Mom died, when he left me to backpack across Europe, I bottled up my feelings because I didn't want him to miss the trip of a lifetime. But someone who knew me, who understood me, would have recognized how much I needed a shoulder to lean on, a hand to hold.

"We'll manage," he said with a careless shrug.

Ugh. Definitely not *compatible.* I shot him a withering look. "I don't want to just 'manage.' With all the options for housing, why can't we start somewhere smaller? Less expensive?"

"Fine!" he retorted. "Then we'll keep looking, but that doesn't explain why you took such a drastic action. Why can't you just admit it's because you want Nate?"

"Because it has nothing to do with Nate!"

He raised an eyebrow. "How can you say that when you just admitted you have feelings for him?"

I buried my head in my hands. "You didn't let me finish."

For a moment, I thought he was going to argue that point as well, but he leaned against the wall and gestured for me to continue.

"I agree with you that I should have spoken about my reservations. There's no excuse for why I didn't. All I can say in my defense is that I've been under a lot of pressure since I arrived to get things squared away with the house."

He didn't respond, and I was grateful to have a moment to organize my thoughts before I went on. "Nate told me about the position, and then I ran into the teacher who's retiring. The town is really struggling to find a teacher to replace her. When you told me about the apartment, something inside of me just snapped." I left out the part about Cassandra and the cardinal. My reasons were already questionable at best. James would have me committed if he thought I was looking for signs in nature. "So, I applied for the position, and they wanted to interview me the same day, but I haven't accepted anything. I haven't even been offered the job."

"But you will be," he muttered. "And it sounds like you've already made your choice."

In that moment, I realized I *had* made a choice, but it wasn't about my professional life. Regardless of whether I stayed in Cedar Haven or moved to LA, regardless of whether Nate and I found our way back to each other, one thing was certain: I needed to let James go.

"I haven't made a choice about the job," I hedged.

He saw right through my half-truth. "So, that's it, then?" His brown eyes were sad as he looked at me. "You're getting back together with him?"

"I don't know what will happen with Nate," I said, and that was true. After the way he'd left that night, I didn't even know if Nate would speak to me again. "But I'm not being fair to either of you."

It was James's turn to put his head in his hands. His fingers riffled through his hair. "This is not at all how I expected this night to go."

"I'm sorry," I said, knowing all too well how inadequate my apology was.

He leaned back on the stairs and slid a hand into his pocket before pulling out a small black box. "I know it's cliché to propose on Valentine's Day, but you sounded so down on the phone, I thought it'd be a nice surprise to lift your spirits." He gave me a rueful smile that didn't reach his eyes. "Guess I misread that situation entirely, huh?"

My heart was heavy as I met his gaze, tears brimming behind my eyes. "I really am sorry, James. I never meant to hurt you." I took his hand. "I was going to tell you everything the next time we spoke."

"Well, I suppose this was better than a Dear John letter or a text."

I bumped his shoulder with mine. "I wouldn't break up with you over text."

"Appreciate that." He sniffled, and I could tell he was barely holding it together.

"Look, why don't you crash here?" I pointed up the stairs. "You can have my bed, and I'll sleep in the recliner. It's too late to drive back into the city."

With a sad smile, he stood. "I need some time alone."

The knot in my stomach grew, but I nodded. I understood why he wouldn't want to be around me right then, but I hoped that I would see him again. I prayed that one day, he would forgive me. He had been there for me through some of my darkest moments, and I didn't want him to disappear from my life completely.

We walked to the door, and he put his hand on the knob, hesitating. When he turned back to me, the tears he had been fighting were streaming down his cheeks.

"I hope you figure it out, Lanie, and that you live the life you want, not one someone else dreamed for you."

I was taken aback by his words, but before I could formulate a response, he stepped into the cold winter's night and shut the door behind him. I didn't know how long I stood there in the empty hallway, staring at that door, but eventually, my back began to ache from lack of movement, and I moved to the kitchen.

Checking my phone, I felt my chest tighten when I saw I had no messages. I debated texting Nate but decided against it. My emotions were chaotic enough after the conversation I'd just had with James. No need to put my heart through the wringer a second time that evening.

I could text Rose, and I knew she would rush right over, hold my hand, and see me through my grief. But the one I wanted to talk to most of all was the person I could never talk to again. My chest ached, and I placed my hand on the wall to hold myself up.

"Oh, Mom," I whispered to the empty house. "What have I done?"

Chapter Ten

Sleep eluded me well into the night. I tossed and turned for hours until I finally gave up and just lay on my bed, staring at the ceiling. What was I going to tell Nate about James? More importantly, *how* was I going to tell Nate? Would he even agree to see me? Would he even care? Last night, he was so cold and distant, even before James arrived. Sure, I should have told him about James sooner, but it wasn't like he'd been clear about how he felt about me either. One minute, he acted aloof and detached, and the next, he gave me one of those sexy smiles that melted my heart.

And he still hadn't told me whatever secret he was keeping about my mom. I'd pushed it out of my mind, choosing to focus on our time together, but it ate away at me. Lately, it felt like my mother was a puzzle I couldn't solve, as if I struggled to piece together the woman I knew and the one I'd discovered only after her death. The puzzle remained unfinished without the information Nate had withheld, a mystery that wouldn't be resolved until that last piece revealed itself.

The pitch-black of my room lightened to a dull gray as if even the sun refused to shine on me that day. I supposed I deserved that. My eyes burned from lack of sleep, and I dragged myself from bed in hopes a cup of coffee or five might help me make it through the day.

When I entered the kitchen, my gaze immediately strayed to the window, searching in vain for my cardinal. The one time I could really use a message from the beyond, and it was nowhere in sight. *Figures.* Maybe the cardinal's absence conveyed a message in and of itself.

After I poured my coffee, a flash of red caught my eye. I hurried over to the window. My little friend perched on the sill, staring in at me with its small black eyes. It chirped, and I could swear I heard a hint of annoyance in the song.

"What do I do now?" I asked.

The bird chirped again then flitted along the windowsill, its feet clinging to the edge. When it reached the end, it fluttered down to the back porch, and I moved to the sliding glass door in the dining room. It hopped closer to the door and cocked its head at me.

"Did I make the right decision, breaking up with James?"

Another chirp came, that time a short syllable. I shook my head. Why did I expect some poor bird to understand the complexities of my life when I could barely make sense of them myself?

My phone pinged, and my heart jumped into my throat. But it was a text from Rose.

Come dress shopping with me.

I laughed, though it sounded hollow. *Don't you already have a wedding dress?*

Not for me. For you. We need to get you an MOH dress.

When I glanced at the window, the cardinal was gone. A shopping trip was exactly what I needed to avoid wallowing all day. And who knew? The cardinal had shown up before I saw Nate countless other times, so maybe I would run into him again that day. I confirmed I'd meet her at the mall that afternoon and rushed to get ready.

After I'd showered and dressed, I checked my phone. But I still didn't have any messages from Nate. With a sigh, I dialed his number, crossing my fingers. It went straight to voicemail. Sinking onto my bed, I debated what I wanted to say.

"Hey, Nate, it's Lanie." I paused. "We need to talk." That was the understatement of the year, but I didn't want to pour my heart out in a voicemail. "Give me a call when you get the chance."

Did my tone convey everything I wasn't saying? Probably not, but at least it was a start. I'd taken the first step. The ball was in his court, which did little to comfort me. I could only hope he would give me another chance, though I had no reason to expect him to. I'd likely exhausted my quota of second chances.

Rose was already browsing dresses when I arrived. The warmth of her embrace chased away the dark thoughts from the morning, and I knew I had made the right decision in escaping the house.

"What are your wedding colors?" I joined her in flipping through the options on the rack in front of us.

"Lavender and blue with pink and yellow accents." Rose's brown eyes brightened whenever she talked about the wedding. "I want it to look like a late-summer sunset."

"Okay." At least I had several options to work with. "What color were you thinking for my dress?"

"Not yellow," Rose said, wrinkling her nose. "I've never been a fan of yellow dresses, and with your skin tone, it would probably wash you out."

A shocked laugh bubbled up in my throat, but I knew she didn't mean anything by the comment. My gaze strayed to a sleeveless dark-blue dress, and I pulled it out and held it up for her to see.

"I was hoping for purple or pink, but I'm not opposed to blue." Rose fingered the material. "But maybe something paler?"

With a nod, I returned the dress and continued flipping through the options. "Is Steven having a best man now that you've chosen me for maid of honor?"

"To be honest, I'm not sure. He has several options, but I think he was leaning toward asking your father."

"Oh, he'd be honored." I smiled. "Well, he may not show it, but I know he would be, deep down."

Rose chuckled. "Your father definitely fits the bill for the strong, silent type." She held up a pink number with ruffles down the front. "Too frilly." As she slipped it back on the rack, she turned. "Do you think he'll ever remarry?"

The question caught me off guard. I chose my words carefully. "Doubtful. It's been so long since the divorce. If he was going to remarry, I expect he would have done it by now."

"Maybe he held out hope your mom would find her way back to him," Rose said. "And now that she's really gone, he'll finally move on."

I shrugged, not entirely comfortable with the direction the conversation was taking. "He's never said anything to me about it, and as far as I know, he doesn't date."

"Speaking of dating." Rose pounced on the opening. "How's James?"

"He, uh, he was here." I walked over to a different rack and hoped my words would be too mumbled for her to make out.

"Wait, James came to visit you? When? Where?" She rushed after me, grabbing my arm and spinning me around. "Why didn't you tell me?"

"He showed up at the Valentine's dance." I shifted away from her, focusing all my attention on the various materials in front of me. The taffeta, silk, and cotton flowing through my fingers kept me grounded.

"Well?" Rose tapped her foot. "What happened?"

I sighed. Since no one else had seen James, I'd hoped to keep his appearance between him, Nate, and me, but I couldn't see a way out of the conversation.

I grabbed Rose's hand and led her away from the sales floor. While the store was technically just outside of Cedar Haven, it was the only bridal store nearby. I didn't want any prying eyes or listening ears to spread gossip about me back in town.

Once we were safely ensconced in a corner, I relayed the whole sordid tale, making sure to include the awkward moment James appeared and Nate's cold shoulder afterward. With every word I said, Rose's eyes seemed to grow wider.

"You broke up?" She yanked me to her and wrapped me in a tight embrace. "Oh, you poor thing. Why didn't you tell me?"

"You have enough on your plate with the wedding." Well, that, and somehow, saying it out loud made the whole situation that much more real.

"Have you told Steven?"

I shook my head. "You're the first person I've told. I want to tell Nate, but he's not speaking to me at the moment."

"Are you hoping to get back together with Nate?"

I pressed my lips into a thin line. "Right now, I'd just like to *talk* to him. Explain what happened with James and apologize for not mentioning him sooner." I glanced behind me, but we were still blissfully alone. "But you can't tell anyone about James. The last thing I need is to add fuel to the fire of my father's campaign to convince me to stay here."

"But will you?" Rose's forehead creased. "I mean, if you and James aren't together, what reason do you have to return to California?"

"I still have my job opportunity." I crossed my arms. "And I did promise my mother I wouldn't settle down here."

She rolled her eyes. "I don't think she can very well hold you to that now."

"I promised her, Rose, and that means something to me." As she opened her mouth to protest, I held up a finger. "I'm not saying I won't stay, but I have some soul-searching to do before I make up my mind." I blew out a breath. "Besides, I can't very well ask her to release me from my promise now."

"Well." Rose smirked. "You could ask the cardinal."

~

Nate still hadn't responded to my voicemail by the time the sun rose Monday morning. He also hadn't responded to my five text messages, two emails, or my failed attempts at telepathy. Could I blame him? Of course not, but I still hoped he would let me explain.

It would have been nice to get that chance before my therapy appointment, but it didn't look likely. With a groan, I dragged myself out of bed and into a hot shower. I was running too late to have my usual leisurely coffee in the kitchen. As I ran out the door with my hair still damp, a spot of red caught my eye. The cardinal was perched on my mother's car, staring at me.

"Here to wish me luck before I face my doom?" I asked it as I opened the driver's-side door and tossed my purse in.

It chirped at me before flying away. Much as I wanted to take the cardinal's appearance as a good omen, Nate's refusal to respond to any of my attempts at communication made me second-guess the purpose of the cardinal's visits. Maybe Cassandra was wrong. Maybe it was just a bird looking for its next meal.

As I drove to the therapist's office, I questioned my decision to forego breakfast. On the one hand, my anxiety had convinced me I wouldn't be able to keep down any food. But on the other hand, the burning in my stomach would only increase the longer I went without.

I almost chickened out. After parking my car, I breathed deeply, trying to settle the panic clawing up my chest. It was just one appointment. If I hated it, I never had to go back. But I didn't want to face my grief. Not yet. Let me get through the sale of the house and probate court. Then, I promised myself, I would take the time to grieve.

Gritting my teeth, I forced myself out of the car and marched with stiff legs into the office. The receptionist gave me a kind smile as I approached the desk.

"How can I help you?"

"I'm here for my appointment," I said. "Lanie McAllister."

She nodded and pushed a clipboard on the counter toward me. "If you'll just fill this out, I'll let Dr. Brooks know you're here."

I took the clipboard and found a seat, grateful that the waiting room was empty. The first few questions on the form were easy, asking about family history and insurance. More difficult to answer were the sections on symptoms. I did my best, unsure whether I was answering things in the right way or if I'd put myself at risk of being committed. When I finished, I stumbled to the reception desk and shoved the clipboard back, wanting to get it as far away from me as possible.

"Thank you," the receptionist said. "Dr. Brooks will see you now." She motioned for me to go through the door behind her.

Every inch of me wanted to run, but it was too late. Dr. Brooks herself opened the door. She was a petite redhead with her hair clipped in a twist behind her head. Her peasant dress flowed loosely down her body, giving her a Bohemian air. I contrasted her appearance with my memories of Dr. Kelvin. Maybe the stark differences were a good sign the visit wouldn't be a repeat of my last attempt at getting help.

"Welcome, Lanie. Come in and make yourself comfortable."

Her office had several different chairs and a couch set up, allowing patients to choose to sit where they were most comfortable. What did a choice say about me? If I sat on the couch, would she expect me to lie down? Or if I chose a chair with a straight back, would she think I was rigid and incapable of change?

I opted for the chair that looked the most comfortable, with green cushions and wooden legs. It sat directly across from the office chair I assumed was hers.

As she settled into her chair, I hid a smile. What did the office chair say about her? Was it simply easy to maneuver back and forth between her desk and the area where her patients sat? Or did it give her a sense of authority?

I shook my head. Maybe I *was* going crazy, thinking so much about nonexistent messages from a stupid chair.

She smiled at me. "Why don't you tell me what brings you in today?"

"Well, my mother passed away this summer—"

"Oh, I'm so sorry," she said. "That must have been difficult." Her face softened, and her tone was kind and genuine.

"Yes, it was. I mean, well, we knew it was coming. She had cancer, and I'd come home to take care of her." I cleared my throat to stop the babble train coming out of my mouth. "Anyway, I'm back now because she appointed me executor of her estate, and I guess I'm struggling?"

Why did I end that speech with a question? "At least, my sister-in-law, who is a nurse, suggested I should go to therapy."

"Have you tried therapy before?"

"Once, while caring for my mom." I hung my head, though I couldn't say why I felt ashamed. Did it count as failing at therapy if I went to only one session? Was it *possible* to fail therapy?

"Why did you stop going?"

I shifted in my seat. "I felt like the therapist was judging me."

She nodded and made a note in her clipboard. *Oh great, now she probably thinks I'm paranoid.*

"I mean, I'm sure she wasn't," I hurried on. "But I was in a vulnerable place, and I didn't take some of her suggestions very well."

Her head tilted. "What did she suggest, if you don't mind my asking?"

"My mom and I didn't always get along." I stared at my hands. "And since she died so young, we didn't get to resolve all of our issues before she was gone." My throat closed, and I swallowed the lump that formed. "The therapist said I should have had it out with her before she died so we could resolve everything."

"Ah, so she thought you and your mother would benefit from closure?" With a frown, she tapped her pencil against her paper. "I'm not sure I agree. While I hope to help you gain closure through our sessions, I don't think it would have been appropriate to spend your mother's last days arguing about things that occurred as part of your shared past."

"That's what I said!" The churning in my stomach settled as a feeling of validation swept over me.

She leaned forward, causing a lock of auburn hair to slip out of her clip. "Sometimes, the person we actually need closure from is ourselves."

I didn't understand what she meant, but something about her words resonated deep within me. I settled into my chair and smiled for the first time since the dance. Maybe therapy wouldn't be so bad after all.

~

The hour flew by faster than I anticipated, and I was disappointed when she announced our time was up. But I made an appointment to see her the following week. Rose would be so proud of me.

We mostly talked about my mom and how it felt to be back in Cedar Haven. I touched on the situation with Nate a little toward the end, and she encouraged me to give myself more time. She said I had just ended a serious relationship and the last thing I should do was jump headfirst into another one.

As I walked to my car, I pulled out my phone and turned it on. My heart leapt into my throat when I saw I had a voicemail. I listened, relief washing over me as Nate apologized for not getting back to me sooner. I dialed his number, and butterflies fluttered in my belly when he answered on the first ring. His voice was gruff and cold, but I focused on the fact he was even taking my calls.

"I need to talk to you about the other night," I began. "Any chance you can come over?" When he didn't respond, I hurried on. "Or I could go there or meet you somewhere. Please just give me a chance to explain."

His silence made my heart pound harder, then he heaved a sigh. "You don't need to explain anything, Lanie. I understood everything when James showed up, and he's come a long way to see you. You should spend time with him."

"James is gone," I blurted out, smacking my forehead as all of my carefully worded arguments floated away. "We broke up Saturday, and he'll be heading back to California tomorrow."

The silence returned, but it seemed different, more shocked than angry. I didn't allow myself to hope it meant he would listen to me.

"Please, Nate," I said. "Just give me a half hour. I promise not to take up too much of your day."

Another sigh. "Now is not a really good time."

Perhaps I had misread the cardinal's visit. Maybe it had come to comfort me, knowing that I'd lost my shot at a second chance with Nate. My breath hitched in my throat, and before I could stop it, my eyes swam with tears.

"Are you... Are you crying?" Nate asked, his voice softer.

"No," I lied, but then I sniffled, giving myself away.

"It's not that I don't want to see you. It's just, um, how do you feel about cats?"

Well, that was unexpected. I frowned. "Cats? Um, half my family is allergic to them, but I don't mind them. Why?"

He huffed a laugh. "It's a long story, but I can show you when you get here if you want to come over."

A grin split my face, and I was so relieved he was willing to talk to me that I brushed off his strange question. "Thank you, Nate. I'll be there in a few!"

On the drive over, I rehearsed my speech, making sure I went over the points I wanted to make to help him understand how I felt about him. And I hoped that in the course of our heart-to-heart, he would finally tell me about making peace with my mom.

When I arrived at his house, Nate nudged open the door, and I peeked in at the large dog he held back. He motioned me in and shut the door behind me, keeping a firm grip on the dog's collar.

"Sorry about him," Nate said as he led me into the living room.

"We don't get visitors often, and Lucky tends to go a little crazy with new people."

"I didn't know you had a dog." I leaned down to stroke Lucky's head. He licked my face and let out an excited bark. His tail thumped heavily on the floor. "What kind of dog is he?"

"A mutt." Nate ran an affectionate hand over Lucky's back. "He's a mix of sheltie, golden retriever, and lab."

I could definitely see the lab in the dark fur and the shape of his face. "Why did you ask me about cats if you have a dog?"

Nate's expression changed, and he released Lucky, taking my hand instead. "Follow me."

We went to the side of his house where the bedrooms were, and he opened a door. The room had a desk and a computer on one side. On the other was a bed, two bowls, and a cardboard box with litter in it. Curled up on the chair by the computer was the cutest little gray kitten I'd ever seen.

"Aww, who is this little guy?" I asked, slipping over and kneeling to let the kitten sniff me. He nuzzled his face into my hand, and I scratched his ears.

"That's Shadow. I found him last night after the dance."

I looked up at Nate. "No mama cat around?"

He shook his head. "Not that I could find. This one was half starved and freezing. I took him to the emergency vet last night, and they said he was fine, just cold and hungry. I picked up a few odds and ends to make him comfortable, but I planned to get more stuff today." He crouched beside me, running a hand over Shadow's fur.

I smiled. "I'm glad to see you never lost your love of animals. Though I wish you'd found a way to turn it into a career."

"I've been thinking about that lately," he said, keeping his gaze on the cat. "While it's probably too late to start a career as a veterinarian, and I wouldn't feel right selling the shop, I've thought about volunteering at the animal shelter."

"That's a great idea! And who knows? Maybe you could find a

position part-time at the vet. They were always seeking assistants when I was growing up."

He ran a hand through his hair. "I don't know. It might not be conducive to keeping my hours at the shop."

I shrugged. "So cut back. You're the boss, after all. And I'm sure Jeff would love to be in charge more often, gain that experience."

"Maybe. Anyway," he said, clearly trying to change the subject, "I've been bottle-feeding Shadow every few hours since I found him. That's why I haven't texted you." His eyes met mine. "Well, that, and I wasn't sure what to say."

I nodded, focusing on stroking Shadow's fur while I worked up the nerve to give my speech. Nate stood and held out a hand to help me up. Each time we touched, that familiar flash of heat traveled up my arm.

He led me to the living room. A black couch lined the back wall, directly across from a television stand. Perched on the stand was a small flat-screen TV, almost as dusty as the one we'd just removed from my mom's house. I supposed he didn't have much time to watch it with his hours at the shop.

"Do you want something to drink?"

"Water would be nice," I said, my throat suddenly very dry.

While he went to the kitchen, I mentally rehearsed once more what I would say as I surveyed the rest of the room. I noted how bare the walls were and how dark the house seemed, even with rays of light peeking in the window on the side. Had he recently moved in? Nate had always been a minimalist, but that was extreme, even for him.

When he returned with the glasses, I took a long drink, buying myself some time. "Have you lived here long?"

"A few months," he said, scanning the room as if seeing it for the first time. "I know it's a bit spartan, but I don't need much."

"So I remember."

He frowned. "You said you wanted to talk."

"I do." A flush crept up my neck as I remembered saying those exact words to James the other night. I cleared my throat and steeled myself. "I'm sorry for not telling you about James sooner. The truth is, I wasn't sure there was any point in it. When I first came home, I planned to finalize the estate as soon as possible and then hightail it to California."

"And now?"

I met his gaze. His eyes were wary, but underneath, I thought I detected a hint of hope. I didn't allow myself to dwell on that, as there were a few things I wanted to explain before I got to where things currently stood.

"James and I had agreed that we would go apartment shopping together. But then, the day you and the guys came over to help us move furniture, he called to tell me he'd found the perfect place for us to live." I twisted my hands. "I don't know exactly why that hit me so hard, but it did." Then I launched into the same things I had told James about feeling like I had so little control over my life and how being part of the process of finding a place to live meant a lot to me.

"I understand," Nate said. "Did you tell him that?"

I shook my head. "Not at the time, but we talked about it after we left the dance." My throat closed, and I swallowed the lump that formed. "He asked me if I still had feelings for you."

Nate went still beside me, as if he was holding his breath, waiting for the answer. I forced myself to look at him, wanting him to see in my face, in my eyes, the truth of what I was about to say.

"I told him I still care for you."

While a light came into his eyes, he didn't comment on my revelation. "What did he say?"

"Well, he wasn't thrilled." I closed my eyes. "He planned to propose to me that night." Nate sucked in a breath, but I went on before he could speak. "Obviously, that didn't happen. But he did say something that's been weighing on my mind."

"What's that?"

I opened my eyes and looked at him. "He said that I shouldn't live someone else's dreams for me, and I can't help wondering if he meant my mom." I dropped my gaze to my lap. "She made it no secret how she felt about you, at least in high school. And she liked James, mainly because she believed he was my ticket out of Cedar Haven."

"Was that why you were with him? For her sake?"

I sighed and stood from the couch before pacing the floor. "I wish I could say no. It's not like I felt nothing for James, but..." I stopped pacing and stared out the window at the back of the room. "I don't know that I would have stayed with him as long had it not been for her encouragement."

He was silent as he digested all of that, and I pressed my lips together to keep from babbling to fill the quiet. I returned to the couch and collapsed against it, preparing for a long wait.

"Is that why you applied for Mrs. Carlisle's position? To have control?"

I shrugged. "Yes and no. Initially, James's revelation about the apartment was a driving force. But something Steven said stuck in my mind as well. He thought I could do more good in a small school like that than in the special school in LA." I took his hand, lacing our fingers. "But I had other reasons."

His face softened, and he squeezed my hand. "Did you mean what you said to James? About... me?"

A laugh bubbled out of my throat, clearly surprising us both. "I wouldn't have blown up my relationship if I hadn't meant it."

He gave me that heart-melting smile then. "And you and James are definitely over?"

I nodded. "He returned to the city, and he'll be flying back to California tomorrow."

One minute, I sat on the edge of the couch, facing him, and the next, he yanked me into his arms and held me close. Once I got over the shock, I laid my head on his chest and listened to his heartbeat, sighing contentedly.

Too soon, he pulled away. "I'm glad you told me, but I want to take this slow, Lanie." I opened my mouth, but he pressed a finger to my lips. "Don't misunderstand me. I still have feelings for you too." He tucked a lock of hair behind my ear. "But you just lost your mother, are in the process of selling your childhood home, and ended a long-term relationship the other night. Any one of those things would cause a lot of upheaval in life, but I can only imagine how hard it's been dealing with all three." He took my hand in his. "So I want to give you the time and space to sort through what you want. You've still got that job waiting for you in California, and you may choose to go."

"I think that's wise," I said, though part of me didn't love the idea.

"But maybe I can help you sort through some things," he said. "Besides your mother, what drew you to James, and what made you decide to move to California?"

"We met at school, freshman year of undergrad," I said, not sure he really wanted to hear any of that. "I was sitting in the cafeteria, having lunch by myself. All of my roommates had classes in the afternoon while mine were mostly in the morning. He was with his friends, and they came over to ask if they could sit with me." I laughed lightly. "Later, he told me he felt compelled to sit with me, like something was pulling him there."

"Fate?" I could see in Nate's eyes how much it pained him to ask.

"I don't know that I believe in fate," I replied. "Not in a universal sense." I couldn't keep the edge out of my voice, and Nate noticed.

"What do you mean?"

I shifted on the cushion and avoided his gaze. "You're going to think I'm crazy."

"I promise I won't."

Little did he know that was a promise he couldn't keep. With a sigh, I pushed myself off the back of the couch and turned to look at him. "Have you ever heard a legend about cardinals?"

He shook his head and gestured for me to go on.

"I went to see my neighbor, Cassandra, the other day," I began. "I've been seeing this cardinal often, particularly before seemingly innocuous events in my life that later prove to be important in some way. I saw it the morning my mom's car had the flat, the day we had lunch at Bea's, the day you came to help with the estate sale, the day of my interview, before the dance, and this morning."

His eyes widened further, but he didn't say anything. Unsure what to make of his reaction, I pressed on.

"Cassandra told me that cardinals are visitors from heaven, our loved ones who have passed away, coming back to check on us, often with a message. She suggested the cardinal might be my mother, and the days she chose to visit were to help convey her message." I glanced at him. "It's like she's pointing me to you. After what you told me this morning, I-I'm starting to believe it."

Every moment that Nate sat there staring at me caused my anxiety to increase. He thought I'd lost it, and I couldn't blame him. My chest grew tight, and I stood to leave, but he grabbed my wrist and pulled me back beside him. I perched on the edge of the cushion, still worried he would have me committed.

"I saw a cardinal this morning before you called," he finally shared.

"You did?" I demanded, raising my eyebrows.

"Briefly. Besides feeding Shadow, I haven't been sleeping well the past two nights," he admitted. "I didn't like how we left things. When I finally gave up and went to get coffee, there was a little cardinal on my back deck."

"What did it look like?" I could barely breathe. *If the cardinal was a messenger, then what message did it convey by visiting Nate?*

Nate's lips twitched as he fought back a grin. "Like a red bird."

I rolled my eyes. "I mean, was there anything about it that stuck out to you? The one I've seen has weird black dots by its beak, almost like freckles."

"I didn't get that close of a look," Nate said. "You saw it this morning too?"

I nodded. "It was the sign I was looking for to call you." We gazed at each other, both digesting the revelations, then I grinned. "My mom is still meddling, even from beyond the grave."

Nate threw back his head and laughed, which was music to my ears. I couldn't remember the last time I had heard him laugh like that, so joyous and carefree. Certainly not since I'd been home.

"Did you tell James about the cardinal?" he asked, and the light in his eyes dimmed.

I shook my head, turning away. "I didn't see the point. Besides, he wouldn't understand."

"Why do you think that?"

"James is... practical... rational. He would explain it away as being coincidental." While I'd once loved James for his directness, he could be harsh, even when he didn't mean to be.

"Well, I appreciate you sharing it with me," Nate said, and his face was sincere.

I grabbed his hand and gave it a squeeze, and I fell back against the couch. The conversation and all the anxiety leading up to it had drained me. Frankly, I could use a nap, but I didn't want to leave him, not yet.

"I don't know about you," Nate said, "but I'm going to need something stronger than water if I have any hope of staying awake for the rest of the day."

We went to the kitchen, and Nate put on a pot of coffee. His house was small but adequate for his needs. The kitchen had all the essentials, but I could tell that the microwave saw the most action. Some of the labels on the buttons were worn down from use. A small window overlooked his postage-stamp yard.

And there on the back deck stood my cardinal. It chirped at me before fluttering closer to the window, peering in at both of us.

"Look! Do you see? I told you I was being stalked by a cardinal!" I pointed.

"I saw, and you're not going to believe this, but I swear when it came this morning, that bird *winked* at me," Nate replied, handing me a mug of coffee.

"Oh, I believe it." I shook my head.

"I think your theory about it being your mother is sound. I can't imagine anyone else being this persistent."

I gazed at him thoughtfully. Making up my mind, I set down my mug and went toward him, biting back a smile at the apprehension on his face. As I wrapped my arms around his neck, I tilted my face toward his, licking my lips. Nate froze, and as I pressed against him, I could feel his heart pounding in his chest. I angled my head closer, but at the last moment, I turned my face away and gazed out the window.

The cardinal perched precariously on the windowsill, staring right at us through the glass. I started giggling, and Nate joined me, though his body sagged against mine, and I wasn't sure if it was from relief or disappointment. But then he leaned down and kissed the top of my head. I sighed and pressed my face to his chest, breathing in his distinct scent of Old Spice and Ivory soap.

"I missed this," I whispered.

His arms tightened around me. "Me too."

Chapter Eleven

THE NEXT MORNING, I WOKE TO THE SOUND OF MY PHONE buzzing beside me. Bleary-eyed, I picked it up and tapped the screen.

The house is under contract.

I blinked. Already? While John had said he'd expected we would get offers soon, I'd thought we'd have to wait a few weeks at least. I sat up in bed and stared at my empty room. Steven said the closing date was to be determined, but I assumed it would be sometime in March. Things were happening a lot faster than I'd anticipated, and it made my head spin.

That also meant I would be moving out soon. I hadn't seen much of my father since the estate sale. Perhaps it was time to fix things with him. I didn't know how long I would be stuck there, and I didn't want us to spend that time at each other's throats.

As tired as I was, I knew I wouldn't be able to fall back to sleep. I stumbled down the stairs and started my usual routine. While I'd cleaned before the open house, I decided to spend the day shampooing the carpets. With most of the furniture gone, it would be easier to do a thorough job.

A few hours later, my phone rang, interrupting one of my favorite songs. When I recognized the number, my eyes widened, and my irritation melted away. Taking a deep breath to compose myself, I answered in my most professional-sounding voice.

"Lanie McAllister speaking."

"Hello, Lanie. This is Principal Wilson. Is this a good time to talk?"

"Yes, this is a good time," I replied, trying to keep the apprehension out of my voice.

"Good. I'm calling about the special education position. We were very impressed with your credentials and would like to offer the job to you."

"Oh, wow! Thank you," I breathed.

"Now, I understand you already have a position you're considering, so I wanted to give you all the details and then give you time to make your decision. Does that sound fair?"

"That works for me."

"While you wouldn't officially be in charge of the students on your own until next year, we're hoping that if you accept the position, you'd start working with Mrs. Carlisle in April so she can train you. The county has granted us a special dispensation to pay for both of your salaries during your training."

I listened as the principal continued detailing the salary and the expectations, nodding along even though Mrs. Wilson couldn't see me. I asked about a start date and was told they would be flexible.

"Before you decide, I'd love to have you work with our students on the Presidents' Day play. Mrs. Carlisle has done a wonderful job with the kids each year, and it would give you an opportunity to see what working in our school would be like. It's completely optional, of course, but I encourage you to think about it."

"That sounds like a wonderful idea. When are rehearsals?"

"After school from three to five. I'll send you an email with the official offer letter and all the details."

"Great! Thank you so much," I said. As I hung up the phone, the first person I wanted to tell was Nate, but I stopped myself.

Was it fair to share the news with him when I hadn't made up my mind to accept? Wouldn't I just be getting his hopes up if I later decided to go to California? As much as I wanted to tell him, I decided to take some time to really consider the offer. Then, if I did decide to accept it, the news would be that much sweeter, as it meant I was staying.

My phone chimed again, and I hated how my heart leapt into my throat when I thought it was from Nate. Instead, my father's name popped up on the screen.

We need to talk. Dinner? 6?

With a sigh, I confirmed I would be there, already dreading the evening. We needed to hash things out, especially since I'd be living with him for the foreseeable future, but that didn't mean I was looking forward to the conversation. He texted me the address of a restaurant outside of town, and I returned to the cleaning with a churning stomach.

Hours later, the carpets were drying, and a knot formed in my belly as I prepared to meet my father. I picked out a simple dress and yanked my hair into a tight bun. A quick dash of lip gloss and mascara, and I was ready to go. After tossing my keys, wallet, and phone into my purse, I headed out and climbed into Mom's car. It ran a lot smoother since Nate's shop had done so much work on it. I knew it would fetch a good price when I sold it, but at the thought of that, I felt a hollowness in my chest. Little by little, I lost more pieces of my mother.

As I pulled into the parking lot of the restaurant, I searched for Dad's car. It sat near the entrance, and I smiled ruefully. He probably arrived early to find a good spot. Max McAllister was a predictable man. I parked in the best spot I could find and went inside. He sat at the bar, nursing a beer.

"Hi, Dad." I gave him an awkward hug.

He grunted what passed for a hello and led me over to the hostess stand. "My party is here, and we'd like to be seated."

"Wonderful," the hostess said. "Right this way." We followed her to a booth in the back of the restaurant. My chest constricted at the distance between us and the rest of the diners. Did he request that spot because he expected a heated conversation?

"Thank you," he said as we slid into our seats.

The hostess nodded and scurried away. I wished I could follow.

"How are you?" I asked, trying to lighten the mood.

He waved his hand. "No need for pleasantries. You know why we're here."

"To have a nice dinner?"

"Don't play dumb, Lanie. We both know that we need to finish our discussion about your choice to leave."

I took a deep breath. Neither Steven nor my father knew that I'd even interviewed for the local position, let alone that they'd made an offer. I'd kept it from Steven for the same reason I hadn't texted Nate that afternoon—I didn't want to get his hopes up. But my father would take it as a win, and I refused to give him that satisfaction, especially since I'd yet to make up my mind.

"I'm not sure what's left to discuss." I kept my tone light and my eyes on my menu. "We've both made our feelings very clear, but as it's my life, I get the final say."

He opened his mouth, probably to respond with some sarcastic retort, but I was saved by the server. She took our orders, though I had to admit, the idea of eating right then made me nauseated. I resisted the urge to glare when he ordered steak and potatoes. His doctor had given him strict orders to avoid red meat because his cholesterol was so high, but we had enough battles ahead of us without adding his health to the list.

"Have you given any more thought to the position at the middle school here?"

I blanched. "How did you know about that?"

"Steven told me. Apparently, Nate told him about it when he came by to help move the furniture." My father raised his eyebrows. "Are you going to answer my question?"

Buying time, I took a sip of water. My best bet was to tell him a half-truth. He wasn't the most social of people, and I doubted he would find out about the offer before I told him. However, I knew he'd probably already heard that I'd interviewed.

"I applied for the position."

"Good," he said, leaning back in his seat with a satisfied smile. "What are you going to tell them when they offer it to you?"

"First, we don't know if they will offer it to me. And second, I have that job in California that I've already accepted—"

"I'm sure if you explain the situation, they'll understand," he interrupted. "Besides, you don't even start until the summer. If you tell that other school you've found a job here, that will give them plenty of time to replace you."

"Dad, we've been over this." It didn't matter that I'd recently begun to second-guess my decision to go to California or that I'd broken up with James. If I decided to stay in Cedar Haven, it had to be because it was *my* choice, not because I'd been bullied into it by my father.

He leaned forward, his thick, dark eyebrows pulling down over his brown eyes. A fire burned in his eyes, and I knew he was working to keep his infamous temper in check.

I stared back at him, rising to the challenge and not blinking. A moment later, he surprised me by lowering his gaze and taking a long drink from his water.

"Heard James came to see you," he said, his voice nonchalant.

I kept my face neutral. "And?"

"Well, as he's not with you, I assume he left in a hurry."

He was trying to rattle me, but I refused to let him see how much he'd succeeded. If he knew James and I broke up, he would use it to further his goal of convincing me to stay, and I couldn't allow him that power.

"He's in DC on business." I shrugged but didn't meet his eye. "He had to return to the city, and he's flying back to LA today."

Our food arrived, and I forced myself to focus on my salad, even though my small appetite vanished as soon as he mentioned James. He harrumphed a thank-you to the server as she set down his plate.

"So, things are still good between you?"

I sighed and set my fork down, finally raising my eyes to his. "Why? Have you heard something different?" Better to ferret out what he knew to avoid being caught in a lie.

"Just that you and Nate seemed to be having a moment in the parking lot before James showed up."

If I still needed a reason to go to California, that was it. In LA, I'd be just another face in the crowd. Small towns were the bane of my existence.

But from the pieces of information he was giving me, I guessed that someone had seen Nate, James, and me in the parking lot. For the first time since that night, I was grateful to have left with James. Our breakup happened in private, and it gave me plausible deniability in that moment, when I needed it most.

"It was a misunderstanding." I forced a smile. "James came back with me to the house, and we talked. Everything's fine."

His eyes widened for a second before he recovered. "Is that so?"

"Of course," I lied.

"I don't believe you," he said, his voice deceptively calm.

"What does that mean?" My carefully crafted cool demeanor cracked.

"I've seen the way you and Nate are together. Steven's seen it. For goodness' sake, the whole town witnessed the love song you sang him the other night!" He pointed at me. "You're still in love with him, and James found out."

I snorted. "You need better sources for spies."

His unwavering stare made me want to squirm, but I kept my body still, hoping the interrogation would end soon and we could talk of other things, safer subjects.

"Have you talked to Nate since James left?"

I blinked. What an odd question. "Of course I've talked to him."

He gave me a strange look. "And what did you talk about?"

I frowned. "I apologized for not telling him about James sooner."

"And that's all?"

What was he getting at? "Should I have discussed something else with him?"

When he didn't respond, I stared at him, trying to read between the lines. What was he hiding? And what did it have to do with Nate? But before I could turn the tables and interrogate *him* for a change, he took a large bite of his steak.

His silence gave me an opportunity to calm the churning in my stomach. I drank my water and force-fed myself the salad, hoping to appear calm and collected.

But when he cleared his throat, I knew the dance we were doing was about to get more complicated, and I already struggled to follow the steps.

"I think you've made your decision, but you just don't want to admit it, even to yourself."

In that moment, all I wanted to do was prove him wrong. I'd grown weary of everyone meddling in my life. James's search for an apartment without me, my father's coercive mechanisms to get me to stay, and even my dead mother's interference in my love life from beyond the grave.

"Why will no one listen to me?" I slammed my fist on the table. "Need I remind you that this is *my* life, and I would appreciate you keeping your nose out of it."

"You're right," he said, undeterred. "It is your life. So why are you willing to throw it away?"

I gaped at him. What did he mean by that? Choosing to pursue a life in California wasn't throwing it away. Even if I didn't have

James anymore, I had a job. I had a future. Why couldn't he see that?

My father sighed and shifted in his seat. "I understand if you're scared."

"Why would I be scared?"

"Your mother's meddling did a number on you, and even though she's gone, I think you're afraid of disappointing her in some way."

I dropped my gaze, fearing my face would give me away. I hadn't told anyone other than Nate about the cardinal or my suspicions about my mother trying to communicate with me.

"I've done everything Mom asked of me. Why wouldn't she be proud?"

"You say that, but I don't think you believe it."

My head shot up. I couldn't even begin to dissect the meaning of those words. "That doesn't make any sense."

He put down his utensils, pushed his plate forward slightly, and folded his hands behind it as he regarded me. The salad turned to stone in my stomach. He certainly lived up to his nickname of *The Intimidator*.

"Your mother has spent years cultivating the Lanie she wanted you to be, and now that she's gone, you're still trying to live up to her expectations. But without her guidance, you're like a ship without a harbor, and you're pushing back on anything that goes against her teachings. Nate is one of those things, and despite how much you care about him, you're afraid to pursue things and end up like your mother."

Sometimes, I forgot how observant my father could be. A man of few words, the present situation notwithstanding, he paid closer attention than most people realized.

"Mom didn't end up so bad," I murmured. "Despite your issues, you two made your peace in the end."

He nodded. "We did. And now it's your turn."

"But Mom and I were at peace." I frowned. "At least, I thought we were." I put my head in my hands.

"It's not your mother you need to make peace with," he said. "It's the version of Lanie your mother has convinced you to be." He shrugged as he scooped up his mashed potatoes onto his fork. "Only then will you be able to make a decision about your next steps."

"And if that Lanie wants to go to California too?"

"Then I'll book your flight myself," he challenged, a gleam in his eye.

I picked at the salad, digesting his words more than the food. Was he right? Had Mom somehow distorted my worldview to the point I didn't know who I was or what I wanted anymore? Our relationship had been strained, especially after my parents separated. Mom had leaned on me a lot, perhaps more than she should have during that time. My father's words painted everything in a different light. I resisted his version, not wanting to think ill of my mom, but deep down, I recognized the truth in what he'd said. In some ways, I'd believed Mom was living vicariously through me, and at the time, I hadn't minded. But now, I could see what havoc Mom's actions had wreaked in my life.

"The school wants me to help with their Presidents' Day play," I said, pushing my food away.

"You should do it," he replied, having no issues polishing off his meal. "It'll give you an idea of what the position here is like."

I nodded. It'd been a while since I last worked with kids, and I missed it. They saw the world so differently than adults did, and I believed some time with them was just what I needed to help me figure out what the "real" Lanie wanted.

A few days later, I stood on stage in the old high school theatre with Mrs. Carlisle. We planned to do a quick run-through before she and I spent one-on-one time with each child to prepare them for the performance. It brought back memories of my own theatre days.

The board of education had organized the event. Several teachers had been chosen to play the role of various presidents, and each class was assigned a president. The students would ask the president questions about his life and contributions to the country. For Mrs. Carlisle's class, the script was more of a suggestion, since some of the students struggled to memorize dialogue. But it had guidelines for the types of questions the children should ask.

"All right, class," Mrs. Carlisle called out. "We're going to begin. As you know, we were assigned Franklin D. Roosevelt, and Ms. McAllister has offered to fill in as our president for practice. Does anyone want to start us off with a question?"

A young boy named Seth raised his hand. "Wasn't Mr. Roosevelt in a wheelchair?"

"I do use a wheelchair, young man," I said in a faux deep voice. "Do you know why?"

Seth shook his head. The other children stared at me with rapt attention.

"Because I got really sick, and when I recovered, I was no longer able to walk." I leaned down and whispered, "But that didn't stop me from becoming president."

Another child, Beth, called out, "What are you most proud of?"

I pretended to think it over. "Let's see. There was the New Deal."

"What's that?" asked Robert, a boy with reddish-brown hair.

"Well, there were several parts to it, but one of the most famous parts that still helps people today was a program where money was provided to people who were too old or sick to work anymore."

"Do you miss being the president?" a sweet-faced girl with pigtails asked.

"Sometimes," I said. "But I served as president for well over a decade."

The children continued to ask questions until Mrs. Carlisle called them back to order. She and I split up the students to work in small groups on memory games. I sat with one group to help them get started.

"Ms. McAllister, I'm scared of being on the stage in front of all those people," Beth said. "What if I forget what I'm supposed to say?"

"Mrs. Carlisle and I will be there to help you," I promised. "But it might help if you pretend that it's just us talking, like we did a few moments ago." I looked at the rest of the group. "Is anyone else afraid of public speaking?"

There were several nods among the students. "I'll let you in on a secret. I'm not a fan, either, though I performed in several plays back in high school." I gave a conspiratorial smile. "But it's easier if you think of yourself as a character. Then it's not you messing up a line, it's the character's fault."

The children giggled, and my heart filled with warmth. I'd missed that. With all of the focus on finishing my master's and then coming home to handle Mom's affairs, I'd forgotten how nice it was to spend time with children. Regardless of where I ended up, I knew as long as I could teach, I would be happy.

I checked in on a few other groups before moving over to where Mrs. Carlisle stood.

"You're doing a wonderful job with them," she said.

"I'm really enjoying helping with the play."

"But you're still undecided on whether you want to take the position." Her words were stated matter-of-factly with no judgment, but my stomach sank anyway.

"I'm still considering it," I replied, though I imagined that excuse sounded as empty to her ears as it did in my head.

She sighed. "I understand, but I do hope you'll make a decision soon. I'd hate to leave in the spring without someone in place to take over."

I nodded but had no response to that. The idea of leaving the children to some stranger gutted me, but if I accepted the position in Cedar Haven, it would mean going back on my word not only to the school in California but also to my mother. The promises I'd made felt more like shackles that I wished I could free myself from. My father's voice echoed in my head. What Lanie did I want to be? What did the *real* Lanie want?

"Anyway," Mrs. Carlisle continued, and I was grateful for the subject change, "we need some help with the set changes the day of the play. If you could put the word out for volunteers, I'd greatly appreciate it."

"Sure, I can do that," I said. "I'll go make some calls."

With a smile, she turned and began making her rounds to the different groups of children. I stepped backstage, knowing exactly who to call first.

"Hey, Lanie, what's up?" Nate's cheerful greeting washed away the awkward conversation with Mrs. Carlisle.

"I have news to share and a favor to ask. Which would you like first?" I still hesitated to tell him about the offer, but I couldn't see a way around asking for his help without doing so. What other reason would I have to be working so closely on the play?

"Hmm, how about the news? That'll tell me whether I should say yes to the favor."

I laughed. "I was offered Mrs. Carlisle's job at the middle school."

The silence on the other end wasn't encouraging. I tapped my foot as I waited for him to respond. Had I made a mistake? He'd been the one to encourage me to apply, after all.

"Lanie, that's amazing, and I'm proud of you."

"But?" I asked, hearing it in his faked enthusiasm.

"Are you going to accept?"

I stifled a sigh. He didn't want to sound too happy in case I didn't stay. While I wished I could give him a more definitive answer, I wouldn't lie to him. "I haven't decided yet, but it does lead into the favor. The school asked me to help with the Presidents' Day play, and we need some volunteers to help with the set changes. Would you be willing to assist?"

"Of course," he said, and that time, there was no hesitation in his voice. "When do you need me?"

I gave him the details for the dress rehearsal and event, and he promised to be there. As I walked to the stage to help the children with their memory games, his question about whether I'd accepted weighed on my mind. I knew I would have to say goodbye to Nate for good if I stuck to my plan to move to California. We'd tried long distance before, and it hadn't worked. His life was in Cedar Haven, and I would never ask him to give up what he'd built. But I also wouldn't allow myself to base such an important decision on a man, no matter how much he meant to me.

Chapter Twelve

SUNDAY AFTERNOON, I STOOD BACKSTAGE WITH THE children, preparing for the dress rehearsal. In addition to Nate, I had roped in several of my friends to help with the set pieces. Trudy and her husband had painted a replica of the White House on a mural, and Steven had worked with Nate to build different platforms on which our presidents would speak to the children.

I went up behind Nate and Steven as they were putting the finishing touches on a set of stairs. "This looks great! How about you both let me take you out tonight as a thank-you for all your hard work?"

They exchanged a glance, and Nate suddenly seemed very interested in hammering a nail. Steven wiped his hands on his pants and gave me an easy smile that didn't reach his eyes.

"Thanks, sis, but I've got plans."

"Oh." I bit my lip to hide my disappointment. "Wedding planning with Rose?"

He scratched the back of his neck. "Ah, something like that."

What a weird response. I turned to Nate. "What about you?"

Before he could respond, someone tugged on my shirt. "Miss McAllister?"

I looked down with a smile. "Yes, Robert?"

"Can you help me run through my questions again?"

With a quick glance at Nate, who refused to meet my eye, I nodded and led Robert to a quiet part of the stage. But Nate's behavior needled me. What was up with him? Had I done something wrong?

I tried to ignore the uneasy feeling growing in my stomach as I helped Robert with the subject matter, giving him pointers on how to remember the questions he would ask. But I couldn't stop myself from staring across the room, where Nate and Steven were still hammering away at the stairs.

After I finished up with Robert, I headed over to Nate. He was alone that time, as Steven had moved on to work on the wheelchair for President Roosevelt. I cleared my throat, and he jumped, spinning around, eyes wide.

"Everything okay?"

He gave a quick nod. "Yep, totally fine."

I cocked my head, not convinced he was telling me the truth. "So, did you want to have dinner tonight?"

"Oh, um..." He cleared his throat. "I would, but I can't."

"Hot date?" I teased, though the idea made me queasy.

He rolled his eyes. "Of course not. I signed up to volunteer at the shelter."

I blinked. Why hadn't he told me that before? "That's great! I'm so happy for you. How long have you been going?"

"Not long. Tonight's my third shift." He smiled at me for the first time all day. "Thank you for encouraging me. I'm really enjoying it."

Third shift? I took a deep breath. While I'd been busy with rehearsals, that was big news. And as he'd said, I'd encouraged him. *So why am I only now learning about it?*

"Well, we should celebrate!" I forced a smile. "I don't mind a late dinner if you want to meet up afterward."

His face fell, and he stared at his hands. "That sounds nice, but I don't know how late I'll be."

"Ah, okay, then." I turned to go, my heart sinking. What wasn't he telling me?

"Wait, Lanie." He grabbed my arm. "I'm sorry tonight's not good, but if you're free for lunch after the play, we could go to Bea's."

Maybe I was being paranoid. He'd just started to volunteer, after all. Perhaps he'd planned to tell me about it after the play, when I had more time.

"That sounds good."

He pulled me in for a hug, and I relished the warmth of his arms around me. But too soon, he let go, and I walked out into the cool evening air, alone.

I had no reason to doubt Nate's word. And I was proud of him for rekindling his dream. Just like teaching was my passion, animals were his, and I hated that he'd lost sight of that when he took over his father's business. But something about his behavior had left me off-balance, and I couldn't quite put my finger on what it was.

The day of the performance, Nate and I stood together in the greenroom, watching the kids changing into their costumes and getting their makeup done. I slipped my hand in his and squeezed. His help with the props and set had meant more to me than I could express.

"This feels like old times," I said.

"I was just thinking the same thing," Nate replied with a warm smile.

When our eyes met, electricity hummed around us. Although we were surrounded by giggling children, it was as if we were the only two people in the room. My heartbeat quickened as his dark-brown eyes melted with heat. I reminded myself that we'd agreed to take things slow, but the urge to kiss him grew whenever he looked at me like that.

"Miss McAllister." Robert, one of my students, tugged on my shirt's hem. "I think it's our turn."

I glanced up to see the eighth-grade class coming off the stage, which was our cue. "Why, Robert, you're right! Let's go gather up the rest of our group."

I gave Nate's hand another squeeze before I formed a quick circle with my students. Nate shot me one of his heart-stopping smiles before heading off to help with the set change.

"All right, everyone, remember what we've practiced. Who is your president?"

Robert raised his hand. "Franklin D. Roosevelt."

"Very good, Robert! And what are we going to ask him?"

"About the New Deal and his wheelchair," Beth volunteered.

"Both good questions, but remember to raise your hand so Mr. Roosevelt can call on you." I put my hand in the middle of our circle, and the students piled their hands on top of mine. "One, two, three, break a leg!"

Robert stared at me in horror. "I don't want to break my legs."

Stifling a laugh, I knelt beside him. "I'm sorry, Robert. It's an expression often used in theatre to wish the actors luck. No actual legs will be broken."

He gave me a quick side-eye before turning and rushing to the stage with the rest of the students. I stood up, shaking my head and laughing. Nate returned and slid his arm around my shoulders.

"You're amazing with them," Nate commented.

"They're such sweet kids." I faced him, and when our eyes met, a spark shot straight through me. He angled his head closer to mine, and my eyelids drifted shut as I closed the distance.

The sounds of the curtain rising and the audience applauding made us both jump. Nate blinked before giving me a sheepish smile and stepping away.

In that moment, I knew what I wanted, what the *real* Lanie needed. *This life, these children, this man, this—no,* my—*town.* Though my chest ached, knowing I would be going back on my promise to my mother, I knew the alternative would break my heart beyond repair. Somehow, I doubted my mother would be angry or surprised to find out I'd broken my word to her.

As I watched the play, in the back of my mind, I considered how to tell Nate I'd made my choice. We were going out to lunch after the play was over. Based on our history, Bea's seemed a fitting location to tell him the good news.

My students did an amazing job, and when they exited the stage with excitement on their little faces, I gave each of them a hug. Nate and I stayed backstage until the last class had performed their scene, then we joined my class onstage for their bow.

After everything was broken down and packed away, we headed to Nate's car. As soon as he unlocked the door, I slid into the passenger seat. He entered chuckling.

"What's so funny?"

"It's nothing," he said, but an amused smile pulled on his lips.

"Tell me!"

He turned in his seat. "It's just... When I picked you up that day on Main Street, you were so tentative around me. But now, you jump into my car like it's where you belong." I bit my lip, and he hurried on. "Not that that's a bad thing. On the contrary, I like that you feel comfortable with me again." His brown eyes softened as he took my hand. "I missed it. I missed you."

My heart melted, and I cupped his cheek with my other hand. He leaned into it, shutting his eyes, and I took advantage of the moment. Leaning forward, I brushed my lips against his.

When I pulled away, his eyes were wide and dark. I swallowed, hoping I hadn't just done something to jeopardize whatever was growing between us before it had a chance to fully bloom.

"I'm sorry," I said, pulling away from him.

"Don't be." He grabbed my shoulder to stop me. "I've been wanting to do that for some time, but I worried you weren't ready."

I grinned and moved close to him again. "So, does that mean we can continue where I left off?"

He huffed a laugh. "Let's not make out in the school parking lot." Then his face sobered. "I still think we should take things slow."

"As long as 'slow' doesn't mean glacial, I'm good with that."

That earned me another laugh as he twisted in his seat and buckled his seat belt. Then he drove us to Bea's. We were silent on the drive there. I was too excited and nervous, replaying the kiss in my mind while at the same time trying to rehearse what I would say.

When we arrived, I chose a booth toward the back of the restaurant. Our conversation didn't need an audience, though the whole town would learn of my choice soon enough.

As soon as we were alone, I slid my hands across the table. Nate eagerly grasped them in his.

"Thank you for today," I said, looking up at him from beneath my lashes.

"It was my pleasure," he replied, his voice growing husky. "I always knew you'd make a great teacher, but I guess I didn't realize how well suited you are for the role until today."

I smiled. "The kids make it easy. They're such a sweet bunch."

"Have you given any more thought to the job offer here?"

"I have, actually." I was brimming with so much excitement, I practically bounced out of my seat. "I'm accepting it!"

His mouth fell open. "You are?" He swallowed and shook his head as if he wasn't sure he'd heard me correctly. "You're staying?"

"I still need to call both schools and tell them my decision, but yes, I'm staying." I grinned, expecting him to congratulate me or say how happy he was with my choice, but he shifted in his seat, and my uneasy feeling from the night before returned. "Aren't you happy?"

"Of course I'm happy," he said, but it came out flat.

"You don't sound like it." He didn't look it either. I tried to catch his eye, but he avoided me, choosing instead to focus on a straw wrapper. What did that mean? Had he changed his mind? Did he not want me to stay? And then my stomach dropped. Was it because I kissed him?

"I-I'm just in shock." He laughed, but it was strained. "What made you decide to stay?"

I cocked my head, studying him. "A lot of things." My excitement deflated, and I stared at my menu with a frown. "Working with the kids has meant a lot to me. My family is here, and I want to be near them." I stopped myself from saying he was part of the reason because it seemed like that would be the last thing he would want to hear right then. And that hurt.

"How did your dad take it?"

I shrugged. "He doesn't know." *This is too much.* I lifted my head and stared at Nate until he looked at me. "You're the first person I've told."

His face softened, but his fist still gripped the edge of the table. "Are you sure you'll be happy here?"

I lost my thin hold on my composure. "Nate, what's going on? I thought you'd be thrilled to hear I'd not only finally made a decision but that I'd chosen to stay. After all, you're the one who told me about this position." I shook my head, trying to wrap my mind around what had happened between then and now. "I understood why you held back when it wasn't clear I would take the job, but here I am, telling you that I'm staying, and it's like you don't want that anymore."

"I just know that part of your indecision stemmed from your mom, and I don't want you to regret staying like she did," he blurted out. His face went red, and he clenched his jaw.

I narrowed my eyes as everything clicked into place. So it wasn't about the job or my decision to stay. *No,* this *is about the secret he's keeping.*

"Enough is enough, Nate." I stared him down. "Spit it out."

He fidgeted with his napkin, and I expected him to change the subject or insist he wasn't hiding anything. But then he gave a defeated nod and sighed. "You know how I told you your mother and I made our peace?"

"I vaguely recall," I said, a hint of sarcasm in my tone. *Like I would ever forget that.*

"Well"—Nate shifted in his seat—"I-I went to see her, your mother, before she died."

"You did?" I racked my brain for any memory of him being at my home, but nothing came to mind. "When?"

"She planned it for when she knew you'd be gone," he continued, staring at his hands. "She wanted to talk to me alone."

My heartbeat picked up its pace, but I worked to keep my expression neutral. "Why? What did she say?"

"She apologized."

"Apologized?" I stilled. I could think of a laundry list of things for which she could apologize. "For what?"

Finally, Nate raised his eyes to meet mine. "For breaking us up."

Whatever I had expected him to say, it wasn't that. I moved my lips, but no words formed, and no sounds came out. My mind reeled from the news. Mom felt responsible for breaking us up? Why? Sure, she had started dropping hints before I left for college about what I would miss out on if I stayed with him, then her hints became more direct the closer we got to my leaving date. And while, yes, she'd certainly never kept her dislike of Nate a secret, I would never have dreamed of blaming *her* for our breakup. I blamed the distance; it was too much for us. I blamed our youth because we were too young to make that kind of commitment. There was even a part of me that still suspected Nate had found someone else, despite his denials then and now. But my mother? I couldn't wrap my head around what he was saying.

Nate searched my face and sighed. "Melody told me things she did to try to convince you to break up with me. Pushing you to have new experiences in college, trying to stop you from making the same mistake she did in marrying your father so young."

I didn't know what to say. None of that made any sense. Nate rushed to fill the silence.

"The weekend she went to visit you, she took a lot of photos. Of you, the campus, but several of the photos of you were with various guys from your college." His brown eyes filled with an emotion I couldn't place. "When she came home, she not only showed me the photos, but she also told me I needed to let you go." His voice broke, and he cleared his throat. "She said that I was holding you back." He reached for me, but I pulled my hand away. "I don't know if she hoped I would think you were cheating on me or if she wanted to prove that you were better off without me, but whatever her motivation, it worked." He looked down, his shoulders drooping. "It's why I stopped responding to your texts and calls. I thought I was doing what you wanted, and when you came home and we argued, it just confirmed what she showed me. That you *were* better off without me." His voice lowered, and there was a wistful note in it. "After she told me all that, she made me promise to tell you. She hoped it might lead us back to each other, without any further interference from her."

Like death would stop her. An errant giggle bubbled up in my throat, and Nate frowned at me. Clearly, he thought I wasn't handling the news well, but the idea that Mom would allow a little thing like her own death to stop her interfering in the lives of those she loved was hilarious. Only Melody McAllister could continue to meddle in my love life from the great beyond. The small giggle morphed into a wide grin, and before I could stop myself, hysterical laughter burst out.

Nate's frown deepened as his eyes darted around the room, like he was debating whether he needed to find reinforcements to have me committed. Somehow, being placed under a seventy-two-hour hold didn't sound like such a bad idea at the moment.

"I'm sorry," I said as I regained control. "It was just... When you said, 'without any further interference,' I found that amusing because she's clearly still interfering by having you be the bearer of this news." I struggled to process what he'd told me, but I felt overwhelmed with all the information. It was just too much. So, my mind homed in on the one thing it thought I could handle. "I still don't understand when you would have had this conversation. I never saw you."

"I told you, she wanted me to meet her when you weren't home," Nate replied. "The nurse set it up." He must have sensed my disbelief because he leaned back and crossed his arms. "After everything I just told you, why would I lie about *that*?"

Before I could respond, the server arrived with our food. I wasn't sure what to believe as I tried to logic my way out of myths, legends, and first loves. I ate a french fry, but it tasted like ash in my mouth. Nothing about the conversation made sense.

I decided to approach it from a different angle. "If she wanted you to tell me, why did you wait so long?"

Nate stared at me as a plethora of emotions crossed his face as if an internal battle raged inside him. A few times, he opened his mouth but quickly closed it again.

"You were already in so much pain. And I thought, well..." He stopped and squared his shoulders as if steeling himself. "At first, I figured things were over between us. As far as I could tell, you had moved on. You planned a new life on the other side of the country, and then, when I learned you had a boyfriend, I didn't see the point." His eyes bored into mine with an unfathomable emotion. "But then, after that song you sang at karaoke, and when you broke up with James..." He shook his head. "I didn't want it to sound like I was telling you these things to manipulate you into staying. I wanted you to choose to stay because you wanted it, not because I wanted you to or because your mother had had a change of heart before she died."

"You're right. It does seem more than a little suspect." I lifted my hand, ticking off items on my fingers as I spoke. "First, you tell me about a job here, and you encourage me to apply even after I tell you I have a job waiting for me in California. Then, we spend all this time together, preparing for the estate sale, fixing my mom's car, and then this afternoon, after the play, we kissed, which would have been the perfect moment to tell me. But you never said a word." I shook my head, trying to clear it. My disbelief was fading as anger took its place.

"I wasn't going to say anything. I thought it would remain something that happened between Melody and me, but then Max told me at dinner last night that he knew—"

What the— "You had *dinner* with my *dad*?" I demanded, a fire building in my belly. Of *course* my father was involved. The one person who had consistently berated me for choosing California over Cedar Haven wouldn't be able to resist any chance to convince me to stay. My skin prickled with rage. His strange line of questioning the other night suddenly made perfect sense. *And what did you and Nate talk about?* Because he knew what Mom and Nate had discussed.

Nate blanched, and it was clear by the expression on his face he hadn't meant to tell me that. "Steven asked me to meet him and Max."

Steven too? I closed my eyes, trying to control my temper. Did *no one* in my family trust me to make my own decisions? Part of me wanted to go to California just to spite them all.

"Is that why you said no to dinner with me? Because you had plans with them?"

At his nod, the thin leash I had on my rage evaporated.

"To what? Conspire behind my back about keeping me here?"

Mixed in with my anger was a sharp pain, twisting in my gut. While I'd expected my father not to play fair, the idea that Nate was in on it cut me to my core. And then he'd lied to me about it. He'd refused to have dinner with me because he would rather collude with my family. Bile rose in my throat.

He dropped his gaze but not before I saw the guilt in his eyes. So, that was what this was all about. A stupid scheme to try to convince me to stay. I hated myself for how well it had worked. I was such an idiot, thinking that I'd figured out what the so-called "real Lanie" wanted. But no, it'd all been a conniving charade so my father could get what he wanted. I shoved my food away and stood, grabbing my coat.

"Wait, Lanie, don't leave," Nate protested, standing as well. "Please let me explain."

"I've heard enough!" I threw some money on the table and glared at him. "Don't follow me." Without waiting for a response, I turned and fled before he could see the tears gathering in my eyes.

Chapter Thirteen

I didn't want to go home. I couldn't bear to sit in that house after what Nate had told me. I wasn't sure which upset me more, my mother's alleged confession or Nate's clandestine meeting with my family. Either way, I needed some distance from anything that would remind me I was a McAllister.

Which was why it made no sense at all when I found myself pulling into the parking lot of the cemetery a few minutes later. I hadn't been there since the funeral. It hurt too much.

As I stood at the edge of the graveyard, that night didn't feel like the right time either. My emotions overwhelmed me, and I didn't know what I hoped to accomplish by going there. Would I confront my mother or at least what was left of her? Was that my plan? Or had I gone there for answers, ones I had little chance of ever receiving? If Nate's story was true, and he had not only seen my mom behind my back but had heard her confession with his own ears, then had everything I'd believed about my mom been a lie?

Fresh tears pricked the backs of my eyelids, and I bowed my head. I could admit there was some truth to Nate's story. I remembered the parents' weekend he referenced. Mom had been thrilled to see me making so many new friends, particularly ones of the male persuasion. I wouldn't have put it past Mom to do exactly what Nate described. And it explained his distance for the last month or so of the semester. It was why I'd thought he'd found someone new but just didn't have the courage to tell me. So it didn't surprise me when we broke up after I returned home. He'd sworn up and down that he hadn't cheated on me, and deep down, I'd always known he was telling the truth. But to learn that it might have all been Mom's doing cut deep.

My hands curled into fists at my side. Mom and I had never had an easy relationship, but that? That was by far the worst thing she had ever done to me. To sabotage my relationship was bad enough, but to not even have the decency to tell me herself? To entrust someone else to share the news? Especially someone who, up until recently, I'd never expected to have in my life again.

Tears blurred my vision as I stomped through the cemetery. I couldn't say whether they were tears of pain or rage. Perhaps it was some of both. But I knew the way. I'd chosen Mom's final resting place myself, and my sure feet carried me directly to the spot.

Though I'd picked out the headstone, I hadn't seen it in person. Seeing her name etched into the cold marble gutted me. In a way, it made it more real. The dates were carved deep into the stone, confirming to the world and to me that she was really and truly gone.

But even that pain couldn't douse my rage. "How could you?" I spat out. "How could you lie to me, for all these years, and then let me find out this way?"

The graveyard was silent. Not even birdsong filtered through the cold winter air. No helpful flash of a familiar red to brighten up the bleak, gray stones or provide me with the answers I so desperately needed. One question echoed in my head, over and over: *Why?* Why didn't she tell me? Why did she involve Nate? And most of all, why couldn't she see how much pain she'd caused by breaking my heart in the first place?

I'd cried for months after that fight with Nate. The only saving grace was going back to Seattle and drowning myself in school. Apparently, I'd never learned a better way to channel my grief, as I'd done the exact same thing when she'd died.

"I was here, for *months*, tending to your every need. You had ample opportunity to tell me this yourself. But you didn't. You *couldn't*." I started shaking. "You're a coward, Melody McAllister."

As soon as the words left my mouth, I slapped my hand over it. I hadn't meant to say that. And yet, I spoke truth. She'd said nothing the entire time I cared for her, and then she left Nate to do what she couldn't and pick up the pieces. I dropped my hand, placing it over my heart as it broke all over again.

"I didn't deserve to find out like this," I whispered. "You should have told me. You should have—" My voice choked off with a sob. I dashed an impatient hand across my tear-stained cheeks and spun away from the grave as I ran to the car. No. I would not break down. Not there, not then. She didn't deserve my tears.

I grabbed my phone and sent an angry group text to Steven and Dad, including Rose for good measure. Somehow, I doubted my future sister-in-law had been involved in the conspiracy dinner. Rose wouldn't have stood for such manipulation tactics, no matter how much she loved my brother. If I had hopes of an ally, my best bet was Rose.

Text sent, I put the car in gear and drove home, determined to discover for myself what was true. I no longer doubted Nate's words, but I needed more. I deserved more than a secondhand message from my dead mother.

When I arrived, I went straight to the file box I'd found. Steven had said it was probably filled with old bills, but I hoped it would hold the answers I sought. Something to explain my mother's actions. I was desperate for any clue that would help me understand why my mother had done that. After rolling up my sleeves, I lifted the lid off the box.

Inside were hanging files. Most were labeled for various bills: Mortgage, Electricity, and the like. But one was labeled Letters. I grabbed that one and opened it. Most of the letters were from my father, friends from a camp my mother attended as a child, or Christmas newsletters from family. There were even a few love notes from old boyfriends Mom would occasionally reminisce about but nothing that appeared recent.

Frustrated, I returned to the box. One folder wasn't labeled. As I opened it, my heart stuttered, and a chill ran up my spine. There were several crisp white envelopes, mostly addressed in Mom's scrawl, but a few were written in a neater hand. Each envelope was addressed to different members of my family. One for me, for Steven, for Dad, for Rose, and... for Nate? I hesitated over the letter to Nate, curiosity getting the better of me. His letter wasn't sealed, as if Mom knew I would find it impossible to resist reading its contents.

My hands shook as I removed a small piece of paper from the envelope and unfolded it.

Dear Nate,

Keep your promise. Take care of her.

Melody

The words were so simple and direct, but they said so much. Tears sprang to my eyes as I read the words over and over, as if they would suddenly change. I yanked out the letter addressed to me and ripped the envelope open. My mother's final words to me took up just one page. She must have written it in her final days. How had she managed to find the energy to do all of that without me knowing?

Dear Lanie,

Of all the letters I've written, yours is the one I struggled with the most. I want to start with two things. I love you, and I'm sorry. I hope Nate has spoken to you by now, but if he hasn't, please give him the chance to explain.

I know you're probably angry with me, and you have every right to be. I should have told you myself. Better still, I never should have interfered in the first place. Unfortunately, I'm afraid you've now learned a difficult lesson and one I'd hoped I'd be able to teach you in time. Parents, like most people, aren't infallible. We often get it wrong.

I've made many mistakes in my life, but none I've regretted as much as this. It was made out of misplaced bitterness, and if I could, I would take it all back.

The simple apology cut through the last remnants of my rage like a knife. The rest of the letter was filled with hopes for my future and how much she wished she could be there to see it. She encouraged me to follow my heart, wherever it led, and to "hold on to your dreams and dream big." Before her signature, Mom wrote: *You have my blessing, whatever you decide.*

I didn't know how long I sat there, clutching my mother's last words to my chest and sobbing. I couldn't move and could barely breathe. It was as if she had died all over again, the pain was so fresh.

Only one question remained for me to answer. My mother had released me from my promise, but maybe I'd been right all along. Maybe the memories I'd made in Cedar Haven were too painful to bear.

Two days later, Steven and my father came over to move me into my father's house. I'd barely spoken to either of them since I'd learned about their secret meeting with Nate. As Dad and Steven packed my things into their respective cars, I pushed my anger deep inside of me. The day would be bittersweet enough without throwing in an argument.

While the closing wasn't for another month, it was the last day a McAllister would live in that house, and it felt appropriate for it to be the day we truly said goodbye. Despite the lingering resentment toward my family, I appreciated that we were all together that day.

But things were awkward. Even Rose gave Steven the cold shoulder. She'd been supportive of me and told both Steven and my dad to back off. It was nice to have someone in my corner, especially as I'd felt utterly alone since that dramatic scene with Nate. While I hadn't reached out to him, he wasn't exactly banging down my door either. I chose to ignore the ache that reverberated in my chest whenever I thought about him.

Besides, I had enough on my plate as it was. Everything was happening so fast; it made my head spin. I couldn't believe how much we'd accomplished in the month and a half since I'd been home.

Once the cars were all packed and ready to trek across town, I stood alone in the driveway, facing the house. Steven and Dad came up on either side of me and slid their arms around me. The three of us gazed at what was once our family home and took a collective breath, remembering all the good memories we had there and the woman who had made it a home.

Then everyone turned and climbed into their cars and drove away, leaving me alone once more. A deep, overwhelming wave of sadness came over me, and I bowed my head under its weight. All the work to get the house ready was over. What would I do with all my free time?

I turned on my heel and walked to the car, my steps heavy and slow. I drove on autopilot to my dad's, and once there, I unpacked my car like a machine. Nobody seemed to notice the change in my demeanor. Well, nobody except Rose.

"Are you okay?" she asked as she carried a box of clothes up to my new room.

"I'm fine," I said, but my voice sounded robotic even to me. I tried to force a smile, but it was like I couldn't feel my face. Everything was numb.

Rose's eyebrows knitted together, but she didn't press the issue. Once all the boxes were unloaded, she and Steven left, and my father settled in to watch television.

I climbed the stairs to my new room and shut the door. Everything about it felt wrong. The sun was too bright, the walls were too bare, and the floor wasn't carpeted. I shut the blinds and closed the curtains. I knew I should unpack, but I couldn't find the energy. Instead, I moved all the boxes off my bed, crawled under the covers, and blocked out the world.

~

There was a soft knock at my door, and I burrowed farther under the covers, trying to muffle the sound. I'd long lost track of the days, but I couldn't bring myself to care. The only time I left my bed was when the persistent gnawing in my stomach told me that I needed to eat something. But even then, I could stomach only a few crackers before the nausea would take over. While up, I would force myself to shower, which really meant standing under the water until it turned cold. I'd worn all my comfy pajamas, though I thought someone had come in at some point to take my laundry. The details were a little fuzzy.

The knock came again, sharper. I opened one eye. The room was dark and unfamiliar with vague shapes standing out in the darkness. I knew I should be doing something, but I couldn't remember what. Whenever I tried too hard to figure it out, tears would leak from my eyes, and sobs would rack my body. So, I didn't try. Besides, all I wanted to do was sleep. I was so tired. But it didn't seem to matter how long I slept. Whenever I woke up, I still felt exhausted. Would I ever feel rested again?

"Lanie!" a deep voice shouted from the other side of the door. "Open this door, right now."

"Five more minutes," I moaned as I flipped onto my side and pulled a pillow over my ears. After a few more muffled shouts and pounds on the door, whoever it was gave up and stomped away. I drifted into a dreamless sleep, my favorite kind as of late.

Sometime later, my phone buzzed. I lifted my arm from under the covers and felt around my nightstand until my fingers brushed the familiar object. I picked it up and slipped my arm back under the covers. The bright screen blinded me, and I winced as I tried to make out the message.

A text from Nate. I groaned, shoving my arm out and dropping the phone back onto the nightstand. I didn't want to talk to him. He'd upset me, though I didn't allow myself to dwell on what exactly he'd done. Despite my lack of response, he refused to take the hint and kept texting. I rolled over, but sleep didn't come easily that time. My brain wouldn't shut off, as if it wanted me to remember.

Glaring at my phone, I threw off the covers. Why did I look at it? I'd successfully avoided it most of the time, picking it up only when the buzzing got incessant. With an irritated growl, I climbed out of bed and turned the phone off before shoving it into a box. There. I wouldn't be disturbed again.

Since I was already awake, I wandered downstairs to the kitchen. It must have been the middle of the night because the house was dark. I tiptoed around the creaky spots on the floor, which I'd memorized during other late-night forages for food. I opened the cabinet doors slowly to avoid the slightest whine of the hinges. A box of toaster pastries sat near the front. That sounded more appetizing than crackers. I gritted my teeth when the metallic wrapping rustled in my hands as I tore the package. After putting the pastries on a paper towel, I crept back up the stairs to my room and quietly shut the door.

I made it through one pastry before I lost my appetite, and I wished I'd thought to get some fresh water. The glass by my bed had been there for a while, possibly days, and tasted stale. But I gulped it down anyway. Then I slid back under the covers and fell into a restless sleep.

The bed shifted, and I startled awake. A gentle hand, warm, soft, and familiar, caressed my hair. I smiled, still half-asleep, and reached up to grab the hand but instead touched my own cheek. Outside my window, a bird chirped. An image of a red cardinal with black freckles near its beak flashed through my mind, but before I could make sense of it, sleep found me again.

"Lanie." A gentle, familiar voice whispered my name. A hand shook my shoulder. "Lanie, it's time to wake up."

I opened my eyes and rolled over, taking in the angular features of my future sister-in-law's face. Rose was smiling, but it didn't reach her eyes. Worry lines creased her forehead.

"Rose," I croaked. I cleared my throat. "What are you doing here?"

"I came to convince you to get out of this bed." When I went to roll over again, Rose grabbed my shoulder and shook it with more force. "No, Lanie. Not this time. Get up. Now!"

Shocked, I stared up at her. "What's your problem?"

"You've been in this bed for a week. Whatever is wrong, whatever has happened, you need to snap out of it."

"You wouldn't understand," I moaned as I buried my face in the pillow.

"Then you're going to have to make me understand." Rose yanked the covers off the bed, and I curled into a ball to escape the sudden cold air. "You're going to get out of this bed, you're going to take a shower—a *real* one with *actual* soap—and then you're going to go downstairs. Your brother and father are waiting for you."

After briefly considering mutiny, I dragged myself out of bed. I wasn't sure if it was the thought of a hot shower to escape the cold after Rose had so rudely ripped away my blankets or if it was my fear of what Rose might do next that drove me to obey. But the moment I was in the shower, I regretted not fighting back. For some reason, the water always helped me to think, and that was the last thing I wanted to do.

When I returned to my room, the curtains had been pushed back, and sunlight was streaming in. Birds chirped outside the window, and I could feel winter losing its grip on Cedar Haven. The promise of warmer days and fresh flowers brought a soft smile to my face. There were still piles of boxes stacked on the floor, and the simple furnishings my father had set up were a stark reminder of the life I had left behind. Dad had moved a few times since he and Mom divorced, and his latest house was much smaller than the one I'd shared with him my last semester of high school.

Voices drifted up from below, and I steeled myself to face the firing squad, a.k.a. my family. My behavior over the last… days? Weeks? I had no idea, but however long I'd spent shut in my room had led to the lovely intervention I was walking into. I took a deep breath and descended the stairs.

"Lanie," Rose cooed as she stood to embrace me as if she hadn't just dragged me out of bed. "It's so good to see you vertical."

Her words caught me off guard, and I laughed in spite of myself. The sound of my laughter quieted the rest of the room as everyone stared at me.

"Why don't you sit here?" Steven pulled a chair out for me. The kitchen was small, with a round table in the center surrounded by five wooden chairs. A little window overlooking the backyard was over the sink. The walls were bare except for a cow calendar Steven had given Dad as a Christmas present. My father didn't do much decorating. He preferred simplicity to style.

I glanced around at the familiar faces of my family. Steven's hazel eyes were clouded with concern, while Dad's thick eyebrows were pulled down in a perpetual frown. Rose kept a smile on her face, though it looked a little strained.

"How are you feeling?" Dad asked, leaning back in his chair.

"Better," I said, my voice still hoarse from disuse. "I didn't mean to worry you." I dropped my gaze to the table. "It's just… a lot happened over a short period of time." My breath hitched in my throat as I fought back tears. "The house selling, Nate's secret, breaking up with James…"

"You broke up with James?" Steven's eyes widened. With a quick glance at Rose, who conveniently looked away, he grabbed my arm. "Why didn't you tell us?"

"Like I said, everything happened so fast." After taking a deep breath, I told the whole story. How James had shown up unexpectedly at the Valentine's dance and I'd subsequently broken up with him. How I'd received the job offer and decided to accept it, but then when I met with Nate for lunch, he told me about Mom and spilled the beans on the clandestine dinner. I glared at Steven and Dad, who, for their part, had the decency to at least look guilty. The more I talked, the more the ache in my chest eased, and my shoulders lifted as if a weight had been removed.

"Once the house sold, I suddenly found myself with a lot of free time. I couldn't go back to California yet because we still have the probate hearings, but there wasn't much for me to do here either. And I had a lot to process." With my head in my hands, I stared at the table. "Mom not only broke up my relationship, but then she also didn't even have the decency to tell me."

For the first time since our awful lunch, my heart went out to Nate. Clearly, we needed to talk. It wasn't his fault he'd been dragged into my mother's drama, though the fact that he'd gone along with her hurt more than I was ready to admit.

My head shot up. "How is Nate?"

They exchanged glances. Finally, Steven spoke. "He's fine. But he's not what's important right now."

"What about the house? Is there anything I need to do to prepare for the sale?"

Steven shook his head. "Everything is on schedule." He exchanged another look with my father. "But there is a matter you need to settle soon."

"You said you received an offer from the local school," Dad said. "But you haven't given them an answer yet."

My teeth worried my lower lip. "I-I haven't made up my mind yet."

"Given what's been going on the last several days, I think it's best if you take some time away from here," my father continued, his eyebrows pulling together in a deeper frown. "We've been looking at flight options, but your breakup with James complicates things." His fingers drummed on the table. "I don't suppose you have somewhere you can stay?"

My pulse hammered in my throat. He wanted me to leave? After conniving to get me to stay, he suddenly couldn't get rid of me fast enough? But I couldn't leave right then, not with everything still so up in the air. How could I do that to Nate? Just leave without a word? I closed my eyes and took a calming breath, forcing myself to focus on the present.

"I had planned to book an Airbnb until James and I found a place to stay," I finally said. "But I don't want to go." I glanced at Steven in hopes he would jump in and say he needed me for the estate, but he refused to meet my eye.

"Steven needs me. Don't you, Steven?" I pressed, trying to force him to engage.

"What I need is for you to get better," Steven said, his voice strained. When he finally looked at me, the pain in his eyes was like a punch to the gut. "And if that means you need to live on the other side of the country, then so be it."

I stared at the table. Since I'd returned, I'd told them I couldn't handle living in Cedar Haven with all the painful memories, and it looked like my family had finally gotten that message just when I wished I could take it back.

When I lifted my head, ready to declare I wasn't going anywhere, all I saw in their faces were worry and fear. My behavior over the last week had scared them, and they were willing to do whatever they could to help me.

Maybe they had a point. The memories I'd avoided had finally caught up with me, and I couldn't afford to spend the rest of my life hiding under the covers. Besides, that wasn't what Mom would have wanted. Regardless of whether I lived her dreams or my own, the point was, I needed to *live*.

"What about probate court?" I asked meekly.

"I can handle the hearings," Steven said, waving a dismissive hand. "And anything I need from you can be done remotely at this point."

My heart squeezed as I thought fast. I needed to buy myself some time.

"I have a therapy appointment tomorrow," I said, squaring my shoulders and looking them each in the eye. "How about I go to that and talk things over with her? That way, I don't make any rash decisions I may regret later."

Steven and Dad looked ready to protest, but Rose nodded. "It'll be good to have an unbiased perspective on the situation."

After exchanging glances, my father and brother nodded. I breathed a sigh of relief, though I knew it would be short-lived. The therapy appointment would grant me a reprieve from the intervention, but I'd have to figure out the rest.

My stomach growled, and I glanced at the refrigerator. "Um, is there anything to eat? I'm starving."

Chapter Fourteen

After my family finished their intervention, I needed to get out of that house. I'd never been more grateful to have my mother's car. Keys in hand, I headed to the grocery store, hoping to find some things to cook for dinner, since I planned to eat regularly again.

I'd barely stepped into the door when Nate appeared in front of me. Startled, I stumbled back a step, and he caught my arm. The spark of heat that I'd felt every time we'd touched was absent, leaving only an unfamiliar iciness in my veins. I yanked my arm back.

He shoved his hands into his pockets, and his eyes roved over me as if searching for signs of pain. But his exploration would be fruitless. My pain was tucked away deep inside.

"Lanie." His voice was soft. "I've been so worried."

"I'm fine." I took another step away from him, and his face fell.

He ran a hand through his hair and stared at the floor. When he raised his gaze back to me, it was filled with questions I didn't want to answer.

"Look," I said, trying to sound forceful. "I know we need to talk, but—"

"You don't need to do anything except take care of you, Lanie."

The sincerity in his dark-brown eyes caused my insides to melt a little, and I hated myself for it. Part of me wanted to escape his intense stare, but I had my own questions. Maybe it was better to talk then, to rip off the bandage and fully allow myself to bleed out before I put myself back together again.

I steeled myself. "Let's go sit in my car." Without waiting for a response, I spun on my heel and headed into the parking lot. The only confirmation I had that he followed me was the sound of his footsteps.

When we reached the car, I unlocked the doors and slid into the driver's seat. The role reversal wasn't lost on me. I couldn't remember the last time I'd driven him somewhere.

"Lanie, I—"

I held up a hand. "No, you've said enough." I turned on him, my lips pressed into a hard line. "My turn."

I hadn't practiced what I would say. Truthfully, I wasn't feeling fully coherent, having spent most of my week hiding in bed. *Just speak from the heart.*

And so I did. "I'm not angry with you for not telling me what my mother did." He visibly relaxed beside me. If I had been in a better mood, I might have laughed at his naivete. "But what I can't forgive..." I stopped and took a breath. "What I don't understand is why you took her at her word. She might have lit the match, but you stoked the fire." I raised my eyes to meet his and saw my own pain reflected there.

The words poured out of me faster than I could process them. "Why didn't you talk to me after she showed you those pictures, after she told you that you were holding me back? She'd tried so many times before, Nate. We even joked about it the other night. The yellow police tape, the tacos, all her subtle and not-so-subtle attempts to break us up." I shook my head. "And none of it worked. At least, not until I left."

His eyes welled up with tears before he dropped his head into his hands. I waited for him to speak, and when he didn't, I pressed on.

"You could have asked me, Nate. You could have point-blank asked me if I was cheating on you, if I had moved on." I threw up my hands. "Hell, *I* asked *you*. That last fight we had, I begged you to tell me who she was. Who had stolen your heart away from me. And you swore there wasn't anyone else. But you never asked me the same." I swallowed past the lump in my throat. "Why was it so easy for you to believe my mother? Why didn't you trust me?"

"I never thought you were cheating on me," he said quietly.

I stared at him as tears streamed down my cheeks. At least that was something, but it didn't explain why he'd stopped calling me. It didn't provide me with an understandable reason for why he just let things fizzle out for months only to explode when we finally saw each other again. All it gave me was more questions.

"Then why? Why didn't you talk to me?"

"Because she was right!" His dark eyes flew to my face, and the rage and pain I saw there took my breath away. "I *was* holding you back, Lanie. You were always meant for bigger and better things than Cedar Haven, and I couldn't bear to be the thing standing in your way." He clenched his hands into fists. "Even now, even after telling you about the position here, even after you told me you were going to accept, I can't bear to think that you're throwing away your life for me."

"I'm not," I blurted out. I hadn't meant to say it, but I recognized the truth in my words. Nate might have told me about the job and given me *a* reason to stay, but it wasn't my only one. I'd fallen in love with those kids, and I hated the thought of leaving them with a stranger. But I also wanted to rebuild my relationship with Steven and spend more time with Rose. I wanted to reconnect with old friends and make a place for myself there, in my hometown.

"In some ways," he continued as if I hadn't spoken, "I think I told you about your mom when I did because I wanted to convince you that you were right all along. That you deserved better than this town. She didn't want you to settle, and I worried that if I didn't tell you, that's exactly what you'd be doing."

I crossed my arms and glared at him. "It doesn't matter what she wanted. What matters is what I want. And I wanted you. I've always wanted you."

When he met my eyes again, they were so filled with hope I couldn't stand it, but I wasn't done. "Which is why learning that you listened to my mother instead of talking to me hurts so much. Her betrayal was bad enough on its own, but coupled with yours—"

His mouth dropped open. "You think I betrayed you?"

"How else would you describe it?"

His throat moved as he swallowed. "I guess I never really thought of it that way."

I turned and stared out the windshield, gathering my thoughts. "Do you know how many nights I sobbed myself to sleep when you wouldn't answer my calls or texts? Do you have any idea what your silence did to me?" I closed my eyes as the memories of my freshman year washed over me. "It was hard enough being in a new city, meeting new people. The pictures my mother showed you were a farce. I met most of those people in classes and never saw them again after that first semester. But I put on a show for her." I opened my eyes and looked over at him. "Had I known what she would do with my performance, I never would have bothered."

He opened his mouth as if to respond, but I cut him off. I was tired of that conversation. I needed to get my groceries and get home.

"My family thinks I should go to California now," I said, unable to keep the bitterness from my voice.

His breath hitched. "You're leaving?"

"I haven't decided yet." I risked a glance at him, which was a mistake because the devastation I found there shattered my heart. I grabbed my purse and tucked my keys inside. "I need some time."

He grabbed my arm. "I'm sorry, Lanie." His voice was hoarse. "I didn't know."

I smiled sadly as I shook him off and climbed out of the car. "Because you never asked."

~

"That's quite a story," Dr. Brooks said when I finished telling her all that had happened since my last session.

I nodded and fell back against the couch, my energy drained. Reliving the last week had taken a lot out of me. But I also felt like a weight had been lifted off me.

"So, what are you going to do?" she asked, cocking her head. She was perched on her office chair again and had furiously jotted down notes while I talked. "Are you going to stay here, or will you go back to the West Coast?"

I bit my lip. Wasn't that her job? Okay, well, maybe she couldn't *tell* me what to do, but couldn't she give me a hint? Some guidance? My decision-making skills weren't exactly stellar, if the last seven days were any indication.

"I don't know." I widened my eyes, hoping she would see the plea in them.

"What do you want to do?"

Stifling a sigh, I dropped my gaze and fidgeted with a string on the cushion. That question was quickly becoming my least favorite. As if it were so easy to say what *I* wanted after spending so long chasing after what *my mother* wanted.

"I don't know that either," I began. Perhaps if I gave Dr. Brooks something to work with, she could steer me in the right direction. "I thought I wanted to go to California. I thought I wanted to marry James and teach at a special school." I stopped and took a deep breath. "But after everything I've learned about my mother, I don't know where she ends and I begin."

"That's understandable."

I glanced at her, hoping she would say more. When she didn't, I ground my teeth and glared at the floor. What was the point of coming for a session if she wasn't going to help me?

"What do you think I should do?" I asked, figuring it couldn't hurt. The worst she might do was give me some psychobabble about how I needed to determine what I wanted for myself and that no one could do it for me. That wouldn't be helpful, but at least I would know that I was on my own.

"Follow your heart."

That caught my attention, and my head shot up. In some ways, it was worse than psychobabble. At least if she'd given me some line about how I was the only one who could figure out what I wanted, she might have assigned some homework to guide me in that process. But her response was so vague. And I doubted she had any worksheets that would aid me in something as intangible as following my heart.

"But how will I know that I'm doing that if I'm so entwined with what my mother wanted for me?"

She was silent, and I shifted under her scrutiny. Then she smiled. "Let's try an exercise."

That sounded more promising than her vague responses so far. I sat up straighter and gestured for her to continue.

"We're going to play a word-association game. When I say a word, I want you to say the first thing that comes to mind. Some of your answers may be skewed due to your mother's influence, but don't worry about that. That's something we can examine later once we have an overall picture."

I wasn't sure I liked that game anymore, but I was willing to try anything. "Okay, let's give it a go."

"Your first word is 'lurk.'"

"Stalker," I blurted out and frowned.

She shook her head. "Don't overthink it. There are no right or wrong answers here." Glancing down at her paper, she continued. "Piper."

"Pied."

After making a note on her clipboard, she read the next one. "Face."

"Consequences." My mouth dropped open. *Where did that come from?*

A sly smile slipped through her professional mask. "We're getting somewhere now. 'Home.'"

"Cedar Haven." I swallowed and closed my eyes, wishing I could go back in time and decide not to play the game. I didn't like where we were heading.

"Good. How about..."

I opened my eyes and found her staring at me with interest.

"Love."

"Nate." Tears filled my eyes, and I covered my face with my hands.

"I think you have your answer," she said quietly.

I did. Despite my mother's influence, despite her dreams for me, even in spite of what I'd recently learned about her, what I wanted, what the *real* me wanted, was to come home. Protests bubbled up inside of me, desperate to claw their way out of my mouth, but I clamped my lips shut. Those were words that echoed in my head, my mother's voice distorted to sound like my own. The words I'd spoken without conscious thought—those came from my heart.

"I have one last word for you, but I'm not sure if it's necessary."

I shrugged as I wiped my eyes. My emotions were already chaotic enough. "Lay it on me."

She grimaced. "Mother."

"Human," I choked out as tears slid down my cheeks. And I knew in that moment that I'd forgiven her. I forgave her for breaking up Nate and me in the first place, for not telling me about her involvement before she died, for making Nate keep that awful promise, and for so many other things that I couldn't voice. As she'd said in her letter, she'd made mistakes, but at the end of the day, she was human. And humans were imperfect creatures.

"My one regret," I said when I had better control of myself, "is that I never got to tell her in person that I forgave her."

Dr. Brooks handed me a box of tissues. "As I said during our first session, we often need closure from ourselves. But there's nothing stopping you from telling her now."

"Except that she's dead." I stared out the window at the new blossoms on the dogwood tree just outside the building. "And heaven is too far away."

"Maybe," she said, and her eyes swam with unshed tears. "I don't consider myself a religious or spiritual person, but even I believe there are signs if we know where to look. So go somewhere you feel closest to her and tell her everything." She lifted one shoulder. "Who knows? Maybe she'll send you a sign."

I thought of the cardinal. What I had originally thought was my mother trying to meddle in my love life suddenly seemed to represent so much more. The bird had kept an eye on me, and I'd found comfort in its regular appearance. Whether my mother intended to steer me toward Nate or to help me find a way to forgive and let go no longer mattered to me. What mattered was that I knew my choice, and I knew what I needed to do.

After I finished with therapy, I went back to my dad's house. I found the number for the school in California and dialed, my hands shaking. Part of me would prefer to do that in an email, and I would send a follow-up message to confirm, but they'd given me my first shot as a teacher. They deserved more than a two-line email.

"Montgomery School, Andrea speaking. How may I direct your call?"

"May I speak to Principal McBride, please?"

"Certainly. May I ask who's calling?"

"Lanie McAllister."

"One moment, please."

The phone rang a couple of times, then a deep voice answered. "Lanie, what a pleasure to hear from you. How are things going in Maryland?"

"Well, sir. The house is under contract. All that's left is to file the finalized estate with the court."

"That's wonderful news. I'm sure you're anxious to get back to the West Coast and settle in before you start."

"Actually, that's why I'm calling." I cleared my throat and squared my shoulders. "I've been offered a position at a local school here, and I've decided to accept it."

The silence on the other end did nothing to help my pounding heart. I felt awful to leave them in a bind, but I knew I was making the right decision.

"I see," he finally said then sighed. "I can't say I didn't see this coming."

I blinked, unsure how to respond to that. "I'm sorry?"

"You're not the first person who returned to their hometown and decided to stick around," he replied with a chuckle. "Much as I think you'd be a great addition to our faculty, I understand, and I hope whatever school you're going to knows what a treasure they're getting."

"Thank you. I really appreciate the opportunity you offered me."

"If you ever change your mind, please feel free to reach out to me directly. I'm sure we'd be able to find you a place here."

I thanked him again and ended the call. One down, one to go. Next, I called the local school. That conversation took a little longer as we discussed the logistics of my start date, having an initial meeting with Mrs. Carlisle before I started officially working with the children, and finalizing the salary offer. When I hung up, I felt lighter and free.

But I wasn't done. I planned to do as my therapist suggested and tell my mother everything, but first, I wanted to clear the air with Nate.

I tried him at the auto shop and at home, but my calls and texts went unanswered. I supposed I couldn't blame him for not responding to me after our last conversation.

Walking into the kitchen, I saw the notes Mom had written,

sitting on the table. The one for Nate lay folded beside mine. It dawned on me that I'd never told him about the note. Would he even want to know? Maybe it was best if he didn't. After all, he'd fulfilled his promise to her.

My head snapped up. As I'd suspected, the cardinal was perched on the railing of my father's back deck, staring at me through the kitchen window. I gazed at it for a moment before my eyes drifted back to the paper in my hand. Perhaps that was a way to reach him. He might avoid me, but I knew him well enough to know he wouldn't ignore a dead woman's last words.

I scribbled my own note to him on an envelope and stuffed the letter inside. After grabbing my coat, I slid my feet into my shoes and raced out to Mom's car. Dr. Brooks had told me to follow my heart, and I intended to do just that.

Chapter Fifteen

I SAT ON THE PARTIALLY FROZEN GROUND, STARING blankly at my mother's headstone. I didn't know how long I'd been there, having lost feeling in my limbs long ago. Overall, I felt hollow and barely noticed the cold. My tears had long since run out, though the cool streaks they left behind were turning into icicles against my cheeks.

After leaving Mom's note for Nate, I went there. Per my therapist's suggestion, I'd gone to the place I'd felt closer to her. Which probably explained why I'd avoided the cemetery for most of my time home.

When I first arrived, I could barely get the words out over my tears. But I told her everything, and I forgave her for it all. While I'd hoped the cardinal would join me, if for nothing else than a sign that my mother heard me, I remained completely and utterly alone. Once I'd said what I needed to, the significance of what I had lost fully sank in, and I finally allowed myself to sit with my grief. No more pushing it away by staying busy or hiding from it under the covers in a darkened room. I let it wash over and through me, feeling everything and not holding back.

A series of images of my future flashed through my mind. The empty seat at my wedding, where my mother should be. Me in a hospital room, surrounded by nurses, with a man standing next to me, holding one hand and encouraging me to push while my other hand was closed in a fist because there was no one else there to hold it. Children's birthdays, first days of school, promotions, anniversaries, and achievements—all things my mother would miss. Graduation was only the beginning. I had a lifetime of events to experience without my mother.

I bowed my head, amazed as tears leaked from my eyes. How I had any water left in my body, I didn't know. And I grieved not only the loss of my mother's life but also the loss of what might have been, how different my future would have looked had she lived.

A sound roused me from my reverie, and I blinked my blurry eyes, attempting to focus. Footsteps crunched over the gravel road that led through the cemetery, and I raised my head, searching for the source of the sound. A figure in a dark coat moved toward me, but I couldn't make out much more than that in the dim light of dusk.

"Lanie?" a deep voice called, and my heart skipped a beat.

"I-I'm here," I croaked.

His pace increased, and soon, he was kneeling by my side. "Are you okay?"

I nodded and stared at my hands, not trusting myself to speak. Though happy to see him, I wasn't prepared to have that conversation then and there.

"Your family is worried sick about you," Nate said as he took my hand. "Your hands are like ice! How long have you been out here?"

I shrugged. My phone was in the car, and I wasn't wearing a watch. Not that I would have checked the time anyway. I glanced at the sky and guessed it had been several hours, based on the gathering shadows.

"I stopped by your house this afternoon, but you weren't there. So I came here," I whispered, unable to find the energy to speak louder.

"Oh, Lanie," Nate cried out as he pulled me to him, wrapping his arms around my frozen ones. "We need to get you inside and warm." He tried to help me stand, but my legs wouldn't cooperate.

"What are you doing here?" I blurted out.

His dark eyebrows pulled down over his brown eyes. "Looking for you. Steven came by my house, asking if I'd seen you. It didn't take long for me to guess where you might be." He stood and lifted me into a standing position, but my legs wobbled, and I couldn't stand on my own. After a moment of assessment, he shrugged and swept my legs out from under me before cradling me against his chest.

Too tired to resist, I rested my head against his shoulder and wrapped my arms around his neck. He carried me to his car and fumbled with the door before he was able to open it and awkwardly set me down in the passenger seat.

"But my car," I protested, trying and failing to stand.

"We'll come back for it tomorrow," Nate promised, resting his hand briefly on my shoulder.

For a moment, I considered arguing with him, but I didn't have the energy. He shut the door and went to the driver's side.

"I need to let Steven know I found you, and then I can take you home," he said as he climbed in beside me.

"Can we go back to your place?" I asked. "If my family is looking for me, they're likely to descend in a worried, frantic mess, especially after how I've acted the last week." I swallowed. "I'd really rather not deal with that tonight."

"I'll take you wherever you want," Nate said with a sideways glance as he pulled out his phone. He dialed Steven and faced the window.

I only half listened to his conversation. He had turned the car on, and I basked in the heat flowing from the vents. I hadn't realized just how cold I was until he tried to help me stand. I held my frozen hands up to the warm air and worked to rub some feeling back into them.

"I told Steven I was going to take you to get something to eat," Nate said as he put his phone away and got the car in gear. "We can stop at a drive-through on the way."

I looked at him then, and all the words that I needed to say to him caught in my throat. Maybe I should have gone home. Dealing with my family couldn't be any worse than the uncomfortable conversation we were about to have.

As if he could sense my thoughts, Nate glanced at me. "Let's just focus on getting you warm and fed. Nothing needs to be decided tonight."

We drove through the town in silence, speaking only long enough for Nate to determine where to stop and what to order. When we reached his house, Nate climbed out first and rushed to help me. The warm car had helped significantly with thawing my limbs, and I was able to stand and walk on my own. I still accepted his offered arm, both to prevent myself from falling flat on my face and to have a reason to touch him. Despite his assurances that we didn't need to talk, I disagreed. And the sooner we had that conversation, the better.

Lucky greeted us at the door, his tail thumping against the wall. Nate helped me out of my coat and led me to the kitchen. When he flicked on the light, Shadow blinked up at me lazily from his bowl, and I bent to pat his gray head.

"Have you given any thought to pursuing your dreams beyond working at the shelter?" I asked.

Nate set our food on the table. "I have." He glanced at me before grabbing some napkins. "I've actually signed up to take a few courses in the fall for a veterinarian tech assistant."

"That's great news!" I sank into a seat on one side of his small table, so he took the chair across from me. "But what about the shop?"

He shrugged, unwrapping his burger. "I talked to Jeff about a promotion. He seemed enthusiastic about the idea, so I could cut back on my hours."

I smiled at him. Regardless of what happened between us, I wanted him to be happy.

He gave me a tentative smile in return then gestured to my untouched food. "Eat. I can hear your stomach growling."

I scowled at him but obeyed. It hadn't occurred to me how hungry I was until I'd devoured my burger and started on my fries. While he tried to be discreet, I could feel his eyes on me, like he thought I might collapse on the spot.

"You can stop looking at me as if I'm going to break," I said, raising an eyebrow.

Nate's wrinkled brow cleared as he gave me a broad grin. "I'm just checking for hypothermia."

I rolled my eyes. Though it was early March, it had been a relatively warm day, and I'd worn a coat. "It's not that cold out."

"You'd be surprised," Nate said, turning serious. "Lanie, what were you doing out there for so long?"

"I-I…" I began, dropping my gaze. "I was… processing."

"But why there?"

"I needed to tell my mother a few things," I admitted, my cheeks heating. Would he think it was stupid? Talking to a dead person?

"I understand," he said, and his face was sincere. "But why didn't you tell anyone where you were going?"

With a shrug, I fiddled with my food wrapper. "I wanted to be alone. And it gave me time to think."

"About?"

I let out a long breath. "My grief." At his puzzled expression, I raked my hands through my hair. "When my mom passed, I didn't really deal with it. Yes, I went to the viewing and the funeral, and I cried, but… I compartmentalized everything." I gestured toward the front door. "It helped to leave this town. At school, I was so busy trying to cram two semesters into one, I didn't have time to grieve. And then when I came home, between the estate, the house, the car, and you…" I cleared my throat. "I was able to distract myself from my loss. But today, I realized how much of my life she'll miss out on."

My eyes watered, and I shook my head. "Like if I get married one day, she won't... she won't..."

"She won't be at your wedding." He slid his hand across the table. I slipped mine into it, giving him a grateful smile. He squeezed my hand, and for a moment, neither of us said anything.

"Honestly, knowing Melody, she'll be there." He chuckled. "And you'll know if she's unhappy with the decorations or venue because something will break or spoil."

I laughed. "You really know my mom!" My smile faded. "But it's not just about a wedding. It's... my whole life."

"I'm sorry, Lanie," he said, bowing his head. "I had no idea."

It reminded me of the last time I'd seen him, and my heart ached. I'd said some harsh things that I regretted. Rehashing the past might have given me the answers to questions that had haunted me for years, but they didn't make me feel any better. If anything, I felt worse.

"You couldn't have known." I waved a dismissive hand. "It didn't really hit me until today." I leaned back in my chair and sighed. "Besides, I didn't tell anyone what I was doing or where I was going, and I turned off my phone."

Nate didn't respond. I wanted to ask him if he'd received the note. I wanted to learn what he thought of my mom's final words to him. But I couldn't bring myself to ask. The elephant between us had returned, and I felt its presence like a crushing weight on my chest.

I stood and crumpled my sandwich wrapper before tossing it into the empty fry container. He followed and pulled out a trash can in the bottom cabinet by the fridge. When I turned back to him, my breath caught in my throat at how close we were, but he took a step back.

My heart plummeted, and I started to move past him. Then I stopped and took his hand in mine, searching his face for answers to the question I couldn't voice. He stared back, his expression neutral, but a spark of heat lit his dark eyes, and I knew it was now or never.

"We need to talk."

Nate started shaking his head. "Not tonight, Lanie. You've been through enough. You need rest. I'll take you home."

"No," I said firmly. "We've been dancing around this for long enough." I pulled him into the living room, where we sat stiffly on his couch, facing each other.

He shifted beside me as if preparing for an argument. "What do you want to talk about?"

"Did you get the note?" I asked, ducking to catch his eye.

He nodded, keeping his gaze on the floor. "But I already knew she wanted me to keep my promise."

"I left it for you because of the other part," I said. "When she told you to take care of me."

"It'll be a little hard to do that when you're in California," he replied, attempting to lighten the mood, but I didn't laugh.

"I'm not going to California."

His head snapped up. "Why wouldn't you go?" His eyes searched mine. "Didn't you already turn down the job here?"

"No, I accepted it. And I let the school in California know I'm staying as well."

He stared at me. "When?"

"This afternoon, before I stopped by your house."

His throat moved as he swallowed. "But I assumed... I mean, after everything's that happened... Why would you want to stay?"

"I love the kids at the school, and I would miss them," I said, lowering my gaze. "This is my home, even if I thought I didn't want it to be for a while." Steeling myself for his reaction, I raised my eyes and met his gaze. "And then there's you."

"Me?" A spark of hope danced in his eyes, but he blinked it away.

"Nate." I frowned. "After everything we've been through these past few weeks, do you really not know how much you mean to me?"

"I know our time together has stirred up a lot of old feelings for you," Nate replied gruffly. "But I don't expect you to forgive me for what I did. As you said the other day, I didn't ask you what you wanted. I let your mother get to me."

"I was hurt and confused. You have no idea how much your actions during my first semester have haunted me all these years." I leaned forward, placing a hand on his arm. "It's not going to be easy, and I imagine we'll have many bumps along the way, but I want to make that journey with you."

"You do?"

"Of course I do. Nate, don't you understand how much I care for you?"

"But that's not the same as—"

I took his hand and traced delicate lines on his palm. I waited for him to continue, and when he didn't, I looked up at him.

"It's not the same as love?" I finally asked. "Is that what you wanted to say?"

Nate nodded. I slid closer to him, wrapping my arms around him and laying my head on his chest.

"I do love you, Nate." My voice was barely above a whisper. I listened to his heart pounding against my ear. "I don't think I ever stopped."

His arms tightened around me. Then he gently grasped my shoulders and moved me back just enough to look at me.

"I *know* I never stopped loving you," he said with conviction. My eyes welled up again but that time with happy tears, and I hugged him, never wanting to let go.

When I pulled back, his eyes met mine with a question, and he reached up and cupped my cheek. I leaned forward and brushed my lips against his. His hands slid into my hair and pulled me closer, deepening the kiss. If I'd had any lingering doubts about staying in Cedar Haven, they melted away.

We stayed up most of the night, reminiscing, talking, laughing, and eventually falling asleep together on the couch, in each other's arms. I woke the next morning before Nate and went to the kitchen in search of coffee.

After brewing myself a cup, I stepped toward the sliding glass door overlooking the back yard. The cardinal perched on a tree nearby, looking in at me.

"I could have used you yesterday," I accused, pointing at it. "Where were you then, hmm?"

The bird lifted its wings in what looked like a shrug and chirped. I shook my head and laughed. When I turned around, Nate stood in the doorway, watching me.

"I see your mom's come to visit," he said, moving into the room and wrapping his arms around my waist.

"So she has," I replied, leaning into him. "I guess this means she approves?"

"I hope so."

I turned to face him before sliding my arms around his neck and giving him a quick kiss. "I know so." When we glanced back out the window, the cardinal was gone.

Epilogue

Two Months Later

I STOOD WITH NATE IN THE HIGH SCHOOL PARKING LOT, watching my students prepare for the Memorial Day parade. I'd been working with Mrs. Carlisle for a little over a month, and soon, the school year would be over, and I would spend the summer preparing for the start of my first year as a teacher. In the meantime, I was looking for a place to live. While staying with my dad had its perks, I was more than ready to move out on my own.

I'd asked Nate to help put together the float, and his mechanical skills had certainly come in handy in making sure all the moving parts worked correctly. The kids had opted to create a fireworks float with lights set up to look like fireworks bursting in the sky.

As the kids prepared to leave to join the parade route, I slipped my hand into Nate's and gave it a gentle squeeze. It seemed the most natural thing in the world. We'd spent so much time together that spring, working on the float, helping Steven and Rose plan their wedding, and just enjoying being back together. With the summer coming, I hoped we might do some traveling as well.

"This feels like old times," I said as I stepped forward to fix a string of lights that had fallen out of place.

"I was just thinking the same thing," Nate replied with a warm smile.

My eyes met his, and the familiar electricity hummed between us. We were surrounded by giggling children, but somehow, it was as if we were the only two people in the room.

"Miss McAllister," Robert said, pulling on my arm. "I think it's our turn to join the parade."

I glanced up to see Mrs. Carlisle waving at me from across the way. "Let's go gather up the rest of our group."

We formed a quick circle as Nate made one last check of the float. I gave my students a pep talk before sending them onto the float to take their places. When I stepped back over to him, he slid his arms around my shoulders.

"You really are an amazing teacher," he said.

As the float began to move, we walked hand in hand with a few of my students. I couldn't imagine being happier than I was at that moment, parading through my hometown with my high school sweetheart by my side.

The parade route was mercifully short, which was a relief in the late-May heat and humidity. Once all of the children were reunited with their parents, I collapsed against the float and let out a sigh.

"I love those kids, but I'm very glad today is over."

"I hope you're not too tired," Nate said as he walked over to me.

"Did we have plans?" I asked, racking my brain. I didn't recall anything specific.

"No, but I have a surprise for you."

I sat upright. A surprise? I loved surprises! "Ooh, where is it?" I searched the storage room.

Nate chuckled. "It's not here. You have to come with me."

"Where are we going?" I asked when I saw we weren't heading toward Nate's car.

"Just trust me," Nate insisted.

We walked up to the building, which only confused me further. He grinned and grabbed my hand again, pulling me toward the auditorium doors.

"Nate, what are you doing? We can't break in."

"We don't have to," he said slyly as he reached in his pocket and pulled out a key.

"What the—" I gasped. "How did you get that?"

"I have my ways." He unlocked the door and led me toward the front of the theatre.

My eyes widened as I took in the stage. It was lined with LED candles, and it looked like someone had sprinkled something over the floor. As we drew nearer, the sweet scent of roses filled my nostrils. In the dim light, he helped me up the stairs and moved to center stage.

"What's going on?" I looked around with wonder. Rose petals were scattered across the stage in the shape of a heart. "Who did all this?" When I turned to him, he wasn't there. "Nate—"

He kneeled before me.

"Oh," I said.

"I wanted to bring you here, to the place where it all started. Where *we* started. To ask you a question."

I stared at him in disbelief. *Is he really...? Is this actually...?* My heart pounded in my chest as butterflies burst into flight in my stomach.

He held fast to my hand while the other reached into his pocket and removed a small blue box. With careful dexterity, he opened the box and held it up. Inside was the most beautiful ring I had ever seen —a white gold claddagh ring, an Irish symbol with two hands holding a heart-shaped diamond topped with a crown.

"Lanie, I bought this ring the summer before our freshman year of college, and despite all that happened between us, I held on to it in the hope that one day, you might come back to me. Will you marry me?"

I nodded, unable to speak around the lump in my throat. He had bought that ring when we were first together and kept it the whole time?

"You have to say yes," he prompted, his lips quirking up in an amused smile.

"Yes," I finally managed to croak out. His smile widened, and he slid the ring onto my finger. I pulled his hand, and when he stood, I threw my arms around him.

"I can't believe you've had this for so long."

"You were worth the wait," he murmured as he kissed me.

We stood on the stage for what seemed like forever but would never be long enough for me. I couldn't stop smiling. Everything about the moment was perfect, from the ring to the location to Nate. I'd never been happier.

"We should probably get to your dad's house," Nate said, his voice reluctant. "I know some people who are dying to know your answer."

"You told them?" I asked.

"I asked your father's permission, and I assume he told Steven and Rose."

I nodded, and we returned to the entrance. "What about all that?" I gestured at the candles on the stage.

"I'll be back for those later," he replied with a twinkle in his eye.

As we walked outside, a flash of red caught my attention. "Look!"

The cardinal perched on Nate's car. In the dim light of the setting sun, it seemed to almost be smiling. Nate reached for my hand, and the cardinal spread its wings and bowed before taking flight. It circled over our heads once before soaring into the sky, beyond where we could see.

~

Enjoyed this story? You can make a difference!
Honest reviews of my books help bring them to the attention of other readers.
If you've enjoyed this book, I would be very grateful if you would consider spending just five minutes leaving a review (it can be as long or as short as you like) on the book's Goodreads' page.

~

When Swans Dance

Dedication

For Mommom,
I promise the pope will approve.

Chapter One

SHAKESPEARE ONCE WROTE, "THE COURSE OF TRUE LOVE ne'er did run smooth." Steven McAllister shook his head with a smirk. No offense to the old bard, but he couldn't have been more wrong. Maybe wedding planning hadn't been going as well as Steven had hoped, but things were coming along, although slower than Rose might prefer. *What's that other saying? Slow and steady something or other?* Whatever it was, it worked for him.

He leaned back in his office chair and rubbed his eyes. A divorce petition glowed on his screen as if mocking him for working late. When had it gotten so dark? Early June usually meant daylight lasted well into the evening, but the sun seemed to have disappeared. He glanced at the clock and groaned. Rose was going to kill him.

As if on cue, his phone buzzed. Stifling another groan, he clicked the message.

Where are you?

To his surprise, it was from his sister. He smiled as he settled deeper into the seat cushion. Lanie was helping Rose with final alterations on her dress before the meeting with the caterer, which put her in the perfect position to stall. He would have to tread carefully, or else he'd press his luck.

Finishing up at work. Be there in 15.

More like a half hour, but Lanie wouldn't mind. The three of them were meeting with the caterer to make final selections on what would be served at the wedding. He could hardly believe that in just over three months, he would be a married man.

But he was ready. He'd never had one doubt about Rose. She'd come into his life just when he needed her the most, stayed through his mother's awful illness, and even helped Lanie through the turbulence of settling the estate. After the past year, they deserved some happiness.

With a sigh, he reread the last stipulation his client had insisted be added. Opposing counsel would never agree to it, with good reason. His client wanted to sell the house, but it was the soon-to-be-ex-wife's childhood home, which she had inherited long before they were married. Steven had tried explaining that, but it had fallen on deaf ears, much like the other legal advice he had given that particular client.

Oh well. He'd promised the client he would try, though it was a waste of everyone's time. As soon as that divorce was over, he hoped to never hear the name Willoughby again. But he knew better. A small-town attorney didn't have a lot of say in who hired him, and Cedar Haven definitely qualified as a small town.

Situated in southern Maryland and about an hour outside of DC, it was barely a pinprick on the state map. But it was Steven's hometown, where he'd been born and raised. And he was proud to have opened his law practice there, despite the lack of choice when it came to his clientele.

Steven raised his arms over his head and stretched, working the kinks out of his back. After saving the latest draft and forwarding it to his client for approval, he closed his laptop and stood. Work had kept him from his beloved long enough.

Just as he reached the office door, his desk phone rang. He stood in the doorway, debating whether to let it go to voicemail or answer it. His staff was long gone, as he should have been. The shrill ring called to him, and he hurried over to answer it.

"It's not enough," a gruff voice said in lieu of a greeting.

Steven stared at the ceiling as he sank into his chair. "What's not enough, Mr. Willoughby?"

"The house. Why should she get to keep part of my retirement while I have to split the cost of a building that's falling apart and not worth much?"

Pinching the bridge of his nose, Steven took a calming breath. As much as he wanted to point out that Mr. Willoughby had specifically insisted on selling the house and splitting the profit, it wouldn't help. He was by far the most difficult client Steven had ever had. Still, Mr. Willoughby's bill would pay Steven's mortgage for the next two months.

"All right," Steven said as he texted his sister that something had come up. "Let's talk numbers."

Better hurry. Rose is on the warpath.

If only it were that easy. But Rose would understand. She wouldn't be happy, but she knew how much pressure he was under to make his law practice a success. He'd spent the last six months building it from the ground up.

Mr. Willoughby droned on in Steven's ear, and though he took notes, his mind was elsewhere. He made the usual sympathetic sounds to ensure his client felt heard, but sometimes, he struggled not to feel like an overpaid therapist. Divorce clients were the worst. If he hadn't found Rose, he might have decided never to get married. The petty things people fought over made the whole institution of marriage sound like a lot of wasted effort.

Rose and I will be different. They'd had a nice long engagement, and he was anxious to have the wedding part over and done with. Who knew that planning what essentially amounted to an extravagant party would take up so much time and cost so much money? Rose and Lanie had done their best to find deals or do whatever they could themselves, but it was still an expensive endeavor.

"Mr. Willoughby." Steven interrupted his client midrant. "We've been over this. I've requested the sale of the house in the paperwork I'm sending opposing counsel, but we've had to offer something in exchange."

"She's going after my retirement, though! I earned that."

As did she. Rubbing his temples, Steven fought the urge to tell his client to shove off. Mrs. Willoughby actually hadn't requested the retirement, despite it being her legal right to do so. She'd been a stay-at-home mom for most of their marriage, which impacted her earning power and ability to save for her future. Steven had suggested offering the retirement as an enticement to sell her childhood home, even though by law, it wasn't marital property. Good luck getting any of that through to Mr. Willoughby, however.

"And as I've said, we are offering it in an attempt to entice your wife to sell the house. You'll more than make up for the loss of retirement in the sale of the home."

His client harrumphed. "I doubt that, and I don't see why I have to give up anything."

Steven had had enough of the circular argument. "Sir, with all due respect, you're lucky she didn't go after your retirement to begin with, and you'll be even luckier if she accepts this offer. Now if you'll excuse me, I must go."

Without waiting for a response, Steven hung up. He would likely pay for that later, but hopefully, Sandra, his paralegal, could smooth things over for him in the morning. She had a knack for knowing exactly how to deal with their more uncooperative clients.

Before Mr. Willoughby could call back, Steven grabbed his things and rushed to the door then locked up. Rose had texted several times while he was on the phone, and he was going to be in more trouble if he didn't get over there soon.

As he pulled out of the parking lot behind the building, he called her and put her on speaker.

"Where are you?"

"Just leaving the office."

The silence on the other end of the line was more deafening than if she had started yelling at him. He cleared his throat.

"I'm sorry, but Mr. Willoughby called and—"

"You stood me up for that philanderer?"

Living in a small town had many perks, but the gossip mill wasn't one of them. "Those accusations are unfounded and—"

Lanie snorted, alerting him to the fact that he, too, was on speaker. "Unfounded my butt. That man has more mistresses than there are blades of grass. I'm amazed he keeps them all straight."

She had a point, though Steven would never tell *her* that. "At any rate, I'm on my way now and should be there in a few."

"You owe me," Rose replied, and though she tried to sound stern, Steven could hear the smile in her voice. Once again, Lanie had saved the day and kept his fiancée distracted. *What would I have done if she had returned to the West Coast?*

"I'll make it up to you, I promise." He hit the end call button and focused on the drive ahead.

As he drove down the darkening street, he pondered how much had changed since Lanie arrived back in town six months ago. Despite her initial determination to leave small-town life behind in favor of the hustle and bustle of Los Angeles and a lucrative position at a prestigious school, she'd decided to stay. He sent up a quick prayer of thanks for her fiancé, Nate. Between telling Lanie about a local teaching job and winning her heart a second time, Nate had done what neither Steven nor his father could do. And his sister was currently engaged and planning a wedding of her own.

If only their mother could see them both, on the verge of walking down the aisle. The smile on Steven's face faded. With the estate finalized and the house sold, he and Lanie had been able to focus on happier things. But the anniversary of their mother's death was fast approaching. Lanie hadn't mentioned it, but she was struggling with it as much as he was. After all, she'd taken a semester off from grad school to care for their mother during those final months, something for which he would be eternally grateful.

Pulling into the parking lot of The Muddy Oar, Steven shut off the engine and pushed the depressing thoughts from his mind. Their mother would want them both to be happy and move on. *What better way to do that than to plan two spectacular weddings?*

He headed into the steak house and to the back of the small dining area. The restaurant doubled as the only caterer in town that could handle large events like weddings, and Steven supposed it could be considered upscale by Cedar Haven standards. Lanie, Rose, and Carissa, their wedding planner, were seated at a round table with more food than he had ever seen before piled around them. His sister's blond head was easy to spot among the crowd. They smiled when they caught sight of him, and Rose stood before running into his arms, her dark-brown hair flying behind her.

"Yay! You're finally here."

"I told you I was on my way." He pulled her close, inhaling her intoxicating scent of jasmine and vanilla.

"You also told your sister you'd be here in fifteen, which was well over a half hour ago," Rose retorted, taking a step back and putting her hands on her hips.

"Fair." Sliding a hand to her cheek, he brushed his lips against hers. "But it's okay if I lie to my sister."

"Sitting right here," Lanie grumbled.

Steven glanced over Rose's head at his very unhappy sister and grinned. "Love ya, lil sis."

"Stop calling me that!" she whined and stuck her tongue out at him, which only further proved he'd chosen the perfect nickname.

Rose led him to the table and sat down. She had a steak and some green bean concoction on her plate. His sister was sampling cake flavors. He hid a smile.

Carissa set a plate in front of him. "Our time is almost up, so you should try what you can before they clear all of this away."

"Thanks," he said before turning to Rose. "So, what do you think so far?"

"I like the steak." Rose took another bite and chewed thoughtfully. "But I'm not as sold on the sides. And we need a vegetarian dish as well."

"The green beans are a definite no from me." Lanie made a face at them.

"I thought the broccoli salad was interesting," Carissa said.

"That's one word for it." Rose sighed and rested her chin on her hand, surveying the table. "I liked the glazed carrots, but Carissa says we have to offer something green."

"What about this?" Steven pointed at a medley of green leaves in a bowl. Leaning forward with his fork, he speared one and brought it to his nose, sniffing it, a move he immediately regretted as the sour scent of vinegar burned his nostrils. "What *is* this?"

"They call it spinach surprise." Rose wrinkled her nose. "None of us are brave enough to try it." Her face morphed into a sweet smile, but he wasn't fooled. "You should do the honors."

I suppose I do owe her. Grimacing, he spooned some onto his plate. He sniffed it again, and the strange combination of vinegar and spice irritated his sinuses. *Here goes nothing.* After taking a tentative bite, he assessed the flavor. The vinegar came through pretty strong, but overall, it wasn't bad. He detected garlic and some sort of creamy substance.

When he looked up, Rose and Lanie were leaning forward as if waiting to see whether he would keep the strange food down. Carissa had a hand over her mouth, probably hiding a smile. With a shrug, he took another bite. "It's not bad, but I'm not sure I'd want to serve it at a wedding."

Rose groaned. "Why is this so difficult? If we'd gotten married in Baltimore, we'd have more options for catering."

Carissa put a hand on her arm. "But you'd pay far more for the experience. I know you want everything to be perfect, but remember, people are coming to see you and Steven get married. As long as you feed them something, they'll be happy."

With a pout, Rose pulled a salad toward her. "This is Caesar salad. It's boring, I'll admit, but at least it's something most people enjoy."

"Maybe you could have a small salad bar where people could make their own," Lanie suggested.

"That's a good idea," Steven agreed. "And then they can put whatever color of vegetable they want on their plates."

Rose smiled, her eyes lighting up. "I love salad bars at restaurants. I'm sure it'll be a big hit."

"That's settled." Carissa tapped away on her phone. "What were you thinking for the entrée? You said steak, but what else?"

Several different dishes sat before him—chicken, shrimp, crab cake, and pork chops—and he sampled each. The savory chicken was a tad on the dry side, and he could only imagine how much worse that would be after sitting over a chafing dish. Crab cakes made sense for a summer wedding in Maryland, but not everyone was a fan of seafood.

"How many entrees are we paying for again?"

Rose rolled her eyes at Lanie. "Typical male. Doesn't pay attention to the details."

"Hey!" Steven protested. "I've got a lot on my plate."

"You sure do." Lanie pointed at his literal plate and laughed.

"The package you picked includes three entrees," Carissa said. "One of which needs to be vegetarian."

Next, he tried the shrimp. The sweet-and-spicy marinade appealed to him but not as much as the crab. After all, the brackish water of the Chesapeake ran through his veins, and blue crabs were practically the state mascot. He reviewed the vegetarian options: wild mushroom risotto, three-cheese ravioli, and meatless lasagna. No matter what they chose, it would be some sort of pasta.

After a moment of contemplation, he tried the mushroom risotto. Good but not quite what he wanted. He sampled the rest of the vegetarian options. The cheese ravioli was better, but the lasagna somehow managed to taste just like it would with meat.

"My vote is for steak, crab cake, and the meatless lasagna."

Rose frowned. "I was partial to the three-cheese ravioli myself."

"The lasagna tasted just like the real thing to me." Steven shrugged. "But I'm not a vegetarian, so I'm not sure that's the goal."

Carissa laughed. "Unfortunately, we don't have time to bring in a vegetarian for their opinion, so why don't we look at it from a price perspective?" After a quick glance at her phone, she continued, "According to the PDF they sent us, the ravioli is cheaper than the lasagna."

"Then let's go with that." Between starting a business and trying to pay off his student loans, Steven hoped to curb the growing wedding costs as much as possible to avoid adding to their already strained finances.

Carissa finished tapping into her phone then stood. "Lanie, would you mind coming with me to talk to the caterer? While we're gone, you two should try the cakes."

Once they were alone, Steven leaned closer to Rose. "I know I complained about the expense of a wedding planner, but she sure is making this easier."

Rose pressed her hand to her chest. "You have no idea. I can't imagine what I would do without her. She's managed to keep everything on schedule, which has stopped me from losing my mind." She shook her head. "Why is wedding planning so hard?"

He rubbed her back. "I'm sorry I haven't been around as much as I promised I would. But now that it's summer, I'm hoping things at the firm will slow down."

Leaning back in her chair, she raised a thin black eyebrow. "I'm not holding my breath."

"I know I keep saying that, but between Sandra and Leslie, I feel like I'm starting to get a handle on things."

She pointed her fork at him. "You need a partner."

"It's too soon."

"Is it?" Her brown eyes darkened. "You've been running yourself ragged for months now, and you're not hurting for profit." He opened his mouth to speak, but she waved a hand. "I know that you've got student loans and bills to pay, but come on, Steven. You can't keep this pace up. You'll work yourself into an early grave."

With a sigh, he sliced off another piece of cake with his fork. Red velvet, if his limited knowledge of cakes didn't deceive him. He took a bite, more to avoid responding to her than because he wanted it. Their conversation had caused him to lose his appetite.

"New businesses always have a hard time getting off the ground. I just want to make sure things are stable before I bring someone else in."

"I understand that." Rose laid a hand on his arm. "But speaking as both your loving fiancée and as a nurse, I'm concerned. I've seen what happens to people who don't take care of themselves, who work too hard. You need to find ways to ease the burden, give yourself some breathing room."

After setting his fork down, he covered her hand with his own. "I promise I'll consider it."

Her forehead creased, but she nodded. "I suppose that's better than a flat-out no."

Just then, Lanie and Carissa returned, and the former grabbed another piece of cake. "Everything's worked out with the caterer. Did you choose a cake?"

"I'm partial to red velvet," he said, even though that was literally the only flavor he'd tried.

"Me too." Rose squeezed his arm.

He breathed a sigh of relief. *Crisis averted.* They were on the same page once more.

Chapter Two

Rose walked quickly through the hospital ward. Rounds were starting soon, and she wanted to check in on her favorite patient before they got underway. Mrs. Winslow was propped up in her bed with the sheet tucked around her legs. Her watery blue eyes struggled to focus as Rose came in, but her smile brightened the room.

"Good morning, Mrs. Winslow," Rose said as she moved to her bedside. "How are you feeling today?"

"Same as yesterday." Mrs. Winslow waved a hand over her face. "My eyesight is still poor, but the doctor said tomorrow's surgery will help."

"I've no doubt about that." After checking her vitals, Rose pulled up a chair. "Any new gossip since I last saw you?"

"I think Dr. Bryant has the hots for Nurse Claire," Mrs. Winslow whispered conspiratorially. "They were canoodling just outside my door late last evening."

Rose laughed. "Oh, that's old news. They've been dating for some time now, though they think they're being discreet."

"Well, they need to find a better dark corner because I could see them plain as day from here." Running a hand through her thinning blond hair, Mrs. Winslow raised an eyebrow. "And what of you and your fiancé? How are the wedding plans coming?"

"Oh, we met with the caterer and made our final choices for the menu," Rose said, forcing a smile. Her conversation with Steven had done little to assuage her constant worrying about him. Since the estate had finalized, she'd hoped he would have an easier time juggling his work and the wedding, but instead, his caseload had only gotten worse. The circles under his eyes grew darker every time she saw him.

"You don't seem as excited as I expected you to," Mrs. Winslow said with a frown.

"I'm excited!" But it sounded fake even to Rose's ears. "Steven has been a bit preoccupied with work lately. I'm afraid he's neglecting his health."

"He's lucky to have you to care for him."

Rose bristled, and she worked to keep her temper in check. Nursing was her job, one she preferred to leave at the end of her shift. Of course she would care for Steven if he needed her, but she would prefer him to take preventative measures *before* he worked himself into an illness.

Stifling a sigh, she stood. "I best get to my rounds." She patted Mrs. Winslow's hand. "I'll check with the doc on whether there's anything I need to do to prep you for surgery, but hopefully, we'll have you seeing clearly in no time."

Mrs. Winslow gave her a grateful smile before leaning back on her pillow and closing her eyes. Rose envied her calm nature. If she was facing complicated eye surgery, she wasn't sure she would be able to appear so serene.

Rose left the room to begin her rounds, mentally counting down the days until she had some time off for the wedding and honeymoon. The last winter had been rough, and she desperately needed a vacation.

As she picked up the clipboard outside the next patient's room, she wondered how much different her life would be once she and Steven tied the knot. They'd discussed children, but with their schedules, she didn't know when they might find the time. And the last thing she wanted to do was add to his stress load by bringing it up.

But she wanted children, at least two and close together. She hoped to start trying for them right away. An only child herself, she had come to the US from South Korea with her parents and had stayed on to finish her nursing degree when her parents returned to take care of her grandparents. Her family was planning to come to the wedding, but part of her worried the travel would prove too expensive. The price of flights had risen substantially in the last year, and she was glad she had locked in their honeymoon tickets when she did.

As much as she loved the McAllisters, relying on them just wasn't the same as having her own family there. While she had no plan to return to her homeland on a permanent basis, she wanted her children to understand their heritage and culture. Maybe once they were more settled, she and Steven could travel to South Korea for a visit—assuming Steven's business ever settled. She sighed and entered Mr. Patrones's room.

He sat up in his bed, staring out the window. The sight of him tugged at her heartstrings. He'd had a mild heart attack a week ago, but no one had been in to visit him. She'd asked about family, but his answers were vague, and she didn't want to make him uncomfortable.

"Good morning, Mr. Patrones. How are we doing today?"

He shifted in his bed, and his sad brown eyes met hers. "Same as yesterday."

Grimacing, she glanced over his chart. He had improved significantly in the last several days, and they would probably release him soon, not that she expected him to take that as good news.

"Your vitals are looking better." She tried to keep her tone cheerful. "I don't think you'll be with us much longer."

His eyebrows drew together, and she realized a moment too late how her words could be misconstrued. She moved to his side.

"I meant that you would be discharged soon."

"Either way, at least I'll be out of your hair."

What a very Eeyore thing to say. She checked his fluids and made a few notes on his chart. All the while, she racked her brain for some encouraging words but came up short.

"Any special requests for lunch?" she asked, wishing she could find a way to reach him. Her patients usually raved about her bedside manner, but with Mr. Patrones, she just couldn't break through the shroud of sadness that engulfed him.

"Does it matter what I request? The diet the doctor has me on hardly allows much wiggle room."

Rose bit her tongue to avoid saying something she might regret. Most heart attack patients struggled with the recommended dietary restrictions, but the ones who refused to follow the diet were at a higher risk of another attack. That probably wasn't the best thing to tell Mr. Patrones.

"All right. Well, push the button if you need anything," she replied, turning on her heel and moving quickly to the hallway.

"Mr. Patrones still as depressing as ever?" a quiet voice asked, making Rose jump.

Rebecca Masters leaned against the wall beside her, clutching a clipboard to her chest. Rose released a breath and nodded.

"He's doing better physically, but I wonder if we shouldn't keep him under a seventy-two-hour psych hold."

Rebecca rolled her eyes. "Dr. Myers will never go for that, especially since Mr. Patrones has never vocalized any suicide ideations. But we should add some recommendations for counseling to his discharge instructions." She glanced behind Rose. "I don't suppose we've found any family members?"

Rose shook her head. "Not that I'm aware of. It's sad. I can't imagine how he's lived alone all this time."

"Ah, well," Rebecca said. "I'll talk to Dr. Myers, but I'm afraid there's not much else we can do."

With a dejected nod, Rose went to complete the rest of her rounds. Other than checking on Mr. Patrones a few more times, she continued her shift uneventfully. At her break, she decided to call Steven to take her mind off things.

"Hey, honey, how's it going?"

"Not bad," Rose said, choosing not to mention her concerns about Mr. Patrones. "I just wanted to confirm we were still on for dinner tonight."

When he didn't immediately respond, her heartbeat quickened. *Not again.* His late arrival to the caterer had been bad enough, but he knew how important their weekly dates were to her. Her parents had maintained date night throughout their entire marriage, which she believed was the secret to their success. While she would never say it, sometimes she wondered whether Steven's parents might not have divorced if they had done something similar.

"Listen," he began.

She squeezed her eyes shut. "You've got to be kidding me."

"I've got a lot of work to finish up tonight." His voice was defensive, and a part of her wished she hadn't pushed the issue. After a beat, he sighed. "But we can go out this weekend instead."

"I work this weekend," she replied, her tone flat.

"Oh."

She rubbed her forehead, resisting the urge to roll her eyes. It was the beginning of June, and their wedding was set for the end of August. They should be spending more time together, not less. But of course, he had a lot on his plate. Sometimes she wished he had kept his job in the city rather than striking out on his own. Then again, some big-city law firms required eighty hours a week. Such a demanding schedule would likely have contributed to his workaholic nature even more.

"When is your next day off?" he asked, a pleading note in his voice. "Maybe I can leave the office early and take you out for a night on the town."

What would a night "on the town" in Cedar Haven entail? Karaoke at Seabreeze followed by a plate of pancakes at Bea's? Not quite on par with the images that phrase brought up. Sometimes she really missed Baltimore.

"I'm off on Tuesday." She braced herself for what she knew he was going to say.

"Ah… I have court Tuesday."

Of course he did. Tuesday was child support day at the courthouse, and he always had at least one client on the docket every week. She clenched her fist at her side.

"Can't you just come out with me for an hour tonight?" She hated begging for his time. Was this what their marriage was going to be like? "The work will still be there tomorrow."

"I'm sorry, babe, but I need to finish this brief. I promise I'll make it up to you."

Empty words. They'd already established that their schedules were both full for the next several days. Oh well, maybe she would have better luck next week, though maintaining their weekly date was becoming increasingly more difficult.

"It's fine," she lied, not wanting him to feel worse than he already did. He'd promised things would let up soon, and he'd said he would consider getting a partner. She needed to be patient. "We can just plan for next week."

"Thanks for understanding, Rose. I really am sorry."

"Promise me you won't stay too late at the office. You need to take care of yourself."

She could almost see him shaking his head, a rueful smile on his lips. Sometimes, despite her best efforts, the line between nurse and fiancée blurred for her, but she couldn't help it. She'd seen too many patients cause themselves avoidable health issues by working too much.

“I love you,” he said, clearly trying to avoid the same old argument.

“I love you too.”

She disconnected and leaned back against the wall, her head in her hands. How had they gotten there? Even when they’d had opposing schedules of law school and nursing school, they’d managed to find time for each other every week.

“Rose?” Rebecca called from behind her, pulling her from her thoughts.

She turned around and smiled. “Hey, I was headed to finish my rounds. What’s up?”

Rebecca’s forehead creased. “About that. Any chance you could stay on? Lisa called out with a sick child again, and I need someone to cover her shift.”

Ordinarily, Rose would have said no. She rarely worked doubles because she tried to maintain boundaries between her work time and her personal life. But aside from Steven canceling on her, she had other reasons to consider accepting an extra shift. There weren’t many opportunities for advancement at the small rural hospital, but she had her eye on the head nurse position that had just opened. What she lacked in tenure, she hoped to make up for with a strong work ethic.

“Sure, I can stay on.”

“Thanks! I owe you one.” Rebecca turned on her heel and headed down the hall.

Taking a deep breath, Rose shook her head. *At least I’ll get overtime.*

A few hours later, Rose was standing at the nurses’ station, reviewing a patient’s chart, when Rebecca appeared beside her. Her coworker’s face was pale, and she breathed heavily as she braced a hand against the desk.

"Have you heard?"

Rose raised an eyebrow. "Heard what?"

"There's been an accident. You need to go to the ICU."

"What? Why?" Rose shook her head. "Nobody told me I was being pulled."

"You're not," Rebecca said, leading Rose toward the elevators. "But you need to get up there. They'll explain when you arrive." She gave Rose's hand a squeeze before hurrying away.

Bewildered, Rose pressed the button, and the elevator doors opened. She stepped inside, chose the ICU floor, and waited, working to swallow her irritation. *What the heck is going on? And why wouldn't Rebecca just tell me?* Worry gnawed at her during the ride up.

The ICU ward was complete chaos as she stepped into the hall. She double-checked that she hadn't accidentally gone to the ER. *Nope, this is the right floor.* Rushing to the nurses' station, she halted when a familiar head of dirty-blond hair rounded the corner on a gurney.

"Steven?" She ran after him only to have someone grab her arm and spin her around.

"Rose, I—"

"Let go of me." She tried to shake free as she met the gaze of whoever had had the audacity to stop her. But Dr. Myers held firm, his blue eyes filled with concern and his expression grim.

"Come with me," he said and half dragged her to an empty office.

Once they were inside, he released her, and she staggered across the room to the desk. She whirled around, ready to march right back out that door, but Dr. Myers blocked her path.

"There's nothing you can do for him right now," he said. "They're in the process of determining the damage and hooking up his IV to start administering medication. I only have a moment."

Her legs gave out, and she sank into the nearest chair. "Oh God. What happened?"

"He was in a car accident, but we think he had a medical emergency that led to the crash." Dr. Myers glanced at her as if assessing how much to say. "Possibly a heart attack, but I'll know more once I get in there and run some tests. You stay here, and I'll get someone to sit with you."

Like hell. "Need I remind you, Doctor, I'm an RN? I'm coming with you."

"And need I remind *you*, Rose, we have a strict policy that prohibits hospital staff from treating family members?" Her five-foot-four stature was no match for Dr. Myers's six-foot frame when he put a firm hand on her shoulder and pushed her back into the chair. "I'll send word as soon as I can."

Without waiting for her response, he spun on his heel and was gone. Rose put her head in her hands. *A heart attack? How? Why?* Steven was twenty-nine years old and one of the healthiest people she knew. She'd joked he was going to work himself into an early grave, but she'd never expected *that*.

The door opened, and Marie, the head RN for the ICU, came in. "So he's told you, then." She handed Rose a cup of coffee.

Rose took a sip, more out of habit than because she actually wanted or needed the beverage. Marie perched in the chair beside her, taking her free hand. The room was dimly lit with a desk lamp, and Rose found comfort in the darkness.

"It'll be all right."

If only she could believe her. But Steven sounded like he was in a bad way. The other half of Dr. Myers's message finally resonated.

"What did he hit?" she asked.

"What's that?"

"Dr. Myers said St—" Her throat closed around his name. "Dr. Myers said he was in a car accident. What did he hit?"

"I don't know the full story," Marie said. "But I gathered from the little the paramedics shared that he lost control of the car and hit a tree."

At least no one else was injured. Small favors. She tried to focus on the good news. Steven was in the best hands in the area. She'd seen

Dr. Myers work magic on patients in worse shape. And Steven was young. He had a better chance than most.

Still, she couldn't just sit there and wait. She needed to *do* something.

"I have to make a call." Not wanting an audience, she stood and raced out of the room. After glancing up and down the hallway, she ducked into a storage closet across from the office. Her fingers shook as she scrolled to Lanie's name in her phone.

"Hey, Rose, what's up?"

"You need to come to the hospital," Rose said in a rush. "It's your brother."

"Steven? What's wrong? What happened?"

"He was in a car accident." Rose couldn't bring herself to tell her the rest, not yet. It still didn't feel real. Besides, Dr. Myers had said a heart attack was possible but not confirmed. There was no sense in getting her future sister-in-law worked up over the phone.

"Oh no! Let me call my dad, and then I'll head on over. What floor are you on?"

"The ICU."

Lanie gasped and promised she would be there as soon as she could, but Rose barely heard her. She disconnected the call and went back to the office. Marie was still there, her eyebrows pulled together in a frown.

"Lanie is on her way, and she's calling her dad." Rose slid into her chair. Her coffee sat on the desk behind it, but she couldn't bring herself to drink it. Instead, she allowed her eyes to take in the details of the room in hopes it would ground her in the moment. A large leather rolling chair was turned to face the dual monitors set up above a docking station on the desk. Mahogany bookshelves towered in the back corner, casting ominous shadows in the soft light of the lamp.

"I'll stay with you until they arrive." Marie grasped Rose's hand again and gave it a squeeze.

Part of Rose wanted to protest, as she imagined Marie had a

million other things to do, but she didn't want to be alone. Her stomach was already in knots, and she feared she would fall to pieces by the time Lanie arrived.

The sounds of machines beeping, muffled footsteps, and whispered prayers wafted into the room as they sat in silence. Rose was literally on the edge of her seat. Her feet ached to move, but her head was spinning, and she feared she would pass out if she tried to stand. With her free hand, she gripped the arm of the chair and stared at the office door, willing it to open with Lanie or Dr. Myers. Though if the latter came right then, it wouldn't mean good news. Not enough time had passed for Dr. Myers to have completed his assessment of Steven. He would run an EKG and assess for internal bleeding as well as broken bones. It was going to be a long night.

Time stood still, and Rose silently prayed for Steven to be spared. If—no, *when*—he survived, he would have to take better care of himself. She wouldn't give him a choice in the matter. Not after that.

Of course, that would all take time, and she hoped she could enlist Lanie and Steven's staff in determining what needed to be taken care of immediately at the law firm. She wouldn't allow him to stress over it, not while his health hung in the balance. They would figure things out. After all, they had the rest of their lives to do so. She refused to give in to despair. Steven *would* live, and they *would* have a life together. She had to have faith.

A knock sounded at the door, and Rose braced herself, but it was only one of the other nurses leading Lanie and Max into the room. When Rose jumped up to embrace them, Marie slipped quietly from the room.

"You made good time," Rose said, fighting back tears that threatened to spill over her cheeks.

"We broke several laws getting here, but we didn't get caught." Lanie cupped Rose's cheek. "How are you?"

Rose blinked. The fact that Lanie's first question had been about her and not Steven caught her off guard. Her face likely betrayed how she felt, but she forced herself to respond.

"Trying to stay positive." She gestured to the door. "There's no news, but I didn't expect there to be."

"He'll pull through," Max said, though it sounded as if he were trying to convince himself. "He's made of stern stuff."

"And he's in good hands." Lanie smiled, but the fear in her eyes was unmistakable.

The same nurse who had brought them to the office returned with two chairs, which she set up in front of the bookshelves. With Marie gone, the chairs weren't necessary, but Rose appreciated her thoughtfulness. When they were alone again, Max collapsed into one of them. Lanie took the seat closest to Rose.

"Do you have any more details about the accident?" Lanie asked.

"They think he had a medical emergency before he lost control of the car."

Lanie frowned. "What kind of medical emergency?"

After taking a deep breath, Rose told them everything she knew, which admittedly wasn't much. And when she mentioned the possible heart attack, their reactions matched her own.

"But he's not even thirty!" Max leaned forward, disbelief blazing from his eyes.

"Stress can cause a lot of health issues, Dad," Lanie said, her tone gentle.

But Max just scowled and faced the wall. Rose opened her mouth to respond, but Lanie shook her head, her message clear. Berating him with medical knowledge would be of little use, especially at that moment.

"What are they doing to him?" Lanie asked.

Rose shrugged. "Dr. Myers is a cardiologist. He's running tests to determine what happened and what damage was done."

Max stood suddenly and walked toward the door. When he reached it, he turned back, his expression blank.

"I can't stand all this waiting. I'm going to grab a coffee. Anyone want anything?"

"Sure, I'll take one," Lanie said, her eyes wide. Rose assumed she was puzzled by her father's erratic behavior. "Rose?"

Instead of responding, Rose gestured to the coffee Marie had brought, not trusting herself to speak. Max closed the door behind him, and she couldn't help the relief that coursed through her at his absence. While he had always been kind to her, something about him intimidated her. She suspected his perpetual bad mood was the cause of her unease.

"He never could handle hospitals," Lanie murmured, her eyes on the door. When she glanced at Rose, she forced a smile. "But he'll be fine, I'm sure."

"I'm sorry to have dragged you both here. Maybe I should have waited until I knew more."

"Nonsense." Lanie shook her head. "We want to be here. Besides, you shouldn't have to go through this alone, not when you've got family to help you through it."

Family. Sometimes Rose forgot what that was like. It had been lonely since her parents moved back to South Korea. But the promise of a future family with Steven had eased the pang. And that was currently in jeopardy. *Oh God, what if he doesn't make it? What will I do without him?*

"He wasn't even supposed to be on the road," she blurted out.

Lanie blinked. "What do you mean?"

"We had plans for dinner, which he canceled." Rose put her head in her hands. "If I'd been with him, maybe I could have prevented this. Or at least been there when it happened."

"Don't think like that." Lanie slid an arm around Rose's shoulders. "He's been working himself sick these last few months. I'd hoped things would calm down for him once the estate was finalized, but instead, he's working harder than ever. He needs to take it easy, especially with all the stress you both must be under from the wedding."

The wedding. Will it even happen now? Depending on his injuries, it could take weeks or even months to recover. There would be rehabilitation, physical therapy, and who knew what else ahead of him. Rose had no idea how that might impact their immediate future, let alone their wedding.

It felt silly to even think about that when his life hung in the balance, but somehow, it was all her mind could handle. Canceling the wedding wasn't the worst thing in the world, but it would be heartbreaking nonetheless. They'd been planning it for well over a year, and she would hate for their hard work to go to waste.

Not to mention that she was ready to marry him. She'd known he was the one for her since that first day they'd met in the library, when she'd accidentally knocked over a stack of books and heard a yelp of pain. She closed her eyes as the memory washed over her.

They had unknowingly chosen to sit at the same table to study. She hadn't been able to see him over the books in her arms. When she'd heard his cry, she'd rushed over to apologize and met the most interesting pair of eyes she'd ever seen—a delicate mixture of green and brown that she wanted to lose herself in. His frown of discomfort quickly morphed into a smile, and he'd brushed off her concern. He'd introduced himself, and the moment their hands touched, a spark shot through her like nothing she'd ever felt before.

A rueful smile pulled at her lips. Even with such a promising first meeting, it had still taken him months to work up the courage to ask her out. They'd met at the library several times and enjoyed each other's company while studying quietly. Her smile fell. With their busy schedules, their relationship had never been easy, but once they'd set a date for the wedding, she'd thought things were looking up for them.

"Hey." Lanie gently shook her arm. "What's going on in that head of yours?"

"Whether or not we're going to need to cancel the wedding." Rose raised her head and met Lanie's eyes. "I know it's the least of my worries right now, but I can't help it."

"I get it. Sometimes it's easier to focus on what you can control.

But I can't imagine we would need to. Dad and I can pitch in more to help fill the gap if Steven needs to back off the planning."

"Assuming he survives this." Rose bit her lip. She hadn't meant to voice her deepest fears.

"He will survive it. McAllisters are made of stern stuff," Lanie said, echoing what her father had said earlier.

Rose nodded mutely. She wanted to believe her future sister-in-law, but she couldn't quite bring herself to do so. And if something happened to Steven... If he didn't make it, she didn't know what that would do to her.

Chapter Three

STEVEN WOKE GROGGY AND IN PAIN. THE ROOM AROUND him was unfamiliar with its fluorescent lighting and antiseptic smell. A repetitive beeping sounded near his head, and he swatted at the alarm with his right hand only to groan as something pulled at his skin. His veins seemed to burn with the movement. Raising his arm took effort, and he frowned at the IV sticking out of it.

What on earth? Am I in the hospital? He remembered getting into his car to drive to Rose's apartment, hoping to surprise her. He recalled the road was slick with rain, then an awful pain had bloomed in his chest. There had been a flash of bright light, but the memory was cut short, as if he'd fallen asleep in the middle of it.

He tried to move his head to search for a call button, but something prevented him from turning it. Breathing became more difficult as he coughed and sputtered. The steady beeping increased in rhythm, matching his heart rate.

A nurse he didn't recognize rushed in, and her eyes widened. "You're awake." She glanced behind him then stepped to his side. "It's okay. This is disorienting, but I'm going to need you to take deep breaths." She inhaled deeply through her nose and exhaled from her mouth in demonstration.

Forcing himself to focus, Steven imitated her, and soon the rapid beeping slowed to a steadier pulse. The panic subsided enough for him to take in more of his surroundings. Lifting his left hand, he attempted to touch his neck, but a brace prevented him from doing so. At least that explained why he couldn't turn his head.

"I'll go get the doctor," the nurse said with a smile before spinning on her heel and leaving the room.

He tried to open his mouth to stop her, to ask what had happened to him, but even his face hurt to move. Frustrated, he settled back against the uncomfortable hospital bed and took an assessment of himself.

His legs were numb with the pins-and-needles sensation he got if he sat on his foot too long. With careful movements, he lifted the blanket draped over him and noted a cast on his left leg. *Must have broken it.* But it didn't hurt. *Strange.* Perhaps they'd given him a great deal of pain medication. If he had to guess, he'd been in an accident. Maybe he'd totaled his car. *Ugh, that's the last thing I need.*

Just as he reached for the call button again, the doctor came in. Steven recognized him as one of the doctors Rose worked with, though he couldn't remember his name.

"Mr. McAllister, you gave us quite a scare. I'm Dr. Myers, though I believe we've met before." He moved a stool over to Steven's bedside and perched on it. "Can you hear me?"

"Yes," Steven croaked out.

"Good. And I assume you can understand me as well?"

Why was the doctor treating him like an invalid? He didn't have brain damage or anything. *Unless... How bad was the accident?*

"Did you understand what I asked you, Steven?" the doctor asked, prompting Steven to focus.

Steven gave a slight nod, as much as the brace would allow, then winced as the motion sent pain radiating through his head.

"Do you remember what happened?"

It took Steven a minute to respond. "I remember... getting in the car to drive to see Rose. My chest hurt..." As he spoke, his chest throbbed, and he rubbed a hand over it. His fingers probed the bandage over his heart. "Was I in an accident? How's my car?"

"Yes to your first question. Unfortunately, I don't know the answer to your second question." After making a few notes on his chart, Dr. Myers leaned forward. "So you remember the accident. Do you remember anything that happened before the accident? How you were feeling?"

Why does "before the accident" matter? His stomach twisted into one big knot, and he gritted his teeth. But to humor the doctor, Steven closed his eyes and tried to focus. Other than the chest pain, he didn't remember anything. Maybe if he said no, Dr. Myers would stop interrogating him and provide answers instead.

"Not really," Steven said, opening his eyes and meeting the doctor's gaze.

"It appears you had a mild myocardial infarction."

A what? Steven stared at Dr. Myers, hoping his expression demonstrated his confusion. When the doctor didn't elaborate, he risked more pain by shifting a fraction of an inch to look at the nurse.

"You had a heart attack," she translated helpfully.

Steven blinked rapidly, trying to digest the words. *Was that even possible?*

"Ah yes, sorry. I should have explained in simpler terms. You had a mild heart attack before you crashed into a tree." He stood and showed Steven a paper with a bunch of lines on it. "We've run an EKG and some other tests. There was a slight blockage in your artery, and I placed a stent."

But Steven barely heard him. *A heart attack?* Wasn't that something that only happened to the elderly? *I'm not even thirty!*

A million questions ran through his mind, but he couldn't articulate any of them. His breathing grew shallower as he tried to organize his thoughts, but they were flying too fast to make them coherent.

The nurse put a hand on his arm. "You need to calm down. You're going to hyperventilate."

It took effort, but Steven forced himself to take several deep breaths. While his heart rate and breathing slowed, the deep breathing did little to quell the panic growing in his belly.

"This is a lot to take in, but there is something else you should know."

"I broke my leg," Steven said, lifting the sheet again to reveal his cast.

"Well, yes, though I imagine it doesn't hurt."

Steven frowned. "I assume that's due to the pain medication."

With a shake of his head, Dr. Myers sat on the stool and moved closer to the bed. "Unfortunately, it's worse than that. You appear to have a spinal contusion, which is impacting your neurological transmitters." When Steven frowned, Dr. Myers pursed his lips. "A bruised spine, which has caused a temporary paralysis."

I'm paralyzed? Steven swallowed, trying to keep a brave face. The doctor had called the paralysis temporary, so perhaps there was some hope yet.

"We need to get you in for an MRI to assess the extent of the damage," Dr. Myers continued. "But I'm hoping there are no indications of tears or permanent damage to your spinal cord."

"What does that mean, though?" Steven tried to lift his good leg, but it wouldn't respond. "Will I be able to walk again?"

"Assuming it's just a bruise and not anything worse, then yes. In time," Dr. Myers assured him. "But it will be a long, hard road to recovery."

That brought up another question. "How long have I been here?"

The doctor stood and moved to the lone window in the room and pulled back the curtain. Steven winced as the bright morning light blinded him.

"Several hours. You were brought in last night, and you've been in and out of consciousness since the surgery." Dr. Myers shook his head. "You were lucky. Although it's rare for someone your age to suffer a heart attack." Moving to Steven's bedside, Dr. Myers folded his arms over his chest. "But Rose told me you've been under a lot of stress lately."

Rose. She must be out of her mind with worry. *Is she here? What about Lanie and Dad?* After what they'd just gone through with their mother, his sister had to be freaking out as well.

"Rose?" he croaked.

"She's here waiting to see you, but I'd like to get an X-ray and MRI of your back before I allow her to visit."

Steven wanted to protest, but there didn't seem to be much point. After all, he'd apparently been there for a while, so a few more hours couldn't hurt.

"I promise it won't take long."

Too tired to argue, Steven gave a quick nod, and the doctor and nurse left the room. Alone again, Steven stared at the ceiling and tried to process what he'd been told. While he would never have claimed to be in perfect health, there was no way he would have expected a heart attack. The stress at the office had been adding up over the last few months, and there were a few times his heart rate was higher than it should be, but he assumed that once he had things more under control, his health would improve as well. Besides, his practice hadn't even been open a year, so there were bound to be some growing pains. He just expected them to be financial, not physical.

The thought of his business made him shiver with cold dread. He looked at his legs again then tried to move one. He thought he saw a twitch, but it could have been his imagination. How long would it take for him to recover the use of his legs? The heart monitor began beeping erratically as realization sank in. *Will my life ever be the same again?*

The nurse came back with an orderly, and soon, he was taken to another area. Already, he was tired of the bed and itching to get up and move around, but he had no idea when that would happen. The fears about his future were enough to distract him from the multitudes of tests the doctor had ordered.

A little while later, he returned to his room, feeling like a human pincushion. Why did doctors always hurt people when they were supposedly trying to help them? What other profession could get away with such awful torture?

"Would you like to see Rose now?" the nurse asked after replacing a bag of fluids and making sure he was comfortable.

"Yes, please."

The nurse nodded before she hurried away. Steven tried to fix his face into a pleasant expression, but every small movement hurt. He could only imagine what he looked like.

When the door opened again, he swallowed his shock at Rose's appearance. Her dark eyes were bloodshot and puffy, with purple circles blemishing her skin. The blue scrubs she must have been wearing for her shift were wrinkled and stained.

And although she gave him a smile, the exhaustion behind it was evident, and a knife twisted in his gut. He'd done that to her—unintentionally, of course—but that offered little comfort. Whatever she'd been going through since the accident was his fault. The doctor had told him stress might have contributed to the heart attack, and Rose had been on his case for several months to take better care of himself. *I should have listened to her. Look where it got me.*

"How are you feeling?" She moved to his bedside and took his hand in both of hers. Her skin was soft, and he relished the warmth she provided to his cold skin.

"Not great." Even moving his mouth hurt, so he tried to keep his words to a minimum. "I'm sorry."

Her dark eyes filled with tears, and she squeezed his hand. "I'm just glad you're okay." She leaned forward and kissed his cheek. "I love you."

"I love you too." He shifted in the bed, trying in vain to find a comfortable position. "Did Dr. Myers tell you what happened?"

"Bits and pieces, but he's been busy." She searched Steven's face. "I know you were in a car accident and had a hea—" Her voice broke, and she covered her face with her hands. Each breathless sob that shook her body was like another knife to his heart.

"Hey," he whispered. "I'm okay." With careful movements, he lifted his left hand to touch her arm.

"I know." She took a deep breath and dashed away her tears. "But when I imagine what might have happened—"

"Shh." He gently pulled her head down to his level and brushed his lips against hers. The pain was worth it.

Too soon, she straightened up. "Lanie and your father are here. Would you like to see them?"

Before he could respond, Dr. Myers returned. "Actually, I think it would be good if we brought them in. You should all hear this together."

Rose left and reentered the room a few moments later with Lanie and Dad in tow. Lanie rushed to his side and gave him an awkward hug, careful to avoid the many wires and tubes that seemed to be coming out of him from every angle. His father's forehead was creased with worry, but he gave Steven a nod and patted his foot. Like Rose, they wore wrinkled clothes and appeared exhausted.

"So, we've run some tests and are waiting on the results, but it's important for you to understand what happened and start considering the next steps in Steven's recovery." Dr. Myers pressed his lips into a thin line before continuing. "The stent I put in Steven's heart should prevent another heart attack from occurring. However, we have another complication that we need to discuss."

Dr. Myers turned to the old-fashioned lighted board on the wall and placed the X-ray into it. "The MRI will tell us more, but I wanted to get an idea of whether anything was broken. It's difficult to get a clear image, likely due to fluid around the injury."

A small gasp sounded beside Steven. Rose squeezed his hand,

clearly understanding something in the doctor's words that he'd missed.

When Dr. Myers turned back, his expression was grim. "I'm afraid Steven will need to undergo surgery to drain the fluid to ensure he has the best chance of healing."

"When will that happen?" Dad asked.

"Well, that's the thing." Dr. Myers scratched his head. "Normally, we prefer to wait to perform surgery on cardiac patients for at least seventy-two hours after the incident because of the increased chance of complications from anesthesia. And Steven has already been through one surgery to place the stent. However, studies have found that patients with spinal contusions have the best prognosis if the surgery is performed within twenty-four hours of the injury."

The room was silent as Steven's family digested the information. While he imagined everyone else was focused on the complications of the surgery, he wanted to know what his odds of recovery were if they waited seventy-two hours to perform it. He would do whatever it took to ensure he could recover and return to his life as quickly as possible.

"I don't want to wait on the surgery," he finally said, breaking the silence.

"It's too risky," Rose protested. "You could have another heart attack during surgery. You could—" Her voice broke.

"I know," he whispered.

"What happens if we delay the surgery?" Lanie asked, shifting her gaze between the doctor and Steven. "Will he recover?"

"I can't say for certain until the MRI results come in. Assuming his spine is severely bruised but otherwise intact, then yes, he should fully recover within six to twelve months."

Six to twelve months? "And how long will it take if we do the surgery now?" Steven asked.

Dr. Myers shook his head. "You're asking me for absolutes when I can't provide those. Every spinal injury is different. The recovery timeline is often shortened if the surgery is performed sooner, but it's impossible to determine at this stage how long recovery will take."

Once again, the room fell into silence. While Steven had made it clear what he wanted to do, he wasn't sure anyone in his family would support him. But at the end of the day, wasn't it his choice?

"Look," Dr. Myers said. "It's not even been twelve hours since the accident. The MRI results should be ready in about an hour, and then we'll know more. In the meantime, I'll leave you to discuss the options and visit with Steven. Once we have the results, we can decide which option is best."

After signaling to the nurse that it was time to go, Dr. Myers left them alone. Nobody spoke, but Steven's increasing heart rate filled the room with sound as the beeping behind him grew in intensity.

"Steven." Rose placed a hand on his shoulder. "Take a deep breath."

Instead of listening to her instruction, he pleaded with his eyes. "Only if you support my decision to go through with the surgery before the twenty-four-hour period is up."

"But—"

His sister stepped into his line of sight. "You heard what the doctor said. Let's wait until we know more before we have this discussion. For now, you should probably rest and relax." Her mouth turned down. "Well, as much as possible."

"I'll relax when you all agree to allow me to make this choice."

Rose and Lanie exchanged glances, but his father gave a quick nod. "I support you, son."

"Thanks, Dad."

Lanie sighed. "Of course it's ultimately up to you. I just wish you would wait until you have all the details so you can make an informed choice."

Though she had a point, Steven doubted there was much that could sway him. He needed to recover as soon as possible to get back to his life, his business.

~

A little over an hour later, Dr. Myers finally returned. Steven's anxiety had reached epic levels, and he was more than a little tired of Lanie and Rose constantly telling him to take deep breaths and calm down. As if they could be calm if they were in his position.

"So, I have good news." Dr. Myers rolled in a cart with a laptop perched on top of it. He turned the screen toward Steven and his family. "There are no tears or signs of permanent damage." Pointing at a shadow near the base of the image, he circled it with his finger. "This is where the injury is located, near the bottom of your spine. As you can see from this darker shadow, there is significant fluid building in the area. This is increasing the compression on your spinal cord, which is part of what is causing the numbness in your lower extremities." Dr. Myers glanced at the door. "Ah, Dr. Bhati, please come in."

A short man with black hair and dark eyes entered the room and nodded to Steven. He moved in front of the screen and studied it for a moment before stepping back.

"Dr. Bhati is a neurosurgeon." Dr. Myers placed a hand on Dr. Bhati's shoulder. "I've asked him to come in to review the MRI results and discuss the surgery option."

"I'm sorry to meet you all under such circumstances. I understand Dr. Myers has already explained the spinal decompression surgery option to you, and I'm sure you have questions. So why don't we start there?"

"What happens if we don't do the surgery within the first twenty-four hours?" Rose asked.

"There are two phases to spinal injuries, with the first phase occurring directly after injury and the second phase beginning a few days later. In the second phase, the body's immune system will sometimes attack the area, causing inflammation as well as a host of neurological problems." Dr. Bhati moved to Steven's side and touched his left leg. "Right now, Steven is only dealing with numbness in his lower body, caused both by the decompression and the shock to his nervous system. But in the second phase, he may start exhibiting more neurological symptoms including slow response time, increased risk of another heart attack, and a higher potential of developing multiple sclerosis."

Steven closed his eyes after hearing the grim future the neurologist had painted. To him, the decision was clear. Surgery, though risky, was worth it when put in such dire context.

"Why is surgery such a risk after a heart attack?" Lanie asked.

"It's not the surgery so much as putting a cardiac patient under anesthesia," Rose responded before either doctor had a chance to. "The heart is already weak from the recent incident, and extra precautions must be taken."

"This is a lot to take in," Dr. Bhati said. "But I assure you that I have performed this surgery several times before with a highly skilled anesthesiologist."

"I want to do it," Steven said. Rose stepped in front of him as if to stop him from speaking, but he wouldn't be deterred. "I understand the risks, but I'd rather avoid additional complications to my spine healing."

With a sigh, Rose moved to his side and patted his arm. His sister didn't look happy, but she held her tongue.

"All right," Dr. Bhati said. "We'll get you scheduled for surgery this afternoon." He glanced at the rest of Steven's family. "Until then, you should give him some time to rest."

Once the doctors were gone, Dad stepped to Steven's left side and gave him an awkward hug. "We'll be back to visit as soon as they let us."

His sister kissed his forehead. "You're either incredibly brave or incredibly stupid."

Steven chuckled. "Perhaps a bit of both?"

With a shake of her head, Lanie followed Dad out of the room. Rose held his hand tightly as if her life depended on it. When he shifted his head toward her, tears glistened in her eyes.

"It'll be okay," he said, though he wasn't sure how convincing he sounded. "I have faith in Dr. Bhati."

"He's a good doctor." But her words did nothing to erase the worry etched on her face. Leaning forward, she brushed a hand over his hair. "You must get through this. I have plans for you."

A small smile tugged at his lips. "Oh? And what plans might those be?"

She kissed his forehead. "Lifelong ones."

Chapter Four

A few hours later, Marie appeared and let them know that Steven was being prepped for surgery. As much as Rose wished she could assist, she had a new appreciation for the hospital's policy on treating family. If something went wrong, she wasn't sure she could handle being in the room and feeling completely helpless.

Still, sitting on the sidelines wasn't any easier. She was used to being part of the action. But at least she wasn't alone. Lanie sat beside her on the uncomfortable chairs while Max paced a trench in the carpet. Mercifully, they were the only ones in the small ICU waiting room. Despite working at the hospital for over a year, Rose had never spent time in that room. It seemed like it had been added as an afterthought. The pale-yellow walls were likely meant to be cheerful, though Rose couldn't imagine they brought much joy to anyone who had to sit there.

"Dad, you might want to take a seat," Lanie drawled. "It's going to be a while."

"I can't just sit here and do nothing." He checked his watch. "I'm going to check on what the cafeteria is serving for lunch. Do either of you want anything?"

"No, thank you," Lanie said.

Rose just shook her head. She couldn't imagine she would be able to keep food down at that point. Her stomach was a bundle of knots that she could only hope would untangle once Steven was safely out of surgery.

After Max left, Lanie turned to her. "What do you think the plan will be for his recovery? I mean, the doctors both said the surgery would speed it up, but they were rather vague on the details."

"Unfortunately, spinal injuries aren't like a broken leg. They're much more complicated and are harder to predict." Rose sighed. "It's more neurological, like a stroke."

"So it could still take six months to a year for him to be fully recovered?"

"It's possible." At Lanie's worried expression, Rose hurried on. "It might help to look at recovery as a progressive timeline rather than a deadline."

"What do you mean?"

Rose debated how to explain it. "Think of it like a baby's development. In their first few years of life, babies learn a lot of new skills. But we don't measure their development by the end goal of them turning eighteen and moving out, right? We measure it by milestones."

"Okay," Lanie said. "I understand what you're saying, but what will that look like?"

"Hmm... I would say Steven's first milestone is this surgery, which will hopefully prevent further complications and allow the healing process to begin. They'll probably put him in a back brace to keep his spine immobile until it heals." Tapping her chin, Rose channeled her training to predict what milestone he might meet next. "In a few weeks, maybe his back will have healed enough for them to remove the brace. Then he'll have some light physical therapy to maintain muscle density. Once the cast is off, he may start working toward walking again, first with crutches then maybe a cane."

"Do you think he'll be walking by the wedding?"

Rose swallowed. She'd pushed aside her concerns about the wedding to allow herself to focus on the details of Steven's diagnosis and recovery. "I guess we'll just have to wait and see."

Lanie nodded and grabbed a magazine, but Rose wasn't easily distracted. Part of her wished Lanie had never mentioned the wedding, as she didn't need to add one more worry to her already filled plate. At the same time, if Steven's recovery was expected to take longer than three months, decisions would need to be made, and the sooner the better.

"I'm going to run to the restroom," Rose said. "I'll be right back."

Once she was clear of the room, Rose bypassed the bathrooms and headed to the nurses' station on her regular floor. She was in luck. Nobody was around. Slipping into the chair, she toggled the computer on with the mouse. She'd saved their wedding contracts in the cloud so she could access them from anywhere. As she clicked through them, a growing sense of dread came over her. Each one included a deadline for canceling for a full or partial refund. Her heart sank as she realized those deadlines had long since passed.

After exiting out of the browser, she sat for a moment with her head in her hands. Perhaps she shouldn't worry yet. Dr. Bhati had said the surgery would speed up Steven's recovery, and it was early June. Maybe Steven would be much improved by the end of August.

With a heavy heart, she headed to the waiting room. Max had returned with an armful of snacks. She chose a bag of rainbow candy and tore open the corner. Maybe a little sugar would take the edge off of her anxiety.

About an hour later, Dr. Bhati finally appeared in the doorway of the waiting room. Rose rushed over to him with Lanie and Max on her heels.

"The surgery was a success," Dr. Bhati said with a weary smile. "We were able to drain the fluid, which should lower the possibility of further complications from the injury. Steven is resting comfortably now. You can see him, but I would prefer you to visit him one by one to avoid overwhelming him."

"Thank you, Doctor," Rose said, relief flooding through her.

"What happens now?" Lanie asked. "Will he be able to come home soon?"

Dr. Bhati pursed his lips. "That will depend a lot on his home environment. There are other options that we can discuss later with Steven when the anesthesia has completely worn off."

The doctor left them, and Rose resisted the urge to run to Steven's room. Although it pained her to do so, she deferred to Lanie and Max to go first. After all, she wasn't quite family.

"Why don't you go in first?" Lanie asked Rose, surprising her.

"But I thought—"

Max waved his hand. "You've been here the longest. Go see him and then go home and get some rest."

The idea of leaving the hospital while Steven was still in it didn't feel right, but Max had a point. She'd been there for well over twenty-four hours, and she was in desperate need of a shower and sleep.

With a grateful smile, she left them and headed to Steven's room. His eyes were closed when she entered, but he must have sensed her presence because he opened them a moment later.

"Rose," he croaked. "I'm still alive."

She glared at him. "Not funny." Her hands shook as she took his. "Are you feeling any better?"

"I honestly don't feel anything from my waist down."

"That'll improve over time."

Steven nodded, his eyes closing again. His breathing deepened as he fell asleep. Her need to stay with him warred with her growing exhaustion, and she squeezed his hand. When he didn't respond to her efforts to rouse him, she leaned forward and kissed his forehead. What he needed most at that moment was rest. The hospital would call her if there was any change.

"I'll come back tomorrow. I love you," she whispered.

~

When Rose arrived at her condo, she sat in her car and stared at the steering wheel. Though exhausted, she was also numb, like the last twenty-four hours had been a dream. The idea of going inside and having nothing but her own thoughts to comfort her was unappealing. Instead, she decided to take a walk around the grounds to enjoy the warm late-spring afternoon. As she headed to the pond near the other end of the property, a pair of swans glided gracefully into view. Their long white necks bent toward each other as if they were sharing some intimate secret.

Rose moved closer, leaning against the fence at the water's edge. The swans paid her no mind, as they were too wrapped up in each other. Their obvious love brought a pang to Rose's heart, and she wished Steven was with her to share in the moment.

"Quite the pair, aren't they?" a deep voice asked beside her.

Startled, she turned to find an older man standing knee-deep in the water. He held a fishing pole.

"They're beautiful," she said.

"At a distance, but don't get too close, or they can turn into some nasty little buggers." He smiled. "But they sure are a sight to behold when they dance."

"Dance?" Rose leaned forward, intrigued by the idea of birds dancing.

"It's a mating ritual." He cocked his head thoughtfully. "Sort of hard to explain. You'll just have to see it."

Rose nodded before returning her attention to the swans. They occasionally dipped their heads below the water before spraying it along their feathers.

A tear slipped down her cheek. *When will Steven and I be together again like the swans?* They had a long path ahead of them, and she had no idea how to traverse that road or where they would be when they reached the end. With worry weighing heavy on her mind, she headed to her condo.

The moment she entered, she sank into her favorite chair in her living room and put her head in her hands. Even with so much up in the air, Rose was clear on one thing. When Steven returned to work, he would have two new clients, including himself. The first thing they would do was draft their wills, especially a power of attorney, so the next time a situation like that occurred, they would be ready.

The next time. She shook her head. After Steven's mother passed, Rose had hoped for a reprieve for him and his family, but now *he* was in the hospital. She still couldn't wrap her head around the idea that Steven had had a heart attack. He was so young. It just didn't feel real.

Her stomach grumbled, and she reluctantly left the plush green cushions and headed to her small kitchen. It was more closet than kitchen, with just enough room for a fridge and oven on one side and a sink and dishwasher on the other. Her limited counter space was cluttered with a spice rack, a toaster, and yesterday's mail.

In no mood to cook, she removed some cheese, crackers, and a bottle of wine. Balancing them in her arms, she returned to her chair. Tears pricked behind her eyes, and she didn't even bother to fight them.

There was so much she didn't know. How long recovery would take. Where Steven would live in the meantime. Dr. Bhati had mentioned other options for when Steven was discharged, but he hadn't specified what they were. Steven's house wasn't exactly equipped for a wheelchair, and all of the beds were on the second floor.

Will he even consent to go somewhere else? While Steven was currently listening to his doctors, she knew her fiancé well enough to know he would be unhappy if anything kept him from the office for very long. In fact, she suspected that he had chosen the risky surgery because a speedy recovery would mean he could get back to work that much sooner.

After she finished her food, she settled back against the chair and sipped her wine. It had been a few days since she'd last FaceTimed with her parents. Part of her wanted to continue to put it off. They would pepper her with questions, first about the wedding, then she would have to inform them of the accident, which would bring a whole host of other concerns. She was in no mood to discuss either. Frankly, she was rather peopled out. But if she didn't call soon, then the worried texts would start.

With a sigh, she picked up her iPad and tapped the app. Plastering a smile on her face, she pressed Call.

A moment later, her mother's face filled the screen. "Rosie. It's been so long. How are you?"

"I'm good, Mom. How are things across the world?"

Her mother's eyes crinkled with her smile. "Oh, there's a lot going on here. And we're missing you, but we can get into that later. How is the wedding planning going? Are you excited for your big day?"

"Mm-hmm," Rose murmured, her lips pressed tight together. She swallowed her pain, not wanting to add to her mother's worry. Her parents had enough stress in their lives caring for her aging grandparents.

She racked her brain to recall the last wedding-related thing she and Steven had done. "We chose the menu for the reception and cake flavors. I'm meeting with the wedding coordinator in a few days to go over the details for the invitations, which should be sent soon."

"Ah, I wish we could be there," her mother said, a wistful note in her voice. "How's Steven? Is he helping with the preparations?"

Rose's thin hold on her emotions broke, and she burst into tears. Her hands flew to her face, but it was too late.

"What's wrong?" her mother asked. "Did something happen?"

"Steven is—" Her voice caught, and she cleared her throat. "He was in a car accident and is in the hospital." Saying the words out loud gave them power.

"Oh my goodness. Is he all right? Why aren't you with him?"

Rose shook her head. "He's... stable." She proceeded to explain what she knew of his condition. Focusing on the familiar medical terminology helped her regain control of her emotions. "I was with him earlier, but I had to come home. When I return tomorrow, they should know more about the next steps."

"When did this happen?"

"Late last night. I'm sorry I didn't have a chance to call you sooner. I've been at the hospital and—"

Her mother waved her hand. "It's fine. You were where you needed to be." She took a deep breath and frowned. "How will this impact the wedding?"

With a sigh, Rose shrugged. "I honestly don't know. Things have been too crazy here. I haven't had time to consider it."

"Is there anything we can do?"

"I doubt it." Rose rested her chin on her hand and studied her mother's face. Moments like that reminded her how much she missed her mother. "You're on the other side of the world."

Her mother raised an eyebrow. "We have friends in the States. They could bring you food, keep you company."

Spending time with virtual strangers wasn't much of a substitute for her parents, but she appreciated the sentiment.

"Lanie and Max were with me. And several of my coworkers brought me food."

"I'm glad you weren't alone." Her mother rubbed her chin. "And Steven is young. He'll heal quickly and be walking again before you know it. Everything is already arranged, right?"

"Yes. With the wedding only three months away, we're only paying the balances due at this point, but between Steven's hospital bills and the fact that he won't be bringing in any money while he's not working, I'm not sure how we'll afford it."

Mom's brow furrowed. "I wish we could send you money—"

"Nonsense. You've got enough on your plate with Grandma and Grandpa. How are they doing?"

"Not well." Her mother sighed. "Your father and I have been discussing finding a placement for them."

"Can you afford that?" From Rose's understanding, the long-term care insurance in South Korea covered more of the cost of a nursing home than insurance did in the US, but it was still expensive.

"I believe so, though it'll be tight." Mom bit her lip. "Actually, that was something I've been meaning to discuss with you."

Something about her mother's demeanor filled Rose with dread. "What's wrong?"

"I'm afraid we won't be able to come to your wedding. Between the nursing home costs and the rising prices for flights, I just don't see how we can swing it."

Could this day get any worse? Fresh tears welled in Rose's eyes, and she struggled to blink them back. Though she'd wondered how her parents would manage her grandparents' care if they were gone for the wedding, it never occurred to her they wouldn't be able to afford to come.

"I understand," Rose whispered.

"But maybe once things are settled, you and Steven can visit us."

"Yeah, maybe." The words sounded hollow. "I should go. I have an early shift tomorrow."

"Should you be working with everything going on?"

The idea of not working hadn't even crossed Rose's mind. With Lisa's daughter still sick, they were short-staffed. And she was going to the hospital anyway to check on Steven.

"I need to maintain some sense of normalcy," Rose said, hoping that sounded convincing enough.

"All right, then. Give our best to Steven and take care of yourself."

"I will. Love you, Mom."

She ended the call and leaned back in the chair, staring at the ceiling. In the span of thirty-six hours, her dream wedding had crumbled before her eyes. First Steven's accident then her mother's bombshell news that her parents weren't coming.

Maybe we should just postpone. She dismissed the thought as soon as it occurred. It was too late to cancel without risking losing all of their deposits and then some. Besides, it seemed selfish to postpone the wedding just because her parents couldn't make it when Steven had lost his mother only a year ago.

The financial aspect was a separate issue but one she and Steven could figure out. At least, that was what she kept telling herself.

Chapter Five

"I'VE CALLED YOU HERE TODAY BECAUSE WE NEED TO discuss next steps," Dr. Myers began.

Steven struggled to draw breath with all the bodies wedged in around his bed. His room in the ICU hadn't appeared so small until his family, Rose, and several members of the medical staff crowded in. He shifted uncomfortably in the tight quarters. At least his neck brace had been removed.

"We've been monitoring Steven since his surgery, and I'm pleased with the progress he's made. If things continue to look up, we plan to move him tomorrow." Dr. Myers gestured to Dr. Bhati, who stood beside him near the door.

"With Steven potentially transferring out of the ICU, it's time to start discussing next steps," Dr. Bhati said.

"What do you suggest?" Rose asked from Steven's right side.

Dr. Bhati frowned. "That will depend on what sort of living arrangement is available to Steven. His injuries will restrict his mobility, even once we're able to move him to a wheelchair. He'll need a lot of assistance, especially in the beginning as he's learning how to compensate for his limited abilities."

"He lives alone." Dad rested a hand on the left-hand bed rail. "In a two-story house where the beds are on the second floor."

"That presents a problem," Dr. Myers said. "Even if his mobility wasn't limited, I wouldn't want him climbing the stairs for a few weeks while his heart heals."

"Can a hospital bed be set up downstairs?" Dr. Bhati asked.

Steven scowled. The last thing he wanted was to continue sleeping in an uncomfortable bed once he was home.

"He could stay with me," Rose suggested. "I have a first-floor condo and a guest room with a twin bed." She glanced at Steven before continuing, "The doors are wide enough for the wheelchair, but the bathroom isn't ADA compliant."

"What about your house, Dad?" Lanie asked. "Could he stay in the den downstairs?"

"It'd be a tight fit for the wheelchair." Dad scratched the back of his head.

Dr. Bhati raised his hand. "These are all good suggestions, but I have another you might consider." After sharing a quick glance with Dr. Myers, Dr. Bhati cleared his throat. "There is a wonderful rehabilitation center just down the road. Dr. Myers and I can easily visit with Steven to keep up to date on his progress."

Rehab? Steven couldn't believe what he was hearing. While he understood his injuries required some drastic lifestyle changes, he hadn't imagined he would be forced to go to *another* medical facility after his discharge from the hospital.

"I can't go to rehab," he protested. "I want to go home."

Dr. Myers blew out an exasperated breath. "Steven, you have a broken leg and a bruised spine, which means you won't be walking for the foreseeable future." He gestured to Rose and Steven's family. "Based on what your family has said, there isn't anywhere you can stay that will meet your needs. If we can't get you the care you require, how do you expect to return home?"

Steven crossed his arms carefully, mindful of both the IV sticking out of his right arm and the bandage over his heart. Truthfully, he didn't have an answer to Dr. Myers's question, but he wasn't going to give the doctor the satisfaction of admitting that.

"Why don't we agree to two weeks?" Dr. Bhati suggested. "It will give you more time to heal and learn how to function with your temporary disabilities. Then we can reassess at that point."

"Are you able to give a better prognosis for how long the paralysis will last?" Rose asked.

Dr. Bhati shook his head. "Draining the fluid helped significantly, but it's difficult to tell the extent of the bruising. We'll run another MRI this afternoon to try to get a better idea. But regardless, he'll need extensive physical therapy, which he unfortunately can't start until his leg heals. The next six months are going to be critical for Steven's recovery."

"And you'll need to make some changes to your lifestyle," Dr. Myers added. "Consider this heart attack a warning. If you don't take care of yourself, it may be worse next time."

"Next time?" Lanie's voice sounded strangled.

"Having a heart attack can increase the likelihood of another one, but there are ways to avoid it."

"Don't worry, Doc," Dad said. "We'll make sure he does what needs doing to get back on his feet."

"If we're in agreement on the rehabilitation center"—Dr. Bhati gave a meaningful look to his patient—"then I can call over there this afternoon to request a bed for Steven. Assuming everything goes well, we may be able to transfer him by the end of this week."

Rose, Lanie, and Dad turned toward Steven. With a sigh of resignation, he nodded.

"I'll go to rehab for two weeks on one condition."

Lanie raised an eyebrow. "Which is?"

He pointed at her. "That you bring me work updates every day so my business doesn't go under."

Rose opened her mouth as if to protest, but Lanie put a hand on her arm to stop her. With pursed lips, Lanie appeared to mull over his request. For a moment, he worried she would say no, but she finally gave him a small smile and a quick nod.

"Fine, but only if you promise to follow the doctors' orders religiously."

"Deal." Steven breathed a little easier. If he could catch up on work while he was in rehab, perhaps he could save his business after all.

Dr. Myers frowned in disapproval before he and Dr. Bhati left. Lanie and Dad followed them out into the hallway, likely to get more information on the rehab facility.

Only Rose remained. At first, she stared at the floor, refusing to meet his gaze. But when she finally looked at him, he was taken aback by the warring anger and fear in her eyes. His stomach clenched as he worried what he might have just sacrificed to save his livelihood.

Steven slept fitfully that night. Despite his exhaustion, he couldn't turn his mind off. Thoughts raced through his head. *How long until I walk again? How am I going to keep my practice going while I'm stuck here? What will happen to my clients?* And the question he didn't dare speak aloud but that encompassed his greatest fear. *Will Rose change her mind about marrying me if I lose everything?*

That last one caused a pain in his chest that had nothing to do with the heart attack or his accident. He'd been looking forward to marrying her for so long. He wanted to start their lives together, and the accident had proved to him that they had no time to waste. Life was short, and he didn't want to lose another moment. They'd planned to start trying for a family soon after the honeymoon. The thought of losing all of that caused an ache that no amount of medication could ease.

Seeing the hurt in her eyes after the doctors left had almost broken through his resolve. He'd agreed to the two weeks in rehab in hopes of softening the blow, but it didn't appear to have had the desired effect. But she knew how important his business was to him —to both of them. Their future depended on its survival, and to ensure the firm survived, he needed those two weeks to fly by so he could return to his office.

Which was likely her other concern. She hadn't brought up him hiring help again, but he suspected it was on her mind. And if he were honest, he could admit bringing on someone to assist with his cases would help lighten his load during his recovery. But he adamantly refused to take on a partner.

Maybe he could hire a law clerk. They worked for dirt cheap, more for the experience than the money. Hiring one would alleviate some of his workload while not costing as much as a partner, which would ease Rose's concerns that he was working too hard without bankrupting his practice. It was a win-win.

The door opened, and a new nurse shuffled into the room. She murmured her apologies for waking him before tying a rubber band around his arm and waiting for a vein to appear. He stifled a sigh. Even if he hadn't been kept up by his own brain, a hospital wasn't the easiest place to rest. The nurses came in several times during the night, and at least one of those visits involved getting a blood sample. His arm was going to be awfully sore when he was finally released.

When the sun peeked through the blinds, he sighed in relief. *Survived another night.* With a shake of his head, he chastised himself for such morbid thoughts. As far as he could tell, he was much improved, and he hoped that meant he would be discharged soon.

The door to his room opened. He sat up, expecting Rose, but instead, his sister entered. She carried a bag over her shoulder and greeted him with a smile.

"Oh good, you're awake." After sliding the bag down her arm, she set it on the bed and removed stacks of paper. "I stopped by your office this morning and spoke to Sandra. She sends you get-well wishes."

He harrumphed, though it came out more as a groan. Lanie didn't seem to notice as she set up various piles on his bed.

"I asked her to help me pull together your most pressing cases so we can determine what needs to be done and how we can do it."

"Thank you," he said as he shifted to sit up in bed. Pain shot through his body from the incision in his back, and he winced.

Lanie put a hand on his shoulder and helped prop him up while she adjusted his pillows. It didn't help, as it was next to impossible to get comfortable after his surgery, but he appreciated the attempt.

"Have you given any more thought to taking on a partner?" she asked.

"No, but I considered hiring a law clerk."

"And that's going to be enough?"

He shrugged. "Maybe."

"What can I do in the meantime? The kids go on summer break next week, and I'll join them a week later. I can pitch in to help if you'll point me in the right direction."

His eyebrows shot up, and he gave an incredulous laugh. "You? What do you know about working in a law office?"

"Hey!" She put her hands on her hips. "I manage unruly children all day. How much harder could it be to corral your clients?"

He thought of Mr. Willoughby and shook his head. "You have no idea."

"Look." She leveled him with a fierce gaze. "You need to reduce your stress level, and I'm offering to do what I can to help with that. If you're not willing to cut back on your hours or hire an attorney with experience, then I suspect you'll be back in this very hospital in a month or less." Her hazel eyes darkened. "Or worse."

He wondered what he could trust her to handle. She'd just finished working through their mother's estate, and he had a couple of clients preparing for probate. Perhaps she could help there.

"Interested in dead people?"

Her eyes widened, and she faltered back a step. When she recovered from his strangely worded question, she stared at him. "You have more estate clients?"

He nodded. "Your experience with Mom's estate may come in

handy. If nothing else, you can hold their hand and help them through probate." Lifting his left hand, he wagged a finger. "But no legal advice. You're not qualified."

Her teeth worried her lower lip as she appeared to consider his request. For a moment, he thought she would refuse, and he couldn't blame her if she did. She'd hated being the executor of their mother's estate. They'd once wondered why their mother chose her when Steven, the lawyer, was the obvious choice. Later, he'd suspected it was the only way their mother could guarantee Lanie would return to her hometown and Nate, her fiancé, would keep the promise he'd made to tell Lanie the truth about Mom's involvement in their breakup. It had all worked out in the end, but if Lanie wasn't in a hurry to get back into the world of trusts and estates, he completely understood.

As he opened his mouth to tell her to forget it, she squared her shoulders. "All right. I'll do it." She twirled a blond lock of hair around her finger. "I'll do my best."

"That's all I ask."

"Before we delve into this stack of papers, Sandra insisted I give you this note." Lanie handed him a piece of paper with a phone message scribbled on it.

Steven rolled his eyes because of course it was from his least-favorite client. Mr. Willoughby was demanding Steven contact him the moment he was back in the office. Sandra had added her own colorful language, detailing her conversation with Mr. Willoughby. She'd tried to offer her assistance, but the client had insisted he must speak to Steven.

"It's my most demanding client," Steven finally said, figuring that sounded more diplomatic than calling Mr. Willoughby a pain in his rear end. "He's still sore at me for hanging up on him the other day when I was on my way out the door."

"Doesn't he know you're in the hospital?"

"I have no idea what Sandra told him." Steven sighed. "But I doubt she would have informed him of my medical issues. She probably said I was out of the office for the foreseeable future."

"Well, I can call him if you'd like—"

Waving his hand, Steven shook his head. "No, that'll probably just rile him up more. I'll deal with him later." He gestured to the papers in her hand. "Let's see what you brought for me."

She gave him a dubious look, and he imagined she was wondering what Rose would say. But she nodded and began handing him documents.

For an hour, they went through the paperwork, with Steven dictating the next steps in each case. By the time Lanie left, Steven's confidence in the state of his law practice had increased, except for the matter of Mr. Willoughby. While nothing would replace going into the office to get work done, he was glad he could handle some of it remotely. He just hoped he could keep up with it all.

Chapter Six

"STEVEN IS BEING TRANSFERRED FROM ICU THIS afternoon," Dr. Myers said.

Rose looked up from her chart. "What time?"

He shrugged. "It depends on when they can find him a bed and get him moved, but I would imagine around lunchtime." When she didn't respond, he raised an eyebrow. "You can take your break then if you want."

As much as she knew she should visit him, part of her didn't want to. As if his reaction to being discharged to a rehab facility wasn't bad enough, he'd then had the audacity to ask his sister to bring work by on a daily basis—right after Dr. Myers had told him he needed to take it easy or risk another heart attack. Though she tried to see things from Steven's perspective, she couldn't help being frustrated. Was he in denial about the reality of his situation?

She understood his desire to go home. He was getting restless after being cooped up in the hospital. And the idea of continuing that existence probably sounded like a prison sentence to him. But throwing himself back into work when he was still healing wasn't going to get him out of a facility any faster. In fact, if he didn't give himself time to heal, his stay might just be extended.

With a forced smile, Rose nodded. "Thanks, Dr. Myers. I'll do that."

He leaned back, assessing her. "Trouble in the love nest?"

"Not at all," she said with feigned sweetness. "We all want him to get better so he can come home."

"It should only be a couple more days here, assuming everything goes well." His expression turned stern. "But I wouldn't expect him to be home anytime soon, and the recovery is likely to take months, if not longer."

"I know." Her tone hardened as her patience wore thin. *Who does this guy think he is?* Like she didn't understand how varied the recovery timeline could be for heart attack survivors, let alone the other injuries Steven had sustained.

"Oh, I have no doubt *you* understand, but does he?"

She glowered at the doctor. "I will ensure he follows all of your advice."

To her surprise, he laughed before turning to leave, calling over his shoulder, "Good luck with that."

"What's that supposed to mean?" she demanded, her hands on her hips.

Glancing at her with an impish grin, he said, "Just that I've seen his type before. Workaholics don't like to be kept away from the thing they love most."

"That shows how well you know him." She stomped away, heading to the nurses' station. His laughter followed her down the hall.

Her irritation rose when she realized Dr. Myers was right. Steven was a workaholic, and he'd already demonstrated that he would resist the changes his doctors had suggested he make. Rose sighed, leaning against the wall. Convincing him to take it easy would be a battle, but she was ready for it. At least, she hoped she was.

But she didn't need to worry about it yet. Steven would be in the hospital for a few more days. With that in mind, she started her rounds, all while mentally preparing herself for when she saw Steven again.

At lunchtime, Rose went up to the ICU and was surprised to find Steven already gone. The nurse at the station gave her his new room number, and she took the stairs to his floor.

Steven was propped up in his bed when she entered, watching something on the television on the opposite wall. His room already had several flower arrangements set up on the limited furniture, and the scent reminded her unnervingly of a funeral home. She knocked lightly on the door, and he turned toward her with a lopsided smile. His face still had angry scratches from where it'd been cut by glass, and a bruise bloomed on his forehead. But they'd removed the IV from his arm.

"How do you like the new digs?" he asked.

The tension in her shoulders eased as she took in his expression. No furrowed brow, no sense of frustration. Maybe moving out of the ICU was what he needed.

"Much less restrictive." She stepped over to his bedside and took his hand. "How do you feel?"

"Not as bad as yesterday." He gestured to his lunch tray. "Is the food served here different? It sure tastes better."

Rose laughed. "It all comes from the same place."

"Maybe it's just that I'm that much closer to freedom."

"You've got a few more days," she warned, trying to keep her tone light.

He waved a dismissive hand. "I'm hoping to be released early for good behavior."

"That's not really how it works." Panic swirled in her gut. "And even if that were true, you agreed to two weeks of inpatient rehab."

His face contorted. "Yeah, definitely not looking forward to that. But I'm not worried."

That made one of them. Swallowing her fears, Rose pulled a chair over and set her lunch box on her lap.

He peered at it. "What are you eating?"

"My usual ham sandwich."

His face clouded. "They won't let me have any meat. Can you believe that?"

"It's temporary," she assured him. "They'll start varying your diet more the better you do in recovery. But don't expect to have steak anytime soon. Red meat isn't good for your cholesterol."

"I *know*," he snapped.

Stop nagging him. He's been through enough. "I'm sorry."

He heaved a sigh. "No, I'm the one who should be sorry." He held out his hand, and she slid hers into it. "I know things are going to have to change, but sometimes, it's a lot to take in. One minute, I'm young and healthy, and the next, I almost die."

"We'll get through it, I promise."

"I don't know what I'd do without you," he said, and the warmth she'd seen earlier returned to his eyes.

"Same here," she said, her throat thick with emotion. The knowledge of how close she'd come to losing him weighed heavily on her heart. Clearing her throat, she tried a lighter tone. "But in order for me to not have to find out, I'm gonna need you to take it easy."

Closing his eyes, he nodded. "I'll do my best."

She squeezed his hand. "That's all I can ask for."

His breathing slowed as he fell asleep. She leaned forward and kissed his forehead before returning to work. At least while he was in the hospital, she found it easier to check on him. She also found comfort in the fact that he was limited in what he could get away with there. Things would be a little more relaxed in rehab, but once they discharged him home, she wouldn't be able to keep as close an eye on him. She suspected he would go right back to working himself into an early grave.

~

Rose drummed her fingers on the table as she stared at the door to Bea's Diner, willing Lanie to walk through it. The longer she sat there waiting, the more she feared she might lose her nerve. Usually, the restaurant was comforting, with its nostalgic 1950s theme and the familiar scent of fried food, but not even the swaying Elvis figure on the wall or the miniature jukebox on the table could distract her that day.

When a familiar blond head cleared the entryway and swiveled to look for her, Rose breathed a sigh of relief before waving her friend over. Lanie smiled and slid into the booth opposite Rose, setting her purse beside her.

"So, what's up?" Lanie asked as she opened a menu, though Rose couldn't imagine why. Her future sister-in-law had been coming to the place her entire life, and as far as she could tell, the options hadn't changed in that time. "More wedding details?"

"Actually, I wanted to discuss that with you." Rose hated how hesitant her voice sounded. She squared her shoulders. "I think we should postpone the wedding."

Lanie's eyes widened. "What? Why?"

"We don't know how long Steven's recovery will take, and it's smarter to start taking action now rather than move forward in the hopes he'll be recovered enough to go through with it." Rose removed her tablet from her bag and tapped the screen until she reached the document that contained their vendor contact information. "I figure between the two of us, we can call everyone this week and—"

Lanie raised her hand. "Wait. Have you talked to Steven about this?"

"Not yet," Rose admitted, dropping her gaze. "I didn't want to add to his stress level. But honestly, postponing the wedding will help alleviate his stress. Then he can focus on healing."

"Except that it may be more stressful for him if you postpone."

Rose frowned. "How do you figure that?"

"I know my brother," Lanie replied with a shrug.

"But he hasn't actually said that, has he?" Worry gnawed away at Rose's gut, but she worked to keep her expression neutral.

"Not in so many words, but he has seemed rather preoccupied with something lately. I thought it was the law firm, but I spent a good hour going over his cases with him yesterday." Lanie frowned. "While he was in better spirits by the time I left, I could tell something else was on his mind." Her hazel eyes narrowed. "You need to talk to him before you do anything."

The mood at the table shifted, and Rose struggled to regain control of the situation. "I'll discuss it with him, but don't you think it would be better if I could tell him I was taking care of it? Then he'd have less to—"

"No. Going behind his back isn't going to help. You need to have a frank discussion with him." Lanie's tone softened. "I know you didn't come to this decision lightly, and I'm sure Steven will understand that."

"You think he'll agree to postpone?" Rose was unable to keep the skepticism out of her voice.

Grinning, Lanie shook her head. "Of course not, but he might at least appreciate a well-reasoned argument." When Rose didn't respond, Lanie leaned forward. "Look, I agree with you that he has a lot of stress, and the wedding planning is unlikely to help, but before you go trying to convince him, I'd like to propose a counterpoint. It's early in Steven's recovery, and we don't know enough at this point to make such a decision. What would you say to monitoring the situation and deciding what to do in a couple of weeks? At the very least, we could talk to Carissa to get her opinion. She might have an idea of how to approach the vendors to give them a heads-up."

"I just hate to leave things up in the air. If it was only the heart attack *or* the spinal contusion alone, that would be one thing. But patient recovery is often unique to each individual. I'm not sure if we'll get a clear timeline, and the wedding is in almost three months."

Lanie pursed her lips. "Are you sure there aren't other reasons you might want to postpone?

That caught Rose off guard. "What other reasons would there be?"

Her future sister-in-law shrugged. "Maybe you're concerned about what Steven will be like once he's released from rehab. How it might place you in a caregiving role again."

Rose swallowed, reminded of the comment her patient had made about her being the perfect candidate to care for Steven. Although there was a trace of truth in Lanie's words, Rose shook her head.

"All I want is for Steven to focus on recovering, and I believe postponing the wedding will help him to do that."

For a moment, Lanie studied her, then she nodded, seeming to accept Rose's explanation. "I agree. But you should still talk to Steven before you do anything. I'll even try to help him see reason." She bit her lip. "Just as long as you remember, his whole world—both of your worlds—have been turned upside down. It's not a bad idea to take some time and let the dust settle before rushing to a decision."

Rose nodded. "I can agree with that."

Lanie turned her attention back to the menu. "Let's discuss our options with Carissa first. Once we have a clearer picture, we can go from there."

The next day, Rose walked into the hospital with her heart pounding in her chest. With Carissa's help, she and Lanie had contacted all of the vendors and had a better understanding of the situation with the wedding. Their responses, though not unexpected, were disappointing.

Most had pointed to the contract and the deadline for cancellation, which had already passed. If she canceled now, she would lose her deposits, which were too large to swallow. The one bright light was many of the vendors were willing to work with her on a postponement using what had already been paid to secure a new date. However, the vendors weren't willing to commit to altering the contract itself until the new date was determined. They all sympathized with her, but sympathy went only so far.

The only place that had extended her a month's grace period to decide was the church. She supposed they were doing Steven and her a favor since he'd been a member of the congregation since childhood.

Though Lanie had cautioned her against talking to Steven about a postponement while he was in the hospital, Rose had decided to go ahead with the conversation. It didn't seem appropriate to wait until he was discharged to the rehab facility. She hoped he would listen to reason. Her arguments were sound, and she'd even chosen a few potential dates for next summer.

But she wouldn't settle on one until they had a better sense of Steven's prognosis or until she spoke with her mother. She hadn't mentioned the possibility of buying her parents' plane tickets herself because she didn't want to risk upsetting anyone. It still felt selfish to postpone the wedding so her parents could attend, and she didn't want people to think her parents were her driving motivation to postpone. Because they weren't. Steven's recovery was her main focus. Yet the more she considered it, the more she hated the idea of her parents not being there for the wedding.

When she entered Steven's room, he was watching television. As he turned his head, his face lit up in such a way that it broke her heart, and she faltered in her resolve. But they needed to have that discussion, and with the wedding date rapidly approaching, the time to decide had arrived.

"I missed you yesterday," he said as she kissed his cheek in greeting. "I thought you'd stop by after work."

"I had a few things to take care of, but I wanted to see you before my shift this afternoon." She nervously pushed a lock of hair behind her ear. "We need to talk."

"The dreaded words," Steven joked, then his smile fell. "What's wrong?"

Steeling herself for his reaction, she took a deep breath and met his gaze. "I want to postpone the wedding."

Several emotions flitted across his bruised face. His eyebrows jumped up in surprise before furrowing with concern. As the reality of what she'd said sank in, his lips turned down, and his eyes widened. "No, Rose, I—"

"Let me finish!" She raised her hands to stop him before he could derail her carefully rehearsed speech. "We don't know what will happen with your recovery or how long it will take. And we're losing money every day you're in here." He opened his mouth as if to protest, but she hurried on, determined to show him she'd considered his counterarguments. "It's not just that you're not working right now." She waved a hand around the room. "The hospital bills are going to be high as well." *Thanks for nothing, US health care.* "We have enough on our plates right now without throwing the wedding into the mix. It makes sense to postpone until things are better. That way, you can focus on your recovery."

"But we've already put so much work and money into planning this wedding. At this point, we're just making final payments to the vendors, aren't we?"

"Yes, but with what? I can't afford to pay for it all myself on my salary, and since you don't have a partner, there's no one who can cover for you while you recover."

"We could ask our families for—"

"We agreed we would pay for this ourselves," Rose retorted. "And I don't need to remind you my parents are struggling to make ends meet as it is on the other side of the world. My mom told me they're putting my grandparents into a nursing home, and the last thing they should be worrying about is funding our wedding."

"I understand, but I'm sure my dad would be more than willing to contribute—er—loan us the money in the meantime."

Her facial expression must have caused him to change direction. But she shook her head. "We can't guarantee we'd be able to honor that loan. What if the law firm doesn't survive without you? That's not something I'm willing to risk or how I want to start our lives together." Without waiting for a response, she continued, "Now, Carissa and I have spoken to our vendors, and most of them are willing to honor the deposits we've made on a new date, provided they're available."

"So, that's it, then?" His voice was filled with pain. "You no longer want to marry me?"

Her heart sank, and she put her hand to her chest. "Of course I want to marry you!"

"Then why wait? If money's a concern, we can cancel some of the more extravagant aspects of the wedding and have a simpler affair." He grabbed her hand and pulled her toward him. "I just want to marry you. I don't want to wait another year to start our lives together."

"It's not that simple, Steven." After rummaging through her bag, she removed a folder filled with vendor contracts and shoved them into his hand. "You're a lawyer, so I know you understand contract law. If we cancel now, we forfeit what we've paid. And in some instances, we'd still have to fulfill our financial obligation regardless of whether we cancel or not."

His heartbroken face caused a chink in the armor of her resolve. Maybe Lanie was right. Maybe postponing the wedding would cause him more stress than forging ahead. But she couldn't see how that was possible when nobody knew what his recovery would look like.

She took a deep breath and pressed on. "Whereas, if we postpone, we might be able to salvage what we've already paid."

They were silent for a moment as she allowed her words to sink in. She hoped he would understand she wasn't backing out of their engagement or putting a pause on their relationship, just the wedding itself.

Finally, Steven sagged back against the bed and stared at the ceiling. "It's still early days. Why don't we wait to make any decisions about this until we know more?"

"I don't think—"

"You said the last day to cancel for a refund has passed, right?" He turned his head so he could look at her.

She nodded. "The only place that isn't holding us to that is the church."

"At least that's something." He sighed. "But if we're already beyond the cancellation date, what would it hurt to wait and see how things go? Maybe my recovery won't take as long as Dr. Myers expects it to."

"We can only hope." Her teeth worried her lower lip. Part of her wasn't ready to give up the fight. First, she wasn't sure the vendors would honor what they'd told her over the phone if she and Steven waited too long to make a decision. And second, she had been so sure he would concede to her arguments that she hadn't considered the very real possibility her wedding would go forward without any of her family there.

But all of her reasons to postpone evaporated as she took in the pleading expression on his face. He'd been through so much, and she couldn't bear to put him through any more pain, even if she believed it was for his own good.

"Please, Rose, just give it a bit more time."

No! She wanted to scream it, but instead, she nodded again, knowing that wasn't the answer he needed.

"And we're okay?"

Her heart panged at the doubt in his voice. "Of course. We're better than okay. Postponing had nothing to do with us and everything to do with aiding you in getting better." She cupped his cheek. "I love you."

"I love you too." He pulled her face down and brushed his lips against hers. “Promise me you’ll talk to me first before you do anything.”

She rubbed his nose with hers. “I promise.” Straightening up, she smoothed her uniform. “I’ll come back on my lunch break.”

“I can’t wait.”

As she left the room, she prayed she wouldn’t have to break that promise.

Chapter Seven

A knock startled Steven awake, and he opened his eyes to find an unfamiliar woman smiling at him. Her eyes were a bright green, and her dark hair was pulled back in a bun. It took him a moment to remember where he was, but when he did, he internally groaned.

He'd hoped the transfer from the ICU meant he would be discharged soon, but three days later and he was still stuck in the hospital. While he was sleeping better than when he'd been attached to a bunch of machines, he missed his comfortable bed at home.

"More tests?" he grumbled, not caring whether he was coherent.

"Worse," the woman said, rolling a cart forward. She typed on the laptop that sat precariously on top of the cart before shoving it to the side and moving beside him. "I'm Lacey Carter, your physical therapist."

Steven smiled, which apparently caught Lacey off guard. But he took a visit from a physical therapist as a good sign. He must be improving if they were going to start helping him regain his ability to move. And he would gladly take physical therapy over being poked and prodded with needles any day.

It took effort, but he shimmied into a more upright position, though his paralysis made it difficult. He hoped by the end of the session he would have a better idea of when he could expect to walk again.

"Where do we start?" he asked, eager to learn.

Her eyebrows pinched together as she studied him. "First, I like to learn what my client's goals are."

He appreciated that she hadn't called him a patient. "I want to be able to walk again. The sooner the better."

When she tilted her head, some of his enthusiasm deflated. *Is she going to tell me the odds are against me?* But she hadn't even examined him yet to determine what he was capable of. *Has Dr. Myers told her something? Or is my broken leg going to be a deterrent?*

"Yes, that's what most people focus on, but we need to start smaller. That can be an overall goal you can work toward over the next few months, but—"

There was that word again. *Months.* Sometimes he wondered if the surgery had even been worth it. While he understood the complications that might have arisen if they hadn't drained the fluid from his spine, the fact that he was still facing months of recovery left a bitter taste in his mouth.

Besides, it didn't make sense to him. Once his leg and back healed, he would regain feeling in both legs. He didn't understand why he couldn't just pick up and start walking like he had before. Surely his body couldn't really *forget* how to walk in such a short amount of time.

As if reading his mind, she sighed. "Relearning to walk as an adult isn't the same as learning to walk as a baby. The damage to your spine has blocked the neural pathways between the lower half of your body and your brain. So it will take time both for your spine to heal and for your body to reestablish that connection." She gestured to his cast. "And until this leg is out of the cast, you're going to be limited in what exercises you can do. I'm here to help you maintain the muscle and dexterity to walk on your good leg."

"Oh," he said. It was as if he'd watched a balloon filled with his hope get torpedoed to smithereens. He worried what that would mean for his business. But that wasn't the only concern that plagued the dark corners of his mind. Try as he might to ignore it, he couldn't help wondering how that would impact his relationship with Rose.

The fear was unfounded. Aside from her suggestion that they postpone the wedding, she'd shown no signs of having second thoughts about him or their impending marriage. Even when she'd brought up postponing, she'd insisted she was only concerned about his health and stress level. And yet... Ever since his parents had divorced, he'd believed their marriage fell apart because his father failed to pull his weight. While he'd brought in enough money, Dad hadn't contributed much to the housework until it was too late.

The last thing Steven wanted was to have a similar dynamic with Rose, even temporarily. And she'd already been through so much after helping Lanie with his mother during her final months. The idea of Rose becoming a caregiver again, especially for him, made his stomach turn. That wasn't at all how he'd envisioned them starting their lives together.

Lacey patted his arm, pulling him from his thoughts. "I know it's a lot to take in, but we've developed exercises to keep your muscles in good working order during recovery. It takes time."

Time. The one thing he didn't have a lot of if he had any hope of saving his business—or his relationship, for that matter.

"For now," she continued when he didn't respond, "I'm going to show you some exercises you can do to maintain function in your good leg. How does that sound?"

Steven inclined his head in his attempt at a nod, though all of his motivation had turned to dust. At the rate they were going, he would be lucky to be back at work by Christmas, let alone walking by then.

~

"I have good news for you today, Steven," Dr. Myers said as he waltzed into the room. "We're releasing you to the inpatient rehab facility. Your transport will arrive this afternoon."

Steven forced a smile. "Great!" And it was, sort of. Progress was progress, he supposed, but it felt like he was leaving one prison and heading to another. "When can I go home?"

That was the wrong question. Dr. Myers glared down his nose at Steven. "As I've told you several times, there is no way to predict your recovery." His expression softened. "But I'm happy to report a decrease in the amount of swelling around your spine. You need to be a little more patient."

I guess that's the most I'm going to get. Steven nodded and returned his attention to whatever mindless soap opera was playing on television. Ever since he'd woken up after his accident, he'd heard repeatedly how unpredictable spinal cord injuries could be. The nonanswer about what to expect during his recovery was getting old. *How hard is it to give a more definitive answer? Is this why they call it "practicing" medicine?* Because doctors were always learning.

He wasn't being fair, especially since most lawyers said they "practiced" law too. There was always some new law to learn, some new case that might provide nuance to a problem a client faced. So he could hardly blame doctors for their inability to predict the future, although that didn't make it any less frustrating.

But the doctor was right—he had made progress over the last week. They'd moved on from cold compresses to a back brace to keep his spine immobilized while it healed. There was still pain, but he managed it better with pain relievers than he could days ago when he'd first met the physical therapist. And he'd come to enjoy his physical therapy sessions, much to his surprise.

As if summoned by his thoughts, Lacey appeared in the doorway. "Ready for another session?"

He winked. "I'm ready for my daily torture appointment."

Lacey laughed as she lowered the rail on his bed and helped him sit on the edge of the mattress. "I know it's painful, but believe me, it'll be worth it."

Gritting his teeth, as any movement aggravated the healing incision on his chest, he worked through the motions of the physical therapy. Some of the feeling was returning to his legs, which was more muscle twitches and flutters. Still, it was more than he'd felt directly after the accident.

"I hear you're leaving us today," Lacey continued when he didn't respond. She lifted his right leg and bent it.

"They're discharging me to rehab."

She must have heard something in his voice because she looked up. "It's not as bad as it sounds. Think of it as similar to what we do here but with a team that's dedicated to your recovery, not just getting you stabilized." After she set down his leg, she held out her hands, and he grabbed them to gently pull himself up onto one leg. "Besides, I hear they have better food."

A laugh bubbled up in his throat, and she shot him a grin. As much as he hated being cooped up in the hospital, he had to admit he would miss her.

"I bet the PT there isn't as awesome as you are."

"Aw, you're my favorite too." She leaned forward and stage-whispered, "But don't tell anyone else."

When the session was over, he was surprised to find Lanie, Rose, and his father enter his room. Lanie and Rose came to either side of his bed and took his hands, but Dad stayed near the door, looking as uncomfortable as ever.

"The hospital has agreed to let us assist with the transport and get you settled in," Rose explained.

Steven nodded, but before he could respond, several attendants came in. One handed Lanie and Dad some paperwork, which he assumed was his discharge papers. Two others moved to his bed with a wheelchair. He resisted the urge to glare at it.

It took both attendants to lift and transfer him to the chair. Rose dutifully took her place behind him and began to push. He hadn't been out of his room except when more tests were needed, and Steven relished the cool air of the hallway. The elevator, on the other hand, jostled him more than he liked, and he cringed with each movement until they arrived on the main floor. When they reached the front of the hospital, a van was waiting for them. It had a wheelchair ramp and myriad belts to strap him in. Steven winced. *Is this really my life now?*

After he was all strapped in, Dad jumped behind the wheel and began the short drive to the rehab center. Steven appreciated the drive through the heart of Cedar Haven, passing Bea's Diner and the middle school where Lanie worked.

Once they arrived at his new home, Steven allowed his eyes to sweep over the building. It didn't look much different from the hospital, though it was noticeably smaller. Two stories tall, the facility had an array of windows on the second floor. He assumed that was where the patients' rooms were. As the attendants unbuckled his chair and took it down the ramp, he noted the circular driveway they had parked in was similar to those he'd seen at hotels.

Rose pushed him toward the doors, which whisked open upon their approach. The lobby area was pristine if a little dreary. The scent of chlorine wafted down a corridor, and Steven frowned. Maybe they had a pool.

"We've found water aerobics to be a great form of physical therapy, especially for those with joint pain," a voice said from beside him. He turned his head to find a man standing to his right in a red polo shirt with the name Chesapeake Rehabilitation on the left breast pocket. The man held out his hand to Steven, his gray eyes twinkling. "You must be Steven McAllister. I'm Marvin Anderson, the director of Chesapeake Rehab."

"Nice to meet you."

"Welcome." Marvin shook his hand before gesturing behind him. "Would you like a tour before we get you settled?"

At Steven's nod, Marvin led them through the facility. In addition to the pool, there was a gym and a cafeteria along with areas for speech therapy, massage, and other treatments that made the place feel more like a medical spa than a skilled-nursing facility.

Maybe this won't be so bad after all. He could certainly think of worse places to spend the next two weeks.

"And this," Marvin said as they came to a stop outside of a door, "is your room."

Rose pushed him through the wide doorway and into what looked like a presidential suite in a hotel. A wave of nausea came over Steven. How were they going to afford that? His insurance wasn't anywhere near as good as what he'd had at the law firm in Baltimore.

She leaned forward and whispered in his ear, "Your father is paying. He insisted."

That sounded like something his father would do. Guilt gnawed at Steven's gut. His father had retired years ago and lived on a fixed income. While Dad had a very comfortable lifestyle, he didn't have the means to throw money around. Steven opened his mouth to protest, but before he could say anything, Marvin began showing off the various features of the room.

"We have a lot of entertainment options to keep you from growing bored, though with the many hours of therapy before you, there's little chance of that." He laughed at his own joke, but no one else joined him. "The bathroom also has some amazing amenities, which you'll be able to enjoy more as you progress in your recovery."

Steven read between the lines. The bathroom amenities were meant for people who could walk. Based on what he'd learned while at the hospital, he doubted he would be able to enjoy any of them. Still, he could barely focus on that as he digested the reality that his father was footing the bill for his recovery. *How can I ever repay him for this?* Tears pricked Steven's eyes, and he wasn't sure if he wanted to thank his father for his generosity or berate him for wasting his money.

Either way, Steven planned to make darn sure he recovered as quickly as possible to avoid becoming a burden. Two weeks should be more than enough time for him to learn what he needed to function. Then he could return home.

"Why don't I let you get settled." Marvin signaled for Steven's father to follow him. "I'll be back to discuss your therapy schedule with you."

When he was alone with Rose and Lanie, Steven leaned back in his chair and sighed. "This is too much."

Lanie snorted. "You have no idea. It would have been cheaper for you to have a roommate, but Dad refused. I'm not sure what's gotten into him, but at least you're going to get the best care possible in Southern Maryland."

Steven smiled. While his sister was making a dig at their hometown, her words had some truth to them. It was no Johns Hopkins, but several doctors in the area had participated in a federal program that paid off their student loans in exchange for them opening medical practices in rural communities. That facility was one example of how well the program had worked out.

"I'm grateful for your father's generosity," Rose said as she wandered through the room. "Hopefully it'll reduce some of your financial stress, knowing this is taken care of."

"If anything, it makes it worse."

"Of course you'd say that. Paying for the wedding is fine, but assisting with your recovery is a deal-breaker," she muttered. With a sigh, she stepped beside him and kissed his forehead. "Unfortunately, I need to go run some errands before my shift. But I'll come by tomorrow. I love you."

When she was gone, Lanie sat on his bed. "And then there were two."

"Did Rose mention the wedding?" he asked.

"She did." His sister turned to the window. "You have a nice view. Would you like to see?"

"Nice try." He smirked. "But you're not getting off that easy."

Lanie glanced over her shoulder. "There's really not much to say.

I convinced Rose to discuss the situation with the vendors. I assume she told you their response was less than ideal?"

"She did. But I told her we should determine areas where we could cut back on expenses."

"I'm sorry, but that's not realistic."

He narrowed his eyes at her, but she didn't even flinch.

"Steven, come on. You're in rehab, for goodness' sake! And no one can give a definitive answer for how long you'll be here or even what exactly happens next. Wouldn't it make more sense to postpone until you're recovered so you can actually enjoy your wedding?"

Shaking his head, he clenched his jaw. His sister would probably see his refusal to listen as stubbornness, but he'd chosen his hill, and he would die on it if he had to.

Dad and Marvin entered then, and Lanie breathed a sigh of relief. Steven hid a smile. If she thought the conversation was over, she had another thought coming. As soon as he got out of that place, he would do whatever was needed to get his life back on track.

The first day of physical therapy at the rehab facility was probably the worst day Steven had had since his heart attack. While Lacey at the hospital had been willing to work at his pace, gently pushing him beyond his comfort zone, Adrian, his new physical therapist, was a drill sergeant. At the end of his physical therapy session, which lasted for two hours, Steven could literally feel every muscle in his body. Well, *almost* every muscle. His legs were still disconnected from the rest of his nervous system.

"You look like you could use a session in the massage room," Adrian said as he laid several bags of ice over Steven's arms and right leg.

Steven could only grunt, too tired to articulate a response. Resting his head against the bed's pillow, he closed his eyes. *Will I even be able to move the parts of my body that weren't broken tomorrow?* Everything felt like a dead weight.

"It'll get easier." Adrian patted his back. "I promise."

"Sure it will," Steven muttered.

Adrian's laugh drifted away as Steven dozed off. But he was abruptly awakened a moment later when Adrian shook him. He opened his eye to a slit, not at all happy to have his well-deserved nap interrupted.

"You can go back to sleep in your own bed," Adrian said, reading his mind. "I need to prepare for my next patient."

"More like your next victim," Steven scoffed, which earned him a grin. He had to admit that despite how much he'd hated every minute of their session, he liked Adrian. And if he wanted to stand next to Rose at the altar and walk with her down the aisle at the end of the summer, he needed to push himself. He just wished the exercises hadn't been so grueling on his first day.

Adrian helped Steven into the wheelchair, then an orderly came and took him away. Once he was settled into bed, his mind was too preoccupied for him to sleep. Lanie had promised an update on how things were going at the office, but he hadn't heard from her yet. It took some shifting and shimmying in the bed, but he managed to grab his phone from the nightstand. His email was filled with messages from Mr. Willoughby, which he ignored. The one nice thing about being stuck in rehab was his ability to avoid some of his more annoying clients, though he would have to deal with Mr. Willoughby eventually.

A knock on the door startled him, but he breathed a sigh of relief when he met his sister's gaze. She had a bag slung over her shoulder and gave him an apologetic smile.

"I'm sorry I couldn't come sooner, but I've been sorting things out at the office."

"How's it going?"

"Not bad, though I'm still getting my bearings." She bit her lip.

"Sandra and I were discussing putting an ad in the paper for a law clerk."

He crossed his arms. "I want to be there for the interviews."

"But the work is piling up without you. Sandra can only handle so much. You need someone who knows what they're doing."

"Bring the work here. I can review it between my therapy sessions."

Her mouth dropped open. "You can't be serious. Rose would kill me if she knew! Besides, we don't even know how long you'll be—"

"I'm only staying here for two weeks," he insisted, interrupting her.

"That was the bare minimum," she retorted, throwing up her hands. "And how long do you think we can hold off your clients? Mr. Willoughby has been blowing up the phone. Poor Leslie looked about ready to quit when I was there."

"She won't," Steven said, though he sounded a lot surer than he felt. He nodded to her bag. "Do you have something for me to sign?"

He thought she would continue to press her case, but she sighed and removed a pile of folders. After setting them on his bed, she flipped the first one open.

"Just a few pleadings. And then Sandra drafted a will and trust she wanted you to review."

It took a few hours for him to review the work she and Sandra had done. But as Lanie slipped the folders into her bag, he had a sense of accomplishment.

"Thanks," he said.

"You're welcome." She checked her watch. "I better go. Visiting hours are almost over."

After a brief hug, she promised to file the pleadings he'd signed with the court the next day, then she was gone. He rested his head against his pillow and stared out the window. As much as he hated to admit it, Lanie was right. The situation wasn't sustainable, but he couldn't allow them to hire someone without his input.

He would have to make the most of the two weeks he was there then continue his recovery at home. It was as simple as that.

Chapter Eight

Rose stared at Dr. Myers with growing annoyance. For the second time in a week, he'd asked her to work a double shift. Despite knowing it was a possibility, she'd hoped to get out of it.

"But I have plans tonight," she protested. She couldn't believe his gall. He knew her fiancé was recovering after a stint in the hospital. *Why can't he find someone else?*

"I'm sorry, but Lisa's daughter is still sick, and Rebecca is out of town." He shrugged apologetically.

Steven wasn't the only one who needed to hire extra help. The hospital had been hemorrhaging staff for ages, and they struggled to replace the nurses who left.

"I promise I'll make it up to you," Dr. Myers continued.

Rose raised an eyebrow. "And how do you plan to do that?"

"You're being considered for head nurse," he said, leaning against the wall. "I can put in several good words for you."

While she appreciated the sentiment, she doubted it would help her in the long run. Dr. Myers had a lot of clout, but he wasn't even on the hiring board. The members might listen to his recommendations, but they didn't mean anything, especially when Rebecca and Lisa both had seniority.

Rather than say any of that aloud, she forced a smile and thanked him before returning to start her rounds... again. She texted Lanie that she wouldn't be able to see Steven before visiting hours ended after all. Maybe it was for the best. Every time she saw him, he and Lanie were discussing some new concern at his office. Rose hated seeing his stress mounting. But she kept quiet to avoid an argument, and quite frankly, she was tired of biting her tongue.

Mr. Patrones was her first stop, and she braced herself for his glum demeanor. She supposed she should be grateful Steven wasn't more like him. But Mr. Patrones had several years on Steven, and his health had been poor even before his heart attack.

Pasting a smile on her face, she knocked then opened the door. "Good afternoon, Mr. Patrones. How are we doing?"

"The same as I was the last time you were here." He blinked at her. "Shouldn't you be off duty?"

"I'm working a double," she said, keeping her voice cheery. Glancing over his chart, she was surprised by Dr. Myers's note at the bottom. *Discharge tomorrow.* "Good news! You're getting sprung tomorrow!"

His eyebrows pulled together. "So soon?"

I thought he couldn't wait to get out of here. "Aw, Mr. Patrones, I'm glad to hear you're going to miss me, but you've made so much progress. You should celebrate."

"With what?" he demanded, his tone acerbic. "I can't have red meat or alcohol, and I'm not much of a cake person."

Rose took a deep breath and released it slowly, counting down from ten. Only that man could make something wonderful like being released from the hospital seem like a chore.

"I'm sure your friends will be happy to see you."

He stared at her, his face expressionless. "I don't have any friends."

Can't imagine why. No, that was unfair. She didn't know

anything about him other than what she'd learned from his medical record and the little he told her. If his heart attack hadn't happened in public, he wouldn't have survived it. When she thought of him returning to the condo where he lived alone, her heart went out to him. She wondered what had happened in his life to cause him to be so utterly alone.

"Now you have a chance to make some," she said, though she didn't know why she was bothering to pretend to be upbeat. Mr. Patrones's defeatist attitude drained the life from her whenever she was in the room with him.

He snorted but said nothing else. After she finished marking down his vitals on his chart, Rose attempted one last smile and hurried from the room.

She took a minute to reorganize her thoughts before moving on to the next patient. As much as she dreaded dealing with Mr. Patrones's depressing comments, she shouldn't judge him. After all, were it not for Steven, his family, and the few friends she'd made since moving to Cedar Haven, her life might not be that much different. Even with all of those people in her life, she struggled sometimes to open up and to let people help her. Her parents had raised her to be self-sufficient and to take care of those around her, which was why being a nurse came so naturally. But she wondered sometimes if she was *too* independent.

The end of her shift neared, and Rose couldn't wait. She dragged herself through her rounds once more. Most of her patients were sleeping, which did nothing to help her pass the time.

"You should grab a quick nap," Dr. Myers said, startling her. She spun around to find him leaning against the doorframe of Mr. Patrones's room with a lopsided grin.

"I've only got an hour left." She shrugged. "Not much point to it now."

He stepped toward her, the grin dissolving into a frown of concern. "Yeah, but you still have to drive home. Take a nap. I can check on your remaining patients."

She quirked an eyebrow. "How are you not dead on your feet? You've been here as long as me, if not longer."

It was his turn to shrug. "I'm used to little sleep." Turning so his back pressed against the wall, he stared at the ceiling. "Before I came here, I was an on-call with the ER in Baltimore."

"Oof." Several of her nursing friends had gone on to work in ERs all over the nation. The last time she saw them, they'd told horror story after horror story. She couldn't imagine the chaos. It'd been hard enough when Steven had come through, and she wasn't even his nurse.

"Yeah," he said. "Oof."

"What made you decide to move to our little town?"

The lopsided grin returned. "Would you believe me if I said a girl?"

That got her attention. "Really?"

He raised his eyebrows. "Didn't you come here for Steven?"

"Well, yeah, but we'd been together awhile by that point." She cocked her head. "You just don't seem the type to go chasing after someone."

His laugh was hollow, bitter. Rose deduced he had quite the story to tell, but she shifted uncomfortably. It wasn't her business, and she wasn't sure she wanted to know the details. They weren't friendly outside of the office like she and Rebecca were. In fact, that conversation was the longest one she could ever remember them having.

He nodded at the chart in her hands. "How many more patients do you have?"

"Just one. Why?"

"If you're not going to take a nap, you should get some coffee in you." When she frowned, he gave a sad smile. "Meet me downstairs when you're done, and I'll tell you the whole sordid tale."

Despite her misgivings, curiosity bubbled up inside her. With a nod, she turned on her heel and headed off to check on her last patient. She didn't know why she cared. Based on some of his cocky behavior at the hospital, she could only imagine what he had done to cause the end of his relationship. But learning that someone else had moved to their tiny town for love intrigued her.

About ten minutes later, Rose entered the cafeteria and allowed her eyes to sweep the room. Though technically the place was closed, a couple of coffee and vending machines were available. A few residents sat around a table by the door, but they paid her no mind. Finally, she spotted Dr. Myers seated at a table on the far side of the room with two coffees set before him.

"Two sugars and a splash of cream, right?" He slid her drink over.

She sank into a seat, dumbstruck by his thoughtfulness. "How'd you know?"

"I pay attention."

Just the scent of the roasted beans was enough to rouse her, but she took a sip anyway. He was right—she needed something to stay awake. Though she lived only fifteen to twenty minutes from the hospital, she always struggled to keep her eyes open after working a double.

"So, tell me," she said. "Who broke your heart?"

His eyes widened. "How do you know she did the breaking?"

"Lucky guess?"

He shifted, his fingers fiddling with the flap on the lid of his cup. "I'd say we broke each other."

When he didn't continue, she leaned back in her chair and sipped her coffee. "We don't have to talk about it if you don't want to."

"No, I want to. I'm trying to think of where to begin." Wrapping his hands around the cup, he stared at the table. "Melissa and I met at Johns Hopkins. I had been accepted into their cardiology fellowship, and she was pursuing her MFA in creative writing." He shook his head, a faint smile on his face. "We came from such different worlds

—it was a wonder ours connected at all. In some ways, it felt like fate."

Rose leaned forward, growing more interested in his tale with each word due to the similarities with her own story. She and Steven had also met in college, and though they'd both gone to the University of Maryland, their programs had almost nothing in common.

"So, how did you meet?" she asked.

He shrugged. "At a party. We had a few mutual friends. Actually, her best friend and my best friend were both 1L's in law school at the time." He coughed a harsh laugh before he continued. "They dated casually. Their schedules made it impossible to make it anything more. But after I saw Melissa, I knew I'd find a way to make it work. And I did." Pausing and draining his cup, he cleared his throat then gestured to Rose. "Did you want another one?"

She blinked then shook her cup. The coffee sloshed around inside, confirming she'd barely drunk any of it. When she declined, he got himself another cup from the machine.

While she waited for him to return, she sipped the now lukewarm liquid, contemplating what he'd told her so far. What had happened between them to cause him to say they broke each other? He sounded like he still cared a great deal for her, if the wistfulness in his voice was any indication.

When he returned, he slid into his chair and grimaced. "So, Melissa and I dated throughout my fellowship and her master's. After we'd completed our programs, we discussed where to live. At first, we got a place in Baltimore, and she got a job at a small publisher while I did a residency at Mercy Hospital.

"But she wasn't happy, and one day, she asked if I would consider leaving the city life for something quieter." He raised an eyebrow at Rose. "I didn't realize how quiet she meant until she brought me down to meet her parents."

"So she lives here?" Rose asked. *Have I ever met her before?* She racked her brain, but she couldn't remember any Melissa from the people she'd met since moving to town.

He shook his head. "A few towns over, but this was the closest hospital."

"Did her parents not like you?"

"Oh no, that wasn't the problem. And my parents loved her." His eyes grew sad, and he sighed. "I guess you could say I took a long time to adjust to small-town life."

"It can be a big change," Rose said, her heart going out to him. "I'm used to living in a city too. But I don't know, Cedar Haven has kind of grown on me."

"That's the thing. I asked her to move here." He brushed his dark hair off his forehead and gazed intently at Rose. "We had rented a little place near her parents, which was quite the hike to the hospital, especially in an emergency."

"She didn't want to?"

"Her father became ill, and she wanted to stay nearby so she could care for him and help her mother."

Rose rested her chin on her hand. "What did she do? Was she still working at the publisher?"

He shook his head. "No. She had decided to pursue writing full-time, so she was working on a novel, which was the other reason I was frustrated she didn't want to move. She had no commute, and I'd already made sacrifices in turning down a lucrative job in Baltimore to move here."

"So, did you move?"

Hunching his shoulders, he nodded. "Briefly. We found a place not far from the hospital." He gave another bitter laugh. "I actually still live there."

"Then what happened? Did she go back to her parents?"

At first, he didn't respond, and Rose wasn't sure whether she should say something comforting. But then he took a deep breath and pushed his coffee cup away.

"As her father got worse, she spent more and more time over there. It got to the point where we barely saw each other." His mouth pressed into a thin line. "Between caring for her dad and comforting her mom, she didn't have much time for me."

"Did you consider moving back closer to her parents?"

He leaned back and nodded. "But I also sat her down and had a long talk about the importance of taking care of her health. She'd become a ghost of her former self. She'd even stopped writing, devoting all her time to her father."

"I'm guessing he didn't make it?" His story was beginning to sound eerily familiar.

Shifting in his seat, he folded his arms on the table. "He did not. She was a wreck afterward. She moved back in with her mother and basically shut herself away."

Rose narrowed her eyes. "And what? You broke up with her?"

He sighed. "Of course not. I tried to talk to her, to pull her out of the depressive funk she was sinking into." Gulping down more coffee, he grimaced. "But she was angry with me for taking her away from her father in the first place, when we'd moved closer to the hospital. And then I couldn't bear to watch her wither away as she poured everything she had into a hopeless case." His eyes shot to Rose's face, and he bit his lip. "I'm sorry. I didn't mean that the way it came out."

She gave him a weak smile. "I know." Then she shook her head. "That's awful."

Leaning forward, he pushed her coffee into her hands and gave her a meaningful look. Dutifully, she raised it to her lips. The cool liquid did little to enliven her as it slid down her throat, but she hoped the caffeine would kick in soon.

"There's a reason I'm telling you this story," he said.

"What's that?"

He cleared his throat. "I'd only recently joined the hospital staff when Steven's mother took a turn for the worse." Rose dropped her gaze, but he continued, "And I saw how you rallied around her, helping Steven's sister and caring for her yourself. While you didn't fade as quickly as Melissa, I could see the toll it was taking on you."

"But Lanie did most of her care," Rose protested. "And they hired hospice nurses, so my contribution was minimal."

"I know." He took a deep breath. "I also know the situation won't be the same with Steven."

She stilled, her heart pounding in her chest. *What does he mean by that?*

"You're a caretaker, Rose. I've seen it here at the hospital with your patients." When she frowned, he hurried on. "That's a good thing. It makes you an amazing nurse. But here, it's easy to maintain boundaries with your patients."

"You think I can't do the same with Steven?" she asked coolly.

"Can you?" He raised an eyebrow. "He's your fiancé, the love of your life, I assume. And I imagine he isn't taking too kindly to staying in the rehab facility." She made a face, and he nodded as if she'd confirmed something. "I know his sister has been going there regularly since the school year ended, which is likely lessening your burden." His eyes narrowed. "But I don't expect that to last much longer."

"So what are you saying?"

He touched her hand, his mouth turning down. "Don't become the next Melissa."

Chapter Nine

AFTER TWO WEEKS IN THE REHAB FACILITY, STEVEN WAS ready to leave, and he didn't care if it happened to be against medical advice. He'd seen through Lanie's lame attempts to hide how much his business was flailing without him, and the longer he remained in rehab, the more the firm would suffer.

Marvin and his medical team were sitting around the conference table opposite Steven, his father, Lanie, and Rose. Everyone's face was grim. Dad was the only one who supported his decision, though Steven suspected that had more to do with how much continuing rehab for another two weeks would hurt his father's bank account.

"You've made such amazing progress," Marvin protested. "Why leave now? Your cast comes off in three weeks, and in another four, we might have you standing again."

"Outpatient therapy can do that as well," Steven countered, keeping his voice cool and detached.

"But these first few months after a spinal cord injury are critical. You'd do better with more therapy than you can receive on an outpatient basis."

"And my firm will fail," Steven retorted. "I've heard the arguments, but they don't take into account the impact to my personal life." With a deep breath, he worked to remain calm. "I need to get back to work."

"Where will you live?" Rose asked quietly. Her brown eyes were filled with unshed tears. It wasn't the first time she'd asked him that question. "Your house isn't equipped for a wheelchair."

"I visited Steven's house yesterday. Despite the concerns expressed at the hospital, I found the door to the house and to the bathroom on the first floor are wide enough to accommodate his wheelchair. But even if they weren't, he'll need a two-person transfer assist to go to the bathroom or to move from the bed to the chair and vice versa," Adrian, his physical therapist, responded for him. "But that can be accomplished with home care aides."

Steven sat up a little straighter. While he hadn't expected his decision to receive much support from his medical team, he was grateful his progress was at least being acknowledged.

"So you support this decision?" Marvin demanded.

"I wouldn't go that far." Adrian sighed. "But determining what's best for Steven depends on all the facts, and quite frankly, the stress of being here, away from his work, isn't good for his spinal injury or his heart." He turned to Rose. "Some adjustments would need to be made, such as placing a hospital bed downstairs until he's able to climb stairs again. I believe, with some adjustments and Steven remaining mindful of his limitations, he could live there." His gaze met Steven's, and his face hardened. "However, there are other things to consider. How will you get to appointments?"

"While I understand being away from the office is stressing you out, how will you maintain a low stress level if you return to work?" Dr. Myers's voice came through the intercom in the middle of the table. He hadn't been able to get away to attend the meeting in person. "I don't need to remind you of the risk of a second heart attack."

Steven gestured to Lanie to speak. She shot him a withering look but nodded and leaned forward.

"We plan to hire a law clerk to help while Steven recovers. An experienced law student, even if they haven't passed the bar, could perform most of the tasks Steven does." Her hazel eyes flashed fire as she glared at him. "But Steven would still have to review the work and sign off on it."

"And the appointments?" Marvin asked.

"I'll drive him," Steven's father said. "I'm retired and have already rented an accessibility van."

The medical team exchanged glances, and Dr. Myers heaved a heavy sigh over the phone. Steven held his breath.

"Again, I state for the record, Mr. McAllister is choosing to leave of his own free will and against medical advice." Dr. Myers's voice was authoritative but resigned. "Marvin, fill out the discharge paperwork and let me know if Dr. Bhati or I need to sign off on anything."

"Thanks for calling in." Marvin pushed back from the table and stood. "We'll prepare everything for discharge."

Rose burst into tears beside him and ran out. Lanie chased her, leaving Steven with his father. Without a word, Dad grabbed the wheelchair handles and guided him back to his room for hopefully the last time.

~

"What's this?" Steven demanded as his father pulled up in front of his house. Several cars were parked along the street and in the driveway.

"Nate and Lanie wanted to welcome you home," Rose said a little too brightly. She'd barely spoken on the way back from the rehab facility, though he'd tried to engage her in conversation. While he understood her fears about his health, he wished she would trust him. After all, he was hiring a law clerk and finding ways to manage his workload. *Why isn't that enough for her?*

Dad cringed but said nothing as he parked and began the complicated process of removing Steven's chair from the van.

Steven raised an eyebrow at Rose. "What's going on?"

"It's just a small gathering of your favorite people to celebrate your release." But she wouldn't meet his eyes.

He leaned back in the seat and crossed his arms. "I'm not leaving this vehicle until you tell me what I'm walking into."

Dad snorted, and Steven flushed. Even he could hear how empty the threat was. Until he was out of that blasted chair, he didn't have a lot of say about where he could and couldn't go. He'd learned to maneuver around in it, but it was easier to be pushed by someone else. They'd recommended a power wheelchair instead of a manual one, but he'd refused. No sense in spending the money if he planned to walk again as soon as possible.

With a sigh, Rose turned in her seat and faced him. "We're holding a family meeting."

His brow furrowed. "Why?"

"Because you're a stubborn workaholic who won't listen to reason," Dad said.

"What he means"—Rose cut in with a glare— "is that we need to discuss how things are going to be now that you're home."

Steven's lips pressed into a thin line. "And if I don't agree?"

Rose opened her mouth, but his father beat her to it. "Then I'll turn this van around and take you right back to the rehab facility."

"You wouldn't dare."

Dad stopped fiddling with the belts strapping Steven in and stepped out as if ready to slam the door. "Try me."

Steven scowled. "Fine. I'll at least listen, but don't think for one minute that I'm going to change my mind."

"Of course not," Rose muttered as she slipped out of the car and headed into the house.

"Let's get this over with," he grumbled as his father pushed him up the sidewalk. His family had had a ramp installed over the stairs. As Adrian had promised, his chair fit easily through the front door.

The scene that greeted him didn't alleviate any of his frustrations. His sister and her fiancé, Nate, sat on the black love seat on one side of the living room. Rose had claimed a matching recliner near the kitchen. Nobody spoke as Steven came in.

"Well, let's hear it," he said, gesturing to Rose. Somehow, he suspected she was the mastermind behind the whole charade.

Dad smirked, raising an eyebrow at Lanie, who simply nodded. Without waiting for an invitation, he sank onto Steven's black leather couch and made himself comfortable.

Nate had moved closer to Lanie, almost protectively, as if he expected Steven to lash out at her at any moment. It took all of Steven's willpower not to throw them out of his house. He'd promised Rose he would listen to what they had to say, even if every instinct told him not to.

"I'm sorry to have ambushed you like this," Rose began, catching him by surprise. "But your decision to leave the rehab center against medical advice left me little choice."

He struggled to keep his emotions in check. "What's wrong with my choice?"

She fiddled with her engagement ring, and he half expected someone else to swoop in and take control of the situation. But no one did, and she seemed to steel herself.

"You aren't taking this seriously," she said. Her tone was firm, but her beautiful brown eyes swam with tears.

His anger faltered, but he tried not to let it show. Perhaps he was being unreasonable, but he couldn't help feeling an intervention was over the top and unnecessary.

"You can't go back to the way things were," she said. "We have to make some changes to not only allow you time to heal but to reduce the likelihood of another heart attack."

"But I'm continuing therapy on an outpatient basis." *Quite reluctantly*, he wanted to add. With his schedule, those appointments would take up a huge chunk of time. "And I'm adhering to the strict diet the nutritionist put me on."

"I'm referring to overall lifestyle changes."

Somehow, he knew the conversation was about his job, and he

clenched his jaw to keep from lashing out. Didn't she understand he needed to work, or he'd lose everything? His business? Their future? Everything was all tied together.

"I've already offered to assist with your business over the summer," Lanie piped up. She glanced at Nate. "And we're happy to help Rose with the wedding planning, as it's a good chance to learn the business before we plan our own."

"But you're going to need to figure something else out soon," Nate said. He took Lanie's hand and fixed Steven with a steely gaze. "Lanie starts teaching on her own in August, so you can't lean on her for too long."

Steven pressed his fingers into his temples. "I already promised I would cut back."

"I'm afraid that's not enough," Rose said, her tone gentle. "And that's what we're here to discuss. How we can pitch in and help you to alleviate as much of your stress as possible."

"Lanie and Sandra are helping me hire a law clerk." He met his sister's gaze. "I'm truly grateful for your help, both while I was in rehab and now. While my staff can handle daily tasks, there's benefit in having someone who knows me and is aware of my..." He couldn't say the words. "Condition."

Rose looked like she wanted to say more, but he held up his hand. "Before you ask me about a partner again, let me explain why that's not possible. The fact is, I can't afford to bring on a full-time attorney right now. There's not enough profit to support something like that at this point." He sighed. "At the same time, there's too much tied into this firm to go belly-up so soon."

"Then what can we do to make sure that doesn't happen?" Dad asked.

"Finding a law clerk is the first step." Steven glanced at Rose. "Though it would be easier if I could go into the office."

"Absolutely not." She crossed her arms. "Dr. Myers said you aren't cleared to return to work yet."

He released a frustrated sigh. "I appreciate everything. And I *am* aware of the risk of another…" He choked on the words again. "Incident." Clearing his throat, he pressed on. "But you also have to understand I have a lot at stake, and there are certain things I'm not willing to compromise on."

Rose clenched her hands into fists. Steven's jaw ached from grinding his teeth. They appeared to be at an impasse, and he had no idea where to go from there.

"Why don't we continue with the arrangement we had while you were in the rehab facility?" Lanie asked in a clear attempt to break through the tension. "I can keep you up to date on the goings-on in the office and bring you things to sign."

Before she finished speaking, Steven was already shaking his head. "I need to start catching up with my clients." At Rose's glare, he added, "But I can do that through phone calls and video conferences."

His sister visibly relaxed and smiled. "That seems fair to me."

All eyes turned to Rose for her verdict. At first, he thought she was going to keep pushing him to stop working entirely, but then she nodded.

"I won't stop encouraging you to take it easy," Rose said, her voice much more tentative than it had been moments ago. "But I understand the need to save your firm." Her teeth worried her lower lip. "Just… promise me you won't overexert yourself."

"I promise." Steven put his hand over his heart, which felt more than a little overdramatic, but he wanted to assure her of his sincerity.

"But you better believe I'll be watching you like a hawk," Lanie said, her hazel eyes darkening.

"I'd expect nothing less," Steven replied drily. He forced himself not to grin. Against all odds, he'd won. Well, he'd won a battle, but if he knew his family, the war was far from over.

~

As happy as he was to be out of the rehab facility, Steven had to admit being home wasn't much better. Despite his pleas, his family refused to allow him to return to the office, not even to visit his staff. And his attempts to convince his sister to bring him work beyond the occasional need for his signature had been met with her threatening to tell Rose. The last thing he needed was another dressing-down from his fiancée. But as the days wore on, his restlessness grew.

To her credit, Lanie was surprisingly lenient with him. She was happy to just sit and talk to him, watch TV together, or play board games. If Rose had stayed, he probably wouldn't get off so easily. She would play nursemaid and insist he follow every recommendation from the doctor. But as long as he didn't overexert himself, Lanie didn't fuss.

"Are you enjoying your summer vacation?" he asked one afternoon while they played Uno.

Lanie shrugged. "I'm not hating it, but since I only got to work a few months before the school year ended, I don't feel like I've earned the break."

He raised an eyebrow as he considered his next move. "I disagree. After everything you've been through this last year, you deserve to relax."

"What about you? How are you feeling about the forced recovery period?"

For a moment, he didn't answer, pretending to concentrate on his cards. "It's nice to be home, but I do worry the work is piling up."

"I've been by the office every day this week to coordinate with Sandra. She said she's handling your cases just fine, though Mr. Willoughby continues to call daily."

Steven rolled his eyes. As much as he missed the office, he had to admit he was in no hurry to return to dealing with that particular client. But he kept that to himself.

"I'm glad Sandra is staying on top of things, but it may be too much for her."

"All the more reason for you to start looking for a law clerk," Lanie said, laying down a draw-four card.

He scowled, both at the insistence he needed help and the move she'd just played. He'd had only two cards left. But his mind wasn't on the game at all, and there were some advantages to letting Lanie win.

"How can I advertise for one if no one will let me work?"

"I've already discussed placing an ad with the newspaper, and I've researched how to advertise at law schools in DC and Baltimore." She glanced at him quickly before hitting him with another draw-four card. "Of course, we'll need your help with the wording."

"Doesn't that count as work?" He winced at how sullen he sounded. His predicament wasn't Lanie's fault, and if he had any hope of convincing her to let him go into the office, even if just for a few hours, biting her head off wasn't the way to do it. He tried a different tactic. "I appreciate your help."

She smiled. "Anytime."

Taking a deep breath, he pushed his shoulders back. "But I'd like to review my files." When she opened her mouth to respond, he rushed on. "It'll aid me in writing the ad if I know exactly what I'll need the law clerk to do."

Her brow furrowed. Whether that was because she was open to his request or debating her next move, he couldn't tell. He fidgeted with his cards while he waited for her response.

With a sigh, she shook her head. "You know Rose will never go for that."

"She's my fiancée, not my keeper," he retorted.

Lanie laughed. "Try telling her that."

"I have," he muttered. *Time to go with plan B.* "You know, I have a special calendar where I track my deadlines and upcoming court dates. I should review that as well."

"Does Sandra not have access to this calendar?"

With a triumphant smile, he shook his head. "It's locally saved on my computer."

"Don't you have a laptop?" Lanie frowned. "Couldn't I bring that home to you?"

Score! "Would you? That would be helpful."

"Sure. I'll swing by the office tomorrow and drop it off next time I stop by."

Steven smiled. Another battle won, and that one was huge. With his computer there, he would be able to work without anyone being the wiser, especially at night, when no one else was around. He was so excited by the turn of events, he didn't even react when Lanie yelled "Uno!"

Chapter Ten

The next day, Rose pushed Steven's wheelchair along the sidewalk near her condo, taking in the late-June evening. It was the first chance they'd had to be truly alone since his accident, and she relished the time with him. For one night, she had committed to put aside all of the uncertainties they faced and just enjoy their time together.

Steven took a deep breath. "This is nice."

"I'm so glad it's summer," Rose said. The recent change in seasons had given her a renewed sense of hope. After all, summer was her favorite season with its long days, warm nights, and plenty of bright sunshine to banish the shadows from her mind.

"And soon, we'll be married."

Rose bit her lip. They hadn't discussed the wedding since that day in the hospital. With everything else going on, she'd tried not to think about it, promising herself they would discuss it later. But the wedding was two months away, and she still wasn't sure what their next steps should be.

"Rose?" Steven called, and she realized she'd stopped walking.

Forcing a smile, she resumed their stroll. "Sorry about that."

The air between them became thick with everything they weren't saying, but Rose didn't want to ruin their evening with an argument. Instead, she angled the wheelchair toward the pond.

"There's something I want to show you," she said.

"Are we going swimming?" Steven joked as they neared the water's edge.

Once they reached the fence, Rose locked the wheelchair's brakes before stepping around to kneel beside Steven. She searched the pond for her favorite birds.

"Look," she said when she spotted them. "Those are our resident swans."

Steven followed her finger and smiled. "They're quite beautiful."

"Aren't they, though?"

The swans glided through the water, seemingly without a care in the world. Rose couldn't help envying them. How simple their lives must be in comparison to hers. Find a mate, raise a brood of cygnets, and live in such a peaceful place.

"Did you know there's an ancient belief that swans sing before they die?" Steven asked.

Rose frowned. "Really? Why?"

He shrugged. "No idea, but that's where the term 'swan's song' comes from. The idea is they're mute most of their lives, but right before they die, they sing a sweet, mournful song."

That didn't sound right to her. "They aren't mute. I can hear them grunting from here."

"I'm sure it's just some old folklore," Steven said with a laugh.

Like Lanie's cardinal. A smile tugged at her lips. She liked having her own legend, especially since she could share it with Steven.

"Did you know swans have their own mating dance?" Rose asked, remembering the man she had seen fishing the last time she was at the pond.

"Most animals do." Steven winked at her. "But I'd rather not sit around waiting to see if they start going at it."

A laugh bubbled up in her throat. "Too true. We should get back anyway. I need to start dinner if we want to eat before midnight."

He took her hand and kissed her knuckles. "I wouldn't mind if it meant I got to spend more time with you."

Her heart melted. She missed moments like that. Sometimes she worried they got too caught up in the day-to-day of life and didn't take time to really enjoy each other's company. With the accident, there had been even less opportunity.

Impulsively, she leaned forward and cupped his cheek before pressing her lips softly against his. He wrapped his arms around her waist and tugged her into his lap, almost tipping over his chair in the process.

Her laughter echoed off the buildings, and she kissed him once more before standing and brushing off her clothes. "Come on. Let's go home."

As she pushed his wheelchair to her condo, the sweet scent of honeysuckle filled her nostrils. She closed her eyes and breathed it in, allowing her mind to be transported back to a special evening two summers ago.

Steven had made reservations at an upscale Irish restaurant overlooking the Inner Harbor. They'd been there plenty of times before, but something felt different about that evening. After a delicious meal of boxtys and fish and chips, Steven had ordered a couple of glasses of champagne.

"What are we celebrating?" Rose had asked as she accepted her glass from the server.

"This," Steven said before sliding off his chair and dropping to one knee in front of her.

Her heart had leapt into her throat as he produced a small black-velvet box and opened it to reveal the most beautiful ring she'd ever seen, a pear-shaped diamond bracketed by a ruby on one side and an amethyst on the other.

"Will you marry me?" His eyes had searched hers as if he didn't already know the answer.

"Of course!" she exclaimed.

He stood, and she jumped into his arms. The rest of the evening was a blur, as she'd spent more time than she cared to admit staring at the ring on her finger. She'd loved that he added their birthstones. It was the perfect representation of their love.

Rose blinked herself back to the present as they reached her door. After unlocking it, she maneuvered the wheelchair into the condo and parked it in the living room.

"Did you want to watch television while I get dinner started?"

He shook his head. "I'd rather sit in the kitchen and talk to you, if you don't mind."

While her kitchen was too small for the chair to fit, she moved it over to the doorway so they could talk without yelling. She grabbed ingredients for stir-fry, one of Steven's favorite meals.

"Any news on the head nurse position?" he asked as he watched her work.

"Not yet. I know they're going to open the application sometime this summer, but I doubt I'll get it. Rebecca has seniority."

"I heard she doesn't want it."

That caught her attention. She turned from the stove to look at him. "Where did you hear that?"

"In the hospital." He grinned. "You'd be surprised how much the nursing staff gossips."

"Actually, I wouldn't," she said with a laugh.

After setting a pot of water to boil and pouring oil into the wok to heat, she began chopping vegetables. But her mind wasn't on the task. Truthfully, she hadn't given a lot of thought to the head nurse position in the last few weeks, for good reason.

"Did Rebecca say why she didn't want it?"

"Just that she wasn't interested in the extra responsibility," Steven said. "I also got the impression she's not that ambitious. She seems happy where she is."

"Hmm." If Rebecca wasn't planning to put herself in the running, Rose might actually have a shot.

"I also heard Dr. Myers say he thought you would be the best fit for the job."

Rose stopped chopping and stared at Steven. "What?"

"You must have made quite the impression on him with all your double shifts."

"Not that I had much choice in the matter," Rose replied through gritted teeth.

"Sounds like I'm not the only one who needs to find a better work-life balance," he teased.

She glared at him. "Not funny." Returning her focus to the vegetables, she racked her brain for a change of subject. She didn't want to get within even a hair's breadth of an argument that evening. "How are things going with the home health aides?"

"Rather well. They're always on time and insanely efficient."

"That's good to hear." Though it did surprise her. While the hospital was understaffed, she'd heard the shortage of home health aides was becoming its own epidemic, particularly in rural areas. As the population aged, more people needed assistance in their homes. That had been one of her main concerns when Steven had insisted on leaving the rehab facility after only two weeks. Knowing he was being well cared for eased some of her worry.

"But I'm not sure I'll need them much longer."

Rose froze. *What could he possibly mean by that?* Clearing her throat, she focused on her chopping. "Why do you say that?"

"Dad and Lanie come by every day, and they help with food prep. The only thing I need the aides for is transitioning, and I'm hoping I'll be able to do more in PT once this blasted cast is removed."

The tightness in her chest eased a little, but she frowned as she dumped the chopped vegetables into the oil and stirred. Something about what he'd said didn't sit right with her.

"The cast isn't due off for at least another two weeks, right?"

"That's what Marvin said." Steven shrugged. "But that's not that far away now."

The pot of water was finally boiling, and Rose added rice to it. Then she removed chicken that had been marinating in teriyaki sauce and added it to the wok.

She glanced over at him and chose her next words carefully. "I would suggest tempering your expectations regarding your recovery. It might not be as swift as you would like."

"It's already slower than I want," Steven grumbled. "But I've been doing some research, and once the cast is off, I expect to make a lot more progress." He leaned his head back against his chair and stared at the ceiling. "And the sooner I do, the sooner things can return to normal."

Warning bells went off in Rose's head. He was so focused on his ability to walk, he seemed to conveniently forget his heart condition. Her desire to keep the peace between them clashed with her concerns about his health. She'd bitten her tongue multiple times that evening, and she wouldn't be surprised if she'd put a hole in it.

Instead of responding, she busied herself with finishing dinner. She stirred the vegetables and chicken together in the wok and checked the rice. Everything was coming along nicely. If only she could say the same about her relationship.

She grabbed two plates and silverware before stepping around Steven and setting the dining room table. On her way back in, he grabbed her hand and gave it a squeeze. She hoped her smile looked more genuine than it felt.

"What would you like to drink?" she asked.

"I'd say a beer, but Dr. Myers would probably kill me."

"And I'd help him," Rose said with a sweet smile. "Water or iced tea?"

Steven sighed. "Water, please."

By the time she'd filled the glasses, dinner was ready. She drained the rice and put it into one bowl with the stir-fry in the other. After setting the food on the table, she unlocked Steven's chair and brought him over.

"This smells amazing," he said before lifting his glass. "To us."

She tapped his glass and took a sip. Then she served Steven and herself. Soon the only sound in the room was forks scraping against plates. She relished the break from cherry-picking her words and pretending everything was fine.

When they finished eating, Steven leaned forward and took her hand. "Thank you for tonight. It was fun being just us for an evening."

Rose's lips turned up in a genuine smile. "It really was. Hopefully, now that you're out of the hospital, it can happen more often."

"From your lips to God's ears."

"The night's not over yet. I made dessert."

Without giving him a chance to respond, she stood and cleared their plates. After dropping them off in the sink to clean later, she removed a pan of brownies from the fridge and plated up two.

She returned to the table and set Steven's plate in front of him. "Enjoy."

"Oh man, you make the best brownies." He took a bite and closed his eyes. "I can't wait to eat your food all the time."

"Hey, mister." She playfully shook a finger at him. "I'm no personal chef. You'll be helping me."

"Of that, I have no doubt." Once he finished his brownie, he brushed the crumbs from his fingers. "I meant it'll be nice to be together every evening. Well, I mean, the evenings you don't have a shift."

And the ones you aren't working late. But she kept that comment to herself. They'd managed to make it through dinner without devolving into an argument, and she was determined to keep it that way.

A knock sounded at the door, and his face fell. "That'll be my dad."

With a heavy heart, Rose stood to answer it. How had the evening passed so quickly? But sure enough, Max stood on the other side.

"Evening, Rose."

"Hi, Max." She stepped to the side to let him in. "He's in the dining room." As she turned to lead him there, Max stopped her.

"How's he doing?"

"Much better. He seems to be happy to be home."

Max searched her face. "And how are *you* doing?"

"I'm okay," she lied.

But her soon-to-be father-in-law wasn't fooled. "I know you worry about him. We all do. He's a hardheaded man."

Rose raised an eyebrow. "Wonder where he got that from."

His face broke into a wide grin, and he laughed. "Fair enough."

"Hey, you two," Steven called. "Stop whispering about me like I'm not here."

"Who said we're talking about you?" Max demanded as he walked into the dining room. "Maybe I was trying to convince your fiancée she's with the wrong McAllister."

"Very funny." Steven crossed his arms. "You're early."

"I'm sorry, son, but the home health care aides had to move your appointment time. They're coming to your house in a half hour."

With a sigh, he nodded. "All right. Well, can you at least turn around? I want to give Rose a proper goodbye."

Max rolled his eyes but did as Steven asked. Rose moved beside Steven and bent down to give him a quick kiss, but that was clearly not what he meant by a "proper goodbye." Instead, he pulled her into his lap and tangled his hands in her hair.

"Have I told you how much I love you lately?" he murmured between kisses.

"No," she whispered. "But now hardly seems the time."

"Then we'll just have to find another time." His final kiss was deep and passionate, almost like a promise.

"You can turn around now," he called to his dad.

Max came over and grasped the wheelchair handles. "You have a good evening, Rose."

"You, too, Max."

She followed them outside and waved as they headed down the sidewalk to the van. Once Steven was secure, Max drove away.

Rose went inside and leaned against the door. Her lips still burned from Steven's fervent kisses, but the fluttering in her stomach wasn't from butterflies. It was guilt. She couldn't keep up the charade of pretending everything was fine between them. Eventually, she and Steven needed to have a frank discussion about their present and their future.

Chapter Eleven

"Here's your computer, as promised," Lanie said the next day as she blew into Steven's house, loaded down with bags of groceries and his laptop.

"Thanks!" He grabbed the computer and eagerly opened it before he caught himself. *Not yet.* He needed to wait until he was alone. Then he could delve into his workload and make a dent. If he tried to do that right then, Lanie would likely rat him out to Rose, or worse, she might return the computer to his office.

With a resigned sigh, he set it on the kitchen table and lifted a few items from the grocery bag. He moved to the pantry and put them on the lower shelves. Although he hated being cooped up and treated like an invalid, he didn't miss grocery shopping. He could get used to having groceries delivered, especially when it didn't cost him any extra in fees.

"I bought stuff to make chicken piccata for dinner tonight." Lanie grabbed the package of chicken and stuck it in the fridge.

"You don't have to do that," he responded quickly. If she stayed for dinner, he wouldn't be able to get to work until late in the evening.

"I know, but I want to." She shot him a smile. "I suspect you miss red meat, but I think you'll love this anyway." Her smile turned wistful. "It tastes just like Mom's."

How can I turn that down? "That sounds great. I appreciate all you're doing for me."

"Rose may be joining us as well," she continued as she filled his pantry with different canned goods. "She wasn't sure whether she'd have to work a double tonight."

Ducking his head into his fridge, he put away some produce, glad for a moment to fix his expression. If Rose came over, he would never get a chance to work. She'd probably stay until the aides came to transfer him to his bed for the night, and then he'd have no way of accessing his computer. For a moment, he hoped she wouldn't be able to get off in time, then he chastised himself. He wasn't being fair.

"That's great," he finally said, hoping he'd added enough enthusiasm to his tone.

"Dad may stop by, although there's a game on tonight."

Sometimes Steven envied his father. Nobody forced him to do anything, mainly because he was stubborn enough to do the exact opposite of whatever anyone wanted him to do. But that might be part of the reason things hadn't worked out between Steven's parents. His father wouldn't bend or compromise, which had led his mother to a breaking point.

That thought sobered Steven up. He refused to fall into the same habits as his father. If Rose stopped by, he would deal with it as best he could. Perhaps he could use the excuse that he needed to compile the ad for the law clerk.

"It's not like Dad can't watch it here," Steven said, coming back to the present.

"Yeah, but you know how he is."

After the groceries were put away, Lanie moved over to where she'd laid his laptop on the counter and pushed it toward him. "So why don't we work on the law clerk ad? We've got some time before I need to start dinner."

He tried to hide his relief as he moved over to her and signed in to his computer. The machine booted up quickly, and he opened his email, skimming through the growing number of unread messages staring back at him. He itched to start reading them in greater detail, but he didn't want to test his sister's patience. The fact that she'd brought him his laptop and was willing to allow him to do some work was more than he could have hoped for.

Instead, he clicked into his files and opened his special calendar, noting with growing alarm that some of the deadlines he'd set were fast approaching. As he surveyed the dates, he debated what cases he would feel comfortable passing on to a law student.

"I need someone who's already graduated," he murmured half to himself. "A 3L might be acceptable, but anyone lower than that is too wet behind the ears."

Lanie gave him a puzzled look. "What does that mean?"

"Ah, sorry." He chuckled. "Basically, a third-year law student, someone who's preparing to graduate."

She nodded and grabbed a pen and paper from the drawer by the fridge. "Do they need to specialize in any area of law?"

"Not really. But their research skills need to be impressive, especially if they aren't familiar with a certain area like estate planning or family law."

After jotting that down, she peered over his shoulder. "That looks like a lot of work. How do you keep up with it?"

"Sandra helps," he said, trying to ignore the growing panic in his belly. "But it's why I work such long hours."

She raised an eyebrow. "Do you expect a law clerk to do that?"

Cocking his head, he considered her question. *Do I expect a law clerk to keep my crazy schedule?* From what he knew of the larger law firms, associates were often expected to work long hours, especially if they hoped to get on the partner track. But he wasn't a large law firm, and he wasn't hiring an associate.

"No, though I do hope they'll be open to working after hours sometimes."

"We'll discuss that in the interview," she said.

He turned to her. "You're planning on joining the interviews?"

"Of course." Her eyes widened. "Why wouldn't I?"

He frowned and glanced at his computer. *What does Lanie know about hiring anyone, let alone for a law practice?* He figured she would assist with the day-to-day, performing more secretarial tasks like editing pleadings or mailing correspondence. But it appeared she had bigger plans for her time with him.

"I didn't expect you to. I mean, no offense, sis, but do you even know what to look for in a law clerk?"

She glared at him. "I know what to look for in an *employee*, regardless of their job title."

After searching her face for a moment, he nodded, though he wasn't convinced. Still, it might be helpful to have another person evaluating the candidates. She might have a different perspective than him, and he wanted to be sure he made the right choice.

"All right. First things first, let's decide what to put in this advertisement to attract quality candidates." He leaned back and crossed his arms. "In addition to research skills, I need someone who's a good writer. Sandra helps draft a lot of my pleadings, but I don't want to rely solely on her. And if I have to spend all my time editing something poorly written, I'd be better off writing it myself."

With a nod, Lanie jotted that down. "But I assume you'll have to review everything since they won't be licensed to practice yet, right?"

"Of course." He waved a hand. "I'd review it even if they were licensed to practice since it's my name on the letterhead." Drumming his fingers on the table, he tried to think of what else might be useful. "Excellent customer service skills."

She frowned. "Won't most of the clients be handled by Sandra or your receptionist?"

"Not necessarily. If I'm not around, they may need to speak to the law clerk if they need something more technical explained. While the clerk can't give them legal advice, they can at least explain the contents of a contract, for example. And they'll likely be in regular contact with the court. I want to make sure they can manage." He ran his fingers through his hair. "Besides, what if Sandra or Leslie are busy? At the very least, the clerk will need to know how to handle clients well enough to take detailed messages."

"Duly noted."

Nothing else immediately came to mind. He glanced at his sister's notes. "Do you think you can draft an ad with what I've given you?'

She nodded, her face breaking into a smile. "I'll go over it with Sandra tomorrow and bring it by when we're done."

"That's great!" The tension in his shoulders eased. He hadn't realized how much it would help to have a plan. "I appreciate your help."

"Anytime." After a quick glance at her watch, she moved toward the kitchen. "I'd better get started on dinner before Rose and Dad arrive."

"If they're still coming," Steven said, crossing his fingers under the table in hopes that they wouldn't. The fewer people there, the greater his chance of getting to work after Lanie left.

"Thanks for dinner." Steven patted his stomach and gave his sister a warm smile.

Rose had been pulled into a double shift, and his father had preferred a night in with pizza and beer to Lanie's cooking. Everything had turned out as he'd hoped. He just needed to see Lanie headed home, and he could get to work.

She shook her head and grimaced. "There's so much food left over. I should have saved some of the chicken for another night."

"Nonsense. I'll have leftovers for lunch and dinner tomorrow."

"True, though I had planned to stop by to make you dinner."

He waved his hand over the table. "Look at all of this. There's really no need."

Her lips pursed as if she wanted to argue with him. He stacked plates and silverware before setting them on his lap and wheeling himself to the sink. His sister jumped up to help him. Between the two of them, they should be able to make quick work of it.

"Did you want to play a game tonight?" Lanie filled the sink while he stuffed the leftovers into the fridge.

Shaking his head, he moved to the table and leaned against it, trying to look tired. "I'm pretty beat. When the home care aides arrive, I plan to have them help me into bed and call it a night."

For a moment, he feared she would see right through him, but instead, she gave a quick nod. "That's wise. You don't look like you're getting enough rest."

"What's that supposed to mean?"

She raised an eyebrow. "Don't get defensive. I'm only saying I'm concerned." Wiping her hands on a towel, she leaned forward and scrutinized his face. "You've got dark circles under your eyes."

"I've got a lot on my mind." He shrugged. "It's hard to turn my brain off, especially with everything I need to do."

"I can understand that, but you've got to try." Her teeth worried her lower lip. "Have you taken any of the sleeping medication the doctor prescribed?"

"You know I hate feeling like I'm drugged. I can't even stand Benadryl."

"But if it'll help—"

"It won't. Trust me."

She shot him a dubious look. "How do you know if you won't try?"

"Look, I appreciate your concern, but I'm fine." When she opened her mouth, he held up his hand. "Or at least, I will be once we find a law clerk and relieve my work burden a bit."

She turned to the sink and grabbed another dish. "It's just, Rose has been talking my ear off every chance she gets about how worried she is. I promised her I would try to intervene."

"Let me handle Rose."

Lanie snorted. "Good luck with that."

I'm gonna need it.

After she put away the last dish, Lanie grabbed her purse, and he followed her to the front door. She leaned down and gave him a quick hug.

"I know you keep telling us not to worry, but we can't help it." She pinched his cheek. "You're the only big brother I've got."

Shaking her off, he smiled. "I'll take care of myself, I promise."

As soon as she was gone, Steven returned to the kitchen and grabbed his laptop. What he'd told Lanie was partially true. When the home care aides arrived, he did plan to have them set him up in bed, but what he didn't tell her was he intended to take his laptop with him.

But it wouldn't help much. Reviewing his emails only confirmed his fears. Due to the amount of work he'd missed, deadlines were pressing in from every direction. With a sigh, he began reading and responding to emails. And he vowed to himself that one way or another, he would find his way back into his office—and soon.

The next morning, Steven woke with a crick in his neck. He'd slumped over while working, and his laptop hung haphazardly off his good leg. He rubbed his eyes and stretched, wincing at the stiffness in his shoulders.

After he righted his laptop, a low groan rumbled in his throat. His emails appeared to have multiplied overnight.

A knock on the door alerted him to the arrival of the home care aides. Two men in scrubs entered the house and helped him to his chair. Neither was very talkative, which was fine with Steven. Their assistance with his morning routine was awkward enough, especially in the bathroom. Once he was showered, dressed, and sitting at the kitchen table, they left, promising to return that evening.

He longed for a cup of coffee, but since his heart attack, Rose had insisted he switch to decaf. That wasn't going to do it this morning. He went to the kitchen to see if Lanie had taken pity on him and stashed real coffee away somewhere.

After searching the cabinets to no avail, he grabbed the decaf canister, grumbling the whole time. But, he reasoned, it was better than nothing, and perhaps the scent of fresh coffee would trigger his brain.

He checked his phone as he waited for the coffee to brew. Lanie had sent him a draft of the advertisement for a law clerk. As he read it, he had to give his sister credit. She'd managed to sum up everything he needed in very few characters. He gave her the go-ahead to post the ad and poured himself a mug of coffee before heading to the living room.

A few hours later, another knock on the front door startled him. When the person didn't immediately enter, he scrambled to hide his computer under a couch cushion before rushing to open the door.

"Hey, big bro." Lanie stepped around him and into the house. Her arms were laden with packages.

"I thought I told you that you didn't need to cook for me tonight," he replied, struggling and failing to keep the annoyance out of his voice.

"I'm not here to cook for you, but I did note you were low on a few things. I took the liberty of picking them up." She side-eyed him. "Don't worry. I'm not staying, so you can return to working on the sly without my interference."

His mouth fell open, but before he could respond, she moved by him and carried her bags into the kitchen. After he recovered from his shock, Steven followed her down the hall.

"Did you tell Rose?" he demanded from the doorway.

She rolled her eyes. "No, I'm not your warden. But *you* should tell her."

Once she put the groceries away, she turned and leaned against the counter, folding her arms.

"I thought you weren't staying," he said, shifting uncomfortably.

"I'm not, but I did want to let you know we already got our first applicant."

His eyebrows shot up. "That was fast." He leaned forward. "Did you have a chance to look over the application?"

She nodded. "I'm no expert, but he sounds perfect. And I'm taking his quick response as a good sign we'll be able to find someone to assist you real soon." She pushed off the counter and stepped toward him. A wave of relief washed over him, and he moved out of her way. When she reached the front door at the end of the hallway, she glanced over her shoulder. "But if you want to interview him in person, you'll have to get the okay from your actual warden."

He waved a dismissive hand. "If it's to help me reduce stress, she won't mind."

His sister's doubtful look made him second-guess himself, but he kept his face neutral as she left. Once she was gone, he retrieved his computer from the couch.

As he reviewed the application, he was buoyed by the credentials of the applicant, a recent Georgetown University graduate looking to gain experience while he studied for the bar exam. Based on the address, he lived in the suburbs, which were about forty-five minutes away from Cedar Haven. Steven hoped that meant the applicant wasn't also applying to the big law firms in DC because there was no way his tiny firm could compete with their salary offers.

After making a few notes on the application, he debated how to approach Rose about his returning to the office to conduct interviews. Lanie had made it sound like Rose wouldn't be amenable, but he couldn't imagine why. After all, the only reason he was hiring a law clerk was to appease her. He couldn't very well hire someone without an interview. And although he could hold a virtual meeting, he was old-fashioned enough to want to meet candidates face-to-face.

There was only so much he could discover about a person over a computer screen.

With any luck, Lanie could schedule the interviews to occur on the same day, which would limit the time he needed to be in the office. Whether that would be enough to appease his fiancée, he didn't know, but if nothing else, it might at least postpone an argument. After crossing his fingers, he sent a text message to Lanie to start setting up interviews.

Chapter Twelve

Rose tapped the steering wheel as she drove to Steven's house. They'd planned to get together to discuss the wedding budget. Since she'd had the morning off, she spent it going over the figures, and things weren't looking good. Although she had made some decent overtime with all of her double shifts, she couldn't say the same for Steven. She planned to ask him about his business's finances, but she didn't expect to hear good news. Their current financial situation had renewed her desire to discuss postponing the wedding again.

She'd spoken to Carissa that morning regarding their upcoming payments. Though Carissa had sympathized with their situation, she told Rose they needed to decide what they were going to do and soon. The vendors were willing to negotiate a new date for the wedding but only if they got paid by the deadline, which was the next day.

When she reached the door, it swung open before she could knock. Steven greeted her with a smile.

"How are you feeling?" she asked as she followed him into the house.

"Better." He maneuvered to the table, where he had set out a pitcher of iced tea and two glasses. "How was work? Is Lisa's daughter better?"

Rose nodded. "Yes, thank goodness. I couldn't handle another double shift this week." After pouring the tea, she squared her shoulders and removed the binder she'd used to track the wedding details and expenses. "So, about the wedding budget."

His body tensed, and he fidgeted beside her. *This is not a good sign.* But she focused on the figures because she needed him to understand what they owed before they discussed his share.

"We've got several items coming due in the next few weeks. Invitations should have been sent this month, but with everything that happened, I ordered them late. I'm hoping to get them out before the Fourth of July." She pushed the binder closer to him. "The next payment to the caterer is due next week, which is fifty percent of the total charge. Our last payment will be due once we have a final head count in August." Then she flipped the calendar page. "The final payments will be due two weeks before August twenty-sixth."

Steven's eyes widened as he took in all of the four-figure amounts. "And how much does this total?"

After flipping back to the previous page, Rose pointed at the equations she'd added yesterday. "It comes down to about fifteen thousand dollars still to pay."

His throat moved as he swallowed thickly, and Rose braced herself for what she expected him to say. But he surprised her when he pushed away from the table and went to the couch. A moment later, he returned with his laptop.

"I'm going to be a little short for my share," he admitted as he opened the computer and signed in.

She pressed her lips together and fought back frustration. She'd known that, expected it, but it didn't make it any less aggravating. While her main focus had been on his recovery, she'd known their finances would take a hit after his accident.

"How short?" She kept her tone even.

He didn't answer immediately. Instead, he seemed to be doing some calculations of his own. His eyebrows knitted together, and he bit his lip.

"Steven?"

With a sigh, he turned the screen toward her. "About seventy-five hundred short."

Her stomach dropped. It was worse than she'd thought. They'd been splitting the wedding costs equally and had opened a joint account to pay for them, with the plan to use that account for joint expenses once they were married. Steven hadn't deposited anything into it since April.

"All of it?"

He gave a grim nod. "And it gets worse."

"How could it possibly be worse?"

"Mr. Willoughby is threatening to find a new lawyer if I can't work on his case."

Though Mr. Willoughby was Steven's biggest client, she couldn't deny she would be thrilled to see the back of him. He was the absolute worst kind of person.

"I'm sure you can find someone to replace him."

He shook his head. "I know he's a pain, but between the drama of his divorce and his real estate business, he's been a very lucrative client, and I'd be underwater without him."

"So what are you going to do?"

When he didn't answer, she decided to try her next strategy. "Can we discuss postponing the wedding now?"

His mouth set in a thin line. "Not this again. We'll lose more money if we cancel now."

"I spoke to Carissa this morning, and the vendors are still willing to work with us on finding a new date next summer." Rose left out the part about needing to pay them by the original deadline. Her share of the cost would cover the payments due in July, and once they had a new date, she hoped to renegotiate a payment plan for the remaining balance.

He searched her face, and she tried to keep her expression neutral while her heart hammered in her chest. She prayed he would see reason.

"I'm doing what you asked, Rose. Lanie and I are setting up interviews to hire a law clerk. And who knows, maybe they'll do well enough to work toward becoming a partner someday. In the meantime, I'm trying to keep my business afloat so we can afford to start our lives together." His chest expanded as he took a deep breath, and she held hers as she waited for whatever he would say next. "I want to marry you. I want a life with you, and I'm doing everything I can to make that happen. So why don't you tell me what's really going on?"

What the—What was that supposed to mean? They were financially strapped and could no longer afford the wedding they'd planned. *What other possible motive could I have? Does he think I* want *to keep having this conversation? Does he think I* enjoy *pushing him on this?*

A cold wave of dread washed down her spine. He couldn't possibly know about her parents' deciding not to attend, could he? Rose hadn't told anyone else about that, and she highly doubted Steven had spoken to her parents since he'd left the hospital. But his insistence that she had some ulterior motive in postponing the wedding was making her paranoid.

Pushing those thoughts away, she glared at him. "What's really going on is that we can't afford to get married the way we planned. And unless you've got seven thousand dollars stashed away somewhere, I don't know how you suggest we pay for the commitments we've already made." When he opened his mouth to protest, she rushed on. "Besides, wouldn't you rather hold the wedding of our dreams when you're fully recovered and able to enjoy it?"

He dropped his gaze to the table as if the fight had gone out of him. Tears pricked behind her eyes because she didn't want to postpone the wedding, but she didn't see any other option.

"I'm not saying forever, Steven. Just a year. One year where you can focus on healing and we can get our lives, and our finances, back on track. Then we can have the wedding of our dreams without bankrupting ourselves." *A year for me to save up for my parents' flights.*

A tear slipped down his cheek. "It's not fair." He raised his head and looked at her. "I don't want to wait anymore. We already put it off for a year because of my mother and opening the law firm. I don't want this to be like Scrooge in *A Christmas Carol* where we keep postponing the wedding until the 'right time.'" He put air quotes around those last words. Sliding his hand across the table, he grasped hers. "It may never be the right time for us to get married, but I don't want to risk losing the right person for me."

Her heart melted. But she looked at Steven, really looked at him, and she could see the toll the situation was taking on him. Dark circles bloomed like purple bruises under his eyes, and his skin was paler than usual. When he'd led her into the house, she could hear his labored breathing as he pushed his wheelchair. It wouldn't take much for him to be right back in the hospital, and who knew whether he would survive another heart attack.

"I want to marry you too," she said in earnest before pulling her hand away. She stared at the table as she spoke the words she'd avoided even thinking let alone saying out loud. "But I don't want to be a widow so soon after becoming your wife."

His jaw dropped open. "Is that what you think is going to happen?" He maneuvered his chair around to her side of the table. His arm slid around her shoulders. "I promise you, I *am* taking better care of myself. Lanie has been buying me healthy food, and I've been getting plenty of rest."

"But some things haven't changed, have they?" She gestured to his computer. "You're still working way more than you should considering you haven't been cleared to return to work. You were already stressed about the law firm's finances, and now the wedding expenses are stressing you out."

"I'm not—"

"I saw the panic in your eyes when I showed you what we owed."

He scratched the back of his head. "We could ask my dad for a loan—"

"You can't be serious." Without another word, she grabbed her purse.

"Where are you going?"

"Home. This conversation is over."

"Come on. Be reasonable." He tried to grasp her arm, but she backed away.

"I *am* being reasonable. Do you really believe it's appropriate to ask your father for money after he just paid for your two-week stay in the rehab facility? He's retired and on a fixed income. He can't afford to throw more money at *our* financial problems."

With that, she turned and fled the house. She jumped into her car and took off, wanting to put as much distance between her and Steven as possible.

Instead of going to her condo, Rose parked by the pond nearby. She breathed in the thick summer air and walked down to the water's edge. Ducks swam near the shoreline, and a lone swan circled near the center. A commotion on the other side of the pond caught her attention, and she hurried over, worried something had happened to half of her favorite bird couple.

Two men were trying to wrangle the swan into a cage but were having quite the time of it. As she approached, the swan was clearly fighting, though it favored one leg over the other.

"What's going on?" she asked.

One of the men coaxed the swan into the cage while the other shut the door. The swan settled into the corner, hissing at its captors.

"This one broke its leg," the man who had shut the door said. He lifted his baseball cap, revealing a bald head, and wiped it with a handkerchief. "We're taking it to a wildlife rehabilitation center where they can set the leg and allow it to heal."

"But we had a time getting it away from its mate," the other man said, wiping his face on his shirt sleeve. He nodded at the remaining swan. It looked lonesome out there on its own.

"Will it be okay without its mate?" Rose asked. She couldn't help comparing their situation to her own.

"Should be," the bald man said. "But swans are one of the few bird species that mate for life. She may grieve as if he's died. We'll keep an eye on her, though, and make sure she takes care of herself for when he returns."

"And when will that be?" Rose asked, unable to hide her interest.

The men exchanged a look, then the bald one shrugged. "Hard to say." He inclined his head toward the cluster of buildings where her condo was. "You live around here?"

She nodded, hoping she wouldn't regret revealing that information to strangers.

"We'll let you know how the male gets on," he promised with a smile. "And you'll definitely want to be here when they're reunited."

Cocking her head, she frowned. "Why's that?"

The other man just laughed. "You'll have to see for yourself."

They loaded the swan's cage into the truck bed and secured it before climbing in and driving away. Rose watched until the truck had driven out of sight before closing her eyes and sending up a short prayer for the swans.

Her earlier anger had dissipated, and she felt hollow. With a heavy heart, she turned and walked to her condo.

When Rose finally checked her phone later that evening, she was surprised to find only two texts and one voicemail. Steven's messages were full of apologies and his insistence that he would be fine. But she'd meant what she'd said about not wanting to be a widow before she'd even had a chance to be a wife. And Steven could wax poetic all he wanted about his dietary changes; the real crux of the issue was the stress load on his heart.

This isn't how I imagined my life when Steven asked me to move to Cedar Haven. It always seemed like something new came up just as she thought they were finally moving forward.

Did I make a mistake? After working for a few years in Baltimore, she'd received a job offer at a prestigious hospital in Boston. But when Steven had learned of his mother's cancer diagnosis, he decided to open a practice in his hometown to be closer to her.

So Rose gave up her dream of Boston and found a position at the small hospital in the middle of nowhere. Of course, there were many things she loved about the town. The hospital's size allowed her to have closer relationships with her patients. She'd become more active in the community, and she had found a best friend in her future sister-in-law. Most importantly, she had Steven.

But sometimes, she wished she'd worked harder to convince him to move to Boston. Several law firms in the city would have snapped someone like him up in a heartbeat. Perhaps he could have found a better work-life balance. At the very least, he would have less stress about finances. Those firms were known to pay very well.

After his mother passed, Rose thought Steven might consider going back, but he had his heart set on opening his own firm. In the end, it hadn't taken much to convince her to stay in Cedar Haven. She was already in town, and the thought of packing up everything to move again sounded exhausting. So they'd stayed.

But he'd never told her how much capital he had sunk into the venture until it was too late. On top of that, he still had to pay off his student loans from law school. The sixty-five thousand dollars he'd inherited from his mother after paying off the estate helped, but it wasn't enough to make a substantial dent in what he owed.

To say they were financially strapped was an understatement. If only they hadn't moved to Cedar Haven so quickly. Maybe if they'd stayed in the city, they could have saved a nest egg to help him build his business.

She checked her phone again but had no new messages. Perhaps he'd decided to give her some time. She grimaced. Or maybe he was doing something he wasn't supposed to be doing, like working. It would be like Steven to take advantage of her absence to dive into his caseload and make some headway. After all, he probably reasoned that if she was mad at him, she would be less likely to stop by and catch him in the act. She hated how well he knew her sometimes.

She'd stewed long enough. She needed to have it out with him, and if she caught him working, it would add fuel to her already simmering fire.

After grabbing her purse and keys, she headed out the door and drove to the house. They hadn't been able to afford much of a mortgage, even that far from the city. But it was enough for them—two bedrooms and one and a half baths in less than sixteen hundred square feet. One of the bedrooms hardly qualified as a full room, but it allowed for a home office. Part of her wondered if she should have insisted Steven use that until they could afford to buy commercial space, but he'd fallen in love with the location of his firm, and his father had helped him secure the loan. It hadn't seemed worth it to fight at the time.

Her hand hovered over the doorknob. Shaking her head, she turned the knob. He always said it was her house too. So she supposed she shouldn't feel weird walking in.

"Steven?" she called. The late-summer-evening sun poured into the room from behind her, basking the hallway in an orangey hue.

No response came, but the distinct sound of keys clacking on a keyboard drifted down the hall. *Unbelievable.* She prepared to catch him in the act.

Sure enough, Steven scrambled to shut his laptop as she entered the living room. He was in his chair beside the couch. His hazel eyes widened, and he bit his lower lip in quite possibly the guiltiest expression she'd ever seen. If she wasn't so angry, she might have laughed.

"What do you think you're doing?" She crossed her arms.

"Nothing," he said a little too quickly. "I mean, it's not what it looks like."

"It looks like you're working." She raised an eyebrow.

"Not really. I mean, I'm trying to catch up on email, I swear." He raised his hands as if in surrender. "I'm not working on any briefs or pleadings, nothing that would cause me undue stress."

She scoffed. "Knowing some of your clients, I find that hard to believe."

With a wry smile, he slid the laptop onto the coffee table. He moved over to her cautiously. When he grabbed her hand and began pulling her into his lap, she stiffened, and he released her with a frown.

"What are you doing here?" He searched her face.

"I came to finish our argument," she said coolly, narrowing her eyes. "But it appears we're about to have another one."

He sighed. "I told you Lanie brought the laptop here so I could catch up on work."

"No." She jabbed him in the chest. "Lanie brought the laptop home to write the advertisement for a law clerk, which you've done. She should have taken it back to the office where it belongs."

"Be reasonable, Rose," he whined. "I can't just sit here day in and day out doing nothing while my business goes to hell." He leaned closer to her, both eyebrows raised in a challenge. "Do you want me to fail?"

That caught her off guard, and she staggered back. "Of course not, but I don't want your heart to either."

Taking her hand, he placed it on his chest. His pulse pounded beneath her palm. "It's still ticking."

A faint smile pulled at her lips before she could stop it. She tried to rearrange her features into a sterner expression. "For now."

But Steven took advantage of her faltering anger and brushed his hand over her cheek. She started to pull away, but he slid his other hand around her waist, pulling her into his lap and kissing her.

"Not fair," she murmured against his lips.

He chuckled and released her. “But the best part of fighting is the making up.”

“You assume we’re done fighting,” she retorted as she stood and put her hands on her hips.

“I took a nap earlier, and I’ve taken multiple breaks. I promise you, even though I’m working, I *am* heeding Dr. Myers’s advice.”

Rose was losing the battle, but she held on to the last shreds of her aggravation at finding him typing away like he hadn’t just suffered a heart attack. “How long a nap?”

His gaze went to the ceiling. “I didn’t time it.” After a quick glance over his shoulder, he turned back to her. “But I’d guess maybe forty-five minutes?”

She pursed her lips and nodded. “I suppose that’s better than nothing.”

“And I have an idea for how to pay off the remaining balance for the wedding, though it might not be easy.”

Despite her apprehension about the direction of the conversation, she laughed. “What do you propose?”

“Mr. Willoughby,” he said. Her face must have betrayed her shock and misgivings because he hurried on. “I spoke to him this afternoon. While he’s still not happy with me for not taking his calls, he was much more focused on the latest response from his wife. She was open to the settlement I had sent her before my accident, but she had some minor adjustments, which he is, of course, blowing out of proportion.” Steven let out an exasperated sigh. “He’s bound and determined to take this to court, and that means if I can keep him happy, he’ll owe me an even larger retainer fee than what he’s already paid.” His teasing grin melted her heart. “The irony is he may single-handedly ensure our marriage through his divorce.”

She giggled, then her face fell. “But he’s your most demanding client.”

“And the law clerk will help alleviate some of that demand.”

“It’s a start,” she admitted.

Slipping his arms around her waist again, he pulled her close. "Can we make up now?"

It would be easy to give in, but she needed to clear the air on one more thing. "First, there's something I need to tell you."

"Oh?"

She took a deep breath. "You were right. I did have an ulterior motive for wanting to postpone the wedding." At his alarmed expression, she cupped her hand over his cheek. "It's not what you think. I promise."

"Then... what is it?"

"My mom told me she and my dad can't make the wedding." Tears pricked behind her eyes, and she tried to blink them back. "They can't afford the plane tickets."

"Oh, Rose," Steven murmured, tightening his arms around her.

"It feels stupid saying this to you." She sniffled.

"Why? I can only imagine how devastating that news was for you. Heck, I'm disappointed, and they aren't even my parents."

"Yes, but you just lost your mom." Rose pulled back to search his face. "It's selfish to want to postpone the wedding so they can be here, especially with the anniversary of your mom's death coming up soon."

His eyes got a little misty. "I'd forgotten that." He took a moment to compose himself. "But my feelings don't trump yours. I wish you had told me."

"Would it have changed your mind about postponing?"

He averted his eyes. "If I'm honest, probably not, but that's because I don't want to wait any longer to marry you. Maybe we can go visit them in South Korea when we're in a better place both physically and financially. How would you like to have a small ceremony there?"

Instead of answering, she knelt beside his chair and wrapped her arms around his neck before peppering him with light, grateful kisses.

Chapter Thirteen

A FEW DAYS LATER, STEVEN ENTERED HIS OFFICE FOR THE first time since his accident. It felt good to be back, like coming home. Despite Rose's protests, he'd managed to catch up on much of what he'd missed from the comfort of his home, but there was something about being physically present that made him feel more productive.

The reception desk sat to the left of the door, though Leslie wasn't in yet. To the right was the waiting room, which he'd furnished with four straight-backed chairs surrounding a small table covered with magazines. A few bookshelves graced the back wall, but the majority of his law books were tucked in his office and the conference room.

"Welcome back, boss," Sandra said as she came in behind him and handed him a coffee cup.

"Thanks, Sandra, but I can't—"

"Chill, dude. It's decaf."

"In that case..." He lifted the cup to his lips and sipped the warm beverage while missing the taste of real coffee. One day, he hoped to get Rose—and for that matter, Dr. Myers—to relent on the dietary restrictions, but… baby steps.

"Lanie texted me to say she was running late but she'd be here in time for the first interview," Sandra continued, moving farther into the reception area and flipping on a light. "Did you want me to sit in as well, or do you think the two of you can handle it?"

"Don't you want to have a say?" He frowned. "You'll be working directly with whomever we hire."

She shrugged. "I can get along with pretty much anyone. Besides, I've got a lot on my plate. I'd prefer to have the time to get through that."

He ran a hand through his hair. "Well, okay, but if we find someone we like, can we bring them to meet you?"

"That works for me." She lifted her cup in salute. "If you need me, I'll be drowning in pleadings."

After checking the mail bin at the receptionist's desk, Steven continued on into his office. A low groan rumbled in his throat as he stared at the mountains of paperwork on his desk. He might have kept up with things electronically well enough from home, but *that* was why he needed to be in the office.

At least he had a couple of hours before the first interview. Maneuvering around was a challenge, but someone had removed the rolling chair behind his desk, and his wheelchair fit well enough in its place. He set his coffee cup on the only clear space he could find and began sorting through the piles, determining what needed his immediate attention and what could wait.

Just as he had finally gotten into a groove, someone knocked at his door. A quick glance at the time confirmed it was almost ten.

"Come in," he called.

Lanie entered the room and carried two coffee cups.

"Ah, thanks, sis, but I've had about all the decaf I can handle for today."

She leaned down and plopped the cup in front of him with a conspiratorial wink. "It's not decaf."

His head snapped up, and he raised an eyebrow. "Real coffee? You're playing with fire."

"I figure you deserved a treat for good behavior."

Chuckling, he sipped and sighed with pleasure. "I'm not sure if Rose would agree with you on that."

"Eh, she worries too much." Lanie slipped into one of the chairs on the other side of his desk and raised an eyebrow. "So, you ready for this?"

"I don't have much choice, do I?" He pulled the pile of applications in front of him. "I just hope there's a true diamond among the rough you found."

She snorted. "Sorry I couldn't find anyone from Yale or Harvard, but somehow, I doubt they would be interested in sleepy little Cedar Haven."

"But you did find a few from decent local schools. I guess I can forgive you."

"There's even a Georgetown in there," she said, separating the pile and pushing a file toward him.

"Yeah, but what are the odds they'll leave DC to come here? I can't compete with the salary, let alone the prestige." He sighed, laying his head back on his chair and staring at the ceiling. "I need someone who can share my vision and is willing to do the work."

A warm hand covered his own, and he glanced at his sister.

"We'll find someone." He must not have looked convinced, because she hurried on. "Maybe not today, but the ad is running for another week."

Leslie appeared in his doorway, her dark-brown hair pulled back in a bun. "Your first interview has arrived."

With a quick nod, Steven focused on Lanie. "I guess it's now or never."

"That's the spirit!" she deadpanned.

He gathered the application for the first interview and motioned for Lanie to head into the conference room, where Leslie had already set them up. The moment they entered the room, the applicant, Jason Gilherst, pushed his chair back and jumped to his feet. His pleasant smile faltered as he took in Steven's wheelchair, and he ran a hand through his disheveled hair. But his eyes widened when they landed on Lanie, and his smile morphed into a leer.

Steven tensed, bracing himself for some inappropriate comment toward his sister. To her credit, she caught on to the man's sudden interest and lifted her left hand to brush her hair away from her face, putting her shiny diamond ring on display.

Well played. Steven bit the inside of his cheek to keep from laughing.

"Mr. Gilherst, this is Steven McAllister," Leslie said. "And this is Lanie McAllister, his sister."

"Do you work here as well?" Mr. Gilherst asked Lanie, clearly undeterred by the prominence of the diamond on her finger.

"I'm just filling in."

"You'd mostly be working with Leslie, our receptionist, and Sandra, our paralegal, until I'm able to return to the office full-time," Steven broke in, hoping to ease the tension and direct Mr. Gilherst's focus elsewhere.

Mr. Gilherst's face fell, and Steven shot a look at Leslie before she closed the door. If her grim expression was any indication, they were in agreement. Their first candidate was a bust.

Still, the interview must go on. He and Lanie went through the motions, which only further confirmed that Mr. Gilherst wasn't a good fit for the firm. He had high expectations of salary with no experience to back up the demand and talked as if he would be running the place in Steven's absence.

When the interview ended, Steven stifled a sigh of relief. *Thank goodness that's over*. His chest tightened. If all of their candidates were like that one, he would be even worse off than if he'd just returned to the office full-time himself.

~

By the time they reached the last interviewee of the day, Steven was ready to throw in the towel. He'd seen one or two applicants he could tolerate, but nobody appeared up to the task. Maybe he was asking too much.

Lanie didn't seem encouraged either. With a sigh, she dragged the last application in front of her and flipped through it.

"Ah, it's the Georgetown applicant," she said with more enthusiasm than Steven could muster.

"He'll probably want a bigger salary than the first interviewee," Steven moaned. The situation was hopeless.

"He can't be any worse than Mr. Gilherst," Lanie said with a wry smile.

A moment later, Leslie knocked on the door and led a young man into the room. He had wavy dark-brown hair and light-brown eyes. His suit was neatly pressed, and he walked right up to Steven and shook his hand. If he noticed Steven didn't stand to greet him, or the wheelchair, he didn't let on.

"I'm Michael Ellerson," he told Lanie as he extended his hand.

"Lanie McAllister, Steven's sister." She gestured for him to sit, and Steven was relieved Mr. Ellerson didn't seem as infatuated with his sister as Mr. Gilherst had been.

Steven and Lanie took turns explaining the job and what was expected. Mr. Ellerson didn't flinch when they informed him of the accident and Steven's limitations, though he did ask some thoughtful questions.

"Will there be a lot of overtime?" Mr. Ellerson asked.

After a quick glance at Steven, Lanie shook her head. "Not necessarily. We do have a substantial workload at present, but we don't anticipate needing someone to work beyond office hours."

"And we likely won't be taking on new clients until I'm fully or at least mostly recovered," Steven added.

"I only ask because I'm still living near DC, and it can be a bit of a challenge to travel if I miss the train."

Steven couldn't help but laugh. "Metro closes at midnight. I can't imagine we would ever need you to stay that late."

Mr. Ellerson nodded, relief apparent in his eyes. "That's good. Some of the law firms I've interviewed at in the city implied I'd be on call around the clock."

"While we can't compete with their salaries, we can offer a better work-life balance," Lanie assured him.

"Honestly, that's more important to me right now. I've heard too many horror stories of first-year associates having nervous breakdowns in the bigger firms." Mr. Ellerson shook his head. "I'd like a bit of a break now school is over." His eyes widened as if he realized he'd implied something negative. "I mean, not that this job isn't hard or that it wouldn't be challenging... I just, er, I only meant—"

Steven raised a hand and smiled. "I worked for a year at a large law firm in Baltimore. Believe me, I understand what you mean, and I can promise you will have that work-life balance you seek here."

His sister raised an eyebrow at him, and he made a face. Just because he didn't have a good work-life balance, that didn't mean he couldn't guarantee his employees had one.

"Would you consider moving here if the job lasted beyond the summer?" Lanie asked, surprising Steven.

Mr. Ellerson glanced from one to the other and cleared his throat. "I wasn't aware that was a possibility, but I'm definitely open to it if the position was extended."

What's she playing at? Steven managed to keep his suspicions off his face. "Of course, there is always room for growth, and that's something we could explore with the right candidate." He wanted to remind everyone no decision had been made yet.

Lanie rolled her eyes at him. It seemed she had made up her mind about Mr. Ellerson and was ready to offer him the job on the spot. While Steven didn't disagree with her, he wanted more time to ensure they made the right decision.

After they finished the interview, Lanie introduced Mr. Ellerson to Sandra before showing him out. When she returned, she leaned against the doorway and crossed her arms.

"Say whatever you're thinking," Steven said, knowing she would anyway.

"He's perfect. You should have offered him the job."

"That's not how I do things." He gathered his notes and the applications before stacking them neatly in a pile. After placing it on his lap, he left the conference room.

"What if someone else snaps him up?" Lanie demanded, following him into his office. "He's the best candidate we've seen."

"So far." As he dropped the paperwork on his desk, he had to admit Mr. Ellerson was probably the best candidate they would see. But in some ways, that made him almost too good to be true.

"You're assuming we'll get more responses to our ad."

He cocked his head. "Weren't you the one who said the ad was still running and we might have more applicants?"

"That was before we interviewed the perfect fit," she scoffed.

"Look, I'll review my notes from today and sleep on it. If we don't have any additional applications tomorrow, then I'll make the decision."

"And hope no one else gets to him first."

In the end, Lanie was right. After letting the ad run for a few more days, no one else applied, and none of the other interviewees could hold a candle to Mr. Ellerson. When Steven called him later that week, he enthusiastically accepted the position. To Steven's surprise, Mr. Ellerson was even willing to start immediately, and they planned his first day for the following week.

Despite not being medically cleared to do so, Steven went into the office that day. He wanted to be there to show the new guy around and make sure everything got off to a great start. Lanie,

Sandra, and Leslie had promised they could handle it, but Steven wasn't leaving anything to chance.

Michael Ellerson arrived promptly at nine o'clock that morning. His suit was freshly pressed, and his brown eyes were filled with excitement as Steven greeted him at the door. Steven showed him around the small office, reintroducing him to everyone before taking Michael to where he would be working.

"Wow, my own office," Michael said, turning in the small space with a wide grin. "I figured I'd get a cubicle."

It wasn't much larger than a storage closet, though at least it had a window. Steven wished he had a better space to offer, but the only larger space available was being used as a conference room. If Steven hired a partner, that would likely change.

"We don't have any of those," Steven replied with a wry smile. "But I hope you can make yourself at home here." He headed to the door. "I'll leave you to get settled. We can meet in my office at ten to go over the cases I want to get you started on. How does that sound?"

"Perfect." Michael set his bag down and pulled out his chair. "Do I need to do anything special to log in?"

"I'll send Leslie in with instructions. Welcome to McAllister at Law."

After stopping by Leslie's desk, Steven entered his office, where his sister was waiting, perched on his desk with a coffee cup in hand. He accepted the cup and took a tentative sip. His lips quirked up as he tasted the robust flavor of real coffee.

"Rose is going to murder you," he said, shaking his head.

"What she doesn't know won't hurt her." Lanie angled her head toward the wall Steven's office shared with Michael's. "So, do you think this is going to work?"

He nodded. "I do." Then he sighed. "Well, I hope so. Do you mind sticking around this morning when I meet with him? You and Sandra need to be aware of his workload so you can keep on top of things when I'm not here."

"Sure thing," Lanie said. "I'll be in Sandra's office. Come get me when you're ready to meet with your new employee."

In the meantime, Steven braced himself for a conversation he'd been dreading. While he had briefly spoken to Mr. Willoughby the other day after Rose had stormed out of his house, he'd promised his client a more in-depth conversation when he was back in the office.

The phone rang once before a gruff voice answered, "Hello?"

"Good morning, Mr. Willoughby. It's Steven McAllister. Is now a good time to talk?"

"It's about time. When do I get my day in court?"

Steven stifled a sigh. "I've drafted a response to your wife's last proposal of settlement, and I'm working on a motion for a pretrial hearing. The judge may order mediation."

"I don't want to go to mediation," Mr. Willoughby growled. "If you can't get me my trial, I'll have to go find someone who will."

Same threat, different day. But since Steven couldn't be sure Mr. Willoughby hadn't already started shopping for a new attorney, he had to play the game.

"Unfortunately, this is how the court system works, sir. In contested divorces, the court would prefer the parties resolve things on their own. Trial is considered a last resort." Steven cleared his throat. "But if you'd like to start over with someone new, potentially delay your divorce another year, and give your wife an upper hand in the proceedings, I have several attorneys I can recommend."

The silence on the other end of the line was deafening, and Steven smiled. The only thing his client would hate more than a further delay of his divorce was giving his wife a win.

"I know my rights," Mr. Willoughby finally said. "And I have a right to a speedy trial."

Steven rolled his eyes to the ceiling. "That's for *criminal* prosecution." Sometimes he wished his fellow citizens had been required to take basic civic and government classes as adults. "A divorce is a *civil* matter."

"Oh," Mr. Willoughby said. "I don't see how it's fair she's been able to drag this out for so long."

Pinching the bridge of his nose, Steven took a deep breath. The fact was, Mr. Willoughby, *not* his wife, had caused the delay. But mentioning that would only aggravate his client.

"I promise, Mr. Willoughby, I'll file the motion for the pretrial hearing tomorrow, and we'll work to get your divorce on the court's docket as soon as possible."

"All right. But I expect you to keep me updated on the process."

Translation: He expects a daily phone call. That wouldn't be easy with Steven coming into the office only sporadically, but he would make it happen. After his discussion with Rose about the law firm's finances, he couldn't afford to lose Mr. Willoughby.

"That shouldn't be a problem," Steven promised.

"And I want to schedule a meeting to go over a real estate dispute I'm having with my neighbor."

"I'll have Leslie set up a time."

"Good," Mr. Willoughby said with a grunt. "Glad you're finally earning your keep again."

"Yes, sir. I'll talk to you soon."

After he hung up the phone, he put his head in his hands. His accident couldn't have happened at a worse time. But he'd managed to salvage his relationship with his client.

He glanced at the clock and groaned. It was almost ten. With a resigned sigh, Steven gathered Lanie, Sandra, and Michael and led them into the conference room. Michael and Lanie sat on one side of the table with Steven and Sandra on the other.

"How are you settling in?" Steven asked as he laid out several folders in front of Michael.

"So far, so good. Leslie got my computer booted up, and I'm logged in. I took a look at your electronic filing system, and it looks similar to what I used last summer during my clerkship."

"That's great!" Steven tapped the folders. "While we've mostly set up everything electronically, we do maintain paper files as well.

These are some of the cases I was working on before my accident." He slid them across the table. "I'd like you to review these today. We can meet either this afternoon or tomorrow morning to discuss any questions you have. There are several deadlines coming in fast, and I'd like to get you up to speed so you can draft the necessary motions."

"Sounds good," Michael said as he flipped open the first folder.

"Sandra is familiar with the cases and has old drafts you can look at to get a feel for how we word things here. But if you have any questions, I'll be in and out of the office this week and available by phone."

"Are you anticipating any court dates in the near future?"

Steven shook his head. "I've filed continuances on all of my court hearings for this month, and I'm not sure if they'll be rescheduled before the summer is up."

Michael's face fell. "Oh, okay, then."

"But if anything does come up, I'll of course be taking you with me."

That perked the law clerk up, and he smiled. "I appreciate that. I haven't had much of a chance to be in a courtroom."

Steven pressed his lips together. How he wished he could say the same. "Don't worry. That'll change soon enough, I'm sure." As he maneuvered out of the room, exhaustion began to take its toll. "Sandra will give you a quick summary of where we are in each case before you start your review, but I'm afraid I need to rest for a minute."

Lanie immediately jumped up and came to his aid, pushing him to his office. Unable to find the energy to protest, he sagged against the back of his chair. Once he was behind his desk, he leaned forward and rested his head on the wooden surface.

"You really shouldn't be overdoing it." Lanie slipped into the chair on the opposite side of his desk. "Maybe I should take you home."

"Stop mother-henning me." He closed his eyes and took several deep breaths as the pain in his chest subsided. "I'll be okay. I just need a minute."

"Are you sure—"

Opening one eye, he glared at her. "Not another word. And don't you dare tell Rose."

She stuck her tongue out at him but didn't argue. After a few more minutes of deep breathing, the pain passed, and he sat up with a groan.

"Do you think he's up for it?" Steven grabbed the water bottle from his desk and took several large gulps.

"He seemed to be. If nothing else, he's eager to learn." Lanie shrugged. "But even if he turns out to be a terrible writer, it's easier to edit a first draft than a blank page."

"True," Steven agreed, albeit reluctantly. "And at least it'll get Rose off my case for a while."

"You hope." Lanie grinned.

He gave a grim nod. "I do."

~

Around five in the evening, Steven packed up his things. How he had managed to work a whole day, he couldn't say, but he was already paying for it. Lanie had arranged for their dad to pick him up, and Steven glanced out the window to confirm Dad had arrived. His spirits lifted at the sight of the van parked outside the building, waiting for him.

Before he left, he popped his head into Michael's office, thrilled to see the law clerk still hard at work. He knocked softly, and Michael glanced up, a proud grin on his face.

"How'd it go?" Steven asked.

"Great so far! I've already finished a rough draft for one of the motions, and I'm hoping to have two more ready for you by tomorrow."

Steven blinked, though he wasn't sure why he was surprised. One of the reasons he had chosen Michael was his can-do attitude and the ambition in his eyes, an ambition Steven had once shared. He hoped it would return once he was fully recovered, but he would be happy if he could find enough motivation to keep his head above water. Drowning in a financial crisis was not something he wished to contend with, especially with his wedding looming.

"Good work." He gave a thumbs-up. "But you should head home and start celebrating the Fourth of July early."

"Sure thing, boss. Just let me save my work, and I'll walk out with you."

While he waited, Steven headed to Sandra's office. She was packing up as well. When she noticed him lurking in the doorway, she motioned him closer.

"You picked a real winner with that one," she whispered, peeking behind Steven as if to make sure Michael wasn't in earshot. "He's been sending me emails left and right with intelligent questions and additional case law he intends to include in his motions. He's going to do nicely here."

"Yeah, I wouldn't mind offering to extend his clerkship into the fall, but I imagine once the bar results from July post, he'll receive more lucrative offers from DC law firms," Steven responded, voicing the thought that had gnawed at him since making the offer.

"Well, Rose wants you to take on a partner. He wouldn't be a bad bet."

Steven bristled. "That's a bit premature, don't you think? I'd like to work with him for more than a few months to make sure he could handle something like that."

"Then it'll be your loss." Sandra shrugged. She straightened as Michael came into view. "Great job today!"

"Thanks for your help," Michael responded with a grin. He turned to Steven. "Mind if I pick your brain on the way out? I had some ideas I'd love to run by you."

"Sounds good." Steven gestured for him to go first. "Lead the way."

"So, what made you decide to set up shop in this town?" Michael asked as they reached the door to the law office.

"I grew up here." Steven lifted his face toward the sky, relishing the late-afternoon sun on his skin. The best part about summer was that it didn't matter how late he worked, the sun was still high in the sky when he left.

"And you decided to come back?" Michael's eyes widened, and a knot formed in Steven's stomach. "There's not much to tempt you here, is there?"

Steven shrugged. "More than you'd expect. I lived in Baltimore for a time, but I'm not cut out for city life. Besides, I prefer the ability to make my own schedule, something I couldn't do at big law firms."

"Ain't that the truth," Michael agreed. "I do love Georgetown, though. Plenty to do nearby or just a short trip downtown." His gaze swept over Main Street. "It's much quieter here."

"You get used to it, and who knows? You may even come to prefer it."

Michael snorted. "I doubt it." Then he seemed to realize how he sounded. "Not that I don't appreciate the opportunity."

"It's fine." Steven chuckled. "A young guy like you needs something more than small-town living. I get it."

"And you have your fiancée," Michael said, shaking his head. "If I had someone to settle down with, I might feel differently."

"None of the women in your class caught your eye?"

"Nah. I didn't have time for dating while in school, and the last few months, I've been studying for the bar." He raised an eyebrow. "Does Cedar Haven have any nightlife?"

"There's Seabreeze." Steven grimaced. "Though it's kind of a dive bar."

"Better than nothing, I suppose."

An idea formed in Steven's head. "If you're looking for a slightly younger crowd, my sister is going out with some of her friends tonight, and several of them are single. If you don't have any plans this evening, maybe you could join them."

"I wouldn't want to impose." Michael frowned.

"Doesn't hurt to ask her." Steven texted Lanie. If anyone could show him what Cedar Haven had to offer, it was her.

A moment later, he received a response. "Is it all right if I give her your number? Then she can add you to the group chat."

"Sure. Why not?" Michael grinned. "Can't hurt, right?"

Chapter Fourteen

"Come on, Rose," Lanie pleaded as she leaned against Rose's kitchen counter. "Come with us tonight. Steven's probably going to bed early. There's no sense going over there to play nursemaid."

Rose bristled at the implication she was *playing* at caring for her fiancé. Her skills were worth more than babysitting or handling his medications, no matter what her future sister-in-law might have thought. Lanie had stopped by to go over some wedding details, but her true purpose appeared to be convincing Rose to go out that night. Crossing her arms, she leveled Lanie with a glare.

"Oh, don't give me that look," Lanie said. "I didn't mean anything negative by that. I'm just saying Steven is doing better. Besides, he's got the home care aides coming by to help him as well." She flipped her blond hair over her shoulder. "Stop searching for an excuse to hide, and allow yourself to have a little fun."

"I have fun," Rose protested. Though she couldn't help finding the situation a little ironic. Just a few months ago, she had been the one trying to convince Lanie to go out. How the tides had turned.

Lanie raised an eyebrow, seeming to read her mind. "Yeah? And when was the last time you went out on the town?"

"Probably for the Memorial Day parade," Rose admitted as she rinsed off the last plate and put it in the drying rack.

"Exactly." Lanie smirked. "So, find something hot to wear and be ready in twenty." Without waiting for a response, Lanie spun on her heel and rushed out the front door.

Rose considered bolting it, but she suspected Lanie wouldn't give up that easily. In truth, Rose probably deserved that treatment since she'd done the same thing when Lanie had wanted to wallow. *What's that saying? Turnabout's fair play or... something?* With a resigned sigh, she flung open her closet to find something to wear.

Flipping through her clothes, she settled on a yellow sundress. The humidity had been ramping up in the last several days, and she could only hope for a thunderstorm to bring them some relief.

Once dressed, she applied her makeup, keeping it light. No sense in going overboard when she was likely to sweat it all off anyway. She brushed her hair back and twisted it against her head before securing it with two sticks.

A moment later, Lanie banged on the front door, and Rose rolled her eyes at her reflection. But she hurried to answer the door before Lanie broke it down. Her neighbors wouldn't appreciate that, not to mention her landlord. As much as she loved her condo, there were advantages to going forward with the wedding and moving in with Steven. The single-family home provided more space and privacy than her current accommodations. And it had plenty of room for a growing family.

When Rose wrenched open the door, Lanie's eyes drifted down her body. Playing along, Rose struck a pose. Though she wasn't in the mood to go out, she could fake it with the best of them.

"You look perfect." Lanie grabbed her hand. "Now, let's go!"

Rose allowed herself to be led to Lanie's car. Well, really, the car she'd inherited from her mother. Nate sat in the passenger seat, and he gave Rose a big smile as she approached.

"You got roped into this too?" Rose asked as she slid into the backseat.

"Lanie's very persuasive," Nate replied.

"Hey, now." Lanie climbed into the driver's seat and glared at Rose in the rearview mirror. "Don't act like I'm some awful bully. I'm just making sure everyone I love has a good time."

"And we appreciate you for it." Nate rested his hand on her knee and gave it a squeeze.

"All right, you two lovebirds. Stop canoodling and let's go," Rose said, though her heart panged a little at the sight. Steven should have been with them, and in another world, he would be. But it would be a while before he was well enough to go out like that again.

When they arrived at Bea's, Trudy and Toccara were waiting for them. Both wore light-colored sundresses that contrasted nicely with their ebony skin. Rose greeted them each with a hug before turning to the newest member of the group, Steven's law clerk, Michael.

"Hi." She stuck out her hand. "I'm Rose, Steven's fiancée."

"I recognized you from your photos," Michael said, bypassing her hand and pulling her into a hug. "I feel like I already know you."

Her body stiffened, not used to such close contact with a complete stranger, and he quickly released her with an apologetic smile.

"Sorry, that was a bit forward."

She waved her hand. "It's fine. Just caught me by surprise is all."

Discreetly, she tried to assess him. He was younger than she'd expected, closer to Lanie's age than her own. But he seemed friendly, and Lanie had told her how impressed she was with his credentials. Perhaps he was the answer to Rose's prayers. At the very least, he might relieve some of the burden on Steven, allowing him more time to heal.

"So, how do you like the office so far?" she asked.

"It's great! Everyone has been nice, and I'm excited to dive in to the cases Steven's assigned me."

Rose smiled, and the tension in her shoulders ebbed away. While she wished Steven would have taken on a real partner, she could be grateful for the assistance Michael provided in the short term. And maybe he would stick around beyond the summer.

Lanie grabbed her arm and pulled her toward the door. "I'm starving. Let's eat!"

The diner was packed, and it took a minute to find a place for them all to sit. As they made their way to the back, Rose caught the owner's eye. Bea's white hair was in a hairnet, and she flashed a grin, signaling that she would stop by their table later.

As they settled into their seats, Lanie immediately started flipping through the jukebox beside her. Everyone else picked up their menus. Rose followed suit, though she wasn't hungry. Lately, she hadn't had much of an appetite, between her worries about the wedding and her concern for Steven.

After the server took their orders, Lanie began laying out the plan for the evening. Once they finished dinner, they would head over to Seabreeze for karaoke and drinks.

Rose couldn't help smiling at the way the tables had turned. The last time she and Lanie had gone to Seabreeze, she was trying to cheer up Lanie, who had spent most of the evening making eyes at Nate.

"Are you going to sing this time?" Lanie asked, giving Rose a pointed look.

"I'm not much of a singer."

"Is anyone at karaoke?" Michael joked.

Rose opened her mouth to respond when she caught sight of a familiar face. Her stomach churned, and she swallowed the bile rising in her throat. Carissa, her wedding planner, was heading their way. Rose should have known she couldn't avoid her forever.

"Rose!" Carissa's gaze swept over the table before settling on Rose. "I've been trying to get ahold of you."

"I'm sorry. I've, uh, had to work a few double shifts lately."

Carissa clicked her tongue. "We have a lot of work still to do for the wedding, you know." She pulled out her phone and tapped the screen. "Since I have you here, why don't we set up an appointment?"

Sweat gathered on Rose's upper lip, and she shot Lanie a pleading look, hoping she would intervene. She was Rose's maid of honor, after all. Lanie took the hint and turned to Carissa.

"Hey, Carissa, I'm glad we ran into you. I've been meaning to ask if you would be available to handle my wedding."

Nate blinked. "You have? I thought we were going to—ouch!" He reached under the table, presumably to rub the shin Lanie had just kicked. Rose bit her lip to hide her smile.

Lanie patted his hand in apology. "We haven't decided on a date yet, but we were thinking late fall, early winter."

"Let me check my schedule," Carissa said, and she seemed to forget Rose was there. "Is tomorrow too soon?"

"Tomorrow's great!" Lanie cleared her throat. "And Rose has her hands full taking care of Steven. But as her maid of honor, I'm happy to go over anything pertinent with you at our meeting."

"Is that okay with you, Rose?" Carissa tucked a lock of graying hair behind her ear.

"Yup, that works for me. Lanie knows my vision better than I do."

"Then that's settled." Carissa gave Rose one last assessing look. "But I do want to chat with you at some point. Give me a call when things slow down."

"You bet!" Rose promised, though it sounded hollow, even to her. She had no idea when anything in her life would slow down.

When Carissa was gone, Nate frowned at Lanie. "What was that all about? I thought we were going to do everything ourselves."

"Rose needed a save." She shrugged. "And besides, it can't hurt to pick the brain of a wedding planner. It's not like we know much about weddings." She gestured to Rose. "What I've learned so far has been through trial and error while helping Rose and my brother."

"Fair," Nate agreed. "But you didn't have to kick me."

She leaned forward and gave him a kiss. "I'll make it up to you. I promise."

Envy needled in Rose's belly at the ease of their interaction. It used to be that way for her and Steven, but lately, everything was a struggle. The accident had exacerbated the problem. She couldn't help wondering if they would ever find their way back to that level of contentedness again.

The rest of the dinner passed without incident. Rose barely touched her salad, her stomach too tied up in knots. She'd planned to go on a diet anyway to look her best for the wedding. At least her growing anxiety was good for something.

When they filed out of the restaurant, she followed Lanie and Nate to the car. Part of her wanted nothing more than to spend the rest of the evening at home, but she didn't want to disappoint Lanie. So she did her best to pretend she was having fun.

Unfortunately, Lanie saw right through it. "Jeez, Rose. We're going to a bar, not a funeral. Would it kill you to smile?"

Rose bared her teeth before sliding into the back seat, which caused both Lanie and Nate to laugh.

"If that's her smile, maybe we'd be better served by her pout," Nate said as he climbed into the passenger seat. "It's way less scary."

Even Rose had to laugh. She'd never considered herself someone who could intimidate people, though sometimes she could make Steven apprehensive, especially if she said words like *we need to talk.*

"I'm sorry," she said, and she meant it. "I don't want to bring down the mood of the evening."

"The point of tonight"—Lanie fixed her eyes on Rose's in the rearview—"was to raise your spirits. If I'm failing at that, I need to either try harder or change tactics." She glanced at Nate before returning her gaze to Rose. "Look, if you don't want to go to Seabreeze, I'm not going to force you. But I'm also not taking you back to your condo. And I'm definitely not dropping you off with my brother." Rose opened her mouth to protest, but Lanie cut her off. "We both know you need a break."

That shut her up, and she nodded. "I can't promise I'll be much company, but you're right." Pushing as much enthusiasm into her voice as she could muster, she continued, "Let's go to Seabreeze!"

"That's the spirit." Nate turned around in his seat and gave her a smile.

The packed bar did little to build her enthusiasm. They found a booth near the back of the bar, far enough from the stage that they could tune out the singers if they wanted to. The outlandish tropical décor was gaudy but somehow fitting. Lanie and Nate went to grab a round of drinks, leaving the rest of them to make small talk.

"How's your baby?" Rose asked Trudy.

"Crawling all over everything," Trudy said with a tired smile, but the pride in her voice was unmistakable. "He's also pulling up on tables. I expect it won't be long before he takes his first step."

"That's exciting!"

"Exciting is one word for it," Trudy quipped. "But it also means we need to double-check our babyproofing." She waved a hand. "Anyway, I came out tonight to escape the baby brain. Tell me all about your wedding planning."

Ugh—the one topic Rose had hoped to avoid. "Everything's booked, but we're struggling a bit financially."

Why did I say that? The last thing she needed was for word of their money troubles to spread throughout Cedar Haven.

"I imagine it's been tight with the opening of the firm." Toccara placed a hand on Rose's arm. "Start-up costs are a nightmare."

Rose blinked, then she remembered Toccara had her own business as well. It made sense that she understood what most people didn't. And her friend was right—the start-up costs had been a huge drain on their finances.

"We'll make do," Rose said brightly, trying to brush away the cloud that hung over her whenever the question of finances came up.

"He's certainly got a robust clientele," Michael piped up. "I'm impressed he was handling the caseload by himself before he hired me. It's a lot for one person to take on, even with his capable paralegal."

A brick settled in the pit of Rose's stomach. She'd known Steven was working with a lot of clients. It helped that he was the only law firm in the tiny town. The last attorney had retired several years ago, and most folks had been forced to venture several towns over to find someone reputable. As much as she wondered if moving there had been a mistake, she recognized the lucrative business opportunity it offered Steven. If only it hadn't been at the cost of his health.

"I've tried to convince him to take on a partner, but he said he can't afford it." She felt disloyal saying the words out loud, especially in front of his new employee, but maybe it would sway Michael to decide to stay.

"Even if that person could buy their way in?" Michael's face held a strange expression, one she couldn't quite interpret.

"I'm not sure what you mean."

Toccara tilted her head as she assessed Michael. "Know someone who has that kind of capital?"

Rose's gaze moved back and forth between the two as they had some sort of silent conversation. After a moment, Michael nodded.

"I might, but I'll talk to Steven directly. Don't want my new boss to think I'm doing something underhanded."

Toccara's face broke into a smile. "I can't imagine anyone accusing you of that." She bit her lip as if she couldn't believe she'd just said that.

But Michael took it as encouragement. "Say, we're at karaoke. What do you think about singing a duet?"

She demurred. "I don't sing."

"Somehow, I doubt that." He raised his eyebrows. "But I'd love to see you prove me wrong."

"You're on."

They hopped up and rushed to the stage just as Lanie and Nate returned with two trays full of drinks. As they set the trays down, Lanie turned to Rose with a quizzical expression.

"What was that about?"

"Looks like those two turned this into their first date," Trudy said with a laugh.

"That was fast." Lanie grinned. "Maybe Steven won't have to worry about those DC law firms stealing Michael away after all." She took a sip of her drink. "What else did we miss?"

"Rose was describing her and Steven's financial situation." Trudy leaned forward. "But I might have a solution to your problem."

Rose frowned. "Oh?"

"What would you say to a fundraiser?"

Lanie's eyes lit up. "Yes! That's a great idea. We raised so much money for the school system after the one you hosted in January. I'm sure we can do the same now."

Heart in her throat, Rose raised her hand. "Wait, I don't want the whole town to know my business."

"Everyone's already heard about Steven's accident. I don't think anyone would be shocked to learn you're facing other struggles." Trudy shrugged. "Besides, after everything you've done for the town since you arrived, nobody would blink an eye at the idea of helping you and Steven have your dream wedding."

Rose bit her lip. It wasn't just about the money, though. Despite his reassurances, Steven still wasn't taking his health seriously. The last time Rose had seen him, the dark circles under his eyes had grown more prominent.

"Come on, Rose." Lanie bumped her shoulder. "You keep saying you want to reduce Steven's stress. Knowing the wedding is paid for would go a long way toward doing that."

"Don't pressure her," Nate said. When Rose glanced at him in surprise, he gave her a sympathetic smile. If anyone else could understand how it felt to be railroaded by a McAllister, it would be him.

"I'm not!" Lanie insisted. "I'm nudging her in the right direction."

Nate rolled his eyes at Rose, and she giggled. She appreciated having someone else on her side for once.

"Talk to Steven," Trudy said. "See what he thinks, and if it sounds like something you want to move forward with, let me know. I'd be happy to help with it."

"Me too," Lanie added.

Rose gave a noncommittal nod. It wouldn't hurt to at least discuss it with Steven. Though she hated the idea of charity, Trudy had a point. Both Rose and Steven had done a lot since coming to Cedar Haven. She had helped with several fundraisers, and Steven had done some pro bono work for townsfolk who couldn't afford legal assistance.

And maybe they could use some of the money raised to help Steven with his law practice. If he was willing to accept help with his business, then she could compromise and accept assistance with the wedding.

Chapter Fifteen

How was your night out? Steven texted Rose when he woke the next morning. Last night had been the best sleep he'd had since his accident, and he felt stronger than he had in weeks. Though he'd pushed himself the day before at the office, he believed it'd done him some good to get out of the house and back to work. Maybe he could convince his doctor to let him go in for half days. Anything to stop being cooped up in the house day in and day out.

More fun than I expected. How are you?

He smiled, glad his sister had convinced Rose to go. She needed a night of fun after everything they'd been through recently. He was just sorry he couldn't join her.

After texting her that he was doing much better, he opened his laptop and began going through emails. Near the top of his inbox was a message from Mr. Willoughby. His heart sank as he read through it. His most lucrative client was only getting more demanding. Steven had drafted the motion for a pretrial conference and planned to file it with the court next week. Apparently, that wasn't soon enough for his client.

With a sigh, he crafted a reply, sprinkling in apologetic language while detailing the strategy he had outlined for the next steps in the divorce. Of all of his current caseload, Mr. Willoughby was by far the most important. Between the contested divorce and his client's plans to sue his neighbors, Mr. Willoughby would rack up several billable hours for Steven's firm.

Steven had never planned to be a trial lawyer, and he expected both cases to settle out of court, but the amount of research and correspondence it required, not to mention taking witness depositions, was sure to help him build his practice into what he wanted it to be. But to do that, Steven needed to be at work. There was only so much he could assign to Michael. Besides, Mr. Willoughby wasn't the kind of client he could leave to a fresh-faced law graduate. Mr. Willoughby needed to be coddled, appeased. And Steven was the only one who could do that. Even Sandra had thrown up her hands the last time she'd had to deal with their most problematic client.

Once the email was crafted, Steven continued working on the case from home. He had access to his files through the VPN, and Rose would be working later that morning. The likelihood of him being interrupted was slim. Though he preferred to be in the office, he figured he could at least schedule depositions and conduct some research he had gotten behind on. Every little bit would help keep his client happy.

Just as he'd started getting into a groove, the front door to his house slammed open. He jumped, almost knocking his laptop over.

"Steven?" Lanie called. "The aides are here."

Since when does she come in without knocking? He pushed the blankets to the side to make it easier for the aides to help him out of bed.

His sister came tearing around the corner, her hair flying, the aides on her tail. For a moment, his heart stopped. Had something happened to Rose? But then he caught the fierce anger in her eyes.

"Lanie, what—"

"I just met with your wedding planner, and do you know what she told me?"

Steven blinked. *This is about the* wedding? "Look, I don't really have time—"

"You're going to make time if you still plan on getting married in August."

Rubbing a hand over his face, he glanced at the aides, who hovered at the back of the room, looking like they wanted to bolt. He gestured for them to come forward and perform the transfer. The sooner they completed the daily morning routine, the sooner they could leave. The fewer witnesses to the conversation he was about to have, the better.

To his relief, his sister seemed to realize her inappropriate behavior. She stepped to the side and tapped her foot while she waited.

Once they were alone, Steven headed to the kitchen. He needed some caffeine if he was going to get through the conversation.

"So, what's going on?"

Lanie removed a stack of papers from her book bag and slammed them on the table. "You're behind on several payments."

Trust Lanie to get worked up over nothing. "Oh, that. Don't worry. Rose and I have already discussed it, and we're handling it."

"With what money?" she demanded, hands on her hips. "I've seen the medical bills that have started pouring in. And have you forgotten that you granted me access to your firm's finances? You're not exactly swimming in dough here."

"I know, but Rose is paying the immediate deposits, and I believe Mr. Willoughby's next bill will pay the rest of what we owe."

She raised an eyebrow. "In time for the August payments?"

He swallowed. Leslie billed their clients at the end of the month, and the clients had fifteen days to pay. When he'd done his calculations, he hadn't accounted for that. It would be tight. Too tight.

He raised his eyes to meet his sister's. "How do you know all of this?"

"I met with Carissa this morning to discuss hiring her for our wedding. We weren't going to have a wedding planner, but she accosted Rose last night, and I thought I'd try to distract her, give you both some breathing room." She gestured to the pages. "But now I think what you two need is a financial advisor."

"It looks bad—"

"It more than looks that way, Steven," Lanie interrupted. "And Carissa said your vendors will cancel their contracts with no refunds if you don't pay them on time." She shook her head. "You should have postponed when you had the chance."

When he didn't respond, Lanie slid into the chair beside him. "What are you going to do?"

"I have no idea." And he didn't. The numbers staring back at him told a story, and if he didn't get them under control soon, that tale wouldn't have a happy ending.

They were quiet for a moment, though Steven could feel his sister's eyes on him. He shifted uncomfortably in his chair. It was bad enough that he had created the situation he was in, but that his little sister had witnessed his failure made it worse.

She sighed. "Look, last night, Trudy had an interesting idea you should consider. Why don't you, me, and Rose meet tomorrow? We can discuss what's going on and formulate a plan."

He nodded, though he had no idea how they would find their way out of that mess. She came over and laid her hand on his shoulder.

"Have faith," she said as if reading his mind. Then she left.

Once he was alone, he covered his face with his hands and groaned. Maybe Rose was right. Maybe putting off the wedding was their best bet. Only by that point, it might already be too late.

The next day, Steven's dad dropped him off at Bea's, where Rose, Lanie, Nate, and Trudy were waiting for him. Nate opened the door, and Rose pushed Steven inside with Lanie and Trudy following her. They found a table toward the back that could accommodate Steven's wheelchair.

"What are you thinking of having?" Lanie asked as she flipped through the menu.

Steven raised an eyebrow. "The same thing I always have—burger and fries." He glanced around at the rest of the table. Everyone was making small talk as they waited to order their food. "When are you going to tell me what's going on?"

"As soon as we order," Lanie whispered.

Shifting in his chair, Steven tried not to scowl. Somehow, it felt like everyone at the table knew what they were there to discuss except him. Even Rose appeared to be completely at ease despite the picture Lanie had painted of their financial situation.

When Bea came around to take their orders, his shoulders sagged in relief. The sooner Bea was done, the sooner he could figure out what on earth was going on.

"Good to see you out and about." Bea leaned down and ruffled Steven's hair. "I've been praying for you." She nodded to Rose and Lanie. "And your family. How are you feeling?"

"A little stronger every day. My cast is supposed to come off next week."

"Then you'll be walking again in no time," Bea said as she moved on to take the next person's order.

I wish. Though he'd attended his outpatient physical therapy appointments religiously, he wasn't seeing a lot of progress. But Dr. Bhati had assured him his spinal contusion was healing well and he'd likely start to regain some feeling in his legs soon.

After Bea had everyone's order, Lanie tapped a fork against her glass. "Let's get down to business, shall we?" She gestured to Trudy to begin.

"The other night at karaoke, I asked Rose to consider allowing us to host a fundraiser. At first, the idea was to help raise money for your wedding, but I think we can agree your financial situation has grown beyond that."

Warmth rushed to Steven's cheeks, and he stared at the table. He couldn't help being ashamed of their situation.

"The one thing everyone in town is asking is how they can help you as you heal." Trudy looked at Steven and smiled. "Even though it's only been open since last November, your law firm has already done a lot to help the town, and folks want to give back."

Steven glanced at Rose, expecting her to protest, but to his surprise, she appeared not only open to the idea but encouraging it. She turned toward him and gave him a smile before refocusing on Trudy.

"So, we're thinking of holding a fundraiser in late July. While it's for both of you, it would make sense to focus on Steven and his recovery." Trudy nodded at Steven. "The town is anxious to help you get back on your feet in whatever manner that requires."

"I don't know how comfortable I am with that," he said. "Won't people think I've squandered my money if I can't afford my own wedding?"

"Everyone knows you've been out of commission for a month while you healed, and you're not back to work one hundred percent," Trudy replied.

"People have asked me every day at the shop how they can help, and I haven't known what to tell them," Nate added. "So unless you want a bunch of questionable casseroles, you should consider the fundraiser."

Steven chuckled. The refrigerator at the law office already held a couple of casseroles and pies that people had dropped off when he was there. Thankfully, very few people had stopped by the house.

"So, how would we do this?" Rose asked, redirecting the conversation.

"While we're here, I plan to ask Bea if we can host it at the diner," Trudy said. "We should focus on raising funds to help Steven in a multitude of capacities. We can either set up various funding options for the wedding, the firm, or medical bills, or we can have everyone contribute to one big pot of money. The latter option provides more discretion on how the money is spent."

"And you aren't concerned people will refuse to help because they think we overspent on our wedding? I don't want this to look like some sort of cash grab."

Trudy cocked her head. "Why would anyone think that?" She glanced at Lanie before turning to Steven. "I believe everyone in town would agree the McAllisters have had more than their fair share of tragedy this year, between losing your mom and your accident."

"And let's be real," Nate said. "If you hadn't had your accident, you wouldn't *need* a fundraiser in the first place. Nobody thinks you and Rose spent beyond your means."

"Right, and even if some people do feel that way, no one is forcing them to contribute." Lanie shrugged. "It's a fundraiser, not a tax."

Their food arrived, and Steven was grateful for a chance to sit with his thoughts. The case they were making for the fundraiser was hard to argue against. But he wanted to hear how Rose felt. After all, she had insisted they pay for the wedding themselves. Would she really be okay with the town financing even a portion of it?

He leaned toward her. "What do you think about all this?"

"If you had asked me when Trudy first brought it up, I would have said 'absolutely not.'" She took a bite of her burger and tilted her head as she chewed, as if considering her next words. "I don't like to accept charity from people. But Trudy makes a lot of good points." Her eyes grew misty as she turned to him. "People love you, and they want to help. This seems like a good way to do that."

He nudged her. "They love you too. You nurse them back to health in some of their darker moments."

"True, but I'm not the prodigal son who returned after earning a law degree."

A laugh bubbled up in his throat. "I wouldn't go *that* far."

They finished the rest of the meal in silence, and Steven had to admit that the idea grew on him the more he thought about it. The fact that Rose was on board spoke volumes.

An idea formed in his head, but he kept it to himself. After all, there were no guarantees regarding how much money they would raise, and he wanted to make sure the funds went to their most pressing problems. But if there was a little left over, it wouldn't hurt to surprise his new bride.

"So, what do you think?" Lanie asked as Bea cleared their plates.

"Well, first things first." Steven gestured to Trudy.

Catching on immediately, Trudy waved Bea over to her side. "We have a proposition for you."

"Shoot," Bea said.

"How would you feel about us hosting a fundraiser in your diner later this month?"

"What's the fundraiser for?"

"Me," Steven said with an embarrassed smile.

Understanding dawned on Bea's face. "Nobody else deserves it more. Of course y'all can have it here. Just give me a date, and I'll be ready."

"How about July twenty-second?" Lanie suggested. "It's a little over two weeks away, which isn't a lot of time, but it's just over a month before the wedding."

Steven and Rose exchanged glances. Two weeks was no time at all to plan an event, but if they kept it simple, it might work.

"Let's do it," Rose said.

As the others set to work planning the event, Steven wrapped his arm around Rose, pulling her close. After everything they'd been through, he was ready for them to have a reprieve and some happiness.

Chapter Sixteen

LATER THAT AFTERNOON, ROSE HEADED INTO THE hospital to start her shift. She'd barely set her things down at the nurses' station when Rebecca came running up. A feeling of déjà vu washed over her on seeing the panic in Rebecca's eyes.

"What's wrong?" Rose demanded. "Is it Steven?"

"No, it's Mr. Patrones. He was brought in a moment ago and is in ICU."

"Mr. Patrones? B-But he was just released the other day!"

Rebecca nodded, her face grim. "Apparently, he didn't heed Dr. Myers's advice to take it easy. According to the neighbor who called it in, he was on a ladder, cleaning his gutters, when he suddenly fell."

"Another heart attack?" Rose covered her mouth with her hand.

"Looks like it." Shaking her head, Rebecca sighed. "I'm sorry to be the bearer of bad news as soon as you started your shift, but I know you were fond of him."

"Thank you for letting me know," Rose whispered.

"I've asked the ICU nurses to keep me posted on his progress. I'll tell you if I hear anything more." Rebecca patted her arm and walked away, leaving Rose alone with her thoughts.

Sinking into a chair, Rose struggled to draw breath. *It's not the same.* Mr. Patrones was an elderly man who had no business being on a ladder at all but especially not right after a heart attack. In contrast, Steven was still confined to a wheelchair. And he was following the doctors' orders. *Mostly.*

Rose closed her eyes. And there it was, her worst fear rearing its ugly head at the news of Mr. Patrones. The truth was, even if he couldn't climb ladders or clean gutters, Steven was still at greater risk of a second heart attack. And his insistence on returning to work the moment he'd left the rehab facility further jeopardized his health.

Images of Steven lying on the floor of his house, cold and unresponsive, came unbidden to Rose's mind. She squeezed her eyes tight, trying to block the thoughts.

Get control of yourself. She forced herself to take deep breaths, trying to calm the erratic beating of her heart. Steven was fine. At the diner, he'd even looked healthier. The circles under his eyes had faded, and he seemed in better spirits.

Shaking off her morose concerns, she stood and wiped her eyes. She could check on Mr. Patrones later. It was time to start her shift.

She began making her rounds, changing fluids, dispensing medications, and catching up on her patients. As she finished up with a new patient, she rounded the corner and almost collided with a wheelchair. She blinked as she met the familiar hazel eyes of her fiancé.

Her heart jumped into her throat. "Steven? What are you doing here?"

He grabbed her hand and pulled her down for an awkward hug. "I had an appointment with Dr. Myers and Dr. Bhati this afternoon. Didn't I tell you?"

Just an appointment. That's all. But she allowed her eyes to rove over him to reassure herself nothing was amiss.

"Rose? What's wrong? You look like you've seen a ghost."

Forcing a smile, she shook her head. "Nothing. I don't recall hearing about your appointment, and seeing you here scared me for a moment. How'd it go with the doctors?"

"Everything's looking good. Dr. Bhati said the spinal contusion has healed enough to where we can increase my physical therapy to help me start walking again."

She frowned. "Is he sure you're ready for that? You don't want to overdo it."

Steven rolled his eyes. "We can trust the good doctor, but you're welcome to interrogate him yourself if it'll make you feel better."

Heat rushed to her face. "That's not what I meant." She swallowed around the lump in her throat. "I'm worried about you. That's all."

He sighed. "I'm sorry. I shouldn't have said that. It's just... I was excited to share the news with you, and I had hoped for a better reaction."

"No, it's my fault." At his questioning look, she continued, "A patient of mine who was discharged the other day is back in the ICU. He had another... heart attack." Her voice broke on the last word.

Steven's expression morphed into one of sympathy and concern. "Oh, Rose, that's awful." His eyes softened. "No wonder you were so frightened when you saw me."

"I certainly wasn't expecting it." She cleared her throat. "Anyway, where are you going for PT?"

"Dr. Bhati gave me a referral for an outpatient physical therapist closer to home. I don't have to go to the rehab center anymore." He held out a small piece of paper.

After scanning the information, she laughed. "Oh, Ronnie. You're in for a world of hurt."

It was his turn to frown. "Why do you say that?"

"Let's just say she believes in getting people back on their feet as quickly as possible." More laughter bubbled up in her throat, and she pressed her lips together to hold it in.

"I'm not sure I like the sound of that. But I'll do whatever I have to if it means you'll smile like that more often."

His words melted her heart, and for a moment, she could pretend all was right in their world. She slipped her arms around his neck and gave him a quick kiss.

"Are you going on break soon?" he asked.

"Unfortunately, no. I only arrived an hour ago."

His face fell. "Ah, okay. What does your schedule look like this week? Maybe we could have a date night."

"I'm off Tuesday and Wednesday."

"Let's plan for Wednesday. I've got a few deadlines on Tuesday."

And just like that, her earlier fears came rushing back, but she swallowed them. After all, he'd gone into the office only a couple of days that week. *And he has Michael now.*

But she still couldn't shake the nightmarish image of Steven on the floor of his house. Bending down, she kissed his forehead so he couldn't see her face. "Wednesday sounds great for dinner. We can figure out the details later. I've got to get back to work." Without waiting for a response, she spun on her heel and rushed away from him.

After her rounds were done, she headed to the cafeteria to grab a cup of coffee. When she returned to the nurses' station, Dr. Myers was waiting for her.

"How's it going?" he asked.

"Everything's great." It took effort, but she was pleased with the cheery tone she'd infused in her voice. "I hear you had an appointment with Steven today."

A wariness flashed in his eyes, but when he blinked it was gone. "I did. I was surprised you weren't there."

A knot formed in her stomach, but she ignored it. "He forgot to tell me, but my shift was starting anyway."

"Mm-hmm," he murmured, his forehead creasing. "Did you want me to tell you what we discussed? He's granted you access to his medical records."

The knot tightened, and she fought with herself. On the one hand, it would be smart for her to be kept informed. But on the other hand, it would be difficult for her to review his medical record with the clinical detachment she'd honed over the years in order to be a good nurse. Her reaction to the news of Mr. Patrones clearly demonstrated she couldn't be impartial when it came to Steven.

The concerned side won over her better judgment, and she nodded. At the very least, it would put her mind at ease to double-check that Steven hadn't left anything out in his vague report on the appointment.

At her nod, Dr. Myers produced a thick file and handed it to her. "He's looking much better, but I'm concerned with the level of stress in his life. I suggested that he consider doing some yoga or meditation classes to help calm him when he's not working."

Her head shot up. "You approved him to return to work full-time?"

A smile tugged at one corner of Dr. Myers's mouth, though he appeared to be trying to suppress it. "I appreciate the vote of confidence, but you know your fiancé. Would my approval really alter the course he thinks is best for himself?"

Pressing her lips into a thin line, Rose returned her attention to the file. *Pigheaded, stubborn man.* Of course, Dr. Myers was right. Steven had argued against most of the medical advice he'd been provided thus far. Sometimes, she wondered if Steven gave much credence to career paths other than his own. *After all, wouldn't he be offended if a client went against his sound legal advice?*

"Look, while I would prefer him to take things a little more slowly, he's doing well considering everything he went through." Dr. Myers put a hand on her shoulder, and she was too shocked by the gesture to flinch. "He's following the diet I prescribed, and as long as he keeps an eye on his stress level, I don't see any reason he can't return to work."

"Thank you," she said, relenting. After all, it wasn't Dr. Myers's fault Steven was being stubborn. Rose laid that character trait entirely at Max McAllister's feet. In the nature-versus-nurture argument, the trademark McAllister stubbornness could be traced to both genetics *and* learned behavior.

"Happy to help." Dr. Myers stepped back. "And if you have any concerns, you can always come to me." That time, he didn't bother to suppress his grin. "Especially if Steven waves them away without fully addressing them."

She found herself smiling back. He might not have known Steven well, but he clearly knew his type.

When Dr. Myers had gone, she pushed aside the files she had pulled to update, then she opened Steven's. As the doctor had said, Steven was progressing at a decent rate. Still, his attitude toward his health hadn't changed, and the similarities between him and Mr. Patrones haunted her. All she could do was continue to keep an eye on him and pray that luck was on their side.

Chapter Seventeen

"I've got the Peterson motion ready to go," Michael said as he entered Steven's office without knocking.

Ignoring his first instinct to chastise the newest employee, Steven gestured for him to take a seat. At that moment, the important thing wasn't manners, it was meeting deadlines.

Sure enough, the document was sitting in Steven's email. He clicked to download it and started skimming through. The arguments were sound, and the case law Michael had found seemed appropriate. Steven frowned. Michael's citations could use some work, but that was something Sandra, their resident Blue Book expert, could handle.

"How's the Harris pleading coming?" he asked.

Michael sighed. "Not great. I'm having a hard time coming up with relevant case law. I've found some persuasive cases in other jurisdictions but nothing that sets precedent here."

Steven looked up from his computer. "Have you asked Sandra for help?"

"I have, and she's not had much luck either."

"Hmm." Steven rubbed his chin. "What do the persuasive cases say?"

After fumbling through the stack of papers he held, Michael set a pile on Steven's desk. "That the hospital's medical negligence doesn't preclude the state's liability since Mrs. Harris fell in their building."

"And there's no Maryland case law backing that up?"

"I mean, there are other slip-and-fall cases, but the facts are distinguishable from our case. For instance, in one case Sandra found, the victim of the slip-and-fall had worn inappropriate footwear, and the court found them comparatively negligent. In another, the company admitted they had just mopped the floor but argued they had put up appropriate signage that the victim ignored."

"That's frustrating." Steven ran a hand through his hair. They were running out of time to file the pleading, but he held out hope of finding some obscure case that aligned closely enough to theirs to bolster their argument. "Keep looking. And double-check the cases you've found. Maybe there's something in there that can help us persuade the jury."

"No problem, boss." Michael stood and left the room.

Once he was alone, Steven put his head in his hands. Going up against a government agency was starting to feel like a fool's errand, but he wanted to get justice for his client. Mrs. Harris was a sweet, grandmotherly type who had tripped on a rug at a state building and fallen down a flight of stairs. As if that wasn't bad enough, the hospital had somehow missed a fracture on her left shoulder, which had caused her pain for days. His firm had sued the hospital as well on her behalf, but since the initial incident had occurred at the state building, he'd had no choice but to go after them too.

Just thinking over the situation caused his heart to beat erratically. Taking a few slow, deep breaths helped, but if Rose walked in at that moment, she would likely murder him on the spot. *With good reason.* He knew he needed to take it easy, but a lot was weighing on him. Once the Harris pleading and the Peterson motion were filed, he promised himself, he would take an afternoon off to rest.

Steven turned back to the will he'd been working on. Sometimes being a small-town attorney wasn't all it was cracked up to be. It required a lot more work than he'd realized. He would get familiar with one set of statutes and regulations, find case law to back up his arguments, then pivot to learn something completely new for a different client.

But he wouldn't trade it for the world because the end reward was worth the sacrifice. Once he'd built his practice, he and Rose would be set for a comfortable life. She might even be able to quit nursing if she wanted, though he would leave that choice to her. Either way, she and their future children would be well cared for.

"Knock, knock," Lanie said from his door. The scent of fast food wafted into his office. "I come bearing sustenance."

"You didn't have to do that." He moved some of the folders from his desk to make space. "I planned to order in."

"In a way, you did." Her hazel eyes danced with amusement. "And don't worry, my delivery fee is reasonable."

He lifted an eyebrow. "Why do I have a feeling you're about to ask me for a favor?"

"Because you know me so well." She smiled. "But first, you need to fuel up if you have any hope of making headway on that document you're writing."

The delicious scent of fries grew as he removed the food from the bag. But Lanie took the burger and fries from him, replacing them with a much less appetizing salad. She handed him a small soda before slipping into the chair opposite him.

He took a sip and grimaced. "Diet? Really?"

"You can't expect me to spoil your well-regimented diet all the time." Her lips pushed out in an unconvincing pout. "Rose would have my head."

As much as he hated to admit it, she had a point. If he was honest, he would rather eat rabbit food than try to figure out how to reduce his stress level at work. Still, he hated diet soda and much preferred water or lemonade.

"You need the caffeine," Lanie said, reading his mind. "I can't justify a coffee this late in the afternoon, but a soda is doable."

"Are you sticking around?"

She nodded. "I figured you could use some help with the research."

The tomato he'd taken a bite of turned to ash in his mouth. "I'm not sure you'll have more luck than Sandra or Michael. They've hit a dead end."

"Ah, ye of little faith."

He eyed her over his food. "What do you have in mind?"

Instead of responding, she gave him a mysterious smile as she popped a fry into her mouth. He hoped whatever she had up her sleeve would help him, though he doubted it would be enough.

After they finished their meal, Lanie gathered the wrappers and empty containers and tossed them into the bin. Since she didn't have an office, she set up her computer on the other side of Steven's desk. He considered telling her to go to the conference room but found her presence oddly comforting. It meant a lot that she was willing to devote her summer vacation to helping him.

"So, what's the favor?" he asked, figuring he'd better get that conversation over with or he would never be able to concentrate.

At first, she didn't respond, and he wondered whether she'd heard him. He was about to ask her again when she looked up from her computer.

"Nate and I are starting to work with vendors, and some of them have sent contracts. Between Mom's estate and helping here, I've taken a crash course in learning the law, but I'm still not quite up to speed on the legal lingo." She took a deep breath. "So I was hoping you'd take a look."

"Of course I'll review your contracts." He gestured to her computer. "You've been a huge help the last few weeks. It is, quite literally, the least I can do."

"Thanks," she said, visibly relaxing.

He cocked his head. "Why would you think I wouldn't do it?"

"It's not that I think you wouldn't. It's more I was afraid you couldn't." She waved a hand around his office. "With everything going on, I didn't want to add to your stress load."

He scoffed. "Of all the things that I'm juggling, contract review is probably the easiest to accomplish." Leaning back in his chair, he smirked. "Though it's probably the most boring aspect of law."

"Hopefully they won't put you to sleep." She started typing again on her computer. "I can bring the contracts over this evening, if that's okay."

"Sure, whenever you're ready. It shouldn't take me long to look over everything and share any concerns, but in my experience, wedding vendors have rather generic contracts just to cover their butts."

"That's good."

"So..." he began. "Does that mean you've picked a date?"

"We have." She kept her eyes on the screen, as if she thought that by not looking at him, he would drop the subject. Surely she knew him better than that.

"And?"

She sighed. "We're planning for November fourth."

He nodded then froze. "Wait..." It was like someone had kicked him in the stomach. "You're getting married on Mom's *birthday*?"

Her teeth worried her lower lip as she gave a stiff nod. "We want to get married in the fall, when there are still leaves on the trees. But October was too soon, and—"

"That's insane," he said, heat rising in his chest. Raking his fingers through his hair, he moved from behind his desk. "And you didn't think to discuss this with me before you made a decision?"

Her eyes widened. "I thought it might be nice to have another reason to celebrate that day."

For a moment, they stared at each other. He opened and closed his mouth as a million thoughts raced through his mind. Last year, he'd visited their mother's grave alone to mark the day. Lanie was in Seattle, finishing school, and Dad had refused to join him. Rose had come to see him after her shift. She'd asked him to wait for her before visiting the cemetery, but part of him had preferred to visit his mother alone.

It had been one of the hardest days since he'd lost her. As they approached July, another hard day was arriving soon—the first anniversary of her death. Lanie's timing in telling him the date she'd chosen couldn't have been worse.

"Find another day," he spat out through clenched teeth.

Her mouth fell open. "What?"

"Choose any day, any other day but that one." He pushed his chair around his desk and glared at her. "I will literally help you find a venue and vendors who can accommodate an October date, if you're insistent on having it fall themed, but choose a different day."

She stared at him. "Why are you being like this?"

He wheeled his chair back and forth, refusing to meet her eyes. "Do you have any idea what the last year was like for me? You were on the other side of the country, barely answering my calls, and Dad was too afraid of his own grief to even share the burden with me. The only one who was here for me that day was Rose, and she had to work for most of it."

"But don't you see?" She closed her laptop and stood. "This year will be different. And instead of being sad, we can celebrate, together."

"No." His tone was harsh, but he no longer cared.

Her eyes filled with tears, and before he could say anything, she grabbed her things and rushed from the room. The anger that had welled up in him dissipated.

"Wait, Lanie. You don't have to—"

But she didn't stop or turn to hear what he had to say. Instead, she ran through the lobby and out the front door, leaving Leslie staring after her.

A lump formed in his throat. He wanted to go after her, but he would never catch her in his chair. Besides, what would he say? He might have been harsh, but he believed she needed to hear it.

How could she think I'd be okay with the idea of making our mother's birthday into anything else? Doesn't she understand that there are two days that will always be dark for me, for both of us?

The one saving grace was that even November was probably too soon to plan a wedding. Maybe he could convince her to wait until next autumn. Their mother's birthday wouldn't fall on a weekend, and he could live with his sister getting married a day or two before it so long as the day itself remained sacred.

~

It took effort, but Steven pushed the scene with Lanie from his mind. He finished filling in the template for the will he was working on, adding the various items the client wished to bequeath. Mr. Rochester had quite the estate, and Steven couldn't help wondering why his client had left it all to chance for so long. The man had to be pushing eighty, and most of Steven's estate clients began the planning in their forties.

Perhaps Mr. Rochester thought he would be the exception to other humans and could beat death. Maybe he saw himself as some Dorian Gray character. *Though if that's the case, what caused him to finally take care of it now?* Steven didn't know, but he was glad for the business.

He saved his changes and closed the file. Mr. Rochester wasn't expecting an updated version for a few days, and Steven liked to let the draft marinate before he went in to edit and finalize it. But it probably wouldn't take many more iterations. During their meetings, Mr. Rochester had been very specific about what he wanted. His questionnaire response was the only one Steven had had to alter because it went over the maximum character count.

With a sigh, Steven stretched before making his way to Michael's office. That neither Michael nor Sandra had interrupted him that afternoon had caught him off guard. When he entered the lobby, he heard whispers coming from Sandra's room.

“Is everything all right in here?” he asked, not bothering to knock.

Sandra and Michael exchanged glances, and Steven crossed his arms. His gaze vacillated between the two.

“Lanie had a breakthrough in the research,” Michael said.

Sandra shot Steven a look. Clearly, she was aware of his fight with his sister. He would deal with that later.

“That’s good news,” Steven replied, waiting for them to elaborate. “Isn’t it?”

“It is.” Michael turned the screen of Sandra’s computer and pointed. “I mean, it’s an old case, but we couldn’t find anything that supersedes it.”

Steven nodded. “More recent is always preferable, but I’ll take what I can get. What are the facts?”

Michael summarized the case, and Steven smiled at how closely it resembled the Harris case. The incident at the center of the lawsuit had occurred at a government building. A coffee had spilled at a stand near a staircase. While the spill had been mopped up, the janitor failed to put up a sign. The victim had slipped on the wet spot and tumbled down the stairs.

“I had actually seen this case myself,” Michael admitted. “But since the victim was an employee and not a member of the public, I thought it was distinguishable. However, the attorneys representing the plaintiff took multiple approaches to ensure victory. They went after workman’s comp but also pointed out the danger to the public, including the testimony of a witness.”

“What did the witness say that was so interesting?” Steven asked.

Sandra’s eyes lit up. “It’s not what they said but what happened to them.”

He frowned, squinting at the screen. “I’m not sure I understand.”

Sandra scrolled down and pointed. “The witness was almost a victim too. They slipped on the same area but managed to avoid a similar fate by grabbing onto the handrail before they tumbled.”

"And the witness wasn't an employee," Michael added.

"Interesting." Steven studied the screen. "Send this to me. I'd like to take a closer look, but in the meantime, feel free to start plugging in the relevant facts to your pleading."

"Sure thing, boss." Michael gathered his papers and headed to his office, though he stopped at the door. "I'll get the pleading to you ASAP as well."

"Sounds good, thanks."

Once they were alone, Sandra leaned back in her chair with a frown. "I heard your argument with Lanie."

He bristled. "I don't want to discuss it."

"So you don't want me to tell you I agree with you?"

That caught his attention, and he raised his eyebrows. "You do?"

She sighed. "Your sister means well, but she's not thinking this through. It's like putting a Band-Aid on a bullet wound. She's trying to change the entire meaning of the day, but it's not going to cover the significance to all of you, herself included."

"Should I try to talk her out of it?"

She snorted. "Not if you're going to scream at her, no. But maybe allow someone with a softer hand, someone who has reached Lanie before when no one else could."

Steven scrunched up his face. "You mean Nate?"

Sandra stared at the ceiling in the way she always did when he was being especially obtuse. "I'm referring to Rose."

Right. "I'll talk to her, but she's got a lot on her mind right now."

"With the wedding?"

"And the fundraiser."

Sandra's eyebrows shot up. "A fundraiser? For what?"

Steven ran a hand through his hair and dropped his gaze. "Um, me? Well, and the wedding. I was supposed to help Rose pay off the final balances to our vendors, but after all the work I missed while I was in the hospital, my finances are dismal at best."

Sandra stood and crossed the room before laying a hand on his arm. "You should have told me. I'd do anything to help the two of you."

"I know," he mumbled, shifting away. "But it's embarrassing."

Her head tilted. "Because of the money?"

"I should be able to support us on my own, but failing that, I should at the very least be able to pay for a wedding."

"Hey." Sandra squatted so they were at eye level. "You've been through a lot. And I can only imagine how the medical bills are piling up. It's okay to ask for help." She smiled. "I planned to pay for my own wedding, but we ended up accepting some assistance from my family. They thought it was the least they could do since both my parents died."

Steven gave a weak smile. "Thanks, Sandra. That means a lot."

"So, this fundraiser..." She raised an eyebrow. "When is it?"

He shrugged. "July twenty-second. Lanie and Trudy are planning it. Er... Lanie was. I'm not sure if she'll do it now."

"She'll do it. And I'll help her."

"You don't have to—"

Sandra held up a hand. "I want to." Leaning against the wall, she peered out the door toward his office. "Did you finish the will?"

He nodded. "I want to go through it again before I send this version to Mr. Rochester, but I've included his latest additions."

"That man has more money than God."

Steven laughed. "Or at least, more money than he knows what to do with."

Her eyes took on a mischievous gleam. "Make sure you send him the latest version before the fundraiser."

His eyebrows pulled together. "Why?"

"Because he'll probably be a lot more eager to donate if you've finished the job he hired you to do."

Chapter Eighteen

"He's being unreasonable," Lanie declared as she sank into the booth across from Rose at Bea's Diner. After shoving her bag into the corner of the bench, she began violently flipping through the jukebox by the wall.

"Who is?" Rose set down her menu and took in her future sister-in-law's uncharacteristically disheveled appearance. Her dirty-blond hair was pulled up into a messy bun, and her cheeks were blotchy, as if she'd been crying.

"Steven." Lanie said it like an expletive instead of a name. "I asked him if he would help me with vendor contracts for my wedding."

"He said no?" Rose couldn't help the incredulity in her voice. Though Steven had a lot going on, she couldn't imagine he wouldn't help his sister.

Waving a hand, Lanie shook her head. "No, he was fine with that. But he asked if we'd finally chosen a wedding date, and as soon as I told him the day we picked, he went ballistic."

That didn't sound like Steven at all. Rose put her hand on Lanie's to stop her frantic search for a song and to keep her from breaking the mini jukebox. With a sigh, Lanie sat back and crossed her arms.

"When's the big day?" Rose asked.

Lanie dropped her gaze and fidgeted with a string on her shirt. Her actions didn't make any sense to Rose. Lanie and Nate had discussed several dates, and Rose expected her to be excited to share the one they'd settled on. But Lanie seemed hesitant, almost guilty.

"Lanie?"

Finally, Lanie met Rose's gaze and squared her shoulders. "November fourth."

After racking her brain to determine why Steven would have objected to the date, a cold chill slid up Rose's spine. There was no way Lanie had chosen her mother's *birthday* to get married.

She was going to have to tread lightly. If Steven had already blown up at her, Lanie wasn't likely to take kindly to Rose tearing into her as well. But somehow, Rose had to make her see reason. Steven had been inconsolable last year on Melody's birthday, and Rose couldn't bear the thought of him forcing smiles and faking joy just to appease his sister.

"Why that day?" Perhaps if Rose asked enough questions, she could lead Lanie to understand not only why her brother had reacted negatively to her news but also why the date was a terrible idea.

"It used to be such a happy day for us, celebrating Mom. So I thought it would be a nice way to honor her memory and give another reason to celebrate the day instead of mourning her loss."

While Rose appreciated the sentiment, she wondered whether Lanie had thought the idea through. It wasn't easy to replace one memory with another. No matter how much she tried to paper over her grief with balloons and décor, the reality of who wasn't at the wedding would lurk in the shadows and pounce when Lanie expected to be happiest.

"How did you spend your mother's birthday last year?"

Lanie set her elbow on the table and, frowning, leaned her cheek against her hand. Then her face cleared as the memory seemed to finally come to her.

"I spent the day researching a specific area of my thesis." She bit her lip. "And trying to forget the significance of the day."

Rose nodded. "And do you think by throwing yourself into planning your wedding and celebrating with everyone you love, you'll be able to forget who *isn't* there to share in your joy?"

Lanie scowled. "I'm not trying to forget her. I thought it would be a better way to remember her."

"I believe your heart was in the right place," Rose said gently. "But have you considered Steven's point of view?"

"It's hard to get my head so far up my own backside."

Rose laughed. "Fair point." She cleared her throat. "I'm sorry Steven was hostile. He shouldn't have yelled at you."

"But?" Lanie raised an eyebrow.

"You can't get married on your mother's birthday." Rose blew out her breath. "At least, not if you want to maintain a good relationship with your brother."

"Maybe I don't," Lanie muttered.

"I don't believe that for a second."

"Fine." Lanie unrolled her silverware. "To be fair, Nate wasn't too keen on the idea either, but he was willing to go along with it if it made me happy."

"Smart man."

"But now I guess it's back to the drawing board."

"Do you have any other dates in mind?"

Lanie pursed her lips. "I thought about Christmas, but I'm not sure that will be received any better by Steven."

Tilting her head, Rose frowned. "Why would he object to Christmas?"

"I don't know. It's a family holiday, and it's kind of cliché."

The server came over and took their orders. Since it was late afternoon, neither of them wanted a full meal. Instead, they split a few appetizers.

Once they were alone again, Rose clasped her hands on the table. "If Nate is on board and you can plan it in time, Christmas is a great day for a wedding. And I'm sure Steven would agree." *At the very least, he'll be more amenable to Christmas than his late mother's birthday.*

Lanie's face broke into a smile. "I'll discuss it with Nate, but I appreciate your support."

"Anytime."

"Now"—Lanie removed a laptop from her bag—"we should probably discuss the fundraiser."

The next evening, Rose stood outside The Muddy Oar, patiently waiting for Max to drop Steven off. Something about their new normal reminded her of being a freshman in high school. Steven's dad playing chauffeur necessitated a curfew they hadn't had previously. While she missed the freedoms they'd enjoyed before Steven's accident, she had to admit the changes made their time together all the more precious.

As Max maneuvered Steven's wheelchair through the parking lot, her fiancé gave an embarrassed wave. The restrictions were taking their toll on him.

"I'll be back in two hours to pick him up," Max said after pushing the wheelchair up on the sidewalk. "The aides will be coming to help him into bed around eight."

"She knows, Dad," Steven said, the irritability clear in his tone.

"Good luck," Max muttered under his breath as he brushed by Rose.

"I heard that," Steven grumbled.

Stifling a sigh, Rose grasped the wheelchair handles and steered Steven into the restaurant. The dining area was mostly empty, though it was rather early for dinner.

"Table for two, please," Rose told the host standing at the podium. He had dark hair and didn't look a day over sixteen.

With a nod, he led them to a table near the back corner. The host removed one of the chairs, and Rose angled the wheelchair into the empty spot. She took the seat across from Steven and accepted a menu.

"Your server will be with you shortly," the host said before returning to his post.

"How was work today?" Rose asked as she opened her menu.

"Not bad. Thanks to Michael, I'm at least meeting deadlines again. Though that may change in a couple of weeks."

"Why do you say that?"

Steven's eyebrows drew together. "He's taking the bar exam at the end of the month."

"But that's good, isn't it?" Rose asked. "He'll be able to do more when he passes."

"He won't have the results until October." Steven sighed. "That won't stop the offers from pouring in, though."

"He's committed to staying the summer, isn't he?"

Shaking his head, Steven set his menu aside. "That's what I advertised for, but we didn't sign any sort of employment contract. He's free to leave sooner if he finds something more permanent."

Then offer him something more permanent. Rose bit her tongue to keep from saying that out loud. They hadn't had a nice evening together in a while, and she didn't want to start a fight.

"Has he said anything about wanting to leave?"

"No, but that doesn't mean he won't."

Worrying her lower lip, Rose raised her menu to hide her face. He was starting to sound eerily like Mr. Patrones. It was making her uncomfortable.

"Anyway, how are things with you? I hear you had lunch with Lanie yesterday."

"Not really lunch, but we met at Bea's to discuss the fundraiser."

"Did she tell you she picked a wedding date?" he asked darkly.

Rose lowered her menu and met his gaze. "She did, and I successfully talked her out of it."

That perked him up. "You did? How'd you manage that?"

"For starters, I didn't blow up at her." She gave him a meaningful look.

"I know." He scrubbed a hand over his face. "I need to apologize to her. She caught me off guard. I mean, Mom's birthday? Really?"

"Although she was misguided, her heart was in the right place." Rose debated briefly whether to tell him the new date Lanie had proposed. Perhaps if she did, he would react better when Lanie told him herself. "She's considering Christmas now."

He rubbed his chin. "That's better, though a bit overdone." He groaned. "And so soon? Why is she in such a rush?"

Rose shrugged. "She and Nate lost so much time after what happened between them, I suppose they don't want to waste another minute."

"I guess." He didn't sound convinced. "Enough about my sister. How's work?"

"The board has scheduled a meeting on August first to discuss the head nurse position."

His eyes widened. "Oh? Do you think they'll offer it to you?"

"It's too soon to say, but Dr. Myers thinks it's likely."

"Wow, that would be quite the wedding present."

Her jaw clenched. *It's not a "present." I worked hard for this promotion.* Breathing in through her nose and out through her mouth, she shook her head. *Don't overreact. I'm sure he didn't mean it that way.*

She was saved from needing to respond by the arrival of the server. Steven gestured for her to go first.

"I'll have the Chicken Chesapeake with a salad," Rose said.

The server nodded and took her menu. "And for you, sir?"

"I'll have a New York strip."

He can't be serious. She stared at him, but he didn't meet her gaze. Her heart thumped in her chest as she willed the server to leave.

"What are you doing?"

Finally, he looked at her and smiled. "Having a lovely meal with my future wife."

"You know what I mean."

With an exasperated sigh, he gestured to the restaurant. "We're in a steakhouse, Rose. What did you think I was going to order?" He took a sip of water. "Besides, I haven't had any red meat since the accident. Dr. Myers said I had to *limit* how much I ate, but he didn't say I couldn't have any."

As much as she hated to admit it, he had a point. Still, it was risky. Especially since he was still in the wheelchair and had limited mobility. It would be better for his heart if he avoided certain foods until he could exercise regularly again.

Once more, they were treading toward dangerous territory. Rose decided to change the subject. "Lanie and I had a good conversation about the fundraiser, though she's going to run our ideas past Trudy before she makes any final decisions."

He leaned forward and took her hand. "I'm glad you're open to the idea. I know how much you hate relying on other people for help."

"It's not about me, it's about us. And we'd do the same for anyone else in Cedar Haven if the situation were reversed."

"Very true." He smiled and squeezed her hand. "Have I mentioned how excited I am to marry you?"

"Not lately," she teased, unable to stop the grin that spread over her face. The tension in her shoulders eased. She'd missed that, how easy things used to be between them.

"Well, I'd tell you my heart skips a beat every time I think about it, but I'd be afraid you'd haul me back to Dr. Myers for another round of testing."

Rose giggled, and a weight lifted as she fell into their familiar banter. "I'll have him do a full workup the day before our wedding just to be sure. Wouldn't want you to faint when you see my dress."

His eyes darkened. "I'm looking forward to seeing you in it... and out of it."

Warmth rushed to her cheeks. "Steven!"

Before he could respond, the server returned with their food. The sight of the steak made her feel like a bucket of cold water had been dumped over her, but she pushed her concerns away. She refused to let them overshadow the evening.

"So, how is physical therapy going now that your cast is off?"

Steven shrugged. "I wouldn't know. I haven't had a session without it yet." He cut a piece of steak and popped it into his mouth, closing his eyes. "Mm, this is delicious. Do you want a bite?"

And just like that, the cold water of reality washed over her again. "No, thank you." Her appetite had disappeared as she struggled to rein in the emotional rollercoaster she'd unwittingly stumbled on. "What do you mean you haven't had a session yet? You were cleared to begin more intensive therapy a few days ago."

"Things have been busy at the office, and I hadn't had time to make an appointment."

Don't make a scene. But the harder she tried to salvage their date, the worse she felt. Her feet ached from tiptoeing around the shattered glass of sore subjects for someone who refused to acknowledge that anything was broken.

He seemed to realize she'd stopped eating and set down his fork and knife. "Rose? What's wrong?"

"I'm worried you're still not taking your health seriously."

His worried expression gave way to a scowl. "I'm not having this argument again."

"It's not an argument," she protested. "It's genuine concern." Without thinking, she gestured to his wheelchair. "I thought you wanted to walk again as soon as you could."

His eyes flashed with anger. "Of *course* I want to walk again. Do you think I enjoy being stuck in this thing? That it's fun to have my dad chauffeur me to dates with my fiancée? To not know if I'm going to be able to walk with her down the aisle on our wedding day?"

She stared at him. "I don't care if you walk, roll, or crawl down the aisle, as long as we're together."

"Well, it matters to me." He waved his hand toward his back. "However, as I've yet to regain feeling in my legs, I can't imagine a few days is going to make any difference in my recovery."

Her clinical training clicked in. "It's about muscle memory—"

"I *know*!"

His raised voice caused something in Rose to snap. "Don't talk to me that way." She took a deep breath to try to calm herself. "Look, I'm sorry if it sounds like I'm nagging you. I *care* about you, and I want you to get better. I want *us* to get better." Tears welled in her eyes, and she furiously blinked them back.

That seemed to sober him. He bowed his head. "I know you do. I'm sorry."

She swallowed around the lump in her throat. *How did we get here?* It seemed only yesterday that their biggest problem was Steven's overworked schedule. In a moment, everything had changed.

With a sigh, he pushed away from the table and maneuvered his chair next to her. "I really am sorry. And I promise I'll try harder to follow the doctors' advice."

How many more times is he going to make that promise? But she didn't feel angry at his empty words. She felt hollow, like the fight had gone out of her.

"This isn't easy for me either. I may not be the one in the wheelchair, but that doesn't mean I'm not having a hard time with this too."

He nodded. "And I appreciate you sticking it out with me." A wry smile stole over his face. "Even when I'm being an insensitive jerk."

"Isn't that all the time?" she joked. While Steven laughed, the words had a ring of truth. Part of her wished she could chalk up his recent poor behavior to the accident, but the fact was, he'd been ignoring her pleas to take better care of himself for months.

After kissing her cheek, he made his way around the table and gestured to her food. "Let's eat before it gets cold."

Rose picked up her fork and knife and took a bite of her chicken, but the food, like her heart, had already cooled.

~

When Rose arrived at her condo, she didn't immediately go inside. Though the sun was low in the sky, it hadn't set, and the evening air hung heavy with warm humidity. Instead, she walked to the pond. She hadn't been by to check on the swans since the injured one had been transported to the wildlife rehab center. But as she neared the water's edge, only one swan remained.

The same man she had spoken to that first day with the swans was standing on the shoreline, watching the lone swan swimming in circles. When he heard her approach, he looked up with a grin.

"Coming back to check on them, are you?" He nodded. "My friend said the male is healing well and should be returned in the next few weeks." Inclining his head toward the female, he continued, "She'll be happy to have him home, I'm sure."

"Does she know he's still alive?" Rose asked.

"I imagine so," the man replied. "She's not gone into mourning."

That caught her off guard. She frowned. "What does a swan in mourning look like?"

"They often don't leave their nest, and I've seen females put their heads under their wings, almost as if they're covering their face while they cry."

I understand how she feels. "I hope she doesn't give up hope," Rose said, her heart going out to the swan. "It must get lonely with no other swans around."

"Oh, she's not alone. You can see her cygnets if you look closely." He pointed at a few small gray blobs in the water.

They were difficult to make out at that distance and with the muddy color of the pond. But when Rose squinted, she could discern three tiny fluffy feathered bodies gliding after the larger swan.

"Aw, they're adorable!"

"Best keep your distance, though. Swans are very protective of their young." He glanced at her. "If you want, I can give you a heads-up when the male is set to return."

Rose nodded. "I would like that very much. Thank you."

After waving goodbye, she headed to her condo, but her thoughts remained with the swans. She couldn't help seeing the parallel between her situation and theirs. Part of her envied the female swan's faith that her male companion was alive and well and would someday return. In contrast, Rose had multiple ways to reach Steven, but no matter how hard she tried, the two of them couldn't seem to connect.

Chapter Nineteen

A few days later, Steven entered his office with renewed hope that he would soon be able to ditch his wheelchair. He had an appointment that afternoon for physical therapy, and he planned to ask when he might expect to graduate to a walker. Though his spine had healed considerably, he still wasn't able to do more than stand for short periods of time with most of his weight resting on his forearms and hands.

Focusing on his physical limitations was easier than letting his mind replay the conversation with Rose the night before. He wasn't being fair, but he also felt she wasn't either. Of course he understood she was going through this with him. Yet he wasn't sure she fully grasped the toll the accident and subsequent recovery had taken on him. Sometimes he procrastinated on scheduling his medical appointments so he could pretend, even for a moment, that everything was normal.

Pushing the thoughts from his mind, he opened his email, and a calendar notification popped up. Michael was out that morning to study for the bar exam. Steven's stomach flip-flopped. While he and Michael hadn't discussed what would happen if Michael passed the bar, Steven had seriously considered offering Michael a more permanent position. But once he passed the bar, he might not be interested in sticking around.

The results wouldn't be released until autumn. Hopefully, Steven had a couple of months to figure that out. He took comfort in knowing Michael had been instrumental in assisting with keeping the lights on.

A few hours later, the front door to the office opened, and pealing laughter filled the silence. Steven glanced at the time, rubbed his eyes, and stretched. Finally, he was through making the last edits to the will, and it was ready to sign. After maneuvering to his office door, he stood and leaned against the doorframe for balance.

"Sandra? That you?"

She came out of her office, and her eyes widened. "What are you doing, standing there like that? You're liable to fall!"

He shifted his back against the wall, though his legs were already shaking. "I've finished the will for Mr. Rochester. Can you set up an appointment?"

"After you sit your butt back in a chair." She rushed over and grabbed his arm before she helped ease him into the wheelchair.

"I can't wait for the day I'll walk again," he said with a sigh.

"You're making good progress, but you've got to be patient. Spine injuries don't heal overnight."

"I know." He leaned his head back against his chair and glared at the ceiling. "But it's frustrating. And I don't want to roll my way down the aisle on my wedding day. I want to stand on my own two feet, head held high." He shook his head. "It's supposed to be the best day of my life."

"I get it. Sometimes life happens in a way we don't expect or want it to. But you have to roll with the punches." Her lips twitched. "No pun intended."

He frowned, not finding her joke as amusing as she did. "Anyway, we're down a staff member today. Michael is at a study group to prepare for the bar."

"Oh, that's right!" Sandra exclaimed. "I'll keep my fingers and toes crossed for him, but I doubt he'll need it." She played with a piece of string on her shirt. "What are we going to do if he passes?"

Swallowing his concerns, he gave what he hoped was a nonchalant shrug. "It's still early summer. We have some time to figure it out."

"Assuming he doesn't find something sooner." Crossing her arms, Sandra released a long sigh. "He's been doing good work. I bet if you offered him something, he'd consider it."

"I can't compete with the DC law firms. He'd make three times what I could offer him."

"Maybe if you take the initiative and make an offer now, he won't consider going back. Or what if you made him a partner?" She sat in one of the chairs across from him. "He might be willing to give up the salary in exchange for an equal part of the firm."

His stomach hardened, but he fought to keep his expression neutral. "The firm isn't ready for that. I need more time to build up the clientele." What he didn't say was he needed to recoup what he had spent to start the business.

But Sandra read his mind anyway. "Look, you're in over your head, but—"

"The answer is no," Steven barked, and he immediately regretted it when Sandra's eyes widened.

"Suit yourself." Her tone had lost its friendliness, and she marched out of his office.

Great. First, he'd hurt Rose, and then he'd upset his best employee. If he wasn't careful, Sandra would be on Michael's heels as he ran out the door. And that would really put Steven in a bind.

~

Around lunchtime, Lanie popped her head in. "I'm here to take you to your physical therapy appointment."

Steven finished what he was typing and hit save before he glanced up and forced a smile. "Yay."

"I know you hate it, but it's good for you."

"Yeah, yeah." He pushed back from the desk and gestured to his chair. "I suppose if it'll get me out of this stupid thing, it's worth it." Without waiting for her response, he maneuvered his chair from behind his desk and out of his office.

"I talked to Rose," Lanie said as she pushed him through the front and headed for the van. "Sounds like you two had another argument because you aren't taking your health seriously."

"Don't start."

"I'm not." After locking his wheelchair into place in the van, she buckled him in. "I'm worried about you two. Maybe you should consider couples counseling or therapy."

"I'm already in enough therapy," he muttered.

Lanie snorted and shut the door. When she climbed into the driver's seat, she shot him a look in the rearview. For a moment, he couldn't breathe. She looked like their mother when she did that, and his heart ached. The first anniversary of her death was coming up fast, and he wasn't ready to face the reality that she had been gone a year.

He closed his eyes, willing his thoughts in another direction. Unfortunately, they turned to Rose. She hadn't said it, but the look in her eyes had told him she hadn't believed him when he'd promised to try harder to take care of himself. Their goodbye had been lukewarm at best, and though he had no real reason to doubt her, his gut told him something had changed between them.

With a sigh, Steven turned away from the window. "Sometimes I've wondered if Rose pushed to postpone the wedding not for my health but because she had an ulterior motive."

When his sister met his gaze in the rearview with a quizzical frown, he tried to think of a better way to word it. For once, the tightening in his chest had nothing to do with his heart attack and everything to do with his jumbled-up emotions.

"I knew after our first date Rose was the one for me. The only reason I waited to propose was because we both wanted to finish our degrees. And then we wanted to establish ourselves in our respective careers." He turned to the window as they passed Bea's Diner. "But I sort of blew that up when I got it in my head to move back here and open my own practice. Rose was doing well in Baltimore, and she'd received a job offer for a position in Boston."

"And now you're afraid she regrets that decision?"

A weight fell off his shoulders. "Yes, exactly. And my biggest fear, the one I can barely bear to think, let alone say out loud"—his voice lowered—"is that if we had put it off any longer, she'd wise up and leave me."

"Oh, Steven." Lanie shook her head as she turned off Main Street and headed toward the parking lot of a large building. "Rose loves you. She may not have promised 'for better or worse' yet, but she meant it all the same when she accepted your proposal."

"I wish I could believe that." When Lanie opened her mouth as if to protest, he hurried on. "Wait, let me finish." He took a deep breath. "Just... look at me. I'm not even thirty years old, and I can't walk, I—"

"But you've made progress in such a short amount of time!" After pulling up to the entrance of the building, she put the van in park then turned and looked at him. "You *will* walk again. You *will* have a beautiful, wonderful, *long* life with Rose."

Tears pricked behind his eyelids, and he blinked rapidly to keep them from falling. "Thanks, sis. That means a lot." He nodded at the clock on the dash. "We'd better go, or I'll be late for my torture appointment."

She laughed. "There's that sense of humor I know and love."

Lanie might have taken his statement as a joke, but Steven had meant it as anything but. No matter how much he tried to convince himself that physical therapy was necessary to reclaim his life and walk again, nothing would ease the sense of dread that grew within him the closer they got to the building. From everything he had heard, Ronnie, his physical therapist, sounded like a sadist. And he expected she would work him until tears literally poured down his cheeks before pushing him some more.

"Ah, my next victim," said a woman with spiky blue hair and a row of earrings climbing each ear. She rubbed her hands together. "I'm Ronnie, and you must be Steven."

Great first impression. Steven shot a pleading glance at Lanie, who shrugged helplessly. When he turned to look at Ronnie, she had a hand on her hip and a smirk on her face.

"Nothing like the smell of fresh fear to start a new session," Ronnie said with a laugh. She smiled at Lanie. "I'll take him from here."

"Good luck," Lanie whispered. After giving him a quick hug, she rushed out to the van. Steven watched her leave, wishing he could follow.

"Come on. It's just an hour." Ronnie steered him into the makeshift gym and over to a bed. "We're going to start you off with some transitions and go from there."

"Transitions?" Steven asked.

She moved in front of him. "You're going to move yourself from the chair to the bed and back again."

"But I'm barely able to stand!"

Instead of responding, she continued, "Watch me first. I'll show you how to support your weight on your arms until your legs are strong enough to hold you." She grabbed a chair and demonstrated using the bars by the bed to pull herself up, then she shuffled to the bed before extending one hand to the bedrail and hoisting herself onto it.

Steven raised an eyebrow. She made it look deceptively easy, but she had full control of her extremities.

With a grimace, Steven gripped the arms of his wheelchair and pushed himself to standing. He grasped the bar and held onto it for dear life as he tried to shuffle his feet. They moved incrementally toward the bed, but it took way more effort than he was expecting.

"That's it. Slow and steady."

He shot her a glare and took another precarious step forward. His leg shook with the effort as he dragged his opposite foot behind him. The weight of the boot on his leg served only to further slow his progress. After what felt like an eternity, he finally made his way to the edge of the bed. He grabbed the bedrail, turned his body, and lifted himself onto the bed with his arms.

"Good, though you need to pick up that back foot more, or else you're going to trip yourself."

"Tell that to my foot," Steven retorted. "It doesn't obey my commands."

She pursed her lips. "It doesn't hear them."

He scowled as he bent down and lifted his legs one by one onto the bed. Once he was securely in the middle, he lay down and stared at the ceiling, struggling to catch his breath.

"Now that you're here, I'm going to have you do some leg exercises."

Steven relaxed, but his sense of accomplishment was short-lived because Ronnie began a series of exercises that worked every muscle in his body. By the time they were done, he was panting.

It had been only fifteen minutes. He still had forty-five to go. *This is ridiculous. I've never been this out of shape in my life.*

"All right. Time to move back to the chair." Once again, Ronnie demonstrated how to transition from the bed to the chair.

His muscles screamed as he lifted himself off the bed and shuffled to the chair. But it took less time than it had to get on the bed, and when he eased into his chair, Ronnie smiled at him.

"Since you're doing so well, I thought you might like to have a bit of fun. What do you say?" Ronnie leaned against the bed.

What could possibly be fun about physical therapy? But he decided to humor her. "What do you have in mind?"

She wriggled her eyebrows. "What do you say we play a round of wheelchair basketball? It'll give you a chance to work your upper body without worrying about your legs."

He snorted. "You know, my grandfather used to be obsessed with me playing basketball because of my height."

She grinned. "But it wasn't for you?"

"I mean, I wasn't against it, but I wasn't really into it either. But I'll try anything at this point."

Her face fell, but she shook it off. "Not quite the spirit I was looking for, but I'll take it."

Without another word, she pushed him out of the room and down a hallway. They entered a gym that reminded him of middle school PE.

To Steven's surprise, the court was filled with other people in wheelchairs. "I thought this was going to be just you and me, one on one."

"What kind of challenge would that be?"

He swallowed, suddenly self-conscious, though he couldn't explain why. Every single person on that court except for the physical therapist was in the same situation as him. They might have arrived there because of different circumstances—Steven noted a few guys with missing limbs—but they would understand what he was going through. Then he realized the real reason Ronnie had brought him out there: to show him that he wasn't alone.

A few days later, Lanie picked Steven up from yet another physical therapy appointment. His muscles ached but nowhere near as much as his heart. The day he'd been dreading had finally arrived, and his sister was taking him to the cemetery.

The weather matched his mood. Dark storm clouds gathered overhead, and he worried Lanie would abandon the plan. He prayed the rain would hold off. It wouldn't feel right not to visit Mom on the anniversary of the day they'd lost her.

As if his sister could read his mind, she increased her speed. If she was trying to outpace the storm, she was fighting a losing battle.

When they arrived, she quickly unfastened his chair from the van. Navigating what had once been a confusing mess of straps and buckles had become second nature since he'd started going to the office on an almost daily basis. After he was safely on the ground, he headed to the grave. It was important to him to show Mom his progress. He believed that even if she couldn't be physically present to witness it, she was watching him from heaven.

"Hey, Mom," he whispered as he stopped in front of the headstone.

Lanie's footsteps sounded quietly behind him, and she placed a hand on his shoulder.

The air had that familiar musky odor that foretold the coming rain. But it was tears that wet his eyes and slid down Steven's cheeks, not raindrops. He sniffled, trying to hold the wave of grief at bay, but when Lanie squeezed his shoulder, he lost all sense of control and let go.

"I miss her so much," he said, both to himself and to Lanie.

"I do too." His sister's voice was hoarse, and she cleared her throat. "But she'd be proud of you. Not just for the law firm but your perseverance, even with all that's happened."

"And to think"—he wiped his eyes—"I almost joined her."

"Don't say that," Lanie admonished, stepping around his chair and kneeling by the headstone. "I like to think she was there that night, protecting you. Keeping you safe so we wouldn't face another loss."

Despite the tears flowing down his face, Steven smiled. "That makes sense. She kept me alive but allowed me to get hurt enough to teach me a lesson."

Lanie raised an eyebrow. "I'm not sure you've learned it."

"I probably haven't," he admitted with a sad laugh.

A car door slammed in the distance, and Lanie stood to see who had arrived. Her mouth opened before she glanced at Steven.

"It's Dad," she said.

Steven shrugged. "I guess it's not surprising. He knew her longest."

When Dad caught sight of them, his steps faltered, then his mouth set in a grim line as he continued toward them. Steven noticed the bouquet of yellow daisies he held.

"Sorry to disturb," Dad mumbled as he moved by Lanie and laid the flowers against the cold stone. "I didn't realize you two were coming."

"Lanie promised we could make a stop after my PT appointment. I wanted to show Mom how much progress I've made."

Dad's dark eyes went a little misty, and he sniffled. "I'm sure she's glad to see it."

Lanie turned to the grave. "It's hard to believe it's been a year."

"Sometimes it feels like a lifetime," Dad whispered.

Whether his father meant since he'd lost Mom as his wife or since she'd died, Steven wasn't sure. But he was compelled to take Dad and Lanie's hands. After a moment, Lanie took Dad's other hand, and the three of them stood in silence.

"One of my last happy memories of Mom," Steven said a few minutes later, "was when she told me I needed to hurry up and propose to Rose because she wanted some grandbabies."

Dad chuckled. "She would have made an amazing grandma."

The words were like a dagger to Steven's heart. He'd had a wonderful relationship with his grandparents while he'd had them, and he'd hoped for the same for his children. Between Rose's parents living in South Korea and the loss of his mother, his kids wouldn't have the same experience. There was something about a grandmother's love that was irreplaceable.

Plop. A drop fell on Steven's head. He raised his face to the sky. The dark clouds were right on top of them, making it seem much later in the day. Thunder rumbled in the distance.

"We'd better get out of here, or we'll get soaked," Dad said, grabbing Steven's wheelchair handles.

"Wait," Steven protested. With effort, he shifted forward in his seat and placed a hand on Mom's headstone. "I love you and miss you."

Lanie laid her hand on top of his. "We all do."

Lightning flashed across the sky, and Steven jumped. "All right, Mom. We get the point."

Dad and Lanie laughed as they pushed him across the graveyard and toward the van. The raindrops increased the closer they got, then a full-out downpour started the moment Dad pushed Steven into the van.

"We'll stay here a moment until it lets up," Dad said. "No sense driving when you can't see five feet in front of your face."

It wasn't how Steven had planned to spend the anniversary of Mom's death, but somehow, it seemed fitting to be huddled in a van in the middle of a thunderstorm with the only family he had left.

Chapter Twenty

Rose stood outside Bea's Diner, trying to find the courage to open the door and walk inside. Looking in through the window, Rose guessed most of the town was in there. The diner was filled to the brim with bodies. And while they were all there because they cared for her and Steven and wanted to give them the wedding of their dreams, she couldn't quite bring herself to take that next step.

What if we don't raise any money because the town thinks we're spoiled kids who should have planned better for a financial crisis? The medical bills were one thing, but it felt wrong to accept money for the wedding. If the fundraiser didn't work, she had no idea how they would pay their vendors. Visions of appearing in small claims court and having her wages garnished danced before her eyes as she struggled to muster up the courage to enter the diner.

The door swung open, and Lanie stepped out. "Are you coming in?"

"Working on it," Rose said, trying and failing to smile.

"Hey." Lanie put a hand on her arm. "Everyone in there has come because they want to help in whatever way they can."

"I don't want them to think we're irresponsible."

Lanie shook her head. "Nobody thinks that." She pointed at the diner. "Everyone in there has faced a hardship at some point in their lives. They've been where you are now, and they survived because people helped them when they needed it." She slid her arm around Rose's shoulders. "In this community, we take care of our own. And that includes you."

Without another word, she led Rose to the door and opened it. As Rose entered the diner, the swath of smiling faces made the situation more bearable. Though she searched each face, she could find no trace of judgment or ridicule, only love and acceptance. She supposed Lanie was right. They'd all been in similar shoes at some point, and they'd survived life's ups and downs by rallying together.

"Rose," Toccara said. "It's good to see you." She kissed Rose's cheek and waved to the crowded room. "Quite a turnout, huh?"

Rose nodded. "Much bigger than I was expecting."

"Just shows how new you are to this town," Trudy replied, coming up behind her. "Where's your dashing fiancé?"

It took her a moment, but Rose located Steven near the breakfast bar. He was with his father, Michael, and Bea. They were laughing at something Bea said. Rose couldn't help comparing the carefree look on his face to the last time she'd seen him in the restaurant. His palpable joy brought a tightness to her chest.

"He's over there. If you'll excuse me."

When he saw her, his face lit up, and he grabbed her hands. It was as if their argument in the restaurant had never happened. He turned her around to face Max and Michael, and each gave her a nod.

"So, are we passing a hat, or how is this a fundraiser and not a party?" Michael asked.

Max rolled his eyes. "If you knew my daughter, you would know better. Nothing is ever that simple."

"It's multifaceted," Steven clarified. "Bea is donating some of the proceeds from sales, a couple of local organizations put together baskets that are up for auction, and there's a donation box for people who want to contribute something without making any purchases."

As if her ears were burning, Lanie stepped up to the counter and tapped a glass until the room quieted. She winked at Rose before hopping up onto a chair.

"First, I'd like to thank you all for coming. The best thing about Cedar Haven is the tight-knit community. When someone needs help, we don't hesitate to do what we can to lift them up, and that is never more evident than during one of our infamous fundraisers!"

A cheer went up through the room, and Lanie grinned. Nate came out of the kitchen, carrying several orders of fries. He broke into a smile at the sight of her before he turned to deliver the food.

"As you know, my family has had more than our fair share of tragedy this last year. After we lost Mom, I thought we might get a reprieve, but Steven gave us all a scare last month." Lanie's smile faltered, and Rose's eyes stung with unshed tears. Her future sister-in-law pressed on. "Thankfully, he's still with us, but unfortunately, it's caused a setback to the wedding with the medical bills piling up. But I refuse to let tragedy stop him from marrying the woman of his dreams." Pointing at the back of the room, she continued, "We've got several baskets up for auction, door prizes, and we'll be having a karaoke contest later. There's a minimal entry fee, but it's going to a good cause."

Turning toward the kitchen, she gestured Bea forward. "And our beloved Bea has offered to donate seventy percent of the proceeds from food and beverage sales."

The room exploded in applause, and Steven's hand tightened around Rose's. It felt a little surreal, seeing so many people there to support her and Steven.

"Without further ado, let's get this party started!" Lanie jumped off the chair to several hoots before disappearing to the back of the restaurant.

Steven signaled to Bea. "Can we get a couple of sodas?" He glanced at Rose, who nodded. "And maybe some food as well?"

"You've got it." Bea turned and headed to the kitchen to put in their order, and Steven maneuvered his wheelchair toward a small table.

"I'm surprised you found a free table with all these people," Rose said as she slid into a chair.

"Lanie reserved this for us," he replied, holding out his hand.

She placed hers into it and smiled. His sister really had thought of everything.

"How long is this supposed to last?"

He shrugged. "I don't know that there's a definite end to it. Sometime before Bea would normally close, I guess, but as long as people want to hang out and order, they'll keep going."

"Is someone keeping a tally of how much money is raised and who's donating what?" Rose bit her lip. "I'd like to send thank-you cards when this is over."

"I'm not sure, but maybe inviting them all to our big day will be thanks enough."

Her eyes widened as her stomach began to churn. "The whole town?"

He laughed. "Okay, maybe not everyone. Still, I'm sure there are other ways we can pay it forward."

The knot in her stomach eased, but she wondered how she would ever repay everyone for their kindness. Lanie's voice echoed in her head. *We take care of our own.* While that might be the case, she would feel unbalanced until she did something to show her gratitude.

Their food arrived, and she dove into her burger, surprised at how hungry she was. Truthfully, she hadn't eaten much that morning because she'd been a bundle of nerves leading up to the event.

But she was glad she'd come. She glanced up from her burger and smiled at Steven. He appeared in good spirits. The lines that creased his forehead when he was stressed had disappeared.

Maybe everything was going to be okay. Maybe *they* were going to be okay. While they still had a lot of things to work through, she had hope for the first time in a long time that things were going to work out.

Lanie popped up at their table with a smile. "We've only been here an hour, and we've already raised enough to pay off the catering bill."

Rose's mouth fell open. "What? Are you serious?"

With a nod, Lanie showed her the tally for the baskets. "People bid a lot higher than I'd expected on these."

"That's amazing!" Steven's eyes were wide. "I suspected we'd be able to at least offset some of the cost, but this..." He shook his head as if unable to finish his sentence.

Lanie beamed. "I'm hopeful the proceeds from food and beverage sales will give us enough to pay off what you owe for the wedding and start working on some of the outstanding medical bills."

"It would be nice not to start our new life together in debt," Steven said. "Thank you for doing this."

"It's not like I planned this alone." Someone called Lanie's name, and she smiled. "Duty calls."

When they were alone again, Rose shifted her chair closer to Steven. "How's physical therapy going?"

"Pretty well. I've been able to successfully perform most of the exercises my therapist has given me, and I practice them at home between sessions." He winked. "Though sometimes, it feels like it should be called physical torture instead of therapy."

She laughed. "How long do you think you'll have to go?"

"I'm not sure. Dr. Bhati has asked my therapist to send an update on my progress in a month, and we'll reassess after that."

At least he was listening to his doctors about something, but she kept that thought to herself. Despite her earlier reservations about the event, it was going well, and she didn't want to spoil it. Instead, she pushed her concerns about the future from her mind and tried to live in the present.

~

"What a success!" Lanie exclaimed as they left the diner. "We've got to wait to find out what Bea raised, but this wedding is practically paid for."

It had been a long day of shaking hands, fielding congratulations, and talking to friends and strangers alike. In some ways, it had felt like the engagement party they never got to have. They'd hoped to have one last summer, but when Melody took a turn for the worse, they postponed it. Then she'd died, and no one was up for a party after that.

The irony of how accommodating Rose had been during that time wasn't lost on her. Whereas when *she* had asked to postpone the wedding, she'd been railroaded. Steven would likely argue the circumstances were different, but were they? Instead of his mother, it was Steven whose health had taken a turn, and while he was on the mend, they still had a way to go.

Although they hadn't done much planning for their engagement party by the time Melody's health failed. So Rose supposed that in that respect, things were much different.

"Thank you for putting this together." Steven pulled his sister in for a hug. "You truly are the best sister ever."

Lanie laughed, patting her brother's back. "I expect my crown to have that engraved on it, but be sure to thank Trudy as well. She helped get the ball rolling." Once Steven released her, she rushed over to Rose. "How are you doing? Has this helped take some of the stress off you?"

Rose nodded. "It has, and Steven's right. We couldn't have done this without you."

"It was my pleasure." After linking their arms, Lanie pulled Rose away and lowered her voice. "And between you and me, there was a special box set up for people who wanted to donate to help Steven's law firm. It didn't raise much, but it might help offset some of the lost income from June. He can protest as much as he wants, but he doesn't realize how much people struggled to get legal advice before he set up shop."

"I won't tell him."

"Good." Lanie flashed a grin, but it fell as quickly as it had appeared. "Though I suppose I can't keep it from him for long. While I've been helping with bookkeeping, he'll eventually notice the extra funds."

"And he'd probably have to account for it come tax season."

Lanie pursed her lips. "True. I'll figure out a way to tell him. Maybe Michael will help me." She glanced over her shoulder and released Rose's arm. "You'd better go. He looks like he could use a nap."

Rose's brow furrowed as she assessed him. While his father buckled him into the van, he rested his head against the back of the wheelchair. Dark circles framed his eyes, and his skin was paler than normal.

As Max stepped away to allow her to say goodbye, she hesitated at the door to the van. Maybe she should ask Max to take him to the hospital and get a quick checkup. Dr. Myers was working, and he likely wouldn't mind.

Steven stirred and reached for her hand. "Will I see you at home?"

"You should get some sleep. You look exhausted." When he opened his mouth as if to protest, she hurried on. "And honestly, I'm pretty beat myself. But I'll stop by tomorrow after my shift is over."

"That sounds good," he replied with a sleepy smile.

Rose leaned in and gave him a quick peck on the cheek before heading to her car.

As she drove to her condo, she felt conflicted. On the one hand, the fundraiser had alleviated some of their financial concerns. But on the other, the exhaustion on Steven's face haunted her. Despite his promises, it looked like he still wasn't taking care of himself, and

Rose was getting more than a little tired of sounding like a broken record when it came to his health. Her misgivings about the wedding had morphed into something more serious. She needed to talk to someone, to sort out her feelings, before it was too late.

Chapter Twenty-One

"Good game, man."

"Thanks for letting me play!" Steven fist-bumped Eric, one of his new friends.

"Anytime."

The rest of the guys left the court to hit the showers, but he stayed behind. He wanted to soak up as much of the moment as he could.

It had been a while since he'd had time to do anything remotely considered fun. Between work and the wedding, there weren't enough hours in the day to finish everything he needed to and enjoy some of his favorite hobbies. For months, he'd promised himself that after he and Lanie finalized their mother's estate, things would change. Then he'd pushed it until after the wedding. And even at that moment, he found himself thinking it would all come together once he'd gotten the law firm off the ground.

Maybe Rose was right. Maybe he was working himself into an early grave. But he didn't know any other way to be. Most small businesses failed within their first year, and he had less than six months to prove that statistic wrong.

Something had to give, and if it wasn't the firm or the wedding, what was it? What ball could he drop or hand off to someone else until he improved?

He didn't have an answer. While Michael had been instrumental in bringing his law practice back from the brink, there was only so much the law clerk could do until he passed the bar. And Steven already felt bad enough about the wedding plans that he'd forced onto Rose's shoulders. He was glad they'd raised enough money to alleviate the financial fears.

His earlier fears rekindled at the thought of Rose. If he lost momentum, if he couldn't keep up with their plans, she might second-guess her decision to marry him. He didn't want to lose her the way his dad had lost his mom.

Images of his parents' fights flooded his brain, and he squeezed his eyes shut to block them out. But they persisted. His father never could live up to his mother's expectations, and Steven's worst fear was repeating that history. He'd tried his hardest to learn from their mistakes. And yet he feared he was headed for the same fate, assuming he and Rose ever made it down the aisle.

"Hey, hot shot, you plan on baking all afternoon?"

He turned to find Ronnie standing by the door, one hand on her hip, the other shielding her eyes from the sun. Only then did he realize how hot the day had gotten.

"Just enjoying the fresh air," he lied as he came over. "I don't get out much."

Her eyebrow rose as she glanced at his ghost-pale legs and arms. "You don't say? You're practically translucent."

"Ha ha," he retorted, but his tone lacked its usual biting sarcasm.

Ronnie noticed. "Something wrong?"

"Lot on my mind is all." He took one last look at the basketball court before he went through the door she was holding open. "Can I do this again sometime?"

"Absolutely!" She grinned. "I thought this would be good for you."

"It was," he said. They were halfway to the waiting room when Steven stopped. "Be honest with me. Will I be able to walk again by my wedding?"

Ronnie gave him a quizzical look. "What brought this on?"

Though she seemed genuinely curious about his change in demeanor, Steven couldn't help feeling like she was avoiding his question. Instead of responding, he stared at her and waited.

"Uh, I mean, it's early yet. Your body is still recovering from your accident, and sometimes it can take up to six months for it to—"

He held up his hand. "I've heard this song and dance before. But you've worked with patients who've been through what I've been through, right? What was their experience? Were they further along in their progress than I am by this time after their injury?"

"Steven, you can't judge your progress by someone else. Spinal contusions are a tricky business, and everyone heals differently. I've had patients who could walk just fine for the most part but would have random bouts of numbness in one or both legs. And then I've had patients who never regained the feeling in their legs."

He winced. That wasn't what he wanted to hear.

"But that's clearly not you," she hurried on, gesturing to his legs. "Your cast is off, and you're already improving in your transitions. Every session, you not only get a little stronger, but I can tell you're gaining more control over your muscles. I imagine you'll regain feeling in your legs before your wedding, but I can't guarantee you'll have total motor control by then."

That was something, at least. With a sigh, he rolled his chair forward. "I'm frustrated. Every day, I feel a little more like my old self. But I'm still in this blasted chair."

"Give yourself some grace and some credit." Her eyes swept over him. "I have absolute faith you won't be in the wheelchair much longer." His face must have betrayed his doubt because she huffed in exasperation. "I understand it doesn't seem that way to you, but as you said, I've been doing this awhile. I've worked with people from all walks of life and with myriad illnesses. Take my word for it."

Before he could respond, the door to the waiting room opened, and Lanie rushed out. The frown on her face faded to a smile of relief when she saw him.

"There you are! I got here a half hour ago, and no one knew where you were." She threw her arms around his neck.

He awkwardly patted her back with one hand while the other stopped the wheelchair from running over her foot. "Sorry for worrying you, but Ronnie banished me outside for my PT."

Lanie straightened and raised her eyebrows. "Oh?"

"Your brother decided to finally pursue the basketball dreams your grandfather laid out for him."

"Figures you'd wait until your height didn't give you an advantage to try to make old Pop-Pop proud," Lanie said with a laugh.

"I'm not sure how proud he would have been," Steven grumbled. "Those guys wiped the court with me."

"But you had fun, right?" Ronnie asked.

He gave a grudging nod. "Yeah, I had fun."

Lanie put a hand over her heart. "I didn't know you knew that word!"

"Oh, hardy har har," Steven retorted. "Come on. Let's get out of here before she finds something new to torture me with."

"See you in a few days!" Ronnie wiggled her fingers in a silly wave before turning to find her next victim.

"So, you had fun, huh?" Lanie pressed.

"Don't make it into a thing." He pushed the chair up to his sister's car.

"I'm not doing anything of the sort!" She tucked a lock of hair behind her ear as she opened the car door. "It's nice to hear that you enjoyed yourself for a change. With everything that's been going on, you deserve to blow off a little steam."

Ronnie was right about one thing. His improvement with performing transfers had made the van unnecessary, and his father had canceled the rental contract. Riding shotgun was a vast improvement to being strapped into the back of the van. With Lanie's help, he pulled himself into the car then busied himself with settling into his seat and buckling in so he had an excuse not to respond. But Lanie wasn't one to give up easily.

"Did you play with anyone I know?"

"I don't think so."

She drummed her fingers on the steering wheel, a clear sign she was getting annoyed with his evasiveness. And really, what was his goal here? She'd asked because she cared, not because she was trying to hold something over his head.

"To be honest, I told Ronnie I'd like to do it again. I can't remember the last time I had such a fun afternoon."

"That's awesome!" The genuine joy in her voice touched his heart.

"And I've been thinking," he continued, unable to resist the excitement in her tone, "maybe Rose is right."

"Uh, what?" Lanie glanced at him out of the corner of her eye. "Could you say that again? She'll kill me if I don't get a recording."

He ignored her antics. "Just that I need to take better care of myself and find a better balance in my life."

"Rose isn't the only one who's been saying that."

It took effort not to roll his eyes. "Yeah, yeah. But the problem is the timing. There's so much going on right now."

"Maybe that's the point," she said.

"What do you mean?"

Her lips twisted to the side as if she was debating how to answer his question. "Health issues often show up when our body is trying to tell us to slow down. If it waited until we weren't stressed, it would kind of defeat the purpose, right?" She glanced at him. "I know you're worried about the firm and the wedding, but it's not as catastrophic as it once was. I've been looking over your financial situation—"

"Again?"

She flipped her hair over her shoulder. "You're the one who gave me access to your accounts."

That was true, though he'd been reluctant to do so. Still, it had freed up some of his time to allow her to take a look at things while he focused on the stuff no one else could do.

"Anyway," she continued when he didn't respond, "Sandra has booked you a few new clients that I don't think she's discussed with you."

"Like who?"

"Our old neighbor Cassandra wants to have a will drawn up," Lanie said.

He stared at her. "Really? I didn't know she had anyone to leave anything to."

"I don't know the specifics." She shrugged. "But she's lived in that house all our lives. I imagine it's paid off by now and is probably worth a small fortune."

"Who else?"

"Nate's parents want wills as well. His father had that heart attack not long after Mom died." Her lips quirked up. "Though I suppose it's more Nate's mom who will be dragging his dad in. And Bea is thinking of taking on a partner for the diner."

"Wow, I thought she was going to sell it."

"So did we all, but she's not ready to give up. She seems to be hoping one of her nephews will be interested in it when they're older."

A moment later, they pulled into the parking lot of the law firm. Steven unbuckled his seat belt and waited while Lanie pulled his wheelchair from the trunk and came around to his side.

"I hope what I told you alleviates some of your stress."

"It does and it doesn't." Steven accepted her hand and shuffled out of the car and into the chair.

Her brow furrowed. "Why do you say that?"

He sighed. *How can I explain this in a way that doesn't sound like I'm ungrateful to her, Sandra, or the town?*

"New clients only help the practice if I'm capable of doing the work for which they hired me. If I can't, they'll move on, and I'll be right back where I started." He patted his legs. "And I barely have enough time now to keep up with my *current* workload thanks to all of my various medical appointments."

"But that won't last forever," Lanie countered as she pushed him into the office.

"No, but the timing is still awful. If this had happened when I was more established, it wouldn't be stressing me out as much."

She snorted. "Oh, please. You'd be stressed no matter when it happened."

He opened his mouth to protest but thought better of it. "Be that as it may, I need to find a better balance between my health and my work. Preferably one that doesn't cause me to go bankrupt or my business to go under."

After pushing him into his office, she stooped and gave him a hug. "I have faith you'll figure it out, and we're here for whatever you need."

Once he was alone, Steven opened the spreadsheet they used to track new clients. Sure enough, Sandra had booked several new ones. She'd set up meetings with them for the following week on both of their calendars. Shaking his head, he couldn't help but smile. If his law firm survived, Sandra deserved a raise.

Chapter Twenty-Two

Rose found herself dragging her feet to her appointment with Carissa to discuss the rehearsal dinner. Time kept flying by, and she couldn't catch her breath.

As she walked through the lobby toward Carissa's office, the sound of raised voices caught her attention. After tiptoeing to the corner, she peered into the room. Max and Carissa sat opposite each other, clearly in the middle of a heated argument.

"You're being unreasonable," Carissa said, flipping her salt-and-pepper hair over her shoulder. "Rose's parents have already paid for the rehearsal dinner. We're just deciding on a location."

Rose sucked in a breath. *My parents sent Carissa money?* They shouldn't have done that. Between her grandparents moving into long-term care and her parents' struggle with employment, the last thing they needed to be worried about was her wedding. *Looks like I have a phone call to make after this is over.*

"It's not unreasonable to want to follow tradition." Max crossed his arms.

Carissa rolled her eyes. "As I told you before, they contacted me privately to pay for the rehearsal dinner because they can't attend or pay for the wedding. It's their wedding gift to their daughter and is important to them. If you want to contribute, I have a binder full of other outstanding items right h—"

"And as *I* told *you*, what is the difference if the money they sent is used toward one of those outstanding items?" He gave a stiff shrug that Rose suspected was meant to be nonchalant. But as she had never known him to be an easygoing kind of guy, it failed in execution.

"If it doesn't matter where their money goes, why does it matter where *your* money goes?"

"Because I'm here. I'm attending the wedding, and I insist on paying for the rehearsal dinner. I want to have a say in where it's held."

Rose had heard enough. The wedding was becoming way more trouble than it was worth. She walked into the room, making sure her heels clicked loudly on the floor to mark each step. Both Max and Carissa turned toward her.

"Rose!" Carissa rushed over, the angry flush on her face dissipating. "I'm glad you're here."

"I hope I'm not interrupting anything," Rose said, keeping her tone neutral. She raised her eyebrows at her future father-in-law, and he shrugged, clearly not at all perturbed at being caught midargument.

"Not at all." Carissa grabbed her arm and pulled her over to the table, where a number of menus were set up. "I've chosen several options for the rehearsal dinner. We need to book one of them soon."

Before Rose could respond, Max angled himself between her and Carissa. "I brought a few menus as well."

Carissa's hands curled into fists. If he saw the death glare she gave him, he didn't let on.

"A little less upscale, perhaps, but much more in line with what the people of Cedar Haven are used to."

"Quaint," Carissa said, her voice deceptively sweet. "But since the guests aren't limited to locals, we should plan for a variety of tastes."

"You mean the dinner my parents have apparently paid for, which you conveniently never mentioned?" Rose asked, narrowing her eyes at Carissa. To the wedding planner's credit, she had the decency to look guilty.

"They wanted it to be a surprise." Carissa's eyebrows pulled together. "They planned to tell you after the wedding. Your mother feels terrible that they're going to miss it."

So do I. With a sigh, Rose sank into the chair that Max pulled out for her and began sifting through the mountain of menus. But her heart wasn't in it anymore. She wished Steven was there, both to act as referee and to help her sort through her complicated emotions.

Like he's helped me talk through my feelings the last few weeks. Heat built in her belly before shooting through her. There she was, tying up loose ends for a wedding she was beginning to wonder if she even wanted anymore. The cracks she'd ignored in their relationship had grown too big to overlook.

Before she could change her mind, she pushed back from the table and stood. "Carissa, I need to talk to you." When Max made a move to go with them, she held up a hand. "Alone."

"If this is about the rehearsal dinner, I should—"

"It's not," Rose said. At his hurt expression, she softened her tone. "I won't make any decisions about that without you, I promise."

Max's eyebrows lowered in suspicion, but something in her face must have told him not to argue. After giving a quick nod, he settled back in his chair and pointedly picked up a menu from a local establishment.

Rose headed outside with Carissa on her heels. The air was stifling, and the blinding heat made her second-guess whether that was the time or place for the conversation, but she needed advice, and she wasn't sure where else to turn.

"So." Carissa leaned against the building. "What's up?"

"What would happen if we canceled the wedding?" Rose asked in a rush, afraid if she didn't ask right then, she would never again find the nerve.

Carissa's eyes widened. "You can't be serious." When Rose didn't immediately respond, she touched her arm. "Rose? What's going on? Is it cold feet or…?"

"I wish it was cold feet." It had taken all of her energy to force the question out. Her back slid down the brick wall of the building until she landed on the sidewalk. Wrapping her arms around her knees, she shook her head. "I don't know if I can go through with it."

After a moment of hesitation, Carissa knelt in front of her. "Talk to me. What's going on?"

Rose wasn't sure where to begin. "It feels like everything that could go wrong has gone wrong."

"The accident was bad," Carissa said. "But Steven's recovering, and I suspect he'll be back on his feet in no time."

"But that's just it." Rose raised her head. "He's so focused on getting back to normal, he isn't taking care of himself like he needs to."

"How do you mean?"

"He had a *heart attack*." For once, the words didn't get stuck in her throat. "He could have died. But he's more focused on his spine and the ability to walk, which I get. It's easier to see the broken parts of ourselves when they're on the outside. It's harder to comprehend when something is wrong inside."

Carissa was quiet. "That sounds like you're talking about more than just his heart."

"I suppose I am." Wiping the tears from her eyes, Rose bit her lip. "I'm sorry. I don't mean to burden you with this. But I don't have anyone else to talk to."

"Hey, don't apologize. You're not the first bride who has had second thoughts." Carissa pursed her lips. "Though you are the first to stump me."

Rose groaned. "That's not what I needed to hear."

"I know." Carissa stood up and brushed off her pantsuit. "Have you tried discussing this with him?"

"Several times. He either blows me off or gives me empty platitudes about how he's 'trying.'" Her throat constricted. "It makes me feel like he sees me as a pest instead of someone who genuinely cares about his well-being."

A throbbing in her head became more pronounced the more she stewed over how Steven had treated her concerns. He'd vacillated between blowing them off and snapping at her for pushing him.

Carissa held out her hand. "Come on. It's doing you no good to sit and stew in that anger. Let's go for a walk."

"But what about Max?"

"He'll probably still be poring over his menus when we get back."

They walked through the parking lot and crossed the street. Then Carissa led the way to a small park with a few trails.

"We won't go far," Carissa said. "But it's cooler beneath the trees, and sometimes, being in nature helps me process my thoughts."

As they walked deeper into the woods, the tightness in Rose's chest loosened. But she had no idea what she was going to do. No matter how much she might try to deny it, canceling the wedding would send a message. And it might also spell the end of her relationship.

"Have you ever been married?" Rose asked suddenly.

The question appeared to catch Carissa off guard, as she stumbled. Regaining her balance, she turned to Rose with a wary expression.

"I was up until five years ago."

"What happened?"

To Rose's horror, tears welled up in Carissa's eyes. "He died."

"Oh my, I'm sorry." Rose shook her head. "I shouldn't have asked."

"No, it's okay." Carissa sniffled and dashed a hand across her face. "I understand why you did." After taking a deep breath, she continued, "Chuck and I had a wonderful marriage, but it wasn't easy. Those last few years, he was sick, and I truly learned the meaning of those vows about 'in sickness and health.'"

"Did you regret it?" Rose couldn't help asking.

But Carissa's face broke into a sad smile. "Not for a moment. I treasure every second we got to spend together." She frowned. "It's not the same as your situation, though. Before Chuck got sick, we had a life together. To face such a challenge so soon in your relationship is a hard pill to swallow. I'm not sure how I would have felt if Chuck had gotten sick before our wedding."

Rose took a shuddering breath. "I know that anyone's health can fail at any time, and I'm not thinking of abandoning Steven because of what happened to him."

Carissa stepped forward and put a hand on Rose's shoulder. "That never crossed my mind."

"But I'm not sure I could bear it if he passed soon after our wedding."

They walked awhile in silence. Rose grappled with the choice in front of her. The idea of canceling the wedding and risking her relationship broke her heart, but the bleak vision of a future with a husband who wouldn't listen to her broke her soul.

When they reached the end of the trail, Rose was surprised to realize they'd completed a circle and were back in the park. Unfortunately, she was no closer to making a decision.

"Rose," Carissa said, breaking the silence. "Can you imagine a life for yourself without Steven?"

Closing her eyes, Rose tried to picture what that might look like. All she could see was the past and the different decisions she might have made. If she had never met Steven, she would have taken the job in Boston. She'd be working at a busy hospital in the heart of a thriving city. But whether she'd be happier in that other life, she couldn't say.

"I'm not sure."

"Give yourself some time to think on it."

They headed to Carissa's office. Once they were across the street, Carissa stopped Rose.

"As far as canceling the wedding, it's likely too late for most of your vendors to rebook the date. That means you'll lose all of the money you've paid thus far, and you'd have to start over from scratch if you decide to reschedule in the future." Carissa crossed her arms. "So I highly suggest you be sure of whatever decision you make before you take action."

Rose nodded. Nothing Carissa said had come as a surprise. "Thank you for listening."

"Do you still love him?"

The question was blunt and caught Rose by surprise. She nodded, not trusting herself to speak.

Carissa's face softened. "That's worth more than you may realize." She pressed her lips together. "But unless you plan to tell your soon-to-be father-in-law that you're no longer marrying his son, I suggest we go back inside and fake it." A rueful smile pulled at her lips. "Though I wouldn't mind taking him down a few pegs."

Laughter bubbled up Rose's throat. "He's not so bad, once you get to know him."

"I've always taken that saying to be a nicer way of telling people 'he's a jerk, but you'll get used to it.'"

"That's probably more accurate." Rose chuckled.

"What's so funny?" Max asked when they reentered the office, his bushy eyebrows pulled down over his dark eyes.

"Nothing," they said at the same time. Rose bit her lip to keep from laughing again. "Why don't you show me the places you had in mind for the rehearsal dinner?" She hoped to keep him from asking additional questions.

His face brightened, though his jaw was tight, probably with suspicion. But he nodded and handed her a stack of menus, all local places. Carissa's tastes couldn't be further from Max's, and they would be hard-pressed to find common ground, but Rose found herself drawn to the local options. It would be easier for Steven, especially if they went through with the wedding they'd already planned. At the same time, those sites were such a vast contrast to the location of the wedding reception, it would almost seem like they were planning two completely different events.

Perhaps that wasn't a bad thing. It would incorporate different aspects of their lives—and their relationship.

As if he could sense her wavering, Max stepped closer. "All of these places have wheelchair access. I checked."

Whether he meant it as a comfort or simply as a fact, she didn't know, but the words weighed heavy on her chest. Those were things she hadn't had to consider mere months ago. How privileged she had been to never have to think about the sort of access a person with a disability might need.

An image of the male swan with its leg wrapped in a splint popped into her mind. If only she could tap into the faith of his mate, she might be able to find the strength to save her relationship.

Chapter Twenty-Three

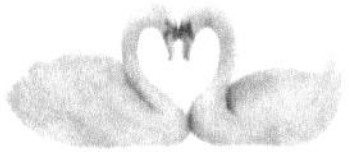

STEVEN STAYED LATER THAN HE INTENDED AT WORK. Lanie had been right about the influx of new clients. Whether it was because the community needed a local firm or because they knew he was in dire straits, he appreciated that they were bringing him business. And Sandra's detailed notes from the initial client interviews she'd done made him think the new wills and estates wouldn't be terribly taxing. Most of them were simple and could be handled without a lot of extra research or effort.

A knock sounded at his door, and he glanced up and did a double take. "Michael? What are you still doing here?"

"I need to talk to you." Michael stared at the floor, fidgeting with his hands.

"Sure." Steven's stomach dropped. Something about Michael's demeanor told Steven it wasn't going to be good news. "Have a seat." After waiting for what seemed like ages, Steven cleared his throat. "So, um, what can I help you with?"

Finally, Michael lifted his head. His brown eyes were wary. "I got a call today from a law firm in DC."

"Oh?" Steven's palms began to sweat. "What did they want?"

"To offer me a job."

It felt like Steven's throat was closing. He attempted to clear it, but it did no good. *Is this it, then? Am I back to square one with my law practice?* Michael had just begun to get into the swing of things. Steven couldn't imagine starting over with someone new, not to mention how much time and energy interviews would take.

"And what did you say?"

"I-I told them I would give them an answer by the end of the week." Michael ran a hand through his hair. "But I don't want to leave here if I can help it."

"Is there anything I can do to convince you to stay?"

"In my interview, Lanie mentioned I might be able to be brought on full-time. And I've heard you might be looking for a partner..."

Steven shook his head. "I'm not ready for that yet."

Michael nodded. "I figured. It's just, well, the DC law firm has a clear partner track, which is rare. And they have openings in areas of law I'm interested in, like environmental and small business."

"It sounds like you've decided," Steven said as his heart pounded. The news was quite literally the last thing he needed right then. Shadows swam before his eyes, and he put his head on his desk. He was vaguely aware of Michael calling his name, then everything went dark.

The next thing Steven knew, a hand was violently shaking him. As he opened his eyes, it took him a moment to realize what had happened and why he was on the floor.

"Steven! Can you hear me?" His sister's hazel eyes, filled with worry, swam into his vision.

"Yes," he croaked. He tried to sit up, but she pushed him back down.

"Don't move. You might have had another heart attack. I've called 911, and they're on their way."

Another *heart attack?* No, it couldn't be. He swallowed and pressed his hand to his chest. It didn't hurt, but that might not mean anything.

"Why are you here?" he asked.

"I was on my way to pick you up when Michael called me." She closed her eyes as if trying to shake the memory of what she'd seen from her mind. "We both called to you, but you were shaking, and then you fell on the floor." Her eyes opened, and she grabbed his hand. "I've never been so scared."

Before he could respond, someone banged on the front door. Lanie squeezed his hand again before hurrying away to let the paramedics in.

He lay there staring at the ceiling and listened as his sister quietly explained the situation. A moment later, a grim face appeared above him.

"Mr. McAllister, can you hear me?"

Steven nodded and made to sit up, but a firm hand grasped his shoulder and held him down. "Don't move, sir, until we assess you."

A small light shone in one of his eyes, and he grimaced but made an effort not to flinch. It felt different that time. While he didn't remember falling to the floor, he was pretty sure he hadn't been unconscious for nearly as long as before.

The man who'd been examining him asked a series of rapid-fire questions. It took a lot of effort to keep up, but Steven did. When the man was finished, he stepped back and held out his hand, which Steven accepted.

"It looks like he might have fainted or had a seizure, but it doesn't appear to be another heart attack." The man turned to Lanie. "Still, we should get him to the hospital so they can run some tests to rule out anything more serious."

Steven squeezed his eyes shut and tried not to dwell on how much the incident would set him back. All those new clients Sandra had found weren't going to make a lick of difference if he couldn't perform the work for which they'd hired him.

"Sir? Are you still with me?"

Apparently, shutting one's eyes and grimacing wasn't the best choice of facial expressions after a possible seizure. Steven opened his eyes and faked a smile to put everyone in the room at ease. But inside, he was a mess.

~

After Steven arrived at the hospital, Dr. Myers had him admitted and started a series of tests, by the end of which Steven felt like a human pincushion. He winced as the orderlies rolled him into his room and bumped into the doorframe. When they left, he took a deep breath and tried to relax, but he struggled to turn his brain off.

A knock at the door startled him, and he braced for yet another test. Rose stood in the doorway—or "clung to it" would be more accurate. Her brown eyes were wide and wary, and she stared at him as if waiting for permission to enter.

"Rose." For once, his voice didn't sound like a croaking frog's.

"Lanie called me," she replied, and the coolness in her tone caught him off guard.

"I'm sorry we're meeting like this again," Steven said in a poor attempt at a joke. "They think I had a seizure and—"

She held up a hand. "I know. I spoke with Dr. Myers."

"But I'm okay," he hurried on. "I mean, at least it wasn't another heart attack."

That was the wrong thing to say. Her mouth twisted before it set in a grim line. She stepped into the room but only so far that she could lean back against the wall next to the door. She crossed her arms.

"Rose? What's wrong?"

Her eyes flashed, and he shrank against his pillow. *Maybe that wasn't the best choice of words, but why is she mad at me?* It wasn't like he *wanted* to be back at the hospital.

"'What's wrong?'" Her voice was incredulous. "Are you kidding?"

"I mean, this looks bad, but—"

"No, Steven, it doesn't just *look* bad. It *is* bad." The rage simmered off her like steam from a pot that threatened to boil over. "I told you. I *warned* you." Her eyes narrowed with barely repressed rage. "I said if you didn't take care of yourself, you would end up back in the hospital." She gestured wildly. "And I was right."

"But it's not as bad as last time," he protested, though it sounded stupid and pathetic even before the words left his mouth.

"So? Does it matter what brought you here?"

"Dr. Myers said it's common to have seizures after a heart attack."

"And did he also tell you excess stress can induce seizures?"

"Not in so many words." Dr. Myers had told him he needed to take it easy, multiple times, but doctors always said things like that. Besides, being a doctor was one of the most stressful jobs there was. *If they can't take their own advice, how can they expect their patients to?*

Of course, Steven said none of those things out loud. One look at the murderous expression on Rose's face convinced him to tread lightly.

"I'm sorry," he said instead, though he imagined that to her, that phrase sounded repetitive and empty. "You were right. I should have taken more time for my health."

She sighed. "At least that's something, though it doesn't change anything."

The muscles along his spine spasmed as he sat up straighter. Something about her tone and the way she had dropped her gaze to the floor told him that whatever she meant by that statement couldn't be good.

"What's that supposed to mean?"

Before she could respond, Dr. Myers came in.

"I suppose it's good that you're here, since it means I only have to say this once."

Chapter Twenty-Four

ROSE BRACED HERSELF AGAINST THE DOORWAY. Whatever Dr. Myers had to say wouldn't surprise her, but it would add to the pain she was about to deliver, both to Steven and herself. Part of her wished the doctor had been delayed. Then she could have done what she came to do and escaped without hearing about Steven's condition. But the other part, the part that had questioned over and over whether she was making the right decision, needed to know Steven was going to be okay.

Dr. Myers moved beside Steven. "You were lucky. It wasn't a heart attack or a seizure but convulsive syncope. Which basically means you fainted due to loss of blood or oxygen to your brain. It can often look like a seizure."

Steven sagged against his pillow, and his lips turned up in a tentative smile. "That's a relief." When Dr. Myers crossed his arms, Steven's mouth tightened. "Isn't it?"

"This was yet another warning sign that your heart is under too much stress. Syncope episodes are common following a cardiac arrest, but it's a bad sign. It means you aren't healing as well as you should be." Dr. Myers took a deep breath. "Stress can be one of the worst things for someone with heart disease. Your body is already in a vulnerable place, and it's trying to heal. But if you don't provide it that time and space to heal itself, you won't survive the next heart attack."

The way he said it, with authority and conviction, seemed to finally break through to Steven. It was no longer a question of whether he would have another heart attack but when and how severe. A hole opened in Rose's chest, and she pressed a hand to it as if it was a gunshot wound and she was trying to stanch the bleeding. But the bleeding was internal and emotional, and there was no way to stop that outpouring of pain.

"I understand." Steven's voice was strained. It sounded so broken and childlike. Rose almost went to his side to comfort him, but she stopped herself.

"I hope you do." The note of doubt in Dr. Myers's voice was unmistakable. Rose peered over his shoulder at Steven, and her breath bottled up in her chest. Maybe he was finally comprehending the seriousness of his situation. She squashed that feeling of hope before it could spread. Even if he did see reason, it was too little, too late.

"We'll be keeping you here for observation for a few days, then we'll discharge you." Dr. Myers glanced at Rose before continuing. "I'm willing to send you home instead of back to the inpatient rehab facility but only if you follow my instructions to the letter."

"I will," Steven mumbled. He shot a mournful look at Rose. "I promise."

Her resolve faltered, especially when Dr. Myers patted her hand on his way out. But once they were alone again, she straightened her shoulders and marched to Steven's bed.

"I'm sorry," he said again, taking her hand. "I should have listened to you. But I promise I've learned my lesson, and I will take better care of myself. What happened was Michael told me he'd been offered a position in DC. He asked me about a full-time position or a partnership, but I told him I wasn't ready for that. When I realized how much finding a new law clerk would set me back, I panicked." He sighed. "But clearly I need more help. I'm going to talk to Michael and see if I can convince him to stay, but I'll also start putting out feelers for a new law clerk so I can get them in before he leaves. It's going to work out. I promise."

Tears pricked her eyes, and she blinked them back. How long had she wished he would take that action? How long had she prayed he would take his health seriously? And he finally had. *Too little, too late* repeated over and over again in her head, like a scratched CD.

"I'm glad you plan to take better care of yourself." She was proud that her voice shook only a little.

"I don't want to be a burden to you." He lifted her hand to kiss it, but the contact would be too much.

She pulled away and stepped back. The hurt in his eyes pierced her heart, but she couldn't back down. The heart attack had been a warning sign, not only for his health but also for where their future was headed. She needed to rip off the Band-Aid and allow her pain to bleed out so she could start over.

Sucking in air for strength, she lifted her left hand and slid the engagement ring off her finger. Steven's eyes widened and flickered back and forth between the ring she held out and her face. It took effort, but she managed to arrange her features into a neutral expression despite the category-five emotional hurricane building inside her.

"Rose." His voice was hoarse and strangled. "Don't do this."

"I'm sorry, but I can't do this anymore." She was amazed at how calm she sounded.

Tears filled his eyes. "Why?"

"I begged you, repeatedly, to take it easy, slow down, take better care of your health." A lump formed in her throat, and she could barely speak. "But you wouldn't listen to me. You blew off my concerns as if they were nothing."

"I'm listening now."

That was probably the worst thing he could have said. Her hands shook as she tried and failed to gain control of her anger. "*Now*? Now that you're back in the hospital?" She gestured to the machines he was hooked up to. "And I suppose you're also finally listening to what your body has been trying to tell you, too, right?" The pounding in her ears increased in rhythm. "But you wouldn't listen to *me*. I may not be a doctor, but I'm not an idiot either. I knew what your workload was doing to you and how stressed you were after your accident. I tried to reason with you. I tried to convince you that you were making a mistake, but you wouldn't *listen*." Her carefully put-together demeanor cracked. "So, now *I'm* done listening to your excuses."

"We can postpone the wedding, if that's what you want! We can reschedule it for next summer or for however long you wish." He reached for her, but she moved farther away. "But don't do this. Don't throw away everything we have because I made a mistake."

"A mistake?" She stared at him. *Is that all he thinks this is?* "A mistake is when you mess up the numbers in a budget or forget an important date. Ignoring your health and brushing off the advice of medical professionals isn't a mistake. It's a choice." He opened his mouth as if to respond, but she didn't give him the chance. "I didn't come here to convince you that it's over but to *tell* you it's over." Tears stung her eyes, but she blinked them back. "I love you too much to sit by and watch you kill yourself."

"Rose, please—"

The pain in his voice might have made her falter at one time, but the more he fought her, the more resolved she became. No matter how much she loved him, she had chosen the right path—for both of them.

"No." For once, she didn't try to temper the finality of the word with excuses or platitudes. It might have been only one word, but it was a complete sentence.

"Please, Rose." His eyes searched her face. "I love you, and I promise, I'll do everything the doctors tell me to do."

"I hope you do." And she meant it. "I hope you listen to Dr.

Myers, to all of your doctors, and follow their advice." Her voice cracked because the alternative was something she couldn't bear to consider. If breaking both their hearts was the only way to get him to understand the gravity of the situation, so be it. At least she could walk away knowing she'd done everything she could to save him. But it was time to save herself.

Her emotions bubbled up inside, and it was only a matter of time before they spilled over. She had to leave before he saw her break down. He would only take it as a sign that he needed to push harder.

With a small smile, she grasped his hand one last time and gave it a squeeze before turning and bolting from the room. She ran past Lanie and Max on her way out, but she didn't stop to speak to them. They would find out everything soon enough.

"Are you sure this is what you want?" Rose's mother asked.

Rose nodded then remembered she wasn't on video chat. "Yes, Mother, I'm sure."

She hadn't wanted to FaceTime her parents, afraid they would see right through her facade, even on the other side of the world. After she'd gotten home, she'd spent a good hour sobbing into her pillow. When her tears ran out, she forced herself out of bed and washed her face.

Her mother sighed on the other end of the line, and Rose braced herself.

"Aren't you being a bit rash?"

She bristled. "I've been asking him for months, even before the accident, to slow down and take it easy. I thought the heart attack would be a wakeup call, but it wasn't." *Calm down.* Getting in an argument with her mother wasn't going to help things. "And now, he's passing out from stress, and I don't know what else to do. I've tried to reason with him. I've tried nagging, begging." She swallowed around the lump in her throat. "He dismissed my concerns or made empty promises. I started to wonder, what kind of future can I have with someone who so easily disregards my feelings? What if that bleeds into other areas of our relationship? What will happen when we have children?" She took a deep breath. "I love him. I do. But sometimes love just isn't enough."

The line was silent, and she held her breath as she waited for Mom to respond, though she supposed it didn't matter whether her mother agreed with her or not. She'd made her choice.

"It's better this way," she continued when her mother didn't respond. "Can you imagine how much worse it would be if we had gone through with the wedding? Now, we can both move on, and maybe I'll go back to Baltimore."

Her mother tsked, and Rose rolled her eyes. That was the other positive point for Steven. Her parents had never liked the idea of her working in a hospital in Baltimore. They hated the city and worried about the things she would witness while working there. She hadn't had the heart to tell them it didn't really matter where she worked, gruesome sights were pretty much universal. In Cedar Haven, she might not have seen gunshot wounds, but she'd seen some tractor accidents that were far bloodier.

"Maybe you can come home to Korea," her mother said.

Rose cringed. The possibility that her mother would mention a return to the home country had crossed her mind, but she'd hoped it wouldn't be during that conversation.

"I'll think about it." Though they both knew that was a lie. "Anyway, it's getting late, and I'm working the early shift tomorrow."

They said their goodbyes, and Rose collapsed onto her couch. The one saving grace in the whole awful situation was that she hadn't moved in with Steven yet. She didn't want to imagine how awkward it would have been to try to find a new place to live when he was released.

She had just flipped on the TV when there was a knock at the door. She debated pretending not to be home. There were only so many people who would have stopped by her house at that time of night.

"Rose? It's Lanie." A pause. "I know you're in there."

With a sigh, she stood and opened the door. Lanie leaned against the wall outside the condo, her eyebrows pulling together. She held up a brown bag.

"Thought you could use some wine."

Rose rocked back on her heels, not sure how to react. Without waiting for a response, Lanie pushed past her and set the bag on the counter before removing two wineglasses from the cabinet.

"You planning to stand there all night, or are you going to join me?" Lanie asked.

Bewildered, Rose shut the door and went into the kitchen. Lanie poured two large glasses of wine and handed one to Rose.

"What are you doing here?"

"Bringing you wine." Lanie shrugged. "And I figured you might want some company."

"So you're not here to convince me to reconsider?"

"Would you listen to me if I was?"

Rose shook her head.

"Then I'm not." Lanie carried her wine into the living room before sinking onto the sofa.

Unsure of what else to do, Rose followed and sat on the other side, keeping some distance between them. As close as Rose had gotten to Lanie recently, she was Steven's sister, and Rose suspected that was where her loyalties lay.

She waited to see if Lanie would start the conversation, but her future sister-in-law... Scratch that, her *former* future... No, that didn't quite work either. While she debated how to define their new connection, Lanie leaned back and gazed out the window. Her face was serene, and she seemed perfectly content to sip her wine and sit in silence.

But Rose was like a firecracker left too close to a bonfire. One small spark, and she would explode. She shifted in her seat, hoping the movement would break Lanie's reverie and force her to speak. When that didn't work, she heaved a sigh to break the silence.

"Something wrong?" Lanie asked before taking yet another unbothered sip of wine.

Rose couldn't put her finger on why, but the nonchalant attitude grated on her nerves more than if Lanie had stormed in demanding answers. The former Rose could have understood, because breaking up with Steven had been like pulling the pin in a grenade. Just because she left before it detonated didn't mean she expected to escape unscathed.

"Why are you really here?" Despite her best attempts at trying to keep her temper in check, the question came out much more harshly than she'd intended.

Lanie blinked. "I told you already. I wanted to be here in case you needed to talk."

"Even if I did need someone to talk to, you wouldn't be my first choice."

To her surprise, Lanie's expression became pained. "Ouch."

"I'm sorry." Rose pursed her lips. "Actually, no, I'm not. Look, I don't mean to be rude, but you're Steven's sister. You may have your differences, but he's your family, and I don't expect you'll understand my reasons for doing what I did."

Lanie leaned forward and set her glass on the table. "Really? You don't think I feel like my brother has brought this on himself?" She lifted her hand and began ticking things off on her fingers. "He left the rehab facility early against medical advice, went back to work sooner than was recommended, worked himself to the bone despite everyone in his life telling him to take it easy, then has the audacity to fight with you about your very reasonable request to postpone the wedding."

Rose opened her mouth to speak but couldn't find the words. Apparently taking satisfaction in Rose's obvious shock, Lanie sat back on the couch with a triumphant smile.

"He may be my brother, but he's being a real knucklehead. I'm hoping the breakup will be the wake-up call he needs."

"But it won't change my mind," Rose insisted.

"Good." Lanie raised her glass and clinked Rose's. "It serves him right."

Is she serious? Her brother was laid up in the hospital as they spoke, but Lanie didn't seem the least bit fazed by that fact. Or by the reality of what Rose had done.

"Though I appreciate your support, I wonder if it's a bit misplaced."

"How so?"

Rose squirmed in her seat. "I mean, he *is* your brother, and he *is* in the hospital."

"As a result of his own actions."

"But don't you feel even the slightest bit sorry for him?"

Lanie raised an eyebrow. "Do you?"

Is this some weird version of reverse psychology? Does Lanie think by acting as if she doesn't care about her brother, she'll get to the heart of how much I do *care?*

"I'm not completely heartless—"

"It's not heartless to call someone out on their actions." Lanie shook her head. "Am I worried about Steven? Of course. But does that mean I don't think he's reaping what he's sown? Absolutely not."

Rose's mouth fell open in shock while Lanie went on sipping her wine as if she hadn't confirmed everything Rose had been feeling for weeks. And Rose had to admit that for once, she didn't feel quite so alone.

"Look, I love my brother. But he can't get out of this one with empty promises. If he wants to live to see his business thrive, he's going to have to make some changes. If he wants a chance to grovel at your feet and beg you to reconsider, which I have no doubt he plans to do, he'll have to prove he's going to do what needs to be done to get better." Lanie gave her signature one-shoulder shrug. "He gambled with his health and the love of his life, and he lost."

"Don't you hate me, though?" Rose pressed. "For kicking him while he's down?"

Lanie snorted. "Are you kidding? I'm surprised you didn't do it sooner."

Frowning, Rose stared at her hands. As much as she appreciated Lanie's support, something didn't sit right with her. While yes, Steven should have paid more attention to his health, she didn't love the idea of him sitting alone in a hospital room.

"That means a lot to me," she said. "But I do worry about him."

Lanie's face softened. "I know you do, and I do too." She laid her hand on Rose's. "And I worry about you."

"Me?" Rose stared at her. "I'm perfectly fine."

"Are you?" Lanie tilted her head. "You broke up with the man you planned to marry." She sniffed. "I wasn't engaged to James, and I still struggled after we broke up."

Tears pricked behind Rose's eyes, but she refused to let them fall. She didn't want to cry, not with Lanie there. She wanted to wait until she was alone, when she could have a full-on wallow fest. Thank goodness she'd had the forethought to stock up on ice cream. The best comfort for a broken heart was a pint of Ben and Jerry's.

But Lanie's probing eyes wreaked havoc on her resolve. Rose cleared her throat. "Okay, maybe I'm not *fine* at the moment." Squaring her shoulders, she lifted her glass and downed the rest of her wine. "But I will be." Her gaze fell on the wedding binder teetering on the edge of the coffee table. "Though while you're here, maybe you can help me. I don't want to bother Carissa, and I should get a start on calling the wedding vendors."

When she moved to pick up the binder, Lanie put a hand on her arm. Rose shot her a questioning look, but Lanie shook her head.

"Not tonight." Lanie stood and retrieved the bottle of wine before pouring them each another large glass. "Tonight, we wallow and let the dust settle."

"But—"

"Trust me, Rose. You'll thank me tomorrow."

Chapter Twenty-Five

STEVEN OPENED HIS EYES THE NEXT MORNING, HOPING IT had all been a dream, but the incessant beeping of the heart monitor betrayed the truth. Not only was he back in the hospital, but he was also single. The ring he had searched for over several months, determined to find the perfect one, mocked him from his bedside table.

If he were honest, he could admit he should have seen that coming. And as if losing Rose wasn't bad enough, his stupidity might have cost him his firm as well.

"Ah, good, you're awake." Dr. Myers popped his head into the room.

I wish I wasn't. The thought came out of nowhere and caught him off guard. Thank goodness he had a filter. Otherwise, he would likely be put on some seventy-two-hour hold. And that was quite literally the last thing he needed.

"I wanted to talk to you about discharge."

That got his attention. "Already? Aren't you keeping me here for observation?"

"Oh, we are," Dr. Myers said. "But I also told you I would discharge you home."

"And you're not planning on doing that anymore?" Steven read between the lines of what the doctor wasn't saying.

Dr. Myers sighed. "If you really want to go home, we can certainly make that happen, assuming everything looks good." For a moment, the good doctor appeared at war with himself, which only amped up Steven's irritation.

"Just spit it out, Doc."

"You won't want to hear this, but you were making significant progress in the inpatient rehab facility." His eyes narrowed as he leveled a stern gaze at Steven. "You should consider going back."

The no was on the tip of Steven's tongue when Rose's face flashed before his eyes. A weight as heavy as an elephant settled on his chest. He would do anything to see her again, anything to convince her to give him another chance.

"You have a better chance of healing and getting back to your life if you spend a few more weeks working through an intensive therapy program," Dr. Myers continued when Steven didn't respond. "I've spoken with the medical team there, and—"

"Okay," Steven whispered as he squeezed his eyes shut.

"They said they can get you Wi-Fi—Wait, did you say yes?"

Opening his eyes, Steven nodded. "I'll do it."

"Well... great!" Dr. Myers's face broke into a broad smile. "That went better than I'd expected." He turned as if to go then glanced over his shoulder. "And just so you know, the facility is making special accommodations to allow you to work from there. You'll still need to focus most of your energy on getting better, but I don't want you to stress about your business. Just... try to find a balance, all right?"

"I will," Steven promised, and the conviction in his words took him by surprise.

~

True to his word, Dr. Myers kept Steven for observation for a few more days, and they were the most boring days of Steven's life. Only his father and a few friends came to visit. He hadn't expected Rose, though he couldn't quite quash the small piece of hope in his heart. After all, she worked at the hospital, so it wouldn't have been difficult for her to swing by.

But the visitor he missed even worse than Rose was Lanie. It wasn't like his sister to avoid him, especially since she'd arrived right after he'd collapsed. He'd thought she would come by every day, but he hadn't seen her since the breakup. To say he was hurt was an understatement. *Doesn't she understand that blood is thicker than water?* Sure, she and Rose were friends, but he was in the hospital. *Shouldn't my needs take precedence?*

Deep down, he could admit, at least to himself, that he understood why she hadn't come. She must have been so angry with him for screwing up the best relationship he could have ever hoped to have. Maybe she was helping Rose cancel the wedding. His throat burned, but he swallowed the pain. Perhaps Lanie believed he deserved it.

"Are you ready to bust out of this place?" His dad entered the room with an uncharacteristic smile on his normally grumpy face.

"More than ready," Steven said. The nurses had allowed him to briefly wander the grounds, but it had been a while since his last outdoor adventure.

"The doc says they'll spring you in an hour or so."

He'd been throwing himself a pity party for long enough. The transition to the rehab facility sounded like just the distraction he needed.

"Have you heard from Lanie?" Steven asked, trying to sound casual.

His father gave him a strange look. "I mean, we keep different hours, but she does still live with me."

So much for trying to sound nonchalant. "I, uh, figured she spent most of her time at Nate's."

"She's been spending several hours at your law firm this week." His father raised an eyebrow. "Hasn't she checked in with you?"

Steven shook his head. Sandra had called and texted a few times, which he appreciated. It helped break the monotony of the hospital stay. But his messages to Lanie had gone unanswered.

"Well, she's meeting us at the rehab center this afternoon, so you'll see her then."

The fact that his father sounded unbothered by Lanie's absence alleviated some of Steven's concern, but the churning in his stomach wasn't likely to subside until he saw his sister.

"I saw Rose yesterday," Dad continued, and there was an edge to his voice.

"Oh?" Steven took deep breaths to calm his racing heart.

"Ran into her on my way here. Seems she's keeping busy with extra shifts at the hospital."

A million questions bubbled on his lips, but he didn't know how to ask them without sounding as desperate as he was. Instead, he nodded and stared straight ahead, trying to look like he didn't care.

Dad ran a hand through his salt-and-pepper hair. "She looked good."

Steven opened his mouth, but nothing came out. What was he supposed to say? That he was happy she was doing well while he wasted away in a hospital bed? That he wished she'd come see him?

"Anyway…" His father shifted his weight to his other foot and dropped his gaze.

Steven took some comfort in the knowledge that their conversation was as awkward for his dad as it was for him.

"Just thought you'd want to know."

"Why?" Steven blurted out without thinking, and he immediately regretted it.

"Look, things aren't good between you two, but I think it's temporary—"

The thin hold he had on his emotions broke. "Temporary? Oh,

okay. So she just temporarily broke my heart. That makes everything better. Thanks, Dad."

"Don't be like that."

"Like what?" And all the pain he had pent up inside since Rose left him erupted like a raging river breaching a dam. "What good does it do me to hear Rose is moving on? That she's doing great while I'm lying here, day after day, with little to distract me."

"You're about to be discharged," Dad protested, though the fact that he wouldn't meet Steven's gaze betrayed how weak those words sounded.

"To an inpatient rehab for who knows how long." When Dad opened his mouth again, Steven held up a hand. "And before you tell me it's good for me, I know. I get that it's what I need, but it doesn't mean I'm happy about it." He stared at his hands, clenching them into fists as he fought to push his anger and pain back down his gut, where it belonged. "I was this close to having everything I ever wanted, and now I may lose it all. So forgive me if I'm having some trouble processing it."

Before Dad could respond, a familiar blond head appeared around the doorframe. "Everything okay in here?"

The joy Steven felt at seeing his sister was tempered by the memory that she hadn't been by sooner. He forced a smile, determined not to let her know how much her absence had hurt. The last thing he needed to do was alienate his entire family in one day.

"Lanie!" Dad said with faux excitement. Steven suspected his father was more grateful for the interruption than he was happy that Lanie had arrived. "I didn't expect to see you here."

"I finished helping Sandra with a major project at the law office. I was able to slip away earlier than expected." She slipped past Dad and wrapped an arm around Steven. "How're you holding up?"

Spiteful words sprang to mind, but he held his tongue. It began to ache with the effort. "Looking forward to getting out of here."

"I'll bet." Her arm tightened around him, and she lowered her voice. "Listen, I'm sorry for not stopping by sooner, but I needed to take care of a few things."

Why is she whispering? "Yeah, Dad said you were working at the firm. I appreciate it."

"Well, yes, I've been at the firm." She glanced at Dad, but he had wandered over to the window and was staring pointedly out at the parking lot. "But I've also been with Rose."

A flash of hot rage shot down his spine as he pulled away. "Seriously? You've been comforting her? Need I remind you *she* broke up with *me*?"

To his surprise, his sister rolled her eyes. "Oh, get over yourself. Don't act like you had no part in her decision. Besides, you should thank me. I was doing damage control."

"What is that supposed to mean?"

"I convinced her not to cancel the wedding."

You did what?

Even Dad spun away from the window, betraying the fact that he'd been listening to their every word. Steven gritted his teeth as he tried to process what she'd said.

"Why would you do that?" he demanded. "She might still be able to get some of the money back if she cancels now."

Lanie stared at him as if he was the one being obtuse. "As long as there's a wedding, you won't lose any money."

Maybe Lanie had lost her mind. "Um, how is there going to be a wedding when Rose broke up with me?"

She lifted her eyes to the ceiling. "Do I have to spell everything out for you?" Shaking her head, she sat on the bed and took his hand. "Rose didn't want to break up with you. She still loves you, but she doesn't trust you to actually follow through on your promises, and she's scared she's going to lose you soon after the wedding."

Pulling his hand back, he scowled at her, but she ignored him.

"Correct me if I'm wrong, but this latest health episode seems to have been the wake-up call you needed."

Steven nodded, not quite sure where she was going.

"Better late than never," she said under her breath.

"Can we cut the shaming and get to the point?"

"If you can prove you're taking things seriously this time *and* that you're doing it for yourself, for your health..." She took a deep breath. "I have reason to believe Rose will give you a second chance and the wedding can move forward as planned."

"But it's barely a month away at this point," their father piped up. "And we don't know how long Steven will be in rehab."

"The doctor said if I follow the advice of my therapists, I could be out in a couple of weeks."

"Perfect." Lanie searched his face. "I assume you'd still like to be able to walk at the wedding as well?" At his nod, she smiled. "Great. And what about the first dance?"

Chapter Twenty-Six

"ARE YOU GOING TO VISIT STEVEN BEFORE HE LEAVES?"

Rose started at the sound of the voice and spun around. Dr. Myers leaned against the doorframe of the nurses' station, one eyebrow raised.

"I doubt he wants to see me." She turned back to her paperwork to hide her face. How she had any tears left at that point was beyond her.

"You'd be surprised." He snatched the patient file from the desk, which forced her to face him again.

After making a few attempts to reclaim her file, she crossed her arms and glowered at him. "Why do you care? Weren't you the one who warned me away from becoming his caretaker? How did you put it?" She tapped her chin. "'Don't become the next Melissa.'"

To her immense satisfaction, he shifted uncomfortably. "That was a different situation."

Her mouth dropped open. "Are you serious?"

For a moment, he wouldn't meet her eyes, but when he finally did, his expression was grave. "I am." He ruffled his hair. "Look, this is going to sound like a line, but Steven has finally seen the light. I expected him to argue against returning to the rehab facility, but he willingly agreed. And he—"

She shoved past him, not wanting to hear another word. Without a backward glance, she raced off to do her rounds. *So what if they aren't due for another hour, and who cares if he has my files?* She would improvise.

But she had barely reached her first patient's room when he caught up to her. "Rose, stop."

"No," she said, and they both blinked at her sharp tone. She'd never spoken to him like that before. Clearing her throat, she tried again. "I understand that as Steven's doctor, you want to reduce his stress level, and I'm sorry if my actions have made your job more difficult." Her eyes burned with unshed tears, and she lowered her head to hide them. "But you can't expect me to go see him. What good would it do either of us? It'd cause more pain, and he doesn't need that right now."

He placed a gentle hand on her shoulder. "What he needs is to be surrounded by people who care about him." Her face must have betrayed her feelings, because he released her and raised his hands in surrender. "I'm not saying get back together with him. Just... talk to him. It'll be less awkward to do it here than at the rehab facility."

Before she could respond, he turned and walked away. With a frustrated sigh, she went back to the nurses' station where he'd left her files and got back to work. But his words needled her.

Isn't it bad enough that I let Lanie convince me to hold off on contacting the wedding vendors? When she'd left the hospital the day of the breakup, she'd been determined to take the necessary steps to cancel everything so that there was no turning back. However, all of her resolve had gone out the window after a night of wallowing with Lanie. She should have started making calls as soon as she'd made her decision, regardless of what Lanie said.

Perhaps it was the way Lanie had approached the situation. Rose had expected her to say she might change her mind or that she should consider giving Steven a second chance. But instead, she'd suggested they repurpose the wedding and maybe throw another type of party. A part of Rose wondered whether Lanie hoped to repurpose the wedding for herself. She and Nate had been having a tough time finding a venue that would accommodate a Christmas wedding since it was less than six months away.

With a sigh, Rose shook her head. No, repurposing the wedding would be out of character for Lanie. Then again, weddings made people do crazy things.

Like end relationships. She closed her eyes. *Has it been only a few days since that fateful conversation with Steven?* It felt like weeks ago, but that was probably because she'd picked up so many extra shifts at the hospital. In some ways, it was counterintuitive to want to spend more time where Steven was, but she hadn't actually seen him. The hospital policy forbidding staff from treating family members had gone from a thorn in her side to a godsend in the span of a couple of months.

Dr. Myers's words replayed in her head. Maybe she should visit Steven, if for nothing else than to check on him. Perhaps even bolster her resolve that she'd made the right choice.

She argued with herself for the rest of her shift. By the time she'd finally worked up the nerve to head to his room, it was empty. He was already gone.

The next day, Rose stepped off the elevator onto her floor, ready to start another shift. But as she approached the nurses' station, her belly fluttered at the sight of a crowd gathered around the desk, their backs to her.

"What's going on?" she asked.

Everyone turned at the sound of her voice and yelled, "Congratulations!"

Some of the nurses held balloons, one had a card, and Rebecca stood in the center of them all with a two-tiered cake. Rose stared, bewildered about what on earth was going on.

"Dr. Myers is going to kill me for planning this," Rebecca said as she set the cake down and walked over to Rose. "But I wanted to share the good news." Her eyes lit up. "You've got the head nurse position."

"What?" Rose could hardly believe her ears. "But... Why? How?" Questions raced through her mind as she digested the news. "Nobody called me."

"Consider this your offer." Rebecca handed her a stack of pages. "It's all detailed in here." At Rose's silence, she frowned. "I'm sorry. Did I overstep? I thought after everything you've been through, it would be nice to receive news with a bit of fanfare."

Rose shook her head. "No, this is wonderful." She raised her eyes to look at the rest of the nurses. "Thank you so much."

"The board would like to meet with you at ten this morning to formally make the offer and discuss any questions you have." With a smile, Rebecca began cutting the cake. "In the meantime, let's celebrate your achievement."

Forcing a smile in return, Rose began skimming the documents Rebecca had given her. A few weeks ago, she would have been ecstatic. The bump in pay alone would have been a welcome addition to the start of her new life with Steven.

But that was then. Since their breakup, Rose had been leaning toward going back to Baltimore or trying to find a position at that hospital in Boston. She'd never dreamed she would stay in Cedar Haven. It was Steven's hometown, and she didn't belong there if she wasn't with him.

"I realize it's a bit early for cake," Rebecca continued. "But I wanted us to have a chance to eat it before things get hectic."

"It's never too early for chocolate." Rose accepted her piece and took a bite. Her heart panged at the realization that it was red velvet, the same flavor she and Steven had chosen for their wedding cake.

Her appetite disappeared, and she set the cake down. "Excuse me."

Without waiting for a response, she rushed to the bathroom. She ran into a stall and emptied the contents of her stomach.

A knock sounded at the stall door. "Rose? Are you all right?"

Say yes. "No." She couldn't bring herself to fake joy for one more moment.

"Talk to me," Rebecca pleaded. "Tell me what's going on."

"I can't take the job," Rose said dully. After hauling herself off the bathroom floor, she flushed the toilet and left the stall. Avoiding Rebecca's gaze, she washed her hands at the sink and rinsed out her mouth.

"What do you mean you can't take it?"

"I'm leaving."

Rebecca touched her arm. "Where are you going?"

The contact almost pushed Rose over the edge, and she stepped back. She needed to keep control of her emotions, or she would never get through her shift.

"I don't know yet. But I can't stay here. Not now. Not with St—" Her voice caught in her throat, and she buried her face in her hands.

Rebecca sighed. "I shouldn't have sprung this on you. I was excited to share the news and hoped it would lift your spirits." She wrapped an arm around Rose's shoulders. "Please don't go. I know things with you and Steven are raw, but leaving isn't the answer. You're needed here. And you're valued."

When Rose didn't respond, Rebecca continued, "At least talk to the board before you decide anything."

Though she wanted to protest, Rose didn't have the energy. "Fine. But I'm not making any promises."

"Keeping an open mind is all I ask."

Chapter Twenty-Seven

It had been a week since Steven entered the rehab facility. Though he hated being cooped up, he appreciated having some distance from his real life. He hoped it might eventually ease the pain of his broken heart.

"Knock, knock," a voice called from his door. When he turned, Lanie stood in the doorway with two cups of coffee.

"I can't have caffeine right now."

She shrugged. "It's decaf."

"Thanks, I think." By that point, he'd gotten used to not having coffee. The facility didn't offer decaf, and tea didn't do it for him.

"Any word from Rose?" Lanie asked.

Steven raised an eyebrow. She knew perfectly well he hadn't heard from Rose since that fateful day at the hospital. He'd long since given up on hoping she would stop by.

"Have you seen her?" he countered.

"Here and there." Lanie dropped her gaze. "She was offered the head nurse position at the hospital."

That wasn't surprising, though it pained him to hear it second-hand. "I'm proud of her."

"Though she's not sure she's going to take it."

Steven frowned as he sipped his coffee. "Why wouldn't she?"

Instead of answering, Lanie stood and walked to the window. "You have a nice view from here."

"Lanie," Steven said. "What's going on?"

With a sigh, Lanie turned to him. "She brought up moving back to Baltimore."

Pain radiated in his throat as he struggled to swallow the news. If she was leaving, that meant things were well and truly over between them.

They needed to change the subject, or he was going to lose it. He'd kept it together pretty well thus far and didn't want to fall apart in front of his sister.

"Are you going by the office today?"

The question appeared to catch Lanie off guard. "Yeah, I promised Michael I'd help him with some filing. Why?"

"Could you ask Michael to visit?" Steven asked. He might have lost Rose, but he still had hope of saving his practice.

His sister's eyebrows shot up. "Uh-oh. Is he in trouble?"

He rolled his eyes. "Of course not. He's been there over a month now, and I want to check in with him."

"And try to determine whether he plans to accept the offer from the DC law firm?" Lanie teased.

Am I that transparent? "That may be part of it."

"For what it's worth, he seems happy to me. They may have offered him more money and a career track, but if you consider bringing him on as, like, a junior partner, he might stick around."

Steven gave a noncommittal nod. Ever since his conversation with Michael, he'd been reconsidering his stance on expanding his business to include a partner. Michael had not only far surpassed his expectations, he'd also shown Steven that he didn't have to do everything alone. While he still had misgivings about sharing his business, if he had to bring on a partner, Michael would be an ideal candidate once he passed the bar.

A knock at the door caused them to start. His physical therapist leaned against the frame and offered a tight smile to Lanie.

"Sorry to interrupt, but it's time for you to head to the gym."

"Ah, my daily torture appointment," Steven quipped. "Lanie, this is Ursula, my least favorite member of my rehab team."

"I guess that's my cue," Lanie said as she stood. Leaning over, she wrapped her arms around his shoulders and gave him an awkward squeeze. "I'll be back tomorrow."

"I'll hold you to that."

When she was gone, the therapist stepped over to his bed. "Want to walk or ride to the gym?"

Steven peered out the door. "Is there anyone else here to see me?"

After glancing up and down the hallway, Ursula shook her head. "Your secret is safe."

"Good." Steven grinned and swung his legs over the bed. With Ursula's assistance, he stood and grabbed his cane.

The next day, Steven was pleased when Michael entered his room, a stack of folders in his arms. He set the folders on the bed and pulled up a chair.

"I brought everything I've been working on for the past week," Michael said as he shuffled the folders into some semblance of order.

Steven waved a hand. "I actually didn't invite you here to go over your workload."

"Oh, sorry. I just assumed..."

"It's no bother. And we should discuss it at some point, but I wanted to finish our last conversation."

Michael shifted uncomfortably. "We can wait until you're out of rehab. Even if I accept the offer, I plan to give a good deal of notice."

"I appreciate that, but it's best if we discuss it now." Steven cleared his throat. The conversation was harder on him than he'd expected it to be. Swallowing his pride and going back to inpatient rehab was one thing, but handing over a substantial share of his business was another thing entirely. "I've given a lot of thought to what you said, and I'd like to discuss what you imagine a track to partnership would look like."

"Well, it would be much different than the typical track at an established firm. But..." Michael scratched his head.

"Yes?" Steven prompted.

"I'd like to be an equal partner, and with that in mind, I'd like to buy into the business."

Of all the things Steven had expected him to say, that was not one of them. "What do you mean?"

"I mean that in addition to sharing the workload, I'd like to invest in the firm." At Steven's frown, Michael hurried on. "My grandparents created a trust fund for me when I was a baby. I planned to use it to open my own firm one day, but this seems like a better opportunity. There's clearly a need in town, and you're a known entity to the people here. So I wouldn't be starting from scratch."

A plethora of emotions shot through Steven. While he'd once feared an established attorney would want to buy his firm or merge it with their own, he'd never considered that someone might own the business equally with him. *And why would I?* Most law school graduates were drowning in student debt. They couldn't afford to invest in an established firm. After all, he'd barely managed to scrounge together the funds to open his own firm.

"So, what do you think?" Michael asked when Steven didn't respond.

The excitement building inside Steven was tempered only by the fear that Michael wouldn't want to be stuck in a small town. "Would that be enough to entice you to stay, though? I can't promise we'll make anywhere near what you would even as an associate in a larger firm."

"I'm not hurting for money," Michael said with a sheepish grin. "And I have other reasons for wanting to stick around."

"Such as?"

The blush that bloomed over Michael's cheeks confused Steven for a moment, then it clicked.

"Ah, this is about a woman, isn't it?"

"I may have gone out with Toccara a few times," Michael admitted.

Steven laughed and raised his hand. "Say no more."

"There is one thing you should know, though." With a sigh, Michael leaned forward. "My father wants me to make a name for myself, and he's one of the main reasons I received the offer that I did."

"I see," Steven said. "It sounds like you have a lot to consider."

Michael nodded. "But I promise to give you an answer soon."

"There's no rush. You'd have to pass the bar before we could make anything official, but I'd love to have you come on board as an equal partner."

"Believe me, if it were up to me, I'd much prefer working in a small-town firm where I might make a difference over slaving away in the big city for corporate cronies who don't even know my name."

Steven laughed. "They're not all bad." His experience was centered in Baltimore, but he didn't miss the hustle. He nodded at the folders. "In the meantime, why don't you bring me up to speed on where you are with things."

Michael seemed eager to change the subject and launched into a detailed presentation on all he'd been working on. While they spoke, a question nagged at Steven. If Michael turned him down, what was plan B?

Chapter Twenty-Eight

What am I doing here? Rose asked herself for the millionth time as she parked outside of the rehab facility and looked at herself in the rearview mirror.

While she could blame it on the need to discuss canceling vendors or even asking for Steven's assistance in alerting his side of the family, the truth was Max had asked her to come. He'd called the night before to check on her and had ended the conversation with a simple request that Rose find it in her heart to visit Steven.

"I'm not asking you to forgive him or to take him back," Max had said. "Only to see for yourself how far he's come."

And so she had. She just hadn't quite mustered up the courage to get out of the car and walk into the building.

"No matter what he says," she told her reflection, "it doesn't change anything."

The doubt in her eyes did nothing to help her resolve. She debated putting the car back in gear and hightailing it out of there, but she'd come that far. She might as well see it through.

Steeling herself for an unhappy reunion, she forced her body from the car and dragged her feet to the rehab entrance. It took more effort than she cared to admit to open the door and step inside.

The receptionist's face lit up when she saw Rose. "He'll be thrilled you're here!"

Did Max tell the whole place I was coming? Ugh, what they must think of her, deserting her fiancé in his condition. She shook her head. *You're overreacting.* The more likely explanation was that the woman had recognized her from her visits when Steven was there before.

She followed the receptionist down the hall. When they reached Steven's room, she moved aside to let Rose pass.

But her feet were frozen to the floor. Her heart pounded in her ears. She'd made a terrible mistake in going there.

Just as she turned to leave, a familiar voice rang out. "Rose? Is that you?"

"Go on," the receptionist urged. "He's been expecting you."

With a sigh, Rose shuffled into the room and closed the door behind her. She held onto the doorknob longer than necessary as she warred with a fight-or-flight reaction. Finally, she peeled her hand away and slowly turned to face him.

She didn't know what she expected to see, but the sight of him sitting up in bed with a smile wasn't it. Part of her wondered if she had dreamed the whole breakup.

"It's good to see you," he said with a slight edge to his voice. It was all the confirmation she needed that the meeting was awkward and uncomfortable for both of them.

"You too." Her feet glided toward him of their own accord, like a magnetic force was pulling them together. *Or a moth to a destructive flame.*

If she wasn't careful, she was going to get burned... again. He didn't give her a chance to react before he reached for her hand as if it were the most natural thing in the world.

Warning bells went off in her head as the warmth that spread up her arm was too much, and she pulled away. There was no missing the disappointment in his eyes.

She cleared her throat. "How've you been?"

"Better, actually." He patted the space beside him, but she shook her head. Things were different between them, and she needed to maintain physical distance if she had any hope of preserving her sanity.

"That's good."

"Yeah," he continued as if he couldn't bear the awkward silence any more than she could. "Dr. Myers is supposed to come by today and talk to my doctors here." A wry smile pulled on his lips. "I might be released by the end of the week."

She blinked. "That soon?"

His face fell. "I'm not sure I'd call it 'soon' after being stuck here for a couple of weeks, but I've improved immensely." His hazel eyes flicked to hers before he returned to pointedly staring at a loose thread on his blanket. "So I'll be leaving with full support from my medical team."

"This time," she said without thinking.

He pressed his lips together. "Yes, this time."

His chest rose and fell as he took a deep breath, and she braced herself for a subject change.

"How are the wedding cancellations going?"

Warmth crept up her neck and into her cheeks, and she bowed her head to hide it. Ever since the night Lanie had stopped by, she'd avoided anything wedding related. Carissa had been blowing up Rose's phone, likely having heard the wedding was off through the town's gossip mill. But she didn't want him to know about her hesitation. It might give him the wrong idea. *Should I lie and say I've already canceled everything?*

"I'm sorry I can't help with that," Steven said, his voice sincere enough to make her look at him. "And I'm sorry that it's... necessary."

So he didn't know. *Good.* It was better that way. No need to get his hopes up that she had changed her mind.

A heaviness settled in her body. On the one hand, she was relieved he seemed to have accepted her decision. It would make their visit more pleasant if she didn't have to worry about defending her choice. But on the other hand, a part of her felt cheated. After all they'd been through, he wasn't even going to fight for her.

I'm not some damsel in distress. I don't need *a man to want to be with me.*

While the truth of those words reverberated through her, a tiny voice inside questioned whether her disappointment was about needing him to fight or *wishing* he wanted her enough to do so.

"Rose?" he prompted. "Are you still with me?"

"Uh, yes, sorry," she stammered. "I have a few things to take care of, but I've almost canceled everything." The lie almost caught in her throat, but she forced it out.

"That's news to me," a voice said from behind her. When she turned, her stomach dropped to the floor as she saw Lanie leaning against the doorframe.

Rose shot Lanie a pleading look. "I haven't had an opportunity to tell you."

"And it's probably going to be news to the catering staff at The Muddy Oar," Lanie continued, her tone cool. "They asked me to request that you call them the next time I see you. Seems they've been having a time getting in touch with you."

Rose's mouth went dry. Her gaze vacillated between Steven and Lanie as she thought fast. Things had been going so well, but if he found out she hadn't canceled their wedding, it might give him false hope.

"They're next on my list." *Play along,* Rose silently begged Lanie.

Steven's face fell the slightest bit, confirming to Rose that he'd held some hope they could mend things. But his sister's eyes glinted with suspicion.

"I see." Though from her tone, it sounded like Lanie didn't

believe her at all. "Anyway, I stopped by to drop off some homemade cookies." She pushed past Rose and set them on Steven's bedside table before kissing his forehead.

"Thanks, sis," Steven said with a stiff smile. "Would you mind giving us a minute?"

Before Lanie could respond, Rose said, "No, that's okay. I need to go anyway." She spun on her heel and practically ran to the door.

She didn't stop moving until she was in the parking lot, the blinding sun blazing down on her head. But she would take the humidity. Anything was less stifling than being in that room.

"Rose, wait!"

Despite every bone in her body telling her not to, Rose turned and faced Lanie. "Why did you do that? Why would you give him false hope?"

"Is it false?" Lanie cocked her head. "In spite of your insistence to Steven, you haven't canceled anything, have you? Instead, you've been dodging calls from both your vendors and Carissa."

There was no point in denying it. If Lanie had spoken to Carissa, then she knew everything.

When Rose didn't respond, Lanie took a deep breath. "I won't pretend to know why. But I can't help hoping that once you hear what I have to say, you'll definitively decide not to cancel the wedding and give him another chance."

Not likely. Rose crossed her arms with a frown but didn't interrupt.

"You know Steven entered rehab of his own accord. But what you don't know is he also offered the partnership to Michael."

Black dots swam before Rose's eyes, and she grabbed onto her car to steady herself. "He what?"

"Now don't get too excited." Lanie hurried on. "Michael received a job offer in DC, and he has to pass the bar before he can accept either opportunity."

While Lanie continued talking, Rose barely heard her. Not only had Steven gone into rehab, but he'd also chosen to find a partner.

Something told her if Michael didn't work out, Steven would find someone else. He was listening and learning like she'd always hoped he would.

Is it enough, though? She couldn't ignore that it had taken her breaking up with him and calling off the wedding to finally get to that point. *If I give him another chance, how far will I have to go the next time he refuses to listen to me?*

"This latest incident shook him," Lanie was saying when Rose tuned back in. "I mean, don't get me wrong, losing you was also a wake-up call." She gave a weak smile. "But the reality that his health issues might actually kill him was ultimately the kick in the pants he needed."

"I'm glad something did." Rose tried to keep her tone neutral. She needed time to consider her next move—and whether she could trust Steven again. "And I appreciate you telling me."

"But it doesn't change anything?" Lanie's face fell.

"I need more time," Rose said.

With a reluctant nod, Lanie threw her arms around Rose and pulled her into a tight hug. "I understand." She stepped back and gave a sad smile. "I'd say if you need to talk, I'm here, but I'm not sure I can play the unbiased third party."

"Nor would I ask you to," Rose said.

They hugged once more, and Lanie moved aside and let Rose into her car. She waved goodbye before heading back into the building.

As Rose left the parking lot, her mind raced. Steven had made many strides in fixing things, and the fact that he hadn't told her all of them meant he wasn't doing it for her. Or at least, he wasn't doing it *only* for her. *And that has to mean something, right?* But whether it was enough for her to give him another chance, she didn't know.

Chapter Twenty-Nine

"I'M HERE TO SPRING YOU!" LANIE RUSHED INTO STEVEN'S room with a huge smile on her face.

"What do you mean? I thought I wasn't leaving until the end of the week."

"Call it time off for good behavior." Dr. Myers grinned as he strode into the room, followed by Dr. Bhati. "Or more accurately, early release for massive improvements." He flipped through Steven's chart. "Your therapists think you can continue on an outpatient basis."

The room was silent as if everyone was waiting for his reaction. He expected to feel excited, but that wasn't the emotion churning away in his stomach. There were too many what-ifs. *What if I relapse? What if I have another heart attack?*

Lanie frowned and took his hand. "What's wrong?"

The old Steven would have brushed her off and insisted he was fine, just in shock. But between his health scares and losing Rose, something had changed within him. He no longer wanted to push people away and pretend he was fine.

"I'm scared."

Dr. Myers's face softened. "That's normal after what you've been through, but I promise you, we wouldn't discharge you if I didn't have the utmost confidence in your continued recovery."

That was something, especially since last time, he'd left rehab against medical advice. The fact that he had the full support of his medical team helped calm his anxiety. But one other thing nagged at him.

"Do you think I'll be able to walk on my own, without a cane?"

Dr. Bhati frowned. "Your physical therapist believes so..."

Steven could hear the hesitation in his voice. "But?"

"But we're not sure when."

"I suppose it doesn't matter anyway," he grumbled. Since the wedding was already canceled, there was no deadline for him to be able to walk again anymore. That was the other reason he wasn't in a hurry to leave. He had no one to rush home to.

"Don't be like that." Lanie squeezed his hand. "You've got to stay positive."

He forced a smile for her benefit, but by the expression on her face, it wasn't very convincing.

"Anyway," Dr. Myers said, clearly trying to keep them on topic, "I've got some discharge paperwork here for you with instructions." His face turned stern. "But just because we're letting you go home doesn't mean you can jump right back into your life. You still need to take it easy and avoid overexerting yourself."

"Understood," Steven said. The last thing he or his business needed was another stint in the hospital—or worse.

"I brought you some clothes." Lanie handed him a bag and hooked her thumb over her shoulder. "I'll wait outside while you change."

"And I'll see you next week for a follow-up appointment," Dr. Bhati said.

They all left the room, giving him some much-needed privacy. He stared at the bag in his hand, trying to ignore the anxiety clawing up his chest. *Am I ready for this? Can I really keep from stressing out once I'm back in my old life? Will the changes I've made stick?*

A part of him wished it had been Rose instead of Lanie who had shown up. He wanted to talk to her again, show her all he'd done to get better. Maybe she would come by once she heard he was home. He crossed his fingers as he dressed.

Less than a half hour later, Steven and Lanie drove away from the facility. It was the first time he'd been in a car in weeks. Despite his misgivings about leaving, he couldn't wait to be home. The rehab bed wasn't comfortable, and while he didn't consider himself an introvert, there was something to being able to shut out the world and enjoy some alone time.

"Welcome home," Lanie said as she pulled into his driveway.

Two cars were parked to one side, and he held his breath as he searched the yard for his visitors. But his ribs tightened when he realized the cars belonged to his father and Michael.

Dad came to the passenger side and opened his door. "How does it feel to be free?"

Steven laughed. "It's not like I was in prison, Dad."

His dad harrumphed. "Might as well have been."

Even though it was pointless, Steven allowed his eyes to sweep over the yard one more time in case he'd missed Rose hiding somewhere. Dad didn't miss the look.

"I'm sorry she's not here, son."

With a nod, Steven grabbed his cane and walked to his front door. On the bright side, he was alive, he was home, and he was no longer confined to a wheelchair.

"We'll bring your stuff in and unpack it," Lanie called from behind.

Michael held the door open. "Welcome home, boss."

Once Steven was inside, he headed to the dining room, where a nice spread of all his favorite lunch fixings had been laid out on the table—ham, turkey, an assortment of cheeses, and spicy mayonnaise. His stomach was churning too much to be hungry, but he decided to humor his family. The last thing he needed was for them to report to Dr. Myers that he wasn't eating.

"Would you like something to drink?" Michael asked, coming into the room behind him.

He nodded and slid into a chair, leaning his cane against the table. A moment later, Lanie appeared and moved it to the corner. He frowned at her, but she rolled her eyes.

"I'll bring it back when you're ready to get up," she said, waving her hand before disappearing with Dad to Steven's bedroom.

He wanted to follow her and not just because he was particular about how his clothes were put away. But he couldn't find the energy to do so.

Michael stared at him expectantly. *Oh, right, he asked if I wanted a drink.* "Water, please."

When Michael left to go to the kitchen, Steven leaned forward and rested his head in his hands. Though he had no reason to do so, he couldn't help hoping Rose would be there to greet him. But he had only himself to blame for the crushing disappointment he felt.

Michael returned with the glass and set it in front of Steven. "So, are you glad to be home?"

"I am," Steven said. "How are things at the office?"

"They're going well," Michael continued when Steven didn't say anything more. "Even Mr. Willoughby seems to be appeased."

Steven snorted. "I wonder how long that will last."

Michael chuckled. "His divorce date is scheduled for September. I give it a month."

Finally, Steven couldn't stand the small talk anymore. "Why aren't you at the office today?"

Michael stared at his hands. "I wanted to tell you I made my decision."

Swallowing his fears, Steven nodded. "And?"

Michael squared his shoulders. "I discussed your offer with my father. At first, he had some misgivings, but when I showed him the good work you're doing, he agreed it would be a good investment for me and a way to make a name for myself."

Steven stared at him, dumbstruck. "Wait, so you're..."

"Accepting your offer to come on as an equal partner?" Michael beamed. "Absolutely."

Once Steven had recovered from his shock, he stood and stuck his hand out. "That's the best news I've heard all day. Welcome aboard, partner!"

Chapter Thirty

When Rose answered a knock at her door, the last person she expected was the bald man from the pond. He tipped his ball cap in greeting.

"Hello there. How can I help you?" she asked.

"I promised I would tell you when the male swan was being rereleased into the pond. My friend is dropping him off in ten minutes if you want to come see."

"Oh!" She'd almost forgotten about the swans. "Of course. Thank you for remembering."

They walked down to the pond, where a large truck had pulled up. The men who had captured the swan were lowering the tailgate, and the bald man went to help them lift the cage from the back of the truck.

After they opened the cage, the bald man reached in and lifted the swan, whose body was secured in a bag. He carefully unstrapped the bag from around the swan, and once the swan's wings were free, it dashed into the water to join its mate. The female swan immediately swam over.

"They're so happy to be reunited," Rose breathed, awed by the scene in front of her.

"Just wait," the bald man whispered with a grin. "The show's about to start."

At first, Rose didn't understand what he meant, but as she watched, the swans bent their necks toward each other as if they were bowing. They started moving their heads in a synchronous motion. Circling each other, they raised their wings and pressed their foreheads together in an intricate ballet.

"They're dancing!" Rose exclaimed in delight.

"That, they are. It's part of their mating ritual. Some say it helps them to rebuild the bond to dance together like this, especially after time apart." The bald man wiped his eyes. "It's one of the most beautiful things I've ever seen."

Rose couldn't think of a response worthy of what she was witnessing. The swans continued their coordinated movements, coming together in the sweetest reunion she had ever seen.

"She never lost faith," Rose whispered, more to herself than the stranger who had brought her there.

"That's true love," the man agreed.

Her heart broke anew. *Why can't Steven and I have what these swans do? Why do humans have to complicate things?* The female swan trusted that her mate would recover from his injury and return to her, and her reward was the swan version of a loving embrace.

But life—well, her life anyway—wasn't like that. Swans didn't have day jobs that kept them from their families. They didn't have a million distractions that prevented them from truly connecting. And Rose couldn't help feeling that swans got the better deal.

As she continued to watch, the swans placed their foreheads together and formed a heart shape with their necks. It was the perfect symbol of their devotion, and her heart longed to have a love like that again.

Ping. Rose removed her phone from her pocket and read the text message from Lanie. It contained only two words: *Steven's home.*

The fact Steven hadn't texted was a message in and of itself. It told her he wasn't going to push her to visit, that he was giving her all the space she could possibly want.

Maybe he truly has changed. The thought gave her stomach a flutter, the first real feeling of hope she'd had in a while.

Turning her attention back to the swans, the knot that had formed in Rose's belly the moment she'd heard of Steven's heart attack loosened, and everything suddenly became clearer. She understood why the female swan had held onto hope her mate would return. She knew what she wanted to do, but she needed to talk to Steven first.

When Steven answered Rose's knock, she wasn't expecting him to stand before her on his own two feet with a cane for support. It took every ounce of control she had not to rush into his arms. He looked much improved from the last time she'd seen him.

"May I come in?" she asked.

Without saying a word, Steven nodded and stepped to the side. Rose took a deep breath and entered the home they'd planned to share. Part of her questioned her decision to speak to him there instead of somewhere less meaningful, but she didn't want to risk having the whole town hear their business.

He led her to the couch and sat stiffly on one side. Her heart in her throat, she sat opposite him. They stared at each other as Rose tried to decide where to begin.

"Not that I'm not happy to see you," Steven said, breaking the silence, "but why are you here?"

Speak from the heart. "Your sister said something the other day as I was leaving the rehab facility, and I wondered if it was true."

Steven's hands clenched into fists. "And what was that?"

She chewed her lip before responding. "That you offered the partnership to Michael."

"Oh." His shoulders visibly relaxed. "Yeah, I did."

"Why didn't you tell me?" she asked in a rush.

He shrugged. "I didn't think you'd care."

With one eyebrow raised, she leaned forward. "I practically begged you to take on a partner. Why on earth wouldn't I care that you finally did so?"

Dropping his gaze, he fidgeted in his seat. "I guess I was worried you'd question my motives."

Though it hurt to hear, she understood. "I suppose I deserve that."

"No." His eyes widened. "You were right. I wasn't taking care of myself, and I'm sorry it took losing you to realize it."

"Well, losing me and going back in the hospital," she joked, though her voice shook.

"Yeah, that too." He gave her a tentative smile. "But I'm better now. I've been making great progress in therapy, and I'm happy to report Michael has accepted my offer."

It was as if a huge weight had lifted off Rose's shoulders. "He did? When?"

"This afternoon. He's coming back over tomorrow so we can finalize the details."

"Oh, Steven, that's wonderful news. I'm happy for you."

"And I hear that the hospital offered you the head nurse position," Steven said. "Congratulations."

She ducked her head. "Oh, um, thanks. I haven't actually accepted it yet." She squared her shoulders and looked him in the eye. "But I intend to tell them when I go in for my next shift, and then I'll start the position mid-September."

"That's good to hear. They're lucky to have you." The smile on his face faltered, and he cleared his throat. "Anyway, now that I'm home, I'm happy to help with any remaining wedding cancelations. I'm sorry you were on your own with that for so long."

Warmth spread across her cheeks. "Um, about that."

He cocked his head with a frown. "What's wrong?"

"Look, I want to say I'm sorry for how I reacted when you went into the hospital this last time." She closed her eyes as she recalled how terrified she was when she got the call that he was being admitted again. "I was hurt and scared. You weren't taking care of yourself, and I couldn't bear to watch you dig your own grave."

He grabbed her hand and squeezed it. "I'm sorry, Rose."

She took a shaky breath. "I just... You're so stubborn." She rolled her eyes. "Your whole family is, and I feared you'd never see reason. But when Lanie informed me of everything you'd been doing..." Her eyes met his, and everything clicked into place. "The fact that you didn't use it to try to win me back when I came to see you showed me how much you'd changed."

"I swear to you, I have." He tightened his grip on her hand. "And I promise I will do anything if you would consider giving me another chance."

"That's the thing. I realized recently how much I miss you."

The smile on his face took her breath away. "I've missed you too. So very much."

"And I've not been fair to you," she continued, dropping her gaze.

His eyebrows pulled together. "You have that backward."

If the situation had been less serious, she might have laughed. "No, I mean it." She cupped his cheek. "You were so hopeful when Lanie called my bluff about canceling the wedding, and I should have decided right then and there if I was going to actually go through with it or not."

"You needed time," Steven said. "And if you still need time, I understand. There's no rush. We can cancel or postpone it until we're ready. We don't have to—"

She held up a hand. "You see? You're bending over backward to make sure I'm okay, but what about your needs?"

He swallowed, and his eyes went a bit misty. "What I need is you. And I don't want to risk losing you by making you go through something you aren't ready for."

Her heart melted. "What I'm trying to say is, I want us to try again, and I'm not going to run away at the first sign of trouble." She bowed her head. "But I understand if you don't trust me because of what I did."

His eyebrows shot up. "Of course I trust you, but I also put you through a lot. So I understand if you're not sure of me."

"But I am sure of you," she said. After a moment's hesitation, she took his hand and pressed it to her heart. "I only broke up with you because I thought I could protect my heart from the pain of losing you if I did it on my own terms. But I was wrong. I know now what a mistake that was because you're the one for me." Her eyes filled with tears. "You're my swan."

"What?" he asked, a quizzical expression on his face.

"Never mind," she said with a watery laugh. "Just know I love you."

"Wait." His eyes widened. "Does this mean—"

She nodded. "Let's make this official."

The joy on his face left her speechless. She wrapped her arms around his neck and pressed her lips to his.

"Rose," he murmured into her hair as they parted. "My Rose."

And they were the sweetest words she had ever heard.

Epilogue

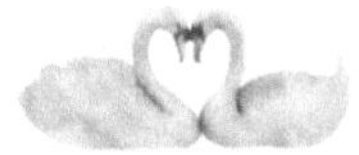

"I can't believe I'm getting married today," Rose said as she sat beside Lanie at the salon.

"And to think, it almost didn't happen." Lanie reached over and grabbed Rose's hand. "But I'm glad you and Steven worked things out. I'm excited to have a sister."

Rose smiled. Her heart was so full that her eyes kept filling up with tears. That was proving to be a problem for the woman working on her hair and makeup. Ellie, Bea's granddaughter, groaned in frustration.

"If you keep crying, you're going to ruin my masterpiece," she complained.

"I'm sorry." Rose blinked rapidly, which only made the situation worse. "This is just such a happy day."

"Better put on some waterproof mascara, El, if you have any hope of that face making it to the picture portion of today," Lanie teased.

Ellie rolled her eyes. "I'm not sure that'll be enough with Ms. Waterworks over here."

"Excuse me, that's *Mrs.* Waterworks," Rose quipped.

"You're not a Mrs. yet, and at this rate, it may never happen." Lanie pursed her lips at Rose in the mirror.

"Fine, fine." It took effort, but Rose managed to control her emotions. When they were both finished, Lanie helped Rose into her dress, a simple white ball gown with off-the-shoulder straps and a sweetheart neckline. Once they were dressed, Ellie had them pose by the window and snapped a few pictures.

"Now at least I'll have evidence of my skill in the event she cries it all off later."

Before Rose could respond, a knock sounded at the door. It was Dr. Myers, dressed to the nines in a tuxedo. He smiled at both women then raised an eyebrow at Rose.

"You ready?"

She nodded and handed Lanie her bouquet. Since her father couldn't be there, she'd asked Dr. Myers to give her away. She'd wanted to ask Max, but when Steven had asked him to be his best man, it didn't seem appropriate.

Lanie gave her arm a squeeze before she left to begin the wedding procession. The moment they were alone, Dr. Myers turned to her.

"I'm glad you decided to go through with it."

"You don't think I'm making a mistake? After what you went through with your ex, I mean."

He shook his head. "If Steven had continued the path he was on, then I would have worried for your welfare. But he's truly gained a new perspective these past few weeks. I have no doubt he'll continue to work at finding a better balance in his life and make his health more of a priority."

She smiled, as she felt exactly the same way. When he stuck out his elbow, she grabbed her bouquet and linked her arm through his. She took a deep breath, and they headed outside.

The church sat on top of a hill, overlooking the river. Closing her eyes, Rose lifted her face to the warmth of the late-August sun. The air was sticky with summer humidity, but when she opened her eyes, there were hints of the coming change in season. Some of the leaves on the tops of the trees had already begun to transition from the bright green of summer to the rich red of autumn. She was glad she and Steven had a weeklong cruise to look forward to, as she wasn't ready to bid goodbye to her favorite season just yet.

They reached the steps outside of the church, and Dr. Myers stopped. "This is where I leave you."

Rose frowned. "What? You have to walk me down the aisle."

With a sly smile, he put his hand on her shoulder and spun her around. There, standing directly behind her, were her parents.

Her heart leapt into her throat. "What? How?" She couldn't form a coherent sentence.

"Steven used some of the money from the fundraiser to buy the plane tickets before you broke things off," Mom explained as she embraced Rose. "When you called and said the wedding was off, I tried to cancel, but he wouldn't hear of it."

More tears welled up in Rose's eyes, and she prayed Ellie's mascara would hold. "I can't believe you're here."

Dr. Myers stepped to her side. "I assume my services are no longer needed. I'll go find a seat inside."

"Thank you," Rose said. "For everything."

With a nod, he climbed the stairs into the church, leaving Rose alone with her parents. Her father held out his arm.

"May I do the honors?"

"You both can," Rose said, taking his arm and grabbing her mother's as well. Together, they climbed the stairs to where Lanie was waiting.

Lanie gave Rose a thumbs-up before she and Max entered the church. As the door swung closed, Rose caught a glimpse of Steven standing at the front, waiting for her. He stood tall and proud and, if she wasn't mistaken, without his cane.

"Is he...?" Before she could finish the question, the door opened again, and the sound of the wedding march filled the room. It was her turn to walk down the aisle. Her heart hammered in her chest as she moved, her eyes never leaving Steven's. It took effort not to run straight into his arms, into her future.

When they reached the front of the church, her parents placed her hand in Steven's before kissing her cheeks and finding their seats. And then, it was as if everyone else disappeared when she looked up into Steven's face. She barely heard the preacher welcoming the crowd and paid only enough attention to what he was saying to know when to say "I do."

Before she knew it, the preacher said, "I now pronounce you husband and wife. You may kiss your bride."

Steven's eyes shone with unshed tears as he wrapped his arms around her waist and dipped her in a kiss. Cheers and whoops could be heard from the crowd, but Rose barely heard them. In spite of the trials they had faced, in spite of almost losing him twice, they had finally done it. And he was hers. Forever.

When he finally released her, breathless and grinning, he turned her to their gathered loved ones and raised their joined hands in triumph. Rose giggled at the silliness of the action. Soon, she found herself jostled away into the arms of her family, both old and new alike.

The first faces she saw were those of her parents, and she pulled them into a hug. Their presence had made the day so much more wonderful.

Lanie embraced her next, and the warmth and joy exuding from her now sister-in-law touched Rose. But she should have known nothing could break their bond. She and Lanie were soul sisters through and through.

Then she threw her arms around Max. Her father-in-law's hug was stilted and awkward, and he shifted away too soon.

"Welcome to the family."

"Thanks," she said with a wry smile. "So, now that your two children are paired up, don't you think it's your turn?"

Lanie laughed. "The day my dad remarries is the day hell freezes over."

Crossing his arms, he shook his head. “I gave marriage the old college try. It’s the bachelor life for me.”

“Pity for the rest of us,” Carissa said as she reached them, a clipboard in hand. “Not to break up this celebration, but we’ve got a schedule to keep.”

Max rolled his eyes. “Not everything has to be planned out to the second.”

“Just because you live life by the seat of your pants doesn’t mean the rest of us have to,” Carissa retorted. Then she wrapped an arm around Rose’s shoulders and led her over to Steven.

Rose grasped his arm and gently pulled him away from his friends. “We’ve got to go get photos taken.”

Her parents and Lanie and Max met up with them outside. Rose wondered whether they shouldn’t have skipped formal shots and stuck with candid photos. Neither of them had a very large family, and there were only so many ways to position their small group.

After posing for several photos, Rose was ready to eat. The photographer told their families to head into the reception hall while he finished up with a few shots of just Rose and Steven.

As soon as they were released to join the festivities, they quickly made their way to the reception for their grand entrance. Rose danced from foot to foot, anxious to get inside and enjoy a well-earned meal.

“And now, ladies and gentlemen, put your hands together for the new Mr. and Mrs. McAllister!”

Their friends and family clapped as Rose and Steven made their grand entrance. Her vision for the wedding was inspired by *A Midsummer Night’s Dream*. Tea lights hung in small globes from the rafters. Scalloped glass vases filled with white and pink roses and rich green leaves sat in the center of each table. Wreaths of hydrangeas and ivy adorned each window and twinkled with hidden fairy lights. The beauty of the room momentarily took Rose’s breath away.

She headed straight for their table, hoping to scarf down some food. But before she got to her seat, Steven grabbed her hand and pulled her to a stop just as the DJ called them back to the dance floor.

"What's going on?" she hissed, following Steven. "We agreed no formal dances." It hadn't seemed right at the time because her parents hadn't planned to attend and Steven's mother was gone.

Instead of responding, Steven smiled. Though he still had a slight limp, she'd been amazed at how steady he was on his feet.

"Are you sure?" Her eyes strayed to his legs, and she worried he would tire if he pushed himself too much.

"I am," he said, drawing her in close and taking her hand. "I've been practicing."

"You have?"

"Lanie and I started before the accident." His lips twitched. "She didn't want me to make a fool of myself for our first dance." He shrugged. "And once I'd made enough progress in PT, Dr. Bhati thought it would be good for improving my dexterity and coordination."

Taylor Swift's *This Love* began to play, and Steven led Rose in a simple waltz. She stared into his eyes, overwhelmed at the realization of how hard he'd had to work to make the moment happen.

"Oh my goodness. I can't believe you did this for me." Tears spilled over her cheeks, and she knew Ellie would kill her if she saw her.

He twirled her before enveloping her in his arms again. "I wanted to make today as special as I could, to show you how much you mean to me."

She rested her head on his shoulder and sighed. "It's just like the swans."

"I'm not sure I follow."

Lifting her head, she placed a hand on his cheek. "Swans mate for life. And when they are separated due to an illness, they perform this beautiful dance together to rekindle their bond."

"I never knew that," he said with a smile.

"I only learned it recently." She tightened her arms around him.

As the last notes of the song played, Steven twirled her once more before lifting her hand to his lips. Their friends and family cheered, and Rose felt on top of the world.

"I know you're hungry," he murmured into her ear. "But how would you feel about taking our dinner down to the river? There's a picnic table by the pier, and we could have a few minutes to ourselves."

A moment alone, just the two of them, was exactly what Rose needed. She grabbed her plate and followed him, slipping out the back door unnoticed.

The sun hung lower in the sky, and the breeze coming off the river held the promise of autumn. They sat on opposite sides of the picnic table near the pier and enjoyed their meal. Just as they were ready to leave, a fluttering of white feathers caught Rose's eye. There in the middle of the river was a pair of swans. Their long white necks formed a heart as they pressed their foreheads together before lifting their wings and circling each other.

"You see," Rose said, pointing. "They're dancing!"

Steven stood and pulled her into his arms again, swaying them back and forth. "And so are we."

~

When Doves Lament

Dedication

To my father and his "love" of brown pasta.

And to my stepmother who indulges his preferences.

Epigraph

"As when the dove laments her love
All on the naked spray
When he returns, no more she mourns
But loves the live-long day"

— Aria from Acis and Galatea
by Handel George Frideric

Chapter One

WHOEVER SAID IT WAS BETTER TO HAVE LOVED AND LOST than never to have loved at all had clearly never been divorced. The moment Max McAllister signed the divorce papers his ex-wife's lawyer had drawn up, he'd sworn off love for good.

Well, romantic love at least. His love for his children was apparent in the way he hoped each of them would have a more successful marriage than he'd had. As his son danced with his new bride, Max sent up a short prayer that the next generation of McAllisters wouldn't screw things up the way he had.

"Your mother would have loved this," he whispered to his daughter, Lanie, as they stood on the sidelines.

"I'm sure she's here in spirit." Lanie's hazel eyes glistened.

It'd been over a year since his ex-wife had died. Despite being divorced for more than a decade, he'd been by her side at the end.

"And I'm sure she's anxious to see you join your brother in marital bliss." Max slid his arm around his daughter and squeezed her shoulders. Her eyebrows rose in apparent surprise, and he pulled away gruffly. He supposed he deserved her reaction. They'd never been particularly close, a reality he was working to rectify since she'd moved back in with him. Besides, as far as affectionate parents went, that had been more Melody's area than his.

"What about you, Dad? Are you sure you don't want to give marriage another try?"

He snorted. "Definitely not. Once burnt twice shy, as they say."

"I believe the saying is once *bitten*."

"Sentiment's the same," he grumbled.

"The bride and groom invite everyone to join them on the dance floor," the DJ announced.

"Want to practice for the father–daughter dance?" Lanie lifted her arms, but Max waved a hand.

"I don't need to practice. I've been dancing since before you were born." As he spoke, his daughter's fiancé, Nate, walked up behind them. "This one, on the other hand, could probably use all the help he could get."

"Thanks for that," Nate muttered, pushing his dark-brown hair out of his face.

"You're better company, anyway," Lanie stage-whispered as she slid her hand through Nate's arm and led him away.

Max crossed his arms and leaned back against the pillar, surveying the reception. The wedding almost hadn't happened. His son, Steven, had suffered a heart attack a few months before. The doctors and Steven's nurse fiancée, Rose, had warned him to take it easy, but Steven hadn't heeded their advice. When he ended up back in the hospital, a frustrated Rose had broken their engagement.

Thankfully, Steven had seen the light and made choices that saved not only his relationship and the wedding but also his life. While he still had a long road to recovery, Max trusted his son would get there in the end.

Watching his children dance with their partners took him back to his own wedding. He and Melody were barely more than children themselves, having married when they were only nineteen. They'd been together since they were thirteen and hadn't seen the point in waiting any longer. But on reflection, he wished they had. Maybe if they'd left the small town of Cedar Haven and gone away to college, gained more life experience, things might have been different.

Well, no point dwelling on it now. Max ordered a soda at the bar. The bartender raised an eyebrow.

"Not much of a drinker," Max said, though he wasn't sure why he felt the need to explain himself. Still, he was probably the only person at the wedding who wasn't imbibing.

Drink in hand, he headed to his seat. Steven and Rose had opted for a sweetheart table, which meant Max had been seated with Nate, Lanie, and—his jaw clenched—that blasted wedding coordinator, Carissa. But as he approached his chair, he breathed a sigh of relief at the sight of the empty table.

If he never saw *that* woman again after the wedding, it would be too soon. After she'd vetoed every one of his suggestions for a rehearsal dinner spot, he'd appealed to his son in hopes that someone would be on his side. In the end, they'd compromised on an elegant restaurant on the edge of town. The cost was more than Max had expected to pay, but he was glad a local establishment had won over one of the many overused chains Carissa had suggested.

He checked his watch, relieved it was half past seven in the evening. About an hour to go before the bride and groom would make their grand escape, then he hoped to make his own. Weddings weren't really his thing, and he was already dreading going through it all over again in a couple of months with Lanie. Two kids married. Who would have thought he would be the only parent to witness it?

"Ah, Melody," he whispered. "They've done you proud."

A few hours later, the hall was clean. Max and Lanie walked outside, and Max took a deep breath of late-August evening air. Soon, the torturous hot and humid days typical of a Maryland summer would give way to the crisp, cool autumn he preferred.

When they reached the car, Max handed Lanie the keys. At her questioning look, he shrugged. "I'm too tired to drive."

She climbed into the driver's side. As they drove home from the church, he glanced at her out of the corner of his eye. In a few months, she would be married as well and leave his home for good. Despite his love of solitude, he wasn't sure what he might do with himself when he was alone again. She'd been living with him for about six months, since her mother's house had sold in March, and he'd gotten used to having her around.

"I can practically smell the smoke from whatever has your head spinning," she joked, turning down Main Street and passing Bea's Diner.

He laughed. "Nothing in particular." The last thing he wanted to do was make her worry about him. Besides, she would only be moving a few streets over. Much better than across the country to California, which was where she'd originally planned to go after settling her mom's estate.

"Could have fooled me," she murmured as she pulled into his driveway.

With a sigh, he unbuckled his seat belt. "I'm going to miss your cooking when you move out." He gave her a wry smile. "Stouffer's has nothing on you."

"I'm sure Nate and I will invite you over all the time." She climbed out of the car, opened the trunk, and grabbed her suitcase after spending the night before with Rose. "And it's not like you don't know how to cook."

"Nate told me you called my burgers hockey pucks once."

A laugh bubbled out of her throat. "Well, he's one to talk. His cooking isn't much better than yours."

"But it is better?" Max followed her up the driveway to the house.

"Only marginally." With a wink, she unlocked the front door and flicked on the light. They both sighed simultaneously, relieved to be home.

"I'm glad that's over." Lanie kicked off her shoes and flung herself into a recliner. "Now, I understand why people only get married once." Realizing what she'd said, she bit her lip and glanced at him. "Er, I'm sorry, Dad. I didn't mean—"

He waved a hand. "Bah, don't worry about me." After sinking into his chair, he propped his feet up. "Besides, I did only get married once."

"Thus far." She nudged his foot with her toe.

As if she hadn't spoken, he asked, "How are the plans going for your wedding?"

"Better now we've switched the date to around Christmas."

"I never saw you as a Christmas bride."

"I didn't expect to be one either," she admitted. "But we wanted to get married by the end of the year."

"Why the rush?"

Her eyes took on a distant look, and a small smile lifted her lips. "Have you ever heard that saying, 'When you find the person you want to spend the rest of your life with, you want the rest of your life to start right now?'" At his head shake, she sighed. "Nate has always been my person. It just took me a few years to realize it. And now that I have, I can't wait to make up for lost time by building a life with him."

Max stared at his hands, unsure how to respond. It brought up memories he would rather forget, like how he'd felt much the same way when he'd proposed to Lanie's mother. How she'd enthusiastically agreed to be his wife. And how those strong feelings his daughter described had led to a marriage for which neither one of them was prepared.

But Lanie was different. For starters, she wasn't nineteen. She'd finished a master's degree, had seen more of the world than he had at her age, and unlike Max and Melody, she'd dated other people.

Still, there was a reason Melody had opposed Lanie's relationship with Nate. Her worst fear was that Lanie would follow in their footsteps, sinking into the same mistakes and patterns that led to their divorce. Melody had wanted a better life for Lanie and made her daughter promise to leave Cedar Haven and never look back.

Then Melody got sick, and Lanie dropped everything to come home to care for her. During that time, Melody had come to regret the promise she'd extracted from Lanie. It was as if the reality of her own demise had caused her to reevaluate her past choices. She'd gone so far as contacting Nate, but in true Melody fashion, she'd taken a situation that required nothing more than a simple apology and explanation and complicated it.

Max shook the thoughts from his head. "I don't want you to rush into anything. You've just started your career."

"We're not rushing into it." She tilted her head. "Like I said, we lost so much time in the intervening years after I left for college."

"But you have your whole life ahead of you."

Lanie took a deep breath, and Max started to worry he'd said the wrong thing—again. The tense silence that followed reminded him of their phone call around the same time the previous year. Lanie had told him she planned to move to California with James, her boyfriend at the time. In the heat of the moment, Max had called her decision a disappointment, which had led to a huge misunderstanding.

"I want what's best for you."

His daughter's face softened. "I know you do. I only wish you'd trust me. Nate and I have discussed the future a lot." A flush crept over her cheeks. "And the past. But, Daddy, I've loved him since before I truly understood what that meant."

It was the way she said "Daddy" that stopped Max in his tracks. She might not be a child anymore, but somehow, she would always be his little girl. Even though she was twenty-four, he still wanted to step in and protect her from the consequences of her decisions.

The conversation was getting too emotional for his tastes. "I'm going to bed." With a grunt, he hoisted himself off the chair and headed toward the stairs.

"Good night, Dad." The disappointment in Lanie's tone caused a pang in his chest.

Their relationship had never been easy. His job required him to work long hours away from home, and he'd missed a lot of her childhood. While he tried to make it up to her with extravagant gifts, making sure she wanted for nothing, his efforts never seemed to be enough.

Then their arguments over the last year about her choice to move to California had exacerbated the cracks in their relationship. He'd pushed her to her breaking point by trying to convince her to stay in Cedar Haven, not because he couldn't bear life without her but because he thought it was best for her. In the end, she'd come around but at a price. Max worried the reason she was in such a rush to marry Nate had less to do with love and more to do with desperation to get away from *him*.

~

The next morning, Max awoke to the delectable scent of fried bacon wafting up from the kitchen. It reminded him of Sunday mornings during his marriage, when his wife would make breakfast for the whole family. Was his daughter trying to recreate those happier days?

When he entered the kitchen, Lanie thrust a plate of scrambled eggs and toast into his hands before returning to the stove. It wasn't the warm greeting he'd hoped for, but she'd made him breakfast, so he kept his thoughts to himself. Still, he couldn't help the way his face scrunched up in disappointment at the lack of bacon on his plate.

"What are your plans for the day?" He pulled out his chair at the end of the table and sat, subtly reaching for the salt shaker.

But Lanie got there first and replaced it with pepper. "Don't even think about it. Your blood pressure can't handle it."

With a harrumph, he sprinkled pepper on his eggs. Maybe her moving out wouldn't be so bad after all. At least then, he could eat whatever he wanted in peace.

"That's the last time you accompany me to a doctor's appointment." He scooped up a bite of eggs and closed his eyes. At least she'd added cheese and a dash of hot sauce, just the way he liked them.

To his surprise, she laughed. "You forget, you signed a HIPAA waiver for me to view your medical records. And I already told Dr. Carson to keep me informed if your blood pressure continues to skyrocket." Before he could respond, she added, "Anyway, to answer your earlier question, Nate and I are meeting with a potential caterer this afternoon."

That caught his attention. He'd been trying to figure out a way to discreetly become more involved in her wedding and thus spend more time with her, but she'd resisted his help. "Mind if I join you?"

She turned from the stove with a raised eyebrow. "Are you only going for the free lunch?"

"Of course not," he retorted, though as he thought about it, that sounded a lot more appetizing than trying to find anything edible on the special diet his doctor had recommended.

"Mm-hmm," Lanie muttered, clearly not convinced.

"I want to make sure you're getting your money's worth." He took a bite of his toast. "Not that you'll let me help you with that."

His daughter visibly stiffened. "Dad, we've been over this." Her voice sounded strained, and she took a deep breath. "Nate and I want to pay for this ourselves. It's important to us to have the wedding we want and remain within the budget we set."

Though she didn't say it outright, he could hear the underlying meaning in her words, and he resented them. "I know what Rose told you, but I did *not* insist their wedding had to be done my way. All I asked that crazy wedding planner for was a say in the rehearsal dinner, which is trad—"

"Traditionally hosted by the groom's family," Lanie finished in a poor attempt at imitating him as she glanced over her shoulder. "And in their situation, I understand why you stepped in. After Steven's accident, they needed the financial assistance. We don't."

Apparently, he'd made that argument too many times before. Perhaps he needed to try a different tactic. He scooped up another mouthful of eggs and chewed to buy him time. When he failed to come up with anything she wouldn't immediately counter, he decided to try honesty.

"Look, I want to spend some time with you. You've been gone for most of the last six years, and even when you were home with your mother, you were busy taking care of her. I barely saw you."

"Okay, you can come today." Then she pointed the spatula at him. "But you better behave."

"I'm not a child," he protested.

As she slid an omelet onto her plate, she mumbled something that sounded suspiciously like she was asking whether he was sure about that.

Chapter Two

Carissa Owens had built her business from scratch. After planning her own nuptials over thirty years ago, she fell in love with everything wedding planning had to offer and wanted to give brides the same joy she'd had on her special day. But despite her best efforts, she'd never been able to branch out beyond Southern Maryland or into other types of events like corporate retreats or even retirement parties.

Still, she considered her work a moderate success, and she had her late husband, Chuck, to thank for that. He'd supported her through those early years of barely making it to her becoming the main breadwinner when he was diagnosed with cancer five years ago. Her work allowed her the flexibility of caring for him during those final months while still providing enough income to replace his when he could no longer work.

As she was fast approaching her sixtieth year on earth, she was faced with a decision: keep trying to break into other markets or throw in the towel and sell her business to enjoy a well-deserved retirement. Chuck would have encouraged her to retire, as he'd always had his eye on traveling the world before they were too old to enjoy it. But without him, she wasn't sure there was much point. Her business was all she had left of the life they'd built together, and she wasn't sure she was ready to give it up.

Thankfully, it wasn't something she needed to worry about yet. Her client for that day had been the maid of honor at the last event she'd planned. After the setbacks with Steven and Rose McAllister's wedding, she hoped Steven's sister, Lanie, would have an easier time. She and her fiancé were planning a Christmas wedding, and Carissa hoped it would be the key to breaking her out of her usual holiday funk. After all, nothing looked quite as beautiful as a snow-white dress against the deep green of a Christmas tree covered with sparkling lights.

But when she entered the door of the caterer, her excitement deflated. There, sitting beside the bride-to-be, was Carissa's least favorite person in the world: the bride's father, Max McAllister.

He'd been a thorn in her side during his son's wedding, and she'd hoped he would be less involved with Lanie's. From what Carissa had seen, Max didn't have a close relationship with his daughter, but she supposed it'd been too much to hope that would apply to wedding planning as well. Usually, it was the mothers of the engaged pair who bickered over the wedding details, but Lanie's mother had passed away the previous year. Carissa reminded herself to tread lightly with her new client. She could only imagine how hard it must be to plan a wedding after such a major loss.

Still, Carissa's job would be difficult with Max around. Part of her wished she could view it as a blessing that a father was involved, and had it been any man other than that one, she might have been able to. He was, without a doubt, the most stubborn, pigheaded man she'd ever met.

Pasting a smile on her face, she sashayed up to the table. Lanie turned just as Carissa reached them, and she jumped up and greeted her.

"Carissa! Thank you for fitting us in on such short notice." She pulled Carissa into a hug.

Nate stood and shook her hand, but Max didn't move. His expression had changed from one of genuine surprise to a cold fury, the warmth in his deep-brown eyes frosted over like a window on a snowy winter day. The feeling was mutual.

"Max." Carissa tried to keep her tone even.

Unfortunately, he didn't repay the favor. "What are *you* doing here?"

She opened her mouth to respond, but Lanie beat her to it. "Dad! You said you were going to behave."

"I didn't know *she* was coming," he replied without a bit of remorse.

Nate pulled out a chair for Carissa, and she gave him an appreciative smile, choosing to ignore Max's less-than-welcoming reception. *You're not here for him*, she reminded herself. It was a mantra she'd developed for the more difficult family members of her clients, but somehow, it had never worked with Max. Something about that man got under her skin.

"It's nice to see you too," Carissa said, surprised by how calm she sounded.

Before Max could insult her further, Nate cleared his throat. "We've been looking over the menu, and we have some ideas of what we want to serve at the reception."

Grateful for his intervention, Carissa nodded. "That's great! Tell me what you envision, and we can look at how it works with your overall theme."

"It's food," Max said, his eyes narrowing at her. "Food doesn't need a theme."

Carissa was tempted to laugh. How little people understood the way weddings worked. From the venue to the decor to the meal, everything needed to fit in with the overall theme of the wedding. Most food was versatile enough to work with any theme, but there were certain ways to finagle dishes to support the overall vision.

But that would be lost on someone like Max McAllister. She'd learned that lesson while planning his son's wedding. Instead of engaging Max, Carissa decided to do what she'd done the last time she'd had to deal with him: ignore him entirely. Nate slid over the printout the caterer had provided, and Carissa's eyes flicked over the choices they'd circled.

"You're going with the traditional Christmas dinner." She pursed her lips. "That's wise, but we need to be careful not to veer too close to Thanksgiving." Her finger slid down the page to the options for sides. "I would forgo the cranberry salad and try for something heartier. How do you feel about squash?"

Lanie and Nate looked at each other and shrugged.

"Depending on how it's cooked, we're fans," Lanie said.

"Good. A maple-glazed butternut squash would offer something colorful and different but still appeal to most of your guests." Something at the bottom of the page caught Carissa's eye. "We could have holiday cookies in addition to your cake." At their dubious faces, she continued, "Having alternative desserts often helps reduce the cost of the cake, as we can make a smaller cake due to the variety of options."

"Who has cookies at a wedding?" Max scoffed. Without waiting for Carissa to reply, he gestured to Lanie. "If the cost of the cake is a problem, I'm happy to pitch in."

A red flush stole over Lanie's cheeks, leading Carissa to believe that was not the first time Max had offered to pay for something. "We've got it covered, thanks."

"Should we add some pies as well?" Nate asked, clearly trying to prevent an argument between father and daughter.

"It's an idea," Carissa said. "But the point of including a variety of cookies would be to reduce the overall cost. If you start adding a bunch of other desserts, you risk paying more than you would have if you just made a cake large enough for all your guests."

"That makes sense." Nate looked at Lanie. "What do you think?"

"I like the idea of having cookies, but I was wondering if we could save even more money by baking them ourselves," Lanie said.

Carissa bit her lip. On the one hand, she didn't want to

discourage her client, but on the other... "That's a lot to take on the week of your wedding."

"Oh." Lanie's face fell. "I didn't think about that."

"But if it's something you want," Max said, "I'm sure Rose, Steven, and I can help bake them."

Nate coughed loudly, and Lanie covered her mouth with her hand. An amused glance passed between them.

"No, that's okay," Lanie replied quickly. "I wouldn't ask that of you."

Carissa kept her eyes on the menu to keep from laughing. From what she'd heard, Max didn't have many culinary skills.

His eyebrows pulled together. "You didn't ask. I offered."

"Perhaps you should talk to Rose and Steven before you offer their services," Carissa said with as much tact as she could muster. "Besides, isn't Steven still recovering? I thought the doctors had encouraged him to continue to take it easy. We wouldn't want to add more stress to his plate."

"And perhaps you should keep your nose out of my family business," Max retorted.

"Dad!" Lanie pushed her chair back and stood. "If you don't knock it off, I'm going to have to ask you to leave."

"Me?" he demanded. "I'm not the one pooh-poohing every idea you have."

If looks could kill, Lanie's furious glare would have slain Max long ago, but luckily for him, Nate intervened. "It's Carissa's job to give her opinion of our ideas. That's why we hired her. She's planned more weddings than any of us, and we trust her."

Carissa's heart warmed. When she'd first spoken to Nate and Lanie, he'd resisted the idea of hiring a wedding planner. They'd originally hired her only for the day of the wedding, but as they'd started putting things together, Lanie had convinced him they were in over their heads.

"Fine." Max crossed his arms like a petulant child. "I'm sorry." But his tone and lack of eye contact suggested he didn't mean it.

Stifling a sigh, Carissa continued to peruse the side-dish options. For a Christmas wedding, she wanted food that embraced the spirit of the season while also providing guests with a hearty meal before they ventured out into the cold at the end of the night.

"What if we did a play on classic Christmas carols for some of the food options?"

Lanie cocked her head. "What do you mean?"

"For instance, they have a fig-and-prosciutto appetizer, which could be a fun play on the line from 'We Wish You a Merry Christmas' about figgy pudding."

Lanie's hazel eyes lit up. "Oh, I see! We could serve roasted chestnuts and maybe have little nutcrackers on every table as a decoration."

"Exactly," Carissa said. "Or we could serve the chestnut-and-rice pilaf as a side dish."

"So more of a subtle nod to the songs than a direct correlation?" Nate asked. "I like this idea."

She braced herself for Max to make a comment, but he didn't seem put off by the plan, even though it was her idea. If she didn't know any better, she would almost think he liked it, though he'd probably never admit that.

"They have towers of garlic bread." Lanie pointed at the option on the menu. "Maybe they can make it look more festive, like a Christmas tree."

"I'm sure we can find a way to make that happen." After pulling out a notebook, Carissa jotted down their ideas, more excited to plan their wedding than she'd been for any event in some time.

Later that evening, Carissa arrived at her home in Hidden River City, a few towns over from Cedar Haven. She'd shared the house with her late husband, and since his death, it'd become both sanctuary and prison. While the house still looked the same as it had when he was there, sometimes, she wished she could bring herself to make it more her own. The constant reminders of his presence weren't helping her to move on, but at the same time, she couldn't bear to give them up.

Setting her bag on the kitchen table, she breathed a deep sigh. "You would love this wedding, Chuck." Her voice seemed to echo off the walls. "Christmas was always your favorite time of year."

Unfortunately, since he'd been gone, it'd become her least favorite holiday. Despite trying for years, they'd never had children, which meant she often spent Christmas alone. Her family had scattered across the country like fallen autumn leaves. Every year, she received invitations to go to her siblings' houses, but she preferred her own company. Instead, if she wasn't working, she blindly picked a place on the map and booked a solo vacation. If she was working, she was usually too busy to notice the holiday.

"This year, I won't be alone," she told the empty house.

In some ways, working with both McAllister children had made her feel like a part of their family—minus their father. She shook her head in bewilderment. Those kids must have taken after their mother because neither one was anything like their dad. Grumpy, pigheaded, and intolerable were just a few of the words she would choose to describe him, and those were the nicer ones that came to mind.

That's how he presents himself, she could almost hear Chuck saying. It was something he'd repeated throughout their marriage whenever Carissa complained about a difficult client or, worse, one of their family members. Chuck believed that everyone had a mask they wore before the world, and his favorite part of getting to know a person was watching that mask fade as the person grew more comfortable with him. Her husband had studied to be a psychiatrist, though he ended up teaching instead of opening his own practice. Still, he'd had a knack for putting people at ease.

If that man has a mask, he's worn it so long he doesn't know how to live without it. She could almost see Chuck's weathered face break into a smile and the way he would shake his head, admonishing her for not looking deeper. Her heart panged at the image, and she closed her eyes.

But her thoughts were interrupted by the shrill ring of her cell phone. Without looking at the caller ID, she answered. "Carissa Owens."

"Hello, Carissa. It's Max."

Closing her eyes, Carissa stifled a sigh. Had her thoughts conjured the phone call? *I thought the saying was* speak *of the devil and he shall appear.* But perhaps thinking about someone was close enough.

"Max, what a surprise. Miss me already?"

A snort sounded on the other end of the line. "Hardly. I spoke to Rose and Steven, per your suggestion, and they're more than happy to help Lanie and Nate bake cookies for their wedding."

She rolled her eyes and was thankful she wasn't on a video call. "Don't you think there will be enough to do for the wedding without adding baking to the list?"

"McAllisters always rise to a challenge."

Pinching the bridge of her nose, she struggled to keep her voice even. "That may be true for you, but I'd prefer to confirm this with my *client* before we make any definitive plans."

He scoffed. "You don't think I discussed it with my own daughter? She does live with me, you know?"

"Not for much longer," she muttered under her breath.

"What was that?"

"Max, I'm in the middle of something right now," she lied. "Don't do anything until I've consulted with the bride." Without waiting for a response, she tapped the button to end the call and tossed her phone onto the counter.

"It's going to be a long four months," she grumbled. First, she'd endured his behavior toward her at the caterer, then came his discussion with Steven and Rose without Lanie's knowledge. It appeared Max was going to be a thorn in Carissa's side once more.

Chapter Three

When Max went out to refill his bird feeder the next day, a sole mourning dove perched on the porch railing, cooing softly. As he approached, the bird fluttered its wings but didn't move, its gaze trained on the ground. Peering over the edge, Max groaned. A pile of feathers was all that remained of the dove's mate.

"I understand how you feel," he said. After descending the stairs, he looked around, trying to determine what had happened. "Must have been a predator of some sort." He glanced up at the dove and found it watching him. "Looks like he put up a hell of a fight, though."

The screen door opened, and Lanie popped her head out. "Who are you talking to at this hour?"

"Myself," Max replied. It probably sounded less crazy than to tell her he was talking to a bird. "Don't come out here. There's a dead bird."

"Aw, poor thing." Ignoring his warning, she stepped onto the porch and approached the dove, which was still perched on the railing. "Was that your mate?"

The bird cocked its head and stared at her before flapping its wings and taking to the sky. Max envied the bird's ability to easily escape uncomfortable conversations.

"Now you've scared it off."

Lanie shrugged, unconcerned. "I seem to have that effect on birds. I had a frequent cardinal visitor when I stayed at Mom's. Whenever I got too close to it, it flew away." Her eyes searched the sky. "I'm sorry for that poor dove. I've heard they mate for life."

"I'm sure it'll find a new mate soon," he said, but it was a sobering sentiment. Humans could learn a lot from birds. He would hazard a guess that divorce didn't exist in the animal kingdom. The animals that chose new mates each year were unlikely to experience jealousy either.

He gestured for her to return to the house, following closely. There wasn't much point to cleaning up the feathers, as they would likely blow away. As he closed the sliding glass door, the lonesome dove returned to its perch on the railing. It glanced at him before bowing its head as if sending up a prayer for its lost mate.

His daughter slid into a chair at the kitchen table and sipped a cup of coffee. She looked exhausted, and he couldn't help wondering if she'd bitten off more than she could chew. Between planning her wedding and beginning a new school year, she had a lot on her plate. It didn't help that it was her first year of officially teaching students with disabilities.

"Got any plans for the day?" he asked.

"Nate and I are meeting to start building a registry, and then I've got lesson planning to do." Her voice lacked its usual enthusiasm.

"You don't sound excited."

"I could use another week or two off," she admitted. "The summer was a whirlwind, between Steven's recovery, helping to plan the wedding that almost wasn't, and now trying to plan my own." She shook her head. "I'm exhausted."

"Maybe you could push your own wedding back a bit." *And find yourself a new wedding planner in the process.* He was still irritated with the reception he'd received from Carissa when he called her last night. The nerve of that woman to suggest she knew his own daughter better than he did. They might not have the best of relationships, but he and Lanie *had* discussed his idea about doing the baking themselves before he contacted Carissa. So what if Lanie had been half asleep when he suggested it? She'd still nodded, sort of. The argument could be made that she'd nodded... off.

She rolled her eyes. "We'll manage, especially with Carissa's help."

"Some help." With a harrumph, he grabbed his mug. The last thing he needed was a third cup of coffee, but maybe it would help spark some idea of how to reach his daughter. If he could convince her to find a new wedding coordinator, or better still, nix that expense entirely, his life would be a lot easier.

"I don't get why you don't like her," Lanie continued. "She was instrumental in getting Steven and Rose down the aisle, and she's been a godsend with finding vendors that were available on such short notice."

"Maybe if you had a longer engagement, she wouldn't be necessary," he muttered under his breath.

Lanie rubbed her temples and took several deep breaths.

A quiet voice inside told Max to drop it. *Change the subject.* Whatever it took to keep his daughter from pulling even further away from him.

"She's too pushy," he said, trying to steer them back to Carissa. "It's as if no one else's ideas are ever good enough for her."

"Well, she has been doing this for her entire adult life."

"But everyone can learn something new," he pressed.

Lanie quirked an eyebrow. "Even you?"

Instead of answering, he drank his coffee to hide his scowl. It wasn't that he *couldn't* learn new things. It was more that he didn't see the point in bothering.

"I'm retired. I don't need to learn anything new."

She laughed. "Learning isn't limited to work. It's something we should strive to continue doing at any age, whether through formal education or not."

He grimaced at her authoritative tone, the one she usually used on students. "I don't need a lecture."

She sighed. "I'm not lecturing you." Tapping her fingers on the table, she appeared to consider a different approach. Before he could redirect their conversation to Carissa, her eyes brightened. "What about woodworking?"

"What about it?"

"You used to want to build furniture. There were several unfinished pieces at Mom's house that we moved here. Wouldn't you like to learn more about that? Develop that skill?"

He didn't have the heart to tell her that his dream had died with his marriage, which was why all his pieces had stayed at the house he'd left behind. Melody had been a staunch supporter of his work, even begging him to refinish the kitchen cabinets and build a matching set of nightstands for the master bedroom. The thought of going back to that, without her encouragement, was one he couldn't quite swallow.

"Woodworking is a young man's business." He drained his coffee cup then stood, hoping that would signal the end of the conversation.

"No, it's not," she countered, not taking the hint or perhaps ignoring it entirely. "And if furniture is too much to start with, you could try whittling."

"I'm no sculptor."

"My point," she said with a sigh, "is that you don't have to have a job to find something worth learning about. Studies show the best way to counteract mental deterioration and prevent illnesses like dementia and Alzheimer's is to continue engaging our brains through learning."

"I'm not *that* old."

She crossed her arms. "You're the one who said woodworking was a young man's business. I was pointing out how hobbies can help avoid the diseases old people such as yourself"—her lips twitched as if she was fighting a smile—"are at risk of developing."

"We're getting off the subject." He waved his hand. "*My* point is Carissa doesn't know everything, and she should listen to her client's ideas with care and consideration."

"Seeing as I'm the client, I'd say she *is* listening to *me*."

"I've invested in this wedding too." He folded his arms on the table. "I paid for your dress."

That was the wrong thing to say. Lanie's eyes darkened, and her lips pressed into a thin line. "I let you pay for *one* thing and only because you kept *insisting* on it. As I've told you several times, Nate and I are perfectly capable of paying for the rest of the wedding ourselves."

"Lanie, I didn't mean—"

"I'd better get moving, or I'll be late to meet Nate." Her eyes flashed to his before dropping to the floor. "We can discuss this later."

Max sank back into the chair at the kitchen table with a sigh. *Strike two.*

Try as he might, Max couldn't get Lanie's suggestion out of his head. It'd been years since he'd done any woodworking. The half-finished pieces were moved to his garage after Melody died, in preparation for selling the house. They'd been sitting there gathering dust. His drive to build and create things had dissipated with the smoldering ashes of his marriage.

It wasn't like the divorce was a shock. He and Melody had been having problems for years before they finally called it quits. While they'd gotten married young, they'd waited to have children. But after they had Steven, things started falling apart. He'd taken on more hours at work to support their growing family, which meant Melody often spent time with the children alone without a break. His absence led to resentment, not just with Melody but with his children as well.

In a last-ditch effort to save his family, Max had planned a trip to Disney World when Lanie was twelve. The trip hadn't gone as expected, as everyone had gotten sick from the heat, and they'd spent a couple of days recovering in their hotel room. Despite the illness, those had been such happy days. Spending time as a family, playing board games, talking and laughing—it felt like things were going to be okay. But once they'd recovered, the bickering started again, and he and Melody knew it was time to let go.

He entered the garage, preparing for an onslaught of unhappy memories as he removed the sheets covering the unfinished furniture. To his surprise, the sad memories didn't come. Instead, as he inspected his handiwork, he realized he was a lot closer to finishing the pieces than he'd originally thought. The intricate designs he'd started would be easy to replicate with practice.

Leaning against the wall, he surveyed his options. He could sell the unfinished furniture or give it away to Goodwill. Maybe someone who had more interest and drive could finish what he'd started. Alternatively, he could buy some scrap wood and retrain his hands, rebuilding his carving skills to what they'd been when he was younger.

A part of him wondered what the point was. His house was fully furnished. Granted, most of it, he'd put together himself with frustrating instructions written in broken English by a Swedish company. But it held together just fine. Why did he need to finish that furniture? Why bother doing all that work when the person it was meant for would never enjoy the completed product?

But another part of him, the part that still loved his late wife, sparked to life at the thought of doing one last thing for her as a tribute to her memory and the love they'd once shared. A love they'd rekindled briefly, only to be snuffed out by a disease that even the strongest of bonds couldn't overcome.

"You look like you're trying to work out a tough math problem," a voice said from the open garage door.

He jumped and banged his knee on a nightstand. As he rubbed the sore spot, he frowned when he met a familiar pair of blue eyes. "What are you doing here?"

Unperturbed by his demanding question, Carissa sauntered into the garage, running a finger over the nightstand. "I came to speak to Lanie." Her forehead creased as she examined the rest of the items surrounding him. "Is this a furniture graveyard?"

He bristled. "No, they're not decrepit. Just unfinished."

"Why did you buy a bunch of unfinished furniture?" Her half smirk gave her a more youthful look. If she hadn't been making fun of him, he might have found the expression attractive.

"I didn't *buy* this stuff," he retorted. "I made it." A rush of satisfaction went through his veins on seeing her obvious surprise.

"You made these?"

The admiration in her voice made his chest swell. "A long time ago."

"Why didn't you finish them?"

That question deflated his ego—and his mood. "They were a gift for my ex-wife. When she served me with divorce papers, it became a moot point."

Her eyes widened. "Oh, I see." Her teeth chewed on her lower lip, and he found the action disturbingly distracting. "Well, they're quite beautiful." She met his gaze head-on. "You should finish them. They'd be a lovely wedding present for Lanie and Nate."

Now, why hadn't he thought of that? Probably because he was so focused on their original intended recipient that he hadn't even considered his daughter might like them. But it made sense. She'd been the one to suggest he return to his former passion, so why shouldn't she be the beneficiary of him doing just that?

"That's a great idea," he said.

His sincerity seemed to catch Carissa off guard. They stared at each other, and his heartbeat quickened. But she broke eye contact first, clearing her throat. The sound brought him back to reality.

"What'd you want with Lanie?" he asked, trying to refocus the conversation.

"To talk to her about the idea you called me with last night." She wore a hint of a smile.

He avoided looking at her directly, fearing a repeat performance of whatever had happened between them minutes before. No way was he attracted to that woman. She was his polar opposite in every way and a real thorn in his side about his children's weddings. Still, he could acknowledge she was pretty. Her ocean-blue eyes were framed with dark lashes, and her silver hair gave her a sophisticated air. He wasn't blind, after all, but that was as far as his attraction went.

"You mean to convince her not to go along with it," he replied, unable to keep the frustration out of his tone.

"Not necessarily." She stepped forward as if she wanted to reassure him. "I want to make sure she understands what an undertaking that would be before she makes a decision." When he didn't respond, she sighed. "I'm not your enemy, Max."

The way she said his name did strange things to his insides. "Oh, really? Is that why you've shot down every idea I've had?"

Her face fell. "I understand why you feel that way, but I assure you, it's not on purpose. I've been doing this a long time, and I know what works and what doesn't."

"That's what Lanie said."

"But I thought about what you said last night, and the fact that Steven and Rose are willing to help with the baking..." She shrugged. "Lanie and Nate are on a budget. If they're on board, then so am I."

A home run! With a nonchalant shrug, he tried to temper his joy at winning. "Glad you're finally seeing the light."

She scoffed. "I wouldn't go that far."

"I'll tell Lanie you stopped by and that we finally agreed on something."

"I bet if you weren't so pigheaded, you'd see there is a lot we agree on."

The way she said it almost sounded like a challenge, and Max straightened his spine, pulling himself up to his full height. "Is that how you always talk to your clients?"

"I thought I made it clear last night you aren't my client," she said, completely undeterred by his attempt at intimidation.

They'd moved subtly closer to each other until they stood a hair's breadth apart. Her flowery perfume filled his senses, intoxicating and infuriating all at once. She lifted her chin. Whether that was a further challenge or an invitation, he couldn't tell. And he wasn't brave enough to find out.

Taking a giant step back, he breathed deeply, relishing the fresh air that wasn't polluted by her scent. As he did so, his senses cleared, and he glared at her. "If there's nothing else you need, I have work to do."

An emotion that resembled disappointment flickered across her face, but before he could fully register it, it was gone.

"Tell Lanie to call me." Then she spun on her heel and stomped down the driveway.

Once he was alone, Max leaned against a half-finished table and ran a hand through his hair. He had no idea what had just happened, but he couldn't help hoping that whatever it was, it might happen again.

Chapter Four

A FEW DAYS LATER, CARISSA HAD MOSTLY PUT HER strange encounter with Max McAllister out of her mind. She'd spoken with Lanie via phone, not trusting herself to meet in person again and risk seeing Lanie's father. The McAllisters were set to bake the cookies themselves, and Lanie had even invited Carissa to join them. But she'd declined, stating she wasn't much of a baker.

Truthfully, her husband had been the kitchen wiz. He loved trying new concoctions, and she'd been a willing guinea pig. Nowadays, she avoided the kitchen like the plague, choosing instead to order takeout and eat on her couch. Her oven probably had cobwebs in it.

Besides, the idea of working in such close quarters with Max wasn't a welcome one. She could only imagine how he would criticize her lack of culinary skills. The last thing she wanted was to derail Lanie's plans for homemade sweets by bickering with Max. If it were up to her, their interactions would be limited to only those necessary.

Unfortunately, she couldn't avoid him forever. In fact, she was preparing for yet another encounter that evening. Lanie and Nate wanted to check out a local band, and they'd invited both Carissa and Max to join them.

A double date, she mused, remembering the way they had inched closer to each other until the scent of his cologne had flooded her senses. That close, she could see the flecks of gold in his brown eyes. Funny how she'd never noticed them before, though she supposed fielding his sarcastic barbs had kept her distracted enough. But for a moment, his eyes had filled with an unfamiliar warmth that made her weak in the knees.

She stopped that thought train before it ran away from her. Or worse, derailed completely. Whatever had transpired between her and Max was fleeting. She needed to focus. Tonight was about her clients and nothing else.

And that became her mantra as she entered Seabreeze, a cheesy tiki bar on the outskirts of Cedar Haven. Lanie, Nate, and Max had already arrived and were sitting at a table near the stage. Max wore a Hawaiian shirt for the occasion, which normally would have looked out of place on him. Somehow, in that bar, with its fake palm trees, tiki torches, and other themed decor, it fit. He appeared less grumpy than normal, and she paused in the doorway to drink him in. Were he not such a grouch, she might even say he was handsome.

"Carissa!" Lanie called when she spotted her. "Come join us."

Shaking off her fascination, Carissa made her way to the table. To her dismay, Lanie indicated the seat between her and her father. Carissa supposed there weren't many options. After all, it would be weird to sit between the bride and groom.

As she took her seat, Max glanced up and met her gaze. Something like electricity went through her, and she quickly broke eye contact.

"What are you drinking?" Max signaled to the waiter to come take her order.

"I'm not sure," she said, grateful for a chance to look at the menu, though the options were disappointing. While she'd been there once or twice before, it wasn't her scene. A classy bar with a piano in the corner and a glass of Chardonnay was more her style. *When in Rome, as they say.* "I'll have a piña colada."

The waiter nodded before heading to the bar. Max was staring at her with the strangest expression. At first, she tried to ignore him, but after a few minutes, she couldn't take it anymore.

"What?" she asked, exasperation coloring her tone.

"You don't strike me as the fruity-cocktail type."

Her face heated, but she kept her tone cool. "Shows how well you know me."

He raised an eyebrow but didn't say anything else. The tightness in her chest eased as the band came onto the stage, and he turned away.

Lanie leaned toward her. "I hope you like these guys. Nate and I saw them all the time when we were in high school."

"You came to a bar when you were in high school?" Carissa frowned.

"Oh." Lanie laughed. "No, they played at the local dances."

"That makes much more sense." Carissa gazed at the stage. The men setting up looked like they hadn't changed much in the intervening years since the two had graduated. "Do they play outside of Cedar Haven?"

"Mostly locally," Nate replied. "They've done a few larger shows throughout the state, but they haven't made it big quite yet."

"Which is why we're hoping they'll do the wedding," Lanie said. "And then if they do become famous, we can say we knew them when."

As the band began to play, Carissa struggled to place their genre of music. It had a pop feel with a slight country twang. She had her suspicions about why they hadn't been able to move beyond the local bar scene, but she understood why Lanie and Nate thought they would work for the reception. They played some of their own songs as well as a few good covers.

She glanced over and was surprised that even Max was tapping his toes to the beat. When he caught her staring, he shrugged.

"I may not get out much, but I can enjoy a good tune as much as the next guy."

"Is this your usual type of music?"

He shook his head. "Not really. I'm more into country and old-school country at that. Alan Jackson, Garth Brooks, and even some Dolly Parton."

"So you won't be suggesting the McAllisters could form a band and play instead," she said dryly, unable to help herself.

"Lanie's about the only one with any musical talent, but she's more into singing than playing an instrument."

"That's right." Nate smiled. "She sings at karaoke sometimes."

Lanie's face flushed, and she mock punched Nate in the arm. "Not now."

Carissa exchanged a puzzled look with Max. It was clear this was some sort of private joke between the engaged couple. For the first time ever, Carissa was grateful Max was there. Were it not for him, she would start feeling like a third wheel.

Though if she were honest with herself, that was a given in her profession, especially since her husband had passed. When she'd first started out, she spent most of her time with the bride. The groom often just showed up to the wedding, happy to have everything planned for him. But the current generation of men was different. Even though Steven had joked that he needed only to show up to say his vows, he'd gone out of his way to make the day special for Rose. And Nate had attended every meeting Carissa had had with Lanie, providing his opinion and brainstorming ideas on his own.

Max's interest in the wedding was a surprise, too, though often more of an annoyance than a blessing. Normally, if the father was paying for the wedding or even a portion of it, he was content to hand over his credit card. It was the mothers who insisted on inserting themselves into every detail. But since Lanie didn't have that option, Carissa assumed Max had stepped in to soften the blow.

Carissa's heart went out to Lanie. She couldn't have imagined planning her wedding without her mother's help. It was a rite of passage for mothers and daughters to have that time together. Between the bickering over every little detail and the tears when they found the perfect dress, it often strengthened that mother–daughter bond.

The band took a break, and Lanie jumped up to seize the opportunity. She grabbed Nate's hand, and they raced to the stage, leaving Carissa and Max alone.

"Any idea what they might expect for compensation?" Carissa inclined her head toward the lead singer, who had jumped off stage to better hear Lanie.

"I doubt it'll be cheap. Don't we have to feed them too?"

"Yes, although we do get a discount from the caterer for vendor meals."

"I suppose that's something," he muttered. At Carissa's questioning look, he sighed. "I tried to convince her to hire a DJ. Figured one person with a sound system would be easier, and then you can hear any song you want." His eyebrows pulled together. "But I suspect you're going to tell me you prefer a band."

"Actually, I agree with you. DJs are less expensive and provide a much smoother experience."

He smirked. "Well, whaddya know? Something else we agree on. What are the odds?"

"As I told you the other day, I expect we have more in common than you think." She laughed, nudging his leg with her knee as she sipped her cocktail.

His eyes widened, and she realized a moment too late what she'd done. *Why am I* flirting *with him? It must be the alcohol.* Her cheeks warmed, and she pushed her chair back.

"I should, uh, go see if they've made any progress on convincing the band." Without waiting for his response, she hurried away.

Ugh, what the heck was that? It didn't make any sense. Just the other day, they were hurling insults at each other and bickering over the wedding. Not to mention, the last thing she needed was to complicate her business with a client's father. She glanced over her shoulder and almost tripped over her own feet when she found Max's eyes on her, watching her every move.

Focus, she commanded herself. When she reached Nate and Lanie, she pasted on a smile and tuned in to their conversation.

"That would be great!" Lanie was saying, her hazel eyes lighting up.

"It sounds like we've got a deal," Carissa said.

Three heads turned in her direction.

"Oh, Dan, this is our wedding coordinator, Carissa," Lanie said.

Dan stuck his hand out. "Nice to meet you."

After accepting it, Carissa raised an eyebrow at Lanie. "So, what did you decide?"

"We'll do the wedding." Dan beamed at Lanie and Nate. "Can't disappoint our biggest fans."

"Thank you!" Lanie gushed. "We haven't talked about compensation, but—"

"Don't worry about that." Carissa handed Dan her card. "Call me tomorrow, and we can discuss terms."

"Sounds great." Dan tucked her card into his pocket. "Now, if you'll excuse me, I need to grab some water before our next set."

Lanie practically skipped back to the table with Nate following closely. Their excitement was contagious, but Carissa dreaded sitting beside Max again. Why had she made things awkward by flirting with him?

But when they got there, he paid her no mind, instead focusing on Lanie. "How'd it go?"

Lanie smiled as she slid into her seat. "They said they'd do it, and Carissa gave them her card."

"That's great," Max said. "One more thing off the list." He took a sip of his beer. "Aren't you going to sit?"

Swallowing her apprehension, Carissa made a show of checking her watch. "Now that everything's settled with the band, I should go."

Lanie blinked. "So soon? But they've only played one set. You should stay and listen to the rest of their stuff."

"Yeah," Nate agreed. "It'll give you a better feel for what to expect at the reception."

Just as Carissa was about to decline, Max pulled out her chair. "I ordered you another drink while you were gone."

With a sigh, she sank into her seat in defeat. Perhaps it wouldn't be as bad as she feared. Max was acting as if nothing had happened, so she could do the same.

"I suppose I shouldn't leave you to third wheel it all on your own," she murmured to him as he moved back to his chair.

He laughed. "I appreciate the sacrifice, but I'm rather used to it."

"Not dated much since your divorce?" Carissa couldn't stop herself from asking. She immediately regretted it. *What is* wrong *with you?*

Max shrugged, clearly not bothered by her impertinence. "I haven't dated at all."

For reasons she couldn't quite articulate, his admission pleased her, but before she could say anything else, her drink arrived—a glass of Chardonnay.

Her lips twitched as she tried to hide her smile. She lifted the glass and swirled the golden liquid before bringing it to her nose. Hints of mango and peach filled her senses, and she sighed.

"How'd I do?" Max arched his eyebrow.

"Not bad." She took a sip, eyeing him over the glass. "Lucky guess."

He shrugged. "Maybe. Or maybe I know your type."

"My type?"

"You don't strike me as someone who gets out much unless it's for work."

Instead of answering, she took another sip of wine and savored the buttery, citrusy flavor. The band was coming back on stage, and Max had returned his attention to the front of the room. She snuck a glance at him. His salt-and-pepper hair was parted to the side, and even in his ridiculous Hawaiian shirt, he had a certain brooding presence. Were he not such a thorn in her side, she would almost call him attractive. Almost.

Chapter Five

THE NEXT MORNING, MAX CAME DOWNSTAIRS WITH MORE pep in his step. He hummed a song he couldn't get out of his head, one that he also couldn't quite place. As he entered the kitchen, he once again found his daughter already there.

She greeted him with a knowing smile. "You're in a good mood."

"Can't a man be happy in the morning?"

"Most men, yes, but you usually don't even crack a smile until you've had at least three cups of coffee."

He harrumphed as he set a coffee cup in the Keurig and pressed the button to brew. While he waited, he grabbed sugar and cream. The whole time, he could feel Lanie's eyes boring a hole in his back.

"So, you and Carissa seemed to be getting along last night. At least, better than usual." Lanie's voice sounded conversational, but Max heard the barely suppressed curiosity.

"I promised you I would be on my best behavior," he mumbled. After his coffee was ready, he searched the cabinets for something to eat. But really, he was stalling.

His daughter snorted. "You've promised that before and not delivered. What was different last night?"

When he could no longer avoid it, he sighed and took his coffee and a bagel to the table. After setting a container of cream cheese out, he sank into his chair and prepared for the Spanish Inquisition.

"I know how important the wedding is to you and how instrumental she has been in helping you to plan it." He slathered cream cheese onto his bagel and took a bite. "So I'm making an effort."

"That's uncharacteristically selfless of you." Lanie peered at him over her cup of coffee.

"Ouch," he muttered into his mug. When Lanie gave an unapologetic shrug, he grimaced, unable to articulate why he'd had a change of heart toward Carissa. It definitely had nothing to do with the fact that he'd briefly thought she was flirting with him. First, that wasn't possible. Carissa had made her dislike of him perfectly clear over the few months they'd known each other. And second, when she returned to the table, she'd acted as if nothing had happened. Clearly, he'd imagined the way her knee grazed his or the way her eyes sparkled when she teased him.

"No offense, Dad, but you've never exactly been one to care what other people think of you." Lanie shook her head. "If I didn't know better, I'd wonder if you were interested in her."

Max choked on his bagel, and he quickly downed the rest of his coffee, ignoring the way it scalded his tongue. *Interested in Carissa? Ludicrous.*

"Hardly," he scoffed.

"You sure?" Her lips quirked into a smile. "You hesitated. Almost like you were debating how to respond."

He scowled. "I figured it would be easier to be nice to her, for your sake." After finishing his bagel, he smacked his hands together to remove the crumbs. "But if you'd rather I continue to fight with her at every meeting, that's fine with me."

Lanie rolled her eyes. She stood and carried her coffee mug to the sink. After rinsing it out, she leaned against the counter and studied him.

"Just... promise me that if you do have any interest in her, you won't pursue it until after the wedding. The last thing I need is her to quit in the middle of planning the event after you break her heart."

"That's the easiest promise I'll ever make," he said, forcing a laugh. But an ice-cold weight settled in his chest, and he struggled to swallow. He cleared his throat before continuing. "You have nothing to worry about. There is not and never will be anything going on between Carissa and me."

"Good. I appreciate that." Lanie's shoulders relaxed. "I've got enough to worry about as it is." She pushed off from the counter. "Though you should consider dating again. I hate the idea of you being alone in this big house by yourself after I'm married.

Lifting a finger, he wagged it at her. "Why don't you focus more on your own relationship and stay out of my love life?" *Or lack thereof.*

Lanie raised her hands in surrender. "I'm just saying it's something to think about." She left the room, calling over her shoulder, "After all, you're not getting any younger."

~

Once Lanie had left for work, Max headed into the garage. The more he thought about Lanie's suggestion to resume work on the unfinished furniture, the more he wanted to try his hand at woodworking again.

But first, he needed to update his tools. Some of them needed sharpening, but most needed to be replaced. Once he made a list, he headed to the store.

After visiting the hardware store and a few other places in town, he had most of what he needed. The rest, he hoped to find online. But instead of going home, he stopped in at Bea's Diner. He hadn't been in a while, and he had a hankering for her chicken-fried steak.

"Max McAllister, as I live and breathe," Bea called out the moment Max entered the diner. Her white hair was covered in a black hairnet, and she wiped her hands on her apron as she approached. "I haven't seen you in a month of Sundays."

"Afternoon, Bea. Been busy with the kids and their weddings." Max gave Bea an awkward hug. "Good to see you."

"Grab a place wherever," she said. "Coffee?"

"Please." Max surveyed the diner. It was a bit early for lunch, and the rush hadn't started yet. Just as he was about to slide into a chair at the breakfast bar, he caught sight of a familiar head of silver hair.

"Hello, Max," Carissa said. "Would you like to join me?"

His first instinct was to decline. After his promise to Lanie, it seemed prudent to avoid Carissa unless it was for something wedding-related. But she had that monstrosity of a binder on the table before her, which meant she was working. Surely, they could get through one lunch without bickering. Besides, he hated to eat alone in public.

"You don't mind?"

Her lips curled in a sardonic smile. "I wouldn't invite you to join me if I minded."

Fair enough. Max walked to her table and slid in across from her. The binder was opened to Lanie's wedding, and he could just make out some calculations on the corner of the page Carissa was studying.

"I'm glad I ran into you," Carissa said, covering the page with her napkin. "I've been struggling with something, and I could use some advice."

He leaned back, crossing his arms. "I would have thought I was the last person you would ask for advice."

"It does concern your daughter, and as you keep reminding me, I shouldn't assume I know her better than you."

Her words surprised him, but he worked to keep his expression neutral. "All right. What's going on?"

"Let's order first." Carissa grabbed two menus from the stand on the table and handed him one. "You strike me as a black-coffee kind of guy."

"I like a little cream and sugar," he said. "But none of that pump of this, sprinkle of that, extra whip stuff they serve at Starbucks. I prefer coffee that tastes like coffee."

Her smile faltered, and he realized a moment too late he'd put his foot in his mouth. Again. "N-not that there's anything wrong with that. It's just not for me."

"I like a sugar rush with my caffeine," she said in an attempt at a joke. It fell flat.

He shifted uncomfortably and was relieved when the server came and took their order. Once they were alone again, he leaned forward and gestured for her to begin.

"So, I spoke to the band this morning, as I'd promised Lanie," she began.

"And?" he asked. "Is there a problem?"

"They're asking for a lot more money than I was anticipating. It's going to blow up the budget Lanie and Nate set."

That didn't surprise him. He still thought a DJ would be the better option, but Lanie had her heart set on a band, that particular band. She would be devastated to learn she couldn't afford it.

He studied Carissa across the table. "Why are you telling me this? As you love to remind me, I'm not your client."

To his satisfaction, her face flushed scarlet. "That's fair, and to be honest, I probably shouldn't be talking to you about this." She pushed a lock of hair behind her ear, which he'd learned was a nervous habit. "But I hate disappointing my clients. I also prefer to offer them options for solutions to problems rather than simply presenting the problems themselves." Her blue eyes bored into his, and the intensity caught him off guard. "You know Lanie better than I do. Would she be content with a DJ instead or even a less-expensive band? Or is this a priority for her? If it's the latter, I can investigate making cuts elsewhere in the budget."

He sighed. "She has her heart set on this band. Beyond the fact she likes their music, they have sentimental value for Lanie and Nate."

With a nod, Carissa moved her napkin and flipped through the binder again. "We could potentially reduce the catering budget by removing one of the entrée options. We've already reduced the cost of the cake because of the cookies you plan to make." She tapped her pen against her lips. "But I'm still not sure it'll be enough."

"What about the photographer?" Max asked. "Could we reduce the number of hours they have to cover? For instance, Lanie's cousin had a photographer for the ceremony and the first hour or so of the reception. They were able to get the formal photos done and several candid photos before the photographer left."

"It's an idea," Carissa said, though she didn't sound convinced. "But we've already signed a contract with them, and I'm not sure we can alter it at this point."

An idea formed in his head, but he pushed it away. After the many fights he and Lanie had had, the last thing he wanted to do was go behind her back and offer to pay for the band. If she found out, she'd be furious, and it would only cause more damage to their already tenuous relationship.

That's assuming she finds out. Max gazed at Carissa, assessing her. Could he trust her to keep a secret from Lanie?

"What would you say to me covering the difference for the band?" When she opened her mouth as if to respond, he hurried on. "That way, I'm not paying for it outright, just the portion that falls outside of their budget."

She chewed on her bottom lip, and he found the action more distracting than he wanted to admit. Shaking his head slightly, he forced himself to focus.

"We should talk to Lanie about it—"

"She'll say no." He sighed. "She's been refusing my assistance from day one."

"Then what are you saying?" Carissa raised an eyebrow. "That we don't tell her you're footing the difference?"

He lifted his shoulders in what he hoped came off as a nonchalant shrug. "What is that saying? 'What she doesn't know can't hurt her'?"

"And if she finds out?"

"We'll blow up that bridge when we get there."

Carissa's lips twitched. "I believe the saying is 'cross that bridge.'"

"Sentiment's the same," Max grumbled, waving his hand.

"I'm uncomfortable lying to a client."

"It's not exactly lying. It's..." Max searched for the right word. "Fudging the numbers a bit. I'd be paying what? A few hundred dollars? That's a drop in the bucket of the overall cost for this wedding." He hoped he sounded more confident about the plan than he felt.

At first, Carissa didn't respond. She seemed to be performing calculations in her head and weighing the pros and cons of his suggestion. Part of him hoped she would refuse. After all, Lanie had made it clear she and Nate wanted to pay for the wedding themselves. And she might be willing to sacrifice in a different area to afford the band.

On the other hand, Max didn't want her to have to sacrifice at all. She'd been through hell, first in caring for her mother during her illness then in learning the truth about what had actually caused her initial breakup with Nate. If anyone deserved to have the wedding they wanted, it was Lanie.

"Look," Max said, breaking the silence. "If Lanie finds out, I'll take the blame. She can add it to the list of things I've done wrong." The last sentence came out more bitterly than he'd intended.

Carissa met his gaze, and curiosity danced in her eyes. But she didn't press. "All right. I'll iron out the details with the band and send you the invoice."

"And you won't tell Lanie?" Max asked.

"I promise, this will stay between you and me."

"Thank you."

Their food arrived, and Max was grateful for the distraction. He hoped the meal would smother the nagging feeling in his gut that he shouldn't be making decisions about the wedding behind Lanie's back, regardless of how well-intentioned they were.

"I'm surprised you didn't tell Lanie about your preference for a DJ," Carissa said a few moments later, breaking the silence.

He shrugged. "I didn't want to dampen her mood, and the band isn't half bad."

Her lips curved into a smile. "I'm surprised you're capable of such restraint."

"Shows how much you know about me," he retorted. After he finished his meal, he paid the bill. "I should get going."

"Hot date?" Despite a teasing lilt to her tone, her blue eyes burned with an emotion he couldn't quite place.

He snorted. "I don't date."

"Ever?" She cocked her head.

"Not recently, anyway," he admitted. "I tried after the divorce, but it didn't take."

Her expression softened. "I understand that more than you know."

That's right. She lost her husband. "Have you dated anyone since your husband...?"

She shook her head. "For a long time, I wasn't ready, and then business picked up." Clearing her throat, she forced a smile. "And now, I'm looking to expand."

"How do you expand a wedding-planning business?" he asked, genuinely curious. "Or do you mean you're expanding to neighboring counties?"

"No. Actually, I'm trying to branch out into corporate retreats." She sighed. "But it's not as easy as I had hoped. Somehow, knowing the perfect color coordination for a specific theme doesn't translate well to team-building activities and seminars. It's been a struggle to even convince a company to give me a chance. That said, I do have a meeting tomorrow with a corporation in DC."

"That's gotta mean something, right?" He leaned forward, folding his arms on the table.

"Yes and no. The client was an acquaintance of my late husband. So he's doing me a favor."

"Maybe he'll pass on your information to other business owners."

"That's the goal."

The server arrived. "Did y'all want anything else?"

Carissa looked at Max. "Do you need to go? I don't want to keep you."

They'd finished eating, and there wasn't anything else to discuss about Lanie's wedding. Yet while he had no reason to stay, he also wasn't quite ready to leave.

"I'd love another cup of coffee."

Carissa smiled. "Me too." After the server left, she placed her elbow on the table and rested her chin on her hand. "What about you? Now that you're retired, do you do any work on the side?"

"Not really." Worried his response would cause the conversation to die, he hurried on. "But as you saw the other day, I'm getting back into woodworking."

Her eyes lit up. "Oh, right. The furniture in your garage. The designs you've carved are beautiful. I'd love to see the finished product."

"Then you'll have to come by when I'm done."

She smiled shyly. "I'd like that."

To his immense surprise, he realized he liked that idea too.

Chapter Six

Carissa didn't stop smiling the rest of the day and into the next morning. Part of her couldn't believe she'd spent an hour talking to the same man who had driven her crazy only a month before about his son's rehearsal dinner. But she knew him better now, and it was clear from their conversation he deeply cared about his children, even if he sometimes had a strange way of showing it.

Stop thinking about Max and get your head in the game. The potential client she was meeting provided the perfect jumping-off point for her new work planning corporate events. They were interviewing several companies for their annual retreat, and she was determined to win the contract. Her desire to expand beyond weddings was twofold. First, she wanted to prove to herself she could plan more complicated events. Second and most important, her wedding clients had dwindled over the last few years.

Some of that was due to technology. Modern brides and grooms had greater access to venues and caterers than they'd had in the past. They could also host smaller gatherings while sharing their special day with friends and family abroad thanks to livestreaming services. The accessibility of technology and direct communication had made

Carissa's job almost obsolete. Often, as Lanie and Nate had initially done, couples would contact her for her "day of" package, which consisted of a few brief meetings before the big day and coordination of the festivities. Though the package was popular, it wasn't as profitable as Carissa's more traditional service offerings.

Her location also limited her ability to attract new clients. Southern Maryland had built up in recent years, but it was still mostly rural with a few small towns sprinkled between vast farmlands. Clients in DC and Baltimore were less likely to hire her because of the distance, and though she'd considered moving, she would rather give up her business than the home she'd shared with Chuck.

For all those reasons, she'd decided to expand to corporate events, and she was excited for her first opportunity with Imaginavigation Enterprises in DC. Of course, driving into the city meant lots of traffic and parking, but she'd built in extra time just in case. The parking price tag was difficult to swallow, but she promised herself it would be worth it if the meeting went well. After leaving her car, she headed to the restaurant.

As expected, she was the first to arrive. She gave the hostess the reservation name and was led to a small table in a back corner. Not wanting to waste a moment, she removed her laptop from her bag and set it up. Then she placed the packets of printed slides at each table setting.

A few minutes later, the hostess approached with three men trailing her. Nervously pulling on her suit jacket, Carissa plastered a smile on her face.

"Carissa, so lovely to see you." Jacob, the CEO of Imaginavigation Enterprises, held out his hand.

She'd perfected her firm handshake after her father had forced her to practice it for years in her youth. He believed the secret to any successful business transaction was in the handshake. In his mind, it could make or break every deal.

"You as well," she said before turning to the other gentlemen who had accompanied him.

"I'd like you to meet Mr. Anthony Westman, our chief financial officer, and Mr. Colin Fields, our activities coordinator."

After shaking both men's hands, Carissa gestured to the table. "Shall we sit?"

The men filed into the three seats opposite her. Colin began flipping through the slide deck while the other two picked up their menus.

Jacob took the slides from Colin and set them on the table. "Let's order first before we get down to business."

Following Jacob's lead, Carissa picked up her menu, though she'd decided before arriving what she would have—a simple chef's salad and a glass of water. Her stomach was churning too much to eat anything heavy, and the water would help counteract the dry mouth she always experienced when nervous.

"Did you have any trouble finding the place?" Jacob peered over his menu at Carissa.

"Not at all. Your directions were thorough, and I used GPS."

He smiled. "I'm glad. The city can be hard to navigate when you're not used to it."

His condescending tone wasn't lost on her, and she gritted her teeth. Part of her wanted to remind him that as someone who had lived in the area for most of her life, she'd visited the city on many occasions. But her father's favorite quote went through her mind: "Better to remain silent and be thought a fool than to speak and to remove all doubt." Besides, she hoped that by the end of the meeting, she would prove not only her competence but also her talent at bringing a vision to life.

"What are you having, Jacob?" Anthony flipped his menu closed.

"A steak, of course. My wife won't let me eat red meat at home. Too worried about my cholesterol."

The other men laughed, and Carissa forced yet another smile, but inside, her heart cracked. How she wished she still had Chuck around to nag about his diet. She swallowed the urge to defend Jacob's wife, but she couldn't blame the woman for wanting to keep her husband around as long as she could.

After the server had taken their orders, Carissa cleared her throat. "Would you like me to get started while we wait for our food?"

Jacob waved a hand. "I don't like hearing a pitch on an empty stomach." He leaned forward. "Besides, I'd like to get to know you a bit better before we get into the business side of things. Have you lived in Maryland long?"

"Most of my life," she said. "My husband was in the army when we first got married, but as soon as he was honorably discharged, we came back to Maryland." She looked over at the other men. "What about you all?"

"Anthony's from New York, and Colin's from Boston," Jacob answered. "I've been in DC most of my life, though I was born on the West Coast." As he took a sip of water, he gazed at her over the rim of the glass. "You've been planning weddings since you moved back?"

"It started as a hobby when we were stationed in North Carolina."

"A hobby?" The skepticism in his voice was unmistakable.

"Quite a few of my friends were getting married at the time, and I had a knack for taking their visions and bringing them to life."

"And you think that'll translate to the corporate world?"

His expression had changed to almost a sneer, though she suspected he was trying to hide his true feelings. *So much for saving the business until after lunch.* But she squared her shoulders and looked him directly in the eye.

"I believe my experience would be a valuable asset for any event planning. Not only am I able to take an idea and turn it into a well-executed event, but I'm also used to working with people in highly stressful situations."

Jacob didn't hide his disdain as he snorted. "Weddings are highly stressful?"

Carissa took a deep breath. She would bet her right arm that Jacob's wife had done all the legwork for their wedding and he'd just shown up, probably drunk, to say his "I do." It was too bad his wife wasn't the one she was pitching to.

"They can be," she said sweetly, forcing a smile. "Especially if there's any rift in the family."

Their food arrived, and Carissa gave the server a grateful smile. Maybe once he had some food in his belly, Jacob would be more amenable to listening to her full presentation instead of degrading her experience. But she had to admit, things weren't off to a great start.

The conversation shifted to a situation the men had experienced in the office, which left Carissa mostly to her own devices. She ate her salad in peace, clicking through her presentation while tuning in every now and again to what was being said in case it might help her pitch.

As soon as Jacob had finished his meal, he pushed his plate away and folded his arms on the table. "All right, Carissa. Let's hear your pitch."

Taking a deep breath, she launched into her presentation. The men were silent as she spoke, flipping through the slides and jotting notes in the margins.

"I believe I can take your ideas for your corporate retreat and create an experience that focuses on team building that's fun and rewarding."

She sat back in her chair and looked at each of the men in turn. For a moment, nobody spoke, and her confidence faltered.

"How much would something like this cost?" Anthony asked.

"That would depend on a few things, such as how soon you want to hold the retreat, if you have a specific location in mind, and how long you want it to last. But I have several contacts throughout the area, which would provide cost savings to the company. Those details can be found on slide fifteen."

"Are your contacts familiar with the corporate world, or are they more geared toward social events like weddings?" Colin leaned forward with a raised eyebrow.

"I have several contacts that work with both social and business events. For example, I often work with local hotels for weddings and parties, but I have seen them host professional conferences." She cleared her throat and snuck a glance at Jacob. "That's why I feel I'm uniquely qualified to do this event because I would come at it with a different perspective."

But Jacob didn't seem impressed by her statement. "We're not planning a party."

"I understand that," she said carefully. "But there's no reason a professional retreat can't include some fun, is there?"

"She's got you there, Jake." Anthony slapped Jacob on the back.

Jacob frowned at his colleagues' antics and flipped through the slides. She held her breath. When he glanced at Colin and nodded, her heart jumped in her throat.

"As I'm sure you're aware, we've been listening to multiple pitches over the last week," Colin said. "We've asked a couple of them to prepare a proposal of three different options for the retreat with a detailed itinerary that includes information such as location, activities, theme, and the like. If you're still interested in working with us, we'd need you to submit your proposal in three weeks."

The tension in her shoulders eased. "That sounds amazing. Thank you for the opportunity."

Jacob signaled to the server to bring the check. "Colin will send you the details for what needs to be in the proposal via email this afternoon."

Her hands shook with excitement, and she tucked them under her thighs before anyone else noticed. She was one step closer to achieving her dream of expanding her business. With a lot of hard work and a little luck, it might be the start of a whole new life for her. And she couldn't wait.

~

As soon as Carissa arrived home, she got to work, hunkering down in her kitchen to brainstorm ideas for her detailed itinerary. Relying on her experience in planning weddings, she believed she could come up with a unique offering others wouldn't think to include.

She thought of how family oriented both Steven and Lanie's weddings were turning out to be. Some of that had to do with Max's insistence that he be involved, but a lot reflected the desires of the bride and groom in each instance. Corporations were always throwing around words about how they saw themselves as "one big family," but what if she could create an event that backed up that statement?

She suspected most of her competitors would focus on the typical corporate week away, one where the company forced its employees to leave home and family to travel to some big city with mandatory participation in team-building activities. Sure, they'd have some social and networking options, but in her experience, it wasn't something the employees looked forward to.

But most people liked going to weddings and parties. How could she bring that fun mindset to a boring corporate event? And was it possible to do so without breaking the bank?

About an hour later, her phone vibrated beside her. She jumped then glanced at the caller ID. "Hi, Max," she answered a little breathlessly.

"Hey, are you okay? You sound like you've been running."

"Sorry. I was in the middle of something, and the phone surprised me."

"Oh, is this a bad time?"

"No, no, it's fine. What's up?"

"I wanted to hear how your pitch went."

She blinked. That was unexpected. Since when did Max McAllister care about her professional life?

"Uh, it went well, actually." She bit her lip. *Should I say more?*

"And?" he pressed. "Did you get the gig?"

A laugh bubbled up in her throat. "I wouldn't call it a *gig*, and I didn't get it. At least, not yet." With a smile, she told him about the meeting and the proposal she had to put together.

"Wow, that sounds like a lot of work. Three different ideas for one event? Are they paying you for this?"

"No." She sighed. "But that's how this industry works. It's highly competitive, and I need to make sure my ideas are top-notch if I have any hope of branching out."

"What do you have so far?"

The blank screen stared back at her. Glancing at the pad of paper on the table in front of her laptop, she pursed her lips. "Fragments of ideas, but nothing that's remotely ready to present."

"Okay." He drew out the word. "Tell me the fragments."

She leaned back in her chair and frowned. "Why do you care?"

After a beat of silence, she wondered if she'd been too abrupt. Still, she couldn't wrap her head around why he'd called her. While she'd enjoyed having coffee with him the other day, she wouldn't exactly call them friends.

"I'm sorry. I don't mean to pry. You sounded excited yesterday about the meeting, and the plans for your company intrigued me."

He's being nice. Why are you giving him a hard time? "No, I'm the one who should be sorry." Their rocky start had put her on edge whenever they spoke, and apparently, even a phone call made her suspicious.

After another awkward silence, she cleared her throat. "But if you're interested in hearing my scattered brainstorming, I'm happy to share."

"Share away," he said.

"I have a few locations in mind, mostly local, but it might be fun to do a more rugged retreat. Like a trip to the mountains, where the participants could go hiking, whitewater rafting, or even rock climbing."

"That sounds... adventurous." He seemed to stumble over the word. "Were you thinking West Virginia? Isn't that kind of far for the DC businessmen?"

"More like Deep Creek Lake," she said. "It *is* quite a drive from DC, but I hear it's beautiful in the autumn." After putting her phone on speaker, she set it on the table and scribbled a few more notes on the page. "I'm hoping for something refreshing and different while still being fun."

"It sounds like you're off to a good start," he said, and his sincerity caught her off guard. "If there's anything I can do to help, let me know."

She smiled. "I appreciate that, and I will definitely take you up on it." Her phone beeped in her hand. "Oh, I've got another call. Can I call you back?"

"I don't want to keep you from your work. I'm sure we'll see each other soon for some other wedding-related event."

Her chest tightened, and she almost ignored the incoming call to stay on the line with Max a moment longer. But Lanie's name was flashing on the screen, and she couldn't ignore her client.

"Thanks for calling, Max."

"Anytime."

Lanie's call had been a request to meet the next evening. As Carissa headed into the school where Lanie worked, she spotted Max crossing the parking lot. His brown eyes crinkled as he smiled at her.

"Fancy meeting you here," he joked as he opened the door.

"Any idea what this is about?"

"I'm as clueless as you."

When they got to the classroom, Lanie was at her desk, poring over papers, and Nate was at a bulletin board, stapling colorful construction paper that had been cut into the shapes of autumn leaves. He glanced up at the sound of their footsteps and waved a leaf at them.

"Thanks for coming. You can sit in the back corner at the table." He pointed toward a small conference table set up with four chairs.

Carissa sat across from Max and pulled out her planning binder. A moment later, Nate joined them and sat beside Carissa, leaving the seat next to Max for Lanie.

"Do you know why we're here?" Max asked Nate.

"Lanie had another idea for the wedding she wanted to run by both of you."

Another one? Carissa pressed her lips together. If Lanie had many more ideas, the wedding was going to get out of hand.

"How much is it going to cost me?" Max grumbled.

"She plans to pay for it herself," Nate said, and Carissa didn't miss the way his jaw clenched. She wondered why they had invited Max if they didn't need him to pay. Surely, this was something they could resolve between the three of them.

"Hi, everyone." Lanie slipped into her seat. "I'm glad you could make it." She placed a collection of Popsicle sticks, construction paper, and string on the table.

Max and Carissa exchanged a look. Were they supposed to do an art project? She'd seen her share of strange ideas but none as odd as that one.

"So, since we're having a Christmas wedding, I thought it would be fun if we gave the kids at the wedding the option to make their own favors." Lanie gestured to the materials she'd laid out. "We could bring a bunch of crafting supplies, and they can make their own ornaments."

At first, nobody said anything. Carissa hoped someone else would chime in. She hated to rain on her bride's parade. When no one did, she squared her shoulders.

"Who would be supervising the children during this activity?" She tried to keep her tone gentle. In her line of work, she'd found the best way to lead someone away from an idea was to have them explain their thought process. Often, they realized they hadn't considered all the work that would go into implementing the idea.

"I would assume their parents would," Lanie said, though her forehead wrinkled.

"But isn't one of your bridesmaids a mother?"

"Trudy has a baby, but he's not old enough to do a craft like this."

"It's a nice idea," Max chimed in. "Though I'm not sure it's the best option to keep the kids busy during the reception."

Lanie sucked in her cheeks. "Why not?"

"Crafts are messy," Max said.

Carissa shuddered as she imagined sticky children with glue on their fingers touching the decor or, worse, Lanie's beautiful dress.

Her client's face fell. "That's true."

"But Lanie thought it would be a nice thing for the families to have." Nate took his fiancée's hand. "Something unique that would allow them to remember our wedding for many Christmases to come."

As much as Carissa disliked the idea, she tried to find a way to salvage it that would keep the spirit of Lanie's desire alive without causing irreparable damage to any aspect of the wedding. She met Max's gaze and raised her eyebrows as if to ask if he had a way to preserve his daughter's vision.

"What about if we have holiday-themed stained glass window kits?" Max asked. "You remember, don't you, Lanie? You used to get kits like that for your birthday, and you'd make one for everyone else."

"Are those less messy than glue?" Carissa asked, hoping to mask the skepticism in her tone.

"They have stickers that fit into the different panes of the design, so it should be." To her surprise, Max winked at her. But thankfully, neither Nate nor Lanie appeared to notice.

"That could work," Lanie agreed, but everyone could hear how halfhearted she sounded.

"Let's keep brainstorming ideas," Carissa suggested. "And I'll research the stained glass things Max mentioned."

"That sounds good." Nate gave Lanie's hand a squeeze.

"Was there anything else you needed to discuss with me?" Carissa asked.

"Where are we on planning? I want to make sure I'm staying up to date on deadlines."

Carissa flipped her binder open. "We're doing fine. I've sent the contract to the band we saw the other night, and we have the cake tasting next week. The wedding invitations should arrive at the beginning of October. We'll need to set aside some time to get those addressed and mailed. But otherwise, we're right on schedule."

Her client sagged into her seat with apparent relief. "Thank you. I'm always afraid I'm going to forget something."

"No worries. That's why you hired me." Carissa made a few notes about Lanie's latest idea in her binder then closed it. "If there's nothing else, I will see you next Wednesday for cake!"

She stood and made her way to the door. A moment later, heavy footsteps sounded behind her, and she turned to find Max hurrying after her. Her eyes narrowed as he neared. "Did you need something?"

He flushed. "Uh, Lanie asked me to walk you to your car since it's starting to get dark earlier."

"Oh." Carissa frowned as Max opened the door. Her gaze strayed to the setting sun in the distance. "That was kind of her but completely unnecessary."

"And I, uh, might have wanted a moment alone with you," he continued.

She cocked her head. "Why?"

If she didn't know any better, she would say he almost appeared nervous. But that didn't make any sense. What would Max McAllister have to be nervous about?

He opened his mouth then closed it as if unsure of himself. Then he sighed. "I was curious about how things were progressing with your proposal for the corporate event."

Although she got the feeling that wasn't why he'd wanted to speak to her, she didn't press. "It's coming along well. I've started to put together the different ideas."

"That's great."

They'd reached her car, and he stood awkwardly beside it as she put her binder and purse into the passenger seat. When she emerged, he ran a hand through his hair.

"I'd love to hear your pitch when it's ready. If you wanted to practice on someone, I mean."

"That'd be really helpful, actually," she said, still unsure why he was acting strangely.

Though the summer humidity was hanging on, it was only a matter of time before the brisk chill of autumn would set in and the trees would begin to put on a colorful show. She shivered both at the thought and at his close proximity. The scent of his woodsy aftershave tickled her nostrils.

"I love the autumn," she said suddenly, hoping to break the weighty silence that had settled between them.

"Me too." He cleared his throat and took a step back as if he, too, had realized how close they were standing. "People hate it because everything is dying, but it's nature's reminder that even death can be beautiful."

In another life, she might have thought his statement morbid, but having lost her husband, she recognized the truth in his words. She felt the loss in every fiber of her being, but she'd come to accept that death was just the final stage of life. And her husband had lived a beautiful life with her.

Nonetheless, an errant tear slipped out of her eye and down her cheek. She turned her head but not before Max saw. With one finger, he traced the trail of water the tear had left. His touch caused an unexpected warmth in her chest, and she leaned closer to him. He cupped her cheek in his hand and leaned toward her.

"Dad?" Lanie called from across the parking lot. "Are you still out here?"

Max and Carissa jumped apart with wide eyes. Without a word, Carissa hurried to the driver's-side door, thankful they had been partially hidden by an SUV. When she was safely ensconced in her vehicle, she pressed her hand to her cheek, which still burned from the warmth of his touch. She didn't know what had happened between them, but she couldn't help wondering what else might have occurred if they hadn't been interrupted.

Chapter Seven

It took effort, but Max managed to keep his expression blank as he walked back to his daughter, but his insides were a turbulent storm. He could still feel the softness of Carissa's skin on his fingers.

"I'm here," he said when he reached Nate and Lanie. "What did you need?"

"Nate and I are getting ready to leave. We wondered if you wanted to join us for dinner."

"No, you two kids go have fun. I've got a steak with my name on it marinating in the fridge."

Lanie raised an eyebrow. "Marinating? Since when do you marinate anything?"

"From what I've heard, you put some butter and pepper on it and call it done," Nate said with a grin as he left the school.

"Oh, ha ha." Max glared at both of them. "Go have your dinner and leave this old man in peace." Without waiting for their response, he stalked off to his car.

The truth was, he'd been making an extra effort to improve his cooking ever since Lanie had set her wedding date. He knew his days of eating well were numbered. After spending the better part of ten years getting his dinners from the frozen food section, he was in no hurry to return to it.

Homemade meals. That was one of the many things he missed about Melody. She'd been a spectacular cook, which had clearly rubbed off on Lanie.

When he arrived home, he sat in the driveway for a moment, staring at his dark, empty house. Since his divorce, he'd thought about dating every now and again but had tried only a few times before swearing it off for good. A part of him was afraid he liked his own company too much to share it with someone new. But he had to admit that ever since he'd started spending time with Carissa, his perspective had shifted.

Climbing out of his truck, he trudged up the stairs to his home and unlocked the door, flipping light switches as he made his way to the kitchen. As he gathered the ingredients, he found himself wishing he and Carissa hadn't been interrupted. Something had clearly changed between them, but he wasn't sure where it was all leading... if it was leading anywhere.

He opened the sliding back door and stepped onto the porch. Evening was rushing in, casting his backyard into shadow. After setting his lone steak on the small table by the railing, he fired up the grill. Once it was hot enough, he set his steak on the grate and closed the lid. Soon, the delicious scent of roasting beef wafted through the air, and he inhaled deeply.

Part of him wished he'd invited Carissa over. The steak was a decent size, and they could have split it. Maybe opened a bottle of wine, though he wasn't sure he even *had* wine in the house. He had a couple of russet potatoes he could have thrown on the grill to make it more of a meal.

Actually, that's not a bad idea. He slipped into the house and grabbed a potato then wrapped it in aluminum foil before placing it toward the back of the grate, away from the flames. His stomach growled. He didn't usually eat that late, but it'd been worth it to spend some extra time with his daughter and to see Carissa again.

In his mind, he replayed the moment the tear had appeared on her cheek. He'd acted on pure impulse, wanting to comfort her in what was clearly a moment of pain. While he and Melody had been divorced for years, it hadn't lessened the pain her death had caused. And yet he could still only imagine how much harder it was for Carissa.

Shaking the thoughts from his mind, he flipped the steak and the potato. He needed to focus, or else he would give Lanie another reason to make fun of him.

Later, he'd finished his dinner and cleaned up the grill and the kitchen. The night was still young, and he had a lot of pent-up energy after his daughter had interrupted him and Carissa earlier.

"Might as well get some work done on that furniture," he told the empty house. He headed into the garage and flipped on a light.

After running into Carissa at the diner the other day, he'd set aside some spare pieces of wood to practice on before he began carving the real thing. He was honestly afraid he wouldn't remember how to maneuver his tools in the delicate way he used to. It took the better part of an hour for him to find his rhythm again, but once he did, he was pleased with what he produced.

A knock on the wall broke his concentration, and he glanced up, irritated. "Don't you know not to sneak up on people wielding a knife?"

Lanie leaned against the doorframe, unperturbed. "I've been calling your name since I got back. Didn't you hear me?"

He shook his head, turning his attention to his work. "Did you have a nice time?"

"Always." She moved into the garage and picked up a piece he'd finished earlier. "Looks like you haven't lost your touch."

"Still rusty but improving with practice."

With a nod, she set it down. "Steven's here."

Max peered toward the door. "He's not coming out?"

"We were hoping you'd come in. He brought you something."

After wiping his hands on his pants, Max headed into the house. His son hadn't come by often since his accident, and truthfully, Max was surprised he was there then. But he took it as a good sign. Steven had continued to improve every day since the wedding, but his doctors were still recommending he take it easy.

He was sitting at the kitchen table with Rose behind him when Max walked in. They smiled at him and gestured to the chair at the end.

"We brought you dessert," Steven said, sliding a plastic container over to him.

Inside was a small piece of chocolate cake. Max raised his eyebrows, but Steven just grinned. Apparently, his son didn't care as much about his diet as his daughter did.

"Did you go out together?" After grabbing a fork, Max dug into the cake. It wasn't as good as a homemade one, but it would do.

"Yeah, we met Lanie and Nate at The Muddy Oar. And then I thought we'd stop by and bring you their cake since I know how much you like it."

"Thank you. I appreciate it." Max took another bite. "How's married life?"

Steven took Rose's hand and kissed it. "Amazing. Rose is almost all moved in, and we're talking about going away to Mexico in the new year."

"Assuming Steven gets the all clear from his doctor," Rose added.

Lanie came in from the garage and shot a look of disapproval at Max's cake. "Steven and I were talking about going apple picking this weekend."

"Apple picking?" Max leaned back in his chair. "I can't remember the last time we went."

"Probably about a decade ago," Steven said. "Before..."

The words he hadn't said hung in the air between them. Before the divorce, before their family broke apart. Max swallowed thickly.

They never really talked about those years, and he wasn't about to start.

"Sounds like fun, though I'm not sure the weather will be great. Were you thinking Saturday?"

"Or Sunday," Lanie said. "We wondered if you might want to join us."

Traipsing through an orchard wasn't exactly his idea of a fun time. In the past, he'd only gone because Melody made him in the name of "quality family time." Then again, as he looked at his children, he realized maybe she'd had a point. After all, nobody had known back then how fleeting that time was.

"Sure, I'll go," he found himself saying. "We used to take you kids in October, as there was usually a greater variety of apples ripening with the cooler weather."

Lanie frowned. "If the weather doesn't cooperate this weekend, maybe we can plan for October instead."

"Sounds good." Max stood and stretched. "I don't know about the rest of you, but I'm beat." He slapped Steven on the back. "Tell me what you decide about apple picking."

"Will do, Dad. Good night."

"Night," Max said.

As he headed up to his room, he had the strangest desire to invite Carissa to go with them. She'd said she loved autumn, and it might be a welcome distraction from the stress she was under with the proposal.

Almost as soon as the thought came to him, he dismissed it. Running into Carissa in town was one thing, but inviting her out with his family would send the wrong message. The last thing he wanted to do was break his promise to Lanie. How strange that when he'd made that promise, not dating Carissa had seemed like the easiest thing in the world. But he couldn't deny his attraction to her.

It won't last, he promised himself. After all, until recently, they'd barely been able to stand being in the same room together. His interest in her was fleeting and would fade in time. Once the wedding was over, they would go their separate ways, and he'd probably never see her again.

~

The weather that weekend was atrocious. They postponed apple picking until later in the season. Max spent the time holed up in the garage instead. By the time Wednesday rolled around, he had almost finished one of the nightstands. As he stepped back to scrutinize his work, he wondered what he would do with the finished piece. Perhaps he could give it to Lanie as a wedding present. The matching set would look great in a master bedroom.

At the same time, Nate had a fully furnished house, and as far as Max knew, Lanie planned to move there after the wedding. While the newlyweds might make some adjustments to better make it their home, he wasn't sure refurnishing it was in the cards.

He crossed his arms and sighed. Maybe he should buy her something off the registry. That was why people made those lists, but that felt impersonal and detached.

Since he wasn't a man of many words, making something with his hands might be the key to showing Lanie how important she was to him. He regretted not making her a larger priority when she was a teen. His initial bitterness over the end of his marriage had caused him to distance himself from his children. By the time he realized how much he'd hurt them, the damage had already been done. Steven was more willing to forgive him, but Lanie... Since Melody had passed, it felt like almost every conversation Max had with his daughter became a battle. No gift, no matter how much time and effort he put into it, would heal the broken parts of their relationship, but it was a start.

After checking his watch, he dusted off his clothes and headed into the house. He didn't have much time before he was supposed to meet Lanie, Nate, and Carissa at the bakery. His stomach flipped at the thought of the wedding planner. They hadn't seen each other or spoken since that moment in the parking lot.

He laid out a fresh set of jeans and a button-down shirt then hopped into the shower. As he rinsed off the sawdust and sweat, he tried to allow the warm water to calm his nerves. Unfortunately, it didn't help. By the time he shut off the water, he was even more wound up than before.

He dressed quickly before moving to the sink to comb his hair. The reflection staring back at him appeared calmer and more collected than he felt.

"You're being ridiculous," he told himself as he combed his hair. "She's just the wedding planner. In a few months, you'll never see her again, and that moment or whatever it was will be a distant memory."

Despite the conviction in his words, he didn't believe a thing he said. Whether Carissa had felt something in that parking lot or not, *he* had. And since then, he hadn't been able to get her out of his mind. He could only imagine what seeing her that day was going to do to him.

Part of him wondered if he should make an excuse, but then he would miss time with Lanie. Besides, he was no coward. He straightened his shoulders and grabbed his jacket, wallet, and keys. Then, taking a deep breath, he headed to his car.

Lanie and Nate had both worked that day, so he was meeting them and Carissa at the tasting. Rose had promised to try to stop by, but with the hospital even more short-staffed than usual, they knew it wasn't likely.

When Max pulled into the parking lot, he saw no sign of Lanie's car. Carissa, on the other hand, was standing by the entrance of the bakery, armed with her *War and Peace*–sized binder. She saw Max and waved before crossing the street.

"Hey," she called as he climbed out of his car. "Looks like you and I are the first to arrive."

Great. He really didn't want to be alone with her again, especially as the cool late-September wind picked up and whipped her hair forward, dousing him in the tantalizing scent of her perfume. Without thinking, he leaned closer to her and closed his eyes.

"Max? Are you all right?"

The confusion in her voice was like having a bucket of ice-cold water dumped over his head. He straightened up and cleared his throat, desperate to find some clean air that didn't fill his head with thoughts he shouldn't be having about his daughter's wedding planner.

"I'm fine," he said, though the words came out strangled. His eyes met hers, and he thought he saw something there beyond the concern. But then she blinked, and it disappeared.

"Lanie texted she's going to be a bit late." Carissa brushed her hair back from her face as the wind picked up again. "If you want, we can get out of this wind and wait."

He led the way to the door. Once he was clear of her scent, he regained control of his emotions. Though that didn't last because he stupidly opened the door for her, and the breeze as she passed made him lose his head all over again.

Get it together, McAllister. It would be a long evening if he couldn't focus.

They headed toward the kitchen, where a large table had been set for the tasting. Carissa gestured to a seat on one side, and she sat across from him. For a moment, he was relieved to have some distance between them, then he realized he would essentially be able to stare at her all night.

While she busied herself with her binder, he did just that. Her graying hair was tousled around her head from the wind, making her appear more relaxed than usual. She shrugged out of her jacket, and beneath was a deep-blue sweater with a V neckline. As she scribbled notes, her small nose bunched up in an adorable way. Then she pulled her bottom lip between her teeth, and suddenly, he could barely breathe.

The sound of his daughter's voice broke through his thoughts, and he jerked his gaze away from Carissa. He stood to embrace Lanie, grateful for the distraction.

His daughter immediately engaged Carissa in a conversation about the wedding plans, and he looked around the bakery. The dining area was small, with only a few tables and chairs set up opposite the counter. It wasn't crowded, but he suspected they did most of their business in the early morning.

On the wall opposite the counter was a cute imitation of the game Candyland but with baked goods instead of candies. Cupcakes, cookies, fudge, muffins, and other pastries were painted in an assortment of colors to bring the mural to life.

A moment later, Nate arrived, and Carissa went to fetch the baker. Max breathed a sigh of relief. The sooner they started the tasting, the sooner he could get some distance from Carissa.

"Welcome to Bakeryland." A woman with short brown hair and green eyes appeared beside Carissa. "I'm JoAnne, the owner of this establishment." She glanced at Lanie with a warm smile. "And I assume you are the bride-to-be?"

Lanie nodded. "And this is my fiancé."

JoAnne took Nate's hand and squeezed it. "Wonderful to meet you both." She turned to Max. "And you are the proud father of…?"

"Lanie." He inclined his head to his daughter. "But I'm mainly here to eat."

Lanie, Nate, and JoAnne laughed politely at his poor attempt at a joke. Carissa gave a tight smile but didn't meet Max's eyes. Perhaps he'd imagined the moment in the parking lot.

"All right. Well, I've spoken at length to Carissa, and I have an idea of what flavors you're considering, but do you have a certain style you want?" JoAnne set a few photos on the table in front of Lanie and Nate. "We can go as fancy or as simple as you like, though keep in mind, we are on a bit of a time crunch."

"We'd like to keep it simple," Lanie said quickly with a glance at Nate. "We definitely want festive colors like red and green to match the Christmas theme."

"So maybe something like this." The baker laid out a photo of a tiered white cake with red and green flowers and other embellishments. "This is a rather simple design that is enhanced with edible flowers." She set down another photo. "If you want a little fancier, we can create a gingerbread house cake with gingerbread cookies and candies as the embellishments. Or we can do something like this"—she laid down one last photo—"where the tiers themselves are either red or green and the embellishments are in other holiday colors."

The photos were stunning. Max had had no idea how beautiful baked goods could be. Then again, he'd never admired a cake for its beauty, as he was more interested in its flavor.

Lanie and Nate exchanged a glance. "And how much would each of these cost?"

"It depends on how many layers you want and the number of guests," JoAnne said. "If budget is a concern, it's also possible to have what we call a dummy tier. It's basically a fake, nonedible cake layer that's used to make the cake seem larger than it is. That's one way to save money on the cake."

"Money isn't a concern." Max waved a dismissive hand.

"Um, yes, it is," Lanie protested without looking at Max, but her hand clenched the photo she'd picked up. "Nate and I have a very specific budget."

Max opened his mouth to interject, but Nate shook his head. "Please don't start."

Carissa cleared her throat. "JoAnne is aware of the budget. We're still hashing out the guest list, but I would assume it would be between one hundred and one hundred fifty people. Right, Lanie?"

"That's correct."

With a nod, JoAnne pointed at the simple tiered cake with the red and green embellishments. "This is going to run you about four hundred dollars for the higher end of your guest list. The fancier cake will be closer to a thousand dollars. If you like the colored tiers, you could save money by having one dummy tier." She smiled. "I've also worked with brides who used two dummy tiers and only had the top tier as a real cake for their first anniversary. Then we had a sheet cake in the back for the guests, which is the least expensive option."

For a moment, Lanie's gaze strayed longingly to the photo with the red bottom tier and the green and gold embellishments. But then Nate picked up the simpler design.

"How about this one?" he asked.

Although Lanie smiled, Max couldn't help feeling it seemed forced. "But that's not the one you really want, is it?"

Lanie shot him a warning look. "This cake is beautiful. It'll be perfect for our wedding."

"Sounds like a good plan. I'll go get the flavors you've requested for tasting." Without another word, JoAnne headed to the kitchen.

"I saw the way you looked at the other cake," Max said the moment JoAnne was out of earshot. "If you'd prefer that one, I'm happy to pay the difference."

Nate glanced at Max with a frown before addressing Lanie. "Is he right? Do you like the other cake better?"

Instead of responding, Lanie took a deep breath and whispered something that sounded suspiciously like she was counting down from ten. Then she turned to Nate with a smile. "All of the cakes were lovely, but it's important for us to stay on budget."

"You wouldn't have to worry about the budget if you let me help you," Max muttered under his breath.

Carissa raised her hand. "Why don't we—"

"Seriously, Dad?" Lanie's eyes narrowed. "Since when do you care how pretty a cake is?"

"I simply want you to have the wedding of your dreams." Max leaned back in his chair. "What's the big deal? I'm helping to pay for the band. Why can't I pay for the cake as well?"

From the corner of his eye, Max saw Carissa drop her head into her hands with a groan. *Oops.* He remembered a moment too late that Lanie didn't know about the band.

"What does he mean he's helping to pay for the band?" Lanie

whirled on Carissa. "I thought you said the band was willing to work with our budget because we're such big fans."

Before Carissa could respond, JoAnne returned with an assortment of different cakes. She set them on the table, oblivious to the tension growing by the minute.

"This is our red velvet cake. I also have a vanilla, a regular chocolate, a peppermint chocolate, which is a seasonal favorite, and a few other options I thought might work with a Christmas wedding." JoAnne beamed at each of them as another woman passed out forks and plates. "Please try all of them and tell me which ones you like best. Depending on how many tiers you get, you can have a different flavor for each tier. Enjoy!"

The moment they were alone again, Lanie opened her mouth to start in on Carissa, but Nate put a hand on her shoulder. They engaged in a silent conversation. Then Lanie nodded, and he cut her a piece of red velvet cake.

For the rest of the evening, they ate the cakes in a mostly tense silence. Only Lanie and Carissa voiced their opinions of the different flavors. Nate seemed to enjoy every flavor and had no preference. Meanwhile, Max kept his thoughts to himself. Apparently, he'd done enough damage.

As the tasting drew to a close, Lanie and Nate chose a more traditional vanilla cake for one tier and the peppermint mocha flavor for another to fit the theme of their wedding. They didn't decide on the third layer, though it was clear they were leaning toward using a dummy tier to save money. It took effort, but Max held his tongue.

Once the cakes were cleared, Lanie grabbed Carissa's hand and dragged her outside. Max slumped in his chair. It seemed no matter what he did, his relationship with Lanie would take one step forward and a hundred steps back.

Nate leaned forward. "You need to stop doing this."

"I'm trying to help."

Nate stared at him. "It's not particularly helpful when you cause

Lanie more stress by constantly undermining her. If she wants you to help her out with the wedding, she'll ask."

"You didn't see her face," Max said. "She looked so wistful at the cake with the red bottom tier." He sighed. "I want to make her happy."

"If you want to make her happy, you might try listening to her."

"I do listen to her."

Nate studied Max. "Has it ever occurred to you why she doesn't want you to pay for the wedding?"

"Because she's stubborn?"

To Max's surprise, Nate laughed. "While that's true, that's not the reason."

"Then why?"

Nate folded his arms on the table. "Because she doesn't want the wedding to be another problem you throw money at."

"What is that supposed to mean?" Max demanded.

Instead of responding, Nate pushed back his chair and stood. "I'm going to go try to calm Lanie down. You have a good night."

Alone at the table, Max tried to push Nate's words out of his mind. But they played on repeat as if to torment him. *Is that what Lanie thinks I do? Throw money at my problems?* Then an awful thought occurred to him. *Is she right?*

Chapter Eight

WITH GROWING ANXIETY, CARISSA FOLLOWED LANIE through the bakery and out the door. *I should never have trusted Max to keep a secret.*

As soon as they were outside, Lanie crossed her arms and leaned against the building, clearly waiting for Carissa's explanation. Carissa stopped, surprised by how much Lanie resembled her father in that moment. The way her eyebrows pulled down over her hazel eyes only added to the stark similarity between father and daughter.

Here goes nothing. "I'm sorry for lying to you about the band." Carissa took a deep breath and launched into the story of what had happened. How she and Max had run into each other at Bea's Diner and started talking about the expense, including whether there were places in the budget that could be cut.

"Your father offered to pay for the band outright, but I knew how you felt about him pitching in with the wedding. So we developed a compromise where he would only pay the difference, and..." She sighed. "We agreed not to tell you, which I acknowledge was wrong and unprofessional of me."

"Why didn't you come to me first?" Lanie asked.

"I suppose I hoped I could come up with a solution that would allow you to keep your dream band without going over budget. And when I ran into Max, it seemed like the best option, and I thought, since he was just paying the difference, it wouldn't be that big of a deal. He is paying for your dress and alterations, after all." Carissa shook her head. "I realize now I was wrong. I'm sorry for not telling you the true cost and for going behind your back with your father."

At first, Lanie didn't say anything. She stared across the parking lot as if gathering her thoughts. Carissa braced herself for the consequences of her actions. While she didn't fully understand why Lanie insisted on paying for the wedding herself when her father was willing to help, Carissa also understood that Max and Lanie had a complicated relationship. Besides, Lanie's reasons didn't matter. Carissa had betrayed her client's trust, which was in direct contradiction to how she'd set up her business.

If Lanie fired her, she would understand. She hoped it wouldn't come to that, though. And she promised herself she wouldn't allow whatever was happening between her and Max to jeopardize her business relationship with Lanie.

Finally, Lanie took a deep breath. She looked calmer, and she even smiled. But Carissa didn't let her guard down.

"I guess I can't blame you for not understanding my insistence on not allowing my dad to pay for things. I don't know that I've ever explained why we have such a turbulent relationship. The truth is it wasn't always this way. Before my parents got divorced, I was very much a daddy's girl. While his work schedule made it difficult for us to spend much time together, we relished the time we had." Lanie's expression darkened. "But after the divorce, he shut down emotionally. Steven and I were supposed to visit with him on the weekends, but half the time, he had to work. And when we did visit, he seemed to think he had to make up the lost time by buying us things." She sighed. "Sometimes, it feels like that's his solution to everything in his life—just throw money at it."

Carissa's heart went out to both of them. "I'm sorry. I had no idea."

Lanie shrugged. "Why would you? We're not exactly known for talking about our feelings in the McAllister clan. That said, I've made a lot of progress with my therapist. She's given me coping mechanisms to help me avoid lashing out at Dad every time he tries to throw money at a wedding problem, but it's not easy."

"Especially since he does it so often," Carissa murmured, earning a laugh from Lanie.

"You have no idea." Lanie sighed. "He means well, but sometimes, I wish he would listen to me." She cleared her throat. "Anyway, how much does the band actually cost?"

Carissa bit her lip. "Uh, around five thousand dollars."

Lanie's eyes grew wide. "No wonder you didn't want to tell me." Her face fell. "There's no way we can afford that. Even if we tried to cut something like the floral budget, it wouldn't be enough."

"Exactly. A DJ is only about a thousand, which is more in line with your budget."

"I see." Lanie ran a hand through her blond hair.

"At this point, it'd be cheaper to keep the band than to find an alternative." Carissa kept her tone gentle but firm. "You'll lose your deposit if you cancel now."

"I suppose you're right." Though Lanie didn't sound happy about that. "Please promise me you'll come to Nate and me first about any future budgetary issues." Lanie leaned against the brick wall of the building. "It's times like these I wish I had my mom as a buffer."

Me too. But Carissa kept that to herself. "I promise to be up front with you in the future about the costs of things."

"Thanks." Lanie pushed herself off the wall and opened the door. "Let's gather the guys and get out of here. Want to grab some dinner?"

Carissa shook her head. "The cake samples were pretty filling, and I've got a lot of work to do for other clients." She followed Lanie into the bakery. Nate was waiting for them on the other side of the door. "I'll be scheduling your dress fittings soon, and we'll have another tasting at the caterer, but otherwise, we're in a good place. Let me know if you need me in the meantime."

"Sounds good. Thanks, Carissa," Nate said as he slid an arm around Lanie.

"See you later." Carissa grabbed her things from the table and spun on her heel, determined to put as much distance as possible between herself and Max.

"Wait!" he called, but she didn't turn.

Her pace quickened when she heard his heavy step behind her, and she practically ran to her car. But she wasn't fast enough. As she reached her door, he put a hand on her shoulder.

"Hey, stop. We need to talk."

She whirled around and glared up into his stupid handsome face. "Haven't you said enough? Why couldn't you keep your mouth shut?"

At least he had the good sense to look chagrined. "I'm sorry. It slipped out." He slid his hands into the pockets of his jeans. "What did Lanie say?"

"She asked that in the future, I talk to her about the budget and leave you out of it." A feeling of satisfaction swelled in Carissa's chest when Max looked as if she'd slapped him. "And I promised to alert her to any more of your shenanigans."

"*My* shenanigans?" Max retorted. "You weren't exactly refusing my offer to pay the difference. We were in on this together."

She hated that he was right, but she wasn't about to admit that. "Be that as it may, I thought I could count on your discretion. Apparently, I was mistaken." Without another word, she sidestepped him and opened her car door. "Now, if you'll excuse me, I have work to do."

"We're not finished here."

"I have nothing further to say to you." After climbing into the driver's seat, she reached for the door, but he blocked her from closing it. "Please let me leave."

Although he stepped back, he put his hand on the door. "I'm sorry for getting you in hot water with Lanie. I didn't mean to mention the band, but if it's not clear, her happiness is important to me." His head dipped, and for reasons she couldn't explain, her heart went out to him. "I don't want her to settle for less than she deserves."

Carissa sighed and leaned back in her seat. "I understand that. Your heart is in the right place, Max, but your methods could use some finessing."

He raised his head with a wry smile that took her breath away. "Ya think?"

Her lips twitched, but she fought to keep the grin off her face. "Maybe try asking your daughter what she wants and how you can help, then actually *listen* to her response. There might be more you can do that doesn't involve solving her problems by throwing money at them."

His eyebrows pulled together as he appeared to consider her words. "That reminds me. I wanted your opinion on a wedding present for Lanie and Nate. I've been working on carving designs into the nightstands in the garage, but Nate has a fully furnished house. I don't want to give them something they don't need."

Her earlier aggravation evaporated as she imagined Lanie's face on receiving such a beautiful gift. His thoughtfulness also surprised and touched her. *Perhaps there's hope for him after all.*

"Are you kidding? I can't imagine a more wonderful gift than something you made with your own hands." Impulsively, she sat forward and cupped his cheek. "I bet she'll love it."

His expression changed as he leaned into her hand. An emotion she couldn't place stirred in his gaze before it dropped to her mouth. Her heartbeat picked up its pace as she struggled to keep breathing.

Is he going to kiss me? More importantly, did she want him to?

She blinked at the thought and dropped her hand. As quickly as it'd come on, the moment passed, and Max shifted away from her car.

"Have a good night," he said, his voice hoarse.

Her stomach flipped, and she hurried to close her door. As she drove away into the sunset, she could no longer ignore the attraction between them, but she had no idea what she was going to do about it.

~

"So, you're planning a June wedding?" Carissa began typing notes into her computer. *So much for Sunday being a day of rest.* "Have you booked anything yet, like the venue for the ceremony or the reception?"

"Not yet," the quiet voice on the other line replied. "We got engaged last week, and I'm already overwhelmed."

"No worries. That's what I'm here for." Keeping her voice professional, Carissa clicked over to her calendar. June was already almost full, but she could squeeze in one more bride. "I'm sorry. I didn't quite catch your name."

"It's Meredith."

Moving the phone to the table and putting it on speaker, Carissa frowned. The woman sounded like she was barely eighteen, but then, most young people sounded like children to her.

"Well, Meredith, I do have an opening for June. If you'd like to meet in person with your fiancé so we can discuss logistics, I'm happy to get started right away."

"Oh, really?" The high-pitched voice let out a squeal that reminded Carissa of a dog whistle, and she was glad she'd put the phone down. Even from the table, the noise made her wince.

Once they'd agreed on a date and time to meet, Carissa assured Meredith she would send over the details in a reminder email, then she hung up the phone. Sagging against her chair, she stared at the ceiling. *Another quick wedding?* As much as she loved new business, she hated short engagements. Steven and Rose had planned a wedding over two years, and she'd relished spending that much time with them. It'd given her a chance to really get to know them and what they wanted. In contrast, Lanie's wedding seemed to age Carissa by the day and not just because of the weird dance she and Max found themselves in.

Any new clients are better than no new clients, she reminded herself. But shorter engagements made her job that much harder and added unnecessary stress. Venues and vendors booked up well in advance, which left few options for those who wanted to get married quickly. Besides, part of her wondered if she wasn't funneling clients to Steven so he could act as their divorce attorney. While she wasn't aware of many clients who had gotten divorced a few years after their marriage, there were enough to almost make her lose faith in the whole idea of love… at least for the new generation.

With a sigh, she pushed away from the table to grab a glass of water before diving back into her proposal. She'd been working diligently on it all morning before the latest call, and she returned to it with renewed purpose. Maybe once she had a few corporate events under her belt, she could be more choosey about what weddings she worked on in the future. Being in high demand would be nice, and it would allow her to focus on events she actually wanted to do instead of working with whoever happened to call that month.

A few hours later, she'd created a decent first draft of her three event ideas, but she couldn't decide how to present them. Should she start with her favorite then go through to the one she liked least? Or was it better to start with expectations low so she could wow them at the end? She drummed her fingers on the table. Humans had short attention spans. It might make more sense to end with the option she hoped they would choose, to keep it fresh in their minds.

She glanced at her watch and was surprised to find she'd lost the whole day. *I'll work on my slides tomorrow.* Though it was late in the afternoon, she needed to go to the grocery store before it closed.

After compiling a small list of items, she rushed out the door.

Sundays in Cedar Haven meant everything closed early, and she had just over an hour to get her shopping done. The store was empty save for a handful of people at checkout. She needed to hurry.

She grabbed a cart and headed to the produce section. The other problem with shopping so late on a Sunday was that everything was picked over from the weekend rush. Perhaps she should have waited until the following day, when things would be restocked, but she had several appointments with her brides, and a presentation to finish.

Her aggravation grew with every aisle she went down. She was about halfway through the store, and they were missing a quarter of the things she needed. At that rate, she would have no choice but to make two shopping trips during the week.

"This is ridiculous," she grumbled as she searched for her favorite spaghetti sauce and then her second-favorite one.

"I've heard spaghetti sauce described as many things," a voice said behind her, "but ridiculous is new."

She spun around and flushed as her eyes met Max's. His amused expression did little to help her bad mood.

"They're out of everything I need." She waved the sauce she'd picked up, the generic store brand that always seemed overly salted. "That's what's ridiculous."

"Ah, I feel your pain. I should have gone out this morning, but it slipped my mind." He shrugged. "It just means another trip later this week."

"Some of us don't have that luxury," she muttered. Her next item was chicken broth, which, mercifully, was well stocked.

"If you want, I'm happy to pick up whatever you can't find when I come back."

Her eyebrows shot up. Max McAllister was offering to do her a favor? "I wouldn't want to put you out."

"You wouldn't. I've already accepted I'll be back here soon. It wouldn't be any trouble to pick up some things for you." His lips curved into a genuine smile, which caused her heart to flutter.

Though she tried not to, she found herself returning his smile. "I must admit, it's tempting to accept your offer. I've got so much going on this week, I'm not sure when I'd have time to come back."

"Then accept it." He gave a playful shrug. "After all, bringing you groceries is the neighborly thing to do."

"Uh-huh." She crossed her arms on the handle of her cart. "We're not actually neighbors, though."

His face broke into a broad grin. "Details."

She studied him as she considered his offer. It *would* help her a lot, but the last thing she wanted was to be indebted to him. "Does your delivery service include no-contact drop-off, or do I actually need to answer my door?"

"Hmm." Tapping his chin, he stared at the ceiling. "I wouldn't want to risk any of your perishables going bad. It's best if I not only confirm you're home but carry the groceries in for you."

A laugh bubbled up in her throat. "Are you planning to put them away as well?"

"That one might cost you."

Is he flirting with me? "Ah, there *is* a fee for your services."

He winked, and her breath caught in her throat. "Not for pickup and delivery, but putting them away, well, that's asking a lot. I mean, I don't even know where you keep all your items. It'd take me a while to figure it out on my own."

They had moved closer to each other, and the warmth from his body poured over her in waves. She tilted her head back to get a better look at him, and his gaze drifted to her mouth. For the second time in a week, she wondered if he might kiss her.

"So," she said, her voice breathy and soft. "Are you expecting a tip, or is it included in the cost?"

His expression changed, and his eyes filled with hunger. "My terms are negotiable."

She pursed her lips. "Fine. What's your starting offer?"

"Have dinner with me," he blurted out.

Did he... Did he just ask me out? She swallowed, but Max looked as shocked by his question as she was.

"I mean, er—" He stared at his feet, avoiding her gaze. "Not like a date, exactly. More... a meal, uh, between friends?" His voice rose on the last word like a question.

The *yes* was on the tip of her tongue, but she hesitated. Besides the fact that she and Max could hardly get through a conversation without bickering, he was her client's father. Her number-one rule was not to mix business with pleasure. And she'd already jeopardized her relationship with Lanie once because of Max. Although, he'd said it would be as friends...

"It may sound crazy," Max continued when she hadn't responded, "but I feel like we've been getting along better, and well, I, uh, don't get out much, as you can imagine." He chuckled nervously. "Besides, I'm sure it would take a load off Lanie if we were friends, and you keep saying we may find we have more in common than we think." He shrugged. "Why not find out?"

The idea of getting to know Max both thrilled and terrified her. Her attraction to him seemed to grow each time they met, and she wasn't sure she would be able to resist acting on it if they were alone together. On the other hand, he had a point. If they could discover more things they had in common, they might butt heads less often. And once the wedding was over...

Don't go there. Allowing herself to even consider Max in that way would only make it that much harder to keep things between them strictly platonic.

Before she could answer, someone came down the aisle. She took advantage of the interruption to search for the next item on her list, a box of wheat pasta. But her emotions were all over the place, and she couldn't seem to focus. Just when she was about to give up, he bent beside her and pointed.

"Is that what you're looking for?"

After grabbing the box, she stood and stared at him. "How'd you know?"

Moving around her, he plucked her list from the seat of her cart.

"I read it right here." His eyebrows pulled together. "Though I can't say I'm much of a fan of brown pasta."

Despite the chaos swirling inside, she laughed. "It's good for you."

"If you say so," he said, clearly unconvinced.

"I-I need to go," she said, turning her cart in the opposite direction. "They're going to close soon."

"Carissa." The way he said her name sent shivers down her spine.

She glanced at him over her shoulder. "Let me think about it."

He opened his mouth, then he nodded. "All right. Text me with what you can't find, and I'll stop by the store on Wednesday."

With a tight smile, she hurried out of the aisle. Thankfully, the next one was empty, and she leaned against her cart while taking deep breaths.

What is this man doing to me? The way he made her feel like some lovestruck teenager. The last time a man had made her feel that way was...

"Chuck," she whispered, surprising herself. But that was crazy. What she and Chuck had was that incomparable, soulmate, once-in-a-lifetime love. She'd considered herself lucky to have found it once, but there was no way it could happen twice, right? And especially not with someone like Max McAllister.

As she finished her shopping and checked out, she kept expecting to run into Max again. But he must have left, because she saw no sign of him in the store. Her emotions swung between relief and disappointment. She only hoped she would have an answer to his invitation by the time he showed up on Wednesday.

Chapter Nine

THE NEXT MORNING, MAX WOKE WITH THE TASTE OF bitter disappointment on his tongue. No matter how much he tried to wrap his head around Carissa's refusal to answer his question, he couldn't understand why she hadn't agreed to join him for dinner. Perhaps his delivery could use some work, but he'd made it clear that the dinner was a friendly invitation and not a date.

Though deep down, he wished he was free to ask her out. His promise to Lanie had seemed trivial at the time, but as his interest in Carissa grew, so did his desire to spend more time with her.

A realization hit him. *Maybe she feels the same and was hoping for more than just a friendship.* He would have to explain about Lanie, but he was sure Carissa would understand. She was a business-woman, after all.

When he came downstairs, he found Lanie in the kitchen and at the stove. The scent of fried bacon wafted toward the doorway, and he inhaled the delicious smell. He hurried to the table and slid into his seat.

A moment later, Lanie placed two plates on the table. His anticipation of a hearty breakfast diminished when he was greeted with an egg-white omelet and a dry piece of wheat toast. Meanwhile, Lanie's plate had two pieces of bacon and scrambled eggs.

"What gives?" he demanded with a frown.

She rolled her eyes. "You can't eat bacon. You're lucky I let you have all that cake at the tasting."

"Lucky," he muttered as he cut into his omelet with a fork. "Like I'm a child instead of a grown man."

"So, how was your evening?" she asked in a falsely cheerful tone. After grabbing the salt, she sprinkled some on her food.

He held out his hand for her to pass it, but she placed it out of reach and handed him the pepper instead. At his scowl, she simply shrugged.

"Nothing of interest to report. I went grocery shopping." He cleared his throat. "I saw Carissa while I was there."

"Oh? How is she?"

Max shrugged. "Fine, I guess. We didn't talk much." That was the understatement of the year, but he had to tread carefully where Carissa was concerned. The last thing he needed was for Lanie to worry he was breaking his promise.

"I'm glad you're at least able to exchange polite pleasantries. A few months ago, that didn't seem possible."

He shifted uncomfortably in his chair. "I'm trying to be on my best behavior. Anyway, how was your night?"

"Nate and I had a good time, though it's always hard to leave him at the end," she said, her face taking on a wistful look. Then she blinked, and it was gone. "He's coming over this evening after work to go over the guest list for the wedding. Oh, and we're planning to go apple picking on Sunday. The weather looks great."

"Who's driving?" Max asked.

"We could all ride up in your truck if you're still coming."

"Just you and Nate?"

"And Steven and Rose."

"I'm not sure I can fit everyone."

She frowned. "Maybe Steven and Rose can drive up separately. His car is a bit more rugged than mine."

"That sounds more doable, but we can figure it out when we get closer to the day."

"I was also thinking," she continued with a quick, almost guilty glance at him, "maybe you could invite someone."

He almost dropped his fork. Tightening his grip, he shoveled another bite of eggs into his mouth to buy him some time before answering. After washing it down with coffee, he raised an eyebrow. "Why would I invite anyone?"

"I don't want you to feel like a fifth wheel."

He scoffed. "I'll be fine. It's not like I haven't gone out with the four of you before."

"True." Lanie placed her elbow on the table and rested her chin on her hand as she studied him. "But don't you ever get lonely?"

The piece of toast seemed to lodge in his throat, and he coughed violently. Lanie rushed to get him a glass of water, and he downed it in a few gulps.

"I'm not lonely, and as I said before, I'm too old for dating."

"No, you're not. That's why they have those dating apps for people your age. Isn't one of them called, like, Our Time or something?"

As much as he hated to admit it, he'd heard of that particular app. But the idea of meeting someone that way didn't sit right with him.

"Or if you don't want to go on an app," Lanie continued when he didn't respond, "you could ask out one of the women in our community."

"You sound like you have a list." A queasy feeling in the pit of his stomach told him she probably did.

"I have a few suggestions." Lanie grinned.

Despite his better judgment, curiosity got the better of him. "Who's on this list of yours?"

Lifting her mug, she regarded him over the rim. "Our old neighbor Cassandra, Bea, and Mrs. Carlisle."

Max's mouth dropped open. "Bea and Mrs. Carlisle are both at least ten years older than me."

"And?" Lanie asked, unperturbed. When he glared at her, she sighed. "Fine. What's wrong with Cassandra?"

"She's too eccentric."

"Or you're too picky." She carried her dishes to the sink. "I'm not saying you have to marry any of them, but it wouldn't kill you to put yourself out there. I haven't seen you go on one date since Mom."

"I don't need to date," he protested. "I have you and Steven."

When she leaned against the table, her eyes filled with concern. "It doesn't hurt to have friends your own age."

"I have friends." He dumped his plate on the counter. "And I don't need my daughter meddling in my love life or lack thereof."

"I'm not meddling. I'm trying to help—"

"Well, don't!" he shouted. "It's not your problem nor your business."

The hurt look on Lanie's face filled him with remorse, but before he could apologize, she grabbed her bag and ran out of the house. He considered going after her, but he knew it would be a futile attempt. With a defeated sigh, he began washing the dishes.

After his argument with Lanie, Max was in no mood to work in the garage. He needed something that required more physical labor than carving. As he glanced out the back door, he debated cutting the grass. It would probably be the last time that season he needed to mow, as October was right around the corner.

He slid the door open and stepped out onto the back deck. The cool September air greeted him, and he closed his eyes. Just being outside lifted his mood. A soft cooing sound caught his attention, and he opened his eyes to find a mourning dove perched on the railing.

"Shouldn't you be flying south for the winter?" His knowledge of birds was limited, but there didn't seem to be many species that stuck around for the cold, snowy months.

The bird cocked its head, and for one crazy moment, Max wondered if it actually understood him. It cooed again, a mournful, poignant sound that tugged at Max's heart. He understood in that moment where the bird got its name.

"Are you the same one that lost your mate?" He moved closer to the bird, careful not to scare it away. Unfortunately, all doves looked the same to him, but it wouldn't be a stretch to think it was the one he'd seen before. Max searched the trees for a nest. Perhaps the bird didn't understand its mate was gone.

"If you're hoping your mate will return, I'm afraid you're out of luck." He sighed. "You should go find someone new."

As the words left his mouth, he had to wonder which of them he was addressing, the bird or himself. The thought brought him up short. But before he could spend too much time brooding over it, his phone beeped.

Does the offer to pick up my groceries still stand?

A smile tugged at Max's lips as he sent a confirmation message to Carissa. That was a good sign. Even if she didn't accept his offer for dinner, at least she seemed more open to him than she had before.

About an hour later, he arrived at her house with several bags of groceries. He gathered them into his arms, trudged up her front stairs, and rang her doorbell.

"Special delivery," Max said, lifting the bags.

"My hero," Carissa teased as she took one of the bags. The warm grin on her face caused his heartbeat to stutter. She'd never looked more beautiful.

He followed her into her house. It was a cozy ranch-style home with an open floor plan that led directly into the dining room. A large bay window jutted out above the kitchen sink with a gorgeous view of her backyard. The marble counters were an eye-catching contrast to the white cabinets.

"You have a lovely home." He marveled as he set the bags onto the small island in the center of the room.

"Thanks." She began to unload them. "And thank you for picking up my groceries. You're a lifesaver." As she put away the groceries, she hummed a merry tune.

Since he didn't know where anything went, Max stood on the other side of the island, out of her way. "What's got you in such a good mood?"

She shot him a smirk over her shoulder. "I finished polishing up my presentation."

"Oh?" A laptop was perched on the dining room table with a pad of paper and a pile of notecards beside it. "Want to practice it on me?"

When she turned toward him, her eyebrows pulled together. "Um, no. That's okay." His face must have given away his disappointment because she hurried on. "I don't want to jinx anything."

"Fair enough." He wouldn't press, though he was dying to know what options she'd put together.

"Thank you again for doing this. I really didn't have time to get back to the store this week."

"Happy to help. Not much else on my plate these days anyway." Try as he might, he couldn't quite keep the edge out of his voice.

"How's Lanie?"

"Busy with school, so I haven't seen much of her." He turned away from Carissa to hide his face.

She laid a tentative hand on his arm. "Are you going to tell me what's wrong?"

"I'm not sure I should."

"Why?"

Running a hand through his hair, he huffed a breath. "It's complicated and embarrassing."

"This is a judgment-free zone," she said. "But I won't twist your arm. Do you want something to drink?"

"Water, please."

She indicated he should take a seat at the table. A moment later, she returned with two glasses and set one in front of him. He wrapped his hands around it and stared at the wall.

Her eyes seemed to search his face. "I'm here if you want to talk."

Instead of responding, he took a sip of water. He wasn't sure he wanted to tell anyone about what had happened with Lanie, least of all Carissa. At the same time, he hated that yet another thing had sprouted between him and his daughter.

With a sigh, he leaned forward. "Lanie has been on my case to date." His eyes flicked to Carissa then back to the wall. "While she's made me promise not to date you, she has offered up other... unappealing options."

"Lanie asked you not to date me?" Something in her voice caught Max's attention. Her eyebrows were pulled together in a concerned frown.

"She didn't want it to complicate things," he said.

"I suppose I should be flattered you find me to be an appealing option," she teased. When he didn't laugh, she cleared her throat. "Sorry, that was in poor taste. Who else has she suggested?"

"Bea, Mrs. Carlisle." At Carissa's bewildered expression, he clarified, "The teacher who Lanie was hired to replace after she retired last year and my old neighbor, Cassandra Winters."

Despite her attempts to disguise it as coughing, Max knew when he was being laughed at. He glared at her. "It's not funny."

"It's sweet she cares so much about you. And the options she gave aren't bad. Cassandra is pretty. Bea and Mrs. Carlisle are a little old for you, but—"

"A *little* old for me?" he growled. "Bea is seventy-two!"

Carissa covered her mouth with her hand to hide her laughter, but her shaking shoulders gave her away. The sound caused his anger to dissipate, and before long, he found himself joining in.

"She means well," Max said. "But sometimes, she's like a dog with a rare steak. She sinks her teeth into it and won't let go."

Tears streamed down Carissa's face from laughing so hard, and she wiped them away. "What did you say to her suggestions?"

"Some things I regret, honestly." His expression sobered. "She caught me off guard, and like I said, her suggestions left a lot to be desired."

"Oh no."

"Yeah, 'oh no' is right." He slid his head into his hands. "I blew up at her. Told her to stay out of my love life."

"I bet that didn't go over well," Carissa said.

"She stormed out of the house, and I don't know if she's going to come home or go stay with her brother." He leaned back in his chair and stared at the ceiling. "It seems like every time I take a step forward with her, I screw something up and end up five paces back."

"But this wasn't your fault." At his incredulous expression, she hurried on, "I mean, yes, you shouldn't have blown up at her, but your reaction is justified. It's not her business whether you date or not."

"She wants me to be happy."

Carissa pursed her lips. "I'll allow that her intentions are honorable, but you know what they say, the road to hell and good intentions."

"Fair." He shifted in his seat. "So, what do I do now?"

"She's at school, so hopefully, being away from you will give her time to cool off. And if she does stay with Steven, don't try to force her to talk to you. Eventually, she'll come home, and you can apologize for your outburst while also making it clear you don't appreciate her meddling."

"Easier said than done."

Carissa's lips twitched as if she were fighting a smile. "I imagine admitting you were wrong is rather difficult for you."

Max scowled. "I'm not *that* stubborn."

"I appreciate the qualification." She bit her lip. "Though now, I understand why you asked me out to dinner as friends."

That caught his attention. He leaned forward, his eyes searching her face. *Is she disappointed it wouldn't be a date?* "Is that why you said no?"

"I didn't say no." Carissa tilted her head. "I didn't really say anything other than to let me think about it."

"And?"

"Dinner is still too..." Her eyebrows pulled together as if she was searching for the right word. "Intimate. I want to respect Lanie's wishes, and dinner would feel like a date."

"Well, how about this?" Since Lanie had already suggested he bring someone, inviting Carissa seemed a safe option. And as it was a group outing, Lanie couldn't accuse him of breaking his word. "We're going apple picking this weekend. Why don't you join us? We can spend some time together socially but without the pressure or intimacy of a solo dinner."

"I wouldn't want to intrude on your family time."

"You wouldn't be," he insisted. "Bringing someone was actually Lanie's idea." He laughed. "She didn't want me to feel like a fifth wheel."

"In that case," Carissa said, her face brightening, "I'd love to."

Max hadn't heard from Lanie by the time school was letting out. But per Carissa's advice, he didn't text her. If she needed space, he would give it, and in the meantime, he would rehearse what he wanted to say to her.

Since he didn't know whether he would be alone for dinner, he decided to prepare something that would make decent leftovers. It also happened to be one of Lanie's favorite meals, or perhaps the better description was that it was one of the only meals he made that she enjoyed. Meat loaf, but not the run-of-the-mill dry meat loaves portrayed on old sitcoms. His included a special sauce that gave it a spicy kick. And he didn't just pour the sauce on top. He mixed it in by hand, which kept the meat from drying out in the oven.

The whole process took a half hour, and it was already after five by the time he slid the loaf into the oven. To his surprise and relief, the front door opened, and his daughter's heels clicked over the linoleum in the hallway.

She entered the kitchen without a glance his way. After removing Tupperware from her lunch box and setting it in the sink, she put the lunch box away. Finally, when she had nothing else to do to avoid him, she faced him. Sniffing the air appreciatively, she met his gaze. "Smells good in here."

"It's meat loaf."

The anxious crease in her forehead disappeared as a small smile tugged at her lips. "My favorite."

"It's going to be about an hour." He shifted from foot to foot. "Gives us time to talk."

Taking a deep breath as if to steel herself, she pulled out a chair. He followed suit, and for a moment, neither of them said anything. But Carissa had told him to start with an apology.

"I'm sorry for blowing up at you this morning," he began. "I didn't mean to react that way, and I know you believe you're helping me."

He hesitated, unsure whether he should wait for her to say something or continue with Carissa's other suggestion. If the conversation turned into a lecture, Lanie might tune him out or walk away before he got through it, but if he could engage her, she might be more receptive.

"I'm sorry too." Her face flushed. "Nate said I needed to butt out of your love life."

Not for the first time, Max sent up a prayer of thanks that Lanie had found her way back to Nate. That man understood him more than most, and Max appreciated how Nate was able to get through to his daughter when he couldn't.

"I understand that you want me to be happy and that your concern comes from a place of love." Max took a deep breath. "But I'm not unhappy. If someone comes along and things happen organically, then I'm open to it." He raised an eyebrow. "Besides, after all the meddling your mother did in your love life, you should be more wary of interfering in others' relationships."

The flush on her face deepened as she dropped her gaze to the table. "That's fair. Though I hate the idea of you being alone again when I move in with Nate."

He waved his hand. "I was alone before your brother came home to start his business, and I was alone before you moved back after your master's." He shrugged. "While I'll miss your cooking, I can get by on my own."

"But I finally got you to stop using paper plates all the time." Her hazel eyes danced with mischief.

"Paper plates conserve water," he retorted. He went over to the oven to check on dinner's progress.

"And clog up landfills."

"Well, I guess no matter what I do, I hurt the environment." As he returned to the table, he raised an eyebrow. "So, are we agreed, then? No more meddling?"

She bit her lip. "Will you at least try going on a dating app? Or maybe joining some local groups?"

"No to the dating app, and maybe to the groups thing." As her face broke into a smile, he waved a finger. "But no promises. I'm not exactly the most social of people."

She burst out laughing. "Understatement of the century."

"Ha ha." His voice dripped with sarcasm. "Still, if it'll make you feel better and convinces you to stop suggesting women almost twice my age, I'll consider it."

"That's all I ask."

Once that was settled, he decided to change the subject to something less uncomfortable. "How was your day?"

That was all the prodding Lanie needed to launch into a lively one-sided conversation detailing what had happened. It sounded like she had a good class, with some of the same students from the year before. Because Cedar Haven was such a small town, they didn't have a lot of options for students with disabilities. Most of them ended up attending the program at the middle school for much of their lives.

"I'm hoping, once I get my bearings, to petition the board to expand the program to allow the students to continue their education with their peers. It's especially hard for the high school–aged students to be stuck in a classroom with the younger kids. I'd like to change that, but I know right now, the budget isn't there."

"Sounds like you need another fundraiser."

She blew out her breath. "I can't fundraise an entire program." Shaking her head, she grabbed a glass from the cabinet then filled it with ice water. "The school system can't support it, and some of the parents end up putting their children into private school when their kids become teenagers because there are more opportunities there." She took a sip of water and sank into her chair. "Mrs. Carlisle and I talked about it at great length before she retired. Apparently, she's been petitioning for the same thing for years to no avail. So now, it's my turn to take up the banner."

"What would the program entail?" Max felt like he was missing something. "Couldn't they hire another teacher and find space at the high school?"

"If only it were that simple. But even if it were, there's no place to put the class at the high school or any of the elementary schools. That's why it's at the middle school. It was the only place with room." Rubbing her temples, she stared at the table. "And as far as hiring someone, well, consider how much it took to convince me to give up that job in California and stick around. And I have family and a fiancé here. There's not much to entice someone who doesn't have roots in this town."

He bristled. It'd been a point of contention between them when she'd come home to settle her mother's estate with the express intent on leaving ASAP. Her view of their little hamlet was in direct contrast to his. She'd insisted there was a whole wide world out there waiting for her, but he struggled to understand why she couldn't go experience the world then return home. Sometimes, he wondered whether she would have ended up in California after all if it weren't for Nate.

"Don't look at me like that," she said when she caught him staring at her. "I'm happy to be home, and I love this town, but even you have to admit it doesn't have much to offer. Sure, cost of living is lower than some places, but the salaries barely cover it. If I hadn't moved in with you, I'm not sure I could afford my own place, even if I subsidized my salary with my inheritance."

"I don't know why you say that. We're not far from DC, and there's plenty to do here."

She raised her eyebrows. "Karaoke nights at Seabreeze and endless town events aren't likely to entice people from my generation."

"Okay," he said, keeping his thoughts about her generation to himself. "Why not hire someone older?"

"Because they'll retire sooner, and we'll be back in the same position we are now." After draining her glass, she shrugged. "Besides, like I said, there isn't any room in the budget even if we could find someone to hire."

For once, he found himself completely devoid of any advice to give her. He knew little of the town budget, having worked as an electrical lineman for a private company for his entire career. The only time he cared about the government's budget was when it came time to pay taxes, and usually, he grumbled about it.

"Anyway"—she waved a hand—"that was my day. How was yours?"

"Uneventful," he said, choosing his next words carefully. "Went grocery shopping, did some woodworking in the garage, and then started dinner."

She smiled. "Sounds like a relaxing day of retirement."

The oven timer beeped, and he took the meat loaf out of the

oven. After setting it on the counter, he grabbed a bag of frozen vegetables and popped them into the microwave. Lanie sighed, and he hid a grin. She'd been on his case to use fresh vegetables since she'd been home, saying they were better for him. But he'd gotten into the habit of keeping things simple, and he figured produce in any form was better than nothing.

Once dinner was on the table, the conversation died as they both dug into the meal. He snuck a few glances at his daughter and couldn't help noticing how tired she looked.

"I'd say a penny for your thoughts, but I expect they're worth more."

Though she smiled, it didn't quite reach her eyes. "I'm worried about the wedding."

That wasn't what he'd expected her to say. "Don't you and Carissa have everything under control?"

"We do, but it's come at a price. And I can't help wondering if I made a mistake picking a date so soon after the engagement."

"What does Nate say?"

A bitter laugh. "He'd be just as happy to elope." Her eyes flicked to Max then back to her plate. "He's like you in that way. Doesn't need or want the pomp and circumstance."

"Hey, now, your mother and I had a big wedding."

"Which I would bet good money was more her idea than yours."

Instead of responding, he harrumphed and focused on his meal. Thinking back, he couldn't remember ever suggesting to Melody that they elope. For one thing, his Catholic mother would have murdered him. But for another, he'd wanted to crow to the world how happy he was that someone like Melody had agreed to marry someone like him.

"I'm sure if you wanted to push the date, Carissa would be willing to work with you," he finally said.

"I don't want to postpone it," she replied, her voice determined. "But I wish there were more months between now and December."

"If there's anything I can do to help, let me know."

"Well, I could use your advice on one thing..." She bit her lip and avoided his gaze.

"Which is?"

Her breath came out in a huff. "Carissa isn't open to the idea of using silk flowers, even though Rose and Steven used them in their wedding. I helped Rose put together her bouquets, and I liked how they turned out."

"What does she have against silk flowers?" Max suddenly wished he hadn't been so willing to help. The last thing he wanted to do was get between Carissa and Lanie when he and Carissa were finally connecting.

"She thinks they're tacky." Lanie rolled her eyes. "But it depends on where you buy them. Some of them are so realistic, you can't tell the difference." She finished the last bite of her dinner and washed it down with some water. "Besides, the flowers I want are expensive. If we did them ourselves, it would save on the cost, *and* I would have something I could keep forever."

"Your mother dried her bouquet and preserved it that way," he said, though he doubted his suggestion was helpful.

"I know that's an option, but it doesn't alleviate my financial concerns."

"All right." He stifled a sigh. "What do you need me to do?"

Her eyes widened. "Do? I don't need you to do anything. I'm planning to talk to Carissa about it again the next time I see her, and I'd love some advice on how to approach it."

"I'm not sure the approach is the problem. It sounds like she's not listening to you."

"For the most part, she does. It's just..." Lanie leaned her chin on her hand. "With her experience, she encourages me to do certain things her way."

That didn't sound right. While Carissa had proven how good she was at her job, what Lanie was saying reminded him of the many arguments he'd gotten into with Carissa during Steven and Rose's wedding. Back then, he'd thought she didn't like him or that she assumed he knew nothing about weddings. But now, he wondered how often Steven and Rose had been pressured to do something that didn't match their vision or budget. "When are you next seeing her?"

"I'm not sure, but probably sometime this week."

"Well, I'm happy to tag along." No matter how he might feel about Carissa, Lanie was his daughter, and he would do whatever it took to make sure she got the wedding she wanted. Especially if doing so helped him build the relationship he wanted with her.

Chapter Ten

CARISSA NERVOUSLY TAPPED HER INDEX FINGER ON THE steering wheel. She was having dinner with the Imaginavigation Enterprises CEO in DC that evening. It wasn't her official pitch yet, but he wanted a preview before she presented to the board the following week. Although it seemed odd, she assumed that was how things worked in the corporate world and decided to go with it.

Which was why she found herself driving to the city on Wednesday evening. Traffic was light since rush-hour commuters were heading in the opposite direction. She hoped parking would be cheaper outside of office hours as well.

When she arrived at the same parking garage as before, she took her time getting out of the car. She'd left earlier than needed, hoping driving would distract her from thoughts about Max. Ever since he'd asked her to dinner, she'd been unable to get him off her mind.

"Buck up, Carissa," she told herself. "Max doesn't matter right now. This meeting could change the course of the rest of your life. Stay focused."

The words sounded empty, but she pretended to believe them.

As she climbed out of her car, she straightened her spine and tried to look more confident than she felt.

The restaurant was rather run-down, especially compared to the place they had met for lunch previously. It had a small storefront she almost walked by, and when she entered, she was directed to a dark set of stairs into the basement below. The space was small, with only a few high-top tables and a bar along the length of one bright-green wall. The other walls sported similar bright colors—orange, yellow, and pink.

Jacob waited for her at the bar. His tie was loosened, and he appeared to have been sitting there for some time. Steeling herself for more condescension, she took a deep breath and marched over to him.

"Mr. Mikelson," she said.

As he glanced at her with a flushed face and bloodshot eyes, he swayed precariously on his stool. "Carissa, you made it. Please, call me Jacob." His words were slightly slurred.

I'd rather call you a cab. How were they supposed to have a meeting with him in that state? Would he even remember her pitch?

"Is this a bad time?" she asked, choosing her words carefully.

"Of course not." He gestured to the stool beside him. "Please have a seat."

"Oh, I thought we were having dinner."

After lifting his glass, he toasted her before draining it. "We are, but eating at the bar is less formal." He signaled to the bartender for a refill. "Plus the service is faster."

Stifling a sigh, she hoisted herself onto the stool and shifted uncomfortably. That wasn't at all what she'd had in mind for that night. Without another word, she picked up a menu and resigned herself to what was sure to be a miserable dinner.

But she'd barely even opened the menu before he snatched it from her hands. "You don't need that. Let me order for you." When the bartender arrived, Jacob continued, "I'll have a medium-rare steak, the most expensive one you've got, and she'll have a salad." A smirk crossed his face as he glanced at her. "Water again as well, or did you want to be more adventurous?"

Swallowing a retort, she forced a smile. "Water is fine."

"Unsurprising," he muttered. Then he shook his glass at the bartender. "And keep these coming."

"About my presentation," she began, hoping to turn the evening around. "I brought my tablet to show you my slides and to go over my ideas at a high level. I wasn't sure if—"

He waved his hand. "No shop talk."

Frowning, she stared at him. "I thought you asked for this dinner because you wanted me to go over my presentation before I meet with the board."

"Wow, you really bought that."

To her horror, he laughed.

"I just wanted to see you again."

Her heart pounded, and her palms grew sweaty. "Why? Aren't you married?"

"I am, but my wife and I have an... agreement." He gave her a once-over.

Repulsed, she leaned away from him. *Is your wife actually aware of this agreement, or is it all in your head?* She pressed her lips together so she wouldn't say anything she might regret, a courtesy she wished Jacob would bestow on her as well.

"I'm sorry, Mr. Mikelson, but I'm not looking to date a married man."

"Perfect." His smirk slipped into a sneer. "Because I'm not looking to date either."

"Then what—"

"Oh, come on, Carissa," he slurred, sliding an arm around her shoulders. "Don't play coy. You were flirting with me throughout our entire last meeting."

She blinked rapidly and pulled away. Was he serious? "I was being polite and professional. I'm sorry if my behavior came across as anything else, but I assure you that wasn't my intention."

Thankfully, she was saved from having to hear his response by the bartender returning with her water and another glass of whatever alcohol Jacob had ordered. In the few seconds it took for the bartender to set down her drink, she debated her options. She could stay there and try to redirect the evening to her proposal, or she could leave and kiss the chance of a lifetime goodbye.

"Excuse me," she said before hurrying off to the ladies' room.

When she got there, she stood in front of the sink and stared at the mirror. She'd been on her share of bad dates before finding Chuck. Back then, she would have suffered through the experience, but she wasn't young and naive anymore. And besides, it wasn't a date. It was supposed to be a business meeting.

The door opened behind her, and a black-haired woman wearing a uniform in bright colors similar to those of the restaurant entered. Carissa dropped her gaze, but to her surprise, the woman walked right up to her.

"Excuse me, ma'am. The bartender sent me in here. That guy you're with was thrown out."

Carissa spun around, her mouth falling open. "He *what*?"

The woman shrugged. "I don't know exactly what happened, but I heard shouting, and then two off-duty cops dragged him outside." She glanced toward the door then back at Carissa. "If you want to catch him, he probably hasn't gone far, but Ricky, our bartender, got the feeling you weren't entirely comfortable with him."

"I wasn't." Carissa exhaled heavily, leaning against the counter for support.

"In that case, it's probably safe for you to leave." The woman searched her face. "Do you need me to call you a cab?"

"No. I drove myself into the city, and I haven't been drinking." Carissa forced a smile. "But thank you."

After the waitress left, Carissa splashed cold water on her face and took several deep breaths. She had no idea what the evening's turn of events would do to her relationship with Jacob's corporation —or her career.

~

When Carissa woke up the next morning, she groaned. She'd hoped last night had been a bad dream. Jacob hadn't contacted her since he'd been kicked out of the restaurant, and she'd waited a half hour before leaving just in case he was lurking, hoping to catch her. By the time she left, there was no sign of him, and she drove home without incident.

Thankfully, she didn't have any client meetings until that evening, and she relished the time to recover from her experience. She couldn't explain why she was shaken by Jacob's behavior. He'd shown how condescending he was at that first lunch, and he probably figured he was doing her a favor by propositioning her like that. Still, it'd been a long time since a man had behaved that way toward her. Even Max, with his grumpy antics during Steven's wedding planning, had never acted inappropriately.

After dragging herself out of bed, she went through her usual morning routine and decided to take a trip to Bea's. It might do her some good to be in a familiar place, surrounded by other people.

When she entered the diner, she caught sight of Max in a booth toward the back of the restaurant. Her first instinct was to avoid him. While Max and Jacob were nothing alike, she wasn't sure she could stomach sitting in close proximity to another man right then. But then he saw her, and the way his face lit up touched her heart.

"Fancy meeting you here," he said as she sat down. "What'll you have?"

"Coffee, black," she said. *Like my mood.*

Max raised his eyebrows and signaled for the server. Once they were alone again, he leaned back and assessed her. "Are you okay?"

"I will be." A moment later, the server returned with her coffee, and she took a sip, savoring the bitterness.

"I'm actually glad I ran into you," Max said when she didn't elaborate. "I wanted to talk to you about the flowers for Lanie's wedding."

Where did that come from? Frowning, she folded her arms on the table. "What about them?"

"Lanie wants silk flowers, but she says you told her they're tacky."

Carissa stared at him blankly. "And? I meant what I said."

His eyes narrowed, and he leaned back, crossing his arms over his chest. "But it's what she wants."

"I understand, but—"

"No 'buts.' If that's what Lanie wants, then that's what she gets. Besides, they're on a budget."

She raised an eyebrow. "You're not supposed to be meddling in Lanie's wedding anymore."

His face flushed, which told her everything she needed to know. "She was upset last night and told me all about it. I had planned to join her the next time she met with you, but since you're here, I figured I'd bring it up now."

This man can't help himself. Taking a deep breath, Carissa wrapped her hands around her mug. "I'm familiar with the wedding budget, and I've given Lanie several suggestions on how to save on the flowers."

"And I assume none of them included silk substitutes?"

"No," she admitted. "They did not." He opened his mouth to respond, but she held up a hand. "Look, I appreciate Lanie's concerns, but she's not my first bride with a small floral budget. I've suggested cheaper versions of the flowers she wants in her bouquet."

"Like what?"

Pursing her lips, she studied him. Would he understand the different types of flowers if she described them? Somehow, he didn't strike her as the type, but since he'd asked, she couldn't see any way around it.

"Gardenias are much like roses and smell just as good." She

began ticking off the rose alternatives she'd used in the past. "Camellias are so similar, you almost can't tell the difference, and like roses, they come in many different colors. Ranunculus would work as well."

As his eyes began to glaze over, she gave up trying to explain. Hopefully, he would realize he was out of his element and let it go. The last thing she wanted to do was go back to the days of fighting with Max over his children's weddings.

"So, let me get this straight. You're willing to use some cheap imitation flower in her bouquet but not an exact replica that happens to be fake?"

She bristled at his characterization. "First of all, they are less expensive, yes, but I would hardly call them 'cheap.' And secondly, have you seen the fake flowers they sell at craft stores? They don't hold a candle to any real flower, regardless of whether it's a rose."

"But Lanie isn't planning on buying flowers at a local craft store. She's ordering them special online."

"Which is more expensive than a craft store," Carissa pointed out.

He frowned. "Is it more expensive to buy silk flowers online than real flowers from a florist?"

"Again, it depends on the flower. Roses would likely be more expensive from a florist, but the less expensive alternatives I—"

"Then you've proved my point," he cut in.

Heat rose up her neck, and she glared at him. "Why do you care so much?"

His mouth turned down. "I'm trying to rebuild my relationship with Lanie. If this matters to her, it matters to me."

Of course. With a sigh, she tried seeing things from his eyes. When Lanie had told Carissa she wanted silk flowers, she'd said she wanted something she could keep forever. If she'd told her father the same thing, Carissa could understand why he was fighting for her.

"You're right. I'm sorry." She took a sip of coffee. "However, there would still be an added cost to have a florist design the silk flowers, just like there would be if they designed real ones."

"What if we did them ourselves? Didn't Rose and Steven do that?"

With Lanie's help. Thankfully, they'd put together the bouquets and boutonnieres before Steven's accident. There wouldn't have been time otherwise.

"They did, but they also had more time to work with than Lanie does."

"What if we all pitched in to help?" Max's voice held a note of pleading.

Wow, he really would do anything for her. A strange feeling of longing welled up in Carissa's chest, and she wondered if that willingness to help applied to everyone he loved. Before that train of thought could derail her, she pushed it out of her mind.

"Are you sure you have time for it? You're already planning on baking cookies for favors."

Max squared his shoulders. "We'll make it work."

Stifling another sigh, she nodded in defeat. "Fine. I'll make the arrangements to get the flowers and assist with making the bouquets. I'll also talk to Lanie about canceling our meeting with the florist."

The slow smile that came over his face took her breath away. Despite the rocky start to their conversation, she was happy to have run into him. Something about him seemed to make all her cares disappear.

"How was your meeting last night?" he asked, and just like that, the night before came back to her in a blinding flash.

She grimaced. "Not great."

His smile faded, and his eyebrows pulled together as if he were concerned. "What happened?"

Squeezing her eyes shut, she counted down from ten to calm the anger that began to rage inside her belly. It wasn't the time or the place to have that conversation. She wasn't sure she ever wanted to talk about what happened with anyone, least of all Max.

"Hey," he said, and when she opened her eyes, he was standing. After tossing a few dollars on the table, he held out his hand. "Let's go for a walk."

She allowed him to lead her out of the restaurant and down the street. Already, the leaves on the tops of the trees had turned bright colors. Reds, oranges, and yellows dotted the otherwise green trees towering over Main Street. A slight breeze brought enough of a chill to remind them autumn had arrived.

Normally, the change of the seasons brought her peace, but instead, it was another reminder of how much her own life hadn't changed. In the five years since her husband had died, she'd lived each day pretty much the same. Wedding planning for several hours, updating her business profile, and grabbing snacks from the fridge. She couldn't remember the last time she'd cooked a decent meal.

Expanding her business would change all of that, but after last night, it felt like a pipe dream. While she could explore other avenues to break into corporate event planning, the idea of canceling her pitch meeting to the board hurt her heart. She'd worked day and night on her proposal, and she was confident in her ideas. To tuck her tail between her legs and admit defeat was too much to bear. She wasn't sure where she would find the energy to start over from scratch. Her husband's name had gotten her the meeting with Imaginavigation Enterprises in the first place. Unfortunately, his contact there had since retired, which was why she was stuck dealing with Jacob.

Max took her hand and settled it in the crook of his arm, drawing her back to the present. They strolled toward Nate's mechanic shop, taking in the sights and sounds of downtown Cedar Haven. Part of her wondered if that was a smart move, walking arm and arm in public like they were, but then she decided she didn't care. The pressure of his arm around her hand helped to center her and made last night feel like a dream... or a nightmare.

But Max, seeming to read her mind, took her to a small street that led to a quiet park. A few children ran and laughed around a playground, but he led her toward a set of picnic tables where they could be alone. When they reached them, he sat on one of the table benches, facing the playground. She settled beside him with a contented sigh and rested her forearms on the table.

"So, do you want to talk about it?" He nudged her with his shoulder.

"No," she whispered, but that wasn't true. She needed to get it out before it could fester, and she could use some advice on what to do.

"Okay, then." His response was simple, so *Max*, that a laugh bubbled up in her throat.

"I don't *want* to talk about it, but I *need* to."

He didn't say anything, clearly letting her take her time. It was weird to think how much his stoicism used to frustrate her. At that moment, she found it comforting.

"The CEO was already drunk when I arrived," she began. "And things went downhill from there."

In painstaking detail, she relived the night before. Max kept silent, but his muscles grew tenser the more she said. When she finished, she took a deep breath and let it out slowly, surprised by how much lighter she felt. She hadn't realized how the events had been weighing on her.

"What a jerk." The phrase was said in a way that was meant to be offhand, but Carissa could hear the edge in his voice. "Someone needs to teach him some manners."

"It's a bit late for that." Impulsively, she leaned against Max, relishing his warmth and strength.

"Are you still planning to pitch his company?"

She picked at her fingernails as she debated her response. "I don't know. I mean, on the one hand, I feel like I shouldn't. The last thing I need is to work with some cheating, entitled creep."

"And on the other hand?" His voice sounded strained, like he was holding something back.

Lifting her head, she gazed up at him. His jaw was clenched, and he stared straight ahead.

"Hey." She squeezed his arm. "I'm okay now."

A flush crept over his face as his eyes narrowed. "Yes, *now*." Shaking his head, he finally met her gaze, and his dark eyes burned with barely controlled fury. "But if you hadn't been in a public place, if he hadn't been thrown out of the bar..." His hands clenched into fists. "He better hope I never meet him."

Max's anger surprised her. Sure, he was protective of his children and their desires. But his reaction then, like he wanted to protect *her*... Well, it was new and different and surprisingly attractive.

She wasn't usually into the overly protective type of guy. Her late husband had always respected her ability to stick up for herself. But she couldn't deny there were times she'd wished he would step up for her. Like when the father of the bride or even a groomsman would get a little rowdy and she'd have to put them in their place. Although Chuck would listen to her rant about the experience and took care to make sure she was okay, he'd never said or done anything that made her feel like he would set the world on fire to keep her safe.

Seeing Max angry on her behalf gave her a heady feeling that both exhilarated and scared her. Max was intense, and she wondered if that intensity was part of what had led to the end of his first marriage. Maybe Melody couldn't stand the heat.

Placing a cautious hand under his chin, she pulled his face around to hers. "I appreciate your concern, but I promise I can handle myself."

Slowly, the angry red color faded from his cheeks, and the fire in his eyes dimmed. "I'm sorry. Just... the thought of someone treating you that way." His hands clenched again. "It makes me see red."

"I didn't love it either." Her hand cupped his cheek. "It's over now, and I'm okay."

He lowered his gaze. "But you're still planning on pitching your proposal to him."

"To be fair, I'd be pitching the *board*, not him. Or at least not *only* him." She searched his face. "But I understand your concern."

"You understand it, but you don't share it?"

"Oh no, I share it." Tilting her head back, she closed her eyes as the warmth of the sun caressed her skin. "I worry that if I don't go through with it, then he wins. I mean, who knows, maybe last night was part of his attempt to convince me I need to stay in my lane and stick to wedding planning. His condescension at our lunch meeting gave me the impression he doesn't think I have what it takes."

Max frowned. "Was it all an act?"

Though she hadn't considered that, Carissa doubted that was the case. "He doesn't strike me as that good of an actor, and I can't imagine he'd purposefully get drunk to sabotage me."

"When is your meeting with the board?"

"Next week on Wednesday."

Max didn't speak as he digested her words. Part of her wondered if she shouldn't have told him, but the relief she experienced on getting it off her chest overcame any misgivings she had. Besides, he'd asked. If he didn't want to know, he would have said.

"While it doesn't sound like a good idea, I understand it's a huge boon for your career. Just... Promise me you'll be careful and you won't allow yourself to be alone with him."

She raised three fingers of her right hand. "Scout's honor."

His lips pulled into a soft smile, and he took her hand, brushing her fingers against his lips. Her heart stopped then raced in her chest. But before she could say or do anything, he stood.

"We should go before I do something reckless." He held out his hand to help her off the bench. Then he took her back to the diner.

For a moment, she thought he might kiss her by her car, but unlike the times before, there was no doubt in her mind she wanted him to. Instead, he squeezed her hand.

"I'll see you Sunday."

Chapter Eleven

THE DOORBELL RANG AS MAX FINISHED LUNCH. HE tossed his paper plate into the trash then went to answer it. His future son-in-law stood on the porch, dressed like a lumberjack—flannel button-down shirt, cargo pants, and work boots with a fleece jacket thrown over his arm.

"It's a bit warm for that, isn't it?" Max nodded to the jacket.

Nate shrugged. "It's colder up in the foothills." He gave a sheepish grin. "But it's more for Lanie. She gets cold easily."

"That makes more sense." Max motioned for Nate to come in. "Lanie's upstairs getting ready. Did you want something to drink?"

"No, thank you. I'm okay."

They went into the living room and sat down to wait. Neither of them spoke, but the silence wasn't awkward or uncomfortable. The one thing Max had always liked about Nate was he was also a man of few words. In that respect, they were cut from the same cloth.

But they weren't alone for long. The front door crashed open, and in walked Steven and Rose. Steven had brought his cane, likely more to help him navigate the rough terrain than because he really needed it.

"Glad you're coming with us, Dad." Steven plopped onto the couch beside his father.

"Where's Lanie?" Rose flipped her black hair over her shoulder. "I'm anxious to get my basic white girl on."

"I heard that!" Lanie called from upstairs. She scampered down and glared at her sister-in-law. "There's nothing wrong with apple picking."

"Of course not," Rose said. "But it is one of those overrated traditions people prop up as the epitome of autumn. Like PSLs."

"Whatever." Lanie rolled her eyes. "It's still fun, and I'll be putting them to good use in several desserts that I bet you gobble up." Turning her attention to the men in the room, she gestured to the door. "Are we ready to go?"

"As soon as we figure out who's driving." Steven pushed himself off the couch.

"Nate and I were planning to ride with Dad," Lanie replied. "We thought you and Rose could come up in your SUV since it's a bit more durable than my car or Nate's Camaro."

Steven grimaced. "I'm still not fully comfortable driving long distances yet."

"Could you drive his car?" Lanie asked Rose.

Pursing her lips, Rose shook her head. "I've not driven it often, and I prefer smaller cars. SUVs make me anxious."

"We're actually waiting on one more person." Max kept his gaze on the floor.

Steven frowned. "Who else is coming?"

Before Max could respond, a tentative knock sounded at the door. He rushed over to answer it, wondering if he should have warned his family prior to Carissa's arrival.

"Carissa," Rose called out, her brown eyes widening. "You're joining us today?"

After a quick glance at Max, Carissa nodded. "If you'll have me."

Max held his breath as he finally risked a look at Lanie. His daughter seemed more surprised than angry, though she did raise her eyebrows at him.

"The more the merrier," Lanie finally said with a tight smile. "Though that does complicate the driving situation a bit more."

"No it doesn't." Max gestured to Nate. "You can drive my truck with Lanie, and I'll take the rest of us up in Steven's SUV."

Lanie looked at her fiancé. "Is that okay with you?"

"If your dad trusts me with his truck, I'm game."

They filed out of the house. Max handed Nate his keys before heading to Steven's car. Steven started to climb into the passenger seat, but Rose stopped him with a meaningful look at Carissa.

"I'm happy to sit in the back with you, Rose," Carissa called.

"Nonsense," Max grumbled beside her, taking her hand. "You're sitting up front with me."

"But Steven might be more comfortable—"

"He'll be fine." Max opened the passenger door. "You're my guest, after all."

Rose and Steven settled into the back as Max closed the door and headed to the driver's side. Once he was buckled in, he started the engine then gestured for Nate to pull out first. Although he'd plugged the address into the GPS, he preferred to follow Nate because he wasn't as familiar with the area where they were headed.

A few minutes into the trip, he started to regret his insistence that Carissa sit up front. Her intoxicating perfume filled his senses, and he struggled to concentrate on the road. He needed a distraction.

"How's work going?" he asked Steven, glancing at his son in the rearview.

"Good. Mr. Willoughby's divorce is finally going to trial."

"Which I hope he loses," Rose quipped.

"That's not very supportive of your husband's hard work," Steven retorted.

"Perhaps not, but that man deserves it."

"Back me up here, Dad," Steven pleaded.

Carissa glanced at Max with an amused smile, and he rolled his eyes. For a couple who'd just had their wedding a little over a month ago, they fought like they'd been married for years.

"I'm afraid I'm with Rose on this one." At Steven's harrumph, Max amended his statement. "But I'm sure you've done a good job of painting what happened in a much different light. It'll probably result in some sort of compromise where neither party is completely happy."

"That's typically how divorces end," Steven agreed with a sigh. "It's not for lack of trying, though. He would have gotten a better deal if he'd listened to me instead of fighting everything I suggested tooth and nail."

"Like I said, I hope he gets what he deserves," Rose said again.

"How's your physical therapy?" Max asked, hoping to change the subject.

"It's... going." Frustration colored Steven's tone. "There are still times where it seems like my legs and brain aren't making the connection, but I'm able to move around without the cane most of the time."

"That's good news."

"Although long trips like this tend to make me stiff."

"If you need me to stop for a break, let me know."

"You? Stop for anything aside from gas or food?" Steven laughed. "Who are you, and what have you done with my father?"

Max scowled. "People can change."

"Can they?" Carissa whispered. At his grimace, she giggled. "To be fair, your father has been somewhat more agreeable the last few weeks."

"Which I'm sure is owing more to your influence than anything else," Steven said.

"Sitting right here," Max muttered. He was grateful when Nate flicked on his turn signal, confirming they were almost to their destination. Maybe for the ride home, he could convince his future son-in-law to drive Steven and Lanie. Somehow, he expected he would have a more peaceful ride without either of his children.

The road into the farm was bumpy, though Max tried to alleviate the jostling as much as possible. Still, by the time they pulled into the parking lot, Steven's face was a mask of pain.

"Do you want to rest for a minute?" Max asked.

"I'll be all right." Steven rubbed his back. "Honestly, getting out and stretching will probably be better than rest at this point."

Max nodded. "If you're sure."

"I have some ibuprofen in my bag if it'll help," Carissa offered.

"Thanks, but I took some before we left."

Lanie and Nate had already headed up to check them in and get the bags for the apples. It made more sense to hang out by the car while Steven stretched than to make him walk all the way up the hill. Rose stepped behind Steven and rubbed his back, which seemed to help with the pain.

"Maybe you shouldn't be pushing yourself." Her eyebrows pulled together as he completed a series of movements.

"Dr. Myers cleared me to come today."

"I know, but—"

"Here come Nate and Lanie now," Max interrupted, hoping to stem another argument.

"We got two pecks." Lanie handed one of the bags to Rose. "Four people can pick a peck." She turned to Max and Carissa. "Did you two want to come with us or go with Steven and Rose?"

After finishing one last bent stretch, Steven straightened up. "Hey, that's not fair. You'll have more people on your team."

Lanie scoffed. "Not everything has to be a competition."

"What are we picking today?" Carissa asked, and Max gave her a grateful look for the distraction.

Lanie lifted one shoulder. "It's whatever you want." Gesturing with the bag, she explained the different types of apples available that day and where they were located. Max hid a smile. She sounded like a walking apple encyclopedia.

"Why don't Rose and Steven pick the Pink Lady and Stayman

Winesap, since those trees are right here? Then the rest of us can go up the hill to pick Crispin, Ambrosia, and Jonagold."

"That sounds like a plan," Rose said. "Meet you back here in about half an hour?" Without waiting for a response, she linked arms with Steven, and they set off into the trees.

The rest of their group headed up the hill. Quite a few people were at the farm, enjoying the cool October day. Several visitors had filled their bags to the brim with apples. Others were sneaking bites between the trees.

"I can't do that," Max murmured to Carissa, pointing at a young boy who had already eaten half of an apple.

"What?" Her eyebrows pulled together. "Eat apples?"

"Not with the skin on," he said. "I'm allergic."

Her eyes widened. "Can you pick them, then?"

"Oh yeah. The skin doesn't bother me unless I ingest it. I have to peel the apples first."

She wrinkled her nose. "That's the weirdest allergy I've ever heard of."

Lanie spun around, a wide grin on her face. "And one he was kind enough to pass on to me. Though at least I can eat strawberries."

"You can't eat strawberries?" The way Carissa looked at him made him feel like an alien. "Do you know exactly what you're allergic to?"

He shrugged. "It could be the pesticides, but I've never been brave enough to try organic."

"What happens?" she asked. "Do you go into anaphylactic shock?"

Despite the fear on her face, Max couldn't help but laugh. "No, nothing that serious. I break out in hives."

"My mom thought it was chicken pox," Lanie said, linking her arm with Nate's. "Which I honestly would have preferred."

"Well"—Nate bent and kissed the top of her head—"at least it's an easy allergy to avoid."

By that point, they had reached the top of the hill. Nate and Lanie took the row of Jonagold while Carissa and Max slipped into the row of Ambrosia. Max had hoped to spend some time alone with Carissa, but as his wish came true, he couldn't think of anything to say.

"Thank you for inviting me," Carissa said. "I can't remember the last time I went apple picking."

His shoulders sagged in relief. "It's been a while for me as well, but we used to go often when the kids were little." He waved a hand. "Nothing wears a kid out more than physical labor."

She laughed. "I can imagine." They walked farther into the row of trees. "What do you do with the apples?"

"It depends. But Lanie loves to bake. I imagine she'll be making all sorts of desserts. The school is having a bake sale soon."

"You don't bake?" Carissa asked, a hint of amusement in her blue eyes.

He grimaced. "Baking was more Melody's area. And as I'm sure Lanie's told you, my cooking leaves a lot to be desired."

"She might have mentioned it."

The conversation died as they focused on picking apples. Max kept track of the number they were picking, as he didn't want to overload the bag with just one type. They each had their arms full when they met up with Lanie and Nate at the end of the row.

After a quick assessment, Lanie nodded. "We've got about ten of each, which means there should be room for a few Crispins. Hopefully, Rose and Steven tried to keep things even on their end as well."

Together, the four of them headed into the last row of trees. The Crispins must have ripened earlier than the rest, as they were pretty picked over, but they each managed to find a couple in good shape.

As they traveled down the hill, Max's body felt heavy. He'd hoped for more time with Carissa, but the activity hadn't taken nearly as long as he'd remembered. Though he supposed that made sense. The kids were young then and had needed a lot more direction and attention.

"How'd you all do?" Steven asked when they met up by the check-in tent.

"Pretty well." Lanie held out their full bag.

"Nice." Steven gestured to the bag in Rose's hand. "Looks like we'll need to find some ample storage space."

"They should fit in the garage," Max said. "And I'm sure Carissa would like to take some home as a reward for her hard work."

"Oh, I wouldn't know what to do with them."

"We should have a baking day," Rose suggested. "Lanie can teach us."

"I volunteer Dad's kitchen," Lanie joked. With a smile, she lifted her bag of apples and gestured to the car. "Shall we go?"

"Are we going home already?" Max asked.

His children glanced at each other, and Lanie shrugged. "The farm has a store not far from here. We could check out what other apple varieties they have."

"If I remember correctly, they have a fall festival as well. We could hang out there for a bit, maybe grab a snack," Steven said.

"Sounds like a plan!" Max could hardly contain his enthusiasm. Spending more time with Carissa was exactly what he'd hoped for, and who knew? Maybe by the end of the afternoon, she would take him up on his offer to go to dinner. The only problem was, he wanted more than a platonic outing, and he had no idea how to reconcile that desire with his promise to Lanie.

Chapter Twelve

CARISSA LOVED THE FARM STORE WITH ITS HOMEMADE décor and desserts, farm-raised meat, and assorted fresh vegetables. While the young couples checked out the festival, she and Max perused the many offerings inside. At first, Max held her growing pile of purchases until an employee quietly offered him a cart.

"Sorry about that." Carissa nibbled her lip. "I wasn't paying attention."

He shrugged as he placed her items in the cart. "It's fine. I was happy to continue carrying everything, but this makes it easier."

They wandered through the store, admiring the various baked goods. Carissa wasn't much of a baker, but she did have a sweet tooth. It was difficult not to put every item into their cart.

Once she was satisfied with her lot, she and Max got in line at the checkout. She looked over her items with a smile. When she glanced at Max, she noticed he hadn't picked up anything for himself. "There's nothing you wanted?"

He shook his head. "I only decorate for Christmas these days."

Lifting a pie, she held it out. "You don't like pie?"

"I do, but Lanie makes the best apple and pumpkin pies. I'm sure she's going to make a ton of delicious desserts with all the apples we picked."

A twinge in her gut caused Carissa to turn around. What she wouldn't give to be able to share a pie with Chuck and his family. Her parents had passed many years ago, but Chuck's parents were still around. While they'd always been kind to her, she wouldn't say they were close. Ever since the funeral, she rarely saw any of his relatives. At first, it had hurt too much, then so much time passed that it didn't seem appropriate to reach out.

"Next!" a cashier called.

Carissa and Max wheeled her cart over to the lane and began removing the items. It took longer than she expected, and she worried she'd gone overboard.

It'll brighten up the house, she told herself. Her home could use it. Returning home alone after spending time with Max and Lanie made her rather lonely.

After she finished checking out, Max helped her carry her bags to Steven's SUV. Steven, Rose, Lanie, and Nate were heading down the sidewalk toward them, each carrying a cup of warm apple cider.

"We grabbed you guys one too." Lanie held out a Styrofoam tray holding two additional cups.

"Thank you," Carissa said, lifting one of the cups and wrapping her hands around it. The sun was lower in the sky than she'd expected, and a chill was in the air.

"We should get back." Max accepted his cup and took a sip.

"You good with me driving your truck again?" Nate asked Max.

Max nodded. "I'll follow you out."

Carissa, Max, Steven, and Rose headed to the SUV while Nate and Lanie went to the truck. When Max opened the passenger door for her, Carissa couldn't help noticing he seemed disappointed, though she couldn't imagine why. The ride home was much quieter than the trip to the farm had been. She hid a smile. It appeared apple picking had had the same effect on Max's adult children that it had when they were little.

When they arrived at Max's house, Carissa felt a pang of regret. She wasn't quite ready for the day to end. Max helped her transfer her purchases from Steven's vehicle to hers, then Steven and Rose headed home.

"Nate and I are going to dinner if you'd like to join us," Lanie said as Nate handed Max the truck keys.

Carissa exchanged a glance with Max and shook her head. "I need to get back. I've got some work to do this evening."

Something flashed in Max's eyes, but before she could decipher the emotion, it was gone.

He nodded to Lanie. "You go have fun. I've got some leftovers calling my name."

"I'll see you for your dress fitting next week," Carissa called as Lanie and Nate walked away.

When she was alone with Max, she smiled. "Thanks for inviting me."

"I'm glad you came."

They stood in an awkward silence as she debated what to say. While she did have work to do, she wasn't quite ready to leave. Deep down, she hoped he would ask her out again.

"So, how'd I do?" Max finally asked.

She cocked her head. "What do you mean?"

"This was our trial run, wasn't it? Sort of a preview before you'd agree to have lunch with me."

A laugh bubbled up in her throat. "Ah, right." His nearness made it difficult for her to think. "And this outing, it would still be just friends, right?"

"I—" Max began then closed his mouth. His eyebrows pulled together.

"What's wrong?"

He ran a hand through his salt-and-pepper hair. "I know that's what I said, but..."

"But?" she asked breathlessly.

"I want... more."

Her heart skipped a beat. "Like a real date?"

"Exactly." His gaze swept over her hungrily before his frown deepened. "But I promised Lanie."

And just like that, the warmth that had been building in her chest vanished. "Right." After such a wonderful day, she'd almost forgotten she was still planning his daughter's wedding. "She didn't seem to mind me tagging along today."

"I'm not sure what she felt," Max said. "But I'm sure if she wasn't happy about it, I'll get an earful later."

Carissa sighed. "She's right to be concerned. If we start something and it doesn't go well, it will make the wedding awkward."

"I suppose we could wait until after the wedding." From Max's tone, Carissa gathered that wasn't what he wanted. In truth, it wasn't what she wanted either, but it seemed their only option.

"It's only a few months away," she agreed reluctantly.

"Or..." He took a deep breath. "We could keep it a secret."

She burst out laughing. "Because that went so well last time."

His harrumph only made her smile wider. "It was an accident. I wasn't thinking." He placed his hand on her shoulder. "This is different. It's not wedding-related, which means I'm less likely to slip up again."

"If she found out, you're not the only one who'd be in hot water. My reputation, my business could be tarnished." Her heart hammered in her chest, both from his proximity and a real concern for what that might mean for her livelihood. Her eyes searched his face. *Is he worth the repercussions I could face if this ends badly?*

"I know, and I hate the idea of sneaking around, but waiting until after Christmas is worse." His fingers tucked a lock of hair behind her ear, and her skin heated where he touched her. Part of her wondered if he would kiss her, and she feared she wouldn't be able to resist him if he did.

Words failed her. Her heart wanted to throw caution to the wind and see if her growing feelings might develop into something real. But as her mind played out the worst-case scenarios, it put a damper on her passion. A cool breeze blew past them, causing her to shiver.

"Do you want to come inside?" Max gestured to the house. "I don't want you to freeze."

"I should go." His face fell, and she hurried on. "But let's plan to grab lunch this weekend."

He smiled. "Saturday?"

"Saturday sounds perfect."

"Until then," he said.

They walked to her car, and he opened her door. She buckled herself in and backed out of his driveway. When she glanced in the rearview, he was still standing outside, watching her leave.

The whole way home, she was on cloud nine. As she gathered her bags and carried them into the house, she practically floated to the door. After Chuck had passed, she never expected to feel this way again and certainly not about Max McAllister. But so much had changed between them in the last month, and she couldn't wait for Saturday.

First, she had to get through her pitch.

When Wednesday finally arrived, Carissa was a bundle of nerves. She drove into the city and parked in the garage under the building where Imaginavigation Enterprises was headquartered. As she took the elevator to the lobby, she kept smoothing her hair and her clothes to keep her hands from shaking.

The receptionist took her name and showed her into a large conference room. A table in the center had somewhere between twenty to thirty chairs stationed around it, though she wasn't sure how many people from the board would be in attendance. A large screen stood at one end, and she decided to set up there.

After plugging in her laptop, she clicked through her slides to make sure everything worked. Once she was ready, she took a seat and sipped from the provided water bottle, trying to calm her nerves.

To her chagrin, Jacob was first to arrive. She kept a neutral smile on her face while she shook his hand and prayed he wouldn't recall their encounter from the other night.

"Carissa, glad you were able to come today." His eyes swept over her body, and she resisted the urge to pull away from him. "I was disappointed our date the other night was cut short."

Bile rose up in her throat, but she swallowed it. "It was unfortunate you had to leave our business meeting so abruptly."

His face darkened, and he opened his mouth to respond, but she was saved from whatever he was going to say by the door opening and the board members filing in. One by one, they shook her hand and introduced themselves before taking their seats.

After everyone was seated, Jacob stood and gave a small introduction. "Now that we've all met Carissa, let me tell you about our lunch meeting last month to give you a sense of what she has to offer. Carissa owns a little wedding business in southern Maryland and has recently sought to branch out into corporate events, including holiday parties and team-building retreats."

She bristled at the description of her business as "little" but worked to keep her smile on her face. As Jacob continued, he couldn't seem to resist firing a jab at her here and there, but thankfully, his remarks mostly went unnoticed by the rest of the board. When he was finished, he sat down with a satisfied smirk.

Determined not to let him rile her, she took a deep breath and mentally counted down from ten before she began. He was one of many who would decide which event coordinator would get the company's business. If she could win over everyone else in the room, she could not only realize her dream but also make him eat crow. The thought thrilled her, and a genuine smile tugged at her lips.

"Thank you for having me today. I've enjoyed learning more about your company." She cleared her throat. "I was asked to present three different options for events that I think will help strengthen the cohesiveness of your company through team building, but first, I'd like to tell you more about me and how I got started in event planning."

Clicking to the next slide, she began the speech she'd rehearsed over the last several days. Her confidence grew as she finished her introduction, and several board members leaned forward, clearly interested.

"The first option I have for you is a trip to a local winery." The next slide showed a beautiful landscape of rolling hills against a deep-blue sky. "For the first night, a wine tasting will be provided for an icebreaker. Then you'll take a horseback ride through the countryside, followed by a special dinner pairing each course with a different wine. Other activities will include a cooking class, a soccer game, and a tour of the winery, during which you will be provided an overview of the wine-making process."

She saw a few nods in the audience, but overall, the reaction wasn't positive. But Carissa had expected that. The winery was her least favorite of her three ideas, and she'd decided to start small and work her way up to the best one, which she hoped would win them over.

Her next slide showed the National Harbor lit up at night. "For the next option, we have a long weekend in the National Harbor. One of the benefits is it's not far from the city. Folks can go home at night to their families or choose to stay in the lovely Gaylord Hotel. The first night will have a welcome dinner cruise. One of the team-building activities will be an escape room. There will also be a rowing contest on the Potomac River."

After she gave a few more details about the second option, she glanced at the board members to gauge their reactions. Some maintained eye contact, but most were losing interest. She started to wonder if she should have presented her ideas in reverse order or discussed her favorite option in the middle to keep their attention.

Quickly clicking to the next slide, she squared her shoulders and paused dramatically. The sudden silence had the desired impact, as many people put aside their phones and focused on her once more.

"And last but certainly not least, the third option is a trip to Deep Creek Lake. As with the second option, there will be an opportunity for water sports but also mountain climbing, biking, hiking, and sightseeing. There are several cabins that can be booked for a week, allowing a perfect getaway with a rustic backdrop while still incorporating modern conveniences like Wi-Fi."

As she finished her presentation, she put her hands behind her back and gazed at the board members expectantly. "Any questions?"

Hands shot up around the room, and her earlier fear about the order of her presentation melted away. She was so busy fielding the questions they fired at her she barely noticed Jacob scowling from across the room. Though her confidence soared, her stomach did a little flip. She worried that even if the board voted in her favor, Jacob would find a way to quash the opportunity.

Chapter Thirteen

THE JOY MAX HAD EXPERIENCED AFTER MAKING PLANS with Carissa dissipated as he considered the logistics of getting out of the house without Lanie learning of those plans. While he and Carissa had agreed to keep things platonic for the time being, it would still seem odd to Lanie that he was having lunch with Carissa on his own. He'd yet to think of a good excuse, and he hoped to avoid the topic entirely by slipping out of the house unnoticed.

Unfortunately, dodging Lanie proved to be more difficult than he'd expected. With it being Saturday, he assumed she would have plans with Nate, but she seemed perfectly content lounging around the house. She'd staked out the living room for the day. When he came downstairs, she already had papers stacked around her and the television tuned to some sappy Hallmark movie.

"What's all this?" He gestured to the mess.

She pointed at the piles one by one. "Lesson plans. Worksheets. Individualized Education Programs, or IEP, I need to review." Her eyebrows pulled together as her hand hovered over the last pile. "Papers to grade." She shrugged. "The work of a teacher never ends."

"Oh, you don't have plans with Nate?" He tried to hide his disappointment.

"Not until later." She cocked her head. "Why? Trying to get rid of me?"

"Of course not," he retorted, turning to the kitchen. But he stopped and glanced back. "Uh, what time is Nate coming?"

Her eyes narrowed. *Wrong question.* If he'd hoped to keep her from becoming suspicious, he was off to a bad start.

"I want to make sure he doesn't block me in," he said, keeping his voice neutral.

Lanie didn't appear to buy his lame excuse, but she didn't press. "Probably not until this evening."

He went to get a cup of coffee. His plan wasn't going to work. He needed to leave by noon to pick up Carissa, which meant he would have to sneak out of the house without Lanie seeing or concoct some plausible excuse for where he was going. And he'd have to give up any hope of dressing nicely for the occasion because that would surely raise her suspicions.

He'd have to make do with something he normally wore. He rolled his eyes. Because that was going to be easy. Maybe he should cancel. Carissa would understand.

But he didn't want to cancel. He'd been looking forward to their lunch all week. Part of him almost wished Lanie had never moved in with him, but he immediately regretted the thought. If she hadn't moved home, he wasn't sure he would ever have the chance to make amends with her. Besides, she'd probably be happy he was putting himself out there again were it not for the person he had chosen to spend time with.

After finishing his coffee, he wandered into the garage. If nothing else, he could make some serious progress on the remaining unfinished furniture. With luck, Lanie would finish her school stuff before lunch and vacate the living room. He crossed his fingers.

As he worked, he tried to get into his normal rhythm. Usually, woodworking helped him to clear his head, but that day, he couldn't seem to concentrate.

Maybe it was because the last time he'd worked on those pieces was before his marriage imploded. Or perhaps it was the fact that autumn always reminded him of Melody because her birthday was in November. Whatever the reason, his mind kept replaying their last argument.

"You need to work on your relationship with Lanie," she'd said. Despite how much the cancer had already eaten away at her, she still had a fierceness he admired, except when she aimed it at him. They were on the front porch of the house they had once shared. Melody sat in a wicker chair in the corner while Max was perched on the stairs.

"Lanie and I are fine," he retorted. "You worry too much."

She raised an eyebrow. "I won't be around to manage your relationships for you. And one day, you may wake up to find yourself cut off from her life."

He snorted. "You're one to talk."

"What's that supposed to mean?"

"Don't think I don't know what you and Nate talked about the other day. Jesus, Melody, you can't put a promise like that on that kid."

Her eyes narrowed. "He's not a kid. He's a grown man. And don't change the subject. We're talking about *your* relationship with Lanie, not mine." Unshed tears glimmered in her eyes as she turned away. "It's too late for me to fix things."

"Don't say that." He stood, hoping to put an end to the morbid conversation.

"It's true, and it's about time you faced it." She sighed. "Let me say my piece, and then I promise not to bring it up again."

"Fine." Leaning against the porch rail, he crossed his arms.

"You've always had an easier relationship with Steven. The two of you are a lot alike in many ways." Her teeth worried her lower lip. "But with Lanie, it's different. When she was younger, she was such a daddy's girl. Since she grew up, it's like you've held her at arm's length."

"It certainly didn't help that she went to college on the other side of the country."

"That was my fault." She stared at the ground. "I leaned on her after the divorce, and I pushed her to get out of this town. I wanted something better for her."

He shifted uncomfortably. Melody had told him about forcing Lanie to promise she'd leave Cedar Haven and never look back. When she'd first told him, he hoped she'd learned her lesson and would make amends before... His mind tripped over the words. Then she'd extracted a very different promise from Nate, and Max wondered if she understood the destruction she'd caused.

"If Nate can't get through to her..." She swallowed. "Then you have to."

"I thought you liked her current boyfriend."

"James is a good guy, and there was a time I believed he was perfect for her." Her eyes misted again. "But I know my daughter, and she's not happy with him. She'd never admit it, but she stays with him to fulfill her promise to me."

"I'm not sure she'll listen to me any more than she would Nate."

She raised an eyebrow. "I wonder where she got that stubbornness from."

His lips twitched as he tried not to smile. "'Cause you're not stubborn at all, right?"

Her answering smile caused his heart to skip a beat, just before a knife twisted in his stomach. They'd lost so much time, and now, she was dying.

"Promise me you'll fix things with Lanie. She's going to need you when I'm—" Her voice cracked.

In an instant, he'd knelt beside her and grabbed her hands. "I promise."

Lanie's laugh floated out into the garage from the living room, interrupting his thoughts. He stared at the wood shavings peppering the floor. What was he doing out there, hiding from her, when he had such precious time left? The wedding was in less than three months, then she would move in with Nate. Had he done enough to fix things with her? Or would she stop by only for the obligatory get-togethers on major holidays?

He didn't want to find out. After putting his tools away, he grabbed a broom and swept the garage. As soon as he was finished, he headed into the house.

Lanie sat in the same spot, but she shifted the papers around her. It appeared she'd made a lot of progress. She looked up and smiled as he came into the room.

"How's the furniture coming?"

"Not bad. I'm still rusty, but I'm getting the hang of it again." He cleared his throat. "I was going to get some lemonade. Did you want some?"

She blinked, seemingly surprised by his offer. "Um, sure?"

Her reaction grated on him, and he hurried into the kitchen before she saw his face. When he returned with two glasses, she accepted hers and patted the empty spot beside her, which he slid into. For a moment, they sipped their drinks in silence as yet another Hallmark movie started.

"How do you watch these things?" He tilted his glass toward the screen. "Aren't they basically the same plot?"

She laughed. "Yes and no. It's the same structure, but the plots and characters are different." His doubt must have been clear on his face because she shook her head. "Okay, sometimes they run together, even for me." She glanced at the screen. "But I like predictability. No matter what's going on in my life, I can watch one of these movies and be guaranteed a happy ending."

"Sounds boring to me."

"Besides," she continued as if he hadn't spoken, "they're easy to follow, so I can focus on something else and have it on in the background."

"I suppose that's true."

After draining her glass, she set it on the small table beside the couch. "Are you planning on working in the garage all afternoon?"

He shook his head. "I'm done for the day. Thought I'd come in and see how you were getting on."

"I've got a few more things to do, but I should finish soon." Her eyes strayed to the papers in her lap, and she picked up her pen.

Normally, he would take that as his cue, but he didn't want to leave. The whole point of him coming in early was to spend some quality time with her, but he didn't want to disrupt her work.

"If you want to change the channel, you can." She nodded toward the remote on the coffee table in front of them.

"Oh, that's okay. There's nothing I want to watch."

Another beat of silence, then she shifted on the couch to face him full-on. "Is something wrong?"

Great. She'd noticed he was acting weird. "No, why?"

"Just... You don't usually hang out here during the day." She shuffled her papers. "If I'm in your way, I can go to my room—"

"No, no, you're fine." *Why is this so difficult?* "I was hoping to spend some time with you."

Her eyebrows shot up, and he wished he'd found a better way to word it. Ah, well, he'd done it. He took another sip of lemonade to buy himself some time.

"Oh," she finally said.

Her teeth worried her lower lip, and it pained him to realize how much she looked like her mother when she did that. "I'm not sure I'll be much company until I finish this stuff."

"That's okay." He peered over at the paper on top of the pile. "So, does the school provide you with a personality profile on every kid?"

She laughed. "You make it sound like the FBI." Then her face grew serious. "It's their school record, with report cards, IEPs, and other pertinent information. I don't have to go through it like I'm doing, but some of these kids were with the last teacher for years. I only spent a little time with them before she left, and I want to make sure I'm meeting their needs."

"You always were a planner," he replied with a wry smile.

"I believe I get that from you," she murmured.

"Me?" He blinked. *When have I ever planned anything?* "I'm not sure I follow."

With a sigh, she set aside the pile and faced him. "I suppose it's not that you're a planner, but you always seem to try to have a firm grasp on any situation."

"Is that a bad thing?"

Her lips twisted as she appeared to consider his question. "Not exactly bad, but it can be frustrating."

His heart sank. "In what way?"

"For starters, you always think you know what's best for everyone. While I'm not saying you're wrong in every instance, it's frustrating because when you're convinced you're right, you don't listen to anyone else's opinion."

"That's not true."

She raised an eyebrow. "Isn't it? You were convinced I belonged in Cedar Haven. You practically badgered me into staying."

"Are you saying I was wrong?"

"No," she admitted. "But I *am* saying you went about it the wrong way." He opened his mouth to protest, but she held up her hand. "Let me try to put it in a perspective you'll understand. Ever heard the saying 'You'll catch more flies with honey than vinegar'?"

He crossed his arms. "In the version I'm familiar with, it's manure, not vinegar."

"Of course it is," she muttered, rolling her eyes. "Anyway, my point is I might have been less resistant to the idea of moving back home if you hadn't continued to undermine my choice at every turn. For example, perhaps instead of calling my decision a disappointment, you could have simply said you wished I would reconsider but you respected that it was my life to do with as I wished."

"Would that have convinced you to stay, though?"

"I didn't need you to convince me to stay, Dad. I needed you to listen to me as an adult and stop treating me like a child."

He scowled. *When have I ever treated her like a child since she's been home?* "I don't do that."

Her lips curved in a sad smile. "Not always, but you often seem to underestimate my capabilities."

The conversation was starting to hit the point where he usually shut it down and left, but something told him he needed to hear what she had to say, regardless of how much it hurt. With a deep breath, he swallowed his retort. "How so?"

A surprised glint lit her hazel eyes. "Take my wedding, for example. You keep offering to pay for things, even though I've told you Nate and I have it handled. Then, to back up your offer, you read into any expression that crosses my face." She raised an eyebrow as if daring him to counter it.

"But you did seem to want that other cake."

"It's a lovely design, but I don't need it." Her mouth turned down. "Sometimes, it feels like you equate money with true emotional connection."

Ouch. He ducked his head to hide how much her words had hurt him. *Is it wrong to want to provide for your children even when they're grown?*

"I'm sorry," Lanie said, clearly realizing her statement had cut deeper than she'd intended. "I shouldn't have said it like that."

"It's okay." He waved a hand and tried to play it off as no big deal, but the words still stung. To give himself a moment to recover, he checked his watch. It was already after eleven. If he had any hope of being on time for lunch, he needed to get ready.

He stood and stretched, ignoring the frown that crossed Lanie's face. As much as he hated to cut their conversation short, he needed some time to process everything she'd said.

"I'm having lunch with an old friend." He headed to the stairs. "We can talk more about this later."

"Okay," she called, her tone dejected. "Have fun."

His chest tightened as he climbed the stairs to shower and change. While he'd known fixing things with Lanie wouldn't be easy, he'd never expected that hearing how she felt would wound him. His mixed-up emotions were only exacerbated by the lie he had just told her. The last thing he wanted to do was cause more issues between them, but he suspected the truth would upset Lanie more.

Chapter Fourteen

Carissa examined her appearance for the hundredth time. Nothing had changed, but somehow, noting her makeup hadn't smeared and her hair wasn't out of place calmed her.

Why am I nervous? It was just lunch between friends. Or at least, that was what she kept telling herself. While they might not be calling it a date, it certainly felt like one. Which meant so much could go wrong. If things didn't work out, the next few months would be awkward until after the wedding. Or if Lanie found out, she might not like the fact that Carissa was mixing business with pleasure.

Carissa was thankful Max didn't have any more children. As happy as she was to have snagged two clients from the same family, she doubted she would survive another McAllister wedding.

The doorbell rang, and her heart leaped into her chest. Taking a deep breath, she swallowed her nerves and opened her door.

Max's eyes traveled down her body, and she bit her lip to hide her smile. The blue long-sleeved dress she wore had been sitting in her closet, gathering dust. She was thrilled to not only have a reason to wear it but also that it still fit.

"You look..." He stopped as if he couldn't find a word that quite fit whatever he saw.

"So do you." Her voice came out much more breathless than she'd intended, but it was true. He wore a leather jacket over a dark-blue button-down shirt, which went nicely with his black trousers. Normally, she wasn't into such dark colors on a man, but somehow, on Max, it fit.

He cleared his throat. "Shall we go?"

After grabbing a light trench coat, she nodded. He held out his arm, and she took it, feeling her fingers warm where they brushed his leather jacket.

When he opened the passenger door, she smiled. "How chivalrous."

He grinned. "What can I say? I'm old-fashioned. Or, you know, just old."

She laughed as she climbed into the truck. The cab was nice and toasty, a welcome change from the chill.

"Won't be long now before we'll be wearing coats and scarves all the time," Max said a moment later, buckling his seat belt.

"Mm, don't remind me."

"Don't you like autumn?"

"Oh, I do." She turned toward him. "But it means we're running out of time to get everything set up for your daughter's wedding."

He scoffed. "If she'd stop coming up with these harebrained schemes, we'd be fine."

"She's excited."

"I'm glad she's happy." As he drove toward the highway, he glanced at her. "But enough about weddings. How did your pitch go? We haven't had much of a chance to talk about it."

"Eh." She closed her eyes, trying to push away the memory of how condescending the CEO had been. "The board seemed interested in the Deep Creek idea, not so much the other two."

"You don't sound very enthusiastic."

"To be honest, I'm not." At his frown, she sighed. "It's not that I don't want the opportunity anymore, but part of me wonders if it's worth it."

"What do you mean?"

"I'd hoped the CEO would have been too drunk to remember our aborted dinner the other night. Unfortunately, he was the first person in the room after I got there, and then during his introduction, he couldn't seem to resist making a few jabs to throw me off my game." She chewed her lower lip. "If I get the event, I may have to work with him directly, and I'm not sure I can handle it."

"Any idea what he has against you?" He glanced at her before returning his gaze to the road.

"I'm sure it has a lot to do with the fact he thinks I'm not qualified for the job." She rolled her eyes. "He keeps referring to my business as 'a little wedding planning.'"

"Which just goes to show he doesn't have a clue about what goes into a wedding. He probably showed up on his wedding day drunk and forgot his vows."

She laughed. "That wouldn't surprise me, but I'm trying not to let his behavior color my perception of the company. While yes, he's the CEO, the event I'd be planning is more focused on his employees. And he doesn't make the ultimate decision. The board does."

"I suppose that's something." A few minutes later, Max pulled into a parking garage. "Still, I'd hate for your first experience in planning corporate events to be with someone who doesn't respect you."

"I've dealt with worse." She raised an eyebrow and patted his hand.

His deep laugh sent butterflies fluttering through her stomach. "I deserve that." Then he climbed out of the truck and came around to her door. When he opened it, he offered her his arm. "Shall we?"

He led her through the busy streets toward the river. Her eyes lit up when she recognized the restaurant they were heading to.

"Oh, McCormick and Schmick's! I do love this place, though it's been years since I've been. Not since—" She stopped herself as a wave of sadness washed over her. The last time she'd come was with Chuck for their anniversary.

"Not since…?" Max paused at the door to the building and searched her face. Understanding dawned in his eyes. "You came here with your husband."

Unable to speak, she nodded once then stared at the ground, taking deep breaths until she'd regained control of her emotions. It had been five years, and still, little things like that could trigger tears.

"It's okay." Max wrapped his arms around her. "I get it. Grief is an unpredictable animal. Just when we think we're moving on and letting go, it jumps up and bites us in the rear."

Despite being on the verge of crying, she burst out laughing at his crazy analogy. As she raised her eyes to meet his, she realized that was his goal.

"We can go somewhere else," he offered. "There are plenty of other restaurants nearby."

"No, I want to go here. It's one of my favorites as well, and it'll be nice to make some new memories."

He stared at her for a moment as if debating whether she was lying to him, then he shrugged and opened the door. The place was busy, and she wondered if they would even be able to get a table, but Max walked up to the host stand with confidence.

"Reservation under McAllister," he said.

She blinked. It hadn't occurred to her to make reservations. So many places didn't even accept them anymore. But the host confirmed the reservation and gathered menus before leading them to a back-corner table with a spectacular view of the Potomac River.

Max pulled out a chair for her on the side of the table closest to the wall. "So you have the best view while we eat."

Her surprised smile coaxed a shy grin from him as he sat opposite her. If someone had asked her months ago how to describe Max, she would have said he was arrogant, stubborn, and overbearing. But in the last few weeks, he'd proved to be thoughtful, understanding, and kind. She began to understand that his gruff exterior was a hard outer shell he'd created to protect his soft heart.

Her eyes swept the room. The walls were covered with dark-wood paneling, with beautiful red flowers adorning each table. When she turned to the window, a large Ferris wheel stood in the distance, just before the rippling water of the Potomac River. "This would be a nice place for a wedding."

His gaze followed hers, and he pursed his lips. "Bit too fancy for me. But maybe an idea for your corporate event."

Tapping her fingers against her chin, she considered that. "It's a bit more expensive than I would like, but I bet the CEO would love it. While the board loved the idea of Deep Creek, he didn't seem as enthused. I imagine he'd prefer to stay close to the city."

"No team-building exercises on a local working farm?"

She snorted, trying to picture any of the men she'd met mucking out a barn, their designer trousers drenched in mud. "I'm afraid not."

"What would a corporate retreat look like in a place like this?" He crossed his arms on the table and leaned forward.

"Probably a lot of boring presentations about how to lead from the bottom." Her smile faded. "Which is exactly like every other retreat they've probably done." She sighed. "I want to stand out, do something unexpected, while still incorporating learning and team building."

He furrowed his brow. "What about sailing? That's a great way to learn teamwork."

"Do you sail?"

"I used to when I was younger. Not so much these days."

The server came and took their drink orders. While Max was giving his, Carissa mulled over what he'd said. Sailing would be a good team-building exercise and something the corporate employees might enjoy. And Maryland was practically surrounded by water between the rivers, the Chesapeake Bay, and the Atlantic. Although it was too late to pitch another location, she could keep that in mind for any future retreats. *Assuming I get another shot at a corporate event.*

"I can practically see the wheels spinning in your head," Max said when they were alone again.

"You've given me ideas for future events."

He raised his eyebrows. "Are you planning on pitching other companies?"

"Maybe. But if I do, it'll be in the new year." She pulled out her phone and typed into her Notes app, where she kept her ideas so she wouldn't forget them.

"Anyway," she continued, "enough about business. Tell me what you've been up to since our trip to the orchard."

"Not much. I did some woodworking this morning, and then I watched a Hallmark movie with Lanie."

She raised an eyebrow. "*You* watched Hallmark?" Shifting forward, she put her hand on his forehead. "Maybe I should take you home. You're clearly feverish."

"Ha ha." His voice dripped with sarcasm. "I didn't say I *enjoyed* the movie."

His expression changed, and he looked so vulnerable, she wished she could take back her joke. "She also said some... things." He cleared his throat, clearly not in the mood to elaborate. "I loved spending that time with her. I don't have much of it left."

Though curiosity burned in her chest, Carissa didn't push him about his conversation with his daughter. Instead, she gave him a gentle smile. "She's not dying."

"No, I know." He sighed. "But she is going to move out as soon as she's married, and, well, we don't have the greatest relationship, as I'm sure you're aware."

Her heart went out to him. "She does seem to have been closer to her mother."

"Yeah, that's my fault." He pushed his hair off his forehead. "I don't know what happened, really. With Steven, it was easier. We're a lot alike, and he's… simpler, I guess." Running a hand over his face, he shook his head. "I'm not making any sense."

"I get it. I mean, I don't have any children of my own, of course, but I can certainly understand the struggle. Every child is different, and I suppose it's natural Lanie gravitated to her mother, especially as she got older. And then, with caretaking, that can forge an even stronger bond."

"If the caretaker and the person being cared for don't kill each other first," he grumbled.

She pressed her lips together to hide a smile. "That's also a possibility."

"Anyway, I promised my lat—er—ex-wife I'd work on rebuilding a relationship with Lanie." He stared at his hands. "And I guess I promised myself that too."

Impulsively, she covered his hand with her own. "You can call her your late wife."

"We weren't married at the—when she—"

"Did you love her?" she asked, her voice soft.

"Of course."

"Then that doesn't matter."

The slow, shy smile that blossomed on his face took her breath away. But the moment was soon interrupted by the arrival of the server with their drinks. They flushed and pulled away from each other.

"Are you ready to order?" the server asked.

After exchanging a look, Max nodded. "Ladies first."

"I'll have the seafood pasta, please," Carissa said.

"And I'll take the crab cakes."

"How very Maryland of you," Carissa teased when they were alone again. "Though I don't recall Steven or Lanie mentioning any crab feasts this summer. Is that because of Steven's accident?"

"No." His eyes darted around the room, then he leaned closer. "I'm not actually into the whole crab-picking thing," he stage whispered.

Her hand flew to her mouth in mock shock. "Isn't that like sacrilege here?"

"The only foods I like to eat with my hands are burgers, hot dogs, and french fries." He shrugged. "Picking crabs is too much effort. But the kids normally do it for the Fourth of July. After Steven's accident, nobody was interested in upholding summer traditions."

"He looked like he was doing well on Sunday."

"He's doing a lot better, though he's still having some balance issues." Max smiled at her. "I'm glad you joined us. I had a really nice time."

"Me too." She smiled in return.

"Maybe we can do it again sometime. The town's fall festival is coming up in a few weeks."

Her heart leapt at the thought, but she took a deep breath to calm her emotions. "I'm not sure that's such a good idea."

The warmth in his eyes dimmed slightly. "Right. While Lanie seemed okay with you coming with us apple picking, two events back-to-back might make her think I'm breaking my word."

"Exactly. Besides, we're just getting to know each other." She took his hand. "Let's take our time and enjoy it."

He lifted her hand and brushed his lips across her knuckles. "Sounds like a plan."

Butterflies exploded in her stomach, and she ducked her head to hide her smile. If she wasn't careful, she might fall for the softer, happier side of Max. And she wasn't sure if she was ready for that.

By the time they finished lunch, it was late afternoon. The sun glinted off the stream of cars on the Woodrow Wilson Bridge, signaling the beginning of rush-hour traffic. Carissa lingered over her glass of wine, savoring the evening and wishing it didn't have to end.

"Did you want dessert?" Max asked, breaking into her reverie.

She shook her head and grinned. "I can't eat another bite."

After signaling for the check, he leaned back in his chair. "This was nice."

"It was," she agreed, trying to hide her disappointment with how quickly the time had passed.

"What's on your agenda for the rest of the day?"

The question surprised her. "Um, I've got a few wedding details to work on for my other brides."

"So..." He hesitated.

"Yes?"

"You don't need to hurry back?"

Where is he going with this? "No. Why?"

"Since we've come all this way, maybe we could check out the harbor."

Her heart skipped a beat, and she nodded enthusiastically. "That sounds good to me."

"Great." He paid their bill. "Let's see what this little city has to offer."

The late-afternoon air was much cooler, though the lingering humidity kept her from being cold. They walked toward the pier, away from the hustle and bustle of the downtown area. As they meandered down the narrow docks, the sound of water lapping against the wood helped soothe Carissa's butterflies.

But the afternoon was starting to feel like déjà vu. She and Chuck had spent a night eating at the restaurant then lingering in the city afterward. It had been their twenty-fifth wedding anniversary, and she'd joked they should rent the private room at McCormick & Schmick's for their fiftieth. Chuck had smiled and told her he wasn't sure it could fit all of their friends and family.

"I'd prefer a more intimate gathering," she'd said.

His arms encircled her waist, and he kissed her cheek. "A big party is more appropriate for such a milestone, don't you think?"

"Fine." She'd relented. "A big party, so long as for our fifty-first, we stay in and have a quiet evening at home."

"Deal," he'd promised.

Her heart ached at the memory. They never celebrated another anniversary. Seven months later, he was gone.

"I'd offer a penny for your thoughts, but I get the feeling they're worth much more." Max had stopped a few feet back and watched her.

"Sorry. I was remembering the last time I came here."

"With your husband?"

She nodded, swallowing the sob that threatened to escape her throat. "For our twenty-fifth wedding anniversary."

"Quite a milestone," he murmured.

If they kept on that track, she was going to lose the thin control she had over her emotions. She changed the subject. "How long were you married?"

"Almost thirty years."

"Really?" She cocked her head, doing some quick math. "How old were you when you got married?"

"Nineteen." His lips pressed into a grim line. "I don't recommend it."

"Still, you lasted longer than most people who marry that young."

"I guess," he said, shifting uncomfortably. "Come on. Let's go check out the Capital Wheel. I'll bet you get amazing views up there."

"Um, I'll pass." She pressed a hand to her stomach as it flipped at the thought.

His eyebrows shot up. "Why? You afraid of heights?"

"A little." That was a lie. She was terrified of them, but she didn't want to tell him that.

"Then what?" His face fell. "Unless... Do you want to go home?"

"No," she said, quicker than she'd intended. "Let's check out some of the shops instead."

"It's too nice out to be cooped up in a shop," he countered. Grabbing her hand, he pulled her toward him. "Come on. It'll be fun." He had a gleam in his eye. "And if you happen to get scared, I'll be there to keep you safe."

The words both frustrated and thrilled her. It was clear he hadn't bought her declaration that she wasn't afraid of heights, but the idea of being in his arms, even if she was terrified, was enough to coax her to go with him.

That was, until they were actually sitting in the gondola, or cage as it seemed to her. What she'd initially believed was excitement soon revealed itself to be paralyzing fear as she gripped the edge of the bench. The ride had no bar or seat belt, and Max sat on the opposite side.

"Where's the safety bar?" She tried to keep the panic out of her voice.

He gave her a weird look. "There isn't one. It's not like a Ferris wheel at the county fair." Her face must have betrayed her fear because he took both her hands. "Keep your eyes on me and take a deep breath."

The first instruction was easy to follow—she'd barely taken her eyes off him all day. But the second... Suddenly, the air seemed too thick, and when she tried to breathe, she started choking on it.

The operator shut the door, and they began to move. She squeezed her eyes shut and bit her tongue to keep from crying out. Max's hands tightened around hers, and he took several loud breaths. After a moment, it dawned on her that he was breathing that way in hopes she would mimic him. She focused on his breathing and matched it, and soon, her fears began to subside.

When she opened her eyes, Max was staring in wonder off into the distance. Then he turned to her and smiled.

"That's better." He nodded to the view. "I can describe what I see if you're too afraid to look."

"Just... give me a minute," she said, still sounding breathless. Her stomach had tied itself in knots, but otherwise, her heart rate was slowly returning to normal.

"Take all the time you need," he said, giving her hands another squeeze.

Chapter Fifteen

As color returned to Carissa's face, a stab of guilt hit Max's gut. He shouldn't have forced her to go. He'd known she'd been lying about not being afraid of heights, but he hadn't imagined her fear ran that deep. Though his hands ached because of how hard she was squeezing them, he never let go, silently pledging to hold on until they were safely on the ground or until Carissa was comfortable, whichever came first.

A moment later, her grip relaxed, and she turned her head the slightest bit. Her eyes widened, taking in the view.

"Wow, you were right. This view is spectacular."

He smirked. "Told you so." At her glare, he ducked his head. "Though I wish I hadn't forced you up here. I had no idea you were that scared."

"I'll be fine."

Her face was still pale, but they'd almost reached the apex of the wheel. Perhaps knowing the ride was about half over was encouraging to her.

They sat in silence, enjoying the breathtaking views. The sun had sunk low over the western shore of the river. It glinted off the buildings and the cars going over the bridge.

Once they were on the ground, the operator stepped forward and helped Carissa exit the gondola. She immediately went to a bench nearby and sat down. Max scrambled out after her.

"Are you sure you're okay?"

She nodded, staring at the ground and taking deep breaths. "I also hate flying. Being up in the air is okay, but the takeoff and the landing are my least favorite parts."

We weren't going that fast. But he kept the thought to himself. Instead, he offered his hand and helped her up.

"I'll take you home," he offered half-heartedly.

Her smile was apologetic. "Yes, please."

His heart sank, but he reminded himself they had a long ride home. At least she didn't seem upset at him, just out of sorts and probably nauseated.

"I promise for our next date, there won't be any heights."

She glanced at him. "Our next date?"

"Er… outing. Friendly lunch?"

Carissa laughed as she stood, still wobbly on her feet. Taking her hand, Max led her to the truck.

As they drove home, he rested his hand on the gear shift. At some point, Carissa trailed her fingers down his arm until she found his hand and curled her fingers over his. Her skin was warm and soft.

"I had a nice time today."

He squeezed her hand. "I did too." Taking a deep breath, he continued, "I meant what I said. I'd like to take you out again and soon."

From the corner of his eye, he could make out a faint blush tingeing her cheeks. She didn't immediately respond, and he tried not to let that bother him. Besides, he had a bigger question weighing on his mind.

In his day, it wasn't necessarily expected to receive a kiss on a first or second date, but times had changed, and he and Carissa weren't a couple of nervous teenagers finding their way through their first romance. Still, they'd agreed it wasn't a date, and he didn't want to pressure her. But the thought of what it would be like, what it would *feel* like, occupied his mind for the rest of the drive to her house.

When he pulled into her driveway, he put the truck in park and climbed out to open her door. She accepted his hand, and he pulled her to her feet. After tucking her hand into the crook of his arm, he led her to her door.

Then, they stood there, the awkward moment growing until he wondered if he should say goodbye and go. He squared his shoulders and met her gaze, but before he could speak, she lifted her hand and cupped his cheek.

"Thank you for lunch."

"My pleasure," he said, his voice hoarse with emotion.

She leaned forward, closing her eyes, and his heart pounded as he closed the distance between them. He could feel her breath on his face as he moved slowly toward her.

Ping.

The sound of his cell phone made them jump. He removed it from his pocket and rolled his eyes.

"Just Lanie checking up on me." He gave Carissa a rueful smile. "Guess she's not used to me being gone so long."

Instead of laughing, Carissa bit her lip. The mood seemed to shift, and he held his breath.

"Max, I had a wonderful time with you."

His stomach flipped, and he braced for whatever she was about to say. "But?"

She sighed. "We're moving into dangerous territory. The apple picking was one thing, though I'm still not sure how Lanie felt about it. Lunch today was wonderful, but we shouldn't be sneaking around behind Lanie's back like this. She made it clear she didn't want you and me to date, and we should respect her wishes."

"We can certainly slow things down until the wedding is over," he said, searching her face. "But why can't we keep seeing each other casually in the meantime?"

"And if she finds out?"

As much as Max wanted to respond with a careless shrug, he knew Carissa wouldn't buy it. Quite frankly, he was terrified of what would happen if Lanie discovered he'd broken his word. While he and Carissa might tell themselves they were just friends, the fact they'd almost kissed proved Carissa's point.

At the same time, he was feeling things he'd never expected to feel again after Melody. Her death had taught him how short and precious life was. Despite how much he didn't want to hurt Lanie, he hated the idea of missing out on whatever was blooming between him and Carissa.

"Maybe she won't mind now that the wedding is mostly planned," he said meekly.

She raised an eyebrow. "You don't believe that's true any more than I do."

"What if I promise not to let our relationship interfere with the wedding?"

"You can't make that kind of a promise." Lowering her head, she stared at their hands. "And it's not just about making things awkward with one client. Wedding planning is my livelihood. And if the corporate gig doesn't work out, I don't want to do anything that risks my professional reputation."

"I understand." For a moment, he wasn't sure what to say. Emotions warred within him. On the one hand, he didn't want to cause her any hardship, financial or otherwise. But was it that selfish to want to be happy?

He ran his hand through his hair. "Listen, if you want to take a step back until the wedding's over, then that's what we'll do." At her growing smile, he held up a hand. "For the record, I don't like it, but I don't want to do anything that will jeopardize your business or my relationship with my daughter."

She searched his eyes. “I’m not saying never. Just maybe not now.”

He nodded, though it killed him to do so. It figured that the first time he’d developed feelings for someone since his marriage, it was complicated. Nothing in his life was ever as simple as he wanted it to be.

“So where do we go from here?” he asked, unable to keep the disappointment out of his voice.

“We can still text and maybe meet for coffee,” she said. “And of course, we’ll see each other for wedding-related events.”

“What about after?”

She leaned forward and kissed his cheek before unlocking the door. Glancing over her shoulder with a sly smile, she winked. “I guess we’ll have to wait and see.”

As he walked to his truck, his emotions were all over the place. On the one hand, he wished December would hurry up and get there so he and Carissa could give their relationship a real shot. But on the other hand, the sooner the wedding arrived, the sooner Lanie would move away and start her new life. His time with her was running out.

He climbed into the car and stared at his reflection in the rearview mirror. “Keep your head in the game, McAllister. Lanie is the priority. Carissa can wait.”

Chapter Sixteen

Carissa's phone rang bright and early Tuesday morning, waking her up. Rubbing her bleary eyes, she answered it on speaker. "Hello?"

"Carissa, hi. It's Colin Fields, the activities coordinator at Imaginavigation Enterprises. How are you?"

Her early-morning brain fog dissipated, and she sat up. "Oh, hello, Mr. Fields. I'm well, and yourself?"

"Very well, thank you." He cleared his throat. "Listen, I wanted to call and thank you for your presentation the other day. The Deep Creek idea you had was a huge hit with the board."

"Does that mean—" She took a deep breath. "That is to say, I'm glad you enjoyed it."

"We did indeed, but we were wondering if you would be willing to allow us to move forward with your idea internally."

She blinked. "Excuse me?"

"We loved your idea, and we're willing to offer you a contract as a consultant."

It took significant willpower to keep her tone even. "Let me see if

I have this right. You liked my idea enough to use it but not enough to hire me as the actual planner?"

"Oh, well..." The cool and confident tone vanished. "Um, you see, we don't believe you have enough experience to pull it off. I'll be leading this event, and Jacob thought you might be willing to collaborate with me."

I bet he did. Her heart pounded, and she glared at the opposite wall. *The nerve.* "I'm sorry, Mr. Fields, but I'm afraid I'm not interested in acting as a consultant. While I can't stop you from planning your retreat in Deep Creek based on my recommendation and pitch, I've no reason to assist you in bringing it to fruition when I'm perfectly capable of leading such an event on my own."

"But you would profit too. Albeit less than you would have if we awarded you the contract outright."

"And that is precisely why I'm not interested in your offer."

"Carissa." Another voice, gratingly familiar, came over the line. "You're making a mistake. This is a way for you to get your foot in the door and gain some experience so that the next time an opportunity like this arises, you'll have this event in your portfolio."

Closing her eyes, she ground her teeth in frustration. Jacob was right. No matter how much it hurt her pride, consulting on the event would give her the experience she needed to break into corporate event planning. Her previous attempts to expand into that world had not panned out, and the only reason she'd had the opportunity to pitch Imaginavigation Enterprises was her husband's acquaintance with the former CEO.

She sighed. *I could end this call right now and never have to deal with this jerk again.* But doing so would mean starting over from scratch, and she was tired of having doors slammed in her face. Besides, she wouldn't put it past Jacob to blacklist her to every other corporation in the DC metro area.

"I'll consider it and get back to you," she finally said as she swallowed her pride.

"You have twenty-four hours," Jacob replied, and she could practically hear his smirk.

The phone beeped three times, confirming they'd disconnected. She put her head in her hands, and tears pricked her eyelids. She'd been confident that she'd nailed the presentation, and she'd hoped her experience in event planning in general would have compensated for her limited knowledge of corporate retreats.

Consulting would help her garner that experience but at a price. She expected she would be working closely with Jacob, and the idea made her skin crawl.

She needed advice, but she wasn't sure who to turn to. Max was the first person she wanted to talk to, but she'd just told him that she should take things slowly, and she didn't want to send mixed messages. Unfortunately, she hadn't told many other people she was pursuing the venture in case it didn't work out.

I need to get out of the house and clear my head. She dressed quickly and headed into the chilly autumn air. The sky was filled with ominous dark clouds that seemed to match her mood. She drove aimlessly until she found herself turning onto Main Street in Cedar Haven and heading toward Bea's Diner.

When she walked in the door, she saw Max sitting at a booth near the back. His eyes lit up at the sight of her, and he waved her over. A warmth blossomed in her chest as she made her way toward him.

"Fancy meeting you here." He lifted his mug in salute. "Care to join me?"

Carissa bit her lip. As happy as she was to see him, they shouldn't be spending time alone together in public.

"I promise I won't bite." A smirk pulled up one side of his mouth, and she couldn't help smiling.

"All right." She slid into the booth across from him. "But just for a minute."

"What brings you out here? Do you have a meeting with a bride?"

Before she could answer, the server came to take her order. She selected a chai tea, hoping the spices would lift her mood.

"No meeting," she said once they were alone again. "I went for a drive to clear my head and ended up here."

He tilted his head. "Something wrong?"

Once again, she hesitated. She'd meant what she'd told him the other day about keeping their distance, but right then, she could really use a friend. "I didn't get the corporate event gig."

His eyebrows pulled together in concern. "Did they tell you why?"

"Apparently, I don't have enough experience." Her hands clenched into fists on the table. "And that's not even the worst part." She proceeded to tell him about the consulting offer and Jacob's smug attitude.

"He knows he's got me. His company only offered me the opportunity to pitch on the recommendation of their former CEO. If I refuse, I'm back to square one."

"If I were you, I'd start over and hope to find someone who isn't such a jerk."

"It's not that simple." She rubbed her temples. "Companies like Imaginavigation Enterprises talk. A lot of event coordinators work on referral. This was supposed to be my ticket into that world. Even if I try to start over, Jacob could blacklist me."

"But why? You've done nothing wrong."

"It doesn't matter. I refused his advances at the restaurant. Men like him have done much worse for less obvious slights."

"Then you should file a harassment charge against him. Or at the very least, report what he did to the board."

"It's my word against his, and they have a relationship with him. Besides, if I reported him now, it would look like I was retaliating for not getting their business."

Max was quiet, and she took a sip of her tea, hoping it might make her feel better. It didn't. The drive hadn't helped either.

Perhaps she would have been better off staying home and wallowing for a bit.

"Why not start with local businesses? Planning holiday parties and the like?"

Max was doing that thing Chuck used to do, trying to fix things instead of letting her vent. Was that just a habit with men from her generation?

"I already plan holiday parties for some local businesses. Corporate retreats are a whole different animal because you're not just booking a location and entertainment, you're planning an entire week of activities as well as lodging, food, and the like."

"What about—"

She held up a hand. "I know you're trying to help, but I didn't come here to brainstorm my next move. I wasn't planning on talking about it at all, but you asked. Let's change the subject, okay?"

It came out harsher than she'd intended, but she didn't have the energy to manage anyone else's feelings that day. A pained expression crossed his face. He gave a gruff nod and stared at the table.

Great. Now she'd upset him too. The day was off to an amazing start. "I'm sorry. Maybe I should go. I don't want to take it out on you."

"No, please stay." He blew out his breath. "Melody used to complain about the same thing. I do better when I have a tangible problem I can fix. But I'm trying, and if you want to vent, I'm here to listen."

"Thanks," she said, and she meant it. But suddenly, all the fire had gone out of her. She was not in a good place for company, and she didn't want to risk taking her frustrations out on Max any more than she already had. "Actually, I'm going home."

He blinked in surprise. "Already? But you just got here."

"I need some time to process this and make up my mind about what I'm going to do." She downed her tea. "Thanks for letting me vent, and I'm sorry I intruded on your breakfast."

He stood and pulled her into his arms before she had a chance to stop him. "I'm here for you. Anytime."

Plastering a smile on her face, she extricated herself from his embrace and waved goodbye. Once she was in her car and driving home, she let the reality of the situation hit her full force. She barely made it home before she fell apart in her car, leaning against the steering wheel and letting the tears fall.

"What am I going to do?" she whispered.

That question haunted her for the rest of the day, and by the evening, she still wasn't sure. She vacillated between taking the consulting gig to garner experience and telling Jacob where he could stick his offer. No matter how hard she tried to convince herself, she wasn't sure she could stomach the idea of working with him.

But the idea of going back to the drawing board and trying to figure out her next plan of attack gave her a headache. She feared her lack of experience would continue to be a barrier, even if her ideas were well received. And if she couldn't expand her business, she wasn't sure what she would do with it when she was ready to retire. She'd hoped integrating corporate retreats into her business would make it a more attractive sale. Without that expansion, she wasn't sure how enticing the business would be to potential buyers.

Her phone rang, and irritation boiled in her belly when she recognized the number. She debated ignoring it, but that wouldn't be professional. With a groan, she picked it up and answered. "Hello, Jacob."

"Actually, it's not Jacob. It's Colin."

"Oh, hello, Mr. Fields."

"Listen, I know Jacob gave you twenty-four hours to decide, but I wondered if there was anything I could do to sweeten the deal to convince you. The position isn't what you want, but it would be a foot in the door with not only our company but the larger corporate world at large."

"Believe me, I'm aware," she said, unable to keep her aggravation out of her tone. "And it's not that I'm averse to coming on as a consultant." Even if it still grated on her nerves that they were more interested in her idea than her ability to implement it.

"Then what's holding you back?" When she didn't immediately respond, he added, "If you don't mind my asking."

She bit her lip. What she wanted to say warred with what she *should* say. Was there a tactful way to tell the activities coordinator that her main aversion was working with his boss? Probably not. And anything she said would likely be relayed to Jacob, which would put her in an even worse situation.

"I'm concerned there will be friction between Jacob and me." Her anxiety eased a little. That sounded vague enough to explain her hesitation without saying anything directly negative about the CEO.

A nervous chuckle came over the line. "I can understand why you'd say that about Jacob." He cleared his throat. "How about this? We can meet outside of the office to limit your interactions with Jacob. I'm happy to set up working lunches at restaurants or even come down to your neck of the woods to discuss things. We can even do virtual meetings if that's easier for you."

He had a hint of desperation in his voice, which only confirmed that he was in over his head. She felt bad for him, and she had to admit his offer was enticing. She could still garner the experience she needed to pitch other companies while maintaining a positive business relationship with Imaginavigation Enterprises. And if she could do that and avoid Jacob, all the better.

"All right," she finally said. "I'll do it. But I want a contract drawn up detailing my consulting fee and terms allowing for that amount of flexibility." Chuck had always insisted she get everything in writing.

"I'll get our legal team on it first thing tomorrow," Colin

promised. “And then I’m hoping to get started as soon as the ink is dry.”

“That works for me.”

After they hung up, the joy she normally felt after closing with a new client didn’t come. She was still too anxious. Even if she never set foot in the offices of Imaginavigation Enterprises again, she doubted she could avoid Jacob altogether. But she’d made her bed, and all she could do was hope Colin was true to his word and kept his boss as far away from her as possible.

Chapter Seventeen

Max spent the next several days working in the garage in the futile hope of keeping his mind off Carissa. It didn't help that he hadn't heard from her since they left Bea's. He wanted to give her space, and if he was honest with himself, he wasn't ready to put it behind him. Her reactions had reminded him uncomfortably of many similar arguments he'd had with Melody. Listening without offering suggestions of how to fix things wasn't how he was wired, but he'd tried, and he wished that counted for something.

Their break from each other would be coming to an end soon. They were supposed to meet for the final caterer tasting that evening, and Lanie was excited about it.

He'd considered not going. It would make things a lot less awkward if he stayed home. But over the summer, he'd made such a fuss about being a part of things that a sudden change of heart would raise his daughter's suspicions. Besides, he wanted to go if for nothing else than to spend more time with Lanie.

As he finished up in the garage, the door to the house swung open, and Lanie came in. Her face was lit up with an exuberant smile he tried and failed to return.

"Are you about done?" she asked as she admired his handiwork.

"Yeah. Just need to clean up the dust and debris, then I'll change, and we can head out."

To his surprise, Lanie grabbed a broom and started sweeping. "I can't believe how fast time is flying. Next week is the middle of October."

"We'll need to pull out the Halloween decorations soon," he said.

"About that." She stopped sweeping and rested her hand on top of the broom handle. "Steven and Rose invited us to the town's fall festival this weekend. In addition to the hayrides and pumpkin patch, I heard there's going to be a haunted house. Would you want to go?"

To buy some time, he busied himself with putting away his tools. Ever since Carissa had turned him down for that very festival, he'd been determined to avoid it. Thinking about it, then, only added to his miserable mood, and he wasn't sure he could muster up the enthusiasm to go in time. The last thing he wanted to do was ruin his children's fun with his sour attitude.

"I'm not sure. When do you need an answer?"

Her smile faded, and she returned to sweeping. "Um, tomorrow, I guess?" She glanced at him. "Maybe you could bring someone." A shadow passed over her face. "But maybe not Carissa."

His heart seemed to stop. "Did it bother you that I brought her apple picking?"

She kept her eyes on the floor. "I suppose I was more surprised. On the one hand, I appreciate that you're trying to get along with her, but on the other..."

"We're not dating." He forced a laugh to disguise the bitterness in his tone.

"Good." Her answering chuckle sounded hollow. "I appreciate you keeping your word."

Instead of responding, he focused on putting away his tools. How would Lanie feel if she learned he and Carissa had had lunch together? Would she believe it was an innocent outing? He shook his head. I *don't even believe that.*

Once Lanie finished sweeping, she helped him cover his pieces. They went into the house together, and he headed upstairs to change.

He stepped into the bathroom and turned on the shower. As he waited for the water to warm, he mulled over his conversation with Lanie.

"What else can I do?" he asked his reflection. "Carissa already said no, and Lanie just reiterated she doesn't want me to date her wedding planner."

Of course, things were already awkward between him and Carissa. He sighed as he climbed into the shower. The tense silence he'd felt since she'd left Bea's would likely get worse once they were in the same room together. Perhaps he should open the lines of communication before he left.

As soon as he was out of the shower, he typed a quick text. He kept it simple since he had neither the time nor the wordsmithing capabilities to make it more detailed. After he hit Send, he dressed and made his way downstairs.

His phone pinged, and he checked the screen. *We're good. Sorry I haven't been in touch. Decided to consult on corporate retreat.*

He frowned. She'd taken the consulting gig after all? Well, he wouldn't ask her about it that night. But he hoped they could get together soon to talk more. He wondered what had made her choose to go forward with it after everything that jerk CEO had put her through.

"Ready to go?" Lanie came into the hallway with her coat hanging over her arm.

With a curt nod, he grabbed his coat and opened the door. They climbed into his truck, and he drove to The Muddy Oar. If nothing else, he had a delicious piece of chocolate cake to look forward to.

When they arrived, Carissa and Nate were already there. The hostess took them to a back room with a private table, where they would have the final tasting. Several hors d'oeuvres were already laid out on the table.

"Help yourselves," the hostess said. "The chef will be with you momentarily to discuss the options he has prepared."

Lanie and Nate sat together on one side of the table, leaving Max to sit next to Carissa. His stomach knotted at the sight of her, but she acted like everything was fine.

"I'm sorry I haven't called," she said in a low voice. "But I have a lot to tell you."

"Maybe we can meet up for coffee tomorrow."

"I was actually hoping you'd be able to stay after and have a drink with me."

"What are you two whispering about over there?" Lanie's eyes narrowed with suspicion.

"Nothing of importance," Carissa said quickly, leaning away from Max.

Before Lanie could press the issue, the chef returned carrying a tray. Max pushed his concerns aside as the delicious scent of roasted meat and herbs washed over him.

"Good evening, everyone," the chef said. "Tonight, I wanted to start you off with lemon-and-herb-roasted turkey with a side of baked parmesan asparagus."

"Ooh." Lanie clapped. "It sounds delicious."

The chef set the tray on the table. Everyone took a generous helping, though Max tried to hide his displeasure at the asparagus.

But Carissa wasn't fooled. "Not a fan?"

"It's not my favorite," he admitted.

"Well, I love it," Lanie said, taking a bite and smiling. "And it'll be a nice change from green beans."

"I may not love the asparagus," Max said after devouring the turkey, "but the turkey has my vote and should be one of the entrees."

Nate laughed. "We still have three other entrees to try." He waved a fork at Max. "Don't fill up on the first option."

As if on cue, the chef emerged again with a tray of steak and an array of vegetables. "We have filet mignon with baked potato and a roasted vegetable medley."

Without waiting for an invitation, Max helped himself to a filet and dug in. He could get used to wedding tastings if it meant he got to eat such delicious food. Maybe he could convince Carissa to allow him to accompany her on meetings with future clients.

"Dad!" Lanie cried out. "You're not supposed to have red meat."

Max harrumphed. "The doctor said I can in moderation."

"You and I have very different definitions of what counts as 'moderation.'"

"Why can't you have red meat?" Carissa asked, her eyebrows pinching together.

Just as Max opened his mouth to respond, Lanie cut in. "Because of his cholesterol."

"It's a little high," Max replied, unable to keep the growing irritation out of his tone.

"A little?" Lanie scoffed. "If you don't get it under control, you're going to have to start taking medication, and we both know how much you hate the side effects."

"I'm fine," he growled, stabbing his fork into the thick cut of beef.

"What do you think of the options?" Carissa asked, clearly trying to prevent another argument.

"I tend to agree with Max on the turkey," Nate said. "And it fits our Christmas theme perfectly."

Lanie pressed her lips together and nodded. Once again, Max found himself silently thanking God for Nate. He only wished his future son-in-law wasn't always needed to step in and defuse the situation between Max and Lanie.

The rest of the meal passed in a tense silence. After the last entree had been served, Carissa handed out scorecards to everyone to help determine which dishes would be included in the final menu. Each card had four options: steak, turkey, crab cake, and ham.

"Rank your favorite dish from one to four, with one being what you liked best and four representing what you liked least. The two entrees with the most votes will be served along with the vegetarian dish we selected last time."

Max ranked his favorites as steak, turkey, crab cake, and ham. Although he enjoyed the crab cake, it was the most expensive option, and he wanted to be mindful of Lanie and Nate's budget. He assumed they would choose either the turkey or the ham for their Christmas theme.

"All right," Carissa said after tallying their responses. "It looks like turkey and steak received the most votes for first and second place."

The chef returned and took the cards from Carissa. After a brief conversation, he signaled for the servers to clear the table.

Carissa checked off the caterer. "We're all set! The last thing the caterer will need from us is a final head count, which is due about two weeks before your wedding. Your invitations arrived yesterday, and we need to get those out by the end of next week." Her face relaxed into an easy smile. "We're right on track!"

Lanie breathed a sigh of relief. "That's good to hear." She hugged Carissa. "We couldn't have done this without you."

"It's what I'm here for." Carissa patted Lanie's back. "Now, why don't you two kids go have some fun?"

"Sounds good to me." Nate grabbed Lanie's hand. "Thanks for everything, Carissa." Without another word, he led Lanie away.

Max stared after them, wondering if that meant he was heading to his house alone.

"How about that drink?" Carissa asked.

Max tore his gaze away from his daughter's retreating back. "Sounds good to me."

They left the small dining area and headed to the bar. The bar was mostly empty, and they had their choice of seats. After they sat near a quiet corner, the bartender came over.

"What'll you have?"

Max glanced at Carissa. "Ladies first."

"I'll have a whiskey, neat."

His eyes widened, but he ordered the same. After the bartender walked away, he stared at her. "I didn't take you for a whiskey girl."

"Normally, I don't drink hard liquor straight like that, but it's been a week, and I want something that's going to burn on the way down."

"Speaking of that," Max said, his tone betraying his hesitation, "do you want to talk about it or…?"

She nodded at the bartender, who was preparing their drinks. "Let's wait until we've had a round."

Once the drinks were in front of them, Carissa closed her eyes and took a sip. "Just what I needed."

"I half expected you to take it like a shot," he joked.

"Don't tempt me." She laughed. Her sips did become more pronounced, and soon, she was waving the bartender over for another.

"You as well?" the bartender asked.

Max glanced at his drink, which he'd barely touched. "I'm good for now."

An amused smile pulled at Carissa's lips. "You need to keep up."

"I'll get there." Max took another sip of his whiskey.

After Carissa had her second glass in front of her, she curled her fingers around it. "So, I'm sure you're wondering why I decided to work with Imaginavigation Enterprises after everything that's happened."

He nodded, saving himself from speaking by draining his glass. The bartender must have expected that because a second later, he'd poured another two ounces for Max.

"It's not as bad as I originally feared. I'd be working mostly with Colin, and I wouldn't have to go into DC unless I wanted to." She proceeded to tell him the entire conversation she'd had with Colin Fields.

When she finished, she downed half her second round of

whiskey. Her eyes watered, but otherwise, it didn't seem to impact her at all.

"At least you're not working directly with the CEO." Max ran a hand through his hair. "But can you trust Colin with your idea?"

She snorted. "I can't trust him to pull it off without me, no. That guy has barely planned a birthday party, let alone something as complicated as a retreat. Still, he's given me no reason not to trust him to serve as an intermediary between Jacob and me. Besides, as I told you the other day, this is the first real chance I've had to branch out and expand my business."

Max twirled his now-empty glass on the bar in front of him. The last thing he wanted to do was discourage her dream, but he couldn't quite shake the bad feeling swirling around in his stomach. From everything she'd said about Jacob, he sounded like bad news, and Max couldn't see any good coming from the job.

But he forced a smile and kept his opinions to himself. "It sounds like you've put a lot of thought into this, and it does seem like a good opportunity."

"I hear a 'but' in there somewhere." Carissa raised an eyebrow.

Biting back a smile, he cleared his throat. "Just... Be careful. Jacob sounds like a real snake."

Her eyes softened, and she took his hand. "I appreciate your concern, and I promise to take it to heart."

"That's all I ask."

"I want to apologize," she continued, running her thumb over his knuckles. "I shouldn't have left so abruptly from Bea's."

"It's okay. I'm sorry I tried to fix it when it was clear you needed to vent."

"I know you meant well." She took a deep breath. "And I'm sorry I've been MIA the last few days. Between receiving the news I wasn't chosen and starting to work with Colin as a consultant, I've had a lot going on lately, and it's important to me to keep my work life separate from my personal life." Her smile faded. "I'm usually better about maintaining a balance."

"It's a new venture for you. It's understandable that it's going to take up more of your time."

"But I'm glad I got a chance to see you again."

"Yeah?" His chest filled with warmth.

"I've missed you."

Impulsively, he lifted his hand and cupped her cheek. "I've missed you too."

Her eyes widened, and her gaze darted nervously around the bar. As it was a weeknight, there weren't many other patrons around. Still, he didn't want to make her uncomfortable. He lowered his hand and shifted away from her.

With a sigh, she placed her glass on the bar and signaled to the bartender. "It's getting harder and harder to keep my distance from you."

"I know what you mean." His voice came out huskier than he intended. "But the wedding is in just over two months."

Her lips quirked up. "I've never been so ready to be done with an event I was planning."

They paid for their drinks and left the restaurant. He walked her to her car and tried to ignore the familiar pull that seemed to draw them together like magnets.

"Will Lanie still be against us dating after the wedding?" she asked as she unlocked her car door.

"Why would she?" Max frowned. "Her fear seems focused on how our relationship might make things more stressful for her if we broke up before the wedding."

"I hope that's the case."

He stepped back to allow her to climb into the car, and once she was settled, he closed the door. As he walked to his truck, he sent up a small prayer that things would work out with her new business venture. But deep down, he feared it was all going to blow up in her face.

Chapter Eighteen

THE NEXT DAY, CARISSA HAD HER FIRST VIRTUAL MEETING with Colin. He warned her Jacob would be sitting in, but she felt confident she could handle it. At least they weren't in the same room, and she wasn't above pretending to have connection issues if he tried to derail the meeting.

She was the first to sign in, and she made sure her audio and video were working well. A few minutes later, Colin popped onto her screen, and she could just make out Jacob in the back of the room. His feet were propped on the conference table, and he scribbled away at a notebook in his lap.

"Good morning, Carissa," Colin said.

"Morning, Colin. How are you?"

"Doing well." The pleasantries out of the way, he got right to business. "So, according to your proposal, we need to contact the cabin rental office to determine when would be the best time for our retreat. Are you able to work on that this weekend?"

Carissa drummed her fingers on her desk. Working weekends was quite normal for wedding planning since most events occurred on Saturdays, but she'd hoped to keep the corporate retreat to normal business hours. While she'd told Max she wouldn't join him for the fall festival in town, she still hoped to go on her own. It was one of the highlights of the season.

"I can give them a call today to set up a meeting for either Saturday or sometime next week, but Sunday, I am unavailable."

Jacob's feet disappeared from view, and he leaned toward the camera. "What do you mean, you're 'unavailable'?"

Before she could answer, Colin intervened. "Now, Jacob, we have a contract with Carissa for a certain number of hours, but there is no stipulation of when those hours must occur. If she doesn't want to work Sundays, that's perfectly fine."

"Says you," Jacob retorted. He moved directly behind Colin. "We need to get this booked ASAP. Whatever weekend plans you have can be canceled, at least until we're further along in the process."

Her mouth fell open. "You can't be serious."

A sinister smile came over his face. "Unless you're not up to the task. I'm sure we can compensate you for the idea, and Colin can handle things."

Colin paled. "Sir, with all due respect, an event this large is beyond my capabilities."

"Then perhaps we need to replace you as well," Jacob said.

At least it's not just me. Jacob had made it clear he didn't see wedding planning as a real business, but watching him interact with Colin, Carissa suspected he was simply a jerk to everyone.

"Excuse me," she called, hoping to regain control of the situation.

Both men turned to the screen but with very different expressions. Colin gave her a pleading look, while Jacob's furrowed brow almost felt like a challenge. Carissa squared her shoulders.

"You're not even planning to host this event until sometime next year," she began, strategically sidestepping the question of her schedule. "While it's important we book the location as early as possible, a few days won't make that big of a difference."

Jacob opened his mouth to respond, but she continued before he could. "I will contact the rental office today and set up a conference call Colin can attend. In the meantime, we should brainstorm a list of ideas for activities we'd like to plan. That way, we are not only fully prepared to discuss our needs with the rental office, but we can also ask if they have suggestions of places to contact."

It was the men's turn to gape at her. Colin appeared impressed, but Jacob's expression was a mixture of annoyance and uncertainty. She smiled pleasantly at the camera, but inside, she was dancing a jig.

Clearly, this man has never had someone tell him no and stick to it. "I'm going to share my screen now and show you what I've been working on over the last few days."

The rest of the meeting went smoothly, in large part because Jacob appeared too dumbfounded by her standing up to him to say anything. After they said their goodbyes, Carissa signed off and pumped her fist in the air. *Carissa: 1, Jacob: 0.*

True to her word, she called the rental office as soon as she finished celebrating. The last thing she needed was for Jacob to start harassing her for updates the moment he recovered from her taking control of the meeting.

"Good morning, The Lodges at Sunset Village, Kevin speaking."

"Hello, Kevin. My name is Carissa, and I'm coordinating a corporate retreat on behalf of Imaginavigation Enterprises. I was wondering if we could set up a call to discuss our options for renting several cabins from you sometime next year."

After a moment of silence, Kevin responded. "Sure thing, Carissa. Let me check my calendar." The clacking of keys wafted over the phone. "I can meet anytime Monday morning between the hours of nine and eleven or Wednesday after one in the afternoon."

Apparently, she wasn't the only one who didn't want to work weekends. "Let's do Monday at nine. Can you provide me with an email address so I can send you the details?"

When she got off the phone, she sent the appointment to Kevin with a carbon copy to Jacob and Colin. Her smile was smug as she closed her computer.

And I thought working with Jacob was going to be hard.

~

By the time Sunday rolled around, Carissa was desperately in need of a break. Despite her prompt scheduling of the appointment to discuss the cabin rental, Jacob had been blowing up her phone for the last few days with the most asinine requests. From an updated list of potential activities, most of which he ended up rejecting, to insisting she put together a detailed itinerary, his demands were beginning to make her regret taking on the project. Ignoring the fact they hadn't even determined the season for the retreat, let alone set a date, she did the best she could with the information she had. Her updated itinerary accounted for things like not being able to take a boat ride in the middle of December or an inability to ski down a mountain in July.

But she wasn't going to let Jacob interrupt her fun-filled day at the festival. She put her phone on do not disturb with a voicemail stating she was unavailable for the day and would respond Monday morning. Although she suspected her decision would backfire and she'd have a million voicemails and texts to deal with, that was a problem for future Carissa.

Her doorbell rang unexpectedly as she was getting ready to head to the festival. When she opened it, Max stood on her front porch with a bouquet of flowers in lovely autumn colors. Red roses, orange lilies, and a couple of sunflowers were interspersed with gold and purple chrysanthemums.

"Well, this is a nice surprise." She accepted the flowers and breathed in their sweet scent.

"I saw these as I was walking past the florist shop on my way to the fall festival, and I thought of you." He shifted his weight to his back foot. "Though now that I'm here, I'm wondering if this is too forward."

"Perhaps, but they're beautiful, so I can't quite bring myself to be cross with you." She smiled and glanced behind him. "You're going to the festival alone?"

"I told the kids I'd meet them there."

A stab of guilt hit her stomach, but she nodded. "Would you like to come in for a moment? I'm going to put these in water."

It took longer than she wanted to find a vase. The last time she'd received flowers was from Chuck for their wedding anniversary. After he died, she'd packed her vases into boxes, not wanting the constant reminder.

The vase she chose was dusty and had a small crack at the top, but otherwise, it appeared in good shape. While she washed it, Max set to work trimming the flowers. When the vase was clean and dry, she began arranging the blooms. Her fingers moved with the familiarity of someone who had successfully avoided bouquet catastrophes at many a wedding. Once she was satisfied, she set the vase near the window.

Chuck would never have gotten her an assortment like that, preferring the traditional dozen roses. But somehow, the arrangement fit Max and their blossoming relationship. The riot of color had a complicated beauty that drew the eye and delighted the senses.

Max placed a hand on her shoulder and gently turned her toward him. "I should get going. I promised Lanie I'd be there for lunch."

"Thank you for the flowers. They're lovely."

His lips lifted in a grin. "Lovely flowers for a lovely lady."

Her face warmed, and she dropped her gaze. "Perhaps I'll see you at the festival."

When he didn't immediately respond, she looked up. A dozen emotions seemed to dance across his face.

"You're going?"

"Of course. I love the fall festival. It's my favorite event of the year."

A muscle feathered in his jaw. "I see."

Too late, she realized he was hurt. "Max, it's not that I don't want to go with you. I do. It's just—you promised Lanie we wouldn't date, and this would be the second outing with your children that I crashed."

"I invited you to go before Lanie brought it up to me. I could have told her..." He appeared at a loss for words.

"Exactly. There's nothing you could have said that wouldn't have made it sound as if you'd broken your word." She smiled sadly. "But if we run into each other there, then it's less suspicious."

The light returned to his brown eyes. "I hadn't considered that."

She touched his arm. "Go meet up with your kids. I'll head over in a few minutes."

After he'd backed onto the street and driven away, Carissa went into her house. She found herself drawn to the flowers like a moth to a flame. Part of her wondered if she shouldn't have refused them. As she'd told Max the other night, it was getting more and more difficult to be around him and not act on her feelings.

At the same time, if she hadn't accepted the flowers, it would have hurt Max, and she didn't want to do that either. She sighed. She was walking a fine line between protecting her business relationship with Lanie and trying not to fall head over heels for Max, and it was getting exhausting.

When she arrived at the festival, the town square was packed. The familiar scents of funnel cake and hot cocoa filled the air. Carissa closed her eyes, remembering the last time she'd come to the festival with Chuck. It was the last big outing he'd had before he got too sick to leave the house.

She opened her eyes as a stab of pain hit her chest. Though she stood in a sea of people, she'd never felt more alone. Perhaps she should have stayed home.

But then, through the crowd, she saw Max, and her heart skipped a beat. She wouldn't approach him yet, as it might look too coincidental. Just knowing he was there helped ease the ache in her heart, and she forced herself to put one foot in front of the other.

"Carissa!" a familiar voice called. She turned to find Rose and Steven coming up behind her.

"It's good to see you both," Carissa said, pulling Rose in for a brief hug. Her gaze swept over Steven. "No cane today?"

"The doctor said I should try to get around without it." He nudged Rose with his elbow. "And she promised not to let me fall flat on my face."

"Provided you behave." Rose's dark eyes glinted with mischief.

"I'll do my best, but no promises," Steven teased, sliding his arm around her shoulders. He nodded to Carissa. "Are you meeting someone?"

"Nope, I'm here by my lonesome." Carissa's voice cracked on that last word, and she forced a smile to cover it.

"We're meeting up with Lanie, Nate, and Dad. You're welcome to join us."

"Oh, I wouldn't want to intrude," Carissa protested, though deep down, she couldn't help feeling a little thrill. Her plan to make it look as if she and Max had bumped into each other was going better than she could have imagined.

Rose scoffed. "There's no intrusion. After working with us for two years, you're practically part of the family." She took Carissa by the hand and led her to the ticket booth.

A moment later, they joined Lanie, Nate, and Max at the entrance. Lanie was purchasing wristbands for the rest of the group.

"Look who we found," Rose said with a smile.

Lanie glanced over her shoulder. When she saw Carissa, her forehead creased, but the frown disappeared before Carissa could decipher it.

"Make that six wristbands, please," Lanie said. Once she completed her order, she stepped out of line and handed them each a band. "This allows you to enter the festival. Everything except food is included."

"Thanks." Carissa put the band on her wrist. "I can pay you back."

"There's no need." Lanie led the way into the festival.

As she followed the group, Carissa's eyes widened as she took in the plethora of activities awaiting them. The entire town square was closed to traffic. The festival offered pumpkin-carving stations and pie-eating contests, hayrides, a petting zoo, a small carnival with questionably safe rides, and even a few demonstrations scheduled throughout the day. Though overwhelming, it was exactly the distraction she needed after dealing with Jacob all week.

"Let's go sign up for a hayride before they're booked up," Lanie suggested.

Carissa swallowed. Hay wreaked havoc on her sinuses, and the last thing she wanted to do was spend the day sneezing and sniffling. "Oh, um, you go on ahead. I'm happy to watch your things."

"Are you sure?" Lanie raised an eyebrow. "The hayrides are a lot of fun, and they take you to a farm not far from here with a pumpkin patch."

"Positive," Carissa said.

"Count me out as well," Steven chimed in. "Not sure I'd be able to haul myself up into that wagon."

His sister's face fell. "Oh gosh, I hadn't even thought of that." She bit her lip. "Maybe we should pick something else to do."

Stepping forward, Max pointed at Lanie. "You, Nate, and Rose can go on a hayride, and Steven, Carissa, and I will scope out the food options for lunch."

"All right," Lanie said, though her disappointment was palpable. "Meet back here in a few?"

"Unless there's a hayride available before then. Just text us if that's the case, and we'll meet you afterward."

After they split into two groups of three, Carissa breathed a sigh of relief, though she worried Max had given up something he might have enjoyed to stay with her and Steven.

"You could have gone," she murmured.

He grunted. "I'm not much into hayrides myself." Leaning closer, he whispered, "Besides, I haven't seen much of you with this new project you've got going on. I want to make the most of the time we have."

"Should I leave you two alone?" Steven asked.

They turned to find him leaning against a light pole, crossing his arms. Warmth spread over Carissa's cheeks, but Steven appeared more amused than annoyed.

"Let's go check out the food stands. I've been smelling funnel cake since we arrived, and I've got a hankering for it now." Max headed toward the food trucks.

"Isn't it a bit early for that?" Steven asked.

"It's a festival," Max replied. "There are no rules."

Several food trucks were parked in a semicircle on the edge of the festival. A funnel cake truck was toward the middle of the semicircle, and Max made a beeline for it, stopping only when his phone vibrated.

"Lanie said they're catching the next hayride and will be about a half hour. I figure we can grab a couple of funnel cakes now for a snack"—Max slipped his phone back into his pocket—"and then make our way over to the petting zoo. Then later, there's a woodworking demonstration I'd like to check out."

Carissa smiled. "You could probably teach that."

"Not quite." Max laughed. "I'm still a bit rusty, but I've about finished all of the furniture I had started before my divorce."

"I'd love to see it sometime."

After glancing back at Steven, who had snagged a picnic table, Max continued in a low voice, "Maybe you can come over for dinner tonight. The kids are going out, but I'm making spaghetti, and I have enough for two."

A laugh bubbled up in her throat. "I've heard horror stories about your cooking."

"Lanie talks too much," he muttered. "Besides, it's hard to burn spaghetti."

"Somehow, I think you could pull it off."

He glared at her. "Now you have to come to dinner so I can prove you wrong."

"That sounds too much like a date." She frowned. "And I don't want to upset Lanie. What if I come by tomorrow while she's at school? You could cook me lunch instead."

Part of her hoped he would insist on dinner. Even burnt spaghetti sounded better than spending yet another evening eating a microwaved meal in her living room. It'd been years since she'd had a home-cooked meal.

But they shouldn't risk it. What if Lanie came home early? How would she react to Carissa having dinner with her father? Carissa snuck a glance at Max. *And how can I resist kissing him if we're alone together?*

"All right," Max said, though she could hear the reluctance in his voice. "How about I make some fried chicken and potato salad?"

Carissa smiled. "That sounds delicious."

Chapter Nineteen

Max couldn't remember the last time he'd had so much fun. After Lanie, Nate, and Rose returned from the hayride, they met the rest of the group at the picnic tables. Lanie and Nate each carried a pumpkin because Lanie had insisted they needed to carve at least two for Halloween. While she'd chosen a taller pumpkin with a more oval shape, Nate's choice was short, squat, and fat. Or as Carissa said, "pleasantly plump."

"We should pick up those pumpkin-carving kits at the store before we go," Lanie said, setting her pumpkin on the table before sliding onto the bench and helping herself to some funnel cake.

Max raised an eyebrow. "You never said anything about carving some intricate design."

Her lower lip pushed out in a pout, and he was reminded of when she was younger and could convince him to do anything she wanted. He could already feel himself caving. Clearly, not much had changed in the intervening years.

"But the triangle eyes and nose with a mostly toothless grin is overdone," she whined.

"Are you kidding?" Steven asked, admiring the pumpkin Rose had gotten for the two of them. "It's a classic."

As his children continued to bicker over the best pumpkin design, Max whispered to Carissa, "Either way this goes, I'm betting I'll be carving all of the pumpkins."

Her eyes twinkled in amusement. "You could have said no."

He sighed. "True." But then he waved his hand. "I'll do anything to see her happy, though."

"Who knew you were such an old softy?" Carissa teased.

"Keep that to yourself," he grumbled. "I've got a reputation to protect."

"So, who's up for the pie-eating contest?" Steven asked as he clambered over the picnic table bench.

Max patted his stomach. "I'm still full of the funnel cake, but you go on ahead."

Rose and Lanie exchanged a look. "How about we cheer you on from the sidelines?"

"Aw, come on," Steven said, his face falling. Then he turned to Nate. "What about you? Are you game?"

Though it was clear from his expression that trying to quickly eat a pie was just about the last thing Nate wanted to do, he gave a reluctant nod. "Sure, I'll give it a go."

"Awesome!" Steven pumped his fist in the air, which almost caused him to lose his balance. Nate, Lanie, and Rose followed him toward the tent where the contest was being held, leaving Carissa and Max alone.

"What would you like to do?" he asked her as he offered his arm.

"Let's visit the petting zoo."

He steered them in that direction. It was one of the more popular attractions, especially among the children. They bought some feed and took it to a couple of goats hanging out near the edge of the pen.

"I've always wanted a goat," Carissa said with a happy sigh.

"That's an unusual pet."

Her eyes remained on the goats. "It is, but they're more than pets. You can milk them, and they can be like miniature lawn mowers, if you think about it."

Max laughed. "I suppose that's true." He cleared his throat. "Chuck didn't want them?"

"He did, but we didn't have the room or the time it would have taken to care for them." She raised her face and met his gaze. "Our retirement plan was to buy some land for goats, a garden, and maybe even a horse."

"Oh," he said, unsure of what else to do. Internally, he cringed. It seemed like one of those moments where he should either say something comforting about her late husband or maybe even change the subject so she didn't have to dwell on the loss. But he'd never been especially good at knowing what to say or do in such situations.

"Anyway, I doubt I could afford something like that on my own," she continued, turning back to the goats.

He shifted uncomfortably. Was she hoping he would offer to help fulfill that dream? Wouldn't that be awkward, since she'd planned to do it with another man? It felt too soon to be talking about the future in that way.

"Did you have a plan like that with Melody?" she asked when he didn't say anything.

"Uh, not really. I looked forward to the day when the kids were grown and it would just be the two of us." He shuffled his feet. "But she was hoping to travel more, and it's not my thing."

Standing, she brushed her hands on her pants. "Well, you're retired now and soon to be an empty nester. Have you made any plans for after Lanie is married?"

He didn't want to talk about how much he was dreading it. When Lanie had announced her engagement, he'd expected the planning to take at least a year. After all, Rose and Steven had taken two years to plan their wedding. Then, Lanie had initially planned to get married on her mother's birthday, which hadn't gone over well. When Rose had recommended December, a part of Max died. So little time left before she would be too busy for her old man.

"I haven't given it much thought," he finally admitted. Forcing a smile, he gestured to the goats. "But I'm not opposed to trying out life with goats." Her face contorted, and he worried he'd said the wrong thing.

"We should probably get back to the others," she said before she walked away.

Stifling a sigh, he trudged after her. *Way to ruin an otherwise perfect day.* Though he wasn't sure exactly what he'd done wrong. Was it the combined future that scared her off or his attempt to co-opt a plan she'd had with her late husband? He supposed either could have caused her negative reaction.

He hurried to catch up with her. "I'm sorry if I came on too strong back there."

"It's okay. You were mostly joking." Her eyes met his briefly before refocusing on the path before them. "It hit a little close to home because I haven't given up on the dreams I had with Chuck, but I'm also not sure I'd want to share them with someone else."

"I understand," he said, and he did, even if it hurt. "Maybe we can come up with some new dreams of our own."

A small smile lit up her face. "I'd like that."

The next day, Max was in the kitchen, putting the breaded chicken in the fryer, when the doorbell rang. He hurried over to let Carissa in.

"Welcome to my humble abode," he said with a smile as he took her coat. His heart stopped as he took in her outfit. Her blue sweater-dress seemed to hug every curve, and it matched the deep blue of her eyes. "You look beautiful."

Her cheeks flushed pink as she stepped around him into the kitchen. "Can I help?"

"The potatoes should be cool enough to mix with the rest of the ingredients." He gestured to the colander in the sink.

She shook out the colander to rid it of excess water before

dumping the potatoes into a bowl. Then she mixed in the rest of the ingredients of the potato salad. They worked together in comfortable silence.

Max realized that was something he and Melody had rarely done. When the kids were young, Melody stayed home with them and cooked dinner around Max's shift work as an electrical lineman. When she went back to work, he took over the cooking whenever he was home. Their schedules didn't allow them many opportunities to cook together. An ache developed in his chest as he supposed that fact basically summed up their marriage. Like their schedules, they were never in sync.

"It's been a long time since I cooked with someone," Carissa said as if reading his mind.

"Oh?" He checked the chicken. "You and Chuck cooked together often?"

"Sort of. He did most of the cooking. I was relegated to side tasks like chopping or putting together a salad." She smiled wistfully. "But I loved spending time with him in the kitchen. It was our way of realigning after being away from each other all day."

The ache in Max's chest grew. From the way Carissa talked, he could tell hers had been a happy marriage, and he envied her. Though he and Melody had parted on good terms, they'd managed to reconcile only right before they'd run out of time.

"But it also caused most of our fights," Carissa continued, a hint of amusement in her voice.

"Fights?" Max turned toward her with a raised eyebrow.

"Oh yes. He was a much more by-the-book cook than I was. If a recipe called for a pinch of salt, he would ensure it had exactly one pinch." She rolled her eyes. "It didn't matter that such forms of measurement are less than accurate or that some recipes suggested adding salt to taste."

"And I take it you were much less stringent in the kitchen?"

She laughed. "That's putting it mildly. I saw a meme on social media recently that said something about adding spices to a dish until my ancestors tell me 'That's enough, child.'" Her smile widened. "That fits me perfectly."

"I've never been much for recipes either, which has been my downfall. At least, if you ask Lanie." He grimaced. "But I've forced myself to learn average cooking times, so I don't burn things as much as I used to."

"For which I'm sure your daughter is grateful."

"I hope so," he said.

The first batch of chicken was done, and Max carefully removed the pieces from the fryer. After placing them on a paper towel to soak up the excess grease, he added the next batch of chicken pieces to the oil. The pan popped and sizzled with each new addition.

While the chicken cooked, he grabbed two plates and silverware before setting the table. The kitchen had warmed considerably with the heat from the stove, and he pushed his sleeves up in an attempt to cool his skin.

"Would you like some wine?" he asked with trepidation. He was more of a beer guy and had no idea what sort of wine should be served with fried chicken, but Lanie had several bottles of red and white in the small wine cabinet she'd insisted on buying after moving in.

"Mm, wine makes me sleepy. I'll stick with water."

A wave of relief flowed over him as he took out two glasses and filled them with ice and water from the fridge. He set them on the table along with the bowl of potato salad.

"The chicken is almost ready," he called. "If you want to grab a seat, I'll bring the platter over."

The sound of a chair leg scraping across the tile rang out behind him. After removing the last of the chicken pieces from the fryer, he set them on the paper towel then unplugged the fryer. Once he'd soaked up most of the grease, he transferred the chicken to a platter and carried it to the table.

They were quiet as they served themselves. Somehow, that afternoon felt different from their lunch the other day, more intimate since they were completely alone. Max snuck glances at her, marveling at the fact that a few months ago, they could barely stand to be in the same room. And yet, there they were, sharing a meal as if it was the most natural thing in the world. The thought made him smile.

"What's going on in that head of yours?" she asked, catching him staring.

"I was thinking of how much we used to hate each other."

She barked a laugh. "Hate's a bit of a strong word." She lowered her gaze then looked up at him from beneath her lashes. "But I'm much happier with where we are now."

"As am I." He cleared his throat. "After we finish up here, I'll show you what I've been working on in the garage, and maybe you can give me some advice on a wedding gift for Lanie."

Carissa cocked her head. "Oh?"

"I wanted to give her the finished pieces I've been working on, but she's moving into a furnished house with Nate. I'd prefer if my gift was both meaningful and useful."

"I'd love to see what you've been working on, though I have no idea what assistance I can provide on a gift idea." She smiled. "I usually pick something off the couple's registry."

"It needs to be special," Max insisted.

She placed a hand on his arm. "I'm sure no matter what you decide to give her, it will be."

Once they finished eating, Max cleared the table before putting the dishes in the sink. "I'll take care of those in a bit," he said as he grabbed her hand and pulled her from her seat. He was eager to gauge her reaction to the pieces he'd finished.

After flicking on the light in the garage, he removed the sheets one by one, glancing at Carissa as he did so. The nightstands were revealed first then a small chest of drawers. Finally, he revealed the table, which hadn't needed much work.

"These are amazing," Carissa said as she moved closer to the pieces.

"Thank you." He dropped his gaze, feeling suddenly shy. Her approval meant more to him than he'd expected.

"What were you planning to give Lanie?"

Stepping around her, he pointed at the nightstands. "These might work in the master bedroom at Nate's house, but he has a pair that match the bedframe and dresser."

"They are striking, but I can understand your hesitation if Nate already has nightstands." She cocked her head. "What about end tables in the living room?"

"Nate's living room is rather small. I'm not sure they'll fit."

With a nod, she turned to the other pieces. "I suspect Nate already has a table as well. The chest of drawers is small enough to be placed on a surface like a dresser or nightstand."

"It seems too small for a wedding gift."

Her head shot up. "Not if you made it. I'm sure Lanie could store her jewelry in there or something similar."

"I guess." As much as he understood Carissa's point, it wasn't enough to show Lanie how much he loved her. He wanted his wedding gift to stand out.

Carissa moved beside him and put her hand on his shoulder. "I'm sure you'll come up with something. You still have two months until the wedding."

"That's not a lot of time to come up with something from scratch."

She smiled. "I have faith in you."

Her words caused a flood of emotions to flow through him. Without thinking, Max slid his hand over her cheek and into her hair. Bending his head, he searched her eyes for a moment before tentatively brushing his lips against hers. He pulled back, afraid he'd gone too far. But before he could move away, she pushed up on her tiptoes and kissed him more fervently. Her arms wrapped around his neck, pressing her body against his.

Every inch of his body felt like it was on fire. His heart pounded as he slipped his other arm around her waist, drawing her closer.

A moment later, she took a ragged breath and stumbled back. The cool air that rushed in from her absence was like a bucket of cold water. As he came back to his senses, he struggled to think of what to say. She'd wanted to take things slowly. He'd promised Lanie they wouldn't date. And yet, there he was, practically making out with her in the middle of his garage.

But he didn't regret it for one moment. Things had changed between them over a month ago, and he'd resisted the urge to kiss her every time they were alone together. However, if he'd hoped that finally giving in to that urge would squelch the desire, he was sorely mistaken. If anything, that kiss made him want her more.

"Carissa, I—"

"Don't," she whispered. "Don't say anything."

"But—"

"School will be out soon. I-I'd better go before Lanie gets home."

Though his lips still burned from the warmth of her kiss, his heart sank. He reached for her, but she shifted away from him. "Shouldn't we talk about this?"

When she finally lifted her head to look at him, her expression seemed to change by the second. First, her eyes filled with longing, then her eyebrows pulled together in confusion. She brought her hand to her mouth.

"We shouldn't have—I mean, I wanted to, but..." She shook her head. "I have to go." Without waiting for a response, she rushed out of the room.

Max stood frozen in his garage. Part of him wanted to run after her, but he couldn't seem to convince his legs to move. The warmth and joy he'd experienced just moments before when she was in his arms felt like a distant memory. In its place was a cold, miserable emptiness. He didn't know what had happened, but he feared he'd screwed up in ways he couldn't yet fathom.

Chapter Twenty

CARISSA STARED AT HER REFLECTION IN THE MIRROR AS she brushed her graying hair back into a clip. Her cheeks appeared permanently flushed, though that might have had something to do with the fact she couldn't get Max's kiss out of her mind.

"Lanie will be here any moment," she told herself. "Focus."

If only she'd had the forethought to postpone the meeting with Lanie, but her mind had been a chaotic mess, and she'd barely slept the night before. She feared Lanie would see right through her thin grasp on her emotions and know what Carissa and Max had done.

All day, Carissa had vacillated between calling Max and pretending the kiss had never happened. They were supposed to be keeping their distance from each other, and she'd assumed, foolishly, that lunch would be safe.

Absolutely careless. They'd had several close calls previously, but something had always interrupted them at the perfect moment. The day before, they'd been alone in Max's house with little chance of anyone or anything drawing their attention away from each other.

Talk about the perfect storm. Still, despite her fears about Lanie learning the truth and how she might react, Carissa couldn't quite bring herself to regret the kiss. She'd wanted to kiss him since things between them had started to change. *And now that I know, I want more.*

A knock at the door sent Carissa's heart racing. She took a deep breath and one last glance in the mirror. Other than the flush on her cheeks, her face didn't betray her guilt.

When Carissa opened the door, Lanie greeted her with a smile. *So far so good.* Carissa led them into the dining room, where she'd set up the piles of cardstock and envelopes that made up Lanie's wedding invitations.

"These look amazing," Lanie said as she lifted an invitation. The design was simple with a white background, dark-green lettering, and a poinsettia at the top of the card.

"I'm glad you like them. I've got my calligraphy pen set up as well as an assortment of pens for writing the addresses on the envelopes."

"Thank you for agreeing to do this." Lanie stared at the table with wide eyes. "I love calligraphy, but I lack the skill."

Carissa waved a hand. "It's no problem at all. I do this as a regular service for all my clients if they request it."

They sat down to work, and Carissa was relieved to have something to focus on. The silence made her uncomfortable, and she wished she could think of something to say.

"Did you enjoy the fall festival?" Lanie asked.

Carissa carefully wrote out a name in her fancy script before responding. "It's my favorite event of the season."

"It's one of mine too." Lanie took the finished inner envelope and slipped the invitation and RSVP card into it. "Though I haven't been in a while due to school." She cleared her throat. "I was glad my father was able to join us."

Warmth rushed to Carissa's cheeks, and she kept her eyes on the next invitation. "You two seem to be getting along better." She snuck a glance at Lanie. "At least, as long as the conversation stays far away from the wedding."

Lanie snorted. "The wedding is only one of many topics we seem to avoid. I can't wait to move in with Nate and get some distance from Dad." She gave Carissa a rueful smile. "It sounds odd, but I'm hoping not living together anymore will give us the space to improve our relationship." Her face darkened. "Though he doesn't agree."

"Why do you think it'll help?" Carissa chose her words carefully.

"I can't explain it." Lanie shrugged. "But I guess I'm hoping having my own space and not seeing him every day will give me some breathing room to come to terms with what has happened between us in the past. Sometimes, I feel like I'm suffocating in that house with him, and new resentments start to build on top of the old."

Carissa set down her pen and studied Lanie. "Have you tried to explain that to him?"

"At this point, I'm trying to keep the peace as much as possible. And besides, whenever we have a conversation that starts to get too deep, he bails." Lanie rolled her eyes. "He's not exactly the picture of emotional maturity."

A couple of months ago, Carissa would have wholeheartedly agreed, but since she'd started spending more time with Max, she'd seen a different side of him. Her heart broke for both him and Lanie. It was clear he didn't want to be that vulnerable with his daughter, though Carissa couldn't quite understand why. It seemed like the key to repairing the hurts of the past and building a strong foundation for the future of their relationship.

"He relied a lot on my mother to communicate with us kids on his behalf," Lanie continued when Carissa didn't say anything. "And I suspect it's a struggle to figure out how to connect with us, especially now that I'm an adult." Her eyebrows pinched together, and she looked so much like Max, Carissa almost laughed. "Well, I should rephrase. He connects with Steven just fine. Which means I must be the problem."

Carissa leaned across the table and put a hand on Lanie's arm. "It takes two to make and two to break a relationship. I believe you two want the same thing, but it sounds like neither of you are sure how to go about it."

"Well, I can tell you, arguing with me about every little detail of my wedding is definitively *not* the right way to connect with me."

Carissa laughed. "Agreed."

"I appreciate that you've been able to mediate between us, though I hate you have to."

A laugh bubbled up in Carissa's throat. "That's a bit of an understatement, but I've grown accustomed to telling your father no. It seemed to be my go-to word during your brother's wedding."

"Rose said as much, and to be honest, I'm amazed at your fortitude." Lanie chuckled. "It takes a strong person to put up with my father's antics."

Carissa hid a smile. While Lanie wasn't wrong about Carissa's ability to handle Max's outbursts, the method she used had drastically changed between Steven's wedding and Lanie's event. "This isn't my first rodeo, and if at any point you feel like your father is overstepping, let me know." She snuck another glance at Lanie. "Though I would like to be clear on something as well."

Lanie blinked. "Oh?"

Carissa set her pen down and folded her arms on the table. "From now on, if you have a problem with how I'm handling something, I would appreciate it if you would come to me yourself."

To her surprise, Lanie rolled her eyes. "I *told* Dad I would talk to you about the flowers myself, but in true Max McAllister fashion, he didn't listen to me."

Carissa chuckled. "Why doesn't that surprise me? Have you ordered the silk flowers yet?"

"No. I was hoping to get your opinion on them."

As she addressed another envelope, Carissa smiled. "Tell me what you're thinking."

The next day, Carissa's phone rang bright and early. Jacob's name flashed on the screen, and for a moment, she debated not answering.

She'd been avoiding the men in her life since her kiss with Max, and she was in no mood to put up with Jacob's antics first thing in the morning.

But she refused to act unprofessionally despite how much the CEO deserved it. "Good morning, Jacob. How can I help you?"

"We need to get eyes on the site," he said, for once jumping right to business. "The pictures on the cabin's website aren't enough. I need someone to go up to Deep Creek this weekend and scope out the cabin."

"All right." She bit back a sigh. "I'll call Colin tomorrow. Perhaps he can meet me there—"

"Colin has other work to attend to," Jacob cut in. "Book something for yourself. Leave no later than Friday."

The phone beeped three times, indicating Jacob had disconnected. Heat rushed to her face as she tossed the phone on the bed. The nerve of that man. Who did he think he was, demanding she drop everything and drive across the state with no notice? Not to mention, it was already Wednesday. What if the cabin was already booked for that weekend? With the fall foliage reaching its peak earlier in the month, she wouldn't be surprised if they were booked solid through the entire month of October.

But what could she do? If she didn't visit the cabin, she risked him firing her. After all, she'd done much of the legwork, researching various activities and setting up the meeting with the cabin rental office. While Colin likely wouldn't fully integrate her vision, he had enough information to make the event happen with a degree of success.

Muttering, she opened her laptop and clicked through to the site. To her surprise, a couple of cabins were available that weekend. As she clicked through to book one of them, her phone rang again. Her stomach knotted as Max's name flashed on her screen.

"Not now." She hated ignoring him after what had happened between them, but she wasn't ready to discuss the kiss. Besides, until she'd established herself in the corporate world, her client had to come first.

Chapter Twenty-One

Max sat back as he finished carving a design into his last piece of furniture. It was hard to believe he'd managed to finish two nightstands, a table, and a couple of chairs in just over a month. Retirement certainly made it easier, but he hadn't expected the skill he'd honed all those years ago to come back so easily.

But something still didn't feel right. None of the pieces seemed worthy of being a wedding gift for Lanie. For one thing, she'd seen all of the furniture in various stages of completion, so there wouldn't be much of a surprise. Then there was the fact she was moving into a furnished house. While Carissa had said the nightstands could be put to other use, Max wanted to give Lanie something meaningful to start her new life.

Carissa. Though he'd tried to sound understanding when she'd called early that morning to tell him about her trip to Deep Creek, he couldn't quite hide his disappointment. He was relieved she'd told him about her plans, but the call had been brief, and they hadn't talked about their kiss. He suspected she'd been avoiding him, and that hurt more than if she'd told him she regretted the kiss.

Shaking his head, he forced his thoughts back to Lanie's wedding gift. *Sitting here staring off into space isn't helping anything.* He headed through the house to the back porch. Perhaps he would find some inspiration in nature.

When he slipped out the back door, a mourning dove was perched on the railing again. He had no idea if it was the same one that had lost its mate, but it seemed likely. The bird cooed softly at him before spreading its wings and taking flight.

It didn't go far, just up into the branches of the tree nearest his house. He could barely make out a small nest settled between a spot where two large branches met. From his vantage point, it resembled an arch.

The longer he stared at the bird's nest, the more an idea began to form. His daughter was getting married. What could be more beautiful for a wedding than an arch for Lanie and Nate to stand under as they said their vows?

Not one of those cheap plastic arches that fell apart in a strong gust of wind but a wooden arch with hand-carved roses and vines. With the right design, he could even create notches in the sides where silk flowers could be wrapped around the wood to give the arch more color.

He closed his eyes as he tried to picture it. A deep cherrywood would work nicely in the church where they were having the ceremony. After the wedding, the arch could act as an elaborate entrance to Nate's backyard. Maybe Lanie could plant a garden using the arch as a focal point.

His excitement grew as he considered the level of detail and work that would be needed for the project. The arch had to be portable so it could be moved first to the church then to Nate's house. He could make it in two pieces that interlocked at the top to allow it to be transported more easily. *What better way to represent their new union?*

"This will require a lot of fresh-cut wood," he muttered to himself, though he would have to figure out the size of the arch and where he might obtain wood pieces that were large enough. There was a time he could have made do with whatever he found in the forest near his house, but a project like the one he was planning would need more than whatever scraps he could harvest.

With one last look at the dove in the tree, he headed into his house. An internet search might help him get an idea of where to start. Then, he would have to figure out how to hide the arch from Lanie until the wedding. Perhaps he could get Carissa involved to help him plan the surprise.

A few minutes later, he was surfing the web for places to buy wood. He found quite a few reputable sources not too far away and sent up a quick prayer of thanks that he'd had the forethought to get a custom truck with an eight-foot bed. Without it, he wouldn't be able to transport the logs easily. A few lumber yards were located not far from him along with a woodworking store that offered classes in whittling and carving. Perhaps they would have a lead on where he could get raw materials for the arch.

After contacting a few places, he leaned back in his chair. Building a wedding arch from scratch was a huge project. Halloween was less than a week away, which meant he had roughly two months to finish the piece.

Am I biting off too much? Maybe I should think smaller, like a vanity or something that would fit in a small corner of the house.

That would certainly be an easier build. But Lanie already had a vanity she'd inherited from her mother. It was old and not in the greatest condition, but she loved it. Would she be open to replacing it?

Max stood and stretched. He would pick up some materials from the hardware store to build a vanity as a backup, but his heart was set on building the arch. It would be the perfect gift—a way to feature his love for his daughter in her wedding then provide a beautiful entryway for a backyard garden.

"She'll love it," he told himself.

~

Two days later, Max drove across the county to meet with a tree-cutting service. They were scheduled to cut down a cherry tree and had told him he could have the wood if he hauled it away.

When he reached the address, the tree service was already there. The cherry tree was in the front yard of an old colonial-style house. Its branches spread across the lawn and were filled with colorful red and orange leaves. Max took a photo with his cell phone. Later on, it might be fun for Lanie to see what her arch had looked like as a tree.

"Are you here about the wood?" asked a young man with sandy-colored hair and tanned skin.

Max held out his hand. "Max McAllister."

"Adrian Lockes." Adrian shielded his eyes from the sun as he gazed up at the tree. "Any idea how much you want?"

"As much as I can fit in my truck. I'm building an arch for my daughter, and I want to make sure I have plenty of pieces to work with."

"Makes sense. My guys are about ready to start cutting off the branches. Just hang back here, and as they bring her down, you can tell us which pieces you want."

"Sounds good." They shook hands again, and Max moved away to lean against his truck. As the men began tying ropes around the tree to hoist themselves into its upper levels, he was overcome with sadness that something so beautiful was about to be cut down. He hoped to do the tree justice with the arch he was planning.

Cutting the tree down took most of the day. After choosing from the multitude of strong branches, Max managed to fill his truck. He checked his watch as the last log was loaded into his truck bed. He needed to hurry if he had any hope of beating Lanie home. But he planned to store the branches in the shed behind the house until he figured out which pieces he would use. Since it was far from the house and filled with all manner of creepy insects, Lanie was afraid to go back there.

As he drove home, he considered calling Carissa before she left for Deep Creek. Part of him wondered if he shouldn't have offered to go with her, but that felt too forward. They hadn't even been on an official date yet, and her silence since their kiss only confirmed she wasn't ready to take their relationship to the next level. It was clearly too soon for a weekend away together, no matter how much he wished it wasn't.

Figuring it couldn't hurt to try to reach her, he slipped an earbud into his ear and pressed Call. To his surprise, she answered on the second ring, her voice a little breathless.

"Hi, Max. I'm afraid you caught me in the middle of packing."

"I won't keep you," he promised. "I wanted to hear your voice."

"It's good to hear yours too." Her tone became wistful. "I'm sorry we haven't had a chance to talk about… things. I needed some space."

"I understand, though I hope we can sit down and talk when you get back." He cleared his throat. "I wanted to tell you I've figured out what I want to give Lanie as a wedding gift."

"Oh?" Curiosity colored her voice. "Are you making her something?"

"Yes, but I'd rather show it to you when it's further along. It's difficult to explain."

"Okay…" She hesitated.

"And you can't tell Lanie. I want it to be a surprise."

Carissa laughed, though it sounded a bit forced. "Won't that be hard since she lives with you?"

"Don't you worry about that," he said as he pulled into his driveway. Lanie's school had let out, but she likely wouldn't be home for another hour. Still, he needed to hurry. "Anyway, I have to go, but I hope you have a good trip tomorrow. Text or call when you get there."

"I will. Try not to kill yourself in that garage of yours while I'm gone."

He snorted. "No promises. Woodworking is a dangerous gig."

They disconnected, and Max smiled as he climbed out of his truck. Though he struggled under the weight of the logs, he made quick work of unloading them and storing them safely in his garage. By the time Lanie came home, he had just finished sweeping out the debris from his truck.

"Hi, Dad!" she called as she climbed out of her car. "How was your day?"

Taking a deep breath, he plastered a smile on his face. *Act natural.* "Not bad. I finished the furniture from the old house the other day, so I picked up some wood for a new project."

She cocked her head. "What are you building next?"

"Maybe a dining room table. I haven't decided yet."

They fell into step beside each other as they walked toward the house. Lanie had a book bag slung on one shoulder and another bag on her arm. The plethora of papers seemed to weigh her down.

"Need a hand?"

"I've got it."

After he opened the door for her, he followed her inside. She took a deep breath, and her shoulders sagged.

"Are we not having dinner?"

Ah, crud. "No, we are. I got home later than expected. You go sit in the living room, and I'll get it started."

With a weary nod, she sank onto the couch and began removing stacks of paper from her bags. Max rushed into the kitchen and removed a packet of chicken from the refrigerator. He preheated the oven then prepared the drumsticks with various spices. It wasn't how he normally cooked, but Lanie had mentioned more than once that his chicken tended to be bland.

A half hour later, dinner was ready. He called to Lanie and set the food on the table. When she came into the dining room, her steps seemed slow and tired.

"Everything all right?"

She gave a one-shoulder shrug. "It's been a long week, and I'm ready for the weekend." After taking a sip of water, she glanced over at him. "Do you have any plans?"

"I'll probably be in the garage all weekend. What about you?"

When she didn't respond, he took a long look at her. Her arm rested on the table as if it were the only thing holding her up. And while she ate with her normal enthusiasm, she seemed to be dragging.

"Are you sure you're okay?"

She sighed. "The stress of the wedding is starting to catch up with me. Carissa and I made a lot of progress the other night, and the invitations are out, but between working all day and then wedding planning at night, I'm exhausted."

His immediate reaction was to offer help, but he didn't want to upset her. Instead, he covered her hand with his own.

"I'll be okay." She gave him a tired smile. "Especially once December has come and gone."

"I don't want to overstep or throw money at your problems." Her earlier words still haunted him. "But I'm happy to help in other ways, even if it's just running errands for you. I *am* retired, after all."

"Honestly, not having to cook dinner is a huge help." She grinned. "Even if sometimes, it's almost inedible."

He folded his arms on the table and glared at her. "I'm improving."

To his surprise, she nodded. "You certainly are. This chicken is delicious."

They fell into silence as they focused on their food, but Max didn't want the conversation to end there. He wracked his brain for something else to say.

"I realize this is probably something you would have preferred to ask your mother," he finally said, choosing his words carefully. He was completely out of his wheelhouse, but he was desperate to connect with his daughter on a different level. "But do you have any questions about, uh, well, marriage itself?"

Real smooth, McAllister. Could you be more awkward? He prepared for Lanie to laugh off his question or change the subject.

"Oh." Lanie's eyes widened. "Um, I have always wondered if there was anything you might have done differently to prevent you and Mom getting divorced."

He'd repeatedly asked himself that very question after they'd first separated. His answers were usually surface level. Perhaps they should have waited until they were older. Or maybe they should have gone off to college, dated other people, then found their way back to each other, much like Lanie and Nate had done.

But faced with the question from his daughter, he forced himself to dig deeper. She deserved more than some flippant response, especially since he could see the fear in her eyes. While he'd thought she'd accepted that Melody had made a mistake in discouraging her relationship with Nate, Max suspected that the damage Melody had done to their daughter went far deeper than even Lanie realized.

"There are many things I could have done differently," Max blurted out, unable to choose only one thing he would have changed. "But what it comes down to is I wish I had gotten out of my own way more often." Seeing her frown, he considered how to better explain himself. "You said the other day I seem to always think that I'm right, and you made it sound like I see the world through a very narrow lens. The truth is I'm so terrified of making a mistake that I stick to something that's worked in the past. With your mother, we defined our roles early on in our marriage. When we had Steven, she quit her job to stay at home, and then when we had you, it made sense to keep things as they were. But as you both got older, your mother wanted to reassess things. She wanted to go back to work, and with that, she wanted me to take on a more active role in the family, particularly with parenting you and Steven."

"Was that such a bad thing?" Lanie asked, and Max didn't miss the hurt in her voice.

"Of course not," Max replied quickly. "But I couldn't just flip a switch. I was gone often due to my job. Even once I had more seniority, I didn't take advantage of the privileges it allowed. I could have taken more vacation, switched my hours to be home more often in the evenings to help with homework or go to your extracurriculars." Remorse filled his chest. "My attitude at the time was if it ain't broke, don't turn over a new leaf."

Lanie burst out laughing. "The phrase is 'if it's not broke, don't fix it.'"

That made a lot more sense, but he waved his hand. "You know what I mean. Your mom and I had a system, and she wanted to change the system because it no longer worked for *her*." He shifted in his seat. "I wish I had removed my blinders and seen what was right in front of me. If I had given the slightest inch, we might have had many more miles in our marriage."

For a moment, Lanie didn't respond, but her eyes glistened with unshed tears.

Max wondered if perhaps he'd said the wrong thing or been too honest. He didn't usually allow his conversations with his children to get heavy, but Lanie had asked, and he would gladly lay his soul bare if it meant they found an ounce of common ground.

"Thank you for sharing that with me." She wiped her eyes. "It gives me a better perspective of what you and Mom went through." She cleared her plate, which he took as his cue that the conversation was over.

"If you want to know anything else, please ask." He stood, and when she turned from the sink, he held out his arms. "I'm always here for you, even if I'm not the greatest at showing it."

She smiled and stepped into his embrace. "Thanks, Dad. That means a lot."

After giving him a tight squeeze, she kissed his cheek and left the kitchen. He watched her go with a full heart. It felt like they had finally made a breakthrough, and he hoped it was the first of many.

Chapter Twenty-Two

CARISSA ENTERED HER CABIN AND COLLAPSED INTO A rocking chair near the fireplace. Traffic had been horrible on the Baltimore beltway, making her second-guess her decision to take such a long drive on short notice.

But the peace of the cabin settled over her, and she breathed in the rich, rugged scent of wood, lingering chimney smoke, and pine. The air was still and cool, as autumn's hand had snuffed out the last remnants of summer warmth there in the mountains of Maryland.

Soon, she would need to start a fire, but for the moment, she allowed the coolness to seep into her bones. It was strangely refreshing.

The cabin was a simple one-room design. To the right of the front door was a full kitchen, complete with an oven, fridge, and plenty of counter space. To the left of the door sat a small wooden table and two chairs. Behind that was a massive stone fireplace. A king-sized bed took up the majority of the center of the room, and Carissa gazed at it longingly. The rocking chair by the fire had been nice, but she was ready for a good night's sleep.

Her lone suitcase was filled with warm sweaters and jeans in anticipation of the cooler mountain air. She threw on a cozy sweater and headed out to the cabin's back deck. A large hot tub sat against the back wall.

Bed or bath? A small smile tugged at her lips. What a privilege to have such simple choices for once. After the last few hectic weeks of planning weddings and a corporate event, coupled with the delicate balance she'd tried to strike between her growing feelings for Max and her business relationship with Lanie, she ached for that simplicity.

Definitely a bath, but first... Her attention strayed to the natural wonder behind her cabin. *Well, not exactly a* natural *wonder*. It was a well-known fact that Maryland didn't have natural lakes. They were all man-made. Still, she could easily forget that knowledge when taking in the pristine view. The fall foliage had peaked there, with the rippling waters reflecting the brilliant reds, oranges, and yellows.

She headed down to the lakefront, listening to the water lapping gently along the shoreline. She tried to remember the last time she'd been up that way.

Chuck was still alive. The thought came to her, unbidden, and in an instant, the peace she'd enjoyed disappeared. He'd always loved to be in nature, and he'd requested they spend one last summer camping. Unfortunately, his illness hadn't allowed for such rugged adventures, so they'd settled for a cabin. It was rustic enough to give the feel of being in the great outdoors but with the modern conveniences his deteriorating body needed.

In that moment, she realized the memory of that trip had inspired her to pitch Deep Creek for the corporate retreat. Her eyes grew misty, and she raised her face to the darkening sky. She could almost feel Chuck with her then, and her heart ached for him.

A small pier jutted out into the lake, and she walked carefully onto its weathered surface. The wood wasn't in the best condition, but it appeared sturdy enough. She stared out across the water for a while, simply watching the few boats that braved the biting autumn wind.

Glancing down, she caught sight of a carving in the railing. Two sets of initials were crudely cut into the wood, surrounded by a heart. *T.S. + T.K.* Though it lacked his level of skill, Carissa's mind immediately went to Max.

She closed her eyes and allowed herself to remember their kiss. Though she'd chosen to avoid him for the past few days, she couldn't help missing him. Part of her had wanted to invite him with her, but it was much too soon. She hoped to use the trip to clear her head and determine what she wanted to do about their relationship. The distance might do them both some good and give them perspective. But she'd promised to tell him when she arrived, so she sent a quick text.

A million other notifications stared back at her, most of them from Jacob. She glared at the screen, fighting the irritation rising in her chest. Was it not enough that she'd come up there on barely a moment's notice? Why couldn't Jacob trust her to do the job she'd been sent there to do?

She pushed off the railing and headed to her cabin. The beauty around her wasn't enough to quell her growing aggravation, but perhaps a warm bath with a glass or two of pinot grigio would do the trick.

The next morning, Carissa woke with a dull headache. Her first instinct was to roll over and go back to sleep, then she remembered the reason for her impromptu trip. Groaning, she rolled out of bed and slipped into the bathroom. After splashing some water on her face, she made herself a cup of coffee and opened the front door. A blast of chilly air would wake her up more than the caffeine could ever hope to.

Once she was fully awake, she showered and set off to start her day. She had a list of possible venues to visit. While most of the retreat would take place either on the lake itself or near the cabins, she'd wanted to infuse some variety into the agenda.

Her first stop was a ropes course with zip-lining. The tour promised tests of agility and required teams to work together with a guide to get everyone through the challenges. As she drove around the north side of the lake, she was surprised by the number of cars she passed. Deep Creek was a perfect summer vacation spot, but the place she was heading to doubled as a ski resort in the winter. She supposed she shouldn't be shocked that other people were drawn to the area for the beautiful fall foliage.

When she reached the resort, she parked and surveyed the building. It was nondescript aside from a sign advertising the zip-lining course. She walked up to the glass door and peered inside.

"Do you have a reservation?" a deep voice asked behind her.

Spinning on her heel, she found a young man with a backward baseball cap on his head. Tufts of blond hair stuck out of the hole in the hat. His gaze traveled over her outfit. "You're not really dressed for climbing."

Straightening her suit jacket, she forced a smile. "I'm not here to climb. I was hoping to talk to someone about bringing a corporate retreat here. Are you the owner?"

"No, but I can take you to him." He moved past her and opened the glass door. "After you."

Once they were inside, the man indicated she should wait in the lobby then left to fetch the owner. While she waited, Carissa wandered around the small area. Instructions were posted in large signs over the check-in desks, and to the right were several small computers where people could view photos of themselves on the course.

Before arriving, she'd checked out their group rates. She was disappointed to learn that they limited the size of each group to eight people. Jacob wouldn't appreciate that. It would take hours to get all of his employees through the course.

"How may I help you, Miss...?" An older man with a receding gray hairline and a scruffy beard walked into the room.

"Owens." Carissa held out her hand. "Carissa Owens. I wanted to speak to you about your group rates."

He clasped her hand briefly and gave it the slightest of shakes. "Ah, do you have a large family on vacation with you?"

"I'm actually planning a corporate retreat for next autumn, and I'm scoping out potential activities to include on our itinerary."

His brow furrowed. "How many people are you expecting?"

She'd anticipated his reaction and took it in stride. "Likely around fifty people."

When his frown deepened, she hurried on. "But that's an estimate, and not everyone will want to participate in every activity. My goal is to provide attendees with a variety of options to explore."

"Well, it would depend on which course you hoped to do." He handed her a brochure. "Because of the size of the group and the time it would take for each person to go through the course, I would suggest one of our shorter courses. The challenges are not complicated, and participants are brought to the zip line portion much quicker, which is usually the appeal."

She cocked her head. "What if we offered all the courses? Could we split the group based on level of preference?"

Scratching his beard, he seemed to deliberate. "I might be able to do that, but I'd need enough notice to ensure we were well staffed."

"I should be able to provide options for dates and times by the end of this year and then numbers of participants by late spring of next year."

"Then we can accommodate you."

Relief washed over her. *One activity secured.* She handed him a card. "Here's my information. I'll be in touch."

By the end of the day, Carissa didn't feel like she'd been on a weekend getaway at all. She'd driven all over the area while checking out restaurants, local hiking trails, and even a white-water rafting company. The latter, she'd visited only on Jacob's insistence. She couldn't imagine anyone would want to risk falling headfirst into the freezing waters of a raging river in the middle of October.

All she wanted to do was soak her aching muscles in her hot tub and open another bottle of wine. Her stomach growled. But first, she needed to grab dinner.

The fast-food restaurants she'd passed on her way back to the cabin didn't appeal to her. However, a small hole-in-the-wall diner caught her eye. Its simple design and homey vibes reminded her of Bea's. A wave of homesickness came over her as she turned in to the parking lot.

The similarities to Bea's ended at the front door. Inside, the diner was decorated in a much more rustic fashion in contrast to Bea's 1950s nostalgia. There was no swaying-Elvis décor and no jukeboxes. Instead, various animal heads were mounted on the walls, and the floor was riddled with peanut shells.

"Sit anywhere you'd like," a woman said as she passed by Carissa on her way to the kitchen.

Carissa surveyed her options. Several booths sat to one side near a huge fireplace, while a breakfast bar was set up on the other side of the room nearest the kitchen. The appeal of the fire was too strong, and Carissa chose a booth closest to it. A sigh escaped her lips as she welcomed the warmth from the hearth into her old bones.

The woman she'd seen earlier stopped by and handed her a menu. "What can I get you to drink?"

"Water's fine for now," Carissa said with a smile.

After the woman left, Carissa flipped open the menu. The options were fairly standard—burgers, chicken-fried steak, and shepherd's pie—but one item stuck out to her.

"Bison burgers?" she asked as a water glass was set in front of her.

"Don't let the name scare ya. They're just like your typical beef burger, but they got a bit of a wilder edge to 'em."

Carissa shrugged. *When in Rome.* Besides, she'd already been to half a dozen fancy restaurants in the area. It would be good to include something local and original for the corporate retreat.

"I'll have that." She glanced at the menu. "And I'll take a beer from one of your local breweries. Whatever goes best with bison."

The waitress grinned as she took her menu. "I love an adventurous soul."

After she left, her words lingered with Carissa. *An adventurous soul. Is that what I am now?* Her wedding business had sometimes taken her to exotic locations when brides requested destination weddings, but the corporate world was opening many more opportunities.

Her phone buzzed in her pocket, and she pulled it out, expecting to hear from Jacob. Instead, Max's name stared back at her.

We need to talk. Dinner when you get back?

Carissa sighed and turned off the phone, in no mood to deal with Max and the repercussions of their kiss. While she knew she couldn't avoid it forever, at that moment, all she wanted to do was enjoy a nice, quiet meal and celebrate how much she'd accomplished. After her excursions that day, she deserved time to relax. Her real life could wait until she was home.

A few moments later, the waitress returned with her food and beer. Carissa took a sip from the cool glass, savoring the mellow and smooth flavor with just the slightest hint of sweetness. The burger was ginormous, which seemed fitting because of the animal it came from. Carissa opted to cut it in half but still required two hands to lift it. Her first bite oozed with delicious juiciness.

Closing her eyes, she chewed quickly before devouring the first half of the sandwich. It was the best burger she'd ever had, and she was ravenous after rushing around all day.

A soft chuckle caught her attention, and she opened her eyes to find the waitress hovering nearby. Carissa set down the burger and wiped her face.

"I take it you're enjoying your first bison burger?" the waitress asked.

"That's an understatement," Carissa said, eyeing the second half. The restaurant would be a perfect addition to the retreat, but she wasn't sure if the small place could accommodate everyone. "Do you ever serve large parties?"

"Like catering?"

Hmm... I hadn't considered that. Which was surprising, since she worked with caterers all the time. "That wasn't exactly what I meant, but that might work too." At the waitress's perplexed expression, Carissa continued, "I'm planning a corporate retreat, and I've been scoping out restaurants and activities all day. The food would be a big hit, but I'm not sure we can fit everyone in here."

"I'd have to ask my boss, but we've catered events before. Maybe she'd be willing to bring the food to you." The waitress opened a notepad. "Where will you be hosting it?"

Carissa provided the details of the cabin rental location. They chatted for a few more minutes, and the waitress promised to give her boss the information.

Once she was alone again, Carissa greedily ate the rest of her burger and licked the grease from her fingers. As she sipped her beer, she promised herself she would stop back by there again for one more burger before she headed home.

Home. She sighed. The weekend was almost over, and she still had no idea what to say to Max. If she were honest, the distance from him had made the possibility of secretly dating more appealing than when he'd first mentioned it. But she couldn't quite stomach the idea of going behind Lanie's back. Besides being unprofessional, it risked ruining any chance Max had of improving his relationship with his daughter.

And yet, keeping Max at arm's length until after the wedding was no longer feasible. After their kiss, she wanted more.

Once she'd paid the bill, Carissa headed to her cabin. When she arrived, she sat in her car and stared at Max's text. With a secret smile, she typed her response.

Chapter Twenty-Three

"I'M BACK IN TOWN." CARISSA'S VOICE CAME OVER THE line, filling Max's chest with warmth. "Are you free for dinner tonight?"

Max surveyed his progress on the arch as he considered her question. On the one hand, he was dying to see Carissa again and catch up on how her planning was going. On the other, he'd planned to show her the arch the next time they met, but it was nowhere near ready. He'd carved one branch into a long curved archway, but he hadn't quite started on the intricate designs he was planning.

"I'd love to," he said, deciding he would show her another time. "There's a place I've been dying to take you. I'll make a reservation."

"Oh, where's that?" she asked.

Shaking his head, Max grinned. "It's a surprise."

They planned for him to pick her up in a couple of hours, and he hung up the phone. In the meantime, he got back to work on the arch. Lanie had said she needed to stay late at school for some parent–teacher conferences, and he was trying to take advantage of her absence. There wouldn't be much time to work on the arch during the rest of the week, as Halloween was the next day, then he,

Lanie, and Steven were planning on spending Melody's birthday together that weekend.

He decided to focus on carving the other side of the arch. It made more sense to make sure the pieces could fit together like he wanted before starting to carve designs into the wood. If they didn't fit right, he would have to scrap one of the pieces and start over. With November just around the corner, he didn't have time to waste.

An hour later, he stood and stretched his aching back. He'd made more progress on the other side of the arch, but he'd run out of time. After grabbing a quick shower, he dressed and headed over to pick up Carissa.

His heart pounded as he parked his car in her driveway and walked to her front door. They hadn't seen each other since their kiss, and he was nervous about how she might act.

She opened the door with a smile. "Hello there, stranger."

He couldn't help grinning in return. "Long time no see."

Without another word, she hugged him. He chuckled as his arms slid around her waist.

"I've missed you," he whispered, though the words were inadequate for the depth of his feelings. In truth, he'd been going crazy and was desperate to find out where they stood.

Too soon, she stepped back, and it took a lot of willpower not to tighten his arms around her to bring her close again. But they had a lot to talk about and a reservation to get to.

He walked around to the passenger side and opened her door.

Her brow furrowed as she looked from the truck to him. "Aren't you going to tell me where we're going?"

Shaking his head, he held out his hand. "You'll see when we get there."

Her lower lip jutted out in an adorable pout, and for a moment, he was distracted by the desire to kiss her. Thankfully, she climbed into the truck before his desire got the better of him. There would be plenty of time for that later, assuming things went well that night.

Instead of heading north toward the National Harbor, Max

turned the truck south. Out of the corner of his eye, he caught Carissa staring at him before she shifted her gaze to the window as if the scenery would help her decipher their destination.

"So, how was your trip?" he asked, hoping to distract her.

"It went really well, actually."

"You sound surprised."

"I am a little. I wasn't expecting everything to come together so easily, but I managed to speak to several different places about possible activities and dining." She smiled. "The event is practically planning itself."

"That's good, though, right? Less stress for you?"

"That's the goal." Her expression darkened. "But I still have to run it by Jacob."

They drove in silence for a few minutes until the landscape opened around them. A minute later, they were crossing the bridge to Solomon's Island.

Carissa gasped and turned to him with wide eyes. "We're going to dinner here?"

He nodded, proud of himself for keeping the secret. Immediately, she began naming potential places, but he refused to confirm or deny any of the options.

"Ugh, this is killing me," she whined, playfully punching his arm. "I can't believe you're not going to tell me."

"Wouldn't be much of a surprise if I did."

When they turned onto a deserted dirt road, her eyebrows pulled together. "Are you taking me to the woods to murder me and dispose of the body?"

He laughed. "Has Lanie been showing you her true-crime shows? Besides, I wouldn't need to drive all the way down here to do that." The road evened out, and a small building appeared in the distance. "This is the island's best-kept secret."

After he pulled into the makeshift parking lot, he grinned at the perplexed expression on her face. He understood her confusion. The building appeared no larger than a boathouse, with blue siding and white shutters.

"Welcome to La Vela." He jumped out of the truck and went around to open her door. "The best Italian food around."

They entered the main area, which had a bar and several small dining rooms that branched off to the right and left. Most of the tables were empty, but it was rather early and a weeknight.

After they were seated, he leaned closer to her. "I wanted something more secluded. Gives us a chance to talk."

Her smile appeared forced, and for the first time since they'd arrived, he wondered if he'd made a mistake. Maybe she preferred somewhere more public.

"I haven't been to this restaurant since they moved locations."

"Well, it is rather out of the way—"

"It's not that," she said quickly. "It's just..." She closed her eyes, and it dawned on him she was trying not to cry.

Oh no, what have I done now? "Do you want to go?"

"Give me a second," she choked out. The server placed two glasses of water on the table then hurried away as if he, too, could sense she was barely holding it together.

Once she'd taken a couple of sips, she gave him a sheepish smile. "Gosh, this is so embarrassing."

"It's okay. We can go somewhere else if you want. There's a seafood restaurant next door."

"No, this is fine, and I'm okay." She cleared her throat. "My husband often came down to Solomon's on business, and I have planned several weddings throughout the island. This was his favorite restaurant."

Oh no. He'd hoped to avoid memories of her husband after their lunch at the National Harbor, and he assumed he would be safe taking her somewhere less well-known. "I'm sorry. I had no idea."

"And why would you?" After she dried her eyes with her napkin, her smile appeared more genuine. "I've always loved this place, too, but I haven't been able to bring myself to come back here." She slid her hand across the table. "I'm glad I'm not doing it alone."

Still, he felt awful. "We should go somewhere else. I want tonight to be about... well, us. And I don't want to bring back painful memories."

"That's just it." She shook her head. "They aren't painful memories. We had a lot of good times at their old location." After giving his hand a reassuring squeeze, she opened her menu. "I want to stay."

He hesitated before opening his menu as well. Part of him wanted to ask her if she was sure, but he didn't want to keep bringing it up either. He hoped maybe tonight would give her a chance to make new memories with him.

"What's your favorite thing to get here?"

"Oh, there's so many things I like," she said. "They have pasta, but I had that the other night. I'll get their duck al vino."

The server returned to take their orders. Max gestured for Carissa to go first. When it was his turn, he ordered the filet mignon.

With a nod, the server took their menus and left. Max sipped his water to buy himself some time before he launched into the discussion they needed to have.

Taking a deep breath, he leaned forward. "Now that we have a moment alone, we should talk."

Her expression became guarded. "You don't waste any time."

"I don't mean to put you on the spot." He cleared his throat. "But it has been a few days since our kiss, and you spent several of them avoiding my calls."

She lowered her gaze. "I'm sorry about that. I wasn't sure what to say or how I felt."

His heart sank. "Then you regret it?"

Her head shot up. "Of course not." The corner of her mouth twitched. "But the timing left a lot to be desired."

"I know." He groaned. "I shouldn't have kissed you, but I couldn't seem to stop myself. I've wanted to do it for a long time."

"Me too." Her voice was almost a whisper.

He heaved a sigh of both relief and frustration. "So what do we do now?"

"I'm not sure what we can do," she admitted. "You gave your word to Lanie, and her wedding is still almost two months away."

"We've kept it from her thus far," Max said, hating himself for even considering betraying his daughter's trust. But she was the one who'd wanted him to put himself out there. And he couldn't help who he'd fallen for.

"I don't love the idea of sneaking around behind her back." Carissa frowned. "Aside from being unprofessional, we're adults, not teenagers hiding our relationship from our parents."

"The role reversal isn't lost on me." Max's chuckle was hollow. "If you want to keep trying to wait, I understand." It would likely drive him mad, but he'd already decided Carissa was worth it.

She squared her shoulders. "I don't want to wait anymore."

"I don't either." He slid his hand across the table, and Carissa grasped it in her own.

Though joy filled his chest, his stomach churned with trepidation. He imagined it was only a matter of time before Lanie found out about them. While the wedding was nearly planned, he hated breaking his word to his daughter. He could only hope everything turned out okay in the end.

An hour later, they tossed their napkins onto their plates at the same time and leaned back. The food was delicious, as always, and Max was greatly enjoying the company as well.

"Would you like dessert?" the server asked as he cleared their plates.

Max glanced at Carissa, but she gave a small shake of her head. "No, thank you. Just the check, please."

"Right away, sir."

"Are you in a hurry to get home?" Max asked.

"Not particularly."

After paying the bill, Max led her outside, and they walked along the streets until they came to the beach. The water of the Patuxent River lapped gently against the shoreline as the sun sank low on the horizon.

"We always seem to end up near water," Carissa said, taking his hand and entwining their fingers.

"It's hard to find a place in Maryland that doesn't have access to water. We're kind of surrounded by it."

"Touché."

"But that sounds like a fun challenge. I'll have to find a place away from the water for our next date."

She raised an eyebrow. "Getting ahead of yourself there, aren't you, Mr. McAllister? I haven't agreed to another date."

"It's too late for your weak protests now. You said you didn't want to wait to be together, so another date is inevitable." He brought their joined hands to his lips and kissed her knuckles. "You're stuck with me now."

Her laugh warmed his heart. "You're quite sure of yourself."

"I know what I want." Wrapping an arm around her waist, he bent to kiss her.

"And what's that?" she murmured against his lips.

"You."

He kept the kiss short, not wanting to get carried away again, especially in public. But it was difficult to let her go. As they continued along the small beach, his heart was full for the first time since he'd lost Melody.

"I've never been here at night," she said. They stopped at the edge of the beach to enjoy the sunset over the water. "Chuck didn't like being so far from home in the evening."

Normally, he might be put off by how much she talked about her late husband, but since losing Melody, he understood. It wasn't the same as being with someone who was still in love with their ex. Death gave a finality that nothing could overcome, and grief was a testament to the strength of love.

"I prefer the evenings here." A chilly breeze made her shiver, and Max wrapped an arm around her. "But we should probably get going. It's a long drive back."

"Just one more minute," she said, leaning into him. "I'm not ready for this night to end."

"Me either."

Time seemed to stop, even as the sky changed from orange to pink and then a deep purple. Her scent wafted over him with the breeze, and he closed his eyes, savoring the moment.

"Would you ever want to get married again?" she asked, her voice barely a whisper.

That wasn't a question he was expecting, and he spoke without thinking. "No."

She stiffened in his arms. He grimaced. Clearly, that was the wrong answer. It might have been the truth, at least up until recently. But despite how he felt about Carissa, marriage hadn't crossed his mind. For one thing, it felt too soon. And for another, he'd been a bachelor for so long, he wasn't sure how he would feel about having a wife again.

"Never?" she asked.

"Uh, I mean, I didn't expect to date again either. I haven't given much thought to marriage." *Ugh.* He wasn't making much sense. "I guess I haven't had much of a reason to consider marrying again, if that makes sense."

Though she nodded and smiled, there was a hint of disappointment in her eyes. "I get it."

"What about you? Do you want to marry again?"

She sighed. "At first, I didn't. I couldn't imagine ever finding what I had with Chuck again, and anything else would be a poor substitute." She gestured toward the street, and he took her hand and led her back up the beach. "But after a few years, I started thinking it might be nice. I've still got a lot of life to live, God willing. And I'd like to share it with someone."

Wanting to share your life with someone doesn't have to mean marriage. But he didn't say that out loud. A comment like that would likely ruin what had otherwise been a pleasant evening.

"It's not something I want to rush into," she continued when he didn't respond. "Right now, I want to focus on my business."

"That makes sense. Expanding it takes a lot of time and effort."

She frowned but didn't contradict him. They walked the rest of the way in silence, but it wasn't as comfortable as before.

When they arrived at his truck, he opened her door. She searched his face briefly before climbing in. As he drove her home, he wished he could find a way to salvage the night, but he kept coming up empty.

Finally, she broke the silence. "I'm sorry if I spooked you with the marriage talk."

"Not spooked," he corrected. "Just caught off guard." He glanced at her before turning his attention back to the road. "I'm not necessarily against getting remarried. It's not something I've had occasion to think about since I wasn't dating."

"I understand." She rested a hand on his knee. "I shouldn't have brought it up."

"No, I'm glad you did." He squeezed her hand. "If we're going to keep seeing each other, it's important we're both honest about what we want, now and in the future." He cleared his throat. "And it's okay if that changes, as long as we talk about it."

A little while later, he pulled into her driveway and hopped out to walk her to her door. After kissing her good night, he spent the drive to his place mulling over their conversation. Though he'd meant it when he said he'd never had occasion to think about marriage, what he hadn't told Carissa was that he'd sworn off marriage the moment the divorce decree was signed. But then, he'd sworn off love too. *And look how that turned out.*

~

Halloween came and went without much fuss. Max passed out candy. Lanie and Nate went with Steven and Rose to a party at Seabreeze. As time marched into November, the pressure was ramping up for him to finish Lanie's wedding present. He needed to show Carissa the arch soon, as he hoped to get her opinion on where it might fit in the ceremony.

But first, he was meeting his children at the cemetery. It was Melody's birthday, and they had agreed to get together as a family.

As he climbed into his truck and headed to the gravesite, he couldn't help recalling how much had changed in the last year. His son was married, Lanie had moved home permanently and was soon to be married, and he'd started to open his heart again for the first time in over a decade.

"Melody," he whispered hoarsely, "you would be so proud."

Lanie and Steven were already in the parking lot when he arrived. While their significant others had offered to join them, they had decided to keep the visit between the three of them.

Lanie was already wiping tears from her eyes, and Max rushed toward her, pulling her into a fierce hug. His son held a small bouquet of flowers in one hand and an angel statue in the other.

A moment later, Lanie pulled away and forced a smile. "Let's go visit Mom."

Together, they trudged through the graveyard. The autumn wind ruffled their hair, and Max liked to think it was Melody showing them she was with them. When they reached the grave, Steven knelt and placed the flowers and the angel figurine in front of the headstone.

"Happy birthday," he said, his voice hoarse from the tears he appeared to be holding back.

Max bent and put a hand on his son's shoulder. He hated seeing his children in pain but knew there wasn't anything he could do for them except offer comfort.

"I'm getting married next month, Mom," Lanie said with a sniffle. "You'd love the dress I picked out."

"It's beautiful," Max agreed before he turned away, not wanting his children to see the tears that came to his eyes at the memory of the first time he'd seen Lanie in that dress. She looked radiant and so much like her mother, it broke his heart.

Steven and Lanie continued to tell their mom about all the things going on in their lives. Max could almost pretend Melody was sitting there listening to them.

"Why don't you tell Mom about your woodworking, Dad?" Lanie called, bringing Max back into the conversation. "She loved the furniture you made for her before..."

She swallowed, but Max could finish the sentence. *Before the divorce. Before everything changed.*

Max shifted closer to the headstone, feeling silly to be talking to a rock. "I'm working on something for Lanie, a wedding present."

"Really?" Lanie asked, her eyes lighting up. "Is it a desk? Nate said I could use the second bedroom as an office for grading papers."

Averting his eyes, Max shifted uncomfortably. Perhaps he should have considered a desk, though he supposed the vanity could double as one, especially if he made the mirror removable. But he was sure she would love the arch just as much once she saw it.

"You'll have to wait and see," he finally said.

They stayed for as long as they could stand the bitter wind, then they headed to the parking lot. After a quick goodbye, Max drove to his house, his heart light. The sun broke through the gathering clouds, and he hoped Melody was smiling down on him.

Chapter Twenty-Four

"Hey, stranger," Max said when Carissa answered her phone.

"I'm sorry I've been incommunicado for the last week." Carissa leaned back in her chair and closed her eyes. For several days, she'd been working on a proposed schedule for the corporate event. "What's up?"

"I was wondering if you could tear yourself away from work to have lunch with me today or sometime this week." When she didn't immediately respond, he continued, "I'm cooking."

"Is that supposed to entice me?" she teased.

"It's a Lanie-approved recipe," he retorted, though she could hear the smile in his voice. "I promise I won't burn it."

Carissa pursed her lips. The timing wasn't great, as she needed to get the schedule over to Colin by the close of business the next day, but she was hungry, and her eyes were starting to cross from staring at a screen. Maybe a break would do her good.

"I can be there in about an hour. Does that work?"

"That's perfect. See you soon."

After they disconnected, she stretched, working the kinks out of her back. She promised herself she would finish the schedule first thing in the morning when she was fresh and closed her laptop. Then she headed straight for the shower.

Forty-five minutes later, she put the finishing touches on her makeup. Covering the dark circles under her eyes was getting more difficult the longer she worked on the event for Imaginavigation Enterprises. But it would be worth it when the clients began pouring in next year.

After donning a heavy coat, she left her house and drove to Max's. The afternoon sun was high in the sky but did little to cut through the day's chill. Before she had even fully exited her car, the front door swung open, and Max stepped out.

"Glad you could make it," he said as he wrapped his arms around her and bent to give her a quick kiss.

But it had been too long since she had last seen him, and she slid her hands into his hair, holding him in place. He chuckled against her lips as he pulled her closer, deepening the kiss.

"I guess absence really does make the heart grow fonder," he murmured when she finally released him. "Come inside where it's warm."

The house smelled of garlic and onion, and her stomach growled in anticipation. She could get used to someone cooking for her again.

"What are you making that smells so delicious?" She slid into a chair at the table.

"Chicken parmesan." He glanced over his shoulder, and her face must have betrayed her skepticism. "It's Lanie's recipe. I'm planning on making it for her later this week for dinner. You get to be my guinea pig."

Pressing her lips together to keep from laughing, Carissa smiled. "Lucky me."

"After we eat, there's something I'd like to show you," he said. "I've been working on a gift for Lanie, and I'd love your opinion on it."

"I'm sure it'll be beautiful."

"But you have to promise not to tell her. It's a surprise."

"I promise."

He served lunch, and Carissa was pleasantly surprised by how well it had turned out. They talked about how their weeks had gone, and Carissa filled him in on the progress she'd made with planning the corporate event.

Once they were finished eating, Max cleared the table and put the dishes in the sink. His excitement about his present for Lanie was palpable.

"I'll take care of those in a bit." He grabbed her hand and pulled her from her seat. Carissa struggled to keep up with him as he led the way to the garage.

After flicking on a light, he moved toward a large object covered with a sheet. With a wink at Carissa, he removed the sheet and revealed a wooden archway. Most of the wood was smooth, but he'd started carving a design featuring roses, leaves, and vines.

Carissa fought to keep her expression neutral as she stared at the monstrosity in front of her. While the arch was beautiful, it was huge. It seemed to almost touch the ceiling of the garage, and it stood about five feet wide.

When she still hadn't said anything, Max cleared his throat. "Well, what do you think?"

Instead of answering, Carissa walked around and through the archway, studying the piece. A million questions ran through her mind. What was his intention with the gift? Did he hope Lanie would use it in the ceremony? She shuddered. *Hopefully not.* She doubted it would fit through the door of the church, let alone in the sanctuary.

Finally, she took a deep breath. "Is this piece going to Nate's house?"

"Eventually, but I hoped it could be included in the ceremony."

Carissa swallowed her horror and kept her tone as diplomatic as possible. "Did you measure the church to ensure this will fit through the door?"

The excitement in his dark eyes dimmed. "No, but the pieces interlock, so they can be taken apart if needed." He pointed at the top of the arch. "See this part here? It disconnects."

Well, at least we can get it in *the church.* She pressed her lips into a thin line as she tried to think of something nice to say.

"Aren't you going to say anything else?" he asked. "I mean, obviously, it's not finished, but I have no doubt I can get it done by the wedding."

Carissa held up her hand. "You should talk to your daughter before you continue wasting your time." The hurt in his eyes made her wish she'd chosen her words more wisely.

"Wasting my time?" he repeated as if dumbstruck.

She sighed. "I'm sorry. That came out wrong." Pinching her nose, she closed her eyes. *How can I get him to understand he's overstepping again?* She opened her eyes and tried a different tactic. "What I meant was Lanie has a specific aesthetic in mind for the ceremony." She stared at the arch. "Honestly, I'm not sure it'll fit the stage area even if we can get it in the door."

"It's a church. I'm sure we can make it work," he insisted, his tone defensive. "Besides, I know my daughter better than you do."

She didn't respond, but her expression must have conveyed her skepticism. While she didn't want to hurt him or make the afternoon any more awkward, she'd promised Lanie to help rein in her father's antics.

Before she could say anything else, Max crossed his arms and stared at the floor. "Maybe you should go."

Her heart sank. She wished she could spare his feelings, but she wasn't sure how else to convey what a terrible idea the arch was. It would be one thing if he'd run it by Lanie, even if he'd offered to make something for her ceremony and left the actual item a surprise. Though given how large the arch was, she doubted that would stave off Lanie's irritation.

Perhaps there was a way to salvage their time together. One

glance at his face disabused her of that notion, and she sighed. She moved past him and went into the house to gather her coat.

He followed her. "Promise me you won't tell Lanie about the arch."

At first, she didn't respond. While she appreciated that Max wanted the arch to be a surprise, she was contractually obligated to tell her client.

"Please, Carissa," he begged, his eyes boring into hers. "It means a lot to me to be able to do this for her, and I want it to be a surprise."

"I understand that," she began. "But you don't understand the position you're putting me in by asking me to keep this a secret. Lanie has entrusted me with this event because she knows I will run everything by her, and we already saw how she reacted when I didn't tell her about the band. You're asking me to lie to her again."

His face flushed. "It's not a lie!"

She crossed her arms. "Lying by omission is still lying."

"I'll tell Lanie before the wedding, when the arch is finished."

"And when will that be?"

"I-I don't know," he admitted. "But I'll try to get it done by the end of this month. Then Lanie can decide what she wants."

They stared each other down as the minutes ticked by. Finally, Carissa nodded. "But if she finds out before then and comes after me, I'm throwing you under the bus."

"Duly noted."

She opened the door and took one last look at him over her shoulder. He refused to meet her gaze. All the warm feelings she'd felt when she'd entered the house had vanished, leaving her with a bleak emptiness. As she stepped out into the cold November day, she wondered if their relationship had ended before it really had a chance to begin.

~

Carissa didn't sleep well that night. After tossing and turning for hours, she gave up around four in the morning and tried to lose herself in event planning. Several emails and calls had come in during her lunch with Max.

Sliding her fingers through her hair, she clasped her hands behind her head and rested her forehead against the dining room table. How had such a wonderful day soured? Had she overreacted to Max's surprise for his daughter? Maybe he was right. Maybe Lanie would love it.

With a groan, she pushed back from the table and began pacing. On the one hand, Lanie had been very enthusiastic about her dad revisiting his old hobby. During some of their meetings one-on-one, she'd gushed about how talented he was. So it was entirely possible she would be thrilled to receive something he'd worked so hard on for her.

But on the other hand, it clashed with the rest of the decor. The church wood was mahogany, and the deep-brown color went well with the rich red-and-green decor they had chosen for Christmas. Meanwhile, the wood Max was carving was cherry, a much lighter brown. Perhaps that wouldn't matter to Lanie, but every time Carissa tried to picture it, she cringed. And as far as she knew, no amount of staining would make the wood dark enough to fit in with the rest of the church.

It also bugged her that he hadn't come to her about it before he started the project. While she had no idea if Lanie even wanted a wedding arch, Carissa could have at least given him pointers on what type of wood would work best, though she hadn't the first clue whether it was even possible to choose different types of wood. For all she knew, he had to work with what was available.

He'd put her in an uncomfortable position, as if she didn't have enough on her plate. Not telling Lanie felt wrong, especially since Max couldn't guarantee when the arch would be done. Which meant Carissa had no idea when he would tell Lanie.

"I didn't need this right now," she muttered as she sat back at the table and stared at her computer screen. "I wish I could trust Max to finish on time and tell Lanie."

Saying Max's name brought up other unpleasant thoughts. She wished she hadn't said he was wasting his time. It had been overly harsh and unfair. At the same time, he'd *just* gotten back into woodworking and was still honing his skills. Why would he decide to take on such a huge project when faced with a tight deadline?

And then he'd asked her to leave. An otherwise perfect day completely ruined because of a pointless argument. She wished he'd never shown her the arch. Then she would be blissfully ignorant, and any fallout between him and Lanie wouldn't land on her.

You can't put the genie back in that bottle now. Her husband's voice rang in her head with one of his favorite sayings. She hated to admit that like all the other times he'd said it, he was right. What was done was done, and what mattered was what she did moving forward.

Shaking her head, she forced herself to focus. As soon as the sun rose, Jacob would start blowing up her phone again, and she needed to address his latest "urgent" nonemergency he'd emailed and called about when her phone was off.

Two hours later, as if on cue, her phone vibrated beside her. Resisting the urge to roll her eyes, Carissa pressed the speaker button.

"Good morning, Jacob."

"I hope you enjoyed your evening off," he said by way of greeting. "Because we've got a lot of work to do."

"We have a call with the board in about an hour to give them an update, so we may have to push off whatever you're hoping to accomplish until after that call."

"Colin sent some talking points he wanted to make sure we covered during the meeting."

Carissa nodded. "I saw those, and I responded with comments of my own."

Following a beat of silence, Carissa lifted her fist in a quiet cheer to have finally been one step ahead of the irritating CEO. After her fight with Max, she needed a win.

"Color me impressed," Jacob said. "You must have been up late last night."

Or early this morning. "Something like that. Anyway, I'll forward you the email thread between Colin and me for your review, but I think we're ready."

"That's good to hear. Can you schedule a meeting with the three of us directly after the call so we can keep our momentum going once the board approves our plans?"

Stifling a sigh, she clicked into her computer calendar and started entering information into an appointment. "Sending to you now."

"All right. I guess I'll talk to you in an hour."

"Sounds good. Bye." She tried and failed to keep the smugness out of her tone. *Score another point for me.* If only she could keep it up.

The next day, Carissa had a meeting with Lanie, Nate, and their preacher at the church. Her part was simple. She was there to go over logistics, but the preacher wanted to have a deeper conversation with the engaged couple about their relationship to make sure the two were ready to enter into matrimony.

They met in the church itself, and Lanie wandered around the sanctuary, taking in all the details. Carissa stayed near the pulpit, hoping once the preacher took the two lovebirds into his office, she would be able to pull out a measuring tape and figure out where they might fit Max's arch monstrosity.

"It'll be even more beautiful when it's decorated for Christmas," Lanie said as she came up behind her.

Carissa forced a smile. "I have no doubt." She waved a hand over the banister that separated the pews from the pulpit. "With the rich red carpeting, it has a natural disposition for Christmas and likely complements the greenery."

"The only thing I don't like is the lack of a center aisle."

Carissa pursed her lips. It was somewhat odd that the church had two side aisles that branched off to pews to the right, left, and center. While it might work well to have the bridesmaids and groomsmen use the two aisles, it would be awkward to have Lanie and her father do the same. But the main door to the church was located stage left, behind the pews.

"You and your father will come down this aisle here." Carissa pointed. "And we can always encourage people to sit in the middle and left pews. That way, they won't miss out on your entrance by being too far away."

"True." Lanie cocked her head. "I don't think the guest list will require the whole room. Maybe we can set up some decorations in front of those seats to mark them as off-limits."

Carissa's mind strayed to the arch. Maybe that was a compromise Max could accept. The arch was certainly large enough to block off the aisle, then it could still be featured in the wedding, perhaps not exactly as Max had envisioned.

"What's wrong?" Lanie asked.

Carissa worked to rearrange her facial expression. "Nothing. I'm brainstorming some options to bring your vision to life."

Guilt churned in her stomach, and she glanced away, hoping Lanie couldn't see through her poor attempt at lying. Maybe she and Max should have stuck to their decision to wait until after the wedding to start dating. Then she wouldn't be faced with divided loyalties.

"Lanie? Nate?" a deep voice called from the front of the church. "Are you ready?"

"We'll be right there," Lanie said before turning back to Carissa. "You'll wait here for us? I'd like to hear your ideas of how to block the aisle."

"Of course," Carissa promised, hoping she sounded more enthusiastic than she felt.

After Lanie and Nate followed the preacher out of the church, Carissa retrieved her measuring tape and set to work. She had to guesstimate how big the arch was based on her memory, but it had stood taller than Max by at least a foot and appeared roughly four or five feet wide.

"Better safe than sorry," she muttered as she measured five feet. Working quickly in case the preacher finished sooner than expected, she measured every place she could think of putting the arch, marking the measurements on a piece of paper.

When she was finished, she slumped into a pew and put her head in her hands. If the arch could indeed be separated, it would fit in the church, but it would stand out as an eyesore no matter where she tried to put it. And if Max's intention was that they would be married *under* it, then Carissa really had her work cut out for her.

As much as she loved the idea of it sitting in the aisle to block people from entering, it would be cumbersome to set up there because of the limited space in the aisle itself. The only other option she could think of was to have it at the entrance to the church. That way, it could be used as a photo opportunity, and it could be displayed in all its glory, but it wouldn't clash with the interior or disrupt the wedding ceremony itself.

But Max probably wouldn't go for that either. With a sigh, she put her measuring tape away. *Maybe my measurements are off.* After all, she hadn't actually measured the arch itself and had relied on estimations of its size.

The door to the church opened, and Lanie and Nate came in, followed by the preacher. Plastering a smile on her face, Carissa stood.

"All set?" she asked.

"Reverend Patrick believes we are fit to be married," Lanie replied, beaming. She took Nate's hand. "But he did want to discuss your idea of blocking the right aisle."

"We have had several couples who have voiced your same concerns," Reverend Patrick began. "And I've found that strategically placed decor seems to be just the ticket to discourage guests from using the right pews without marring the beauty of the sanctuary." He gestured behind him. "Come with me, and I'll show you photographs from past weddings."

"He showed them to us already," Lanie said. "But you might have a better idea of how to incorporate what others have done into my vision."

Carissa followed the preacher. His office was small and simply set up. A wooden desk sat a few feet out from the back wall with a simple upholstered chair that had seen better days behind it. On the other side were two straight-backed chairs. In one corner was a bookshelf with several versions of the Bible, a few hymnbooks, and some devotionals.

On the desk lay several photo albums that had been opened to specific collages of weddings, and beside those was a document entitled Marriage Contract. She hid a smile. Though she didn't see it often these days, it had been more popular when she'd first started in wedding planning. The document wasn't legally binding but was meant to serve as a vehicle to talk to couples about what marriage was like and what was expected of each party. Unlike the Catholic version of premarital counseling and the agreement of a covenant, it was a symbolic gesture to demonstrate a couple's willingness to enter into matrimony.

"Have a seat," Reverend Patrick said.

She took the seat nearest the door. "Do you keep photos from all of the weddings you host here?"

"If the bride and groom are willing to donate them," he replied with a smile. "But we respect their wishes if they do not want to provide photos, and we don't take our own." Leaning forward, he pointed at a photo at the top of the album page. "Here, they strung tulle down both sides of the aisle to block the seats. While that's not exactly what you're going for, it would signal to guests to return to the main aisle." He flipped a page. "And here, they put up a simple sign asking people to sit on the other side of the church."

Both options seemed appropriate for what Lanie hoped to accomplish, but the image of the arch kept intruding on Carissa's thoughts. She studied the reverend. Max had forbidden her from telling Lanie, but he hadn't said she couldn't discuss it at all. Reverend Patrick would know better than anyone whether such a thing would work in his church.

"What about an archway that directs people down the aisle we want them to use?"

Reverend Patrick raised an eyebrow. "What sort of archway?"

A ridiculous one. But she kept that comment to herself. "A large wooden one. Roughly seven feet high by five feet wide." When he didn't immediately answer, she continued, "I can get more accurate measurements and a photo to give you a better idea."

He leaned back in his chair and tented his fingers. "Lanie didn't mention an archway."

"That's because she doesn't know." Now, she was treading on dangerous territory. Technically, if the reverend told Lanie, it wasn't necessarily Carissa's fault. However, since he knew about the archway only because of her, she doubted Max would see it that way. "Her father is a skilled woodworker, and as a surprise gift, he's decided to build an archway. He wants to incorporate it into the ceremony, but it likely won't fit at the front of the church, nor do I believe Lanie would want it there. However, if it would fit, putting it in front of an aisle may be a compromise he's willing to accept."

Pursing his lips, Reverend Patrick stared at the ceiling. Carissa wondered if he was consulting God, but she assumed he was just considering the request.

"It's hard to say without actually seeing the structure." Shifting forward, he rested his hands on the desk. "Get a picture and the precise measurements, and we'll figure out a way to make it work."

"Thank you, Reverend." She stood to leave then glanced back. "Please keep this between us. I'd hate to ruin the surprise for Lanie."

He smiled. "My lips are sealed."

As Carissa left the office, she felt like a weight had been lifted from her shoulders. At least she could say she'd done everything in her power to help Max with his surprise and maintained her client's vision. A small smile tugged at her lips. In some ways, she supposed she'd left the situation with God.

Chapter Twenty-Five

DESPITE HIS ATTEMPTS TO THROW HIMSELF INTO CARVING the arch, Max hadn't quite been able to ignore the bitter silence that hung between him and Carissa. As the days turned into one week then two, Max tried to accept that whatever had been building between them was over.

Her harsh words still echoed in his head every time he worked on the arch. *Before you waste any more time.* A few times, he'd considered leaving the arch unfinished and giving Lanie the desk she'd mentioned. He'd even started building a desk just in case. But his heart wasn't in that. The arch was not only different and unique, but it was also a symbol of the marriage he hoped his daughter would have—two halves that could stand completely on their own but worked together to make something truly beautiful.

Of course, he couldn't completely avoid any mention of Carissa. Lanie kept him informed of the wedding planning progress, and from their conversations, he learned bits and pieces about how Carissa's life was going.

One night at dinner, about a week before Thanksgiving, Lanie propped her chin on her hand. "I was thinking of asking Carissa to

Thanksgiving." At his expression, she frowned. "Don't look at me like that. She doesn't have any family here, and I bet she gets lonely during the holidays. Besides, the two of you seemed to be getting along better."

"It's your first Thanksgiving since you graduated," Max said, avoiding responding to his daughter directly. "I'd rather keep it to family."

"But we always have more than enough food," Lanie protested. "I'm sure Rose and Steven won't mind."

"*I* mind," Max cut in more forcefully than he'd intended. Lanie's eyes widened, and he was filled with regret. "I'm sorry. It's not a good idea."

"Why not?"

He shoved a forkful of chicken into his mouth to buy himself some time. *Why, indeed.* He would have to tread lightly, or Lanie would get suspicious.

Since Lanie wasn't aware of their many outings together, he figured it couldn't hurt to pretend he and Carissa meant nothing to each other. "While I've tolerated her for your sake, I suspect I'm the last person Carissa would want to spend a holiday with."

"That's an assumption on your part. You don't know it for sure."

"Trust me, it's not an assumption," he muttered. The memory of Carissa's face when he'd asked her to leave flashed through his mind.

"You don't even have to talk to her. She'll sit at the other end of the table with Rose and me." She leaned forward, and her hazel eyes pleaded with his. "Please, Dad. No one should have to spend the holidays alone."

His resolve faltered. The last thing he wanted to do was have an awkward dinner on one of his favorite holidays, but Lanie was right. After the divorce, he'd spent too many holidays alone when Melody had the kids. He remembered how lonely he'd been back then, and he wouldn't wish that on anyone.

"Fine," he said reluctantly. "You can ask her, but don't be surprised if she says no."

Lanie brightened. "Thank you."

Max grumbled a response, but inside, he was a mess. His only hope was that Carissa would want to avoid an awkward family dinner as much as he did. Otherwise, he suspected the night would only end in disaster.

The Monday before Thanksgiving, Max headed to the grocery store to grab the last few items he planned to serve at the feast. Lanie hadn't mentioned whether she'd spoken to Carissa yet, and he wanted to make sure they had plenty of food.

The store traffic was light. One of the many benefits of retirement was the ability to shop on a weekday morning. After grabbing a cart, Max steered it toward the produce aisle.

"Hello, Max," a familiar voice said behind him.

Max froze. Squeezing his eyes shut, he held his breath. As if he could make Carissa disappear. Or at the very least, make himself invisible. But when she tapped her foot, he realized his actions were futile, and he slowly turned to face her.

"I haven't heard from you in a while," she said when he didn't speak.

"I could say the same about you." His back was ramrod straight, which made him appear even taller than normal. Some people might be intimidated by his height, but Carissa didn't seem to notice.

At the sight of her, a wave of emotions ripped through him. Her gray hair was pulled back from her face in a messy bun, and her eyes seemed duller than usual, like she hadn't been sleeping well. His hands ached to touch her, but he crossed his arms to keep from giving in to temptation.

"That's fair." She bit her lip. "I'm sorry for how I reacted to the arch."

"Did you tell Lanie about it?" he asked, cringing at how desperate he sounded.

"Of course not." Her eyes rose to meet his. "I promised I wouldn't."

For a moment, they stood in uncomfortable silence. He knew he should ask her about Thanksgiving, but he couldn't quite bring himself to do so. When he couldn't bear her presence anymore, he slipped behind the handle of his cart and aimed it at the other end of the aisle.

"Wait," Carissa said, so softly that he thought for a moment he'd imagined it.

He glanced back at her. His hands tightened on the plastic handle, causing it to squeak under the pressure. "Yes?"

"I spoke to the reverend at the church." Her hands fiddled with the plastic on a bag of bread sitting in the top of her cart. "We're trying to figure out how to incorporate the arch into the ceremony."

"You told him?" Max's heart sank. The more people who knew, the more likely Lanie would find out and the surprise would be ruined.

"He promised he wouldn't say anything," she said as if reading his mind. "But I was wondering if it would be okay if I stopped by to measure it. We need an accurate understanding of how much space is required."

Max hesitated. That moment was simultaneously the perfect opportunity to ask Carissa to join them for Thanksgiving and the worst possible time to do so. They were barely able to speak to each other. Spending more time with him was clearly the last thing on her mind.

And yet... Seeing her there, he realized how much he missed her. While her initial reaction still stung, realizing she'd spent some of their time apart brainstorming ways to blend his gift into Lanie's vision of her wedding touched his heart. Perhaps olive branches came in unexpected ways.

"Max?" Carissa prompted.

"That would be fine." He cleared his throat. "How would you like to spend Thanksgiving with the McAllisters?"

Her eyes widened with what he hoped was surprise. “I wouldn’t want to intrude on your holiday.”

“It’s no intrusion. We would love to have you.” Lanie’s words came back to him, and he repeated them to Carissa. “No one should be alone for the holidays.”

Her lips curved into a tentative smile. “Thank you for thinking of me. I would love to.”

Though her response lacked the enthusiasm she’d had the last time he’d invited her over, Max’s chest warmed. “Great. Dinner is at five.”

She chewed her lower lip, and Max was distracted by the movement. Desire swam in his belly at the thought of kissing those lips again, but he forced himself to refocus.

“Do you need me to bring anything?”

“Only if there’s something you’d like to bring.” He gestured to the cart. “We’ve got the rest covered.”

“Sounds great. I’ll see you then.”

On Thanksgiving Day, Max was up with the sun to start preparations for the feast. Every year the kids were with him for the holiday, he and Lanie had the same routine. The day before, she would make deviled eggs and pumpkin pie. In the morning, Max would get up and set the turkey out to rest on the counter while he made pumpkin pancakes for breakfast. Then, once the turkey was in the oven and breakfast was cleaned up, they all gathered in the living room and watched the Macy’s parade.

After the parade, he planned to spend the rest of the afternoon helping Lanie in the kitchen. She made the rolls from scratch, while he made the other sides. He had a buffet server Crock-Pot that he used to make slow-cooker macaroni and cheese, green beans, and stuffing. When the turkey was almost done, Lanie would boil sweet potatoes and make a casserole. The minute the turkey came out of the oven, the casserole and the rolls would go in. They were like a well-oiled machine.

Of course, last year, Lanie hadn't come home. With Rose's help, he and Steven had tried to recreate the tradition, but it had turned into a huge mess. Somehow, the turkey was both burnt and undercooked, the sweet potatoes exploded in the oven, and each boiled egg had ripped apart when he tried to pull the yolk out. Max was glad Lanie was back and hoped things would go more smoothly.

As he removed the turkey from the fridge, a door opened upstairs. A moment later, Lanie appeared in the kitchen doorway, rubbing her eyes.

"Have you started on breakfast yet?" she asked with a yawn.

"Was just about to." Max set the turkey on the counter and preheated the oven. "If you want to start frying the bacon, that would be great."

With a sleepy nod, Lanie poured herself a cup of coffee before setting up the griddle on the stove. As he worked quietly next to his daughter, a sense of peace washed over him. Thanksgiving was his favorite holiday for many reasons. Although Christmas was also a family holiday, he found the rampant consumerism associated with it off-putting. In contrast, Thanksgiving was a more relaxed get-together.

He chuckled to himself. *Well, if you don't count the stress of cooking and the cleanup.* Still, the expectations were different, and people tended to linger, whether because they were too full of the feast or simply able to enjoy the company of family.

Just as he flipped the last pancake, the front door swung open. Steven's voice carried through the house as he and Rose made their way to the kitchen. Rose carried an apple pie, and Steven had several grocery bags in his hands.

"Lanie asked me to pick up a few things," Steven said as he set the bags on the floor. He sniffed the air appreciatively. "Did you make enough for us?"

"Of course." Max carried the plate of pancakes and set it on the table next to the bacon Lanie had made. "There's fresh coffee in the pot."

"Don't mind if I do." Steven poured mugs for Rose and himself and took them to the table. "No Nate this morning?"

"He'll be by later." Lanie passed him the butter. "He planned to visit his parents first."

"And he didn't invite you?" Rose asked.

Shaking her head, Lanie took a bite of pancake. "He did, but I told him I have too much to do here." She turned to Max. "This is delicious, Dad."

"Don't act so surprised," Max grumbled, though he couldn't help smiling.

After finishing one pancake, Steven reached for another. "Is it just the five of us, then?"

Instead of answering, Max lifted his coffee and drained the liquid. Lanie bit her lip, and Max wondered if she hadn't had a chance to talk to Carissa.

"Um, we might have one more," he finally said.

Rose tilted her head. "Who?"

Keeping his eyes on his food, Max answered, "I asked Carissa to join us."

While Lanie's eyes lit with a happy surprise, Steven exchanged a wary look with Rose. "You two are spending quite a bit of time together."

"I've been making an effort to get along with her," Max said. "For Lanie's sake."

"You two seemed pretty cozy when we were at the festival." Rose gave him a secretive grin that suggested she knew he wasn't being entirely truthful.

"We're just friends," he insisted, though he wasn't even sure that was true anymore. But Carissa had agreed to join their holiday festivities, and that gave him hope.

Before anyone could further comment on his and Carissa's relationship, he stood. "I, uh, need to start on the dishes if we want to watch the parade."

Thankfully, his children didn't push him on the issue, and the rest of the day went as planned. As the clock ticked closer to five, his stomach began tying itself in knots. The meal was on schedule, and everything had turned out beautifully, thanks to Lanie, but Max couldn't help worrying about what might happen when Carissa arrived. Would they be able to move past the arch-shaped elephant that stood between them?

A few minutes before five, the doorbell rang. Max wiped his sweaty palms on his jeans and prepared to answer the door, but Lanie got there first. He stood in the hallway as his daughter wrapped Carissa in a warm hug.

"Happy Thanksgiving!" Lanie cried.

"Happy Thanksgiving." Carissa's voice was more subdued as her eyes met Max's. "I brought a pecan pie and homemade cranberry sauce." She shifted her weight to her other foot. "I hope that's all right."

"Homemade cranberry sauce?" Steven turned in his chair in the living room and raised an eyebrow. "Doesn't everyone eat the kind that comes in a can?"

Carissa gave a nervous laugh. "It's my mother's recipe."

"I'm sure it'll be delicious." Lanie took the bags from Carissa and led her into the kitchen. "I'm glad you were able to make it."

"Thanks for inviting me." As she stepped into the kitchen, Carissa's eyes widened. "Wow. That's a lot of food." Her gaze found Max's again. "You really go all out."

"We haven't eaten since breakfast," Max explained. "We save our calories for the meal. Did you want something to drink?"

"White wine if you've got it."

Max removed the bottle from the fridge and poured Carissa a glass. He was thankful to have an excuse to turn away from her. She looked absolutely radiant in a simple blue dress with a matching jacket. Her hair was pulled away from her face with a clip, showing off her high cheekbones. It had taken everything in his power not to reach for her the moment she set foot in the house.

As he handed her the glass, their fingers brushed, and a jolt of electricity shot up his arm. He wished he could have a moment alone with her, to hash out what was wrong between them as well as to kiss her senseless.

She stared at him, and the same yearning he felt was reflected in her eyes. The beep of the oven timer broke the spell, and they glanced away from each other.

"That's dinner!" Lanie removed the sweet potato casserole and rolls from the oven and set them on the counter.

Grateful for a distraction, Max rushed to help her carry the food into the dining room. Steven and Rose came in from the living room and took their seats on one side of the table with Lanie and Nate on the other. That left Carissa and Max to sit at opposite ends.

A flash of memory shot through Max as he realized no one had occupied that seat since Melody. Seeing Carissa sitting there caused an avalanche of emotions to come crashing through him all at once. Sorrow at what he'd lost after his divorce. Joy at seeing the seat filled once more with someone who had stolen his heart. Hope that Carissa's presence was the promise of something new and beautiful. And fear that he had already screwed it up.

"Dad?" Lanie prompted, bringing him back to the present. "Are you going to carve the turkey?"

With a gruff nod, he picked up the carving knife and a fork and began slicing the meat from the bird. Everyone passed their plates and called out whether they wanted light or dark meat. Once everyone had turkey, other sides were passed around. Max finished carving the last of the turkey and tossed out the bones.

His children and their partners had already begun digging into the food when Max finally had a chance to fill his plate with the rest of the sides. As he lifted his fork, he caught Carissa staring at him.

"Everything all right?" he asked.

She glanced at the two couples sitting on opposite sides of the table before clearing her throat. "Do you not say grace?"

"Um..." Lanie set down her silverware. "Not usually, but we can if you'd like."

Steven smiled. "Our tradition is to say what we're thankful for after the meal."

"But Carissa is our guest." Rose gestured to her. "Would you like to say grace?"

The way Carissa's eyes widened suggested to Max she was wishing she hadn't said anything. He had opened his mouth to save her when she nodded.

"Dear Heavenly Father." She bowed her head. "We give thanks for this bountiful feast prepared by loving hands. We give thanks for this time with our family and friends. We ask that you bless those who are gathered here and those we have lost but still hold in our hearts. Amen."

As Max raised his head, he fought back the tears Carissa's words had brought forth. Despite being raised Catholic, he'd never been a religious man. But the simple prayer Carissa had offered reminded him so much of Melody that for a moment, it'd felt like she was still in the room with them. Her faith, even at the end, had been steadfast.

Everyone began eating again, but a much more somber mood filled the room. Carissa gave him an apologetic smile, but he shook his head. Her prayer was beautiful in its simplicity. And it made him realize that while he missed Melody terribly, there was no doubt in his mind he was ready to take a second chance at love—and all that came with it.

Chapter Twenty-Six

After dinner, Carissa offered to help with the dishes, but Steven and Nate shooed her and everyone else out of the kitchen.

"Since we didn't help with the cooking, the least we can do is the cleaning," Steven said as he filled the sink with soapy water.

Rose and Lanie claimed the couch and talked excitedly in low voices. While Max sank heavily into his recliner, he kept his gaze on Carissa.

"Take a load off," he said, gesturing to the other recliner.

But she couldn't sit still. As happy as she was not to have to spend another holiday alone, she couldn't ignore the last time she'd been in that house with Max and all the things they'd said. They needed to talk.

"I need to burn off some calories," she said with what she hoped was a lighthearted smile. "Want to go for a walk with me?"

To her surprise, he jumped out of his chair. "Absolutely."

She started for the door. *Don't be rude.* With a sinking heart, she turned to Lanie and Rose. "We're going for a walk. Do you want to join us?"

The two women exchanged a glance then looked at Max. Their eyes widened, and they shook their heads as if Max's expression had made their decision for them. But when Carissa glanced at him, he had a pleasant smile on his face.

"Shall we?" he asked.

They grabbed their coats and headed out the front door. Once they were safely on the sidewalk, Max tentatively took her hand.

"I'm glad you came tonight." He kissed her cheek. The slightest peck, but it sent shivers down her spine. "I don't like how we left things the last time."

"Me either," she breathed, momentarily forgetting her apprehension about the evening.

"I should have reached out." His eyes were filled with sorrow. "Our first contact after the argument shouldn't have been in a supermarket, though I hope to make it up to you."

Her heart fluttered. "What did you have in mind?"

A slow smile stole over his face, but he shook his head. "We'll get to that later. For now, we should probably talk."

"I'm sorry for what I said about you wasting your time with the arch," Carissa began. "I'm concerned we either won't be able to fit it into the church or it won't be done in time to do so." She frowned. "I wish you had told me before you started working on it. I could have helped you."

Max sighed. "In retrospect, I should have included you in my plans. I was so focused on keeping it a secret from Lanie, I didn't think about the impact it would have on your work."

"I appreciate that." They strolled through Max's neighborhood, and Carissa took a deep breath of cool air. "Before I leave tonight, I'd like to get the measurements of the arch. I can take them to the church tomorrow."

"As long as we can wait until Lanie is otherwise distracted, that sounds fine."

She gave a short nod. While she appreciated how much Max

wanted to surprise his daughter, logistically, he couldn't keep it from her for much longer. For one thing, he was storing the arch in their garage, and it wouldn't take much for Lanie to stumble upon it. Then there was the fact he'd promised to tell Lanie before the wedding, and as they were approaching the end of November, time was running out.

Carissa supposed she could come back on Monday when Lanie would be at school, but the longer she put off measuring the arch, the less time Max would have to make something else. Though at that point, she wasn't sure he *could* do something else even if he wanted to, which he clearly didn't.

When they got back to the house, Lanie and Nate were already cutting into the pies. Steven and Rose sat at the table, enjoying a glass of wine.

"Welcome back," Lanie said as Carissa and Max entered the kitchen.

Carissa detected a hint of suspicion in Lanie's eyes, but she only asked, "Pumpkin, apple, or pecan?"

"Apple," Max said without hesitation.

"I'll try the pumpkin." Carissa had never been a fan of apple pie.

After Lanie handed them their plates, they took their seats at the table and dug in. The pie was the perfect blend of sweet and savory. She was surprised at how quickly she gobbled it up considering she was still full of dinner.

When everyone had finished their desserts, their little group began to break apart. Steven and Rose said their farewells and headed home. Lanie and Nate finished cleaning the last of the dishes.

As Carissa left the kitchen, Max took her hand. "Perhaps now is a good time for you to measure the arch."

She allowed him to lead her into the garage. The moment he removed the sheet from the arch, she gasped at the progress he'd made. One side was almost finished, with intricate roses and vines. The only part he hadn't carved was the top of the curve.

Without a word, he handed her a tape measure, a notepad, and a piece of paper. She got to work measuring the arch and comparing it to the measurements she'd taken at the church.

"So, what's the verdict?" Max leaned against one of the finished nightstands.

She flicked her gaze back and forth between the measurements she'd scrawled on the paper and the ones from the church. It didn't look good.

He raised an eyebrow. "Does it pass muster?"

To buy herself some time, she remeasured a few sections just in case, but they only confirmed what she already knew. Her mind raced through different tactful ways she could explain her concerns.

"I need to go to the church to measure the doors and one other area where it might work," she began before shaking her head. "But I can tell you that even if we can get the pieces inside the church, it's not going to fit."

"Even though the pieces can be separated?"

"It's too wide." She handed him both the paper with the arch measurements and the church measurements. "The church's aisles are narrow. It would fit near the handicap entrance, as that is wide enough for a wheelchair, but that's on the other side of the stage from where the ceremony will take place."

He waved a dismissive hand. "I'm sure we'll find a way, but I'm happy to come to the church with you to troubleshoot."

"That won't be necessary," she said quickly. "Besides, it might look suspicious if we're both there. Wouldn't want it getting back to Lanie and ruining your surprise."

His eyes narrowed in apparent suspicion, but he nodded. "Fair enough. Let me know what you find."

"I will. I promise."

~

Carissa wasted no time getting to the church the next day to compare the measurements. The church was empty when she arrived, though she assumed most people were Black Friday shopping. She'd called ahead to Reverend Patrick to make sure the building was open, and she'd hoped she could get in and out without too much fuss.

After setting her purse on a pew, she walked to the railing that separated the sanctuary from the congregation. At Steven and Rose's wedding, they had stood on one side of the railing in the center, and Reverend Patrick was on the opposite side on the slightly elevated platform.

Lanie wanted to be married at the small opening to the right of the elevated area near the choir loft, but Carissa might be able to convince her to move to the center. *Best to measure both to be safe.*

After surveying the measurements and looking at the spaces, Carissa determined the arch would fit better nearer the congregation, but it wouldn't leave much room in the front pew for people to sit. As she'd suspected, the only other place it would fit was near the handicap entrance, which would allow it to be in the church but not part of the ceremony.

On the other hand, if Max could narrow the arch, it would fit in that small opening by the choir. The preacher could stand on the step, and the arch could be placed where Lanie and Nate would stand. She tilted her head. *Though they might have to stand in front of it if it's too narrow.*

With a sigh, she headed to the back of the church and measured the entryway just to be sure. The moment she began measuring, the door to the church opened, and in walked Lanie.

"Carissa, I'm glad I ran into you. I want to—" Her eyebrows pulled together. "What on earth are you doing?"

"Uh, I-I needed to measure the church."

"For what?" Lanie asked, her frown deepening.

Carissa's mind raced, but she couldn't come up with a lie fast enough. Besides, she didn't *want* to lie to her client, even if it meant breaking her promise to Max. Her reputation was built on being forthright and honest no matter the circumstances.

Lowering her arms in defeat, Carissa took a deep breath. “I’m not supposed to tell you this, but I imagine you’ll find out soon enough anyway.” She gestured to a pew, and Lanie sat, her bewildered expression growing more pronounced.

“Your father is building you a wedding arch.” Carissa sank into the pew beside Lanie. “I tried to talk him out of it, but it’s a surprise wedding gift for you.” She then explained why she was there and what she was doing by measuring the church.

“And he didn’t think to discuss this with me?” Lanie’s face reddened.

“He was going to tell you when he finished it.” Carissa put a hand on Lanie’s shoulder. “I’m sorry. I shouldn’t have told you.”

“No, you did the right thing.” Lanie’s eyes flashed as she glared at the front of the church. “Of course he would pull something like this. First, he bullies his way into paying for Steven’s rehearsal dinner. Then he has to put his two cents into everything we’re doing, despite repeated requests from both of us that he back off. And now, he’s completely changing the decor of my wedding without even asking me.” She scowled. “Clearly, we need to have a come-to-Jesus meeting.”

“He’s not going to be happy I told you,” Carissa warned.

“Is he working on it in the garage?”

“Yes. He covers it with a sheet, but its height is impossible to miss.”

“Then it’s easy enough for me to happen upon it myself.” Lanie glanced at Carissa, her expression softening. “He never needs to know you told me.”

At first, Carissa breathed a sigh of relief, then she shook her head. “No, it’s better if you tell him the truth. I’ll deal with any fallout later.”

With a nod, Lanie stood. “All right. Well, wish me luck.”

Carissa blinked. “You’re going now?”

"I'm hoping to catch him in the act." Without another word, Lanie spun on her heel and stalked out of the church.

Lord help us. Bowing her head, Carissa sent up a prayer she hadn't just blown up two relationships. But she wasn't holding out much hope.

Chapter Twenty-Seven

MAX WAS METICULOUSLY CARVING A HEART INTO THE SIDE of the arch when the door from the house to the garage swung open. His heart stopped when he caught sight of his daughter's face.

"Lanie, wha—" Although he knew it was too late, he threw the cover over the arch in a half-hearted attempt to hide it.

"It's true, then?" she demanded as she rushed into the room and yanked the sheet away. "You've been building this behind my back?"

"H-how'd you find out?"

Instead of answering, she took a deep breath as if to calm herself. "Does it matter? The fact is, I know, and I don't appreciate you trying to make such a major change to the layout of the ceremony without consulting me."

Max held his hands up. "Now, hold on. I'm doing something nice for you." He touched the wood. "It's a gift."

"That you decided to create without any forethought into whether it would fit into the church, let alone with the rest of the decor?"

Something about the way she spoke sounded suspiciously like Carissa. He narrowed his eyes. "She told you, didn't she?"

"Again, it doesn't matter how I found out, though I would love to know why you told her and not me." Lanie crossed her arms. "But we'll deal with that later. Right now, we're talking about *you*. What were you thinking?"

"I wanted to do something nice for my daughter," he retorted. "Though I didn't realize how ungrateful she would be to receive it."

"Ungrateful?" Her eyes widened in disbelief. "This isn't like a table or chair Nate and I could incorporate into the wedding and then use in our future home." She held up her hands to try to capture the sheer size of the arch. "How are we supposed to fit this in Nate's house, let alone the church?"

Pain stabbed in his gut at her sharp words. Of all the reactions he'd expected Lanie to have, he'd never expected that one.

When he didn't say anything else, she let out an exasperated sigh. "Why couldn't you have at least talked to me before you went to all this trouble? I love what you've done with the pieces you recently finished. I would have been happy to have something similar as a wedding gift."

"But I wanted to be part of your big day," he blurted out as he spun around. The realization of what he'd said hit him, and he hurried on. "I mean, I wanted *it* to be part of your day. The arch."

The flush of anger on her cheeks faded as she bit her lip. "You didn't need to make anything to be part of the day." She moved toward him and placed a hand on his arm. "You're walking me down the aisle and dancing with me at the reception."

"I know," he said gruffly, shaking her off. "I wanted to give you something that showed how much I love you." He glanced at the arch. "I could try to make it smaller—"

"It won't work, Dad," she said sharply. But he must have flinched because her face softened. "I'm sorry to be harsh. This isn't what I envisioned, and it doesn't go with the rest of the aesthetic."

"Fine." He threw the cover over the arch and stomped out of the garage, calling over his shoulder, "I'll figure something else out."

But his attempt to get away from her was thwarted when she

followed him. "Why did you tell Carissa and not me?" She grabbed his arm. "Is something going on between you two?"

He froze before slowly turning to meet her gaze. "Why do you ask that?"

She frowned. "Something Rose said at Thanksgiving, that you two would make a cute couple. Then you went for a walk alone at dinner, and you were gone for a while." She studied his face. "There is something, isn't there?" Tears sprang to her eyes as the realization fully hit. "You're dating? After I specifically asked you not to?"

"You wanted me to put myself out there," he mumbled, shoving his hands into his pockets.

"With anyone but her!" Lanie's hands balled into fists at her sides. "I can't believe you did this to me. I thought we were getting closer. I thought—"

"It doesn't matter anyway because clearly, she and I aren't going to work out." He was unable to keep the bitterness out of his tone, but at least it masked the pain.

"Great." Lanie put her hands on her hips. "The whole reason I asked you not to date her was to *avoid* making things awkward at the wedding. So thanks for ruining that plan."

"Well, you won't have to worry about that," Max said, his anger getting the better of him. "Because I'm not going to your wedding!"

The words came out before he could stop them. Lanie's face crumpled, and without another word, she fled the room. The front door slammed, and a moment later, an engine started.

Max leaned against the counter and buried his head in his hands. The arch was supposed to be symbolic, a way to bridge the divide between him and his daughter.

Congratulations, old man. You just burned that bridge.

An hour later, Max had stewed in his emotions long enough. He grabbed a coat and headed out into the chilly autumn air to confront Carissa.

On the way to her house, he rehearsed what he wanted to say. But the more he recalled her betrayal, the angrier he became. By the time he roared into her driveway, he was practically spitting fire.

He didn't even make it to the front door before she swung it open and came out. Her hands were lifted, whether in surrender or to fend him off, he couldn't tell.

"I'm sorry," she said quickly. "I ran into Lanie at the church, and I couldn't lie to her about why I was there."

"Why not?" he demanded. "There are a million reasons you might be at that church that had nothing to do with her. Why couldn't you have said you were there for another bride? Or you needed to check in with the reverend about something?" He glared at her. "You promised me you wouldn't tell her."

Instead of cowering under his berating questions, she lifted her chin. "Lanie is my client. She is paying me to assist her with her wedding. It's one thing to ask me not to say anything to her, but it's quite another to insist I lie when directly questioned."

"So it's okay to lie to me, then?"

Carissa's eyes flashed. "I didn't lie to you. I did everything in my power to keep your secret." She crossed her arms. "But it was a fool's errand to expect Lanie wouldn't find out about the arch. You live with her for goodness' sake. You don't think at some point she might have grown curious about what you were working on in the garage?"

Warmth rushed to his cheeks, but Max shook his head. "She hasn't yet, and I've been working on the arch for over a month now."

"And we've still got about a month until the wedding. A lot can happen even in that short amount of time."

"Well, count me out."

Her mouth fell open. "What is that supposed to mean?"

"I'm done with it." At Carissa's bewildered expression, he continued, "All of it. If my work isn't good enough for her wedding, then clearly, neither am I."

Carissa pursed her lips. "Did Lanie say she didn't want you in her wedding?"

"She might as well have." Max ignored the heaviness in his stomach. It wouldn't surprise him in the least if Lanie decided not to have him at her wedding after the way he'd behaved. But Carissa didn't need to know that part.

"Give her time," Carissa said. "I'm sure you both said some things you didn't mean and—"

"Don't lecture me about how to handle my daughter."

Her mouth turned down. "I'm not." She gestured behind her. "Look, why don't you come in, and we can talk about—"

"No, thank you." Max straightened his spine. "As you said, Lanie is your client, and it wouldn't be appropriate." He headed to his car.

"Max, wait!"

But he didn't stop. As he drove away, he tried to hold on to his anger to counteract the pain.

When he returned home, he wasn't surprised to find Lanie wasn't there. She would probably stay the night with Rose and Steven. Guilt needled his belly, though he tried to ignore it.

His phone vibrated. At the sight of Carissa's name, he almost turned it off, but the beginning of the text message caught his attention.

FYI, the arch won't fit in the church. Not sure it matters at this point, but here are the measurements.

When he tapped the message, he saw that the arch was about two feet too wide. He sighed and leaned his head back against the seat. She was right. It didn't matter now.

For a moment, he considered burning the arch. Then he imagined chopping it into smaller pieces and using it for firewood. He climbed out of his truck and went into the house as visions of destruction danced in his head.

Though it was nearing dinnertime, he wasn't hungry. And he'd had more than his fair share of cooking for one after his divorce. He headed into the garage and leaned against the wall, allowing his eyes to move from the arch to the desk and back again.

The desk likely didn't need half as much work as it would take for him to remove two feet of wood from the arch. But even if he hadn't blown up two relationships in one afternoon, he couldn't quite bring himself to work on the desk. While Lanie was right in that the desk would be useful beyond the wedding, it didn't feel big enough for what he wanted to do.

A car door slammed on the other side of the garage door, and Max rushed into the house with his heart in his throat. The crushing disappointment was only slightly buoyed by the sight of his son.

"Steven," he said. "What a nice surprise."

A muscle feathered in Steven's jaw as he entered the house. "I'm afraid it's not a social call."

Max's smile faded, and he gestured for Steven to go ahead of him into the living room. "I assume Lanie visited you."

"Well, she came to talk to Rose," Steven corrected. "But I closed the office for Black Friday, so I was home." With a sigh, he sank onto the couch. "Dad, what were you thinking?"

Crossing his arms, Max prepared to dig in his heels once more. "I wanted it to be a surprise."

"I'm not talking about the arch, though I'll get to that in a minute." Steven leaned forward. "I mean telling your only daughter you don't want to be at her wedding. She's already struggling with the fact that one parent *can't* be there, and now the other parent is choosing not to be."

A lump formed in his throat. In all his righteous anger, Max hadn't once considered how hard planning a wedding must be for Lanie without her mother. Melody had had such grand plans for her children's weddings, including a dance with both of them.

"I didn't mean it," he said. "Her reaction upset me, and I spoke without thinking."

Raising one eyebrow, Steven shook his head. "That seems to be your MO lately."

"What's that supposed to mean?"

"Exactly what it sounds like." Steven raked a hand through his hair. "You could have talked to me about the surprise you were planning. I would have been happy to steer you in a direction that would have both fit her wedding theme and served a functional purpose in her new life." He rolled his eyes. "I've heard more about floral arrangements and color coordination than I ever expected to in my young life, but it's all she and Rose talk about."

"I didn't want to tell people because I was afraid Lanie would find out," Max said, feeling like a broken record.

"And I would have kept your secret. You could have even stored it at my house."

"What if Rose found out and told her?"

Steven's expression darkened. "First, I don't appreciate your lack of faith in my wife. And second, I have my hiding places. Rose rarely goes into the basement because she thinks it's creepy."

"But my tools are here," Max protested feebly. It became clearer with each passing moment that he wasn't going to win the argument.

"All I'm saying is you could have handled this differently." Steven's eyes softened. "You and Lanie haven't always had the best of relationships, and I understand why you wanted to do this for her." He took a deep breath. "But a true gift shouldn't be about you and your desire to fix things. It should be about the person receiving the gift." A quiet chuckle. "Believe me, I learned that the hard way with Rose. I almost worked myself into an early grave trying to give her what *I* thought she needed rather than letting her tell me about her needs in her own way."

"It's a bit late for that now," Max grumbled.

"It's never too late to fix a mistake. Take Rose and me. It took her breaking off our engagement for me to see reason, but I did." Steven smiled. "And now we're married."

As much as Max hated to admit it, his son had a point. Still, Steven had had an easier time mending his relationship with Rose. They'd been together only a few years, and the conflict they faced was a recent development. In contrast, Max's relationship with Lanie had been steadily deteriorating for over a decade.

"And what's this I hear about you and Carissa?" Steven asked when Max didn't respond.

Pressing his lips together, Max stared at the floor and refused to answer. But if his son's groan was any indication, he didn't need to.

"I'm glad you're dating again, but I don't understand why you couldn't tell me everything."

With a sigh, Max raised his head and met his son's stare. "I promised Lanie I wouldn't date her wedding planner, and honestly, when I made that promise, Carissa was the last person I ever considered dating. But... things happened."

"Is it safe to assume you blew things with her as well?"

Max crossed his arms. "Only because she broke her promise not to tell Lanie about the arch."

Steven stared at him with wide eyes. "Are you for real? She's employed by Lanie. It's her job to keep the bride up to date about the goings-on of her wedding. You literally asked her not to do what Lanie is paying her for. If she'd lied to Lanie, she would have risked her position over it. Her livelihood."

"A text message warning me Lanie was on the warpath would have been nice."

"Perhaps, but you aren't her client. She's under no obligation."

"But we're in a relationship. Shouldn't that count for something?" The argument sounded worse out loud than it had in Max's head.

Steven grimaced. "Well... You *were* in a relationship."

That's enough hard truths for one evening. Max made his way to the kitchen. "Since you're here, would you like something for dinner?"

"I could eat."

Grateful to have something to distract him, Max removed some leftover turkey from the fridge and diced it. Once the turkey was cut up, he mixed it with a can of cream of chicken soup and frozen vegetables. After assembling the mini turkey potpies in the muffin pan, he placed the pan in the oven and left it to cook.

While he waited on the potpies, he stepped outside for some fresh air. The little mourning dove was eating at one of the bird feeders. When it saw him, it flew to the railing.

"Hello again."

She cooed in response and cocked her head as if she understood him. Her gray feathers ruffled in the cool evening breeze.

"I've really done it this time." Lifting his face to the heavens, Max closed his eyes. *If Melody were here, she'd know what to do.* A soft chuckle bubbled up in his throat, and he opened his eyes. "If Melody were here, she'd probably tan my hide for treating Lanie so poorly."

The bird cooed as if in agreement, and the chuckle developed into a laugh. Max turned to look at his feathered companion.

"You have the right idea, staying single and true to your love for your lost mate." He shook his head. "Relationships are more trouble than they're worth."

Shaking its wings, the dove suddenly took flight, startling Max. A moment later, another dove joined it. They circled each other before swooping into the nest he'd seen the other day.

"Well, I'll be," Max said as the birds nestled down together. "I guess you moved on after all."

He'd never felt so alone.

Chapter Twenty-Eight

"I WANT TO THANK YOU FOR ALL YOUR HARD WORK ON this," Colin said as they finished their virtual meeting late Monday evening. "I couldn't have done it without you."

"We make a good team." Carissa leaned back in her chair and rubbed her temples, grateful that Colin didn't force her to turn her camera on when it was just the two of them. Her love life might have blown up in her face, but she was kicking butt at planning the retreat. It helped that Jacob had been caught up with another project in his office and hadn't joined the last few meetings. Working with Colin was easier when the CEO wasn't breathing down his neck.

"If you can make the latest changes to the schedule, I'll forward our slides to Jacob for approval." Colin sighed. "And then maybe you and I can take a well-deserved break for the holidays."

Her heart panged. The last thing she needed right then was a break. Staying busy kept her mind off the problems with Max. They hadn't spoken since he'd shown up at her house on Friday, but Lanie had a dress fitting the next day. She was torn between hoping Max would show up and praying he'd stay away. She wasn't sure she was ready to see him again.

"I'll get those over to you by close of business tomorrow," Carissa promised. As she disconnected from the call, she put her head on the table, promising herself she'd rest for only a moment.

The buzzing of her phone woke her, and she blinked bleary eyes into the bright morning sun. Her neck and back ached from being hunched over the table all night, and her throat was bone dry. With a groan, she stretched and glanced at her phone.

"Oh no." She was late for Lanie's fitting.

Be there in twenty, she texted. Then she ran upstairs to take a quick shower. When she left the house ten minutes later, her hair was damp. The cold wind blew the wet strands against her bare neck, making her shiver. As soon as she started the car, she cranked up the heat and prayed her hair wouldn't form icicles on the way to the dress shop.

Minutes later, she raced into the bridal shop, where Lanie stood on the pedestal in front of the mirror. Only Rose and three of Lanie's other friends sat on the benches by the pedestal. Max was nowhere to be seen.

"I'm sorry I'm late," Carissa said. "I overslept."

"That's all right. You have a lot going on." Lanie smoothed the satin skirt of her white dress. It had a sweetheart neckline with off-the-shoulder lace sleeves. "What do you think?"

Carissa put her hand to her heart and smiled. "It's perfect." Tears sprang to her eyes, and she dashed them away. *What on earth is wrong with you?* She never cried when seeing a bride in her dress.

"Should we shorten the hem?" Lanie asked, oblivious to Carissa's sudden onset of emotions. "I don't want to trip."

"Maybe just an inch?" Rose suggested as she lifted Lanie's skirt. "If you go too much shorter, it might look awkward."

The seamstress pulled Carissa aside. "We've got the bridesmaids' dresses ready for final fittings as well. Did you want us to bring those out?"

"Since the bridesmaids are here, we might as well. It'll save us a trip later." Carissa clapped. "Ladies, your dresses are ready. If you're game, we can have you try them on now to determine if there are any additional alterations needed."

"Oh, that's wonderful!" Lanie cried, hugging herself. "I can't wait to see them."

The seamstress beamed at her. "While they're changing, let's pin up your hem."

Once the room had emptied of all of Lanie's friends, Carissa sat heavily on one of the benches. Her neck and back still ached from sleeping at the table, and she wished she'd had time to grab a cup of coffee.

"I'm glad to have a moment alone with you," Lanie said. She glanced at the seamstress. "Well, semi-alone, I suppose."

"Oh?" Carissa asked, immediately on high alert. "Something on your mind?"

"I wanted to talk about my dad."

Keeping her eyes on her own reflection, Carissa nodded. "What about him?"

Lanie sighed. "We haven't spoken since he said he didn't want to go to my wedding, and now, I'm worried I won't have anyone to walk me down the aisle."

"I'm sure he just needs to cool off." Carissa tried to sound more confident than she felt. A memory of the anger and pain in Max's face flashed through her mind, and she winced. "He wouldn't miss your wedding."

"Turn, please," the seamstress said.

"You don't know how stubborn my dad is." Lanie shifted to her right.

Carissa snorted. "I have a pretty good idea."

"Would it be weird if I asked Steven?"

With a sigh, Carissa shook her head. "It wouldn't be weird, but you should give your dad some time. The wedding is still a few weeks away."

"But we're not even speaking," Lanie said mournfully. "I have no idea what to say to him anymore. He hasn't apologized for what he said, which makes me think he's stubborn enough not to attend my wedding." She sniffled. "And that really hurts."

"Maybe start with how you feel." Carissa moved beside Lanie, taking her hand. "He needs to know how this is impacting you."

"What if he doesn't care?"

A laugh bubbled up in Carissa's throat. "The man built you a seven-foot arch. Actions speak louder than words, and that action tells me he cares."

Lanie rolled her eyes. "Is it really that tall?"

"I've got the measurements right here." Carissa patted her purse.

That brought a grin to Lanie's face, but it quickly faded. "I'm struggling to get past him not telling me about the arch or the fact that you two are dating."

Carissa squeezed her hand and worked to keep her emotions in check. "For my part in that, I'm sorry. I should have kept things more professional until after your wedding was over. As for your father, give him a chance to apologize. If he won't come around, we'll figure out a contingency plan for the wedding." Her eyes filled with tears for the second time that morning. "Just know there's no replacement for your father."

The truth of her words hit her harder than she'd expected. There was no replacement for Max for her either. He'd touched her heart in a way she'd never expected, and she wished they could find a way to mend what they had broken. But at that moment, it seemed hopeless.

"All done," the seamstress said as she stood.

Lanie turned in the mirror, checking her reflection at all angles. "What do you think?"

"You look beautiful."

Chapter Twenty-Nine

MAX FELT LIKE HE'D GONE THROUGH ALL FIVE GRIEF stages since his confrontations with both Lanie and Carissa. But at least he'd made progress with Lanie. She'd agreed to have dinner with him that night, and he was determined to mend things between them.

Carissa was a different story. Every time he tried to see things from her point of view, his emotions got all mixed up again. He understood why she hadn't wanted to lie to Lanie, but would it have killed Carissa to give him a heads-up?

Steven's words echoed in Max's head. Lanie was Carissa's client, and Max was not. In the last few days, he'd realized he would always come second to her business, and he wasn't sure how he felt about that.

Her branching out into the corporate world would only make things worse. Her business was her priority. If she was successful, how long would it be before she had no time for him? *Better to rip the Band-Aid off now, forget her, and move on.*

Unfortunately, that was easier said than done. Despite how upset he was, he missed her. And the pain of missing her was sharpened by each day that passed when they didn't speak.

All those thoughts were running through his head as he parked at the supermarket to buy ingredients for his dinner with Lanie. As much as he hated to admit it, he half hoped to run into Carissa. But every time he went down an aisle, he was met with another wave of crushing disappointment.

With a sigh, he finished his shopping and headed to the checkout. Since the weather had taken a turn for the worse, a nice hearty meal of shepherd's pie might help thaw his daughter's frosty countenance toward him. He suspected Lanie had accepted his invitation only because Steven had encouraged her to.

After he checked out, he scurried to his car, anxious to get to the house. Aside from getting dinner started, he'd been splitting his woodworking between the desk and the arch. Perhaps he was a glutton for punishment, but he wasn't ready to give up on the gift he'd intended for Lanie.

Besides, Carissa's measurements had given him renewed purpose. If he could narrow the archway, it would fit in the church right where Lanie and Nate would stand. He hoped to discuss the possibility with his daughter over dinner—after he apologized profusely, of course. But since the arch was no longer a surprise, he could get her perspective. And if she hadn't warmed to the idea, then he would force himself to let go of his plans and focus on the desk instead.

When Max arrived home, he still had a few hours before he needed to get dinner started. He headed into the garage and continued his efforts to decrease the width of the archway. Inch by inch, he'd been shaving the wood on both pieces where they would meet in the middle. Once he was sure he'd narrowed the arch to the correct size, he planned to carve two heart pieces that would interlock when placed together.

As he worked, his mind kept returning to Carissa. *Wouldn't kill her to send a text.* The smooth, rhythmic movement he used to shave the wood morphed into a frenzied back-and-forth motion as his mind raced.

After all, I'm *not the one who broke the trust in our relationship.* He frowned as he recalled the way her lips had twisted when he accused her of breaking her promise. The argument was reminiscent of several he'd had with Melody during their marriage.

That was the trouble with women, and his own daughter was no exception. They seemed to think they could do no wrong, and when called out on their behavior, they flipped things around to paint the man as at fault.

Not this time. It would be a cold day in the devil's house before he would take the blame. All he'd tried to do was create something beautiful for his daughter. Max's conversation with Steven had convinced him he hadn't handled things well, but it didn't change the intent of his gift.

Max's renewed fervor paid off when he stepped back an hour later and surveyed the arch. He'd shaved off a foot on each side. After checking his measurements against Carissa's, he smiled for the first time in days. The arch was the right size. All that was left was to finish the intricate designs and the interlocking hearts.

But that would have to wait. He needed to start dinner. He headed into the house to get cleaned up. After washing his face and changing clothes, he went into the kitchen and drizzled oil into a skillet then set it on the stove to heat. Then he filled a pot with water and placed it on a burner to boil. While he waited, he chopped an onion.

Just as he'd added the onion to the pan, the front door opened. Max frowned as he stirred the onion. Lanie was early.

Her heels clicked on the linoleum in the hallway. A moment later, she peered around the wall of the kitchen and sniffed the air. "What's for dinner?"

"Shepherd's pie." Max glanced at her and stifled a sigh at the way her shoulders seemed to hug her ears. The tension in the air between them grew. *Maybe this is a bad idea.*

But he was determined to make things right with his daughter. For too long, they'd had an arm's-length relationship. He'd tried many different tactics to grow closer to her, but they all seemed to blow up in his face. He cringed whenever he recalled their dinner at The Muddy Oar when Lanie was still planning to go back to California. And he'd come to accept that her decision to stay in Cedar Haven had had nothing to do with him. If anything, his actions had almost sent her running back to the West Coast.

"Seemed a decent meal for a cold day," he continued when she didn't respond. "I'm a bit behind, though. I wasn't expecting you until later."

"I can leave if you want."

"That's not what I meant," he ground out then closed his eyes. Taking a deep breath, he opened them and turned to look at her. "I had simply hoped to have things set up by the time you arrived."

Her expression softened. She nodded at the potatoes he'd set on the counter. "Want me to peel those?"

"You don't have to," he said. "I can manage."

"Nonsense." She went to the sink and washed her hands. "I'm here now. Might as well put me to work."

"Thanks," he said. They worked together in silence. Once the onions were ready, Max added the lamb and the herbs, sautéing the meat mixture on the stove. The water in the pot began to bubble.

"Shall I add these now?" Lanie held out the peeled and chopped potatoes.

Max couldn't help the smirk that came over his face. "You don't have to ask. You probably know how to cook this better than I do."

Her tentative grin took him back in time. She looked so much younger when she smiled like that, and when her hazel eyes lit up, he could almost see the little girl he remembered.

Once she'd added the potatoes to the pot, she stepped back. He finished browning the lamb before draining the grease. Then he added the rest of the ingredients to the meat, stirring to combine them.

"So, how's school?" he asked, hoping to fill the silence.

"It's going well. The first couple of months were a bit of a struggle. A lot of the students didn't remember me from my brief time with them in the spring. They missed Mrs. Carlisle. But we're finding our groove now."

"That's good." He leaned against the counter and smiled. "I'm glad that all worked out."

"I've had to get up earlier than usual, though, since Steven's house is farther away." She gave him a pointed look.

"You're welcome to come back anytime. You know that."

She arched an eyebrow. "Do I?"

His face flushed. "I'm sorry for what I said—about not wanting to go to your wedding." He ran a hand through his hair. "I didn't mean it."

"It sure sounded like you meant it."

The pain in her voice cut through him, and he sighed. "I'm sorry I didn't tell you about the arch." He finally met her gaze. "It's just... You and I haven't always had the easiest relationship."

She snorted. "That's the understatement of the century."

His chest tightened. "Ouch." She opened her mouth as if to respond, but he shook his head. "No, I deserve that. But that's why I was building the arch. I wanted it to be something meaningful to you in hopes it might show you what I've always struggled to say."

"I know you love me, Dad." She gave a rueful smile. "Sometimes, you have a strange way of showing it, but I know you do, in your own way."

A splash sounded from the stove, and she hurried over to lower the burner heat for the potatoes. When she turned away, he impulsively pulled her to him in an awkward hug. She stiffened, clearly surprised by the contact, but she shifted slightly to face him and wrapped her arms around his waist.

"I hope you know I do appreciate the thought behind the gift," she mumbled into his shoulder. Too soon, she moved away. "I wish you would have talked to me about it, and your feelings for Carissa. It might have saved us both a lot of heartache."

His face must have changed at the mention of the wedding planner's name because Lanie's eyes narrowed. "Have you spoken to her?"

Max vigorously stirred the meat mixture, hoping Lanie would drop the subject. But he knew his daughter better than that.

"Aren't you being a little unfair?"

"I don't want to talk about her," Max grumbled.

"All right. I won't press."

Spinning around in surprise, Max gaped at Lanie. She gave a one-shoulder shrug before testing the potatoes but didn't volunteer anything else.

Soon, both the potatoes and the meat were ready to be combined. Lanie drained the water before mashing the potatoes with some sour cream, butter, salt, and pepper. After Max poured the meat into the casserole dish, Lanie dolloped potatoes on top. Then he slid the dish into the oven.

"Want something to drink?" he asked.

"Wine would be nice."

He poured Lanie a glass of wine and got himself some ice water. They sat on opposite sides of the table and sipped their drinks. The silence was stifling, and Max struggled to find a safe topic of conversation.

"So, what are you working on these days?" Lanie asked.

So much for safe subjects. Max braced himself for her reaction. "Well, I've been splitting my time between working on a small desk and... finishing the arch."

Her throat moved as she swallowed her wine and stared at him. A fire lit behind her hazel eyes, but she took a deep breath. It bothered him that she seemed to be carefully choosing her next words.

"We agreed the arch wouldn't work."

If things hadn't been so tense between them, he might have laughed. After all, from where he was sitting, there was no "agreement." Lanie—and Carissa, for that matter—had *told* him to ditch the arch idea.

It was his turn to take a breath and measure his words. "While I understand your concerns about the size, I've taken Carissa's measurements into account, and I'm altering the arch to fit the parameters of the church." When she opened her mouth, presumably to start yelling at him again, he held up a hand. "But I'm also working on the desk. If you don't like the arch, you can use that instead."

That seemed to catch her off guard. "You're giving me a choice?"

"I didn't want to leave another project unfinished, but I also don't want to force you to incorporate something you don't like into your wedding."

Her eyes became misty. "Dad... I—thank you."

The conversation was becoming too emotional for his tastes. "See there? I do listen..." He gave a sheepish grin. "Well, sometimes."

Her laughter warmed his heart. Then the oven beeped, and he rose to remove their dinner. He set it to rest on the counter, and Lanie grabbed dishes and silverware. As she slipped by him to set the table, she put a hand on his shoulder and squeezed it. And for the first time in a long time, he believed things were going to work out after all.

Later that evening, Max sat in his living room, reflecting on the conversation he'd had with Lanie. She'd been open to the idea of incorporating the arch into the ceremony, but she'd insisted that Carissa be part of the process. Her reasoning had left him doubtful and suspicious.

She'd requested that Carissa view both pieces to determine which would work best. That way, they could still salvage some of the surprise, as Lanie hadn't seen the desk yet, and she hadn't viewed the arch since that day she found out about it.

Though he wasn't thrilled at the idea of Carissa coming to his house again, he'd agreed. He'd also reluctantly promised his daughter he would reconcile with Carissa, at least as far as the wedding went. The last thing he wanted was to cause Lanie more stress before her big day. They'd left things on good terms, with Lanie promising to move back home that weekend. He suspected that had more to do with the distance between Steven's house and Lanie's job than anything else. Still, he would take what he could get.

Something Lanie had said at dinner nagged at him. She'd danced around his issues with Carissa, but at one point, she'd told him she missed the happiness he'd shown after he started spending more time with Carissa.

"I can't remember the last time I saw you so…" She seemed to struggle to find the right word. "Content. Carefree."

The words had stuck with him because they weren't ones usually associated with him. *Grouchy, grumpy, irritable, pigheaded, and stubborn. That's what most people say about me.*

After she'd said it, he'd thought back to before the whole arch drama. Things with Carissa had been simple, easy. Mixed in with that heady feeling of a new relationship was an unexpected familiarity. *Almost like coming home.*

In all his righteous anger at Carissa for breaking his trust, he'd pushed aside those feelings to protect his heart. He'd developed that defense mechanism during the final years of his marriage. He found it easier to stay mad, which served only to push him further from what he really wanted—love and acceptance.

His ex-wife's voice echoed in his head. *I told you so.* But there was no malice or anger behind it, only gentle teasing.

"You were right." He smiled sadly. "And now I'm about to make the same mistake twice."

Oh, your count is much higher than that. He could almost picture her making that retort while her hazel eyes, so much like their children's, flashed, her hands on her hips. Then he imagined her face softening. *You never understood how to be vulnerable. Always had to be the strong one, even when you were falling apart.*

Max shook his head, and the image of Melody's ghost faded. Yet the ache in his chest remained. Melody had warned him that his lack of emotional availability would cause his downfall. She'd meant it regarding his relationship with their children, but he now understood that it applied to other aspects of his life too.

For the first time since their fight, he began to understand Carissa's perspective. In his quest to save his relationship with his daughter, he'd put Carissa's professional reputation at risk. Although he couldn't imagine that Lanie would have bad-mouthed Carissa or her company, he recognized why it concerned Carissa.

Her reputation and business are important to her, but what about me? That was the one question he couldn't answer. They hadn't spoken since he'd blasted her after she told Lanie about the arch. While he could, begrudgingly, admit his mistakes and contribution to their falling out, he needed to know if there was space in her life for him.

With a groan, he stood and stretched before heading upstairs to get ready for bed. Lanie had said she requested a meeting with Carissa sometime that week. Her plan was to have Carissa stop by the house and assess the two pieces to determine which one would work for the ceremony.

And then, I'll know if my arch and my relationship with Carissa have a future.

Chapter Thirty

When Carissa entered Bea's, Lanie was waiting for her. To Carissa's surprise and immense relief, the man sitting beside Lanie was Nate, not Max. Still, she covertly searched the rest of the restaurant to make sure he wasn't lurking somewhere.

"Good morning, Lanie. Nate." Carissa smiled. "I'm sorry I couldn't meet sooner, but my schedule has become rather busy as of late."

"It's fine," Lanie said, her voice higher pitched than normal.

Immediately, Carissa was on high alert. Something, or perhaps someone, was making Lanie nervous. Carissa took another cursory glance around the diner but saw no sign of Max.

"We wanted to discuss revisiting the arch," Nate said, bringing Carissa's attention back to the conversation.

"Oh?" Carissa's stomach flipped. The only thing worse than having Max attend the meeting was talking about that blasted arch. If she never had to think about wedding arches again, it would be too soon.

"I had dinner with my dad last night, and we had a long talk,"

Lanie said, and Carissa was relieved to hear her voice return to normal. "While he still hasn't shown me the arch, he said he's working with your measurements to make sure it fits in the church." Lanie took a deep breath. "But he's also been working on a desk that we can use for the ceremony in case the arch won't work."

"How accommodating of him," Carissa said, unable to keep the sarcasm out of her voice.

Lanie stiffened. "I know you aren't on good terms."

The talent of understatement must be a family trait. Carissa waved a dismissive hand. "That's not important right now. What matters is what *you* want for *your* wedding."

Lanie and Nate exchanged a glance.

"Well, that's the thing," Lanie said. "We want to keep the final arch a surprise." She gave a nervous laugh. "I mean, I saw it in its unfinished monstrosity when everything came out the other day, but Dad's keeping both the smaller version and the desk under wraps until the big day."

A silence fell over the table as Carissa digested their words and what they likely meant. Her lips parted, the *no* on the tip of her tongue.

"And so," Nate hurried on before Carissa could say anything, "we were hoping you would view them both and decide which one would work best."

"I don't think—"

"As our wedding planner, your opinion matters." Lanie gave her a meaningful look. "And you would know best what works with our vision."

Carissa stifled a groan. What Lanie hadn't said was they were paying Carissa to bring their vision to life, which meant she needed to view the arch to determine whether it would work.

Still, she wasn't about to give in without a fight. "I would suggest you forgo adding any unnecessary distractions to the ceremony space. The church is beautiful as it is."

Lanie frowned. "But my father wants to be a part of the day—"

"Which will happen without including his hobby." Carissa hated herself for being so cold, but she didn't want to spend any more time alone with Max McAllister than was absolutely necessary.

Nate's eyes vacillated between Lanie and Carissa, and he shifted uncomfortably in his seat. It was clear he wanted to be there even less than Carissa did. But she presumed Lanie had insisted he attend to present a united front.

Is avoiding Max worth upsetting a client? The thought came unbidden to Carissa's mind, but she pushed it away. She saw no reason they couldn't continue with the wedding without such an unnecessary hiccup.

Then Lanie bit her lip and lowered her gaze. "He won't say it, but he misses you."

A knife to the heart would have been more subtle. Carissa took a calming breath in through her nose and released it through her mouth. "I appreciate your concern, but my relationship with your father is not up for discussion."

"That's fine," Nate said suddenly, catching both Carissa and Lanie off guard. "But as your clients, we are telling you we want one of Max's wood pieces in the wedding ceremony." He slid an arm around Lanie's shoulders. "It's important to her that one of her father's handcrafted pieces be a part of our day, which means it matters to me, and it should matter to you."

Darn it. How could she argue with that? While she'd never fully bought into the saying about the customer always being right, in the current instance, he was. Were they any other clients, she wouldn't have even blinked at such a request. She had to admit that the only reason she was resisting was because of Max.

Stifling a sigh, she nodded. "You're right. I'm sorry. This is unprofessional of me." Though the words burned her throat, she continued, "I will contact Max and set up a time to see the pieces. Then I'll get back to you with my recommendation."

Lanie's eyes lit up. "Thank you. We really appreciate it."

"Now, let's talk about the seating chart," Carissa said, desperate to change the subject. "While we're still waiting to hear from a few people, we have a pretty good guesstimate of the head count."

~

Though she tried to put off calling Max for as long as possible, by Thursday, Lanie had begun sending her daily text messages asking for a status update. While Carissa could try to blame it on Max, his daughter wouldn't buy that since she'd probably seen Max since the meeting.

Carissa planned to call him that afternoon, once she'd finished her weekly grocery shopping and tied up a few loose ends with the retreat. Fate must have had other plans because when she turned the corner to the bread aisle, she almost ran smack into Max.

His eyes met hers, and several emotions flashed through them. Some, she expected—anger, resentment, and even fear. But as all of the other reactions faded away, a look of longing stayed.

Her heart skipped a beat, and she put a hand to her chest. "S-sorry. I didn't see you there." Spinning the large cart around in the aisle was no easy feat, but she tried to make as hasty a retreat as she could.

"Carissa." Her name on his lips felt like a caress, and she squeezed her eyes shut as if she could make him disappear.

He shifted forward and put his hand lightly on her arm. "We need to talk."

She shook her head, stepping away from him. "Not here."

"I can come by your place—"

"No," she said quickly, opening her eyes. The last thing she wanted was that man in her personal space. Besides, she'd promised Lanie and Nate she would assess the arch and desk. "Let me drop off these groceries at home, and then I'll come to you."

There was a beat of silence, and she held her breath. Part of her hoped he would say it wasn't convenient, which was stupid since he'd just offered to meet at her house.

"All right," he finally agreed. "I'll see you soon."

The words were said kindly, but it felt like a threat nonetheless. Once she was sure he wasn't going to add anything else, she tore back down the aisle. Not wanting to risk running into him several more times, she abandoned her cart and rushed out of the store.

Instead of heading home, she drove twenty minutes across town to another store. She felt silly for going to all that trouble to avoid him, but she needed time. Seeing him there had shaken her more than she wanted to admit.

The relief she felt at entering the new store was palpable. But as she shopped, she was reminded why she never went there. Their selection left a lot to be desired, and everything was overpriced.

Oh well. At least I can get my groceries without a side of drama. She lingered over each item on her list. The longer she stayed in the store, the less time she would have to spend in Max's presence.

Yet even as she dreaded the moment she would have to abandon the pretense of shopping and head over there, she also yearned for it. In their brief meeting, she'd realized that the longing she saw in his eyes was reflected in her own. The simple fact of the matter was she missed him.

When she finally ran out of stalling tactics, she checked out and went home. It took her no time at all to put everything away. Taking a deep breath, she grabbed her keys and purse before forcing herself to walk to her car.

The drive over seemed to simultaneously last forever and end in the blink of an eye. To her surprise, the garage door was open, revealing Max's woodworking shop in all its dusty glory. As she climbed out of the car, she steeled herself for another argument.

At the sound of her car door slamming, Max stepped out of the garage and waved. "Come on in. I've got the arch uncovered and ready for your inspection."

She followed him into the garage, and as he'd promised, the arch was unveiled in all its glory. Even without closer inspection, it was clearly narrower than the first time she'd seen it. After digging in her bag, she removed her measuring tape and her phone. Then she refreshed her memory on the measurements of the church and measured the arch.

"I took about a foot off each half at the top," Max said. His voice shook, and Carissa breathed easier, knowing he was having a rough time with her visit too.

Once she finished taking measurements, she leaned back and pursed her lips. As he'd promised his daughter, Max had managed to alter the arch to fit into the church. But it was still a huge inconvenience.

"And the desk?" she asked, keeping her tone professional and detached.

"It's here." He gestured to a small rectangular table.

She hesitated, not wanting to be in such close proximity to him. As if reading her mind, he took a few steps back.

Goodness, this is awkward. But she kept her emotions in check as she examined the table. To her, it made the most sense for the wedding. Lanie and Nate were having a unity candle ceremony, and the piece was just the right size to hold the two individual candles that would join a flame on a large candle in the center.

And yet... Turning back to the arch, she could understand why Max had insisted on creating it. The piece was striking, with intricate leaves and flowers carved into the wood. Though it didn't go with Lanie's aesthetic, it had enough indentations and curves to make it easy to decorate with garlands and other Christmas décor.

"We could drape it with cloth to make it less one-dimensional," Max suggested. He lifted the cover and twisted it to demonstrate what he meant.

"Flowers and garland would work better." Carissa pressed her lips together. She hadn't meant to say that out loud. Until she'd determined which option was best, she didn't want to give him false hope.

He tilted his head as he surveyed the arch. "I could see that."

Glancing back at the table, she leaned closer. "Unfortunately, we'd be covering much of the design on this with a cloth to protect it from the wax."

"Oh." He frowned. "I hadn't thought of that."

A small smile pulled at her lips. "That's why I'm here." He gave her a tentative smile in return, which made her heart flutter. "At the same time, I'm still not sold on the arch. It does appear to fit the measurements I gave you, and I believe it will physically fit into the church, especially since it's in two pieces." She tilted her head. "But it's going to be difficult to transport, and we'd have to move it in and out of the church the day of the wedding."

When Max didn't immediately respond, she risked a glance at him, expecting to find his face flushed with anger. Instead, he stared at the arch as if assessing it from a different perspective.

"What if I take full responsibility for moving it?" he asked. "It'll fit in my truck, and I can get Steven to help me carry it the day of the ceremony."

Carissa tapped her chin. "I hate to ask this, but could you haul it over to the church now? It would help me to visualize how it would look the day of the wedding."

Max's face lit up. "I can get it in my truck and bring it over."

"Uh, maybe find someone to help you lift it," Carissa advised with a rueful smile.

He pulled himself up to his full height. "I'm stronger than I look."

"Be that as it may, I don't want to have to tell Lanie you won't be able to walk her down the aisle on her wedding day because you threw your back out." She began typing on her phone. "I'll ask Nate if he can spare a few guys once I get the go-ahead from the pastor to stage this in the church."

"Sounds like a plan." Max shuffled his feet. "Do you have a minute? I can make us a cup of coffee."

Her immediate instinct was to say no, but something about his demeanor made him appear more vulnerable and open than she had ever seen him. Against her better judgment, she nodded.

Max moved toward the entrance to the house and pushed the button to close the garage. Then he led her out of his workshop and into the kitchen. He indicated a seat at the table while he made the coffee. A few minutes later, a piping-hot cup was placed in front of her.

"Thank you," she said, keeping her eyes on the steam swirling out of her mug.

Sinking into the chair opposite her with a sigh, Max set his mug on the table and wrapped his hands around it. Neither of them said anything.

"I'm sorry for the way I acted after Lanie found out about the arch," Max said, breaking the silence. "I didn't handle the situation well, and I said a lot of hurtful things to both you and Lanie."

"I appreciate your apology," Carissa said.

He seemed to wait for her to say more, and when she didn't, he continued, "But it doesn't change anything?"

She met his gaze. "I didn't say that."

A spark of hope flashed in his eyes. "I'd like to start over—"

"I'm not ready for that."

He frowned. "Why not?"

Why not, indeed. A war waged inside of her, and she had no idea which would win—her head or her heart. On the one hand, she missed Max. When she lost Chuck, she expected to spend the rest of her life alone. But the more time she'd spent with Max, the more she wondered if it was possible to have two great loves in her life.

On the other hand, Max was stubborn and set in his ways. While she was glad he and Lanie had made up, they were family, and kin tended to overlook shortcomings because of the whole *blood is thicker than water* belief. Carissa wasn't sure she could get past the things he'd said and the way he'd treated her.

She chewed her lip as she debated her next words. Max was laying his cards on the table. It made sense for her to do the same.

"I'm not sure you fully comprehend what could have happened as a direct result of your actions." She leaned forward. "Lanie may just be one client of many, but she's a pillar in this community. The wedding side of my business is based mostly on word of mouth at this point. I enjoy the privilege of not having to reinvest my profits into advertising dollars, which has freed that money up for the expansion into corporate events." She shook her head. "One bad review from a client can devastate small businesses like mine, and by putting me in the middle of your relationship with your daughter, you risked that livelihood."

He put his head in his hands. "I realize that now, and I'm sorry." But when he raised his head again, she recognized the stubborn lines forming around his mouth. "At the same time, it might have made more sense for you to tell me that you couldn't keep the secret from Lanie rather than going forward with seeing the arch."

That was a fair argument. She had no excuse for why she hadn't refused to keep the secret when he'd asked. Perhaps things would have worked out differently if she'd insisted on telling Lanie from the start.

"I understand your work is important to you," Max continued. "Sometimes, I wonder if you had the right idea in the beginning."

Although she could guess what he meant by that, she wanted clarification. "I don't understand."

He sighed. "About holding off on any sort of relationship until after Lanie's wedding. If we weren't dating, I wouldn't have roped you into seeing the arch surprise, and maybe we could have started with a fresh, conflict-free slate. But what's done is done, and now I must ask if there's room in your life for anything beyond your expanding business."

She blinked. "What is that supposed to mean?"

"It means I want to be with you." He gestured between them. "You and I have a good thing going here, or at least, we did until everything blew up. I understand how important your business is to you. I need to know if that's always going to be your priority."

"Like I said, it's my livelihood."

His forehead wrinkled as if he was struggling to find the right words. "Can you see yourself building a future with me?"

That caught her off guard, especially given his reaction when she'd asked about marriage. "We've only been on a few dates."

He laughed. "I'm not proposing." His expression turned serious. "But I'm also not getting any younger, and, well, I want to give us a real shot."

If he'd said something like that over the summer, she would have laughed. The Max she'd known then was not like the Max she'd come to know since. He'd opened up to her, shown her his vulnerabilities. And there he was, asking her not only to forgive him for his mistake for his daughter's sake but also to give their budding romance another chance.

She sipped her coffee to buy some time. As much as she'd missed him, she wasn't sure she could trust him. He might be questioning her priorities, but she'd already seen how he put family before anyone or anything else.

"I need time," she murmured, pushing back from the table to leave.

The disappointment in his eyes almost made her reconsider, then he nodded.

"Take all the time you need."

As Carissa had expected, the rest of the month leading up to the wedding was filled with hectic last-minute plans. Unlike Rose and Steven's wedding, which had been planned for two years, Lanie had given Carissa less than six months. That she had been able to pull it together at all still felt like a miracle. The McAllisters had even come through with their cookie plans. Lanie and Rose had dropped off the homemade favors the night before.

But they'd finally made it. It was the day before the wedding, and

Carissa was getting dressed for the rehearsal. The pastor had agreed to let them set up the arch and desk that afternoon, and Carissa was excited to see Lanie's reaction.

After Max had taken the arch to the church, Carissa had finally been able to envision what it would look like on the day of the ceremony. The moment he'd set it up at the front of the sanctuary, all her objections died on her lips. The piece was truly beautiful.

While Carissa had suggested they wait until the day of the wedding to allow Lanie to get the full effect with all her guests, Max had insisted that his daughter see it beforehand in case she wanted to make any changes. His care and concern for Lanie's happiness had helped dissolve Carissa's remaining doubts about him. She couldn't wait until the wedding was over because she hoped to give their romance a second chance.

Once she was dressed, she headed to the church. She wanted to get there early to make sure everything was set up for her bride-to-be.

As she climbed out of her car, she grabbed a small bouquet of fake flowers she always used for brides during their rehearsals. A lone familiar truck sat in the parking lot near the church entrance. She climbed the stairs, anticipation building as she entered the doorway.

Max sat alone in a pew, staring at the arch. She quietly crept down the aisle and slid in beside him. If he was surprised by her sudden appearance, he didn't show it.

"What are you doing here so early?" she asked.

"What do you mean early?" he scoffed. "I never left after the guys helped me bring in the arch."

"Why?"

He shrugged. "Lanie wanted the house to herself for her and her bridesmaids. I didn't want to be in the way." His gaze slid to her. "Besides, I figured you'd come before everyone else and we'd have a moment alone."

"Something on your mind?"

"Just you," he said simply, turning to face her. "And a question you asked me once."

"Oh? What's that?"

"Whether I'd get married again."

She stiffened. His reaction to her asking that question hadn't endeared him to her. While she understood him better now, his immediate rejection of the idea had stung at the time.

He covered her hand with his. "I was wondering if I could change my answer."

She swallowed, unsure of what to say. "Um... Sure?"

"After my divorce, I swore off relationships entirely. I didn't want to even date, let alone consider marriage again." His eyes searched her face. "Maybe it was watching my children find their own joy in matrimony. Or maybe it was spending this time with you, but I would like to get married again." He smiled. "Someday."

The emotions coursing through her were overwhelming. She tried to lighten the mood. "You'll have to let me plan your wedding."

"Hmm, I was thinking more of a destination type of deal."

"Really?" She raised an eyebrow. "To where?"

"Well, I'm not one for traveling, as I hate flying. But maybe somewhere drivable." A sudden gleam came to his eye. "Deep Creek, perhaps?"

Her heart in her throat, she opened and closed her mouth but couldn't find the words. She was saved from responding by laughter outside the church door. Taking a deep breath, she tried to calm her pounding heart.

"Oh my goodness!" Lanie squealed from the back of the church. "It's gorgeous." She rushed to their pew.

Max gave Carissa's hand a squeeze before he released it and stood to greet his daughter. Together, they stepped out of the pew, and Lanie threw her arms around her dad's neck.

"Thank you, Daddy. I love it."

"I thought you would," Carissa said with a smile. Her mind still whirled from what Max had said, but she had a better handle on her emotions. "I ordered a few garlands and poinsettias from that silk flower site you sent me. We could wrap them around the arch to make it more Christmasy."

Lanie nodded with enthusiasm. "That sounds perfect!"

Several people filed into the church with Nate, Steven, and Rose leading the way. The wedding party and some out-of-town guests Carissa had yet to meet moved toward the arch.

"Wow, Mr. McAllister," Nate said. "That's quite a talent you've got there." His dark eyes examined the arch with appreciation.

"Isn't it about time you called me Max? You're about to be family, after all."

"Would 'Dad' be too forward?" Lanie teased as she stepped away from her father and grabbed her fiancé's hand.

"Let's not push it."

Then the pastor came through the side door. "Welcome, everyone." He gestured to Lanie and Nate. "Are you ready to begin?"

Lanie exchanged a glance with Nate then nodded. "Let's do it!"

For the next hour, the pastor and Carissa worked together to line up the processional and walk through the ceremony. They went through it all a couple of times to ensure everyone knew when to enter and where to stand.

"All right. Everyone appears to have a better idea of what to expect tomorrow," the pastor said. "I'll open the church around eight in the morning for decorating, but please tell me if you need anything between now and then."

Before everyone dispersed, Carissa clapped. "Bea is holding several tables for us at her diner. Please make your way there as soon as possible."

She waited until most of the party had left before grabbing her things to leave as well. While Bea's was not her first choice for a rehearsal dinner, Lanie and Nate had insisted. It held sentimental value from their many dates there as teens.

When she came out of the church, Max was sitting on the stairs, hunched over seemingly to protect himself from the bitter December cold. He looked up at the sound of her footsteps.

"You didn't have to wait for me."

He shrugged. "I wanted one more moment alone with you before everything gets crazy."

They descended the church stairs together and went out to the parking lot. She opened her car door and put away her wedding binder before facing him. "I have an answer to your question."

His eyebrows pulled together. "My question?"

"About whether I could see a future with you."

"Oh." He swallowed. "And?"

Her heart pounded as she took a deep breath. "I want to *make* room in my life for a future with you."

The way his whole face lit up caused her stomach to flip. Without a word, he leaned forward and cupped her cheek. Then he brushed his lips gently against hers. Warmth spread from her face, down her neck, and to the tips of her toes.

Too soon, he pulled away, but he didn't release her face. "I was wondering..."

She raised an eyebrow. "Yes?"

"How would you feel about me tagging along on your corporate retreat in October?"

Her mouth fell open in surprise. October was months away. Why was he thinking so far ahead?

"Um... It shouldn't be a problem, but I expect I'm going to be very busy. We may not be able to spend much of that time together."

"That's okay. I'd just like to be there with you, and for you. To help where I can."

Her heart melted. "That would be lovely."

He kissed her again before stepping back with apparent reluctance. "We'd better go."

As he turned to leave, she called out to him. "Save me a dance tomorrow."

"I'll save you all of them."

~

As much as Carissa loved working with her brides and planning their big days, she tended to hate the wedding itself. The planning was fun because everyone was usually relaxed and excited. But the day itself never failed to cause her a big ball of stress. Something always went wrong, and she had so much to keep track of, she sometimes felt like she momentarily had gone insane.

Lanie's wedding was no exception. Carissa had gotten to the church early with a few volunteers to start decorating the church. Another team, mostly Nate's friends, worked in the reception hall. Thankfully, the caterer was overseeing that, though Carissa would swing by before everything got started.

Meanwhile, the bride and groom were in their respective homes, getting ready. Max had texted multiple times, complaining about the level of estrogen in his house. He'd begged to assist Carissa, but she kept telling him he needed to be there for his daughter. Based on his grumpy replies, that wasn't what he wanted to hear.

The morning passed quickly as Carissa ran around making sure everything was perfect for her clients. For a few moments, she forgot it was Christmas Eve. Usually, it was one of her favorite holidays, but she'd barely had time that month to go shopping let alone enjoy the holiday season.

Luckily, the church was already decorated for Christmas with a large tree covered in gold and white ornaments. A swag with pine cones and red ribbons adorned the pulpit, while green garland with red bows wrapped around the altar railing. But Carissa had added more greenery to the arch itself as well as red roses, white lilies, and holly berries.

Before she knew it, it was half past two. The wedding was due to start at three. Nate and his groomsmen milled about the church as guests arrived. There was no word on the bride yet, but Carissa had told Max to keep Lanie at the house until the last minute to avoid any opportunity for the groom to sneak a peek before the wedding.

As the clock ticked closer to three, Carissa suggested the groom and groomsmen get into place. Her phone buzzed in her pocket with a text from Max confirming he, Lanie, and the rest of the wedding party had arrived. The time had come.

The guests were ushered into their seats, and the pastor entered the church through the side entrance, just as he had the night before. At his nod, Carissa headed to the back of the church to begin the processional.

As she stepped out into the bright afternoon sun, she lifted her hand over her eyes. Lanie stood at the bottom of the staircase with one of her bridesmaids fussing about her train. Her blond hair was pulled up on the sides and curled in the back. A simple lace veil cascaded gently over her curls.

Carissa put a hand to her chest. Seeing a bride for the first time on her wedding day always brought a tear to Carissa's eye. But something about that particular bride stuck with her. Perhaps it was her involvement with the family, having planned Steven and Rose's wedding as well. Or it could have been her feelings for Max and what she hoped the wedding signified for their future. Whatever the reason, it took her a moment longer than usual to compose herself, but once she had, she descended the stairs.

"Lanie, you look beautiful." Carissa allowed her gaze to sweep over the rest of the bridesmaids. As the maid of honor, Rose wore a stunning green gown with cap sleeves and a V-neckline. The other bridesmaids wore similar gowns, but their sleeves were long and sheer. Each dress had a red sash to coordinate with the Christmas décor.

When Carissa finally turned to Max, her breath caught in her throat. He wore a black tuxedo with a red tie. A boutonniere of a red silk rose surrounded by green leaves and holly berries hung loose and lopsided on his lapel.

Without asking, Carissa went to him and straightened the flower before pinning it more securely. She didn't miss the way his eyes traveled over her. Glancing at her outfit, she was pleased with the way her simple red dress suit hugged her curves.

"That dress is going to put the bride to shame," Max whispered, grabbing her hand and pressing his lips to her knuckles.

"Don't say that," she scolded playfully. "Your daughter is beautiful."

"She is," he agreed, giving Carissa another once-over. "But you're gorgeous."

"You're distracting me." She addressed the rest of the wedding party. "All right, ladies. It's time to start the processional." After searching for the flower girl, she found one of Lanie's students standing wide-eyed near the bridesmaids. "Beth? Come here, please. And where is Robert?"

"Here." Robert stepped forward.

"You two are up first." Carissa handed the ring bearer pillow to Robert and a bouquet to Beth. "Are you ready?"

They nodded, and Carissa led them up the stairs to the church door. She peeked inside and signaled the pianist, who began to play the music Lanie had chosen, the traditional Irish ballad "Red Is the Rose." She gave each child a gentle push, and they began their procession to the front of the church.

Next, Carissa sent Trudy then Tocarra down the aisle. Finally, it was Rose's turn. Carissa gave her a quick hug.

"It's hard to believe only a few months ago, we were at *your* wedding."

"And maybe in the not-so-distant future, we'll be at yours," Rose quipped with a meaningful glance back at Max.

Carissa's face warmed, and she averted her gaze before gesturing for Rose to make her way to the front of the church.

Once everyone was assembled, Carissa again signaled to the pianist, and the music changed from "Red Is the Rose" to "A Thousand Years" by Christina Perri. Tears pricked behind her eyes as her latest bride began her walk down the aisle to her future. Max glanced back and winked at her before focusing on the task before him.

As the wedding continued and Lanie and Nate promised themselves to each other, Rose's words echoed in Carissa's mind. *And maybe in the not-so-distant future, we'll be at yours.* The idea of getting married again both thrilled and terrified her. It was too soon to even consider that with Max. They'd only just begun. But if the past year of spending time with the McAllisters had taught her anything, it was not to take anything for granted and to make the most of the time she had.

Epilogue

October of the following year

If Max had thought weddings were hectic, he was completely unprepared for how insane a corporate retreat could be, at least for the person planning it. Luckily, the people attending the event seemed to be relaxed and enjoying themselves.

As much as he tried to help, he often felt like more of a nuisance than an aid. Carissa was like a well-oiled machine, which was no surprise after watching her handle both of his children's weddings. Still, he hoped he was at least a comfort to her if nothing else.

It was the last day of the retreat, and Carissa was run ragged. They'd just sent the group off to a restaurant for dinner. They had a few loose ends to tie up before everyone went home, but overall, it'd seemed a smashing success. Even the jerk of a CEO, Jacob, had begrudgingly complimented Carissa on her work. They planned to book future retreats with her, and she'd already had a few calls from potential clients. Between her wedding business and the new venture, she was doing well.

Max had made a point of becoming more involved. While he was often out of his element with the wedding stuff, Carissa appeared to appreciate that he provided a male perspective on the activities and ideas she had for the events. They made a pretty good team, and working together had only brought them closer.

So much so that he was hoping to find a moment alone with her before they headed back to Southern Maryland. He had a particular question he wanted to ask her, and he'd been planning how to do it for months.

After making sure she was still in the shower, he snuck the ring box out of his pocket and opened it. A brilliant solitaire diamond glinted back at him from the velvet cushion. It was simple but elegant. Truthfully, the ring had been burning a hole in his pocket ever since he'd bought it, and he'd had to restrain himself from popping the question multiple times. But the trip meant a lot to Carissa, and it seemed the perfect way to end what had been a long and exhausting road.

The shower turned off, and he slipped the box into his pocket. He'd debated asking her that night, but she'd been so tired when she got back to their cabin. Without telling her, he'd extended their reservation for one more night. He'd reserved a picnic basket and a wine tasting at a local winery for the next day. He hoped once the hubbub of the retreat was over, she would relax and enjoy their time together.

But that night, they were planning a quiet evening in. He'd bought some steaks for the grill and had already opened a bottle of red wine to breathe. As soon as she was dressed, he would get started on their meal.

As she entered the room fully dressed, her graying hair wrapped in a towel, his breath caught in his throat. She was more beautiful to him than ever before. His hand slid into his pocket, and he caressed the velvet box. *I should ask her now.*

He shook his head, pushing the thought from his mind. *Not yet.* Everything needed to be perfect. Her eyes met his, and she smiled.

"You look like you're struggling with something."

He swallowed and waved a dismissive hand. "No. I was caught off guard by how beautiful you are."

She scoffed. "I look like death." After walking over to the mirror, she unwrapped her hair and began towel drying it. "As happy as I am with the success of this week, I'm glad it's over. I need a vacation."

"I can't give you a whole week, but I extended our stay by another night. We leave Sunday."

She spun around, eyes widening. "What? Why didn't you tell me?"

"I wanted it to be a surprise." He moved toward her and wrapped an arm around her waist. "You worked hard this week, and you could use a day to relax before returning to the realities of home."

"Wow." Her face lit up with a smile. "A whole day here with just you." The smile morphed into a smirk. "Whatever will we do with ourselves?"

He laughed and kissed her briefly. "How does an afternoon at a winery sound?"

She closed her eyes and drew a deep breath. "Like heaven."

The urge to ask her bubbled up inside him again, and he forced himself to step back and put some space between them. "You hungry? I've got the steaks ready for the grill."

Opening her eyes, she nodded. "Famished."

He made his escape, carrying the steaks with him. After firing up the grill, he waited for it to get hot before he tossed the steaks on with a few vegetable kabobs and closed the lid. Drinking in the cool autumn air, he tried to clear his mind.

A moment later, Carissa joined him with a glass of wine in each hand. She handed one to him then clinked it with her own.

"To the best unexpected assistant I've ever had," she said with a wry grin.

"To us." His eyes never left her face.

She sipped the wine and frowned at him over her glass. "Something's gotten into you."

His heart skipped a beat, and he almost blurted out the question, but he bit his tongue to keep from speaking. When he recovered, he raised his hands.

"I don't know what you mean."

After setting her glass on the table next to the grill, she crossed her arms. "You've been jumpy all week. At first, the stress seemed to be getting to you, but the retreat is over. Everyone goes home tomorrow." Her lips quirked in a smile. "Well, except us."

"It was more stressful than I expected."

She raised an eyebrow. "There's more to it, though, isn't there?"

Lie. Tell her you're tired or missing the kids. But if the whole arch debacle had taught him anything, it was that he shouldn't hide things from her.

"I have something I want to ask you," he began.

"So ask me."

He sighed. "It's not something you just blurt out."

A light of understanding dawned on her face. "Oh."

Darn it. There goes the surprise. He grimaced and turned to the grill to check the steaks.

Then she leaned closer and took his hand. "I don't need some big romantic gesture."

He rolled his eyes. "You might not *need* it, but I want to give you one." He harrumphed. "Or I did, but once again, my surprise is ruined."

Cupping his cheek with her other hand, she held his gaze. "It's still not something I was expecting. And you know my answer is—"

Before she could continue, he dropped to one knee. *No way is she going to beat me to the punch.* With a shaky but determined breath, he removed the box from his pocket and opened it.

"Carissa Owens," he began. If nothing else, at least he could give the darned speech he'd been practicing for weeks. "I can't say we had love at first sight." Her laughter urged him on. "Or even second, third, or fourth sight. But it's been a long time since I felt this way about someone. I never saw myself getting married again, but then I fell in love with you, and I can't imagine spending the rest of my life without you." His voice cracked. "Will you marry m—"

"Yes!" she squealed before throwing her arms around him and sprinkling sweet kisses all over his face.

"You didn't even let me finish the question," he protested, sliding his hands into her hair and pressing his lips to hers.

She pulled back just far enough to look at him, a twinkle in her eye. "I wanted to prepare you for what a lifetime with me will be like."

He narrowed his eyes, hoping to appear stern but mainly to keep from laughing. "You mean you plan to ruin all of my surprises?"

"Pretty much."

She stepped back and helped him stand. Then he slipped the ring onto her finger. It was a perfect fit. While she admired her ring, he flipped the steaks then gazed toward the lake. He blinked. Sitting on the picnic table across from him was a pair of mourning doves. One of the birds cocked its head at him before preening its mate. A slow smile spread across his face.

"Looks like we both found someone," he whispered.

"Did you say something?" Carissa asked.

Max cleared his throat. "Uh, do you have a date in mind?"

She moved beside him, a mischievous grin on her face. "What about a West Virginia wedding? They have a drive-through service."

A laugh bubbled up in his throat. "That's not quite what I had in mind for a destination wedding." When he glanced at the birds, they took flight, soaring above the deep orange and red hues of the leaves on the trees as the sun set in the distance. His heart felt lighter. "But I could see getting married here."

"Hmm." Her brow furrowed. "Same time next autumn?"

He kissed her again. "Let's do it.

~

Finished The Love Birds series and ready for what's next? Read on for a sneak peek at my next book, The Tides That Bind, book one of the Heartstrings and Hops duology. Coming Spring of 2025.

The Tides That Bind

Around eight in the evening, things were slowing down. Cassie took advantage of the lull in customers to wipe down the bar. It would make closing easier if she started cleaning early. The door to the pub opened and a light breeze followed a new customer. She looked up as he approached the bar. A baseball cap covered his head and obscured his face, though strands of blond hair peeked out from the sides.

"What can I get you?" she asked as he sat down.

"You're new," he said, raising his head and giving her a quick once-over.

"Actually, I'm not," Cassie said. "I'm filling in. My family owns the place."

He did a double take. "You're a Gallagher? Emily or Cassie?"

Wow, personal much? Cassie took a giant step back as she folded her arms across her chest. "Who are you?"

He gave her a sheepish grin. "My apologies. I'm Ryan Caulfield. I'm the mayor of Blue Heron Bay, thanks in large part to your father." He held out his hand, and she hesitated before she took it.

"Your dad meant a lot to me, and I like to stop by and check on the place whenever I can."

She worked to swallow past the lump that still formed in her throat whenever someone spoke of her father. Her father mentioned working on a local campaign, but as she'd never much cared for politics, she hadn't paid attention to who the candidate was.

"I'm Cassie," she said. "The youngest of the Gallagher brood."

"It's wonderful to meet you. Did you move back?"

Cassie shook her head. "My siblings and I came home to help our mother, but I'll be leaving at the end of the summer."

"That's too bad, though I'm glad your mother found help." He folded his hands on the bar. "I was afraid I'd asked too much of her when I told her about the hotel group I've pitched to build here."

Cassie nodded absently. She vaguely recalled Emily talking about a hotel during their FaceTime the other day, but truthfully, she'd been more focused on the time off from work than the reason it was needed.

"Now that you're here, I hope to make the most of your time," Ryan continued with a wink.

She blinked, unsure what to make of it. Was he flirting with her? She, of all people, should be able to tell, especially after spending much of the evening flirting herself. But he was different, more sincere, more... purposeful, like he had set a strict path for himself and refused to deviate from it.

"So, can I get you anything?" Cassie asked again.

"Sorry, yes, I'll have a Sam Adams."

She nodded and grabbed a glass before heading over to the taps. The weight of his gaze followed her every move, and she shifted from foot to foot. Not that there was anything wrong with him, but he wasn't her usual type. For one thing, he appeared much older than her—maybe mid-thirties?

"Thank you," he said as she set the glass in front of him. "Are you planning to go to the town's Memorial Day parade?"

Cassie gave her one-shoulder shrug. "I'm not sure. I only arrived today."

"And you're already working?" he asked with raised eyebrows.

"I wanted to," Cassie said. "Besides, it was a long drive. Feels good to move around."

"How far away are you?" Ryan asked.

She stared at him. Again, with the personal questions.

As if he read her mind, he hurried on. "I mean, if you don't mind my asking."

"I'm right outside of D.C.," she said, not wanting to give out too much information. A girl could never be too careful, regardless of his connection to her late father.

"Wow, that's quite a change of pace from here. Do you prefer the city?"

"Usually," Cassie said, the tension in her shoulders releasing. "I love being able to walk most places and there's so much life there. Every day, I meet new people. But I do miss the ocean."

"What do you do?"

Cassie rolled her eyes. Of course, the inevitable professional question. Sometimes it seemed like that's all that mattered to some people: a job, a profession, a neat and tidy box into which they could categorize someone.

"I'm sorry. Did I say something wrong?" Ryan asked as his brows furrowed.

"Not exactly," Cassie said with a sigh. There wasn't much point in explaining it to him. He struck her as a stuffed shirt, and he was clearly established in a career path if he was mayor. He wouldn't understand. "I'm a paralegal."

His face cleared, as Cassie expected it would. Now that she fit into a box in his mind. Typical. And before he spoke again, she knew exactly what he was going to ask.

"Have you ever considered going to law school?"

There it was. She'd known his type from the second he walked in, and he hadn't disappointed. This was the question she was most often asked by business professionals. The question had been the bane of her existence since she'd finally finished her legal studies degree. Everyone wanted to know what her next move was, her career goals, her ambitions. The truth was, she didn't have any. Why did everyone else adhere to a strict timeline of events for their lives: college, career, marriage, then family? Cassie swallowed another sigh.

"Probably not," she finally said. "I barely finished my bachelor's, so the idea of more school doesn't appeal to me."

Instead of pressuring her, as people often did, he laughed. "I don't blame you. I've thought about going for a J.D. with a focus on tax law, but I don't need to take on more student loan debt."

She couldn't help wrinkling her nose. "That sounds incredibly boring."

Ryan grinned. "It is, but it's also very lucrative." He took a swig of his beer before setting it back on the counter. "I like to keep fallback options in mind, especially since politics is hardly a stable career."

Stability wasn't really a word with which Cassie was well acquainted. She flew by the seat of her pants and this method hadn't failed her thus far. The idea of having a fallback option more boring than her current job was about as appealing as getting a root canal.

"It was nice to meet you," she said as she moved away. "But I better check on my other customers."

He nodded. "I'm sure I'll see you around while you're in town."

Cassie wasn't sure if that was a threat or a promise.

Preorder *The Tides That Bind* today!

Acknowledgments

As always, I want to start by thanking my mother, who encouraged me to pursue my dream of writing from the tender age of eight. I want to thank my husband and daughter, who have provided me with so much love and support throughout the whole process. My deepest thanks to my father and step-mother, who have supported me through all the ups and downs of my life and who served, at least in part, as the inspiration for the final book in The Love Birds seres! A huge debt of gratitude to my sister and sister-in-law who have helped spread the word about my books! And huge thanks to my brother and his partner who cheer on my writing from across the country.

I'd be remiss not to thank Rashida and Angela McRae at Red Adept Editing for their assistance with making all three of these stories shine!

Finally, thanks to all my friends who have offered feedback on my writing over the years, especially those of you who were unfortunate enough to read my angsty teenage poetry. They say it takes a village to raise a child, and I think it takes at least that, and so much more, to raise a writer.

Also by Katie Eagan Schenck

A Home for Christmas

The Love Birds Series

When Cardinals Appear

When Swans Dance

When Doves Lament

About the Author

Katie Eagan Schenck writes sweet romance and women's fiction that warms the heart and gives all the feels. She has an MFA in creative writing from Queens University of Charlotte and her debut novel, A Home for Christmas, was released in October of 2022. When she's not writing she's either drafting regulations for the federal government, baking delicious treats, or binging Hallmark movies. She lives in Maryland with her husband, daughter, and their three cats.

Connect with Katie on her website or via social media.

www.ingramcontent.com/pod-product-compliance
Lightning Source LLC
Chambersburg PA
CBHW020720310726
48979CB00004B/998
9781965807903